Murder Most Scottish

Murder Most Scottish

SELECTED BY STEFAN DZIEMIANOWICZ,
BOB ADEY, ED GORMAN, AND
MARTIN H. GREENBERG

BARNES
&NOBLE
BOOKS
NEW YORK

Contents

Introduction

urder for political advantage. Murder for love. Murder for profit. Scotland can claim them all as part of its colorful history. In all fairness, Scotland probably boasts no more than any other country's share of criminal killings as part of its heritage, but the incongruous juxtaposition of deeds so dastardly to a society so romantic and inviting makes them stand out in sharp relief.

This contrast of the dark and light sides of Scotland has fascinated writers for centuries and inspired a host of stories not only by distinguished native sons and daughters but also observers beyond the rugged Scottish shores. *Murder Most Scottish* taps the rich vein of literature they have created, offering twenty tales of mystery drawn from two centuries of fiction that explore both the murder theme and the country from a variety of angles.

Doug Allyn and Rafael Sabatini both depict murder as an element inextricable from Scotland's historical past. Stories by Ian Rankin and Peter Turnbull are unabashedly contemporary, set in modern urban environments and pervaded by issues that include cutthroat business competition and modern domestic crises. James Hogg, Catherine Sinclair, and Sir Walter Scott offer tales that are rich embellishments of Highland folk tales. Elizabeth Ferrars and Michael Innes deliberately invoke folk superstitions to complicate their rigorously logical plots. Robert Louis Stevenson, Hugh B. Cave, and Christopher N. Johnson all flavor their murder stories with a dash of the supernaturalism indigenous to Scottish lore. Bill Knox (in a full-length novel) and Edward D. Hoch provide a counterbalance in stories steeped in coldly rational Cold War espionage.

P. M. Hubbard and Sir Arthur Conan Doyle both delve into the psychology of the criminal mind. Guy N. Smith and Basil Copper are more concerned with the process of detection that drives the wheels of justice, as is George Goodchild, whose detective hero McLean reminds us that, in addition to having clever murderers, Scotland is the namesake of that paragon of criminal justice institutions, Scotland Yard. Antonia Fraser's detective heroine Jemima Shore, like Knox's Chief Inspector Thane and Turnbull's Detective Inspector Donoghue, are among the most highly regarded series characters in contemporary mystery and suspense fiction whose adventures involve them in Scottish intrigues.

The murderers on parade in these stories constitute a veritable rogues' gallery, driven by motives as different as lust, greed, patriotism, maternal instinct, revenge, financial desperation, and jealousy. Their methods involve a number of imaginative variations on the classic blunt and penetrating weapon, and their ingenuity invites a variety of storytelling approaches ranging from the classic cozy to the historical melodrama, the deductive procedural, the weird thriller, the locked-room mystery, and the hard-boiled crime caper. Each story blends history and regional atmosphere into powerful narratives leavened with insight into the character and culture of the country.

There is something to suit every mystery lover's taste here, whether you're blood of the glen or just a vacation Scots sympathizer. So take the high road to homicide, and let *Murder Most Scottish* be your travel guide.

STEFAN DZIEMIANOWICZ
New York City, 1999

The Dancing Bear

DOUG ALLYN

he inn was a sorry place with walls of wattle and daub and a lice-ridden thatch roof in dire need of repair. The light within was equally poor, no proper candles, only tallow bowls and even a few Roman lamps that were probably cast aside when the last legions abandoned these Scottish borderlands to the Picts six hundred years ago. Still, logs were blazing in the hearth, the innkeeper had recently slaughtered a hog, and there were guests to entertain. I was content to strum my lute and sing for sausages and a place near the fire. The few coins to be earned in such a hovel weren't worth the risk. With five kings contending in Scotland and the Lionheart abroad, banditry ruled the roads.

The guests were a mixed lot, a pedlar of tinware, an elderly man and his wife on a pilgrimage to Canterbury, a crew of thatchers drifting south in search of work, two farmboys taking an ox to market.

The only person of any substance was a young soldier, a returned crusader from the boiled look of him. He wore a well-crafted chain mail shirt beneath his linen surcoat, and his broadsword was German steel, carried in a bearskin sheath across his back in the old Scottish style. He was tall with unkempt, sandy hair and a scraggly blond beard. His skin was scorched scarlet as a slab of beef, and his eyes were no more than slits. Perhaps they'd been narrowed by the desert sun. Or perhaps they'd seen too much.

He kept to himself, away from the camaraderie of the fire, though he did applaud with the others when I made up a roundelay that described each of the guests in a verse. But his countenance darkened again when I sang "The Cattle Raid at Cooley," an Irish war ballad popular in this border country. The innkeeper was an affable fellow, but I noticed he kept a weather eye on the moody young soldier. As did I.

But he was no trouble. As I gently plucked the opening notes to "The Song of Roland," the crusader lowered his head to the table and dozed off. The ballad is a hymn to the fallen stalwarts of mighty Charlemagne who died for honor. It's a song I sing well, but barely a quarter through it, I noticed the eyes of my listeners straying. Annoyed, I followed their glances.

In the shadows in the corner, the young soldier was on his feet. And he was dancing, shuffling round and round in the smoky darkness. At first I thought he was responding to my music, but his eyes were clenched tight and his steps were graceless. If he was hearing music, it was not mine. My voice died away, but still he danced, lost within himself. And we watched, in silence, bewitched. And for just a moment I felt a feather touch of a memory. There was something familiar about his movements, something I'd seen before. But I could not call it to mind. After a time I quietly took up my song again, though to little effect. I doubt anyone heard a word.

The young crusader stumbled back into his seat and his slumber before I finished singing, but the sense of fellowship around the fire was gone. Uneasy, avoiding each other's eyes, we each of us found places, wrapped our cloaks about us and so to sleep. But not for long.

Living on the road has sharpened my senses, if not my wits. Sometime in the night I heard a muffled footstep and snapped instantly awake, my glance flicking about the room like a bat.

Movement. In the corner. As my eyes adjusted to the dark, I could see the young soldier. Dancing. His eyes were partly open, but there was no light in them, no awareness. And his face was a twisted mask of anguish. And yet he danced shuffling in a mindless circle like a . . .

Bear.

And I remembered where I'd seen this dance before. In the marketplace of Shrewsbury when I was a boy. It was a feast day and there was a fair, with jugglers and minstrels and a puppet show. And near the village gate was a man with a chained bear, a great brown hulk of a brute with a mangy coat. The man would prod it with a stick and sing a doggerel verse, and the bear would rear upright and shuffle in a circle, pawing the air. And the man would swat it and caper about as though the two were dancing.

I was enchanted, awed by the power this ragamuffin minstrel had over his monstrous beast. When he worked the crowd, I paid him my only copper to see the bear dance again. And I gradually lost my fear of the animal and moved closer. Only then did I realize why the minstrel had no fear of it. The bear's claws had been ripped out, and his eyes seared with coals. He was blind.

I cried all the way home and poured out my heart to my father. Who cuffed me for whining. Perhaps rightly. But later that night I hid a blade beneath my jerkin and skulked back to the marketplace, determined to rescue the bear somehow. But the fair was finished and they were gone. I never saw him again. Until tonight. For the young soldier's dance reminded me strongly of the ghost bear of my boyhood. He too shuffled in his circle, blind to his surroundings. The difference was that if the soldier opened his eyes, he could see.

When I opened mine again, he was gone. As were the thatchers and the farmboys and even their ox. Only the old pilgrims and I had slept past the dawn, and they were packing to leave as I stirred myself. Perhaps I could have stayed another night, earned another meal, but the inn felt haunted to me now. I slung my lute o'er my shoulder, bade the innkeeper good day, and set out.

The day was fine, a brassy October morn, heather crunching beneath my shoes and curlews crying. I'd summered to the north in Strathclyde, singing in inns and village fairs, but winter was on the wing, and I wished to be far south of these border hills when it came. In England. Perhaps even at home in Shrewsbury.

Or perhaps not. A mile or so from the inn, I came to a fork in the trail. The young soldier was resting there, seated comfortably on a knoll above the path, his blade across his knees.

"Good morning, minstrel," he nodded. "I've been waiting for you."

"Good morning to you," I said. In the light of day he seemed older. Not his face, which despite his beard was boyish and unseamed, but his eyes. . . . "Waiting?" I said. "Why?"

"To offer you employment," he said. "I journey west to the Clyde, to a town called Sowerby. A small place, but lively. I should like to hire you to perform there, and a troubador of your skill will surely find other work as well."

"Thank you, no," I said. "I'm traveling south."

"To those of us who drift on the wind, one road is much like another, is it not? Come with me. I have need of your talent, and I can pay. In advance if you like." He rose, blotting out the sun with his shoulders. And for a moment he was again the blinded bear of my boyhood. And my dreams. And he was asking for my help.

"Keep your money," I said with a shrug, offering him my hand. "I'm Tallifer of Shrewsbury, minstrel and poet. And the price of my company is a riddle. Why does a man dance like a bear in the dark when no music plays?"

"I am Arthur Gunn," he said, accepting my hand. "Of Clyde, and the Holy Land. I, ah, danced last night?"

"That you did. A curious thing to see," I said as we set off on the path to the west. "Tell me the story of it."

"You should have taken the coins," he smiled. "There's nought wondrous about it. I followed the cross and King Richard to Acre, and I was captured by Saracens in a raid in '91 south of Caesarea, myself and a dozen more."

"People say they are cruel captors."

"Not unlike ourselves," he said dryly. "They led us east, into the wastes. By chance, one of the captured was a bastard son of Hugh of Burgundy, and so a band of French horse dogged us like hounds.

"And after a few days, the Saracens began to kill us. Not from malice, but to save water. Each night when we camped the guards would look us over and slaughter those who looked too weak to go on before giving water to the rest. I was young and very afraid, so when they approached me, I would rise and shuffle about to show I was hale. And worthy of a sip of water. Of living another day. As the chase stretched on, we all went half mad from thirst and exhaustion. And if a man fell on the trail and was killed, I would dance over him. To prove I was stronger, you see. That I was still alive. So my friends died, and I . . . danced."

He fell silent, his face dark with memories.

"It must have been terrible," I said. "What happened?"

"On the twelfth day, young Burgundy died, and I knew the pursuit would end when they found him. I had wasted a bit so my shackles were not so tight, nor did the guards check as closely as before, for they were exhausted, too. That night I chewed my arm and dripped blood onto my ankle till it was oily enough to slip my chain. I must've fled into the desert, though I honestly don't remember. The French said I was dancing when they found me. Alone, on the sand."

"Perhaps it will pass now that you are returned?"

"It has abated somewhat," he agreed. "It only happens when I drink too much, or get overtired. With luck the winds of Scotland will blow my ghosts away altogether."

"I hope so," I said earnestly. "A happier question. What song do you wish me to sing? To your family? Or a lass, perhaps?"

"I've no family, and as for a lass, I'm not sure," he said, brightening. "Before I left, my best friend and I fought over a woman, a tanner's daughter we'd both lain with. Nearly killed each other, but by God she was worth the fight. Hair dark as a raven's wing, eyes like opals, and a heat about her . . ."

"You still care for her, then?"

"Who knows?" He shrugged. "It's been long years. I lost to Duncan fair and square and went off crusading. I expect they are married now with a brood. Whatever their situation, I want you to make up a song to suit it as you did last night. And whether it's a wedding gift or a peace of-fering, say the trouble between us is forgotten, and I would be his friend again."

"And if he chooses not to forget the trouble?"

"Then perhaps you'll have to sing a dirge for one of us," he said mildly.

"That's all very well for you," I grumbled. "But dirges are difficult to sing. And if you kill each other, who will pay me?"

Sowerby was larger than I expected, a walled market town sprawled hap-hazard along a riverbank, with a branch of the Clyde running through it. The village gate was guarded but open, and we passed through without being challenged. Within, all was abustle. There were two smithies with hammers ringing and sparks dancing aloft, a tannery, an alehouse, and a pottery shop with goods displayed on planks in front. A water-driven grist-mill was built into the town's outer wall, rumbling like distant thunder as its great wheel turned.

The village houses were mostly thatch or wattle and daub, with a few built of stone. In the south corner, the castle keep loomed above all, a crude but substantial blockhouse built of stone atop a natural hill in the Norman style. Its corners were outset so archers could sweep its walls.

Two herds of horses were tethered just outside the inner ward gate, with guardsmen and merchants looking them over.

"Horse traders," Arthur offered, "from Menteith and Lennox if I recall their livery right. We've come at a good time, minstrel. There will be celebrating—"

"Arthur! Arthur Gunn?" A guards captain stepped away from a group of traders and strode toward us. He was a striking man, half a head taller than Gunn, bearded and dark as a Saracen. He wore a brimmed steel helmet and the livery of Sowerby over a mailed coat. His fist grasped the hilt of his broadsword as he came, from habit, I hoped.

He halted in front of Arthur, looking him over, his face unreadable. And then before Arthur could react, the captain seized him by the waist and lifted him aloft.

"God's eyes, Arthur," he grinned, "I thought you'd be dead with your head on a pike by now."

"I may be yet," Arthur said. "Or have you forgotten what happened the last time we spoke?"

The smile remained on the captain's face, but it no longer lit his eyes. "No," he said, lowering Arthur to the ground. "I've not forgotten. A word, Arthur, alone."

They wandered off a few paces, heads together, the captain whispering earnestly. I busied myself examining a row of pots, trying to appear uninterested, but I whirled about with my hand on my dirk when I heard Arthur shout.

But he was laughing. Both of them were, arm in arm, tears streaming, laughing like boys at the greatest joke in the world. I think Arthur would've fallen if the captain hadn't held him up. It appeared my song of peace wouldn't be needed. Just as well. Yet I'd have felt better about it if the burly guard captain's laughter had been less fierce.

"Tallifer, this is the old friend I told you about, Duncan Pentecost. A captain now, Duncan?"

"Aye. Promotion comes easy when the best men are off to the Holy Land. You've come at a good time, minstrel. Laird Osbern and his lady have come down from Pentland to look at stock. There's a feast tonight, and our steward's beside himself trying to organize an entertainment. His name's Geoffrey. Tell him I sent you and that you come highly recommended."

"You're most kind," I said.

"Not at all. Arthur says you're a fine singer, and his word has always been good with me. And now I'd best get back to the mounts before Simon of Lennox skins my lord's marshal out of his house and first-born daughter. I'll see you both tonight at the feast. And, Arthur, welcome home."

He strode back to the horse traders.

"A fair-sized man," I observed.

"So he is," Arthur agreed. "If we'd had trouble, it might have ended as it did before. Still, I was glad for your company, Tallifer. And I wish to pay you for the song, even though you didn't have to sing it."

"No need," I said. "With your friend's help I'll find profit enough to make my trip worthwhile. And as you said, to those who drift with the wind, one road's the same as another. I'd better be off in search of Geoffrey the steward."

"And I'll find our lodging," Arthur said. "Duncan offered us beds in a barracks room in the castle. You'll stay with me?"

"Are you sure you want me to? Isn't there someone else here you must see?"

"Someone else?"

"The woman, you clot. The one you and Duncan fought over. Is she his wife now?"

"No," he said, trying not to grin and failing. "He's unmarried. And the woman . . . is dead, minstrel. Forget her. I'll see you later."

He strode off, chuckling quietly to himself. Crazed by grief over his lost love, no doubt. Hair dark as a raven's wing . . . I shook my head and set off to find Laird Osbern's steward.

The evening feast was a small one, a courtesy to the traders who'd gathered rather than a display of wealth by the Laird of Pentland and

Sowerby, Solmund Osbern. There was food aplenty, but plain. Cold plates of venison and hare and partridge, wooden bowls of thick bean porridge flavored with leeks and garlic. The laird and his family sat at the linen-draped high table, a small army of them, four grown sons, their wives, the local reeve, and a priest. Two low tables of rude planks extended from the corners of the high table to form a rough horseshoe shape, which was appropriate since horses were the topic of the day.

In England, strict protocols of station would have been rigidly observed, but these Scots were more like an extended family, with jests and jibes flying back and forth between high and low tables. Indeed, I'd seen Laird Osbern himself that afternoon haggling like a fishmonger with a red-bearded trader from Lennox over a yearling colt. The laird was on in years, nearly sixty, folk said. He was gaunt of face and watery-eyed, but still formidable for all that. He'd gotten the best of the bargaining without adding the weight of his title to the scales.

His sons were a dour crew, wary and hard-eyed as bandits. They were dressed in coarse wools, little better than commoners'. They conversed courteously enough with their guests but kept wary eyes on them. They were fiercely deferential to their sire, though less so to his lady, I thought.

Lady Osbern was clearly not the laird's first wife, for she was a strikingly handsome woman younger than his sons. Richly clad in fur-trimmed emerald velvet, she had the canny eyes and grace of a cat. She stayed demurely at Osbern's elbow, saying little and that only to her husband, but I doubt there was a man in the room who wasn't aware of her. Or a woman either.

As I'd been hired last, I sang last, for such are the protocols of minstrelsy. I wasn't displeased at the order of things, since Scots afeeding can be a damned surly audience. Later, with full bellies and oiled with ale, they're a ready and roisterous crowd. I won them over early with a maudlin love ballad I'd learned in Strathclyde, then followed with "The Cattle Raid at Cooley." Even Laird Osbern joined in at the last chorus, with a full, if unsteady, baritone, and the guests roared their approval at the finish.

To a wandering singer like myself, such times are the true compensation for my craft, fair payment for the chancy life of the road, the loneliness, the lack of home and family. I was glowing like a country bridegroom, singing at my best, the circle of rowdy Scots cheering me on. And so chose my best tune next, "The Song of Roland." A mistake.

Half through it I began to hear murmurs and muffled laughter. I glanced behind me as I strolled the room. It was Arthur. He'd been sitting at low table with Duncan Pentecost, but now he was up, his face flushed with wine, eyes closed, dancing his mindless shuffle, round and round, my bear on a chain. It would've been funny if it were not for the agony so plain in his face. I skipped to the last verse of the song, thinking that if I ended it quickly, he might end his dance. But I was too late.

A trader from Menteith, a wiry rat of a man, staggered from his seat and began capering about Arthur, making sport of him. With a roar, Duncan Pentecost vaulted a table, seized the wretch by the throat, and hurled him back amongst his friends.

In a flash men were up, blades drawn, squaring off, ready for slaughter.

"*Hold!*" Laird Osbern roared. "I'll hang the first man who draws blood in my hall. Sheath your blades, sirs, or by God's eyes, ye'll answer to me and my sons."

"Your captain struck me for no good reason," the rat-faced trader complained.

"You were mocking a better man than you'll ever be," Duncan said. "And if you and your lot want satisfaction, come ahead on, one at a time or all together—"

"Shut your mouth, Duncan," Osbern snapped. "These men are guests. I've given you no leave to fight anyone. Now, what's wrong with this lad? Is he mad?"

"No, my lord," I said hastily, seizing Arthur's arm. He had stopped circling and was looking about, confused. "He's newly home from the Holy Land. He has no head for wine."

"Then see him to bed and let him sleep it off. As for you, Duncan, hie yourself up to keep tower and relieve the watchman there. The night air will cool your temper."

For a moment I thought Pentecost was going to refuse and charge into the traders. But he didn't. He visibly swallowed his anger, then nodded. "Yes, my lord. As you say." He wheeled and stalked out.

"And that, sirs, is the end to it. We can't fall to brawling in front of our good ladies like a pack of damned Vikings. We're friends here. So," he said, raising his tankard, "will you join me, gentlemen? Here's tae us. Wha's like us?"

In the hallway I heard the roar of approval as Osbern's guests answered his toast. The din seemed to startle Arthur into awareness.

"What's happened?" he mumbled, blinking.

"Nothing," I said, leading him into the barracks room and easing him down on a pallet. "Everything's all right."

"The laird was shouting at Duncan," he said, frowning, trying to remember. "Was there trouble because of me?"

"Nothing that can't be mended. Go to sleep, Arthur, we'll put things right in the morning."

But apparently he couldn't wait. Later that night, I woke to the scuff of a footstep, and saw Arthur go out.

In the morning his bed was empty. I stirred myself and set off for the kitchen, in search of news and perhaps a crust of bread. But before I reached it, I heard shouts of alarm, and a guardsman pounded down the corridor past me. I followed him at a walk. Trouble finds me quick enough without hurrying toward it.

A crowd was clustered near the milltower in the outer bailey wall. I threaded through them close enough to see. It was Arthur, my bear. He lay crumpled against the stone wall, his limbs twisted at impossible angles, his body broken like a crushed insect in the muddy street. His cloak was torn and bloodstained, and his poor face was shattered, bits of bone and teeth gleaming bloody in the morning sun.

There was a stir behind me as Duncan Pentecost thrust his way through the crowd. He was hatless and bleary-eyed, doubtless roused from sleep after his long nightwatch. He knelt beside Arthur's body and gently closed his friend's eyes with his fingertips. Then he tugged Arthur's bloody cloak up to cover his head and turned to face the crowd. And those near him took a step back at the killing rage in his eyes. The others parted as Laird Osbern strode up with two of his sons and several of the Lennox and Menteith traders. "What's happened here?" Osbern asked.

"My friend's been beaten to death," Duncan said coldly. "And I tell you now, my lord, the cowards who did this will not see their pigsty homes again."

"You accuse us of this killing, captain?" the red-bearded Lennoxman said, outraged.

"Perhaps not you personally, Simon of Lennox. But my friend was a soldier. It would take several men to break him like this. And he had no enemies here but your lot."

"We had no trouble with him, Pentecost. Only with you."

"But I was out of your reach last night. Perhaps some of you chanced on Arthur and took out your anger on him."

"Gentlemen," I interjected quietly. "Before this goes further, I think you should look at the body more closely. Arthur was not killed here."

"What do you mean?" Duncan said, whirling to face me as I knelt near the corpse. "Of course he was. And what would a singer know of such matters anyway?"

"I was a soldier before I was a singer," I said, rising. "I've seen death many times in many guises. And I tell you Arthur was not killed where he lies now."

"I don't care if he was killed in Araby," Simon of Lennox said. "I'll not have my men accused of murder by——"

"Curb your tongues and tempers a moment," the laird snapped. "You, minstrel, why do you say he was not killed here?"

"He's been brutally savaged, my lord, and his limbs are broken. If it had happened here, there would be blood spattered on the wall and the ground. But only his cloak is bloodsoaked."

"He's right," Laird Osbern's eldest son put in. "There is no blood about, or at least not enough for the damage done."

"True enough," the laird said, eyeing me shrewdly. "You arrived with the dead man, didn't you, minstrel? He was your friend?"

"Yes, my lord, he was."

"And you know no one else here, no friends or kinsmen?"

"No, lord."

"Then perhaps I see a way past this," Osbern nodded. "The traders planned to leave at midday. If I delay them, it might be said I'm making an excuse to seize their property. Since you are a stranger here, with neither friends *nor* allies," he added pointedly, "perhaps you can be relied on to give a fair accounting. My son Ruari will stay with you to lend you authority. Go where you like, question whom you like. If you discover who has done this to your friend, they shall pay dearly for it. But, minstrel, take care not to accuse anyone falsely. For that would be as great an offense as this. Do you understand?"

"Yes, my lord," I said, swallowing. "I will do what I can."

"And do it quickly," Osbern said. "I'll not risk war with Lennox over one death, however unfortunate. At midday, we'll have done with this whether you discover anything or no. And now, shall we see to our break-fast, gentlemen? I'd hate to hang a man on an empty stomach."

He strode off, trailed by the others. Duncan held back a moment, but at Osbern's pointed glance, he followed.

Young Osbern and I looked each other over warily. He was a bull of a youth, beetle-browed and round-shouldered, with a shaggy mane of dark hair. He wore the plain leather jerkin and pants of a yeoman. Save for his boots, which were finely made, he looked quite ordinary. He'd spoken up boldly about the blood, though, and his eyes were clever as a ferret's.

"So, minstrel," he said, "whom shall we talk to first?"

"The dead man," I said, kneeling beside Arthur's body. I pulled his cloak away from his face and swallowed. It was terrible to see. His skull was crushed, the bone showing clearly through the gash.

"His face has been smashed like a melon," Ruari said, wincing.

"And yet there's very little bleeding from it," I said. "I think he was probably dead already when this occurred."

"His cloak is quite soaked," Ruari said, reaching past me to tug the cloak from beneath the body. Beneath it his coat of mail gleamed dully, except in the small of his back, where it was darkly stained. "Odd. His armor appears intact."

"So it does," I said, tugging the mailed shirt up above the bloodstain, to reveal a puncture wound in the small of his back. "There. That is how he was killed."

Ruari knelt, gingerly touching the hole with his fingertips, in part, I think, to show he wasn't afraid. "I've seen this sort of wound before," he said slowly, "or one similar to it. A spike dagger, needle-bladed to slide through chain mail. That's why his armor is unmarred."

"Who would have such a blade?"

"I don't know," Ruari said. "It's an uncommon weapon. I doubt any of the traders own one."

"What about your father's men?"

"Nor them either," he said. "The blade's too thin to be of use in a fight. A man at arms might carry one into battle to finish a fallen enemy, but it's good for little else."

"Aye," I said. "And Arthur wore no helmet. Since he was struck from behind, he could have been killed as easily with a broadsword, or even with a cudgel. Why use a dagger at all?"

"Or break his bones after? Someone must have hated him greatly."

"Perhaps not. Perhaps he wasn't beaten. His bones could have been broken in a fall."

"From the milltower, you mean? Not likely. A man might break a limb, but not much more."

"But suppose he fell from the castle keep, and struck hard on the slope above us? He might tumble outward to land where he lies now."

"The keep? But what would he be doing there?"

"I don't know. What's directly above us?"

"The armory. But it would've been locked last night."

"Then perhaps I'm wrong. But if he did fall from above, there should be a mark of some kind on the rocks. He would have struck with great force."

"Aye, so he would," Ruari nodded thoughtfully, looking up at the rocky face that slanted steeply down from the stone towers above. "And it would have to be somewhere near the foot of the wall . . ."

He was climbing before he finished his thought, scrambling up the cliff face like a Barbary ape. A few rods below the ashlar facing of the wall he paused, glanced down to get his bearings, then began inching to his left among the rocks.

And then he stopped. He turned cautiously and looked down at me. And raised his hand. And even in the deep shadows of the keep above, I could see his palm was stained with blood.

It was still an hour until noon when Ruari and I strode together into the great hall. The tables were as generously laden with cold game and trenchers as they had been the previous evening, but the mood was taut as a strung bow and no one was eating much. The traders from Lennox and Menteith were seated together, shoulder to shoulder, as though they were ringed by wolves.

And perhaps rightly, for there were a half dozen men at arms arrayed behind Laird Osbern, Duncan Pentecost was guarding the door, and armed yeomen were posted at intervals around the room. Save for Lady Osbern, who sat at her husband's left, no women were present at all.

"Father, gentlemen," Ruari began, but the laird waved him to silence.

"Have you discovered the truth of what happened to the crusader?" he asked.

"I'm not sure. Perhaps."

"Then let the minstrel tell it. If trouble comes from what is said here, on his head be it. Come, stand by me."

Ruari glanced at me, shrugged, and did as he was bid. Leaving me alone in the center of the room. "Now, minstrel, what did you find?"

"We found, my lord, that Arthur Gunn was murdered, struck from behind with a thin blade. A spike dagger."

"A spike dagger?" Osbern echoed, frowning.

"Yes, my lord. And further, he was not killed in the street where he was found. He was killed in the keep, either in the armory or near it, and his body thrown from the wall there."

"The keep? But there was no one up there, save my family and—"

"And Duncan Pentecost," I finished, "who was on duty there." I sensed a movement from behind me, where Duncan stood at the door.

"But Duncan was the lad's friend," Osbern scoffed. "He stood up for him at the feast, ready to fight half the room on his behalf."

"That is true, my lord. Duncan was his friend. In fact, he was the only close friend he had here. And thus the only one he would likely have gone to visit in the night. Where Duncan stood watch. In the keep tower."

"But the stairway guard—"

"Admitted to me that he had a bit too much ale last night," Ruari put in. "He likely was asleep when the crusader went past."

"But even so, Duncan and the crusader were friends."

"And sometimes even friends can fall out," I said quietly. "Over a woman."

"Enough!" Lady Osbern's voice cracked like a whip. "Duncan, will you just stand there and let this English vagabond dirty your name with his lies? He's all but called you murderer—"

"Gentlemen, I am not armed," I said, backing away. "Nor have I accused anyone."

"Duncan! Hold your place, sir!" Laird Osbern snapped. "Madam, forgive me for being such a lout. You're quite right, our hall is no fit place for such talk. And as you gentlemen of Lennox and Menteith have been found blameless, you are no doubt eager to be on your way, are you not?"

"Yes, my lord," Simon of Lennox said hastily, arising. "We have imposed on your hospitality too long already. By your leave we shall be off straightaway."

"Of course. Godspeed to you, Simon, and to all of you. My dear," Osbern said, smiling benignly at his lady, "all this talk has upset you. Perhaps you should retire and rest a bit. Alwyn! See your stepmother to her rooms. As to this other matter, Ruari, minstrel, Duncan, come with me."

He turned and stalked from the hall. I followed, and Ruari pointedly fell into step between Pentecost and myself. Osbern led us a considerable distance from the great hall to a tower guard room with arrow slits for windows and an oaken door.

"Ruari, wait out here and see we're not interrupted. By anyone." He closed the door and turned slowly to face us.

"And now, sirs, we are quite alone. And I will have the truth, from both of you. Minstrel, what did you find up there?"

"Bloodstains on the stones, my lord, near the armory. And on the wall. Arthur was killed there, and his body thrown down."

"I see. And you, Duncan, what have you to say?"

"It was . . . as the minstrel says, my lord," Pentecost said, swallowing. "Arthur and I fell out years ago, before he went crusading. And last night . . . we argued again."

"And you stabbed him from behind? Dishonorably? With a spike dagger? Is that what you are telling me?"

"Yes, my lord."

"I see. And you carry such a blade ordinarily, do you?"

"No, lord, I was . . . he found me in the armory, and we argued, and as he turned to leave, I, ah, seized the dagger from a workbench. And struck him."

"You seized the dagger. You didn't draw your own blade and order your friend to defend himself? And yet a few hours earlier you were ready to fight *for* him. But never mind. This Arthur Gunn came upon you in the armory, you argued, and you killed him. From behind," Laird Osbern said, moving closer to Pentecost until their faces were only inches apart. "And was there, by chance, a witness to any of this, Duncan?"

"Witness, my lord?"

"I'm asking if you were alone when he found you?"

"Yes, my lord," Pentecost said, avoiding the old man's eyes. "Quite alone. I'd gone there to get out of the wind."

"Enough," Osbern said, turning away. "You've killed a man who was my guest, Duncan. I could have you gutted in the courtyard for that alone. But that would only cause my—family further upset. So I offer you a sporting chance, Pentecost. Go from this place, now. Take a mount, but no weapons. In two hours' time, armed men will follow. With orders to kill you on sight. Unless, of course, you have something further to offer in your defense. A mitigating circumstance, perhaps?"

"No, my lord. I have nothing more to say. Now or ever."

"Then be off. Forgive me if I don't wish you luck."

Duncan turned without a word and stalked out. Osbern eyed me for a moment in silence, then shrugged. "So, minstrel, are you satisfied that justice has been done for your friend's death?"

"Yes, my lord. And he wasn't a friend, really, only a companion of the road."

"I see. He behaved strangely last night, but he seemed harmless enough. People tell me you've been at court, minstrel. In London?"

"Yes, lord."

"Then you must have seen many beautiful women. And what do you think of my lady?"

I hesitated a heartbeat. I've been wounded in battle and once I was trapped in a burning stable, but I've never felt nearer death than at that moment. It was in the old man's eyes. I wondered if I would leave the room alive.

"Your wife is truly lovely, my lord. Her hair gleams like a raven's wing, her eyes glow like opals."

"Spoken like a poet," Osbern said dryly, "but that wasn't my point. Any fool can see she's beautiful. It's her . . . deportment that troubles me.

Speaking out of turn as she did today, for example. She's not nobly born, you see. She was only a tanner's daughter. But as my sons are grown and the succession is assured . . . I indulged myself and married for love. And even now, God help me, I do not regret it. Still, a man of my station must maintain certain standards, must he not?"

"As you say, my lord."

"I have an aunt," he said, musing to himself more than to me. "A horse-faced old crone, married to the church. She is abbess of a grim little convent in the highlands north of Pentland. Perhaps I'll send my lady there for a rest. And to learn proper behavior. A few months with my aunt would teach a mule manners. As to the matter of your friend's death, there's still one minor point that troubles me. This woman Duncan and his friend fought over. What do you know of her?"

"Only that she is dead," I said carefully. "Arthur told me she died long ago."

"Did she indeed? What a pity. She must have been very comely to cause all this trouble from beyond the grave."

"We do not know for certain that the argument *was* over the woman, my lord. We have only Duncan's word for that. Perhaps they fought over something else. Men sometimes kill each other over a penny or a look. Or nothing at all."

"So they do," he nodded, satisfied. "You've a glib tongue, minstrel. And you're quick with a song as well. And will you sing of what happened here?"

"No, my lord," I said positively. "A friend murdering a friend over a trifle is no fit subject for a song. It's best forgotten."

"Truly," he said, gazing out the arrow slit. "Best forgotten. Will you be tarrying long in this country, do you think?"

"No, lord. My home is far to the south, and winter is coming on. I'd best be on my way."

"Very wise," he said, without looking at me. "Godspeed to you, minstrel."

I strolled out of Sowerby that afternoon at a leisurely pace, whistling as I went. Until I was out of sight of the watchtower. Then I plunged into the wood and struck hard to the east, running full out as long as I could, then slowly to a steady, mile-eating trot. I found a stream just at dusk, but instead of using the ford, I waded downstream until well after moonrise, finally leaving it many miles below where I'd entered.

Was I being overcautious? Perhaps. But I'd seen Ruari and a band of men-at-arms set out after Duncan in far less time than the two hours the old laird had promised. And I had little doubt that when they'd finished with him, they'd be hunting me.

The old laird knew damned well Duncan hadn't killed his friend over nothing. Arthur had gone to the keep looking for Duncan in the middle of the night. And found him in the armory. But not alone. He was almost certainly with Lady Osbern. Perhaps she'd even struck the blow that killed him. And now Arthur was dead, and Duncan soon would be. And I was the last one who might spread the tale. A proud old man with a young passionate wife fears the sound of laughter more than death itself. He will do anything, even murder, to stop it.

I maintained my killing pace all through the night and the next day. Late that evening, I forded the Tweed into England. Perhaps Osbern's men would not pursue me so far south, but the Tweed is only a river and the border only a line on a map. And Laird Osbern was a tall man with a long reach. I pushed on through the night.

The morning broke clear, a golden October dawn that melted away the shadows and my fears. As the sun climbed slowly through the morn, my spirits rose with it. I was exhausted but too numb to feel much pain. And so I walked on.

And just before midday, a breeze came wafting out of the east, swirling leaves and dirt into a dust devil that seemed to dance ahead of me on the road, leading me on. On a whim, I tried to join in with it, whirling round and round, capering about like a mating partridge. Or a dancing bear.

I shuffled in a circle until my legs finally gave way and I sank to my knees in the road. Still the dust devil danced on ahead. Beckoning me to follow. But not to the south and home.

To the west. Toward Ireland. A land of poets, they say.

I knew of no towns that lay in that direction. But there was a path of sorts. And to those who drift with the wind, one road is much like another.

Vanishing Point

HUGH B. CAVE

hen this Adrian Budd Colby fellow first came to our little mountain village of Wendel, none of us knew who he was. Even if he'd told us his name, I don't believe it would have meant anything to most of us. We've never had a bookshop or library.

Wendel, I have to tell you right off is not the real name of our village. For reasons, as they say, that will become apparent before you finish reading this, I'm not about to tell you its real name, or my name either, or the names of my chums. I will say this much: the village I'm calling Wendel lies not too far from Fort William, in Inverness-shire, from which climbers often tackle the highest peak in our Scottish Highlands, Ben Nevis.

Now, then, what happened is this: old Tom Gurney's wife Ethel, she died, and Tom's daughter in Aberdeen persuaded him to come live with her. Tom was seventy-seven. So he put his house in the hands of some real estate people in our nearest town of any size, and folks began turning up to look at it. Not a whole lot of people, you understand. It isn't everyone wants to live in a place like Wendel, where you have to fence deer and other wild beasties out of your vegetable garden or go hungry, and where the nearest shopping mall is so far away you don't even think of driving to it.

But a few people did come, and decided they didn't want the place, and then this Adrian Budd Colby showed up. As I've said, most of us didn't know who he was at first. Arriving alone in a fancy car, he walked himself into Rosie's, our village restaurant, and introduced himself to Rosie's daughter Mabel, who was only sixteen then.

It's kind of funny the way Luke Wallace tells it. He was there that morning. The feller says, "Good morning, Miss. I'm Adrian Budd Colby," and then just stands there smiling at Mabel, and Mabel stands there with a rag in her hand—she'd been dusting the counter—staring back at him like he'd stepped out of a movie. That's what he looked like, one of those handsome movie stars. There were six or seven people in Rosie's at the time, some eating at the tables and some shopping for stuff on the shelves, and they all sort of stopped what they were doing and watched. And finally the fellow laughs and said, "Well, never mind who I am. For now, anyway. Can you tell me where the Gurney estate is, Miss?"

"Estate?" said Mabel, still staring up at him as if she was mesmerized.

"Well, now," said he, "it *is* quite large, isn't it? I was told it's twenty acres or more."

"Oh," said Mabel. "I see what you mean." And then she told him how to get to the Gurney place, which is half a mile from Rosie's, on the river, and he thanked her and walked out.

He spent the whole rest of that day looking the house and the town over, and stayed with John and Francie Upchurch that night. Francie was taking in overnight guests then and had a sign in front of their house. Next morning, after he'd driven off in his fancy car, Francie and John walked down to Rosie's to report that he was buying the Gurney place.

"Adrian Budd Colby," Francie said. "That's his name, and he's a writer, he said. Does that ring a bell with any of you?"

It did with me, because I read quite a lot for a man who never got to college. "He writes mystery stories," I said. "He's one of the real big names in that field. Well, what do you know? We're going to have a celebrity living here!"

"You mean you've read some of his things?" someone asked.

"Well, I read one book of his. It was too raunchy for my taste, so I never tried any others. But he's big, believe me. He's real big."

Mabel, behind the cash register, frowned at me as if she didn't care for my remark. "He didn't look like a nasty man to me," said she.

"Never said *he* was nasty," I told her. "Just said he wrote nasty stories."

"Well, I liked him," she said. "And I hope he does come here to live."

"Even if he's married, Mabel?" Enid Burns asked with a laugh.

"He isn't married unless it happened just lately," I said. "He got divorced last year. I read about him in some magazine only last month. An interview. The person interviewing him asked why he writes the kind of stories he does, and he said because it satisfied his craving for *real* mystery. He loves real-life mysteries. They challenge his mind, he said."

"Well, I hope he does buy the Gurney place," said Rosie, bagging some groceries for Enid. "It'll be good for business, having a celebrity living here."

"He won't be living here year round," said Francie Upchurch. "Only in summer, he said."

"Never mind. The word'll get out that he comes here, and that'll draw tourists."

Well. This happened in May, in case I haven't said so before. And soon after this first visit of Adrian Budd Colby to our village of Wendel, workmen began arriving to do the Gurney house over. They came every day for the rest of the month and took their meals in Rosie's—where else?—and talked a good deal about what they were doing, and it sounded pretty impressive. "Would've been cheaper for him to tear the place down and build a new one," one of the carpenters, a fellow named Lathan, remarked one time. We got friendly with them—or some of us did—and were able to get in to see what they were up to.

No point in my going into detail, because this isn't about the house; it's about Adrian Budd Colby and a certain place in the mountains known only to five of us. But I can say this: The old Gurney place was the finest-looking house in the village by the time Colby arrived to spend the summer with us. It had a fresh coat of dark gray paint on it, and the yard was neat as a pin, and the workmen had even planted new flowering shrubs all along the front by the road.

"I need someone to cook and keep house for me," Colby said in Rosie's that very first afternoon. "Can I find someone around here, do you suppose?"

The way I heard it, five girls—or young women if you like that term better—applied for the position before nightfall. After all, he was single and rich, and we all knew by now that he was famous. And, as I've said before, he was *handsome*.

He hired Ned Picken's daughter Judy to keep house and Luke Wallace's daughter Leila to do the cooking. Judy was nineteen and Leila twenty, and both were single. You don't have to remember those names. As I told you at the start of this, I can't use any real names in telling this tale.

So then, the first week in June, Adrian Budd Colby moved into his new-bought house planning to spend six or eight weeks honoring us ordinary country folk with his presence, and things began to happen.

Right off, we discovered he had an eye for women. Not just for one or two, but for every blessed one in Wendel who wasn't too old. If it didn't have nothing between its legs, Colby figured he was the one to put something there.

And he hadn't been living in Wendel two weeks when he heard about the door.

He heard about it, I found out later, between seven and seven-thirty one Monday evening when Luke Wallace stopped by to pick up his daughter Leila after she'd finished her day's work. At three minutes to eight that evening, just when my wife and I had settled down to watch a show on our television set—which at that time there were only a handful of in the whole village—we heard a car in our driveway, and our doorbell rang.

Trudy said, "Oh, damn," and went to the door, and there stood Colby.

"Good evening," said he with the smile that our womenfolk were all talking about. "Have I come at a bad time, Mrs. Snowden?"

"Oh, no, no, not at all," said Trudy, like we hadn't even thought about watching the telly. "Come right in, Mr. Colby!"

We don't have an entrance hall like some people. Took it off when carpenter ants got into it one time. Our front door opens directly into our sitting room. So he came in and just stood there waiting to be told to sit, and of course that's what Trudy invited him to do after she'd got through looking at him like he was a movie star in person.

He sat down and looked at me and said, "Mr. Snowden? Ben? May I call you Ben? What's this door that Leila's father has been telling me about?"

"Door?" I said, tightening up. The five of us, you understand, had sworn not to tell a soul.

"Some door in the mountains that you and he and some other men stumbled on last deer-stalking season."

I'm not one to hide my feelings. Trudy told me afterward that my face just about turned to stone. "What—exactly—did Luke tell you?" I said when I got my voice back.

"Not much, actually," he admitted. "But he did say it was a genuine mystery that none of you had ever really tried to solve. We were talking about my work, how I love to chase down such things. What's this about your seeing a *dinosaur?*"

I laughed. "You say you and Luke were talking about your work? You mean those books you write?"

"Yes, and—"

"Well, there's your answer, right there," I said, and laughed again. "Far as I know, Luke Wallace's only read one book in his whole life, and that was *The Lost World* by a fellow named Arthur Conan Doyle. Same man that wrote the Sherlock Holmes stories." I threw that last bit in just to let him know I was better read than some of the folks in Wendel. "I guess if you and Luke were discussing *your* books, Luke just tossed *The Lost World* into the conversation to make it lively. It's not about Scotland, though. It's about a bunch of people exploring some kind of prehistory world they discovered in South America, if I remember it right."

Adrian Budd Colby lowered his head and peered at me from under his half-closed eyelids for a while. Then he said in a real quiet tone of voice, "Is that all you're going to tell me, Ben?"

"That's all there is *to* tell," I said. "*I* don't know about any door in the mountains."

"Well," he said, standing up, "it's probably too soon for me to come around with such questions. After all, I'm new here, and there's no reason for you to trust me." He smiled at my Trudy again. "So I'll just say goodnight then, Mrs. Snowden. But maybe another time . . ." And he departed.

We didn't turn the telly back on. After his car had rolled out of our driveway, we just sat there looking at each other. Then Trudy said, "How much do you suppose Luke told him, Ben?"

"Depends on how much Luke had to drink."

"Should we go over there and ask him, do you think?"

Luke and his wife and daughter lived only a little way down the road from us. We wouldn't even need to get the car out. So I said, "All right, let's just do that," and we walked on down.

They were listening to a program on their big radio, but when we told them what we'd come for, Luke shut it off.

"I admit I mentioned the door to him," he said when I started to give him hell for it. "It just sort of slipped out. We were sitting there while Leila was gathering up her things to come home with me, and he started talking about how fond he was of chasing down mysteries—how solving them was a challenge to him—and I forgot myself. But I barely mentioned it."

"You must've mentioned the dinosaur," I said. "What else did you tell him?"

"Well, I—" Sitting there on his sofa, Luke put his hands on his knees and spread his knees apart and looked down between them at the floor. He shook his head. "I guess I blew it," he admitted. "I told him how it happened."

"The whole thing?"

"Well, not the *whole* thing, Ben. We didn't talk long enough for that. Just how the five of us were stalking deer that day and Martin walked in between those two big rocks . . ."

He went on talking a while longer, but I wasn't listening. In my mind I was back there that afternoon, the previous October, watching my deer-stalking chums disappear.

There we were, the five of us, talking about what a poor day it'd been and how we'd better call it quits and head for home or we'd be caught on the mountain in the dark. We had a three-hour walk ahead of us. But Martin said, "Wait a sec, fellers," and unzipped his fly as he walked toward those two rocks, about twenty, twenty-five feet from where we were standing. And when the rest of us got through talking—which, as I remember it, was about our lack of luck—and I turned and yelled at Martin to shake a leg, come on, let's get moving, well, he just wasn't there any more.

"Now, what the hell is he up to?" Ned Picken said, and went striding over to those two big rocks—which were taller than a man, you understand—and disappeared between them calling out Martin's name. And *he* didn't come back.

That left Luke Wallace and John Upchurch and me standing there wondering what in the world was going on, and Luke said, "You suppose they spotted a deer back in there? Let me go look, and if they did, I'll signal you."

So *he* walked in between those two high rocks, and whole minutes went by, and *he* didn't come back.

John and I yelled a lot then, but nobody answered us. It was like those three men had vanished off the face of the earth.

"There must be something on the other side of those rocks," John said to me. "I hope to God it isn't some kind of precipice they fell down, or some deep hole they dropped into. You know these mountains."

He was right about our mountains, of course. The peaks in our Scottish Highlands may not be as sky-scraping as some others in the world, but they can be treacherous, and people hiking through them quite often get hurt. So John and I were pretty careful walking over to those rocks.

When we got to them, we saw how the space between them was like a tunnel about four feet wide, and real dark because the rocks themselves shut out the afternoon light. So after we'd gone in a way, with me in the lead, I stopped and laid down my rifle. If there was any sort of pit a man could fall into, I didn't want that gun going off by accident and hurting someone. Besides, it was an almost new one and I didn't want anything to happen to it.

So I laid it down, as I've said, and the damnedest thing happened. We were only part way through the tunnel between those rocks, you understand, with me in the lead and nothing out of the ordinary in front of me that I could see, but when I leaned forward and put that rifle down, the whole front end of it disappeared.

Just vanished, as if it had been chopped off with an ax!

I stopped, of course, and John, who was right on my heels in that dark place, didn't see me stop and bumped into me, sending me stumbling forward. And suddenly I wasn't on our mountain any more but in some world I'd never seen before. I was in a crazy world full of strange-looking trees and God-awful rock formations and a lake of some sort that appeared to be covered with green slime. And all at once John Upchurch was there beside me, grabbing at my arm and saying, "For God's sake, Ben, what is this? Where are we? What's happened to us?"

All I knew was that I wanted out of there, fast. But at the same time I kind of knew that Martin and Ned and Luke must be there somewhere, and we oughtn't to leave them. So I started yelling to them and, sure enough, the three of them came running. Or rather they came stumbling toward us through all that creepy vegetation, scared half to death and out of breath when they finally got to us.

"My Lord, Ben," Luke Wallace said, shaking all over like he'd seen a ghost. "There are dinosaurs in there! We saw them!"

Well, I wasn't about to argue. All I wanted was to get out of that place and back into our own world or our own time or whatever. But he was right, and I know he was right because I'd read about dinosaurs. And when I saw something huge and shadowy moving among those weird trees off to our left as we ran back the way we'd come, I knew what it was. Yes, sir, I sure did.

Well . . . all this went through my mind while Trudy and I sat there in the Wallaces' living room listening to Luke explain how he'd so stupidly told Adrian Budd Colby about our finding what we called "the door." In fact, I snapped out of my reverie, if that's the proper word for it, just in time to hear Luke say, "Of course, I explained to Mr. Colby that it wasn't a door, exactly. 'It's more like a doorway,' I told him. 'A doorway into some other world or some other time.'"

"And I suppose he wanted you to take him there," I said.

"That's right, Ben. He even offered me money to guide him. A whole lot of money, in fact. 'You name the figure,' he said. But I said no, I couldn't do that without consulting with you and the others first. Besides, I told him, I wasn't sure we could find the place again. We'd never been back there ourselves."

"And I'll bet he said he didn't believe you," I said.

"Well, he didn't say it outright. But by the look on his face I could tell he didn't." Luke stared down at the floor and shook his head again. "Ben, I'm real sorry. I been a jackass and I know it. What are we going to do?"

"I can't answer that by myself," I said. "I guess we ought to hold a meeting, the five of us." And with that, Trudy and I went on home.

Well, the famous new resident of Wendel kept after us, of course. He approached us one at a time and did his damnedest—his charming damnedest, I have to admit—to win us over. What we'd done, he said, was stumble upon a time warp. That was the expression he used, a time warp.

And being a writer, he just had to investigate it. "If it really exists," he said, "I'll do a blockbuster book about it and make you all famous."

Och aye, we said to one another, he'll make us and our village famous, and every scientific Tom, Dick, and Harry from the whole wide world will come here to explore that "Lost World." Not to mention a few million other people just wanting to rubberneck. And we natives of the village of Wendel would never again have a moment of peace.

No, no, we said among ourselves—we didn't want to be rich or famous at such a terrible cost.

So after a while, as you might expect, Adrian Budd Colby stopped pestering us. And things in Wendel got back to normal. Or would have, except that—as I said before—Colby had all that charm and was so filthy rich and looked like a movie star. Women in a backwoods village the likes of Wendel don't get to see many men who look like movie stars.

You couldn't blame some of them for losing their heads over him.

What happened next was that our women began buying his books by mail, and reading them. Before long almost every house in Wendel had one or more of those books, and almost any time you'd walk into Rosie's Restaurant you'd hear them being talked about. I'm not speaking of plain, ordinary mystery stories, you understand, but about books so raunchy that some of them had been banned in parts of Scotland. And, so help me, some of our women were devouring them.

Also, they were talking to the author of them every time they got a chance. Wherever you saw Adrian Budd Colby you'd see one or more women hanging onto him, laughing and giggling and looking up at him in a way most of us men never got looked at even in our bedrooms. As time went on it got worse and worse, and we men talked about it a lot.

Trudy and I got to talking about it seriously one evening, and Trudy said, "I'll be glad when this summer is over and he goes back to Edinburgh, Ben. There's going to be trouble here."

"You mean there's more to it than hero-worship?" I said.

"I mean he's too big a temptation for some of our younger women, anyway. Like Leila Wallace and Judy Picken, who see him every day in his own house."

"He's over forty," I said. "He wouldn't go for girls that age."

"He isn't the kind of man to say no if they go for *him*, Ben," she said. "Would you believe me if I told you he made a pass at *me* one day last week?"

I just looked at her. My Trudy didn't lie to me, ever.

"It's true," she said. "I was walking home with some groceries and he offered me a lift in that fancy car of his. We got to laughing about how almost everyone in town was reading his books, and the next thing I knew he had a hand on my knee and was telling me I was really too pretty to be wasting my time in a mountain village. I ought to come visit him in Edinburgh this winter, he said, so he could show me a different kind of life."

"What did you say to that?"

"Laughed, of course. What else could I do? But if he made such a pass at me, you can bet I'm not the only one. Lots of women in Wendel are prettier than I am. Just to name one of them, what about Francie?"

She meant Francie Upchurch, and a funny thing happened a week or so later. Adrian Budd Colby called on us one evening with what he said was an advance copy of his newest mystery novel, and while he was sitting at our diningroom table, signing it for us, he just casually dropped the name of John Upchurch into what he was saying. If I remember rightly, it went something like this:

"This particular book of mine might interest you more than some of my others, Ben. It's about a man who finds the key to his nightmares and can enter them at will. And speaking of other worlds, John Upchurch told me yesterday he remembers where the doorway to *your* other world is."

I just looked at him.

"So . . . don't you think we might talk again about your taking me there, Ben?" he said. "I'll make it worth your while, believe me."

I shook my head.

"Why not?" he said. "What harm can it do?"

"We like our village the way it is," I said. "We don't want it overrun with hordes of crazies." In fact, I thought, we'd like it to be the way it was before *you* came here and began seducing our womenfolk.

"Well, think about it, Ben," he said with that smile of his. "My offer is still open. If I walk through that doorway of yours into the world that's been described to me, I'll put this place on the map and make all of you filthy rich."

I called on John Upchurch the very next day and said, "All right now, John. What exactly did you tell Colby about our doorway?"

"Only that I remember where it is and could take him there."

"Why'd you tell him that, for God's sake? Don't you realize you've opened up the whole bag of worms again?"

John just sat there in his easy chair and stared at me. We were alone, the two of us. His wife Francie had gone down to Rosie's for some groceries.

Have I mentioned before that John Upchurch was forty-four years old and a real nice, down-to-earth fellow with the misfortune of having a wandering eye? I don't mean an eye for the ladies—with a wife as pretty as his Francie was, he'd have been stupid to look at any other woman. I mean the kind of an eye that actually keeps looking off to one side.

Well, sir, for the next ten minutes or so, while he told me his suspicions, that wandering eye didn't wander. It stared at me as straightforwardly as his good one. And what he told me made me a little sick to my stomach.

He'd actually seen his Francie and our famous writer *doing* it, if you know what I mean. In the man's car, at the far dark end of Rosie's parking lot.

But we didn't take Colby to our doorway then. When I pointed out that it was nearly time for the fellow to return to Edinburgh for the winter, John agreed to wait and see what would happen when summer came again. And he wasn't to blame his Francie, I told him. "My Lord, John, half the women in Wendel would probably do the same if he asked them to. Ordinary men like us don't stand a chance."

So Adrian Budd Colby returned to the big city, and winter came, and things were almost normal for a while. But in May, Lord help us, he came back.

And within a week he was at it again.

The whole of Wendel was watching him this time, because we'd spent the winter talking about it. First he had an affair with nineteen-year-old Judy Picken, who was keeping house for him again. Then with Leila Wallace, who was cooking for him like before. Then with two or three older women. Then with John Upchurch's wife Francie again, not in Rosie's parking lot this time but in his own home, for God's sake. And then he invited Martin Burns's wife Enid to go to Inverness with him, shopping. And Martin followed them and saw them go into a motel there.

The next day Martin called on each of us and asked for a meeting, and we got together that evening at Ned Picken's house. Ned's wife and daughter had gone for an overnight visit with his wife's folks in Fort William.

We talked for about an hour. Then Martin said, "Well, are we all agreed?"

One by one we nodded or said we were.

"And are we agreed on when to do it?" Luke Wallace asked.

"This weekend, if he's willing," said Upchurch.

"Oh, he'll be willing, all right," Ned Picken said. "If he was here right now, he'd want to start up there this minute."

Next morning I called on Adrian Budd Colby and told him we'd agreed to show him our doorway. His eyes lit up like stars over Ben Nevis peak on a clear summer night, and he all but wrung my hand off.

"I'll write you out a check," he said.

We had agreed not to take any money from him, so I shook my head. "Later, maybe," I said. "After we've taken you up there and you're convinced there really is such a place. Can you be ready at daybreak?"

"Ready and eager!" said he in a loud voice.

"So be it," said I, and went on home.

Well.

This was in July, when it gets to be daylight real early in our mountains. So the five of us and Adrian Budd Colby set out from his house about quarter to six. And I want to tell you, that man was excited. He did all the talking. The rest of us just hiked along, speaking only when we had to answer his questions.

We didn't do much of that, either. Answer his questions, I mean. We'd agreed among the five of us to say as little as possible. So mostly what we said was, "You'll see, Mr. Colby. Just be patient, and you'll see when we get there."

Now it's no easy climb up to where those big rocks are. Takes a good mountain man maybe two hours, and with Colby along we didn't come close to doing it in that. Oh, he was strong enough. I said before, didn't I, that he was six-foot-three or thereabouts, and built solid? But he was a city man, after all. Half a dozen times, on his account, we had to stop and rest. And while we were resting, he'd ask questions.

"Now let me get this straight," he said once. "What you saw when you passed through this doorway of yours was a kind of primeval forest. Right?"

"You'll see," I said.

"Somebody—you, Luke, I think—mentioned Conan Doyle's *The Lost World*. Said you'd read that book. And was it like that, this place you found yourselves in?"

"Something like that," Luke said.

"A forest? Strange trees you didn't know the names of?"

"And a lake," Martin said, "all green with slime, and big things swimming in it."

"What kind of things?"

"Couldn't see them too well. Just the wakes they made, and their big scaly heads stickin' up out of the slime. Somethin' like the Loch Ness monster, maybe."

Colby could hardly control himself. "And dinosaurs? You said you saw dinosaurs!"

"Yeah," Ned said. "Those, too."

Colby jumped up, so excited his face seemed on fire. "Then come on, come on!" he shouted. "What are we wasting time here for?"

So we finally got there, and the place was just as I remembered it: those two tall rocks with a dark tunnel running in between them, and both the rocks and the forest blocking out the light so much that even at nine in the morning you couldn't see very far into the tunnel.

We stopped there in front of the rocks to get our breath, and then I stepped forward. I say I stepped forward because the five of us—Martin, Luke, John, Ned, and I—had cut a pack of cards the day before to decide who would take him in, and I'd drawn the two of spades.

"All right, Mr. Colby," I said. "Just follow me now, and I'll show you."

And I was scared.

I was scared because I wasn't carrying a rifle this time. You remember I had one the other time I went in there, and laid it down just before I stepped through the doorway, and the whole barrel of that gun disappeared as if it had been chopped off with an ax? You remember that? Well, this time all I had was a plan of action.

So when I reached the exact same spot where I'd laid down my gun before, I took only one more step and froze. Not for all the money in Adrian Budd Colby's bank account would I have taken a second step. There I was, just one step inside that other world or time warp or whatever it was—and Colby was all at once there beside me.

"God in heaven!" he said in a kind of raspy whisper, then let out a crazy yell and went racing off to explore the place.

As I've said, I didn't move. Not even a muscle. I just stood there and watched him go tearing into that weird forest, with all those strange vines and things dangling from trees I couldn't put a name to, and that slimy looking lake in the distance, and—yes—another of those big, shadowy dinosaur things down at the lakeshore, drinking.

Then when Colby was out of sight and I couldn't hear him any more, I took a single step *backward*, praying to God I hadn't made a mistake in my calculations, and found myself on the right side of our doorway again. With Martin and Luke and John and Ned crowding around, asking me what happened.

"He tore off into the forest there," I said. "Never even glanced back to see if I was with him."

"It figures," Martin said.

"We ought to wait around, though, just in case," said Luke. "We shouldn't ought to go home right off."

"Och, aye," I agreed. And so we did. In fact, we hung around there until four o'clock. But Colby didn't come out.

"Remember how it was when we went in there?" Luke said. "How everything in that crazy forest looked the same, no matter which way we turned? All those trees and vines and weird-looking blossoms, and not a clue to tell us where the doorway was?"

"How we searched for hours and hours and thought we'd never find the way out?" Ned said. "My God, I was scared. I still have nightmares about it."

"Me, too," said John. "Sometimes I wake up thinking I've been wandering around in there for years, with no chance of *ever* getting back to this world. One morning the bed was so wet, Francie asked me if I'd peed in my sleep."

"And we just *might* be there yet if it hadn't been for me laying my rifle down just before I happened to step through the doorway," I said. "You remember the yell I sent up when I finally discovered the rifle barrel in that mess of stinking yellow flowers in there, showing us where the doorway had to be?"

They remembered, all right. For a while they just sat there looking at me. Then we decided it was time to go home. Home to our womenfolk, who we wouldn't have to worry about any more.

So.

Writing all this down now, I'm eighty-seven years old and the last one left of the five of us. The doc tells me I have maybe three months left— my lungs are gone—and my Trudy's been dead for six and a half years, so I'm more than ready. But I figure the world is entitled to know what really happened to Adrian Budd Colby, and that's why I'm telling this.

The tale we told at the time was good enough to keep us out of trouble, you understand. We just said he'd wandered off and got lost and most likely fell into a ravine somewhere. That happens in our mountains, as I've said. They searched for him for days without finding any body, but that happens, too.

None of us ever had any regrets about showing him our doorway, I want you to know. After all, he claimed to be keen about solving real-life mysteries, and all we did was give him a real good one to work on.

The Adventure of the Callous Colonel

BASIL COPPER

1

hat on earth are you doing there, Pons?"

I paused on the threshold of our sitting-room at 7B Praed Street in astonishment. It was a bitterly cold morning in early February and I had just come in from a particularly fatiguing case.

On opening the door I was immediately confronted with the spectacle of my friend Solar Pons, his lean, angular figure recumbent on the carpet, his right hand holding the gleaming barrel of a revolver flat against a bolster taken from one of our armchairs. Beyond the bolster was a plaster bust of Napoleon which normally lived on top of a bookcase in the far corner.

Pons laughed and got up, dusting the knees of his trousers.

"Just indulging in a little amateur theatricals, Parker."

I glanced down at the mess on the carpet, the rich crimson firelight glinting over the pale surface of the bust. To my astonishment I saw there was a small hole in one side of it and a distinct smell of burning.

"It looks as though your services will be in demand at the Lyceum, Pons, if this goes on," I said somewhat tartly, noting that there was a hole drilled clean through the bolster.

My companion chuckled, his right hand softly stroking the lobe of his right ear.

"*Touché*, Parker. You are developing quite a pretty wit of late. I see I shall have to be on my mettle."

He looked down ruefully at the bolster and the bust.

"But you are right in one respect. I fear my little drama will not be greatly appreciated by Mrs Johnson. If you had been but five minutes earlier you would have heard the muffled explosion."

I looked at him in astonishment.

"Good heavens, Pons! You don't mean to tell me you have actually fired that thing in here?"

My friend shook his head.

"Oh, I can assure you, Parker, there was little danger. I had carefully worked out the possible impact. The bullet has just penetrated the surface of the bust, the greater force of the blow having been taken by the cushion. That explains both the crushing impact of the wound, consistent with the unfortunate man having apparently shattered his head upon the stony ground, and the lack of any sound for people who were passing the edge of the Forest only a few hundred yards away. It also had another advantage in that there was no scorching of the wound which would have given the game away in short order."

I put my medical case down on my armchair and my overcoat on top of it and drew nearer to the fire. I looked at Pons with rising irritation.

"I wish I knew what you were talking about."

"I am sorry, Parker. I sometimes forget that you are not always *au fait* with my cases. I was merely conducting a little experiment in ballistics. Though the characteristics of a bullet striking plaster are different from that of flesh, I fancy my theory will stand up in court. Sufficiently, I trust, to put paid to the unspeakable activities of the abominable Mr Horace Mortiboys of Epping."

His deep-set eyes looked so angry and vengeful at that moment that I was quite taken aback. Then he seemed to recollect himself and stirred as I spoke again.

"I did not realise, Pons. One of your cases, eh? I trust you have now brought it to a successful conclusion."

"I think we may say so, my dear fellow. Come and sit near the fire. Lunch will be served in a quarter of an hour or so."

"I must say I could do with it," I returned. "Just give me a few moments to put my things away and wash my hands."

When I returned to the sitting-room Pons had tidied the carpet, the bust was back *in situ* on the bookcase, the damaged side away from the viewer; and the rumpled bolster on one of the chairs. Pons had evidently returned the revolver to his bedroom for there was no sign of it. He sat in his own chair to one side of the fire indolently reading *The Times* as though he had not a thing in the world on his mind.

After a few minutes he put down the paper and turned his deep-set eyes on me.

"What do you know about Colonel Alistair McDonald, Parker?"

I glanced up from the fire in mild surprise.

"Not a thing, Pons," I admitted. "Should I?"

My companion shook his head, a faint smile on his face.

"Your field is altogether too specialised, Parker. You have been missing something. Explorer, big-game hunter, stalker, collector of esoteric objects, he also has regrettable criminal tendencies which have made him a good deal of money. At the present time I should class him as the third most dangerous man in Europe."

Solar Pons tented his slender fingers before him and stared broodingly into the fire.

"In fact he has twice tried to kill me, the most recent occasion being yesterday."

"Good heavens, Pons! You cannot mean it?" I spluttered.

Solar Pons shook his head.

"I wish I were not serious, Parker. A parcel came for me yesterday. If I had not been on my guard, I should not be sitting here talking to you now."

He glanced over at his desk in the far corner.

"Just take a look at that. But please do not touch the thing. I should burn it, by rights, but I am retaining the ingenious toy as possible evidence."

I got up and crossed the room to stare down at the brown-paper parcel which sat on my friend's blotter. It had been opened out and a strange wooden idol figure sat in the midst of it. It had a curiously shaped base, with a marked indentation in the front, obviously to fit the thumb of a person holding the image by the base. I saw now that there was a small steel needle protruding from the front of it.

"I do not understand, Pons," I remarked, as I resumed my seat.

"It is simple, Parker," Solar Pons commented. "I might have picked it up from the cardboard box but for the fact that I noted a minute hole in the shallow depression in front of the thing. I procured a pair of pliers with which to hold it and with the aid of a heavy ruler I applied pressure. The result was quite dramatic, the needle stabbing forward through the hole. After analysis I found that the needle, which is of the ordinary sewing variety, had been impregnated with a solution of curare, which I need not tell you is a deadly poison, which speedily produces paralysis and death."

I gazed at Pons open-mouthed.

"But why should this Colonel McDonald wish to kill you, Pons? And how do you know he sent the idol?"

Solar Pons chuckled drily.

"It has all the hallmarks of the Colonel's ingenious mind, Parker. The thing is entirely hand-made. The carving, the staining with red varnish, the glass-eyes, the skilful painting of the features, and the heavy spring-mechanism, typical of the skilled toy-maker, bear all the signs of the Colonel's ingenuity. The parcel was post-marked Putney by the bye, so he and his agents are not far away."

"I still do not understand, Pons."

"Tut, Parker, the matter is simple enough. A few months ago I was instrumental in exposing a gross public swindle, involving a non-existent housing scheme on the Riviera. The company responsible was headed by puppets, of course, but I have no doubt the Colonel's hand was behind the thing. He lives in Inverness, incidentally, and the intricate machinations of these schemes are peculiar to him. In fact I am informed by Scotland Yard that inquiries into the fraud may take two years or more, with no guarantee of conviction. The directors of the scheme are figureheads and the police have so far found no visible trace of McDonald in the affair. But I have no doubt my interference has rankled."

Pons twisted down the corners of his mouth and looked mockingly over at the parcel in the far corner.

"Just peruse his entry in that current volume of *Who's Who*, if you would be so good."

I brought the weighty volume to my armchair and studied it. I soon found the item I wanted. McDonald's entry was impressive indeed. He lived at Ardrossan Lodge near a small village about twenty miles from Inverness. I went down the article with increasing puzzlement.

"He is a scholar too, Pons."

"Is he not, Parker."

"Publications include, 'The Sphere and the Triangle' (1914) and 'The Dimensions of Ecstasy' (1923)," I said.

Pons chuckled drily.

"Oh, yes, the Colonel has a great deal to him. The Dimensions of Ecstasy indeed. He is as much at home among the shelves of the library and the higher philosophy as he is at a rough shoot or on one of the crags of his native heath."

I put down the volume on the table.

"You intrigue me, Pons. This business is serious."

Solar Pons looked at me sombrely.

"Serious indeed, Parker. It can only end one way or another. We have been conducting a struggle at long-distance for the past six years or so. I really must take up the challenge."

I looked at him sharply.

"You have something in mind?"

"There is a matter in train which bears the unmistakable stamp of Master McDonald," my friend went on. "I fancy he sent me the parcel because he wished to clear the decks before putting it in motion."

His eyes were fixed somewhere up beyond me at the ceiling.

"I really would give a great deal to checkmate him."

He broke off abruptly.

"Ah, there is Mrs Johnson's motherly tread upon the stair. We will take up this matter again after lunch."

2

My sick calls took me out again in the afternoon and it was not until the early evening that I once again set eyes on my friend. A thin fog was swirling about the streets and I was glad to get indoors. When I entered the sitting-room I found Pons in consultation with a tall, fair-haired girl of about twenty-five, whose pink cheeks and flashing eyes bespoke some degree of agitation.

"Ah, this is my friend and colleague, Dr Lyndon Parker," said Pons, rising from his chair and effecting the introductions. "Allow me to pre-

sent my client, Miss Jennifer Hayling of Wortley Hall, Norfolk, and Inverness."

"Inverness, Pons!"

I could not resist an involuntary start and Miss Hayling paused in shaking hands, before favouring me with a brief smile.

"This is connected with Colonel McDonald, then, Pons?" I asked as I took off my overcoat and drew my chair up to the fire.

"Indeed it is, Dr Parker," said the young lady indignantly, "though I cannot prove it. But a more thorough-going rascal it has never been my misfortune to encounter until now."

I looked at her in surprise.

"I really must press upon you the necessity of telling your story again, Miss Hayling," said Pons quickly. "That is, if we are to persuade the doctor to accompany us to Scotland for I certainly cannot do without him."

My surprise grew.

"Scotland, Pons! Good heavens! It is a long way in such inclement weather."

"It is indeed, Parker," said my companion smoothly, "but it is vitally urgent that I travel there. It is a matter of life and death."

I sat looking from one to the other for a long moment.

"I will certainly come, Pons, in that case. Though what my locum will say I cannot tell."

"There will be time enough to make arrangements, Parker. We shall not need to depart until tomorrow."

"Leave it to me," I said, with a reassuring smile at Miss Hayling.

Our visitor, who was elegantly dressed in a well-cut overcoat with a fashionable fur collar, now resumed her seat at the fireside, removing her outer garment to reveal a full-fashioned figure clad in a thick jersey dress. On her head she wore a West End milliner's version of what passes in the South for a Scottish lady's tam-o-shanter with a knitted bobble.

The young lady smiled as though she had guessed what I was thinking.

"I have only just returned from Scotland, Dr Parker, and I like to give some token respect to the land of my adoption."

"Certainly, Miss Hayling," I returned. "I was thinking it most becoming."

"You are extremely gallant this evening, Parker," said Pons gravely.

"But I fear these sartorial notations are coming between us and the young lady's story."

With a brief smile at both of us, our attractive visitor plunged into her tale without more ado.

"As I already told you in my letters, Mr Pons, I am an orphan, living mainly in the Norwich area. My mother was Scottish and the family once owned considerable estates near Inverness. During the time of my parents' marriage they divided their time between Glen Affric and Norwich, where my father had business interests. Both my parents were killed in a tragic accident a little over a year ago."

A cloud passed over her face and she paused, as though the recollection were painful to her.

"I am so sorry, Miss Hayling," I mumbled, with a quick glance at Pons.

He sat with his brows knitted, as though concentrating fiercely, several sheets of paper, evidently his client's letters, spread out on the table at his side. At the girl's extended permission he lit his pipe and was soon contentedly wreathed in aromatic blue smoke.

"I would not have referred to it again except that Mr Pons seems to think the matter of some significance," the girl resumed.

"It may be, Miss Hayling, it may be," Solar Pons interjected. "There is a wealth of difference. Pray continue."

With a shy smile in my direction, our visitor went on, "You would not, of course, know Glen Affric or the terrain thereabouts, but it is, as you might imagine, hilly, with steep winding roads, often little more than lanes. The road from the main gates of Glen Affric is extremely steep and winds down through rather forbidding pine forests. It is well enough in summer but in winter, especially during icy conditions, can be extremely dangerous.

"I had often told my parents to take the car and they usually did so but they were inordinately fond of driving about the neighbourhood in a pony and trap, as my father, who was not a Scot at all, loved to pose as a laird, which caused both him and my mother great amusement."

The girl smiled reminiscently, as though she could see her dead parents' images rising before her once again in the flesh and I must say I was touched at the warmth of her expression.

"The road turns at right angles across an old stone bridge, which spans a ravine through which a stream runs. It was there, just at the bridge entrance, that the accident happened. The shafts snapped on the turn, the pony went on, but both my parents and the vehicle crashed through the wooden guard-rail into the ravine below."

Our visitor was silent as though re-living the horror of the moment and I broke the silence, tactfully, I thought.

"I see, Pons. In the wintry conditions, no doubt the horse slipped at the turn and the unwonted strain on the shafts broke the wood, thus precipitating the tragedy."

"Perhaps, Parker," said my companion softly, his eyes flashing me a discreet warning. "The point is that it was unusually mild spring weather at the onset of April last year and the road was firm and dry."

I must have sat with my mouth open for a second or two and by that time the young lady had recovered herself.

"It was after my parents' death, Mr Pons; some months in fact, when I had come back to Scotland and was going through their papers, that I found the letters from the Scottish Land Trust, signed by their President, Mungo Ferguson."

"Mungo Ferguson," said Pons through the thin banners of smoke, his voice soft and almost dreamy.

"Tell me about him again, Miss Hayling."

"He is a loathsome creature, Mr Pons. A bully and a braggart. A great, red-bearded man who thinks he can ride roughshod over other people's rights."

Solar Pons smiled, taking his pipe out of his mouth.

"He did not ride roughshod over you at any rate, Miss Hayling," he observed. "For you took a whip and showed him off the estate, did you not?"

The girl flushed and there were little sparks of amusement dancing in her eyes.

"Indeed I did, Mr Pons!" she said spiritedly, "and I believe I have adequately described the incident in my letters."

"Good heavens, Miss Hayling!" I exclaimed. "And this is the brute we are up against?"

Solar Pons shook his head, smiling at me through the coils of smoke.

"Hardly, Parker. You have surely not forgotten our earlier conversation. Ferguson is merely the cloak for something far more sinister. Let us hear something of the letters, Miss Hayling. You did send me a sample and I have in fact already checked on the registration of the company in question. The Scottish Land Trust, with Ferguson as President was first registered something over eighteen months ago and has a paid-up capital of £100."

I looked at Pons in surprise.

"That does not sound very impressive, Pons."

Solar Pons chuckled drily.

"You have not seen their notepaper, Parker. That is impressive enough at any event."

"Then you think the whole thing a swindle, Mr Pons?" said the girl impetuously. "They have offered a good price for the house and land."

"Too good, though it is genuine enough, at any rate," said my companion sombrely. "I think you would find the money forthcoming readily enough if you were to agree to their request."

"But fifty thousand pounds, Mr Pons! The whole estate is not worth a fraction of that. The house is well enough but the rest is just 300 acres of woodland, with some coarse grazing. There is not even any shooting or a trout stream or anything of the sort."

My astonishment must have shown on my face.

"Fifty thousand pounds, Pons?"

"Interesting, is it not, Parker. This is why Miss Hayling's little problem intrigues me so. Have a look at this."

My friend passed me an impressive, blue-tinted deckle-edged sheet of stationery, which had very elaborate headings in flowing script printed on it.

The legend, Scottish Land Trust, Registered Offices, Carnock House, Inverness, was followed by a list of directors whose names meant nothing to me. The letter, addressed to Miss Hayling's parents, was an offer, couched in unctuous terms, of fifty thousand pounds sterling for the estate known as Glen Affric. It was dated more than a year earlier and signed by Mungo Ferguson. I passed it back to Pons with a non-committal grunt.

"We are rather running ahead of ourselves," said he. "Just let me *précis* the situation. Mr and Mrs Hayling were made an astronomical offer for

Glen Affric estate, which is worth only a fraction of that, about eighteen months ago. They refused, as they had a great affection for the place, which is nevertheless worthless from a commercial development point of view.

"Mungo Ferguson, the President, persisted with the offer, however, and said that the Trust wished to develop the property as a leisure and holiday centre and the site was the only place suitable for many miles around."

"There may be something in that, Mr Pons," the girl muttered, searching Pons' face with attentive eyes.

"A short while after the last of these letters, Mr and Mrs Hayling died in the tragic accident with the pony and trap," Pons continued. "Following the funeral Miss Hayling returned to Norwich and the Scottish house, with a reduced staff of three, remained in her ownership. But about six months ago the Trust's offers were repeated by letter, at the lady's Norwich address. What could be the reason behind such persistence?"

"I have no idea, Pons."

"Nevertheless," my companion returned. "It raises a number of interesting possibilities. This company seems inordinately concerned with this piece of ground. However, it is something which cannot be fully appreciated without seeing the terrain."

"You think the company genuine, Pons?"

Solar Pons tented his thin fingers before him.

"Oh, it is genuine enough so far as it goes, Parker. Miss Hayling, nothing if not a persistent young lady, has been to the Trust's headquarters in Inverness. They have a proper office there, which is open at fixed hours on five days a week, though the one clerk employed there has little to do. But I am holding up Miss Hayling's narrative. There are far more sinister overtones to come."

"You have put the situation admirably, Mr Pons," said the girl. "This was how things stood until I returned to live again in Scotland back in the autumn."

"You had been called there by your old servants, had you not?"

"Yes indeed, Mr Pons. By Mr and Mrs McRae, steward and housekeeper respectively. They are the only staff now apart from Mackintosh, the outside man and gardener."

"Something strange had happened, I understand."

The girl nodded, her eyes worried.

"Strange enough, Mr Pons. After I had received McRae's letter I thought I had better get the first available train."

Solar Pons blew a little eddying plume of blue smoke up toward the ceiling of our sitting-room.

"It began with noises in the night, did it not?"

"That is so, Mr Pons. Neither Mr McRae nor his wife are what you might call sensitive or over-imaginative people. They are, on the contrary, stolid, strong-minded and dependable. Mackintosh likewise."

"The house is a lonely one, I understand?"

"You could say that. The nearest habitation is about five or six miles away but that is irrelevant as the property itself, in extensive grounds, is approached by a long private road and well screened by heavy belts of trees."

"There were noises at first, you say."

"Yes, Mr Pons. Odd scratches, as though someone were trying the shutters at dead of night. McRae got up and ran out, but though it was a fine moonlight night, saw nothing. Another time there were footsteps and after odd banging noises a window was found open, as though it had been forced. On yet another occasion Mackintosh found a set of heavy foot-marks across a flower-bed after rain. They had obviously been made during the dead hours of the night, for they were not there the eve-ning before."

Solar Pons nodded.

"Which brings us to the fire."

"Yes, Mr Pons. Though not serious it might well have been. Some out-houses, which stand between the main house and the stable-block, caught fire. Fortunately, Mr and Mrs McRae together with Mackintosh, who lives in a nearby cottage, were able to contain the outbreak with a garden hose but two of the sheds were completely destroyed."

I looked at my companion.

"An accident, Pons?"

The girl shook her head.

"They found a three-quarters empty petrol can near the scene of the fire. It was obviously deliberate. The police were called in but found nothing."

Solar Pons blew out a little plume of smoke from the corner of his mouth.

"What do you make of that, Parker?"

"Why, coercion, Pons," I said. "The Land Trust wants Miss Hayling's property badly. Now they are putting on pressure to force her out."

"Splendid, Parker," said Solar Pons, a twinkle in his eye. "You really are improving all the time. Those are my thoughts exactly and though the conclusion is a trite and obvious one it appears to me that my training is beginning to bear fruit. The question is, what does the Land Trust really want? And why should anyone desire such a remote and isolated property, which has no obvious commercial value."

"Exactly, Mr Pons," put in Miss Hayling. "Farming is a depressed industry anyway and despite the Trust's explanations, the one obvious use to which the land could be put is ruled out, because the estate is unsuitable for that purpose. The timber might be of some value, if it could be cut and marketed, but even that qualification is doubtful."

"There is more to come, Pons?" I asked.

"Oh, a deal, Parker, a deal. I must apologise for these constant interruptions, Miss Hayling, but such sifting and evaluation of points as they arise, together with the comments of my good friend the doctor here, are a valuable factor in refining the ratiocinative processes."

There was a dry and humorous expression on Pons' face as he spoke and I saw little sparks of humour dancing in the girl's own eyes.

"Well, Mr Pons, as I have already informed you by letter, things got rapidly worse. I had no sooner been apprised of the fire when something even more serious occurred. Mackintosh, the gardener surprised someone in the shrubbery one dark evening a few days afterwards, and was attacked in consequence. He struck his head on a stone bordering the driveway as he fell and briefly lost consciousness.

"But he is a strong and vigorous man, fortunately, and came to no permanent harm. As soon as he was himself he roused the household, the police were called and a search made of the neighbourhood. But the terrain is hopeless as there are so many places of concealment and the perpetrator of this outrage was never found. On receipt of that news I immediately made my way from Norwich and took up residence at Glen Affric."

"When even more serious events took place, Miss Hayling."

"Indeed, Mr Pons. But not before being preceded by two letters, both signed by Mr Mungo Ferguson, and both repeating the original offer of the Land Trust."

"You took no notice of them?"

"Of course not, Mr Pons. On these occasions I did not even bother to reply. But one afternoon, a fortnight ago, I had returned from a brisk walk on the hillside when I heard voices from the stable area. I found Mr McRae, my steward, having a fierce argument with a huge, red-bearded man dressed in riding clothes. He had come up in a dog-cart and the pony had been tied to the railings. McRae had found him wandering about the property uninvited, which had led to words. But he raised his hat civilly enough to me and introduced himself, asking for a private interview. I did not wish to invite him into the house and decided to keep McRae within earshot, so we walked a few yards away to talk.

"He introduced himself as Ferguson and again repeated his offer from the Land Trust and when I refused, somewhat vehemently, he became abusive. I think he had been drinking and it was then, in the course of the interview, that he made an improper suggestion."

Miss Hayling paused and her cheeks were pink, her eyes gleaming with the recollection. Solar Pons' own deep-set eyes turned on her sympathetically.

"An improper suggestion, Miss Hayling?"

"Yes, sir. It was one no lady could repeat to a gentleman. I am afraid I lost my temper completely. Ferguson was holding a riding crop loosely in his hand as we talked and I seized it and beat him about the head and shoulders with it. He was so surprised that he retreated rapidly. I threw the whip after him, he got quickly up into his trap and with many curses drove rapidly off and good riddance to him."

"Well done, my dear young lady," I could not resist saying and Solar Pons looked at the pair of us, a slight smile playing around his lips.

"And what did McRae do all this time?"

"He was as astonished as Ferguson, Mr Pons. But there was no doubt he approved."

"Which brings us to three days ago."

"That is correct, Mr Pons. I felt thirsty after retiring to my room and came down to Mrs McRae's kitchen to get a glass of milk. It was late—or what passes for late in the Highlands—just turned half-past eleven, and I was passing a side-door to get to the kitchen when I heard a sound outside. There was only a dim light burning in the far hallway and the rest of the building was in darkness.

"I distinctly heard a foot grate on the stone step outside and then the iron door-latch was lifted once or twice as though someone was testing to see whether it was locked. I can tell you, Mr Pons, it was somewhat unnerving at that hour of night in such a lonely place to hear and see such a thing."

"I can well imagine, Miss Hayling. You called out, I believe?"

"I shouted, 'Who is there?', more to keep my courage up than anything else. The latch was abruptly released and I heard the sound of hurried footsteps on the flagged path outside. I put on the outside porch light and went out to see who it was, but there was nothing."

"That was a brave thing," I said.

"But extremely unwise, Parker," Solar Pons admonished.

And to the girl.

"You did nothing further that night?"

"No, Mr Pons. I re-locked the door, got my milk and went to bed. But I was much troubled in my mind though I did not mention the matter to Mr and Mrs McRae. All the staff had been greatly disturbed by these incidents and I had no wish to lose their services. Which brings me to yesterday afternoon."

Pons' client paused as though recollecting her thoughts and went on in a low, even voice.

"I had been out for a walk after lunch and my ramble had taken me to the northern portion of the estate, which abuts Glen Affric, a wild and lonely place, bordered by one of our local mountains of the same name. It was cold, grey and overcast and I had heard shooting earlier."

"Surely it is not the season?" I said.

Miss Hayling shook her head.

"No, but there are many local people who shoot rabbits and other small creatures for the pot during the winter months, so I took no particular notice. I was standing on the path, looking up the glen, taking in the romantic charm of the scene and thinking about nothing in particular when there came another shot, much closer this time. Mr Pons, it was aimed at me and the bullet passed through the bushes only four or five feet from my head!"

3

There was a long silence which I felt incumbent upon myself to break. "Good heavens! This is serious indeed!"

"Is it not, Parker," said Pons, rubbing his thin fingers together, suppressed energy evident in every line of his frame.

"What did you do next?"

"I am afraid I panicked, Mr Pons. I took to my heels down the path and did not rest until I was safe in the house again."

Solar Pons nodded sombrely.

"You have done wisely, Miss Hayling. This is a black business. That shot was undoubtedly intended for you."

"But what does it all mean, Mr Pons?"

"That is what I intend to find out. I have formed tentative theories but must wait until we are upon the ground before testing them. That was when you sent me the telegram?"

"Yes, Mr Pons. Some weeks earlier I had remembered my father once speaking of you in connection with some case you had solved. It was then I first wrote you and apprised you of the situation and our ensuing correspondence has been the only thing which has strengthened my resolve in this business. I had Mackintosh get the trap and take the telegram into the village post office for transmission."

"Which was undoubtedly known to McDonald within the hour. He would know you had an interview at Praed Street this afternoon. You saw nobody when you took the London train last night?"

His sharp eyes held the girl's transfixed.

She shook her head worriedly.

"No, Mr Pons. Though I had a strange feeling that I was followed all the way from Scotland."

"You undoubtedly have been. We must be on our guard."

Solar Pons puffed furiously at his pipe, the aromatic blue clouds surrounding him in thick whorls.

"You haven't told us about Colonel McDonald, Miss Hayling," I said.

"I am sorry, Parker. It is my fault. I am *au fait* with the story and had forgotten it was quite new to you."

"I went to the station that evening, Mr Pons, as I told you. I had to pass the Affric Arms to get to the forecourt. There is a small private bar near the pavement and the window was uncurtained. I glanced in as I went by. Mackintosh was carrying my luggage and had noticed nothing but I could see Ferguson inside, in deep conversation with a man in front of a roaring fire. There was no mistaking him, Mr Pons. The flaming red hair drew my attention to him. The man with him glanced up though I am convinced he could not see me at the window as it was dark in the street. It was undoubtedly Colonel McDonald."

"You know him?" I said.

"Of course, Dr Parker. Everyone in Inverness-shire knows the Colonel. He is a celebrated, not to say notorious figure. I must say I was alarmed to see him in such intimate circumstances with such an odious person as Ferguson."

"Why was that, Miss Hayling?"

"Somewhat obviously, Mr Pons, I immediately gained the impression, rightly or wrongly, that he and Ferguson were in collaboration. Or, not to put too fine a point on it, that Ferguson was acting as McDonald's agent in putting pressure on my family to get our estate."

"Have you or your family ever had any personal contact with the Colonel, Miss Hayling."

"So far as my parents are concerned, not that I am aware of. In my own case I have never met the man, though I have read a good deal about him, mostly in the financial press."

"And you do not like what you read?"

"No, Mr Pons. He is certainly not a sympathetic figure."

"I see."

Pons was silent for a moment, his head resting on his breast, his eyes half-closed, as though deep in thought.

"And you have no idea why such a man as Colonel McDonald would have an interest in a small estate like Glen Affric?"

Our visitor shook her head.

"No, Mr Pons."

"Very well, Miss Hayling. You have done well to come to me. There is little point in further discussion. However, I should be very careful while you are in London. Dr Parker will accompany you back to your hotel and I want your promise to stay there until we come to fetch you tomorrow. I believe there is a midday train from King's Cross, is there not?"

"That is correct, Mr Pons. But you do not believe I am in danger here in London?"

"It is as well to be on our guard, my dear young lady. I would like your promise, if you please."

"You have it, Mr Pons."

The girl got up from her chair, her eyes shining. We both rose also.

"Thank you so much, gentlemen. I feel very much better already."

"I can promise nothing except that I will exert my best endeavours in your interests, Miss Hayling."

"One could not ask for more, Mr Pons."

"If you will just wait a moment while I get my coat, we will be off," I said.

The girl was silent as we took a taxi to her hotel, a comfortable, middle-class establishment conveniently situated near King's Cross Station, but she reiterated her promise to remain in her room before we parted. She was to be ready at a quarter past eleven the following morning when we were due to pick her up by taxi. I saw her into the hotel and waited until she had locked herself within her room. She would dine in the hotel restaurant and would have no need to go out again until we caught the express north.

When I returned to 7B an hour later I found Pons sprawled in his armchair in front of the fire in a brown study. Judging by the swathes of dense smoke which filled the room he had been smoking furiously.

"Well, Parker," he observed on my entry. "What is your opinion of Miss Hayling and her problem?"

"A brave young lady, Pons," I answered, laying down my overcoat and thankfully seating myself opposite him in my favourite armchair in front of the fire.

"But a dark and difficult business. Though it seems obvious that the crude and murderous activities of the Scottish Land Trust were directed toward the purpose of obtaining Miss Hayling's estate, I confess I cannot see the point. From what both you and she tell me it has no possible commercial value."

Pons regarded me through the smoke with very bright eyes.

"You have hit it, Parker. I have already been to Companies House and set my own inquiries afoot. The Trust has ostensibly been set up for the innocuous purpose of recreation and leisure, as they have already suggested to Miss Hayling. They have no need to be more specific than that."

"You think McDonald owns the company and has set it up for some other purpose?"

"There is no doubt about it, Parker. The scheme bears all the traces of his ferocious methods, though his normal native cunning seems to have deserted him. These crude and blunt tactics with Miss Hayling are not typical of him."

"Perhaps the man Mungo Ferguson whom he appears to be using as his agent . . ."

"Perhaps, Parker, perhaps. He may overstep himself. A scoundrel like McDonald has to use the tools to hand and following some of his recent experiences his more genteel and respectable associates may well have been frightened off."

He smoked on in silence for a few more minutes, while I went to the telephone to let my locum know of the situation. When I had arranged for my leave of absence, I returned to the warmth of the sitting-room to find him immersed in a gazetteer and large-scale maps of Scotland which he was studying intently with the aid of a powerful magnifying glass. As soon as I reappeared he swept everything briskly off the table.

"I must apologise for monopolising our quarters with my little problems. We will leave it over until the morrow. In the meantime if you would be good enough to ring for supper, I would be greatly obliged."

4

The weather was, if anything, even more inclement when we set off next day. Though there was no rain an acrid fog hung about the capital which gave the streets a deceptively mild air but the biting cold came through, catching one unawares, so that I had to catch my breath and draw the collar of my heavy overcoat about me. We carried only valises so it was only a moment to engage a cab and with the good Mrs Johnson braving the elements to see us off from the top of the steps we had shortly collected Miss Hayling and were en route to King's Cross.

We had engaged a first-class compartment to ourselves and were soon speeding through the suburbs, the sun attempting to break through the iron-grey clouds which hung over the city. Once north of Welwyn the great locomotive got into its stride and the only indication of our immense speed was the rapid passage of the shadows of the telegraph poles across the carriage windows.

"There is something almost mystical about a great machine," Pons observed. "And the Scotsman is such a locomotive even in an age which has grown blasé over steam power. Eh, Miss Hayling?"

"You are certainly right, Mr Pons," said the girl.

She looked very becoming today in a smart tailored suit. She had put her overcoat and luggage on the rack and still wore the bobbled hat, which gave the carriage something of the atmosphere of our destination.

The trip passed uneventfully; we took lunch and high tea in the dining car and long before darkness fell we were well on our way. Pons spent much of the time studying his maps and occasionally scribbling notes, while I wracked my brains over *The Times* crossword, which I finally threw down in disgust.

"It is digit, Parker," Solar Pons observed with a smile.

"Eigh, Pons?"

"The answer to nine across, my dear fellow. I solved it almost immediately but refrained from filling it in as I did not want to spoil the problem for you."

"You have not done that, Pons," I observed grimly, picking up the paper and scanning the clues. It seemed blindingly simple once my companion had pointed it out and I was conscious of the fair girl's quiet amusement as I somewhat savagely inked the answer in.

I had noticed, as the journey progressed, that my companion, though apparently engrossed in his calculations, had cast sharp glances about him from time to time, particularly at people passing the door of the compartment. Now I was astonished to see him suddenly leap to his feet. We had in fact drawn the blinds as dusk fell, in order to ensure privacy, and Pons strode to the door and swiftly slid it open. A small man dressed in a salt and pepper suit with a bow-tie slid into the compartment with a muffled exclamation.

"Dear me," said Solar Pons gently, as he closed his hand over the elbow of the little man, ostensibly to steady him.

"I beg your pardon, sir," the latter stammered, blinking about him.

"It is rather a squeeze in the corridor here."

"It is rather a squeeze in here also," said Solar Pons, clamping his fingers on the other's arm and propelling him back into the passageway. The fellow howled with pain and tears ran down from beneath his horn-rimmed spectacles.

"You may tell your master that we are *en route* to Scotland," said Pons crisply. "That will save you a good deal of time and trouble. You may also add—though that is expecting rather too much of human nature—that you are doing your job extremely incompetently. There is an art to observing people without being noticed and you have not yet mastered it."

He slammed the door in the other's face and resumed his seat with a dry chuckle, oblivious of my astonishment and that of Miss Hayling.

"What on earth was that about, Pons?" I asked.

"That little man was obviously one of Colonel McDonald's agents," he observed soberly. "But, as I indicated, he is not very good at his job. I have noticed him no less than a dozen times during the day, giving our compartment an extremely close degree of attention. I happened to observe that the door had been slid back an inch or so, though I secured it firmly after tea. He was obviously listening in the corridor."

"Good heavens, Pons," I said. "This is serious. So we are expected at Glen Affric?"

"Of course, Parker," my companion said calmly. "We would have been in any case. I would have expected little less of the Colonel. He is leaving nothing to chance. You forget he has already made several attempts to remove me from his sphere of influence."

He pulled thoughtfully at the lobe of his left ear.

"The question is whether he will try anything before we reach our destination."

He turned to the girl.

"I take it we shall be breaking our journey in Edinburgh this evening?"

"Oh, certainly, Mr Pons. I took the precaution of booking rooms at one of the best hotels as soon as I left Dr Parker last night."

"Hmm."

Pons continued to look grave.

"We must be on our guard this evening, that is all. I think we must stay indoors tonight, Parker. An accident before we reached Glen Affric would suit McDonald's purposes nicely. But I do not think even he would be fool-hardy enough to try anything on a crowded train in broad daylight tomorrow."

And he immersed himself in his documents until we had arrived at our destination. I noticed his eyes were extremely watchful and alert as we alighted in the great, steam-filled vault of Waverley Station. He chuckled as the little man of the dramatic interview scuttled away.

"I fancy we have seen the last of him at least, Parker."

The evening was well advanced by this time and the air raw and damp and he hurried us out to the taxi-rank. In a few moments we were bowling swiftly down Princes Street to the elegant, not to say luxurious hotel Miss Hayling had engaged for us.

Pons glanced back through the rear window several times but as far as I could make out we were not being followed by any other vehicle. As though he could read my thoughts, Pons nodded grimly and put his empty pipe between his teeth.

"Unless I miss my guess, Parker, McDonald would know our destination in advance. He has a big organisation."

"Then why would he set someone to watch us on the train, Pons?"

"He wants to make sure we three have arrived at Waverley. Once we are in the city he can pick us up again without much trouble."

The girl shivered suddenly, though it was warm in the interior of the cab. We were screened from the driver by a heavy sheet of glass and I had already noted that Pons had given the man a very careful scrutiny, being at some pains not to choose the first vehicle in the station-rank.

"I am afraid I have involved you in a very black business, Mr Pons. I would never forgive myself for leading others into danger if something dreadful were to happen."

Solar Pons' eyes rested reflectively on the girl's face, now lit, now dark as the lights from shops in the great thoroughfare glanced across her expressive features.

"Do not disturb yourself, Miss Hayling," he said, solicitude in his tone. "You are forgetting I am operating within my own milieu. The danger and excitement of the chase are like meat and drink to me and the Colonel is an opponent worthy of my steel. My own concern was for your welfare."

The girl smiled winningly.

"Oh, I am safe enough in your company, Mr Pons," she said confidently. "I feel so much better already."

By this time the cab was crunching into the hotel forecourt and the discreet lights of the vestibule were beginning to compose themselves from the thin mist which lay about the city. Gas-lamps bloomed in the square and marched in stately rows along Princes Street until they were lost in the hazy shimmer. At any other time such a noble prospect would have gladdened my heart but our errand and the mortal danger in which Pons' young client stood filled my mind with foreboding.

We lost no time in paying off the cab and while the luggage was being carried in, we hurried the girl through into the warm luxuriance of the hotel lobby.

The evening passed without incident. After we had registered and taken possession of our respective rooms, we dined *à trois* at a side-table in the great elegant Edwardian restaurant with its crystal chandeliers and afterward took coffee in a cavernous smoking-room which had an enormous fire of logs blazing in its huge stone fireplace. Pons sat slightly apart from us, his eyes apparently directed toward the dimly-glimpsed façade of the square through the fog which seemed to have thickened at the long windows hung with filmy gauze. For some reason the hotel servants had not pulled to the thick velvet curtains in here but even as I noted the fact an elderly man in dark blue livery appeared to make a solemn, stately ritual of the drawing.

Pons swilled the whisky round moodily in his glass and turned toward me as the servant withdrew. The girl was facing away from us as the coffee-room waiter poured her another cup from the silver-plated pot and Pons lowered his voice as he spoke.

"I am worried about the young lady's safety, Parker. I am convinced the Colonel will make some attempt against her before we reach our destination. With her removal goes the last obstacle to him obtaining her property. You brought your revolver, as I requested?"

"Certainly, Pons," I replied. "It is securely packed in my luggage. Do you wish me to stand guard tonight outside the young lady's room?"

Pons glanced at me sharply and then gave me an affectionate smile.

"Hardly that, Parker, though it is good of you to discount your comfort in such a manner. I do not think the danger will manifest itself directly and Miss Hayling is safe enough among such surroundings. But there are a number of ways in which she may be approached."

I looked round quickly at the coffee-room waiter, who was exchanging a few commonplaces with Pons' client.

"Good heavens, Pons. Not through her food and drink, surely?"

Solar Pons shook his head, his eyes fixed thoughtfully on the old waiter.

"I hardly think so, Parker. It would be far too difficult for a stranger to penetrate the kitchen of such a hotel as this. And then there would be the difficulty of ascertaining which dish was intended for which guest. I fancy such an approach as I envisage would come from one of two sources. A fellow guest, perhaps . . . ?"

He broke off as if something had occurred to him, and then listened intently to the girl's explanations of our intended travel arrangements for the morrow. We would travel by train to Inverness, catching the ten o'clock fast and the gardener from the estate would meet us at Inverness with a pony and trap.

"That seems perfectly satisfactory, Pons," I said.

"As far as it goes, Parker," he said slowly. "Frankly, I do not like this weather and the thicker it is likely to get the farther north we go, particularly among the mountains."

"There is little we can do about it," I returned.

He shook his head.

"You are quite right, Parker. But a wise general makes his dispositions accordingly, taking account of both the weather and the movements of the enemy."

The girl turned very bright eyes on my companion.

"The danger is not past then, Mr Pons?"

"Not yet, Miss Hayling. I have no wish to alarm you, but we must still remain on our guard. I would like your promise that you will lock your room door tonight and not stir from it, except for any personal request from myself or Dr Parker."

Miss Hayling looked puzzled.

"I am not even to open to the hotel servants?"

Pons shook his head.

"Not even for the servants. In such an event please telephone to my room and I will come along. We will attend your room at eight o'clock to-morrow morning to escort you to breakfast."

The girl rose.

"Very well, Mr Pons. Goodnight."

When I had returned from seeing Miss Hayling to her room I found Pons sprawled in the smoking-room chair, a hazy cloud of smoke about him, a re-filled whisky glass at his elbow.

"Well, I think that about takes care of everything, Pons," I said with satisfaction.

My companion turned sombre eyes to me.

"We shall see, Parker, we shall see," he said slowly.

And he picked up his whisky glass again.

5

I was up betimes in the morning but early as I was, passing through the hotel lobby to fetch a newspaper, I was astonished to see Pons coming in from the open air. It was a bitterly cold day and mist had quite closed in the square outside and beads of gleaming moisture were stippling my friend's overcoat as he strode in through the main entrance.

"What on earth, Pons . . ." I began, when he rudely interrupted me.

"I have just been outside reconnoitering, Parker. A brief conversation with the Scottish taxi-driver, for example, is extremely rewarding. They do not often miss much of importance which takes place outside a large hotel."

"And what did you learn, Pons?"

"Very little, Parker. There has been nothing out of the ordinary. Which has me worried."

"Worried, Pons?"

Solar Pons' lean face was furrowed with concentration. He shook his head toward the misty street outside the vast glass doors.

"I shall not breathe easily until Miss Hayling is once again safe within her own four walls."

"Why do you think, if danger does threaten, that she was not molested on her way down to see us?"

"Because, Parker, it was not in the Colonel's interests to do anything precipitate. And the girl's telegram may have caught him off balance. Now that we are in the field he has nothing to lose."

He glanced up at the clock.

"Ah, it is five to eight. We have just time to collect Miss Hayling for breakfast."

We were ascending the great ornamental staircase that led to the upper floors when the hotel porter came down and met us at a turn in the stair. His face brightened.

"Ah, Mr Pons, I could not find you. I have just delivered the parcel to Miss Hayling's room. She would not open at first until she had identified my voice."

I had never seen such a change as that which came over Pons' face.

"Parcel? What parcel?"

"Why, sir, the parcel for Miss Hayling which came by special messenger a few minutes ago."

"And you have just delivered it to her?"

My friend did not wait for the porter's answer. He was electrified into action.

"Come, Parker! We have not a moment to lose!"

He took the stairs two at a time so that I was hard put to keep up with him. A few seconds later he was beating a tattoo at the girl's door.

"Miss Hayling! It is imperative that you do not open the packet which has just been delivered."

"Oh, Mr Pons. What is the matter?"

To our relief there came the grating of the key in the lock and the surprised face of the girl appeared in the opening of the door. Pons unceremoniously brushed by her and strode into the room, every line of his body denoting energy and purpose.

"Ah, there we are!"

I crossed quickly to Pons' side and looked at the small sandalwood box which the girl had set down on a side table. It bore a plain white label with Miss Hayling's name and hotel inked on it. It was about six inches square and had small holes drilled in the sides. I bent down close to it and it may have been my imagination but I sensed I could hear a faint rustling noise from inside.

Pons turned back to his client.

"You have made no attempt to open it?"

The fair girl shook her head.

"No, Mr Pons. I would not even let the porter in at first, as I remembered what you had told me."

"Excellent!"

Solar Pons rubbed his thin fingers together. The girl's eyes opened in surprise and she turned white.

"You do not think there is any danger in that packet?"

"We shall see, Miss Hayling. In the meantime I suggest you descend to the dining room and order breakfast. We will join you in a few minutes."

I could see by the spirited look in the girl's eyes that she was inclined to argue but the tense expression on Pons' face silenced her. She left us quickly and I stood in the open door of the room until she had descended the stairs.

When I turned back I could not see Pons for a moment and then I heard him call out from the adjoining bathroom.

"Just come in here for a moment will you, my dear fellow."

I found Pons with his sleeves rolled up, a grim look on his face. He started running hot water into the bath.

"What on earth are you up to, Pons?"

"I do not like cruelty to living creatures, Parker, but I fancy there is something abominable in this box. As I have no wish to risk our lives to indulge Colonel McDonald's sadistic instincts I intend to scald and drown whatever is within. There is no doubt it is a living creature for why otherwise would the air-holes be there."

"We do not even know it came from McDonald, Pons."

Solar Pons shook his head with a grim smile, reaching out one lean arm to turn off the tap.

"No-one knew we were at this hotel, Parker. I have Miss Hayling's word for that. It bears all the stamp of McDonald's work. We know we are under surveillance by his emissaries. Why the special box and the special messenger. Just pass me that long-handled scrubbing brush, if you please."

I did as he suggested and watched in silence as he dropped the box swiftly into the boiling water, holding it under with the brush. There were some noises coming from it now but Pons swiftly blotted them out by turning on the taps. He held the box under the surging water for perhaps a minute his face grim and tense.

"Now, my dear Parker," he said eventually, pulling out the drain-plug with the head of the brush. "We have need of your specialised knowledge, if you please."

He was searching around the bathroom as he spoke and grunted as he came across a thin metal spanner at the head of the bath. He held it in his hand, waiting as the last of the water swirled down the drain.

"Let me do it, Parker. We do not want any accidents."

I held the box, while he levered up the lid. There was paper inside, which had been made soggy with water, and we waited a moment to allow it to drain away. Cautiously, Pons parted it with the end of the spanner, his face concentrated and absorbed.

"There is no danger any more, Parker, I fancy."

I stood looking sickly down at the monstrous, bloated thing which was curled in death at the bottom of the box. It resembled nothing so much as a huddled mass of brownish-black fur, though I knew it was the biggest spider I had ever seen in my life.

"What on earth is it, Pons?"

"You may well ask, Parker. A tarantula. One of the most deadly creatures known to man. One bite could have been fatal, had Miss Hayling been unwise enough to open the box."

"Good heavens, Pons! I thought they inhabited only tropical climates."

Pons shook his head, his face set like stone.

"They are found mainly in Southern Europe, Parker. But you are right. This could not have existed long in a place like Edinburgh in January. Hence the warm packing. McDonald is a specialist in such things. I hear on good authority that he has an esoteric private zoo at his Scottish estate."

"Then this came from there, Pons?"

"Undoubtedly, Parker."

My companion became brisk in his manner. He got up, unrolled his sleeves and resumed his jacket. Carefully, he eased the sodden mass out of the box and swirled it down the drain-hole of the bath. He had to force it through the grille with the end of the spanner. He let the water run for a minute or two, his eyes expressing his anger. When he had cleaned the bath to his satisfaction he replaced the spanner and the long-handled brush and rinsed his hands thoughtfully. Then he turned to me.

"Miss Hayling must know nothing of this, Parker. She is worried enough already."

"But what are you going to tell her?"

There were little glints of amusement in my companion's eyes now.

"I shall think of something, Parker. Have I your word?"

"You may rely upon it, Pons."

"Good. And now, I think we have already done a good morning's work. It is more than time to join Miss Hayling for breakfast."

<h1 style="text-align:center">6</h1>

The train shuddered and came to a halt. Thin mist swirled around the platform. I huddled more deeply into my overcoat and handed out the cases to Pons after he had assisted Miss Hayling from the carriage.

"So this is Inverness, Pons?"

"It would appear so, Parker, if one can rely upon the station sign-boards. I believe you said you had a trap waiting, Miss Hayling?"

"There should be one, Mr Pons. I specifically ordered Mackintosh to be here. Ah, there he is!"

A tall, bearded man with a ruddy, good-humoured face was material-
ising through the groups of passengers who hurried toward the station
exits. Carriage doors were slamming, there was the hiss of steam and all
the bustle that I invariably associate with travel. Mackintosh, who wore a
heavy caped tartan overcoat gave Miss Hayling a respectful salute and
took our cases, looking curiously at Pons and myself.

"This is Mr Solar Pons and Dr Lyndon Parker," she explained. "They
have come to help us in our problems."

"You are welcome indeed, gentlemen," said the gardener in a rich,
smooth burr.

He extended a strong hand to Pons and myself.

"I have the trap just outside here, Miss."

We handed the young lady through the gate of the smart equipage
drawn by a sturdy cob and Pons and I settled ourselves down opposite her
while Mackintosh stowed the baggage. Then the gardener took his seat at
the reins as we busied ourselves enveloping ourselves in the thick travelling rugs provided.

As soon as we had left the town the mist seemed to encroach more
strongly and the cold bit to the bone. Pons had been extremely alert all the
time we were at the station and in the inhabited streets of Inverness and I
noticed that the girl always walked between the two of us, so that we
shielded her on either side. But now that we were on the country road that
wound up between frowning shoulders of hill, Pons relaxed somewhat
and sat leaning forward, a thin plume of smoke from his pipe billowing
over his shoulder to mingle with the mist, his lean, aquiline features
brooding and heavy with thought.

The atmosphere into which we were going obtruded itself more and
more and was not conducive to conversation, so we travelled in silence, the
gardener Mackintosh skilfully handling the reins, the sure-footed cob
sturdily breasting the rises with its heavy load. We were still going in
a northerly direction, despite the twisting and turning of the undulating road and it was soon obvious that we were straying into strange and
lonely country.

Not that we could see much of it for the mist clung clammily to tree
and hedgerow; but beyond the white blanket, which occasionally drew
aside momentarily in currents of air, I could see bleak pine forests and the

shaggy shoulders of mountain. The road itself dipped and fell so that Mackintosh eased the cob back to a walk and we jolted on through the damp, bitterly cold winter morning, each of us lost in his or her own thoughts.

Only once was there a change in the landscape and that was when another momentary break in the mist showed us the dark, sullen surface of a large black lake or loch which lay in a vast hollow beyond a fringe of trees to the right of the road. In response to my interrogatory look, Miss Hayling broke the long silence.

"Loch Affric," she said. "We shall not be much longer before we arrive at our destination."

"It is indeed a remote spot," I ventured.

The girl gave a wry smile, her eyes fixed beyond our little group in the trap, as though she could penetrate the mist which had again descended, blotting out the dark and brooding aspect of the loch.

"Just wait until you have seen the estate, Dr Parker. Then will you and Mr Pons fully appreciate the situation in which I found myself."

Pons nodded sombrely, his pipe glowing cheerfully as he shoveled smoke out over his shoulder at a furious rate. But I noticed that his eyes were stabbing glances all around and his whole attitude reminded me of a terrier or game dog whose very sense was attuned to this strange and bizarre atmosphere into which every beat of the horse's hooves was leading us.

The land by now was excessively hilly and the lonely road wound crazily this way and that, bordered by dark plantations of firs and pines so that it was inexpressibly gloomy. I felt my own heart becoming oppressed by the surroundings and marvelled at the girl and her family choosing to make their dwelling in this outlandish place.

As though he could read my thoughts Pons observed to the girl, "Tell me, Miss Hayling, this country, as you have already told us, is almost impossible for farming. It looks equally forbidding for leisure pursuits."

"That is correct, Mr Pons," said our hostess earnestly. "Now that you see it for yourself I am sure you will agree the notion is quite preposterous. There is some fishing, certainly a little shooting but hereabouts forestry with some grazing is about the only possibility."

Pons nodded, puffing thoughtfully at his pipe.

"This Colonel McDonald, Miss Hayling. Do his estates adjoin yours in any way?"

Mackintosh turned round in his seat at mention of McDonald and I saw him and the young lady exchange a long look. The latter nodded vigorously.

"Oh, yes indeed, Mr Pons. You might almost say we are encircled by his property."

Pons' eyes flashed beneath the brim of his hat as he glanced across at me.

"That is extremely interesting, Miss Hayling, and could explain many things."

"I fail to see, Pons . . ." I began when we were interrupted by a lurching movement of the trap and Mackintosh applied the brake. I saw that we were travelling down a steep hill into a valley so deep that it appeared to be nothing more than a vast bowl half-filled with mist.

"This is the river hereabouts, Mr Pons," said the girl. "It is a gloomy place, I am afraid."

I hung on to the rail at the side of the cart and prayed that nothing would happen to the brakes as the cob was having some difficulty in keeping its feet. A few moments later Pons and I, by tacit consent and without speaking descended, and Pons went to take the horse's head. I walked with him and we proceeded like this for some way. It was indeed an awe-inspiring place and we seemed to be descending an interminable distance down the narrow, twisting road.

Presently the slope eased out and Mackintosh brought the cob to a halt to give him a rest. He slipped down to give the beast a knob of sugar.

"Thank you, gentlemen," he said. "The hill is a very difficult place and yon slope the other side is little different."

As a breath of wind slightly cleared the mist I saw that we were almost on a right-angle turn leading over a large rustic bridge, which had white-painted railings protecting the edges. Pons and I walked across and after a short while the trap followed. Pons paused at the far edge and rested his two hands on the edge of the palings. Far away and below us, apparently at a vast distance, came the rushing of water. The trap was now level with us and Mackintosh drew it up obediently. Pons turned to Miss Hayling.

"I am sorry to revive sad memories, Miss Hayling, but is this the spot where your parents met their fatal accident?"

The girl shivered, though not with cold, and a dark shadow passed across her face.

"That is so, Mr Pons. Just a little farther along. The carriage is still down there."

Pons' languid air was transformed.

"What do you mean?"

"Why, Mr Pons, the place is so steep and the slopes either side so precipitous that it still rests on the bed of the stream."

"Indeed."

Solar Pons' eyes were glittering with excitement and he puffed smoke furiously from his pipe.

"So there was no evidence about the carriage produced at the inquest?"

"I do not quite follow you, Mr Pons."

"No matter, my dear young lady. If you will excuse me for a few minutes I will just satisfy my curiosity."

To my astonishment he walked a little farther over the bridge, skirted the railing where it re-joined the road at another steep turn and disappeared into the dark, misty woodlands which led down to the invisible stream below. For some while I could hear the swishing of his shoes among the leaves and then they died out in the noise of the river. Mackintosh sat politely, his eyes in front of him, though I could sense he was as astonished as the rest of us. In the event more than a quarter of an hour had passed before Pons reappeared, dusting himself down absently.

"You will forgive me, I am sure, Miss Hayling, but I always like to see things for myself."

"And what did you see, Pons?" I asked as we re-seated ourselves in the trap.

"Oh, the vehicle is there all right, Parker. The stream is quite shallow and I could see it clearly through the dark water. We can have it up, if necessary."

"Have it up, Pons?"

Solar Pons nodded but further conversation was again interrupted by the necessity of descending once more as the way again became extremely steep and dangerous, leading upward eventually from the other side of the bridge toward the estate of Glen Affric. We passed two lichen-encrusted gate-posts surmounted by stone heraldic griffins and were then on a sort of plateau which contained the park. Miss Hayling pointed off to the right, where the blank white wall of mist skirted the driveway.

"In good weather one has an excellent view of our local mountain, Ben Affric, in that direction, gentlemen."

"Indeed."

Pons looked musingly about him but it was obvious that even had the air been clear his thoughts were far away and absorbed with calculations that were obscure to me. The road led steeply up the drive which wound between a gloomy avenue of trees, now dank and dripping moisture in the bitingly cold air. Twice Pons glanced back behind him and I thought at first he feared we were followed but then realised he was reconstructing in his mind the tragic scene as the late Mr and Mrs Hayling's trap bowled down that steep hill and through the main gates for the last time.

At length we came up through a dark, almost threatening mass of rhododendron and evergreen shrubbery into a gravelled concourse beyond which lay the long, low granite mass of the house. With its yellowed walls and lichen; the heraldic devices repeated on stone shields below the turret-like roofs; and the Gothic stable-block beyond, it was a forbidding sight and my heart sank at the lonely and oppressive atmosphere of the place, lost in these dank and dripping pine woods.

But Pons sprang alertly down to assist the lady, merely observing, "You will note, Parker, that Miss Hayling has spoken correctly. The estate is the only flat land for miles around. I commend that factor to you."

"I cannot see its significance, Pons," I confessed.

But my companion had already turned to the massive figure of Mackintosh as his client hurried toward the front steps of the house.

"I should like to have that trap up from the stream-bed by tomorrow, Mackintosh, if it is at all possible."

The gardener scratched his head, looking thoughtfully at the horse which was staring wistfully toward the stable-block.

"Well, sir, it would be possible if you are really determined on it."

"I am so determined," said Solar Pons.

The grave eyes were appraising my companion now.

"Well, sir, if it is to help Miss Hayling, I would do anything for the leddy. We have a tenant who farms a few acres just below here. In fact there are two farmers who manage to scrape some sort of a living from the skirts of our land. If he and his boy are not too busy we might try to get it up."

"I would be obliged. It will not be necessary to recover the equipage, merely to raise it from the water in order that I may make a brief examination."

"It shall be done, sir."

Mackintosh raised his whip in salute and rattled off to the stables at a brisk pace.

"What do you hope to find, Pons?"

"Evidence of crime, Parker," said my companion grimly as we hurried across the concourse with our hand baggage to where the slim figure of Miss Hayling waited at the head of the steps.

The house was indeed sombre and lonely though Miss Hayling's hospitality was lavish and Mr and Mrs McRae were kind and attentive. It was obvious that the atmosphere had lightened with Pons' arrival and as we were served a late lunch in an old oak-panelled dining-room Miss Hayling's manner was bright, almost gay at times.

She answered all Pons' questions in great detail and the events at the house and in the grounds were gone through again, this time with the benefit of Pons being on the spot. So dark did it get in these northerly latitudes in winter-time that it was almost dusk by the time we had finished at table but despite this Pons insisted on seeing round outside and listened to our hostess's explanations of the estate with keen attention.

If anything, Glen Affric, the girl's property being named after the nearby glen, was more bleak and remote than before in the fading light. The chill mist persisted but despite this Pons tramped about the stable-yard and the adjoining paths through the fir-plantations with energy and gusto, occasionally asking questions of Mackintosh, who accompanied us, and at other times darting aside silently on small expeditions of his own.

It was during one such that we temporarily found ourselves alone,

Miss Hayling having gone in search of her black Labrador which was engaged in chasing an imaginary rabbit.

"I have already spoken to the tenant farmer about that matter, Mr Pons," the gardener said diffidently. "There should be no difficulty. We will try and get the cart up by midday tomorrow."

"Excellent," said Pons crisply, turning his head as the girl came up with the dog at her heels.

"This must be the spot hereabouts, where you were attacked, is it not?"

The good Mackintosh' face turned brick-red and he knotted his thick fist.

"Aye, Mr Pons, a little farther down here. As you can see the shrubbery comes quite near the edge of the path. The black villain sprang on me as my back was turned or I'd have given him a hard fight of it, sir."

"I have no doubt of that," I said encouragingly.

The girl smiled at the gardener's expression, calling to the dog, which was sniffing about in the bushes. But she stopped when Pons held up his hand, an alert expression on his face.

"I believe he has found something."

The dog was in fact snarling at this point, as though he had discovered something particularly unpleasant. I followed Pons as he strode into the clump of bushes. It was still light enough to see clearly and I could make out an area of muddy ground which looked as though someone had trampled over it.

"Have you been through here lately, Mr Mackintosh?"

"Not I, sir," said the gardener in his sturdy manner. "When the villain hit me I lost consciousness and came to myself in the driveway. I must have staggered some yards and I had no idea from what direction my attacker had come. There was no point in searching the shrubbery at any particular point. Of course, the police were called and went all over the place, but the rain would have blotted out their tracks weeks ago."

Solar Pons shook his head, his deep-set eyes searching the ground. "I do not think the police would be involved. Someone has been standing here for a long time, as though watching the house."

He looked thoughtfully at the blanket of mist which pressed upon us.

"Can one see the house from here in normal conditions?"

"Most certainly, Mr Pons," the girl said. "It is only a few hundred yards."

Pons had stopped now and was going over the ground carefully, his thin, sensitive fingers raking in the icy mud. He gave a muffled exclamation and came up with two yellowed slivers of something that looked like wood or cardboard. He held them up to Mackintosh.

"You know what these are?"

"Of course, Mr Pons. Swan Vestas."

Solar Pons nodded.

"Exactly. Someone stood here smoking and watching the house, dropping his matches from time to time and stamping them out on the ground. Perhaps you surprised him when you came along the path in the dusk. He may have dropped something else in his hurry. Hullo!"

I looked round, startled by the urgency in his voice.

"I fancy the dog has something there in his mouth, Miss Hayling."

The Labrador had, in fact, a black bedraggled object which it was shaking and worrying with a dreadful intensity. The animal rolled its eyes and I thought it was going to bite the gardener as he bent to take it from him. When he had wrested it away from the Labrador he handed it to Pons.

"Nothing but an old oilskin tobacco pouch, Mr Pons."

"Mmm."

Pons studied it in silence.

"Half-full of Coronation Mixture, I see. And the initials M.F. in gold lettering on the side. What does that suggest to you, Parker?"

"Mungo Ferguson, Pons!"

"You have not quite lost your ratiocinative touch, Parker. The name fits rather too pat it would appear."

"I do not follow you, Pons."

"Do you not, Parker. We have every reason to believe that Ferguson is the tool of McDonald."

"You mean the Colonel left the pouch here, Pons!"

"Possibly, Parker. Or he has his own reasons for employing a hot-headed and unreliable tool."

The girl's eyes blazed and she looked at Solar Pons in amazement.

"The dog hates Ferguson, Mr Pons. No wonder he was growling."

She paused, controlling her emotions.

"Are you suggesting Colonel McDonald is using the man Ferguson as a scapegoat, Mr Pons?"

My companion looked at her mildly, putting the oilskin pouch into his pocket.

"Nothing is impossible in these romantic surroundings, Miss Hayling. But it is a cold and inclement night, with darkness fast approaching. We can do little more here. I propose we adjourn to the house where we may plan our strategy for the morrow."

7

I was late abed the next morning, possibly because I slept soundly after our journey and the strange change of scene, and it was past nine o'clock when I joined Pons at the breakfast table. Miss Hayling was in the study discussing some matter with McRae and Pons was alone, his head wreathed in tobacco smoke, frowningly studying large-scale maps of the area. He seemed oblivious of my presence but as Mrs McRae smilingly appeared with silver breakfast dishes on a tray he abruptly waved his hand to disperse the tobacco smoke and moved his charts to one side.

"Forgive me, my dear fellow. My manners are abominable when I become absorbed in these problems."

"Think nothing of it, Pons," I said, falling to with a will on the great platter of bacon, eggs and sausages Mrs McRae had prepared.

"I have such an appetite your pipe does not bother me at all."

"It is indeed good of you, Parker," said my companion with a sly smile at Mrs McRae. "Yes, thank you, Mrs McRae, I will have another cup of that excellent coffee if there is enough to spare."

"There is plenty here, Mr Pons," said that good lady, pouring for us both. "And if there were not I would be glad to make a third pot."

I studied Pons between mouthfuls.

"You have made some progress?"

"A little, Parker. Tell me, Mrs McRae, how is your knowledge of these parts?"

"Extensive but not exhaustive, Mr Pons."

"Excellent. Pray sit here for a moment or two, if you please."

Mrs McRae sat down opposite, looking with puzzled eyes at my companion.

"Can you read a map at all with any accuracy, Mrs McRae?"

"Tolerably well, Mr Pons. My husband and I did a great deal of walking in the old days, when we were young."

"I see."

Solar Pons tented his thin fingers before him, his deep-set eyes fixed on the housekeeper.

"The large-scale map of this area in front of you, for instance. Would you be able to indicate to me roughly, using this thick black crayon, the boundaries of Colonel McDonald's estates."

"I think so, Mr Pons."

Mrs McRae sat with pursed lips, studying the map intently while Pons sat quietly smoking, his eyes studying her face. I had finished my bacon and eggs and had started on the toast and marmalade before she stirred. Then she seized the crayon and started etching boundaries over a large section of the map.

"That, to the best of my knowledge, is the extent of the Colonel's lands, Mr Pons. I have no doubt Miss Hayling would corroborate, though I could not vouch for fine detail. The land by the stream there and the more mountainous parts may be inaccurate by a quarter of a mile or so."

"A quarter of a mile or so, Mrs McRae!" said Pons, surprise on his face. "You are a paragon among female cartographers!"

"You make fun of me, Mr Pons."

"By no means, Mrs McRae. I have never been more serious. Those lines you have drawn are invaluable. My grateful thanks."

"You are welcome, I'm sure."

Mrs McRae rose, the surprise still evident on her face and with a re-iterated statement that if we required anything further we were to ring, withdrew.

Pons sat for some minutes, studying the map, his eyes glittering with suppressed excitement. I sat back in my chair and finished my second cup of coffee. It was still almost dark outside, but the strengthening light showed only dim outlines of soaked coppices through the thin mist.

"You have found something, Pons?"

"It has confirmed my suspicions, Parker. Except for the main roads,

Colonel McDonald's lands completely surround the estate of Glen Affric. More significantly, Miss Hayling's property is the only flat land of any size in these parts, the remainder consisting of bleak hillside, rough glen and undulating forest-land, most of it extremely inhospitable indeed."

"Is that of significance, Pons?"

"Absolutely vital, Parker. It is an essential clue to this bizarre business. Look here."

I drew my chair over, following the tip of the crayon, and carefully examined the map. By using the figures given for contours I was able to see it was indeed as Pons had said. Much of the land owned by the Colonel was precipitous and most of it lay at an altitude of over 2,000 feet.

"Let me have your thoughts on the matter, Parker."

I frowned at him through the pipe-smoke.

"I have not many, truth to tell, Pons. Perhaps it is as the girl says. The Land Trust want Miss Hayling's property for holiday development."

Solar Pons narrowed his eyes thoughtfully through the smoke.

"I fancy there is a good deal more to it than that, Parker. However, McDonald is an expert at floating bogus companies. We will see what the Land Trust office has to say. They are located at Inverness, are they not?"

"I believe Miss Hayling said so, Pons."

I studied the map again but the more I looked at it the more puzzling the problem became. We were interrupted at our occupation by the entrance of Pons' client. She was dressed in a thick sweater, a long skirt and stout boots so it was evident that she was prepared for some heavy walking about the estate.

"I am just off to the Five-Acre Wood with Mr McRae, gentlemen. If there is anything further you require, Mackintosh or Mrs McRae will be glad to look after your wants."

"We are quite well provided for, Miss Hayling," said Pons equably. "And I have my day planned out, thank you."

The girl smiled.

"Very good, gentlemen. Lunch is at one. I will see you then."

We both stood as the girl left the room, her slim, lithe body the picture of health and energy.

"A very brave young lady, Pons," I observed.

"I believe you have already said so, Parker. But it is a truism worth repeating, nevertheless."

A few moments later we saw our hostess walk past the window with McRae.

"You do not think she is in any danger, Pons?"

My companion shook his head.

"Not for the moment. I fancy McRae can look after himself. She is in good hands."

As soon as the couple had disappeared along the misty drive Solar Pons was galvanised into action.

"Now that the young lady is away, Parker, we can set to work. We must first find Mackintosh and I must then descend to the stream at the bottom of the ravine. It is imperative that we get that dog-cart up."

"Just give me a minute or two, Pons," I said. "I need my thick walking boots and an overcoat."

"Very well, my dear fellow, but do hurry."

When I bustled downstairs five minutes later Pons was already standing impatiently on the drive before the house, obviously eager to be off. We could not find Mackintosh at his cottage or the stable-block. It was now full daylight and Pons looked at his watch anxiously.

"I think we will make our own way there, Parker."

I followed him down the drive. The mist had lifted a little but it was still a bleak and inhospitable day.

"Perhaps Mackintosh is already down there, supervising the lifting operations," I suggested, as I fell into step with him.

"Perhaps, Parker. We shall see."

And he said nothing further until we had arrived at the bridge. The way down was indeed steep and precipitous and I must confess my heart sank when I thought of our errand and the terrible end of the girl's parents in their headlong dash to destruction over this very road.

Our footsteps echoed hollowly in the mist and only the harsh cry of some bird broke the eerie stillness. Moisture pattered faintly from the dripping foliage and the bitter air rasped in one's throat while our breath smoked out of our mouths. Pons had thrust his pipe into his pocket and walked along grimly, his brows frowning over his deep-set eyes. I had rarely seen him look so serious. For some reason he had seized a thick hawthorn stick from the hall-stand as he left the house and he slashed moodily at various pieces of foliage at the roadside as we descended.

We had reached the bridge and the sombre gorge now and I could hear the faint fret of the river in the far depths below. It struck with a chilling note to the heart. Pons glanced keenly about him.

"You have your revolver, Parker?"

I tapped the breast-pocket of my overcoat.

"You insisted on me bringing it north, Pons. You told me we were on a dangerous business. I have it here."

A faint smile curled the corners of his lips.

"Excellent, Parker. You are running true to form."

He had turned aside as he spoke and plunged downward between the dark boles of the trees as though he had known the place all his life. I followed rather more hesitantly, as it was slippery underfoot, and I was more than once thankful for the thick cleats on the soles of my heavy boots.

8

It was a dark and gloomy place and the incessant fret of the water, which grew even louder, only emphasised its sombreness. Pons led at a fast pace, winding downward through the shadowy boles of the trees, the water roaring in our ears now. I saw as we came level with the stream that it tumbled over boulders below the bridge and then flowed level, though swiftly, in a calmer manner.

Pons plunged forward along the bank, following the curve of the stream, until he arrived at a point just below the falls where there was deep, fairly agitated water. He looked up toward the bridge, which was hidden from us by the thick matting of undergrowth and tree-boles.

"A bad place, Parker. They would have hit the head of the waterfall and then come down the fall into the deeper water here."

"You mean Miss Hayling's parents, Pons. An awful business."

I stared at the white, broken water but was roused from my reverie by a sharp exclamation from my companion.

"Extraordinary though it may seem, it has gone, Parker. Mackintosh has been true to his word."

I followed his gaze. Though dark, the stream was clear here and I could see to the bottom. There was certainly no sign of the wreckage of the dog-cart. Pons was already moving again and I followed him across large boulders which made a series of stepping-stones. They were wet and slippery and the water ran surging and deep between them so that I was glad to reach the far bank without a ducking. There were dark runnels torn in the soil here, where the cart had been dragged up the bank. Pons looked sharply about him.

"I shall be surprised if this is Mackintosh' work, Parker," he said drily.

He slashed moodily at the undergrowth with his stick.

"I do not follow you, Pons."

"Do you not, Parker. It is crystal-clear. But it merely confirms what I wished to know."

He turned as there came a crashing noise in the bushes. The angry figure of Mackintosh appeared, with a puzzled-looking farm-worker in corduroy behind him.

"It is disgraceful, Mr Pons! I have never heard the like!"

"I take it you did not remove the cart, Mackintosh."

"Not I, sir," replied the other grimly. "It has been taken out by the people from the neighbouring smallholding and burned in their yard! Despite the fact that this is private property!"

"By whose orders?"

"Mr Mungo Ferguson's sir!"

Solar Pons smiled grimly. He turned to me.

"This promises to be rather interesting, Parker. Let us just find out the situation. Is Mr Ferguson there?"

Mackintosh nodded gloomily, falling in at Pons' side as we walked uphill, away from the babbling stream.

"Aye, Mr Pons. Supervising the burning. I gave him my tongue and he is in no better temper for it. I thought it best to come away for he is a formidable man when the anger is on him. I know not what you wanted to prove, Mr Pons, but there was little left of the cart when I last saw it."

Pons nodded, his deep-set eyes gleaming.

"It was of oak, I should have said."

"That's right, Mr Pons. It had lasted well, despite the action of the water."

"How on earth did he burn it?" I put in.

Mackintosh turned a puzzled face to me over his shoulder.

"He poured petrol over it, Dr Parker. If ever a man seemed determined to destroy another's property, it was Mungo Ferguson."

"Destroy evidence, rather," said Pons, a hard expression in his eyes. "Well, he has played right into our hands."

He increased his pace and as we came up from that gloomy valley I could see thick black smoke billowing across the trees, where low, poor-looking farm buildings jutted from the landscape. Mackintosh turned to speak to the man in corduroy and he went back across the fields, presumably to his own farm.

Within a very few minutes we had come upon an extraordinary scene. In the midden within the three sides formed by the stout stone walls of the farmhouse, byre and stable, were a group of wild-looking men, standing round a great fire of bracken and wood. They were labouring types obviously and the dominant figure among them, who stood a little apart and directed them, was a gigantic figure in hairy tweeds with flaming red hair and a thick beard. Pons chuckled quietly to himself.

"Mr Mungo Ferguson," he said with satisfaction. "Well, Parker, the best means of defense is attack, is it not?"

And without more ado he strode across to the group round the fire, who watched with a sort of sullen fascination as we came up. The huge man, who had a coarse, inflamed face, had been shouting at the men about the fire and I now saw that it contained the remains of a carriage, obviously the one with which we were concerned. It was almost all consumed and the shafts had evidently been the first to go, for there was no sign of them. Two petrol cans stood at a distance from the bonfire and it was obvious that they had been used to ignite the sodden wood.

"Who is responsible for this?" said Solar Pons, coming to a halt near the group of men, but glancing sidelong at the figure of the bearded man who toyed with a shooting-stick in one gigantic hand. The men stirred uneasily but before they could reply the big man came to life. He stamped forward menacingly, holding the metal stick in his hand, and glared at my companion.

"You are on private property. You are trespassing."

"I am well aware of that," said Solar Pons evenly. "You are burning private property, are you not?"

Ferguson had a loud, coarse voice and his eyes flamed with anger, but there was something about Pons' quiet, resolute manner, that made him pause and choose his words with relative care.

"The carriage has been blocking yon stream for a long time. We thought it was time to have it out."

Solar Pons smiled thinly.

"An odd coincidence, was it not, that you chose the very day we had decided to remove it ourselves?"

"Maybe," Ferguson snapped.

He came closer, his manner bristling and prickly.

"You have a name do you?"

"Solar Pons. And you, judging by your coarseness and lack of manners must be Mungo Ferguson."

There was a hoarse burst of laughter from the men round the fire and Ferguson drew himself up, his red-rimmed eyes filled with hatred.

"Solar Pons!"

He bit the words off savagely.

"The London detective! The meddler and pryer into other people's affairs!"

Solar Pons stood quietly, perfectly at ease, a smile on his lips. His assured attitude seemed to enrage the red-haired man.

"Well, we have a way with meddlers in these parts, Mr Solar Pons! We pitch them down the mountainside, head first!"

Solar Pons drew himself up, his right hand firm and steady on the stick.

"You are welcome to try, my vulgar fellow, but I would not advise it."

With a bellow of rage Mungo Ferguson lurched forward, raising the shooting-stick. Mackintosh had started forward in alarm and I was before him but our assistance was not needed. The stout hawthorn stick moved round so quickly it was just a blur in the air. There was a dull crack as it connected with the giant's shin and he gave a low howl of pain.

Pons turned swiftly as the red-haired man staggered, falling forward; he brought the shooting-stick round in a vain effort to support himself but he had not even reached the ground before my companion caught him two resounding blows across the thick of the body. He fell with a tremendous crash and there was blood on his chin as he scrambled to his feet, a burning madness in his eyes.

"I have some little experience of bar-room brawls," said Solar Pons coolly, "and am able to meet you on your own terms. I would advise you to cut your losses."

There was an enraged bellow from the giant and he came forward, his huge fists flailing. Light as a ballet dancer, Pons moved to one side so that the man's mad rush took him past. The stick came round again, tripping him this time. When he regained his feet, his face plastered with mud and green from the grass, he had lost much of his confidence, but he still came forward with a low growl.

"This has gone far enough, sir," said Mackintosh in a concerned voice, though he could not erase the delight from his features.

The huge man thrust him aside and leapt at Pons for the third time. His blows met only empty air. Then Pons had thrown the heavy stick down; Ferguson staggered as Pons' left caught him on the point of the chin. My companion's second blow, from his right, clipped him exactly in the classic textbook spot and his eyes glazed. He went down, his body square in the heart of the fire, red-hot ashes, cinders and sparks erupting into the air like fireworks.

I rushed forward with Pons to drag him clear and soon saw that though he was unconscious, there was little damage done, except for a scorch-mark on the breast of his overcoat and a smouldering coat-tail. The awed group of men tending the bonfire moved to let us pass. Pons retrieved his stick from the ground, his eyes sparkling, his breathing even and normal, his voice good-tempered.

"You may tell Mr Ferguson when he comes to himself that the Colonel now has me to deal with. He will understand."

He looked down thoughtfully at the unconscious giant.

"If I were you I should lose no time in getting him to his home. He will catch a chill lying on the ground at this time of the year."

And with a dry chuckle he turned on his heel and made his way back across the fields, re-tracing the route we had already followed. Mackintosh caught up with us before we had gone ten yards.

"That was champion, sir. Just champion. I have never seen the like. Allow me to shake you by the hand, Mr Pons."

The old fellow was so sincere in his admiration and delight that Pons smilingly extended his hand.

"It was nothing," he said carelessly. "I was quite a good amateur boxer at one time. But the affair was a single-stick bout for the most part and I must confess I rather pride myself on my prowess in that direction."

I fell into step alongside him.

"At any rate it has demoralised friend Ferguson and thrown the enemy into disorder," said Pons reflectively. "I have no time for such bullies and there is no doubt in my mind that it was Ferguson who downed you in the coppice that dark evening, Mackintosh."

The old man's face was clouded with anger.

"Then you have made ample restitution, Mr Pons, and I am doubly grateful to you."

"You have made a bad enemy, Pons," said I.

"Tut, Parker, he is a tool, merely, and as such of no importance. But unless I miss my guess the incident will bring some reaction from the Colonel. The thing is as plain as daylight to both of us. Each reads the other like a book."

"I do not quite follow you, Pons."

"Ah, here we are at the stream again," said my companion, as though he had not heard my comment, and he was silent and preoccupied with his thoughts until we had again regained the comfortable quarters assigned to us at our hostess' estate.

9

Smoke and steam obscured the platform as we descended from the carriage in the biting air.

"But why are we returning to Inverness, Pons? And by such a roundabout route? That long journey in the dog-cart and then the change of train and boring wait?"

"Tut, Parker," said Solar Pons impatiently, as we gave up our tickets at the barrier.

"It is elementary, surely. The Land Trust offices are at Carnock House, Inverness. Therefore, to Inverness we must go."

"But Mackintosh could have driven us here direct, just as he did when we came," I protested.

Solar Pons shook his head, impatience showing in his deep-set eyes.

"You are not using your brain, Parker," he said crisply. "And give away our destination? The thrashing I gave Mungo Ferguson would have reached the Colonel's ears very quickly. Before he has time to react, we have made our move. I wanted to reach Inverness secretly, before he has an inkling of what we are about."

"I see, Pons," I said, as we hurried down a side-street opposite the station. "But where is Carnock House?"

"I have already looked it up," said Solar Pons, shifting his valise from one hand to the other. "It is a pity that we have to leave Miss Hayling for one night like this but there was no alternative if I was to find out what I wanted. But with Mackintosh sleeping in the house tonight and the McRaes on the alert, she is safe enough for the moment."

"But what do you expect to find here today, Pons?"

"The Land Trust is the key to the whole thing, Parker. I must find out what sort of statements they are issuing. The girl's property is the crux of the matter. This is where you come in, Parker."

"Me, Pons?"

I looked at him in some alarm, as we turned into a broad, impressive-looking thoroughfare, crowded with shoppers and traffic.

"Your grammar is going to pieces in your agitation, Parker, but I follow your drift. I want you to play out a little comedy in the main office and keep the clerk they employ busy."

"What will you be doing in the meantime?"

Solar Pons chuckled.

"Breaking into their private quarters, Parker."

I gazed at him in horror.

"You cannot be serious, Pons!"

My friend stared at me sombrely.

"I was never more serious, Parker. The young lady's life is in danger.

McDonald will step up his campaign against her now that I am on his home territory. You surely have not forgotten that creature at the hotel?"

I shivered and drew my overcoat collar closer round me.

"You are right, as ever, Pons. But what are we to do if we are caught? There may be others on the staff."

Solar Pons shook his head as we turned into a large, imposing-looking court, crowded with offices and commercial buildings.

"I have already deduced from what our client says, Parker, that the office is a sham, merely designed to give respectability and credence to the Colonel's operations. It is imposing enough, I give you, but if we are to believe Miss Hayling it is not even on the telephone. The young fellow McDonald employs as a clerk is respectable enough, and no doubt believes in the reality of the brochures and literature he sends out. But he is the only person on the premises so my scheme should not be too difficult to put into operation."

I looked at him with pursed lips.

"Let us hope you are right, Pons. Otherwise we shall not need our hotel reservations while spending the night in police cells."

Pons was still chuckling when we came in sight of the discreet gilt lettering of the Scottish Land Trust offices. They were respectable-looking premises in a narrow-chested building of clean-cut granite, whose bow windows were filled with impressive cabinet photographs and printed literature drawing-pinned to green baize boards. I paused and pretended to examine the windows while Pons turned aside under a small archway which immediately adjoined the building and led to a cobbled courtyard at the side.

He was back again in a few moments, his face bright and alert. He handed me the valise.

"It is just as I thought, Parker. There is a small private office with a glass door which a child could unlock. There are filing cabinets and desks and I should be able to find what I want there. Now listen carefully, because I want you to follow my instructions implicitly."

A few minutes later, as I entered the office, there was no sign of Pons in the street outside. I had begun my task in doubt and uncertainty knowing that we were engaged in illegal, perhaps even criminal proceedings, but the young man with dark hair who rose eagerly from his desk at the

back of the office to come to the counter on my entry, was so naive and unversed in the profession for which he was so obviously unfitted that I
rapidly regained my confidence.

The elaborate and searching questions about the Scottish Land Trust
with which Pons had primed me, soon had young Wilson in a tangle and
he had shortly retreated to his desk, pencil in hand, while he searched for
a slip of paper on which to note his mumbled calculations. When he re-
joined me at the counter, there were little patches of pink on his cheeks
and his manner was agitated and nervous in the extreme. But I think I
carried out my task with commendable thoroughness. With the brochures
and other literature spread out on the countertop between us, I plied the
young clerk with searching questions so that the quarter of an hour Pons
had stipulated had seemingly passed in a flash.

Twenty-five minutes had ensued before Wilson had extricated himself from the morass of questions and another five before I had gathered
up all the material he had placed before me. I finished up by giving the
young man an entirely fictitious name and address and he was so pleased
to get rid of me that he actually ran round the counter-flap to open the
street door.

I walked on briskly down the road, in the thickening mist, in case he
was still looking after me and at the next corner came across Pons indolently studying the contents of a tobacconist's window. He turned to me
with a welcoming smile.

"Excellent, Parker. You played your part to perfection. That question
about investments overseas was shrewdly phrased."

I looked at him in puzzlement.

"How would you know that, Pons?"

"Because I was the other side of the door to the inner office watching
you both," he said quietly, falling into step as we wended our way back
through the narrow streets.

"You had some luck, then?"

He nodded, putting the stem of his empty pipe between his teeth.

"It has been a most fruitful expedition, Parker. We have only to visit
Mr Angus Dermot at Culzean Lodge and we are free to return to Miss
Hayling's estate."

"Mr Angus Dermot, Pons?"

My companion nodded. He drew two heavy sheaves of documents from his pocket.

"He is a geologist and mineralogist who fortunately lives quite close by in Inverness. If he is at home we will have saved a good deal of time and trouble."

And he quickened his pace as though trying to outstrip his racing thoughts. When I caught up with him at the next corner, he had turned into a quiet street of broad-fronted, respectable-looking houses whose trim front gardens led to carved mahogany doors whose brassware winked welcomingly through the mist.

His ring at the bell was answered by a trim, short man of about thirty with dark, tousled hair and a good-natured face. His eyes expressed surprise behind his steel-framed spectacles.

"Mr Angus Dermot?"

"Yes. What can I do for you, gentlemen?"

"My business is private, Mr Dermot, and cannot be discussed in the street. My name is Solar Pons and this is my friend and colleague, Dr Lyndon Parker."

The young man's cheeks flushed slightly and he shifted nervously on the door-step.

"Mr Pons! The famous detective. Forgive my manners, gentlemen. Come in by all means though what you can want with me I cannot fathom."

"We will get to that in a moment, Mr Dermot," said Pons smoothly, standing aside for me to precede him into the hall. Dermot shut the door behind us decisively and led the way into a cheerful study in which a coal fire blazed in a brick surround. With his thick brown tweed suit he looked out of place in the room, as though farming were his natural vocation. He waved us into two leather armchairs set in front of a raised construction which was part desk, part drawing-board. A green-shaded electric lamp was suspended above it and its surface was littered with papers and map-tracings. Pons wasted no time in coming to the point.

"Mr Dermot, you are a geologist and mineralogist, are you not?"

The young man stared at us in frank puzzlement.

"Among other things, yes, Mr Pons. There is no secret about that."

Solar Pons tented his thin fingers before him.

"Just so. I would like you to cast your mind back some time. You made a report, did you not, for the Scottish Land Trust, regarding a property known as Glen Affric."

Dermot was leaning against his drawing-board but now he drew himself up as though he had been stung, indignation on his features.

"That was a highly confidential report, Mr Pons. How you came to know of this is beyond me."

"We will leave that aside for the moment," said Pons calmly. "You confirmed the presence of certain minerals, I believe. I would hazard the guess that there was something strange about the commission. You were employed by Mr Mungo Ferguson, were you not?"

Dermot stared defiantly at Pons for a moment, then lowered his eyes sheepishly. He broke into a chuckle.

"Your reputation has not been exaggerated, Mr Pons. This was a highly confidential report. My sample drillings were carried out by night, in areas of woodland. The whole thing was most unusual but the arrangements were made, I was told, because of the secrecy necessary for a profitable commercial enterprise."

Pons' lean, aquiline features were alive with interest.

"Hmm. This is something you have met before in your experience?"

"Sometimes, Mr Pons. Though it is comparatively rare it is not unknown."

"You have a high reputation in your profession, I understand. One you would not wish to hazard."

Dermot's frank, open features showed his thoughts clearly.

"I have never yet broken my word, Mr Pons. And my reputation is as dear to me as your own."

"Well said, Mr Dermot," I could not forbear adding and Pons glanced at me with amusement, giving a dry chuckle.

"I was not imputing any slur on your reputation, Mr Dermot. But your report—your highly confidential report—revealed the presence of shale oil in great commercial quantity."

Dermot's face bore a puzzled expression again.

"I cannot see how that can be, Mr Pons. My test drillings confirmed the presence of low-grade shale oil, but hardly in commercial quantity. It would not be worth anyone's while to attempt to extract it and I made the matter clear in various letters which accompanied my reports."

My companion was smiling now.

"Excellent, Mr Dermot. Everything is quite clear. You have told me all I wish to know."

"That is all very well, Mr Pons, but I am in some confusion. We cannot let the matter rest here. You have somehow come into possession of a secret document intended only for the eyes of my clients."

Pons nodded.

"You are perfectly correct, sir. You have been open with me. I will be equally frank in return."

He drummed with restless fingers on the arm of his chair.

"I must in turn impose a pledge of secrecy upon you."

"You have my word, Mr Pons," the young man replied quickly.

"I have reason to suspect your work is being used as the basis of a gigantic swindle. A young lady's estate is the key to the whole business, and murder and attempted murder are only some of the ingredients."

There was nothing but shock and suspended disbelief in Dermot's eyes.

"You cannot be serious, Mr Pons?"

"I was never more serious, Mr Dermot. I hope to bring this business to a successful conclusion within the next few days but in the meantime nothing of what we have discussed here tonight must go beyond these four walls."

"I have already given my word, Mr Pons."

My companion looked at our host approvingly.

"Excellent. It goes without saying, Mr Dermot, that your part in this affair is nothing more than that of an innocent person whose work has been made the basis of fraudulent misrepresentation. You may rely upon me to bring the true facts before the police authorities."

"Thank you, Mr Pons."

Young Dermot came forward impulsively and shook my companion's hand.

"You may rely upon me for every assistance."

Solar Pons nodded.

"We will be in touch, Mr Dermot. Come, Parker."

And he strode from the room so briskly that I was hard put to it to keep up with him.

10

"All is well, Parker."

Solar Pons opened the door of the telephone booth outside the station and emerged, rubbing his hands. It was a bright, cold morning with just a hint of mist, and our journey back from Inverness had been uneventful.

"Mackintosh is already on his way and should be here shortly. But let us go into the waiting room. There is a fire and we will be more comfortable than in the street."

I followed him into the small chamber with its leather and horsehair benches, where a glowing coal fire gave off a cheerful radiance that gleamed on the brass fire-irons and coal-scuttle in the fender. I glanced at a coloured poster advertising the attractions of the Isle of Skye as I warmed my hands at the fire. Pons put his valise down on a corner of the bench and busied himself lighting his pipe.

We were alone in the room which shook and vibrated as a fast train went through on the down-line outside. Pons sat frowning for a moment and then fixed me with a steady eye.

"Well, Parker, I take it you have easily seen through Colonel McDonald's little scheme."

I shifted uncomfortably before the fire.

"I get the general drift, Pons, but I am not so sure I see the specific purpose of this blackguard's operations."

Pons stabbed the air with the stem of his pipe, a little furrow of concentration on his brow.

"Tut, Parker, it is simplicity itself. I had a good idea of what lay behind the sinister events enmeshing Miss Hayling before ever we left London. Her letters had apprised me of most of the details and I lacked only the motive. That McDonald was behind it was obvious. Not only did it bear all the hallmarks of his shifty schemes but Miss Hayling's glimpse of him with that scoundrel Ferguson clinched the matter."

He looked reflectively at the black-bearded porter who was vigorously sweeping the platform with a twiglet broom in the hard winter sunshine on the other side of the line.

"Unfortunately, there was little deductive prowess called for, though it was an exercise not without its points."

"You talk as though the whole thing were over, Pons."

"So it is, Parker, so it is," my friend remarked dreamily. "Though I must confess that I am at some pains as to how to bring him out into the open. And I am still going to find it difficult to prove anything against him."

He rubbed his thin fingers together and turned his eyes on the fire as though he could read the answer in the small blue and green flames which leapt and danced and sang as the coals shifted as they burned deeper into the grate.

"Ferguson is a danger to McDonald, Parker," he said almost absently. "Something will happen or my name is not Pons."

I came to stand in front of him.

"What do you mean?"

"We wanted to get that dog-cart up from the stream. Ferguson bungled it by having the thing burned."

"But how did he know?"

"Tut, Parker, the simplest thing in the world. There are two small tenant farmers with properties adjoining. Mackintosh gives his farmer instructions about raising the cart yesterday morning. The other farmer, who is McDonald's tenant, lives in a house only a few hundred yards away. It is my guess that we have been under observation through field-glasses in daylight hours during every journey we have taken in these parts since our arrival. They would have seen me at the stream and McDonald would have known soon after."

"You cannot mean it, Pons."

"I do mean it, Parker. It was only by going far off in our journey to Inverness that we have come close to the truth."

"I am apparently excluded from it," I said somewhat bitterly.

Pons glanced at me with sympathetic eyes.

"Surely not, Parker. We have both had the same set of circumstances before us. McDonald wanted the Haylings' land. He failed by legal means to obtain it so he achieved his object, or so he thought, by the crude methods of Ferguson. That precious rascal or one of his minions half-sawed through the shafts of that unfortunate couple's dog-cart. It had been carefully done and gave at the moment of greatest stress, the right-angle turn across the bridge. But McDonald had not bargained for Miss Hayling and her stubbornness. He found he still could not get hold of the land."

"But why did he want it, Pons?"

My friend looked at me quizzically.

"You have already told me the reason, my dear Parker," he said patiently. "It was surrounded by the Colonel's property and was the only flat piece of land of any size for miles around. The Colonel had to have it for the latest gigantic swindle he was floating."

"This is all supposition, Pons."

My companion shook his head.

"Not at all, Parker. It is as plain as day. It was all there in the brochures and prospectuses I stole from the Scottish Land Trust offices. That gives a glowing and entirely erroneous picture of things, based on young Dermot's report."

My puzzlement must have shown for Pons' face creased in a smile.

"Oil, Parker, oil! An oil boom which, to mix a metaphor, the Colonel wishes to convert into a gold-mine."

I looked at him blankly.

"But there is only low-grade shale-oil there, Pons!"

"Exactly, Parker. McDonald is relying on this to give credence to his fantastic scheme. He is floating hundreds of thousands of shares in a specially set-up company, based on misleading statements from Dermot's confidential report. It is all here. He wants the girl's land for his drilling operations and plant to give the whole thing a plausible basis."

He tapped the breast-pocket of his overcoat.

"There are thousands of gullible fools in this world who will invest in anything providing it promises them a reasonable return. This, if we are to believe the literature, promises them a hundredfold for each share. If

McDonald owns Miss Hayling's property and floats his company, I estimate at a rough guess that he will make something in excess of three million pounds before the bubble bursts."

"Good heavens, Pons!"

I stared at my companion for a long moment.

"Exactly, Parker," said Pons succinctly. "The problem is, how are we to stop it, with nothing concrete to lay before the authorities. This was the reason the Colonel was so anxious to get rid of me when he learned I was coming northward at Miss Hayling's behest. And he is equally obviously behind the attempts on Miss Hayling's life, using an odious tool like Ferguson, whom he employs as a figurehead and smokescreen."

"But supposing Ferguson exceeds his authority, Pons?"

My friend smiled thinly.

"McDonald is relying on that, Parker. Ferguson, crude, violent and bad-tempered is ideal for his purposes. If anything goes wrong he would be the scapegoat. McDonald would have covered his tracks perfectly. No-one at the office of the Director of Public Prosecutions would be able to link him with the Land Trust in any way."

"He must be a devil, Pons."

"He is, Parker."

"Then he left Ferguson's tobacco pouch in Miss Hayling's grounds?"

"Not in person, Parker. But he would have given the instructions from far off."

His brooding eyes looked into the heart of the fire.

"I would not like to be in Ferguson's shoes when the Colonel reacts to our latest moves."

He broke off as there came a grating noise from the forecourt outside the little station.

"Ah, here is the good Mackintosh now."

The sturdy form of the gardener was indeed striding toward the station entrance and we hurried out to him for there was something grim and stern in his usually good-natured features. He came to the point straight away.

"A bad business, Mr Pons, though a relief for Miss Hayling. Mungo Ferguson has been found dead in a ravine near Glen Affric."

Pons' face became sharp and alert.

"Ah! I am not surprised. The development we have been waiting for, Parker."

I nodded.

"You believe the Colonel to be responsible?"

Solar Pons' face was as grim as Mackintosh' own.

"I know he is, Parker. When and how did this happen?"

"Early this morning, Mr Pons. The body has been taken to the mortuary in Inverness. I met a local constable on my way to fetch you and he gave me the news. Apparently Ferguson slipped at a steep part of the ravine, fell and broke his neck. Foul play is not suspected."

A bitter smile twisted Pons' lips.

"It bears all the ear-marks of the Colonel. He is a worthy opponent, however evil and warped. Ferguson had served his purpose and had become too dangerous, Parker."

"Even so, Mr Pons," said Mackintosh steadily. "It is a bad business."

"You are quite right, Mr Mackintosh," my companion observed evenly. "I accept your implicit moral judgment. Now, we must put final matters in train."

"What are you going to do, Pons?"

"Send a telegram to the Colonel at Ardrossan Lodge, Parker. I have a mind to bring him into the open. My challenge is one he will find it difficult to avoid."

I felt somewhat alarmed at his words and looked at him anxiously as we took our seats in the trap.

"I would like you to find the local post-office and send this telegram for me," Pons told Mackintosh, who had now clambered into the driving seat.

"Certainly, Mr Pons. It is only a few hundred yards."

Pons pulled an old envelope from his pocket and sat smoking furiously as we rattled down the narrow street, his brows furrowed and concentrated as he wrote with a stub of pencil on the back of the envelope. He looked at it with satisfaction as we drew up in front of a large granite building. Mackintosh' eyes opened wide as he glanced at the envelope when Pons handed it to him. My companion rummaged in his pocket and gave him a guinea.

"Please keep the change."

"Thank you, Mr Pons. Would you like me to go to the village for a reply when we arrive back?"

Pons shook his head.

"I think not. It is my belief that the Colonel will come in person."

My astonishment re-echoed Mackintosh' own as the gardener hurried into the post-office.

"What on earth did you put in the telegram, Pons?"

"Something he could not resist, Parker. I appealed to his vanity."

And with that I had to be content as Mackintosh soon returned and in a few moments we were rattling on our way back to Glen Affric. Pons was silent for most of the journey, only breaking into conversation once.

"Tell me," he said to Mackintosh when we were within a mile or two of our destination. "Does Miss Hayling have a radio at the house?"

The driver glanced at him in surprise.

"Oh, yes, sir. There are two at the main house and I myself have one at my cottage."

"Excellent. You did not listen to the weather forecast this morning, by any chance?"

"Indeed I did, Mr Pons. Such things are vital to country folk in areas like this."

Pons smiled faintly, taking the pipe from his mouth.

"Do you happen to remember what was predicted for Scotland?"

The gardener hunched his shoulders, his eyes fixed forward over the pony's back.

"Fine in the morning with local mist in mid-afternoon, thickening at nightfall."

"Good," said Pons with satisfaction.

He rubbed his hands.

"It is certainly fine this morning. They might be right for once, eh, Parker?"

"Of course, Pons," I agreed. "But I fail to take the point."

"It would not be the first time," said he, with a twinkle in his eye. "It was just a notion which had occurred to me when sending the telegram, but it could be a vital one. I would stake my life that the Colonel would go for rifles. He is a crack-shot and a master of the stalk."

"Really, Pons . . ." I began when we started our steep descent of the hill near the stream, and we had to alight to assist the pony. Our arrival at the house had been noted and Miss Hayling herself stood on the front steps to greet us. She looked pale but her manner was collected.

"A friend has just telephoned from the village to say that Mungo Ferguson is dead."

She put her hand impulsively on my companion's arm.

"Oh, Mr Pons, what does it mean? Goodness knows I have no reason to mourn his death but it is a dreadful thing nevertheless."

"Your sentiments do you credit, Miss Hayling," said Pons, a kindly look in his eyes. "But unless I miss my guess this business will soon be over. I must just ask you to be patient a little longer."

"But what does it all mean, Mr Pons?"

"It means that Colonel McDonald will be here shortly," said Pons sombrely. "I have sent him a telegram this morning which should resolve the business."

There was a look of shock in the girl's eyes but she forbore to question my companion further.

"No doubt you know best, Mr Pons. In the meantime lunch is waiting."

And she led the way into the house.

11

All through lunch Pons had been silent and abstracted and he sat watching the windows which commanded the driveway as though he expected something to materialise at any minute. The sun shone brightly despite the cold and threw the shadows of the mullioned windows across the cheerful, panelled room in which we ate.

The girl had been restrained though her curiosity was obvious and we had chatted desultorily on a number of mundane topics. Afterwards, we took coffee in a small room which overlooked the front porch. We had eaten early and it was still only a quarter to one when I became aware of Mackintosh' sturdy form hovering on the front steps. I glanced at Pons and realised instantly that the gardener had taken up his position on my friend's instructions. He took the pipe from his mouth and addressed himself to our hostess.

"Miss Hayling, you have been extraordinarily patient and trusting in the extreme. In all my long experience I have known few persons of your sex who have exhibited such courage and character."

The short speech was an unusual one for Pons and I saw the girl flush with pleasure while Mrs McRae shot a glance of approval at Pons.

"I know you have my welfare at heart, Mr Pons," the girl said in a low voice. "I am content to leave the explanations for later."

"You shall have them in full, Miss Hayling," said Pons. "In the meantime I shall have to ask you to trust me a little longer. I would like you and Mr and Mrs McRae to withdraw to the upper floors of the house and leave this matter to Dr Parker and myself."

"By all means, Mr Pons."

The girl got up obediently and followed the housekeeper out of the room.

"What on earth, Pons . . ." I was beginning when my friend rose to his feet with astonishing alacrity and put his hand on my arm.

"Ah, he has risen to the bait, Parker."

I followed his glance through the window to find the shimmering image of a white Rolls-Royce Silver Ghost purring to a stop in front of the main entrance. By the time Pons and I had joined Mackintosh a tall, military figure was descending.

"Just stay within earshot, if you please," said Pons to Mackintosh sotto voce and the burly gardener withdrew a dozen paces or so to the bottom of the steps.

There was no sound in all the great park except for the cawing of rooks in some ancient elms in the distance and the measured tread of feet in the gravel as the tall figure came toward us. I don't know what I had expected but the actuality was a shock. A smartly-dressed but almost emaciated old man with a gaunt face, hook-nose and iron-grey moustache. The only things alive in the dead white face were the burning yellow eyes which were fixed unwinkingly upon Pons. Colonel McDonald came to a halt at the foot of the steps, without a glance at myself or the gardener.

"Well, Mr Pons," he said in a low, soft voice. "We meet at last."

"We do indeed, Colonel," said my companion, descending the steps so that they were on the level, almost face to face. "You have not wasted much time on receipt of my telegram."

"The opportunity was too good to miss," said the other in the same low, unemotional voice. "You have not lost your dexterity in dealing with my little toys."

"Neither you your ingenuity, Colonel. Spring catches operating surprises were always your specialty, were they not."

A muscle started fretting in the Colonel's cheek but otherwise he and Pons might have been calmly discussing stock-market prices.

"You have been interfering with my operations, Mr Pons. And when you come upon my own home ground I find it intolerable."

Solar Pons shrugged.

"It was a clumsy business, having the wreckage of the dog-cart burned. Though I have no doubt I should have discovered that the shafts had been sawn through."

The Colonel nodded absently.

"That was a tactical error on Ferguson's part."

"But one you have soon put right," Pons observed.

McDonald gave a harsh, mirthless laugh.

"I heard about the accident just before I left to come here. A tragic business."

"Murder is always tragic," said Solar Pons evenly.

McDonald was still standing stock-still but now the muscle in his cheek was twitching almost uncontrollably. That and his blazing eyes were the only indications of the anger within.

"Strong words, Mr Pons," he said in that uncannily soft voice. "Strong words. And ones you are going to find difficult to prove."

"I am not trying to prove them," said Pons with a faint smile. "I am merely speaking my thoughts aloud."

The Colonel nodded again, his yellow eyes now glancing from me to Mackintosh.

"Your telegram implied a settlement between us, Mr Pons. I am in agreement."

"I knew I could rely upon you," said Solar Pons slowly. "Your courage has never been in question."

Colonel McDonald drew himself up stiffly and bowed slightly at the compliment.

"Perhaps we could walk to the car."

"You have no objection to my friend and colleague, Dr Parker, accompanying us?"

"By no means, Mr Pons. I am quite alone."

I hurried down the steps and followed as the two men strolled toward the white Rolls-Royce. The Colonel opened the spring-loaded boot which came up gently with a scarcely audible click. Within I could see two long leather cases.

"Matched sporting rifles, Mr Pons. Neither of us will be at a disadvantage. You accept the challenge?"

"Certainly. After all, it was I who issued it."

As the import of their words sank into my brain I found my tongue. "This is madness, Pons! Are you suggesting something as barbaric as a duel? The Colonel is a crack-shot and an experienced stalker."

"I am well aware of that, Parker. I am not entirely a novice myself with the sporting rifle."

The Colonel bowed again, reluctant admiration on his face.

"Then you accept, sir?"

"Most certainly. But on certain conditions."

"And those are?"

"That Dr Parker be allowed to accompany me to act as my second— and see fair play. You to have a companion also. Unarmed I might add."

The Colonel chuckled.

"By all means. I shall not need a companion for I would find him a hindrance. The only conditions of mine are time, place and the question of ammunition."

Solar Pons looked steadily at the other.

"Ammunition?"

"Five rounds each. No more, no less. That should be ample to settle the matter."

"Agreed. And the time and place?"

McDonald looked up at the sun.

"It is now one-thirty P.M. Darkness comes down swiftly in these latitudes. Both parties to be in position on the field by not later than two-thirty."

Pons nodded.

"Agreed. And the venue?"

McDonald slid out one of the leather cases and handed it to Pons before closing the boot. He glanced across at Mackintosh.

"There is a rock called The Sentinel in the glen near the edge of Miss Hayling's property just before the land rises to the skirts of Ben Affric."

"Ah, the mountain beyond the glen. I will find it."

"The gardener will tell you how to get to it. It is only a mile or so from here. I will meet you there. Until two-thirty, then."

"Until two-thirty."

We waited in silence as the Colonel got behind the wheel. The Rolls-Royce glided sedately round the concourse and disappeared down the drive, a thin plume of exhaust smoke hanging behind it in the frosty air. Pons was already opening the case, looking at the sleek, polished rifle within. He broke open the breech.

"Fortunately, I am familiar with this model. It is a beauty. One of a matched pair, as McDonald said. The Colonel goes in for nothing but the best. There are five cartridges, as agreed."

"This is madness, Pons," I repeated, looking at the stolid form of Mackintosh as if for support. "I will not be a party to murder."

"Tut, Parker," said Pons chidingly. "You exaggerate, as usual. I do not think it will be as bad as that."

He glanced up at the sun.

"Come, we must hurry. I have a few preparations to make before we reach the killing-ground."

12

We walked uphill in silence, the sun throwing long shadows on the heather, a faint mist rising, the beauty of the blue-green mass of Ben Affric in the distance making our sombre errand seem like some wild figment of imagination. I still could not quite believe the whole incredible circumstance and walked in silence across the rough ground behind Pons, sick at heart and afraid for my friend.

Pons must have sensed my mood for he looked back at me with a smile, the harshness of the sunlight strongly accentuating the clear-minted lines of his face.

"My dear Parker. You look as though you are on your way to a funeral. Did I not tell you that things were not so serious?"

"That is all very well, Pons," I said. "But there is likely to be a bloody outcome to this business. How do you know that Colonel McDonald will keep his word. He is sure to be up to some treachery."

"I am relying on it, Parker," said Pons gravely, taking his pipe-stem from his mouth. "I have not come unprepared."

He patted the large canvas bag he carried as he spoke. I myself had the loaded rifle McDonald had left with us, slung over my shoulder by the strap and I was finding our progress over the rough terrain rather heavy going. It had now turned two o'clock and we had cleared Miss Hayling's estate and the humped mass of the mountain Ben Affric threw a vast shadow over the glen before us, so that it seemed as though we were advancing into the valley of the shadow. I looked at my companion in surprise.

"I do not follow you, Pons."

He chuckled.

"All will be made clear to you shortly, Parker. Ah, that must be The Sentinel."

I followed his gaze and saw the great hump of rock rising from the plain before us. Already, its base was lost amid the haze.

"What do you intend to do, Pons?"

"Indulge in a little deception, Parker. Normally, I would abide by the rules but I have myself no compunction in being devious when dealing with such a person as McDonald."

We both saved our breath for the next ten minutes, as the going was difficult underfoot. Slowly the huge splinter of granite set in the middle of the lonely glen grew before us. By twenty-past two we were only a few hundred yards off.

"There is no sign of McDonald, Pons," I observed as we stumbled the last few yards across the boulder-littered ground.

"I would not expect there to be, Parker. Unless I miss my guess he is up on the skirt of the mountain there, where the ravine runs, watching us through glasses. That would be a perfect vantage-point."

"Good heavens, Pons!"

"There is no danger for the moment, Parker. The Colonel will not make his move until he is absolutely certain."

We were within the shadow of the rock now and scrambled, by means of broad ledges to a position just below the top. As Pons had hinted the place was empty and there was no sign of the Colonel. It was bitterly cold here in the shadow and the surface of the granite was damp and slippery. I put down the case and busied myself in unstrapping it and removing the rifle. Pons had his back to me as he knelt and rummaged in the canvas bag he had brought.

When I turned I was amazed to see what appeared to be a dummy, dressed in old tweeds. Pons produced a crumpled deer-stalker and jammed it on the figure's head. He surveyed it critically.

"I think that will do nicely, Parker."

"But what are you doing, Pons?"

"With the aid of a few bolsters borrowed from Mrs McRae and an old suit of her husband's I am making a passable facsimile of myself. I think it will pass muster, even through the Colonel's glasses, if I pull the hat well down."

Pons put the finishing touches to his creation and then carried it to a position a few feet below the ridge of the rock. Then he cautiously hoisted it there, with its back to the mountain, and pinned it with a dead branch he had broken from a stunted tree which projected from the rocks just below the sky-line. It stood up well and the silhouette so presented must have been visible for miles around. Pons dusted his hands in satisfaction and then came back to me.

"It is almost half-past two, Parker. I do not think we shall have long to wait."

He took the rifle from me and went cautiously back. In a niche in the rock below the summit, where I joined him a few moments later, I found I could see right up the glen to where the purple-brown mass of Ben Affric was becoming slowly rinsed with haze. Nothing moved in all the vast expanse of the glen before us.

"You see, Parker," said Pons calmly. "Colonel McDonald never had the slightest intention of keeping this appointment. At least in the way we intended."

No sooner had he spoken than there came a bright flash from the sombre darkness of the mountain before us and a moment later the echoing crash of a high-powered rifle which thundered about the glen. At almost the same instant the tweed-clad figure which sat on the summit of the rock above us somersaulted in the air and landed some yards from us. Feathers floated down after it. I ran across and was stupefied to see the large hole torn in the material of McRae's jacket.

"It would have been right through the heart, Pons!"

"Would it not, Parker."

Solar Pons was lying in the niche of the rock, his keen right eye sighting along the rifle, his cheek close in to the stock.

"The flash came from the head of the ravine. Ah, there he is!"

He squeezed the trigger gently and the rifle cracked, the stock jerking against his cheek while blue smoke curled from the breech and barrel.

"You have not killed him, Pons!"

My friend looked at me with a grim smile.

"Hardly, Parker. I have no wish to appear as the principal figure in a murder trial. I fired to frighten him. As near as I can judge the bullet struck the rocks a dozen feet away from him."

No sooner had he finished speaking than the most dreadful cry sounded from the head of the glen and went echoing round the heights. Pons started to his feet but I put my hand on his arm.

"Careful, Pons! It may be a trap to lure us out. He cannot be wounded and we shall be at his mercy in the open."

Solar Pons smiled.

"His rifle is useless now, Parker. The weather is closing in. I relied on it in my calculations of the risk involved."

I soon saw what he meant. Already, as we had moved off The Sentinel heavy banks of mist were gathering around the skirts of the mountain.

"So that was why you asked Mackintosh about the weather, Pons?"

"Naturally, Parker. I do not believe in taking unnecessary chances in face of such an enemy. It is no bad thing to enlist the help of nature when possible."

Pons was scrambling down the base of the rock now and I followed, carrying the rifle, which he had cast aside. As I gained the ground I could see Pons striding away at a great pace among the scree and boulders. By dint of great effort I caught up with him and we went forward side by side through the rapidly thickening mist.

As we mounted up the flank of Ben Affric the air grew ever more raw and dank. The mist was breast-high now and Pons guided us over toward the right of the mountain.

"Be careful, Pons. We are coming near the area of the ravine."

"I am well aware of that, Parker. I am endeavouring to memorise the salient features of the terrain before the weather closes down completely."

Even as he spoke we seemed to walk into an impenetrable white wall. A few yards behind us the sun had been shining; now, it was almost as though we were in the middle of the night, as the great fog-bank rolled on, borne inexorably forward from the heights above by the wind at its tail. Instinctively I had faltered, but Pons' hand was on my elbow, guiding me on as though all were daylight and absolutely clear to him.

"It is only a few yards now, Parker. Please be extremely careful. Ah, here we are!"

A few seconds later I saw what his keen eyes had already noted; the matching rifle to the one I carried was lying on the damp rock floor of the gully we had been mounting. On top of a flat boulder from which McDonald had obviously fired, were four spare cartridges.

"At least the Colonel kept his word in one respect," said Pons grudgingly. "Keep behind me and mind your footing."

He went forward slowly and I followed, anxious not to lose him for the mist had grown remarkably thick. Our journey did not take long. After only a few yards the terrain shelved steeply on to slippery rock. Pons stopped and held up his hand.

"We can go no farther, Parker. This is the edge of the ravine."

As he spoke there came a terrible groan from the chasm before us; the sound was so unexpected that I felt an indescribable thrill of horror run through me. Pons' reaction filled me with alarm. He went forward on the steep slope and lay down, supporting himself by a small nodule of rock which rose from the precipitous surface.

"For heaven's sake be careful, Pons!"

"If you would come here and hold my legs, Parker, I would be obliged," he said in a low, almost gentle voice. "And pass me the rifle if you would be so good."

I did as he bade and came forward, lying down in a flat place by a boulder and leaning forward to grip his ankles. Pons was slowly extending the rifle and its sling before him.

"My shot startled him and he obviously slipped into the ravine," he said musingly.

At that moment there was a sudden breeze and the mist parted briefly. I think I shall never forget the sight it revealed. The Colonel's gaunt face with the burning yellow eyes glaring savagely over the iron-grey moustache was suspended in the blackness. He did not see me, for his intense, malevolent gaze was fixed entirely on Pons. I could see only his head and the upper part of his shoulders; his body must have been hanging almost vertically in space.

His fingers were frenziedly locked in a clump of heather which was growing from a crevice in the rocks in front of him. I could see now where his heels had scored a distinct passage in the damp, mossy surface of the gorge. Inch by inch Pons advanced the rifle toward him. Pons' arms were extended to the limit in front of him and I felt his ankles vibrate beneath my hands.

The end of the rifle sling was still a foot short. The Colonel opened his mouth as if to say something, then shut it with a snap. Little flecks of saliva dribbled down his chin. There was a mixture of anger, pain and regret in his eyes. Then the stems of the heather tore out with a convulsive movement and the head and arms whipped backward out of sight into the mist. The dreadful cry which echoed and swelled from that terrible abyss I hear still in my dreams to this day.

Then it was cut off abruptly and we heard the sickening impact of broken flesh on rock as the body bounced from boulder to boulder until the sound died away in the distance. For a long time there was nothing but the patter of scree and small rocks rattling down the sombre depths.

Pons slowly dragged himself back to safety. He was white and trembling. Despite his efforts the rifle slid over to join its owner in the chasm below. I got up and we two sat on the edge of a boulder for several minutes to collect ourselves. Pons lit his pipe and soon had it drawing comfortably, his head wreathed in tobacco smoke.

"Well, Parker," he said eventually. "Poetic justice, though I would not have had it happen like that."

"You could not have helped it, Pons," I said. "That dreadful creature would have murdered you in cold blood."

He nodded without speaking, his eyes hooded and brooding as he stared into the misty deep before us.

"Fate is unpredictable, Parker," he observed presently. "Unless I miss my guess it is somewhere hereabouts that McDonald's tool Mungo Ferguson met his end."

I stared at him, still too shocked to say anything. He looked at me sympathetically and roused himself.

"We must get back and inform the police, my dear fellow."

I nodded, my thoughts still elsewhere.

"What did you put in that telegram, Pons?"

"THIS MATTER MUST BE SETTLED BETWEEN US. YOUR TERMS OR MINE. PONS. I knew he could not resist the challenge. I accepted his terms, with the result we have seen."

Pons sighed and I looked at him sharply.

"Unfortunately there was little in the case which appealed to my ratiocinative instincts, but it was not without interest. And it has disposed of one of the most dangerous opponents I have ever come up against."

I nodded.

"The Colonel's was an ingenious scheme, Pons. The shale-oil report was a stroke of genius."

"Was it not, Parker."

Solar Pons stared at me with a far-away look on his clear-minted features.

"Who knows, Parker, there may well be oil beneath Scottish soil and Scottish seas. Whether it will come in our time is another matter. We shall have to wait and see."

He turned abruptly on his heel.

"Now we have a tidy step before us and it will soon be dark. And I really owe a most gallant young lady some detailed explanation."

Our Midnight Visitor

SIR ARTHUR CONAN DOYLE

I

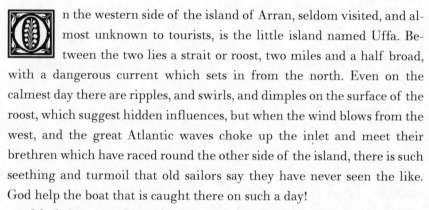

On the western side of the island of Arran, seldom visited, and almost unknown to tourists, is the little island named Uffa. Between the two lies a strait or roost, two miles and a half broad, with a dangerous current which sets in from the north. Even on the calmest day there are ripples, and swirls, and dimples on the surface of the roost, which suggest hidden influences, but when the wind blows from the west, and the great Atlantic waves choke up the inlet and meet their brethren which have raced round the other side of the island, there is such seething and turmoil that old sailors say they have never seen the like. God help the boat that is caught there on such a day!

My father owned one-third part of the island of Uffa, and I was born and bred there. Our farm or croft was a small one enough, for if a good thrower were to pick up a stone on the shore at Carracuil (which was our place) he could manage, in three shies, to clear all our arable land, and it was hardly longer than it was broad. Behind this narrow track, on which we grew corn and potatoes, was the homesteading of Carracuil—a rather bleak-looking grey stone house with red-tiled byre buttressed against one side of it, and behind this again the barren undulating moorland stretched away up to Beg-na-sacher and Beg-na-phail, two rugged knolls which marked the center of the island. We had grazing ground for a couple of cows, and eight or ten sheep, and we had our boat anchored down in Carravoe. When the fishing failed, there was more time to devote to the crops, and if the season was bad, as likely as not the herring would be thick on the coast. Taking one thing with another a crofter in Uffa had as much chance of laying by a penny or two as most men on the mainland.

Besides our own family, the MacDonalds of Carracuil, there were two others on the island. These were the Gibbs of Arden and the Fullartons of Corriemains. There was no priority claimed among us, for none had any legend of the coming of the others. We had all three held our farms by direct descent for many generations, paying rent to the Duke of Hamilton and all prospering in a moderate way. My father had been enabled to send me to begin the study of medicine at the University of Glasgow, and I had attended lectures there for two winter sessions, but whether from caprice or from some lessening in his funds, he had recalled me, and in the year 1865 I found myself cribbed up in this little island with just education enough to wish for more, and with no associate at home but the grim, stern old man, for my mother had been dead some years, and I had neither brother nor sister.

There were two youths about my own age in the island, Geordie and Jock Gibbs, but they were rough, loutish fellows, good-hearted enough, but with no ideas above fishing and farming. More to my taste was the society of Minnie Fullarton, the pretty daughter of old Fullarton of Corriemains. We had been children together, and it was natural that when she blossomed into a buxom, fresh-faced girl, and I into a square-shouldered, long-legged youth, there should be something warmer than friendship between us. Her elder brother was a corn chandler in Ardrossan, and was said to be doing well, so that the match was an eligible one, but for some reason my father objected very strongly to our intimacy and even forbade me entirely to meet her. I laughed at his commands, for I was a hot-headed, irreverent youngster, and continued to see Minnie, but when it came to his ears, it caused many violent scenes between us, which nearly went the length of blows. We had a quarrel of this sort just before the equinoctial gales in the spring of the year in which my story begins, and I left the old man with his face flushed, and his great bony hands shaking with passion, while I went jauntily off to our usual trysting-place. I have often regretted since that I was not more submissive, but how was I to guess the dark things which were to come upon us?

I can remember that day well. Many bitter thoughts rose in my heart as I strode along the narrow pathway, cutting savagely at the thistles on either side with my stick. One side of our little estate was bordered by the Combera cliffs, which rose straight out of the water to the height of a couple of hundred feet. The top of these cliffs was covered with green sward and commanded a noble view on every side. I stretched myself on the turf there and watched the breakers dancing over the Winner sands and listened to the gurgling of the water down beneath me in the caves of the Combera. We faced the western side of the island, and from where I lay I could see the whole stretch of the Irish Sea, right across to where a long hazy line upon the horizon marked the northern coast of the sister isle. The wind was blowing freshly from the north-west and the great Atlantic rollers were racing merrily in, one behind the other, dark brown below, light green above, and breaking with a sullen roar at the base of the cliffs. Now and again a sluggish one would be overtaken by its successor, and the two would come crashing in together and send the spray right over me as I lay. The whole air was prickly with the smack of the sea. Away to the north there was a piling up of clouds, and the peak of Goatfell in Arran looked lurid and distinct. There were no craft in the offing except one little eager, panting steamer making for the shelter of the Clyde, and a trim brigantine tacking along the coast. I was speculating as to her destination when I heard a light springy footstep, and Minnie Fullarton was standing beside me, her face rosy with exercise and her brown hair floating behind her.

"Wha's been vexing you, Archie?" she asked with the quick intuition of womanhood. "The auld man has been speaking aboot me again; has he no'?"

It was strange how pretty and mellow the accents were in her mouth which came so raspingly from my father. We sat down on a little green hillock together, her hand in mine, while I told her of our quarrel in the morning.

"You see they're bent on parting us," I said; "but indeed they'll find they have the wrong man to deal with if they try to frighten me away from you."

"I'm no' worth it, Archie," she answered, sighing. "I'm ower hamely and simple for one like you that speaks well and is a scholar forbye."

"You're too good and true for anyone, Minnie," I answered, though in my heart I thought there was some truth in what she said.

"I'll no' trouble anyone lang," she continued, looking earnestly into my face. "I got my call last nicht; I saw a ghaist, Archie."

"Saw a ghost!" I ejaculated.

"Yes, and I doubt it was a call for me. When my cousin Steevie deed he saw one the same way."

"Tell me about it, dear," I said, impressed by her solemnity.

"There's no' much to tell: it was last nicht aboot twelve, or maybe one o'clock. I was lying awake thinking o' this and that wi' my een fixed on the window. Suddenly I saw a face looking in at me through the glass—an awfu'-like face, Archie. It was na the face of anyone on the island. I canna tell what it was like—it was just awfu'. It was there maybe a minute look-ing tae way and tither into the room. I could see the glint o' his very een—for it was a man's face—and his nose was white where it was pressed against the glass. My very blood ran cauld and I couldna scream for fright. Then it went awa' as quickly and as sudden as it came."

"Who could it have been?" I exclaimed.

"A wraith or a bogle," said Minnie positively.

"Are you sure it wasn't Tommy Gibbs?" I suggested.

"Na, na, it wasna Tammy. It was a dark, hard, dour sort of face."

"Well," I said, laughing, "I hope the fellow will give me a look up, whoever he is. I'll soon learn who he is and where he comes from. But we won't talk of it, or you'll be frightening yourself tonight again. It'll be a dreary night as it is."

"A bad nicht for the puir sailors," she answered sadly, glancing at the dark wrack hurrying up from the northward, and at the white line of breakers on the Winner sands. "I wonder what yon brig is after! Unless it gets roond to Lamlash or Brodick Bay, it'll find itself on a nasty coast."

She was watching the trim brigantine which had already attracted my attention. She was still standing off the coast, and evidently ex-pected rough weather, for her foresail had been taken in and her topsail reefed down.

"It's too cold for you up here!" I exclaimed at last, as the clouds cov-ered the sun, and the keen north wind came in more frequent gusts. We walked back together, until we were close to Carracuil, when she left me, taking the footpath to Corriemains, which was about a mile from our bothy. I hoped that my father had not observed us together, but he met me at the door, fuming with passion. His face was quite livid with rage, and he held his shotgun in his hands. I forget if I mentioned that in spite of his age he was one of the most powerful men I ever met in my life.

"So you've come!" he roared, shaking the gun at me. "You great gowk—" I did not wait for the string of adjectives which I knew was coming.

"You keep a civil tongue in your head," I said.

"You dare!" he shouted, raising his arm as if to strike me. "You wunna come in here. You can gang back where you come frae!"

"You can go to the devil!" I answered, losing my temper completely, on which he jabbed at me with the butt-end of the gun, but I warded it off with my stick. For a moment the devil was busy in me, and my throat was full of oaths, but I choked them down, and, turning on my heel, walked back to Corriemains, where I spent the day with the Fullartons. It seemed to me that my father, who had long been a miser, was rapidly becoming a madman—and a dangerous one to boot.

II

My mind was so busy with my grievance that I was poor company, I fear, and drank perhaps more whisky than was good for me. I remember that I stumbled over a stool once and that Minnie looked surprised and tearful, while old Fullarton sniggered to himself and coughed to hide it. I did not set out for home till half-past nine, which was a very late hour for the island. I knew my father would be asleep, and that if I climbed through my bedroom window I should have one night in peace.

It was blowing great guns by this time, and I had to put my shoulder against the gale as I came along the winding path which led down to Carracuil. I must still have been under the influence of liquor, for I remember that I sang uproariously and joined my feeble pipe to the howling of the wind. I had just got to the enclosure of our croft when a little incident occurred which helped to sober me.

White is a colour so rare in nature that in an island like ours, where even paper was a precious commodity, it would arrest the attention at once. Something white fluttered across my path and stuck flapping upon a furze bush. I lifted it up and discovered, to my very great surprise, that it was a linen pocket-handkerchief—and scented. Now I was very sure that beyond my own there was no such thing as a white pocket-handkerchief in the island. A small community like ours knew each other's wardrobes to a nicety. But as to scent in Uffa—it was preposterous! Who did the handkerchief belong to then? Was Minnie right, and was there really a stranger in the island? I walked on very thoughtfully, holding my discovery in my hand and thinking of what Minnie had seen the night before.

When I got into my bedroom and lit my rushlight I examined it again. It was clean and new, with the initials A.W. worked in red silk in the corner. There was no other indication as to who it might belong to, though from its size it was evidently a man's. The incident struck me as so extraordinary that I sat for some time on the side of my bed turning it over in my befuddled mind, but without getting any nearer a conclusion. I might even have taken my father into confidence, but his hoarse snoring in the adjoining room showed that he was fast asleep. It is as well that it was so, for I was in no humour to be bullied, and we might have had words. The old man had little longer to live, and it is some solace to me now that that little was unmarred by any further strife between us.

I did not take my clothes off, for my brain was getting swimmy after its temporary clearness, so I dropped my head upon the pillow and sank into profound slumber. I must have slept about four hours when I woke with a violent start. To this day I have never known what it was that roused me. Everything was perfectly still, and yet I found all my faculties in a state of extreme tension. Was there someone in the room? It was very dark, but I peered about, leaning on my elbow. There was nothing to be seen, but still that eerie feeling haunted me. At that moment the flying scud passed away from the face of the moon and a flood of cold light was poured into my chamber. I turned my eyes up instinctively, and—good God!—there at the window was the face, an evil, malicious face, hard-cut, and distinct against the silvery radiance, glaring in at me as Minnie had seen it the night before. For one moment I tingled and palpitated like a frightened child, the next both glass and sash were gone and I was rolling over and over on the gravel path with my arms round a tall strong man— the two of us worrying each other like a pair of dogs. Almost by intuition I knew as we went down together that he had slipped his hand into his side pocket, and I clung to that wrist like grim death. He tried hard to free it but I was too strong for him, and we staggered on to our feet again in the same position, panting and snarling.

"Let go my hand, damn you!" he said.

"Let go that pistol then," I gasped.

We looked hard at each other in the moonlight, and then he laughed and opened his fingers. A heavy glittering object, which I could see was a revolver, dropped with a clink on to the gravel. I put my foot on it and let go my grip of him.

"Well, matey, how now?" he said with another laugh. "Is that an end of a round, or the end of the battle? You islanders seem a hospitable lot. You're so ready to welcome a stranger, that you can't wait to find the door, but must come flying through the window like infernal fireworks."

"What do you want to come prowling round people's houses at night for, with weapons in your pocket?" I asked sternly.

"I should think I needed a weapon," he answered, "when there are young devils like you knocking around. Hullo! here's another of the family."

I turned my head, and there was my father, almost at my elbow. He had come round from the front door. His grey woollen nightdress and grizzled hair were streaming in the wind, and he was evidently much excited. He had in his hand the double-barrelled gun with which he had threatened me in the morning. He put this up to his shoulder, and would most certainly have blown out either my brains or those of the stranger, had I not turned away the barrel with my hand.

"Wait a bit, father," I said, "let us hear what he has to say for himself. And you," I continued, turning to the stranger, "can come inside with us and justify yourself if you can. But remember we are in a majority, so keep your tongue between your teeth."

"Not so fast, my young bantam," he grumbled; "you've got my six-shooter, but I have a Derringer in my pocket. I learned in Colorado to carry them both. However, come along into this shanty of yours, and let us get the damned palaver over. I'm wet through, and most infernally hungry."

My father was still mumbling to himself, and fidgeting with his gun, but he did not oppose my taking the stranger into the house. I struck a match, and lit the oil lamp in the kitchen, on which our prisoner stooped down to it and began smoking a cigarette. As the light fell full on his face, both my father and I took a good look at him. He was a man of about forty, remarkably handsome, of rather a Spanish type, with blue-black hair and beard, and sun-burned features. His eyes were very bright, and their gaze so intense that you would think they projected somewhat, unless you saw him in profile. There was a dash of recklessness and devilry about them, which, with his wiry, powerful frame and jaunty manner, gave the impression of a man whose past had been an adventurous one. He was elegantly dressed in a velveteen jacket, and greyish trousers of a foreign cut. Without in the least resenting our prolonged scrutiny, he seated himself upon the dresser, swinging his legs, and blowing little blue wreaths from his cigarette. His appearance seemed to reassure my father, or perhaps it was the sight of the rings which flashed on the stranger's left hand every time he raised it to his lips.

"Ye munna mind Archie, sir," he said in a cringing voice. "He was aye a fashious bairn, ower quick wi' his hands, and wi' mair muscle than brains. I was fashed mysel' wi' the sudden stour, but as tae shootin' at ye, sir, that was a' an auld man's havers. Nae doobt ye're a veesitor, or maybe it's a shipwreck—it's no a shipwreck, is't?" The idea awoke the covetous devil in my father's soul, and it looked out through his glistening eyes, and set his long stringy hands a-shaking.

"I came here in a boat," said the stranger shortly. "This was the first house I came to after I left the shore, and I'm not likely to forget the reception you have given me. That young hopeful of yours has nearly broken my back."

"A good job too!" I interrupted hotly, "why couldn't you come up to the door like a man, instead of skulking at the window?"

"Hush, Archie, hush!" said my father imploringly; while our visitor grinned across at me as amicably as if my speech had been most conciliatory.

"I don't blame you," he said—he spoke with a strange mixture of accents, sometimes with a foreign lisp, sometimes with a slight Yankee intonation, and at other times very purely indeed. "I have done the same, mate. Maybe you noticed a brigantine standing on and off the shore yesterday?"

I nodded my head.

"That was mine," he said. "I'm owner, skipper, and everything else. Why shouldn't a man spend his money in his own way. I like cruising about, and I like new experiences. I suppose there's no harm in that. I was in the Mediterranean last month, but I'm sick of blue skies and fine weather. Chios is a damnable paradise of a place. I've come up here for a little fresh air and freedom. I cruised all down the western isles, and when we came abreast of this place of yours it rather took my fancy, so I hauled the foreyard aback and came ashore last night to prospect. It wasn't this house I struck, but another farther to the west'ard; however, I saw enough to be sure it was a place after my own heart—a real quiet corner. So I went back and set everything straight aboard yesterday, and now here I am. You can put me up for a few weeks, I suppose. I'm not hard to please, and I can pay my way; suppose we say ten dollars a week for board and lodging, and a fortnight to be paid in advance."

He put his hand in his pocket and produced four shining napoleons, which he pushed along the dresser to my father, who grabbed them up eagerly.

"I'm sorry I gave you such a rough reception," I said, rather awkwardly. "I was hardly awake at the time."

"Say no more, mate, say no more!" he shouted heartily, holding out his hand and clasping mine. "Hard knocks are nothing new to me. I suppose we may consider the bargain settled then?"

"Ye can bide as lang as ye wull, sir," answered my father, still fingering the four coins. "Archie and me'll do a' we can to mak' your veesit a pleasant ane. It's no' such a dreary place as ye might think. When the Lamlash boats come in we get the papers and a' the news."

It struck me that the stranger looked anything but overjoyed by this piece of information. "You don't mean to say that you get the papers here," he said.

"'Oo aye, the *Scotsman* an' the *Glasgey Herald*. But maybe you would like Archie and me to row ower to your ship in the morn an' fetch your luggage."

"The brig is fifty miles away by this time," said our visitor. "She is running before the wind for Marseilles. I told the mate to bring her round again in a month or so. As to luggage, I always travel light in that matter.

If a man's purse is only full he can do with very little else. All I have is in a bundle under your window. By the way, my name is Digby—Charles Digby."

"I thought your initials were A.W.," I remarked.

He sprang off the dresser as if he had been stung, and his face turned quite grey for a moment. "What the devil do you mean by that?" he said.

"I thought this might be yours," I answered, handing him the hand-kerchief I had found.

"Oh, is that all!" he said with rather a forced laugh. "I didn't quite see what you were driving at. That's all right. It belongs to Whittingdale, my second officer. I'll keep it until I see him again. And now suppose you give me something to eat, for I'm about famished."

We brought him out such rough fare as was to be found in our larder, and he ate ravenously, and tossed off a stiff glass of whisky and water. Afterwards my father showed him into the solitary spare bedroom, with which he professed himself well pleased, and we all settled down for the night. As I went back to my couch I noticed that the gale had freshened up, and I saw long streamers of seaweed flying past my broken window in the moonlight. A great bat fluttered into the room, which is reckoned a sure sign of misfortune in the islands—but I was never superstitious, and let the poor thing find its way out again unmolested.

III

In the morning it was still blowing a whole gale, though the sky was blue for the most part. Our guest was up betimes and we walked down to the beach together. It was a sight to see the great rollers sweeping in, overtopping one another like a herd of oxen, and then bursting with a roar, sending the Carracuil pebbles flying before them like grapeshot, and filling the whole air with drifting spume.

We were standing together watching the scene, when looking round I saw my father hurrying towards us. He had been up and out since early dawn. When he saw us looking, he began waving his hands and shouting, but the wind carried his voice away. We ran towards him however, seeing that he was heavy with news.

"The brig's wrecked, and they're a' drowned!" he cried as we met him.

"What!" roared our visitor.

If ever I heard exceeding great joy compressed into a monosyllable it vibrated in that one.

"They're a' drowned and naething saved!" repeated my father. "Come yoursel' and see."

We followed him across the Combera to the level sands on the other side. They were strewn with wreckage, broken pieces of bulwark and handrail, panelling of a cabin, and an occasional cask. A single large spar was tossing in the waves close to the shore, occasionally shooting up towards the sky like some giant's javelin, then sinking and disappearing in the trough of the great scooping seas. Digby hurried up to the nearest piece of timber, and stooping over it examined it intently.

"By God!" he said at last, taking in a long breath between his teeth, "you are right. It's the *Proserpine*, and all hands are lost. What a terrible thing!"

His face was very solemn as he spoke, but his eyes danced and glittered. I was beginning to conceive a great repugnance and distrust towards this man.

"Is there no chance of anyone having got ashore?" he said.

"Na, na, nor cargo neither," my father answered with real grief in his voice. "Ye dinna ken this coast. There's an awful undertow outside the Winners, and it's a' swept round to Holy Isle. De'il take it, if there was to be a shipwreck what for should they no' run their ship agroond to the east-'ard o' the point and let an honest mun have the pickings instead o' they rascally loons in Arran? An empty barrel might float in here, but there's no chance o' a sea-chest, let alane a body."

"Poor fellows!" said Digby. "But there—we must meet it some day, and why not here and now? I've lost my ship, but thank Heaven I can buy another. It is sad about them, though—very sad. I warned Lamarck that he was waiting too long with a low barometer and an ugly shore under his lee. He has himself to thank. He was my first officer, a prying, covetous, meddlesome hound."

"Don't call him names," I said. "He's dead."

"Well said, my young prig!" he answered. "Perhaps you wouldn't be so mealy-mouthed yourself if you lost five thousand pounds before breakfast. But there—there's no use crying over spilt milk. *Vogue la galère!* as the French say. Things are never so bad but that they might be worse."

My father and Digby stayed at the scene of the wreck, but I walked over to Corriemains to reassure Minnie's mind as to the apparition at the window. Her opinion, when I had told her all, coincided with mine, that perhaps the crew of the brig knew more about the stranger than he cared for. We agreed that I should keep a close eye upon him without letting him know that he was watched.

"But oh, Archie," she said, "ye munna cross him or anger him while he carries them awfu' weapons. Ye maun be douce and saft, and no' gain-say him."

I laughed, and promised her to be very prudent, which reassured her a little. Old Fullarton walked back with me in the hope of picking up a piece of timber, and both he and my father patrolled the shore for many days, without, however, finding any prize of importance, for the under current off the Winners was very strong, and everything had probably drifted right round to Lamlash Bay in Arran.

It was wonderful how quickly the stranger accommodated himself to our insular ways, and how useful he made himself about the home-steading. Within a fortnight he knew the island almost as well as I did my-self. Had it not been for that one unpleasant recollection of the shipwreck which rankled in my remembrance, I could have found it in my heart to become fond of him. His nature was a tropical one—fiercely depressed at times, but sunny as a rule, bursting continually into jest and song from pure instinct, in a manner which is unknown among us Northerners. In his graver moments he was a most interesting companion, talking shrewdly and eloquently of men and manners, and his own innumerable and strange adventures. I have seldom heard a more brilliant conversa-tionalist. Of an evening he would keep my father and myself spell-bound by the kitchen fire for hours and hours, while he chatted away in a desul-tory fashion and smoked his cigarettes. It seemed to me that the packet he had brought with him on the first night must have consisted entirely of tobacco. I noticed that in these conversations, which were mostly ad-dressed to my father, he used, unconsciously perhaps, to play upon the weak side of the old man's nature. Tales of cunning, of smartness, of various ways in which mankind had been cheated and money gained, came most readily to his lips, and were relished by an eager listener. I could not help one night remarking upon it, when my father had gone out of the room, laughing hoarsely, and vibrating with amusement over some story of how the Biscayan peasants will strap lanterns to a bullock's horns, and taking the beast some distance inland on a stormy night, will make it prance and rear so that the ships at sea may imagine it to be the lights of a vessel, and steer fearlessly in that direction, only to find themselves on a rockbound coast.

"You shouldn't tell such tales to an old man," I said.

"My dear fellow," he answered very kindly, "you have seen nothing of the world yet. You have formed fine ideas no doubt, and notions of delicacy and such things, and you are very dogmatic about them, as clever men of your age always are. I had notions of right and wrong once, but it has been all knocked out of me. It's just a sort of varnish which the rough friction of the world soon rubs off. I started with a whole soul, but there are more gashes and seams and scars in it now than there are in my body, and that's pretty fair as you'll allow"—with which he pulled upon his tunic and showed me his chest.

"Good heavens!" I said, "How on earth did you get those?"

"This was a bullet," he said, pointing to a deep bluish pucker underneath his collar bone. "I got it behind the barricades in Berlin in '48. Langenback said it just missed the subclavian artery. And this," he went on, indicating a pair of curious elliptical scars upon his throat, "was the bite from a Sioux chief, when I was under Custer on the plains—I've got an arrow wound on my leg from the same party. This is from a mutinous Lascar aboard ship, and the others are mere scratches—Californian vaccination marks. You can excuse my being a little ready with my own irons, though, when I've been dropped so often."

"What's this?" I asked, pointing to a little chamois-leather bag which was hung by a strong cord round his neck. "It looks like a charm."

He buttoned up his tunic again hastily, looking extremely disconcerted. "It is nothing," he said brusquely. "I am a Roman Catholic, and it is what we call a scapular." I could hardly get another word out of him that night, and even next day he was reserved and appeared to avoid me. This little incident made me very thoughtful, the more so as I noticed shortly afterwards when standing over him, that the string was no longer round his neck. Apparently he had taken it off after my remark about it. What could there be in that leather bag which needed such secrecy and precaution! Had I but known it, I would sooner have put my left hand in the fire than have pursued that inquiry.

One of the peculiarities of our visitor was that in all his plans for the future, with which he often regaled us, he seemed entirely untrammelled by any monetary considerations. He would talk in the lightest and most off-hand way of schemes which would involve the outlay of much wealth. My father's eyes would glisten as he heard him talk carelessly of sums which to our frugal minds appeared enormous. It seemed strange to both of us that a man who by his own confession had been a vagabond and adventurer all his life, should be in possession of such a fortune. My father was inclined to put it down to some stroke of luck on the American goldfields. I had my own ideas even then—chaotic and half-formed as yet, but tending in the right direction.

It was not long before these suspicions began to assume a more definite shape, which came about in this way. Minnie and I made the summit of the Combera cliff a favourite trysting-place, as I think I mentioned before, and it was rare for a day to pass without our spending two or three hours there. One morning, not long after my chat with our guest, we were seated together in a little nook there, which we had chosen as sheltering us from the wind as well as from my father's observation, when Minnie caught sight of Digby walking along the Carracuil beach. He sauntered up to the base of the cliff, which was boulder-studded and slimy from the receding tide, but instead of turning back he kept on climbing over the great green slippery stones, and threading his way among the pools until he was standing immediately beneath us so that we looked straight down at him. To him the spot must have seemed the very acme of seclusion, with the great sea in front, the rocks on each side, the precipice behind. Even had he looked up, he could hardly have made out the two human faces, which peered down at him from the distant ledge. He gave a hurried glance round, and then slipping his hand into his pocket, he pulled out the leather bag which I had noticed, and took out of it a small object which he held in the palm of his hand and looked at long, and, as it were, lovingly. We both had an excellent view of it from where we lay. He then replaced it in the bag, and shoving it down to the very bottom of his pocket picked his way back more cheerily than he had come.

Minnie and I looked at each other. She was smiling; I was serious.

"Did you see it?" I asked.

"Yon? Aye, I saw it."

"What did you think it was then?"

"A wee bit of glass," she answered, looking at me with wondering eyes.

"No," I cried excitedly, "glass could never catch the sun's rays so. It was a diamond, and if I mistake not, one of extraordinary value. It was as large as all I have seen put together, and must be worth a fortune."

A diamond was a mere name to poor, simple Minnie, who had never seen one before, nor had any conception of their value, and she prattled away to me about this and that, but I hardly heard her. In vain she exhausted all her little wiles in attempting to recall my attention. My mind was full of what I had seen. Look where I would, the glistening of the breakers, or the sparkling of the mica-laden rocks, recalled the brilliant facets of the gem which I had seen. I was moody and distraught, and eventually let Minnie walk back to Corriemains by herself while I made my way to the homesteading. My father and Digby were just sitting down to the mid-day meal, and the latter hailed me cheerily.

"Come along, mate," he cried, pushing over a stool, "we were just wondering what had become of you. Ah! you rogue, I'll bet my bottom dollar it was that pretty wench I saw the other day who kept you."

"Mind your own affairs," I answered angrily.

"Don't be thin-skinned," he said; "young people should control their tempers, and you've got a mighty bad one, my lad. Have you heard that I am going to leave you?"

"I'm sorry to hear it," I said frankly; "when do you intend to go?"

"Next week," he answered, "but don't be afraid; you'll see me again. I've had too good a time here to forget you easily. I'm going to buy a good steam yacht—250 tons or thereabouts—and I'll bring her round in a few months and give you a cruise."

"What would be a fair price for a craft of that sort?" I asked.

"Forty thousand dollars," said our visitor, carelessly.

"You must be very rich," I remarked, "to throw away so much money on pleasure."

"Rich!" echoed my companion, his Southern blood mantling up for a moment. "Rich, why man, there is hardly a limit—but there, I was romancing a bit. I'm fairly well off, or shall be very shortly."

"How did you make your money?" I asked. The question came so glibly to my lips that I had no time to check it, though I felt the moment afterwards that I had made a mistake. Our guest drew himself into himself at once, and took no notice of my query, while my father said:

"Hush, Archie laddie, ye munna speer they questions o' the gentleman!" I could see, however, from the old man's eager grey eyes, looking out from under the great thatch of his brows, that he was meditating over the same problem himself.

During the next couple of days I hesitated very often as to whether I should tell my father of what I had seen and the opinions I had formed about our visitor; but he forestalled me by making a discovery himself which supplemented mine and explained all that had been dark. It was one day when the stranger was out for a ramble, that, entering the kitchen, I found my father sitting by the fire deeply engaged in perusing the newspaper, spelling out the words laboriously, and following the lines with his great forefinger. As I came in he crumpled up the paper as if his instinct were to conceal it, but then spreading it out again on his knee he beckoned me over to him.

"Wha d'ye think this chiel Dibgy is?" he asked. I could see by his manner that he was much excited.

"No good," I answered.

"Come here, laddie, come here!" he croaked. "You're a braw scholar. Read this tae me alood—read it and tell me if you dinna think I've fitted the cap on the right heid. It's a *Glasgey Herald* only four days auld—a Loch Ranza feeshin' boat brought it in the morn. Begin frae here—'Oor Paris Letter.' Here it is, 'Fuller details;' read it a' to me."

I began at the spot indicated, which was a paragraph of the ordinary French correspondence of the Glasgow paper. It ran in this way. "Fuller details have now come before the public of the diamond robbery by which the Duchesse de Rochevieille lost her celebrated gem. The diamond is a pure brilliant weighing eighty three and a half carats, and is supposed to be the third largest in France, and the seventeenth in Europe. It came into the possession of the family through the great grand-uncle of the Duchess, who fought under Bussy in India, and brought it back to Europe with him. It represented a fortune then, but its value now is simply enormous. It was taken, as will be remembered, from the jewel case of the Duchess two months ago during the night, and though the police have made every effort, no real clue has been obtained as to the thief. They are very reticent upon the subject, but it seems that they have reason to suspect one Achille Wolff, an Americanised native of Lorraine, who had called at the Château a short time before. He is an eccentric man, of Bohemian habits, and it is just possible that his sudden disappearance at the time of the robbery may have been a coincidence. In appearance he is described as romantic-looking, with an artistic face, dark eyes and hair, and a brusque manner. A large reward is offered for his capture."

When I finished reading this, my father and I sat looking at each other in silence for a minute or so. Then my father jerked his finger over his shoulder. "Yon's him," he said.

"Yes, it must be he," I answered, thinking of the initials on the handkerchief.

Again we were silent for a time. My father took one of the faggots out of the grate and twisted it about in his hands. "It maun be a muckle stane" he said. "He canna hae it aboot him. Likely he's left it in France."

"No, he has it with him," I said, like a cursed fool as I was.

"Hoo d'ye ken that?" asked the old man, looking up quickly with eager eyes.

"Because I have seen it."

The faggot which he held broke in two in his grip, but he said nothing more. Shortly afterwards our guest came in, and we had dinner, but neither of us alluded to the arrival of the paper.

IV

I have often been amused, when reading stories told in the first person, to see how the narrator makes himself out as a matter of course to be a perfect and spotless man. All around may have their passions, and weaknesses, and vices, but he remains a cold and blameless nonentity, running like a colourless thread through the tangled skein of the story. I shall not fall into this error. I see myself as I was in those days, shallow-hearted, hot-headed, and with little principle of any kind. Such I was, and such I depict myself.

From the time that I finally identified our visitor Digby with Achille Wolff the diamond robber, my resolution was taken. Some might have been squeamish in the matter, and thought that because he had shaken their hand and broken their bread he had earned some sort of grace from them. I was not troubled with sentimentality of this sort. He was a criminal escaping from justice. Some providence had thrown him into our hands, and an enormous reward awaited his betrayers. I never hesitated for a moment as to what was to be done.

The more I thought of it the more I admired the cleverness with which he had managed the whole business. It was clear that he had had a vessel ready, manned either by confederates or by unsuspecting fishermen. Hence he would be independent of all those parts where the police would be on the look-out for him. Again, if he had made for England or for America, he could hardly have escaped ultimate capture, but by choosing one of the most desolate and lonely spots in Europe he had thrown them off his track for a time, while the destruction of the brig seemed to destroy the last clue as to his whereabouts. At present he was entirely at our mercy, since he could not move from the island without our help. There was no necessity for us to hurry therefore, and we could mature our plans at our leisure.

Both my father and I showed no change in our manner towards our guest, and he himself was as cheery and light-hearted as ever. It was pleasant to hear him singing as we mended the nets or caulked the boat. His voice was a very high tenor and one of the most melodious I ever listened to. I am convinced that he could have made a name upon the operatic stage, but like most versatile scoundrels, he placed small account upon the genuine talents which he possessed, and cultivated the worse portion of his nature. My father used sometimes to eye him sideways in a strange manner, and I thought I knew what he was thinking about—but there I made a mistake.

One day, about a week after our conversation, I was fixing up one of the rails of our fence which had been snapped in the gale, when my father came along the seashore, plodding heavily among the pebbles, and sat down on a stone at my elbow. I went on knocking in the nails, but looked at him from the corner of my eye, as he pulled away at his short black pipe. I could see that he had something weighty on his mind, for he knitted his brows, and his lips projected.

"D'ye mind what was in yon paper?" he said at last, knocking his ashes out against the stone.

"Yes," I answered shortly.

"Well, what's your opeenion?" he asked.

"Why, that we should have the reward, of course!" I replied.

"The reward!" he said, with a fierce snarl. "You would tak' the reward. You'd let the stane that's worth thoosands an' thoosands gang awa' back tae some furrin Papist, an' a' for the sake o' a few pund that they'd fling till ye, as they fling a bane to a dog when the meat's a' gone. It's a clean flingin' awa' o' the gifts o' Providence."

"Well, father," I said, laying down the hammer, "you must be satisfied with what you can get. You can only have what is offered."

"But if we got the stane itsel," whispered my father, with a leer on his face.

"He'd never give it up," I said.

"But if he deed while he's here—if he was suddenly—"

"Drop it, father, drop it!" I cried, for the old man looked like a fiend out of the pit. I saw now what he was aiming at.

"If he deed," he shouted, "wha saw him come, and wha wad speer where he'd ganged till? If an accident happened, if he came by a dud on the heid, or woke some nicht to find a knife at his thrapple, wha wad be the wiser?"

"You mustn't speak so, father," I said, though I was thinking many things at the same time.

"It may as well be oot as in," he answered, and went away rather sulkily, turning round after a few yards and holding up his finger towards me to impress the necessity of caution.

My father did not speak of this matter to me again, but what he said rankled in my mind. I could hardly realise that he meant his words, for he had always, as far as I knew, been an upright, righteous man, hard in his ways, and grasping in his nature, but guiltless of any great sin. Perhaps it was that he was removed from temptation, for isothermal lines of crime might be drawn on the map through places where it is hard to walk straight, and there are others where it is as hard to fall. It was easy to be a saint in the island of Uffa.

One day we were finishing breakfast when our guest asked if the boat was mended (one of the thole-pins had been broken). I answered that it was.

"I want you two," he said, "to take me round to Lamlash to-day. You shall have a couple of sovereigns for the job. I don't know that I may not come back with you—but I may stay."

My eyes met those of my father for a flash. "There's no' vera much wind," he said.

"What there is, is in the right direction," returned Digby, as I must call him.

"The new foresail has no' been bent," persisted my father.

"There's no use throwing difficulties in the way," said our visitor angrily. "If you won't come, I'll get Tommy Gibbs and his father, but go I shall. Is it a bargain or not?"

"I'll gang," my father replied sullenly, and went down to get the boat ready. I followed, and helped him to bend on the new foresail. I felt nervous and excited.

"What do you intend to do?" I asked.

"I dinna ken," he said irritably. "Gin the worst come to the worst we can gie him up at Lamlash—but oh, it wad be a peety, an awfu' peety. You're young an' strong, laddie; can we no' master him between us?"

"No," I said, "I'm ready to give him up, but I'm damned if I lay a hand on him."

"You're a cooardly, white-livered loon!" he cried, but I was not to be moved by taunts, and left him mumbling to himself and picking at the sail with nervous fingers.

It was about two o'clock before the boat was ready, but as there was a slight breeze from the north we reckoned on reaching Lamlash before nightfall. There was just a pleasant ripple upon the dark blue water, and as we stood on the beach before shoving off, we could see the Carlin's leap and Goatfell bathed in a purple mist, while beyond them along the horizon loomed the long line of the Argyleshire hills. Away to the south the great bald summit of Ailsa crag glittered in the sun, and a single white fleck showed where a fishing-boat was beating up from the Scotch coast. Digby and I stepped into the boat, but my father ran back to where I had been mending the rails, and came back with the hatchet in his hand, which he stowed away under the thwarts.

"What d'ye want with the axe?" our visitor asked.

"It's a handy thing to hae aboot a boat," my father answered with averted eyes, and shoved us off. We set the foresail, jib, and mainsail, and shot away across the Roost, with the blue water splashing merrily under our bows. Looking back, I saw the coastline of our little island extend rapidly on either side. There was Carravoe which we had left, and our own beach of Carracuil and the steep brown face of the Combera, and away behind the rugged crests of Beg-na-phail and Beg-na-sacher. I could see the red tiles of the byre of our homesteading, and across the moor a thin blue reek in the air which marked the position of Corriemains. My heart warmed towards the place which had been my home since childhood.

We were about half-way across the Roost when it fell a dead calm, and the sails flapped against the mast. We were perfectly motionless except for the drift of the current, which runs from north to south. I had been steering and my father managing the sails, while the stranger smoked his eternal cigarettes and admired the scenery; but at his suggestion we now got the sculls out to row. I shall never know how it began, but as I was stooping down to pick up an oar I heard our visitor give a great scream that he was murdered, and looking up I saw him with his face all in a sputter of blood leaning against the mast, while my father made at him with the hatchet. Before I could move hand or foot Digby rushed at the old man and caught him round the waist. "You grey-headed devil," he cried in a husky voice. "I feel that you have done for me. But you'll never get what you want. No—never! never! never!" Nothing can ever erase from my memory the intense and concentrated malice of those words. My father gave a raucous cry, they swayed and balanced for a moment and then over they went into the sea. I rushed to the side, boat-hook in hand, but they never came up. As the long rings caused by the splash widened out however and left an unruffled space in the center, I saw them once again. The water was very clear, and far far down I could see the shimmer of two white faces coming and going, faces which seemed to look up at me with an expression of unutterable horror. Slowly they went down, revolving in each other's embrace until they were nothing but a dark loom, and then faded from my view for ever. There they shall lie, the Frenchman and the Scot, till the great trumpet shall sound and the sea give up its dead. Storms may rage above them and great ships labour and creak, but their slumber shall be dreamless and unruffled in the silent green depths of the Roost of Uffa. I trust when the great day shall come that they will bring up the cursed stone with them, that they may show the sore temptation which the devil had placed in their way, as some slight extenuation of their errors while in this mortal flesh.

It was a weary and awesome journey back to Carravoe. I remember tug-tugging at the oars as though to snap them in trying to relieve the tension in my mind. Towards evening a breeze sprang up and helped me on my way, and before nightfall I was back in the lonely homesteading once more, and all that had passed that spring afternoon lay behind me like some horrible nightmare.

I did not remain in Uffa. The croft and the boat were sold by public roup in the market-place of Ardrossan, and the sum realised was sufficient to enable me to continue my medical studies at the University. I fled from the island as from a cursed place, nor did I ever set foot on it again. Gibbs and his son, and even Minnie Fullarton too, passed out of my life completely and for ever. She missed me for a time, no doubt, but I have heard that young McBane, who took the farm, went a-wooing to Corriemains after the white fishing, and as he was a comely fellow enough he may have consoled her for my loss. As for myself, I have settled quietly down into a large middle-class practice in Paisley. It has been in the brief intervals of professional work that I have jotted down these reminiscences of the events which led up to my father's death. Achille Wolff and the Rochevieille diamond are things of the past now, but there may be some who will care to hear of how they visited the island of Uffa.

The Dreadful Bell

ELIZABETH FERRARS

elen Benson had known what the stairs would be like. She knew those old Edinburgh houses. She had spent her childhood in one of them. But what she had not realized was that the furnished flat that Colin had rented for them while she was in hospital was on the top floor.

He told her that only when they were on their way through the town in a taxi from the airport. He had met her there and had helped her out of the wheelchair that the airline had laid on for her and into the taxi and they were already past the suburbs and entering the region of tall, formidable, dark stone houses before he mentioned that she would have three flights of stairs to climb.

'*Three* flights?' she said in a startled, disbelieving voice. 'But, Colin, I can't! How can I get this thing up *three* flights of stairs? '

She used one of her sticks to hit the plaster on her leg.

He looked apologetic and distraught, a look that always made it difficult for her to hold anything against him for long. It frequently appeared on his face when he was compelled to deal with anything practical.

'But honestly, I couldn't find anything else,' he said, 'and the rent's so low and it's really quite pleasant when you get there. I'm sure you're going to like it. The thing is to take the stairs slowly. You'll manage all right.'

'I'll have to, shan't I?'

She looked out of the taxi window. There had been a powdering of snow in the night, which had turned to dirty slush on the pavements. A sky of tarnished grey hung low above the rooftops, promising more snow. After five years in one of the small, new, African countries where the sun shone every day and flowers bloomed all the year round, it felt bitterly cold.

'I did my best,' Colin said unhappily.

'I'm sure you did.' She patted his hand. He was wearing his defensive face now, which made him look as if he were preparing to be deeply, un-justifiably hurt, but bravely to put up with it. Only the trouble was that he never did put up with it bravely when he was hurt. He could lose his tem-per in a flash and be far more deadly than Helen ever was to him. Or that was how she saw it herself, perhaps mistakenly. But the last thing that she wanted at the moment, when they were trying so hard to make a new beginning, was one of their scenes. She had enough to put up with with-out that.

The taxi turned into a street that she remembered from her child-hood, though she did not think that she had ever been into any of the houses. They were tall and stark, with two centuries of grime upon them, yet with a good deal of dignity, although the street, which might once have been considered a fine one, now had a depressing air of decay. There was a seedy-looking tobacconist at one corner, opposite a greengrocer, whose goods, outside his window, spilled out of their boxes on to the pave-ment. The stone steps up to the doorways were worn and looked slimy with the morning's slush. As the taxi stopped at one of the houses the first big, damp flakes of a new snowfall drifted waveringly down.

Colin jumped quickly out of the taxi, paid the driver and turned to lift Helen's two suitcases out of it. Then he reached up to help her down. She gritted her teeth at the pain as she moved. He handed her two sticks to support her weight as she stood on the pavement, where he left her for a moment while he carried her luggage into the house. She realized that the effect of the pills that she had taken before she started on the journey had worn off. She would take two more as soon as she reached the flat, but first she had those three flights of stairs to face. She felt a little dizzy when she thought of them, wondering if in fact there was any possibility that she would be able to climb them.

But what would she do if she could not? The taxi was already moving off. It was too late to call it back and say that she wanted to be taken to an hotel, one with a lift and no stairs to trouble her. And the snow was com-ing down faster. There was nothing for it but to try to reach the flat.

The stairs were just as she had imagined them, bleak stone worn hollow by two hundred years of footsteps. The house was of a type common in Edinburgh, with the two lower storeys a self-contained dwelling with an entrance of its own, and with these stairs mounting at the side of it to the flat above, without any doors opening on to any of the landings where the stairs turned back on themselves. Each flight was long, because all the rooms in the lower house were very high. There was a cold, iron handrail.

Colin left the suitcases at the foot of the stairs, put an arm round Helen's waist, and while she put an arm round his shoulders, took most of her weight as she hobbled from step to step. After every few of them she paused to draw a shuddering breath, trying to pretend that it was not hurting as much as it was.

'Once I get to the top I'll never be able to come down again,' she said as they reached the first landing.

'You won't need to,' he said. 'I'll see to everything. Just take it slowly. You're doing fine. And really, you'll like it when you get there.'

She knew that that was possible. When this house had been built, staircases like this were regarded as part of the street and most of them were bare and unlovely. But often the flats opening off them had rooms of the greatest magnificence, with nobly lofty ceilings, finely proportioned windows and Adam fireplaces. She tried to hope for the best, and somehow, after she did not know how long, reached the top landing.

There were evidently two flats there, for there were two doors, side by side. Colin let go of Helen to feel for the key in his pocket. As he did so, one of the doors opened a few inches, as far as the chain holding it would allow, and singularly blue eyes in an aged, wrinkled face peered out at them. Red hair in a tangle hung over the lined forehead. A thin hand held the collar of a green quilted dressing-gown close up to the withered neck.

'You won't ring the bell, will you?' the old woman said abruptly. 'If you ring it, she comes, but she doesn't like it. Remember that.'

The door closed.

Helen looked at Colin in astonishment. 'What was that?'

'Just a lonely old body, gone a little peculiar,' he said. 'She's quite harmless. In fact, she's been very kind to me since I moved in last week.'

'But why should we ring the bell? There's no one to answer it.'

'Why indeed?' He fitted the key into the lock and opened the door.

'Now just a little further,' he said, 'then you can sit down and be comfortable and I'll bring you a drink.'

'What about my luggage?'

'I'll get that in a minute.'

He helped her forward into the flat.

Except for the smell of dry rot that was wafted to her as soon as she entered, it was more or less as she had expected. There was a spacious hall, with an elegant archway half-way along it and a polished floor of thick, broad old boards with a narrow runner of red carpet up the middle of it. Several doors opened off the hall, immensely solid-looking. Colin pushed one of them open and led Helen into a big room with two tall sash windows, a high ceiling with a cornice of delicately moulded plaster and a fine marble chimneypiece.

There was no fire in the old black basket grate, but an electric fire stood on the hearth in front of it, with three bars alight, and in spite of the snow now beginning to swirl thickly against the windowpanes, the room felt pleasantly warm.

'I turned the fire on before I went out to meet you, so that it'd be nice when you got here,' Colin said, 'but actually the place is surprisingly easy to heat. The walls are about a yard thick and once you've managed to warm things up inside, they keep it in.'

Helen took off her coat and lowered herself into a chair beside the fireplace.

'That old woman next door,' she said, 'are we going to have trouble with her?'

'I told you, she's just mildly eccentric,' he said. 'Actually she's helped me quite a bit. She told me where the best shops are locally and advised me about getting in supplies, and when she knew you were coming she brought round a chicken casserole that we've only got to warm up when we want it. Now I'll go and get your things. I shan't be a moment.'

He went out, closing the door behind him to keep the warmth in the room.

Helen leant back in her chair and looked round her, taking in the room with its curious mixture of grandeur and decay. Once, she thought, it must have been beautiful. It would have been a fine background for elegantly dressed ladies with hoops and powdered hair and patches. But in those days it would not have been filled with shabby Victorian furniture, sufficiently comfortable and not positively ugly, but without any particular character. It would not have had that faint, pervasive smell of mildew. Other smells, perhaps, even more disagreeable, for the sanitation would have been primitive, but that would have been normal and would have gone unnoticed. Exhausted by her climb up the stairs, she closed her eyes for a moment, then, opening them, suddenly noticed the bell beside the fireplace.

It was the kind of bell that consists of a circle of painted china, with a handle at the side of it, with a small china knob that would have to be pulled downwards to set wires jangling and bells ringing in the kitchen. The bell was white and its decoration was a pretty little wreath of rosebuds. It was a dainty, charming object, but it had probably not been in use for fifty years. On an impulse, Helen reached out and pulled the handle.

There was only silence. No bell rang. The wires that the handle had once set working had, no doubt, been broken long ago.

Opening her handbag, she took out the bottle with her pills in it and swallowed two, then closed her eyes again. The pills took some time to work. It would be at least half an hour before they began to give her any relief from pain, but meanwhile it would be pleasant to doze. But suddenly she became aware of a draught on the back of her neck, a very chill draught, and looking round to see where it was coming from, she saw that the heavy door, which she remembered Colin had closed, was standing open.

He reappeared in the room a moment later, carrying the suitcases. He closed the door. Then, after one look at Helen, he asked quickly, 'What's the matter?'

'Nothing,' she said.

'Is the pain bad?'

'Just about average. I've just taken my pills. They'll help soon.'

'But you look as if—I don't know what—something had happened to you.'

She gave an uncertain laugh. 'It's just silly. I don't know why, but I suddenly took it into my head to ring that bell there, and of course it's broken and doesn't work, but a moment afterwards the door opened by itself, and I felt just as if—no, it's too silly.'

'What was it?'

'I felt just as if someone had answered the bell and come into the room.'

He hit his forehead with the back of his hand. 'Oh God, are you going to take it into your head that the place is haunted? Don't you like it? Won't it do till we can look for something together? We'll do that as soon as you can walk.'

'It's fine,' she said. 'I like it very much.'

'That door's got a way of opening by itself,' he said. 'I've noticed it before. I think the latch probably needs a drop of oil. I'll see to it.'

'Yes, of course that's it.'

'And perhaps you were a bit upset by what Mrs Lambie said.'

'Mrs Lambie?'

'Our neighbour. What she said about not ringing the bell. I expect the journey and then climbing those stairs were a bit too much for you. I've blundered, haven't I, taking this flat? Somehow I can never manage to do the right thing. I'm sorry, I'm sorry!'

He was beginning to work himself up into one of his states of self-accusation, which were really a way of accusing Helen of failing to understand him. She flinched at the thought of the scene that could develop now if she did not manage to stop it in time.

'You're quite right,' she said placatingly. 'I told you it was silly of me, didn't I? Of course it was just the awful state of nerves I've been in ever since the accident. Perhaps I ought to be on tranquillizers.'

'We'd better get you a doctor as soon as possible, anyway. Mrs Lambie gave me the name of one who lives quite near, who she says is very competent.'

'You seem to have been seeing a lot of her.'

'I told you, she's been very helpful. She's given me dinner a couple of times and told me a great deal about the neighbourhood. She's got all sorts of stories about it. She seems to have lived here most of her life. In her way, she's very interesting. By the way, she's our landlord. I got the flat through a lawyer who'd advertised in the *Scotsman*, but when I got here it was she who showed me round. Now I'll get those drinks. And don't worry if the door opens. I'll get some oil this afternoon and see to it.'

He meant it when he said it, but it was the kind of thing that he forgot to do, and by the afternoon the snow was coming down thickly, covering the pavements and the dark slate roofs of the houses, and Helen did not feel inclined to send him out again into such weather. It turned out that the door would stay shut if it was slammed hard enough. They had an omelet for lunch, and after it Helen went to lie down. The pain in her leg had been dulled by the pills and she soon drifted off to sleep.

Colin did not wake her until six o'clock, when he told her that he had sherry waiting for her and that he had put Mrs Lambie's chicken casserole to warm up in the oven. They sat by the electric fire in the living-room, with the faded red velvet curtains drawn over the windows, shutting out darkness and snow, and Helen, to her own surprise, found herself in a mood of quiet contentment that she had not known for a long time. Not for many months before they had decided to return to Europe. Not for at least a year, when that woman Naomi had come into their lives.

But she was thousands of miles away now and Helen had Colin to herself, and at last he seemed satisfied that it should be so. The unfamiliar, gracious room, with the dim light almost concealing the cracks in the plaster and the patches on the wallpaper where someone else's pictures had hung, began to feel strangely homelike.

Mrs Lambie appeared in it next morning, carrying a plate of beautifully-cut little three-cornered sandwiches. Colin was not there. He had gone out shopping with a list that Helen had made out for him. He was not working at present. He was a schoolmaster, a teacher of history, and the Christmas holidays had begun. So far he had said very little of how it felt to be facing the teaching of Scottish children in one of Edinburgh's more distinguished schools after five years of teaching in East Africa, but it was Helen's impression that he was looking forward to it with some eagerness, though the thought of it intimidated him a little.

The snow had stopped, but there had been a heavy frost in the night and the roofs of the houses opposite were a shining white, in which small rainbows of colour were trapped, under a blue, cloudless sky. Helen had stood at the window to watch Colin set out and had seen him skid and nearly fall on the icy pavement. Apparently it was the morning that the rubbish van came round, for there were two rows of dustbins along the edges of the pavements, some of them with their contents spilling out into the gutters. They detracted from the dignity of the street and gave it an air of squalor. At one of the bins a lean, black cat was trying to extract what looked like the backbone of a herring, and at last succeeding, sat there, chewing it with great satisfaction. It was as she saw this that Helen heard the front doorbell ring.

Using her two sticks, she hobbled along the hall to answer it, and found Mrs Lambie standing there, holding the plate of sandwiches.

'I do hope I'm not intruding, but I thought these might help you with your lunch,' she said, 'though I'm not sure if they're substantial enough for a gentleman. There's just pâté inside them, which I made myself, so I can assure you there's nothing unwholesome in them.'

Her accent took Helen back to her childhood in Edinburgh. Fully dressed, Mrs Lambie seemed a different person from the grotesque figure who had peered out from her doorway the morning before and had spoken so mysteriously. She looked about eighty, with a small, pointed, deeply wrinkled face, but a straight back and slim, straight legs with excellent ankles. She was a small woman and very trim, and was dressed in a neat grey tweed suit with a cameo brooch on her lapel and a string of small pearls round her throat. The red hair, which yesterday had fallen in a tangle over her forehead, was brushed smoothly back from it into a small bun. To Helen's surprise, she realized that its colour was its own. The day before she had assumed that it was dyed, but now she could see that there was enough white mixed into it for that not to be possible.

'You're very kind,' she said. 'Won't you come in? My husband's out at the moment, but he'll soon be back.'

The old woman accepted the invitation with an air of eagerness, walking ahead of Helen into the sitting-room.

'He's so charming,' she said. 'I took a fancy to him at once. And you're both young. I like that. I like having young people living next to me. But of course you won't stay. Nobody stays long in this flat, isn't it strange? I've made it as nice as I can and the rent isn't high, but still they don't stay. Sometimes I wonder if it's something to do with that old murder, that there's still a feeling of evil in the place. Do you think that could be possible? Do you believe in that sort of thing?'

She spoke in as matter-of-fact a tone as if she had just mentioned some minor fault in the plumbing, but her blue eyes, on Helen's face, were watchful. They were very fine eyes. Helen thought that when Mrs Lambie had been young, she had probably been very striking to look at.

Hoping that she too sounded calm about it, Helen said, 'Murder? In this flat?'

'Yes, indeed. Of course it happened long, long ago. These houses are very old, you know. All kinds of things must have happened in them.'

Helen had taken the plate of sandwiches and put it down and they both sat down on either side of the fire.

'About two hundred years old, aren't they?' she said.

Mrs Lambie nodded. 'And in those days these two flats were all one. I had it divided myself when I bought it after my dear husband died, because of course it was far too big for just me, but it was cheap and really so handsome, I couldn't resist it. And I've always liked this part of Edinburgh. It's got a special sort of character of its own. And I thought I could make a little extra income by letting this half, but people don't stay. Yet I've never felt anything wrong in my own flat. I'm very fond of it.'

'What happened?' Helen asked. 'Who was murdered.'

'A young woman, the wife of a young advocate. He was very handsome and she was very jealous, because she was older than he was and rather plain, and consumptive too, as so many people were in those days, and they had a maid who was very beautiful, with whom he soon fell in love. And the lady of the house did everything she could to get rid of the maid, but her husband wouldn't have it, so the lady did her best to make the maid leave of her own accord, ringing that bell for her over and over again, and abusing her, and at last the girl told her master that she couldn't stand it any more and was leaving, and he fell into a great rage and threw his wife down the stairs, and she broke her neck and died.'

'And what happened to him and the girl?' Helen asked.

'Well, he was executed, naturally. They hanged people in those days. And the girl went nearly mad with grief, and the story is, as it was once told to me long ago by an old neighbour, that if you ring the bell there, she answers it, because she wants revenge on her mistress.'

'But it was her mistress who was killed,' Helen said. 'Wasn't that revenge enough?'

'But it was all her fault, don't you see, because she was so jealous? Jealousy's a terrible thing.'

'So that's why you told us not to ring the bell.' Helen was rather wishing that she had not heard the story.

The old woman gave a cheerful little laugh. 'But of course it wasn't necessary. I can see you aren't at all superstitious. I've never felt at all worried here myself. But then I'm not in the least bit psychic, and I don't know what to think about the people who say they are. Is there any truth in it? I honestly don't know and I should never go so far as to deny it's possible that some people experience things that the rest of us don't. But I thought the story would interest you anyway. Tell me about your accident now. Your husband mentioned it, of course, and told me how helpless you'd be for a time, so that's why I've been trying to help. I believe in helping other people whenever I can. I'll always do anything for anyone.'

'It was my own fault really,' Helen said. 'When we got to London we bought a second-hand car and drove up to stay with some friends of ours who live in a village near Birmingham. I was doing the driving, and I had a feeling there was something wrong with the brakes, not seriously wrong, but I thought we ought to have them seen to. And my husband said he'd attend to that, and I thought he had, and I took the car out one day and its brakes went and I went slap into a lorry that was coming out of a turning when I had the right of way, and I couldn't stop myself. The car was a write-off, of course, and I was lucky to get off with only a broken leg and shock. I was taken to hospital, then I stayed on for a time with our friends, but I didn't feel it was fair on them to stay with them for ever, so I came after Colin, who'd come on ahead of me to find somewhere for us to live.'

Mrs Lambie looked at her thoughtfully. 'And he found something for you at the top of three flights of stairs, and he hadn't had those brakes seen to when he said he was going to. I'm afraid he isn't the most practical of people, is he? But so charming. I understand how easily you can forgive him when that accident certainly wasn't your fault, but his.'

'Oh, I don't think so,' Helen said. 'He'd never told me he'd had the brakes put right, I just took it for granted he had.'

'But didn't he know you were going to take the car out? Shouldn't he have warned you?'

Helen gave a worried shake of her head. 'I can't really remember. Perhaps he did and I forgot about it. Everything about that time's a bit hazy.'

'Yes, of course. Most natural. But such a misfortune, when you were coming to start your new life here. Well, let me know if there's ever anything I can do to help. I can easily go shopping for you. It isn't the sort of thing that gentlemen like to do, though of course they do it much more willingly now than they did when I was young. And I know your husband would do anything for you, even if he's a little thoughtless sometimes. Such very attractive young men sometimes get just a wee bit spoilt and grow up a little irresponsible. But you mustn't hold it against him. I'm sure he can't help it. I hope you enjoy your sandwiches.'

With further offers of help, she left.

Soon afterwards Colin returned, having omitted to buy the oil for the latch of the sitting-room door, although Helen had put it on her list, but with everything else that she had written down. When he realized that he had forgotten the oil, he offered to go straight out again to buy it, but he had snow on his shoes and looked so cold that Helen assured him that it was unimportant, and urged him to come to the fire.

'I've had a visit from your friend, Mrs Lambie,' she said. 'She's overcome by your charm.'

'Splendid,' he said, sitting down and holding out his hands towards the glowing bars of the fire. 'I'm glad I've not lost my touch with aged ladies. I thought it would be a good idea to get on the right side of her, since you'd be stuck up here alone so much and she might easily be useful.'

'She told me we've got a resident ghost—did she tell you that?' Helen asked.

'No,' he said. 'What kind of ghost?'

'Believe it or not, a live-in maid, who comes when you pull that bell.' She nodded towards the pretty little bell-pull, with its wreath of rosebuds. 'Which reminds me, what are we going to do about cleaning this place? I don't know how soon I'll be able to cope with it.'

He did not answer at once, but after a moment, looking at her with a troubled frown, he said. 'You're worried, aren't you? You're pretending to laugh at it, but yesterday you pulled that bell and the door opened and you were quite frightened, and you're remembering that now.'

'No, that was nothing,' she said. 'I was just startled.'

'Why is this woman supposed to haunt the place?' he asked.

Helen told him the story of the old murder, as Mrs Lambie had told it to her.

The frown deepened on Colin's face. 'I wonder why she told you that story, not me,' he said. 'The other night, when I had dinner with her, she told me a number of fairly gruesome stories about Edinburgh. She seems to like them. She told me the old Burke and Hare yarn, of course, and how the senate room of the University is built over the site where they murdered Darnley, and a particularly nasty story of how some idiot son of a local nobleman roasted a scullion on a spit. And sometimes I got the feeling that her sense of time was all mixed up and that she wasn't sure these things hadn't happened yesterday. But she never told me anything about our domestic ghost.'

'She may have been afraid she'd frighten you off the place. As I said, she's really taken to you.'

'But she doesn't mind frightening you.'

'Or even enjoyed it. Actually I am more afraid of being haunted by Mrs Lambie herself than by her ghost. She says people never stay in this flat. It could be, couldn't it, that they have to put up with just a bit too much of Mrs Lambie?'

'But she *is* awfully helpful,' Colin said. 'You were asking what we're going to do about cleaning the flat. Well, of course, I can manage that, but I met her on the staircase just now and she told me the address of an agency where we may be able to get a daily. I'll go and see them this afternoon—no, I'll have to leave it till tomorrow. This afternoon I'm going to go and see that doctor she told me about. We want him to come and see you as soon as possible.'

'Damn the woman, is she going to run our lives?' Helen exploded, suddenly unaccountably angry. 'Can't we do anything without her?'

He gave her a startled look, and they stared at one another blankly, then Colin's face assumed his deeply-hurt look, which changed almost at once into one of rage, and in a high, furious voice, he cried, 'Christ, you're jealous of her! She's eighty at least, but you're jealous of her! You can't stand it if I talk to anyone. If this sort of thing goes on, don't you realize what it's going to do to us? I can't stand it—get that into your head—I can't stand it!'

'But of course I'm not jealous of her,' Helen said, 'and I'm sure she means well. It's just that if I have too much to do with her, I may go slightly mad.'

'That's the kind of thing you said about Naomi. And that's why we're here—just to get away from Naomi. I told you she meant nothing to me—'

'You meant plenty to her,' she interrupted swiftly.

'Did that matter? Could I help it? And didn't I agree to come here just to satisfy you that the thing wasn't important?'

'I thought we came here because we'd agreed there was no future for whites in Africa.'

'Oh yes, that's what we told everyone else. But Naomi was the real reason. And now you're jealous of an old woman of eighty, who's only been doing her best to help us.'

'Well, d'you realize she tried to put it into my head that my accident was your fault, even though I'd told her it was mine? Is that helping us?'

'So that's it! That's the grievance you've been nursing against me all this time! I knew there was something. But didn't I tell you not to take the car out till I'd had the brakes checked?'

'You know I thought you'd had them seen to. You didn't try to stop me taking it out.'

'I didn't know you were going to.'

'I could have been killed.'

'And you think I wanted that!'

They were equally angry, but while Colin's voice had stayed loud, Helen's was low and bitter. As she always did, once she had become involved in a quarrel with him, she almost at once started wondering desperately how to put a stop to it. She could have drawn back from it herself in an instant, apologizing, even grovelling, but once Colin was sufficiently angry, it took hours, sometimes even days, to persuade him to forget it. He was looking at her with a strange look in his eyes, which she found peculiarly disturbing.

'I'm not a murderer,' he said, suddenly speaking only just above a whisper, 'but for God's sake, don't provoke me too far.'

Then he picked up the overcoat that he had dropped on a chair, struggled into it and walked out of the room. Helen heard the outer door slam as he let himself out of the flat.

She knew that he would be gone for most of the rest of the day, perhaps going to a cinema, or pottering about bookshops, or merely walking along the slushy streets, encouraging the black mood that had gripped him, assuring himself over and over again that he was in the right, which, as it happened, this time he really was, or so Helen thought, as she turned her anger, once he was gone, against herself. Of course Naomi had been the real reason why they had come home. And hadn't she sworn to herself that whatever happened she would never blame him for her accident? If she loved him, she had to accept him as he was, moody, casual, forgetful, but after his fashion loving her.

Or could that be wrong?

Sooner or later, after one of their quarrels, she always arrived at this point. Did he really love her, or did he merely feel entangled in something from which he could not break free? Was that the explanation of his moods? Did they mean something far more important than she had ever let herself believe?

She ate most of Mrs Lambie's sandwiches for her lunch. She was half-way through them when she heard the rattle of the letter-box, and leaning on her sticks, made her way along the hall to the front door to see what had been delivered. One letter lay on the mat inside the door. She picked it up, looked at the address on it, then grew stiff with shock. It was addressed to Colin, and the handwriting was Naomi's, and the postmark was London.

For a moment Helen could not believe it, thinking that she must be mistaken about the handwriting. But she knew it well. There had been a time when Naomi, who had been a secretary working for the High Commission, had been her friend rather than Colin's, and Helen had often had notes from her. It was distinctive writing, not easily mistaken.

Limping slowly back to the sitting-room, she put the letter down on a table, where it would catch Colin's eye when he came back again, then returned to the sandwiches.

Dusk came early, only half-way through the afternoon. The days were just at their shortest. Going to the windows to draw the curtains against the deepening darkness, Helen stood for a moment gazing down into the street, which just then was empty of traffic. She thought how noble the old houses looked when the light was too dim to show up their state of decay. It was easy to imagine coaches driving along the street, and fine ladies alighting from them and sweeping grandly in at one of the handsome old doorways.

But then, as she drew the curtains, she found herself thinking of a young woman who had once lived here, and who perhaps had worn a hoop and powdered her hair, and who might have stood at this window long ago, just as Helen was doing now, watching for her husband to come home, then perhaps seen him hurrying along, but not for her sake. A young woman who had gone to her death down the long stone stairs, because of her jealousy.

Helen looked at the envelope lying on the table and felt an impulse to destroy it and say nothing to Colin about its having arrived. But the impulse was followed by a chilling little tremor of fear. Leaving the envelope lying where it was, she sat down and picked up a newspaper that Colin had brought in with him and did her best to read.

The doctor called soon after four o'clock. Though Colin had not returned, he had not omitted to call on the doctor recommended by Mrs Lambie and ask him to visit Helen as soon as possible. He was a short, square man, with a loud, hearty manner, full of reassurance. He wanted the address of the doctor who had treated Helen after her accident, so that he could send for her X-rays and records, then he stayed chatting for a little, commiserating with her for living at the top of a staircase that would keep her virtually a prisoner until the plaster came off her leg, and for the weather that had welcomed her to Edinburgh. Then he went away, saying that he would call again in a few days.

Colin returned about six o'clock, with a parcel of fish and chips for their supper. He said nothing about how he had spent the day and looked tired and sullen. Seeing the letter on the table, he ripped it open, read it quickly, then held it out to Helen.

'Here, d'you want to read it?' he asked.

'Not unless there's some reason why I should,' she answered, looking away.

He tucked the letter into his pocket and said no more about it.

He was not openly antagonistic to her that evening, but he hardly spoke. They went to bed early. In the morning, soon after he had washed up the breakfast things for her, he left the flat, without telling her where he was going or when he would be back. Helen would have given a great deal at that time to be able to leave the flat too, to be able to go rapidly down the stairs and along the street to investigate the local shops and perhaps take a bus to Princes Street and see how much everything had changed since she had been here last. She felt restless and tense. There had been a partial thaw in the night and most of the white covering of the roofs had slid down on to the pavements, lying there in dirty heaps, but the sky looked low and heavy, as if more snow might be coming soon. Helen sat down in her usual place, near to the electric fire, and wondered how she was going to pass the time.

It was only a few minutes later that she felt the draught on her neck which meant that the door behind her had swung open. It did it so silently that she still found it eerie. Looking towards it and gripping the arms of her chair, she started to heave herself to her feet so that she could go and close it. But as she did so, a slim, ethereal figure in grey moved into her line of vision in the hall. She dropped back into her chair, wanting to scream, and shuddering from head to foot in helpless panic.

The figure moved forward.

'Did I startle you, dear?' she asked. 'I'm sorry. The gentleman gave me the keys and said it would be all right if I came straight in, else I might disturb you.'

She was a young woman of about twenty-five, tall and vigourous-looking, with short auburn hair and a bright healthy complexion, and she was wearing a transparent white plastic raincoat, which she started to un-button as she came into the room. Under the coat she was wearing dark brown slacks and a heavy Aran sweater. She was not in the least ghostlike.

'I said tae the gentleman, I said I'm not sure you should give me the keys,' she said. 'Who kens, I might be anybody, you never ken what I might do with them, but he said it would be better than having me ring the bell and making you come tae the door with your sore leg, and he seemed tae thing he could trust me. So I came in, like he said, and if you'll just tell me what you want me tae do, I'll get ahead with it.'

'Who are you?' Helen demanded. 'What are you talking about?'

'My name's Mrs MacNab,' the girl answered, 'but most folks call me Fiona.'

'Why have you come?'

'Because I just happened tae meet the gentleman in the agency yes-terday afternoon, when I went in tae see if they'd a wee job for me, and he said how you couldn't get around yourself because of your leg being bro-ken, and he wanted someone tae keep the flat clean and I said I could manage, and he gave me the keys and I let myself in, like he said. Were you not expecting me?'

'Yes—yes, of course I was,' Helen said. 'I'd just forgotten about it. I don't think he told me what time you'd be coming, or if he did, I didn't remember. It's very good of you to come.'

'He was so awful anxious about you, I couldn't say no tae him,' the girl said. 'Now where will I start?'

'Oh, anywhere you like. If you can, just give the place a general clean-up. That would be fine.'

'Will do,' the girl said cheerfully and disappeared to the kitchen to look for brooms and dusters.

Helen found herself wanting to laugh helplessly, but she felt that there was a danger of hysteria getting into the laughter and took hold of herself, not to let it escape her. How like Colin it was to have taken the girl on after only a few minutes' talk in an employment agency, almost certainly without asking a single question about her references, and then, on the spot, to have handed over the keys of the flat, and then to have said nothing to Helen about what he had done. That had probably been because when he had returned to the flat the evening before he had still been angry with her, and had half-hoped that the girl's sudden appearance would frighten her. He could sometimes be remarkably cruel. But also it demonstrated to her that even when the two of them had quarrelled, he could still be magnanimous enough to go to the trouble of finding this girl to help her.

And of course he had charmed the girl. It had not been concern at Helen's helplessness that had brought her here to work this morning, but Colin's smile, his diffidently courteous manner, his appearance of interest in her. Helen had seen this in operation so often that she could imagine exactly how the scene had gone. She herself was the only person on whom he hardly ever troubled to exercise his charm, and when he did, she found that she had lost the ability to respond to it. She preferred him to be what she considered his natural self, with all his difficult moods, since she was accustomed to them and thought that she understood them reasonably well.

Half-way through the morning Fiona brought her a cup of coffee, then stayed to chatter about herself for a time. She was an unmarried mother with a child of five, she said, whom she had left for the morning in a nursery school. She spoke of the child's father with an amused kind of contempt, but no bitterness, seeming to be glad that he had removed himself from her life. With only a little more warmth she mentioned someone whom she called her boy-friend. Her attitude to men seemed to be placidly uncomplicated. Helen envied her. When the girl had gone, promising to come again in three days' time, Helen thought how comic it had been to confuse someone so robust, even for a moment and in the dim light of the hall, where she had looked grey and wraithlike, with the beautiful maid of long ago, who had been the cause of murder.

Colin again returned to the flat at about six o'clock in the evening, bringing with him some packages of Chinese carry-out food, and told Helen that he had spent the day in the National Library, reading up on Scottish social history.

'It's appalling how little I know about it,' he said. 'If you're educated in England, it's extraordinary how little you learn about the rest of the British Isles. I've a lot to catch up on.'

He seemed to be in a better mood this evening than he had been the evening before, glad that Fiona MacNab had arrived to clean the flat, as she had promised, and he presented Helen with two paperback thrillers that he had bought for her during the day.

'You must be getting pretty bored', he said. 'Isn't there anyone here that you used to know in the old days whom you could ask to come and see you?'

'I thought of trying that,' she said, 'but it's more than ten years since we moved away and I haven't kept in touch with anyone.'

'Let's see, all the same.'

But something gave Helen the feeling that he was forcing himself to be amiable, to make up for their quarrel the day before, and when they had eaten their king prawn chow mein and drunk some tea, he seemed to have forgotten his suggestion. Helen did not remind him of it. When she thought about the schoolgirls whom she had once known in Edinburgh, they seemed utterly remote. Even if they still lived here, they had very likely got married and changed their names, and if she tried to find them in the telephone directory, there would be no trace of them. In any case, the chances were that they had completely forgotten her. She must face it,

her only acquaintance here was Mrs Lambie. She settled down to read one
of the thrillers that Colin had brought her, while he picked up a history
that he had bought for himself, but which he left unopened on his knee,
while he gazed broodingly at the fire.

After a little while Helen glanced up at him and found that that
brooding gaze had been transferred to her face, as if he were asking himself some profound question about her. She smiled and asked him what he
had on his mind.

He muttered, 'Nothing,' and opened his book. But he went on staring
at the first page for so long that she knew he was not reading it.

At breakfast next day he told her that he was going back to the library, and
as soon as he had done the washing-up he left the flat again. He had
hardly spoken at breakfast, but once he had gone, the complete silence in
the flat seemed suddenly unbearable. Limping from room to room, she
tried to fight off a new and terrifying sense of claustrophobia. She had
never suffered from it in this way before. It felt as if the walls of the flat
were closing in on her and were going to crush her.

The kitchen seemed specially sinister. It had a modern sink and a gas
cooker, but the floor was of great, uneven blocks of stone, which must
have been there since the house was built, for at no later time would a
floor so many storeys up have been paved with such slabs. They were very
cold to stand on. Helen found herself thinking of the maid of long ago, so
beautiful and so dangerous, who had probably had to live in this kitchen,
feel the chill of the floor through her shoes and get down on her knees to
scrub it. The thought of her sent Helen back as fast as she could to the
sitting-room, wishing that somehow, if only for a little while, she could
get out of the flat and talk to the butcher and the greengrocer and the
baker, flesh and blood ordinary people who had never driven any man or
woman to their deaths.

Going to the window, she wondered if, after all, if she made up her
mind to it, she could get down the stairs alone and breathe in some of the
fresh, cold air of the streets. Getting down should not really be too difficult. She could do it sitting down, manoeuvring herself from step to step
without ever putting any weight on her painful leg. It was the thought of
trying to get up again without Colin there to support her that she found

intimidating. She might actually find it impossible and might have to stay below in the cold for she did not know how long until, if she were lucky, she could persuade some kind passer-by to help her up again.

While she was thinking of this, she saw an old man on the far side of the street slither and fall and lie helplessly where he had fallen on the pavement. It was then that she realized there had been another heavy frost in the night, and that the half-melted snow of the day before had hardened into a sheet of ice. A passing milkman helped the old man to his feet, brushed him down and made sure that he had not hurt himself before leaving him to go on again down the street, holding tightly to the iron railings of the areas as he went. But the sight had put Helen off any thought of trying to go out herself. She must accept the fact, she was imprisoned here in this silent dwelling.

If only it had not been so silent! If only she could have heard other people moving about!

Knowing how foolish she was being, but all at once exasperated beyond bearing, she crossed to the fireplace, grasped the bell-pull beside it and wrenched it over and over again, feeling as if, sooner or later, if only she went on long enough, it would make some sound. Then suddenly it did. A bell pealed clearly in the silence.

She snatched her hand back from the bell as if it had burnt her. Then she realized that of course it was not this bell that had rung, but the front doorbell. Leaning on her sticks, she made her way along the hall to the front door and opened it. As she had expected, it was Mrs Lambie who stood there, dressed in her neat grey tweed suit and holding a saucepan.

'I've just been making a pot of lentil soup,' she said, 'much too much for just myself, and I thought in this weather you might find it acceptable. There's nothing like a good soup when the weather's so inclement. Do you care for it?'

'How very good of you,' Helen said. 'Won't you come in?'

'Are you sure it's not inconvenient? I don't want to intrude.' Mrs Lambie was already inside the door by the time she spoke. Helen closed it behind her. 'You'll find there's nothing unwholesome in it, none of that tinned stuff, just good ham bones and lentils and plenty of vegetables. I hope you enjoy it. And I hope you and your delightful husband are happy here. I know it isn't very grand, but I did my best to make it comfortable.'

'It's fine,' Helen said, taking the saucepan and carrying it to the kitchen, then rejoining Mrs Lambie, who had gone into the sitting-room and sat down by the fire. She was patting her red hair, so bizarre above her aged face.

'Yes, I did my best,' she said. 'But you aren't happy here, are you? I can always tell. You won't stay.'

'Well, of course we never meant to stay for long,' Helen said. 'As soon as I can get about better we want to find ourselves a small house some-where and have our own furniture moved in. We had it sent to Edinburgh when we left to come home, and it's in store now.'

'Yes, yes, your husband made that quite clear to me when we signed the lease,' Mrs Lambie said. 'I knew you'd only be here temporarily. But when I said you aren't happy here, that isn't what I meant. It's nothing to do with the flat, is it? There's trouble between the two of you, anyone can see that. So sad, when you're both so charming. And you're both trying so hard to make a success of things now. I think that's what I noticed first, how hard you were trying. It didn't seem quite natural. Of course I realize you may think I'm very interfering, but I'm a very old woman and I al-ways say what I think now, and I know that sometimes it's a help to have someone to talk to, even someone like me. So tell me, my dear, was the trouble another woman? Was that the real reason why you left Africa, and why you think your husband let you take that unsafe car out on purpose?'

'On purpose?' Helen said sharply. 'Whatever made you think that?'

'It's the truth, isn't it?'

'No, of course not. I've never thought of such a thing.'

'Dear, dear,' Mrs Lambie said with a sigh. 'How very sad. Because it's what your husband thinks himself, you know. He says you blame him for your accident. He told me so himself only yesterday.'

'Yesterday?' Helen said.

'Yes, when he dropped in for a drink with me when he got back from the library. I happened to be coming up the stairs myself when he got home and I asked him in for a chat. And we had a wee drink together. I do so enjoy company for a wee drink. It isn't the same when you're by your-self. And he told me how you blamed him for not having had the brakes of the car seen to, just as I was saying to you the other day. And he said how angry you were with him for taking a flat at the top of so many stairs and how you'd stopped trusting him in any way. And I asked him if the real trouble was another woman, because that's what it generally is, and he didn't answer, but I could tell from the way he coloured up that I'd hit on the truth. Oh dear, it's so sad. He's so very unhappy about it. If only I could persuade you not to blame him, because young men like him can't help attracting women, you know. They'll always pursue him. There are people who are like that without meaning any harm, women as well as men. They can't help it. So if you can't make up your mind to put up with it, you'll never be happy yourself. Do take my advice and try to conquer your jealousy. There's been enough unhappiness in this flat because of jealousy. I told you all about that, didn't I—about the young advocate and the beautiful maid? Yes, I remember I did. Well, we don't want any more tragedy here, do we?'

Helen had been only half-listening to what the old woman had been saying. She had taken in the fact that Colin had visited Mrs Lambie the evening before when he returned from the library, he apparently unburdened himself to her, and then had said nothing about this to Helen. And the fantastic thing about this was that what Helen felt about it was a kind of jealousy. That he should have kept the visit to himself made it seem important, overwhelming her for a moment with as deep a fear of losing him as she had ever felt when she had known that he was with Naomi. For if he was afraid to tell her such a thing, it must mean, surely, that she had completely lost his confidence.

Determined above all things that the old woman should not see how she had been shaken, she asked, 'Wouldn't you like a drink now, Mrs Lambie?'

'No, no, thank you, it's much too early in the morning for me,' Mrs Lambie replied. She stood up. 'I hope you enjoy the soup. I'm very fond of a good lentil soup myself, and it's as easy to make a big potful as a small one. And think over what I've been saying, because I've had a great deal of experience of life and I know what I'm talking about. Goodbye for now. Don't bother to come to the door. I'll let myself out.'

Helen let her do so, then got to her feet and poured out for herself the drink that Mrs Lambie had refused. Before she drank it, she took two of her pills. Her leg was hurting more than usual. Nerves, she thought. She had actually let that old creature upset her.

Colin came home earlier than he had the day before, bringing with him a cold roast chicken and the makings of a salad. It would have been a chilly meal for such an evening, if it had not been for the lentil soup. As they sat drinking sherry before it by the fire, Helen told Colin how Mrs Lambie had brought it to her in the morning.

He smiled and said, 'She's a kind old thing really, isn't she?'

'I think she's horrible!' Helen said with sudden violence. 'She's been doing her best to put evil thoughts into my mind.'

'Aren't they there already?' he asked with an edge on his voice.

'Don't, don't!' she exclaimed. 'I'm getting the feeling she's putting us against one another. And we'd made up our minds to stop quarrelling, hadn't we? We wanted this to be a really new start.'

'Of course, but it isn't her fault if it isn't, it's our own.'

She gave a sigh. 'I know you're right. It's this being cooped up with the snow and everything that's making me unreasonable. I'm sorry, Colin. But d'you know, it was rather funny this morning. I was in a vile mood and I started pulling that bell, as if it would ring if only I pulled it hard enough— and suddenly *she* came—Mrs Lambie—just as if I'd summoned her.'

'Coincidence.'

'Of course.'

'Anyway, the bell there wouldn't have been the one that that woman who got murdered used to ring. I'm pretty sure this is a Victorian thing, not Georgian. The works may be original, the wires and so on, but the bell itself isn't really old.'

Helen turned to look at the pretty, painted bell-pull, and her face became thoughtful.

'The fact is, you know,' she said, 'Mrs Lambie's never told me when that murder happened. She said it happened long ago, but that could mean anything. It doesn't have to mean two hundred years. Suppose it was only fifty, she might actually have been in Edinburgh herself at the time, and remembered quite a lot about it. Perhaps she even knew the people.'

'You're letting it obsess you,' Colin said. 'I wish you wouldn't.'

'It obsesses her.'

'Because it's nice and dramatic and she's lonely and old and hasn't much else to think about. Now I'll get that soup, and let's forget the ghosts.'

'But if it *did* happen only fifty years ago . . .'

But Helen did not finish her sentence. She was not sure what she wanted to say. It was a new thought to her that Mrs Lambie might have more knowledge of the murder that had happened here in this building than she had implied, and that that perhaps was why she had such a pressing need to talk about it. Perhaps, now that she was old and her own death was close to her, she even wanted to confide in someone some secret that she had nursed all these years.

Helen sipped her sherry and tried to adjust her picture of the people who had once lived here in this flat from the hoops and powdered wigs of the eighteenth century to the brief skirts, flesh-coloured stockings and shingled hair of the nineteen-twenties.

Next morning Colin said again that he was going to the library. Helen nearly asked him to stay at home for a change, partly because she was afraid of the mood of yesterday morning returning once she was left alone, but she knew that he would have nothing to do in the flat, and that if he had nothing to do he would soon become restless and irritable. It was fortunate really that he had found something to interest him in the library.

But was it true that he had?

The question sprang so abruptly into her mind that for a moment it made the room spin about her. But once she had asked it of herself, she realized that it had been troubling her since the day before. For if Naomi had arrived in London, as it had been plain from the postmark on her letter that she had, might she not have come the small distance further to Edinburgh? Might Colin not be spending his time with her?

The thought filled Helen with sudden terror, more because she felt that she was losing her grip on herself than because she really believed in it. Yet it might be right. Why should it not be right? And if it was, what was to become of her?

In a mood of needing to distract herself at any cost, she fetched from the kitchen the saucepan that had contained the lentil soup, let herself out of the flat and rang Mrs Lambie's bell.

There was silence for a little while, then the door opened a few inches and Mrs Lambie peered out cautiously, just as she had when Helen had first arrived. She was dressed as she had been then, in an old quilted dressing-gown, with her red hair tangled about her face. For a moment she gazed at Helen as if she did not know her, but then she gave a vague little smile and said, 'Oh, it's you. I couldn't think who it could be. I'm sorry, I'm not dressed.'

'I just came to bring you back your saucepan,' Helen said.

'Oh dear, you shouldn't have troubled. Any time would have done. But do come in, if you don't mind everything being in a mess. I haven't started to tidy up yet.'

It looked to Helen, when she went into the flat, as if Mrs Lambie had not tidied up for a long time. The room into which she took Helen was very like the sitting-room next door, and it was furnished in much the same way, but there was thick dust everywhere and cobwebs trailed from the ceiling. There were heaps of old newspapers on the floor and stuffing showed through slits on the worn upholstery of the chairs. A small table had been drawn close to the electric fire and had a cup and a coffee-pot on it.

'Really I'm just having my breakfast,' Mrs Lambie said. "I don't get up very early. I've nothing to get up for. But you'll join me in a cup of coffee, won't you?'

Holding her dressing-gown closely about her, as if it might reveal nakedness if she let it go, she went away to the kitchen to fetch another cup.

Sitting down, Helen looked with interest at a row of photographs on the mantelpiece. All but one were of young men, one in the uniform of a subaltern in the first world war, two or three in the plus-fours of the nineteen-twenties, a few more who looked as if they belonged to ten years later, and one who was in the timeless wig and gown of an advocate. The one exception to this parade of youth was the photograph in the place of honour in the centre of the mantelpiece. It was of a man of at least seventy, with a plump, mild face, a bald head and vague, troubled eyes, as if, even at his age, he had not got over finding life a bewildering puzzle.

Mrs Lambie, returning from the kitchen, saw Helen looking at this photograph.

'Ah, you're looking at my picture of my dear husband,' she said. 'He was a wonderful man, so good and kind and generous. We'd only been married three years when he had a stroke and died, but I'd been his housekeeper for years before that, and understood him perfectly. The rest . . .' She gave a little laugh. 'Well, we all have our memories, haven't we? And they keep me company. They were all very dear to me at different times. It may surprise you now, but I was often told when I was young that I was very beautiful. Now how do you like your coffee? Cream? Sugar?'

Helen said that she would like it black, without sugar.

'Ah, you're worrying about your figure,' Mrs Lambie said with a smile. 'I never had to do that.'

She handed Helen her cup. Like all Mrs Lambie's cooking, the coffee was excellent.

She went on, '"But beauty passes; beauty vanishes; However rare, rare it be . . ." I kept my looks till I was well into my sixties, you know, and even then I had distinction. So that's why I can tell you so much about the dangers of jealousy, my dear. Women were always jealous of me. It used to make me very unhappy, and truly it wasn't my fault. I couldn't help it if men pursued me. It was just something about the way I was made and not my fault at all. Why, one man even died for me.'

Suddenly Helen could not drink any more of her coffee. She put the cup down abruptly. Looking at the photograph of the advocate, she asked, 'On the gallows?'

The old woman stared at her blankly. 'What did you say?'

'Didn't he die on the gallows? Wasn't he convicted of murdering his wife? Didn't he throw her down those stairs out there, and weren't you the maid who caused all the trouble? Fifty or sixty years ago. And didn't you come back here when the flat was for sale because you couldn't keep away from it? It was the scene of your greatest triumph, the most wonderful memory of all.'

Mrs Lambie let her mouth fall open. She also let her dressing-gown fall open, and Helen saw that under it she was wearing a transparent black nightdress, frilly with lace, a private fantasy of youth and beauty.

'Are you mad, woman?' Mrs Lambie demanded, her voice trembling a little. 'What have I ever done to you since you got here but try to help you? Why do you hate me?'

'You've done all you could to turn my husband and me against one another,' Helen said. She stood up, grasping her sticks. 'You keep giving us advice, but all it comes to is dropping horrible thoughts into our minds.'

She hesitated. 'I'm sorry—I shouldn't have said that. Perhaps you don't mean to do it. I'd better go.'

Mrs Lambie was on her feet, facing her. "Yes, yes, go. I know your type. You're a wicked, jealous woman, that's what you are. You're jealous of me, even at my age. You're jealous of my past and all that I've had. You've never known what it is to be adored, worshipped. You're a plain, ordinary woman who isn't even sure she can keep her husband's love.'

'But you were the maid for whom the handsome young advocate was hanged, weren't you?' Helen said. Suddenly she felt absolutely certain of it. 'Isn't that true?'

'Go!' the old woman shrieked at her. 'Go!'

Helen turned and limped as quickly as she could to the door.

When Colin came home that evening, she told him what had happened. By now she felt quite detached from the scene in the flat next door. It was almost as if it had never occurred.

'I'm sorry,' she ended. 'I don't know what got into me, but at the time it seemed quite obvious to me that she must have been the maid in the story of the murder. I'm not sure what made me so certain of it—something to do with your pointing out that that bell there isn't really old, and then the photograph of the lawyer. But of course I've no evidence. Only the way she took it makes me feel I may have hit on the truth.'

Colin had brought home fish and chips again for their supper. He carried the packages out to the kitchen and put them in the oven to keep warm, then returned to the sitting-room with an unusually grim look on his face. He poured out sherry for them both.

'Tomorrow I'm going house-hunting,' he said. 'I don't know, perhaps this place *is* haunted. Anyway, I've got to get you out of it, because I think you're going mad. If we stay on, I don't know what'll happen.'

'I'm not mad,' she said. 'Don't you see, it's because of her part in the story that she's so obsessed with it and can't let it rest.'

'Did you say that to her?'

'More or less.'

'For God's sake, don't say it to anyone else,' he said. 'It's slanderous in the extreme.'

'I never see anyone else,' she said.

'No,' he said thoughtfully. 'Perhaps that's the trouble. Anyway, it's obvious I've got to get you out of here. I don't know what'll happen next if you stay. I'll go looking for another flat tomorrow, and try to find one on the ground floor, so that you can get out for a little when you want to.'

'Don't bother,' she said. 'I'm quite all right here.'

'You don't seem to understand,' he said. 'You're making the situation intolerable.'

'But suppose I'm right.'

He gave his head an impatient shake. 'No, something's got to be done. We can't go on like this, or I'll go crazy myself. Perhaps we ought to talk to that doctor. Anyway, I'll see what I can do tomorrow.'

He went out to the kitchen to fetch them their fish and chips.

In the morning he repeated that he was going out to hunt for another flat, and when Helen tried to dissuade him, his face took on a set, obstinate look, which meant, she knew, that there was no chance that he would listen to her. And after all, she realized, it might be that he was doing what would be best for them both. Even if she was totally wrong about Mrs Lambie, there was not much chance that the old woman would forgive her for what she had said, and living next door to her, with no one else at the top of the long stairs, would become more and more impossible. But when Colin left the flat, saying that he was going straight to a house-agent, Helen followed him out on to the landing.

'Please leave things as they are,' she pleaded. 'I'm not sure that I could face another move.'

'You might have thought of that sooner,' he said. 'But don't worry, I'll pack our things and get you down the stairs.'

'But, Colin—'

'No, we've got to go.' His voice began to rise.

'But haven't we signed a lease or something?'

'Oh, we'll lose some money, but what's that compared with peace of mind? I'll try to find something that'll suit you better.'

Her voice rose to match his. 'Ask Naomi to choose it for you then. She may know better than you what a woman wants.'

He had been about to start down the stairs, but he checked himself, turning to stare at her with a startled look of understanding.

'So you think she's here,' he said. 'That's been the trouble all along, hasn't it? You think I deliberately got you cooped up here so that there'd be no danger of your finding out that we were meeting.'

'Haven't you been meeting?' she asked. 'At least since she wrote to you.'

'You should have read that letter when I offered to show it to you,' he said, 'but you were too bloody proud. You tried to pretend you didn't care. Well, what it told me was that Naomi's come home to get married and it said goodbye—quite finally. You need never be afraid of her again. And if you don't believe me, the letter's in the waste-paper basket in our bedroom. Get it and read it for yourself. And get it into your head that if you can't trust me, we can't go on. I may be a hopeless, useless character, but try to realize that I love you, you damned woman, that I always have! There's never been anyone else.'

He turned back to the stairs and went running down them.

Helen stumbled towards them.

'Colin—wait!' she called out. 'Please wait! Don't go like that!'

But she heard only his running footsteps on the stone stairs, then the slam of the outer door as he reached the bottom.

Then she felt a pair of hands in the middle of her back and a violent thrust. Her scream as she fell echoed in the empty stairwell, where there was no one to hear her.

It was Fiona MacNab, arriving just afterwards to clean the flat, who found the body. She went out, screaming for the police, who arrived in a Panda car after only a few minutes. She told them that she had passed Mr Benson in the street, that he had been almost running, had been muttering to himself and had seemed to be in a state of extreme excitement.

Mrs Lambie, when they questioned her before the ambulance arrived, said that she had heard the Bensons quarrelling violently on the landing that morning, that they often quarrelled and that it was very tragic, because they were such an attractive young couple. There had been some trouble about another woman, she believed. Colin was picked up later in the National Library, where he had gone after two or three unsuccessful visits to house-agents. Later Mrs Lambie went into the flat next door and wandered round it, wondering what she ought to do with the belongings that the Bensons had left in their flat. There were only a few clothes and a few books. If no one appeared to claim them, she decided, she would send them to the Salvation Army.

She felt an agreeable sense of peace. During her long life as maid, as housekeeper, and finally as wife, she had committed several murders, the first of them, of course, having been that irritating, ailing woman, who kept on ringing the bell for attention, and whose good-looking young husband had been Mrs Lambie's first love. A pity that they had hanged him, he had really been very attractive. But how could she have helped it? And no one had ever come near to guessing her secret but that wretched girl with her broken leg, who had had too much time on her hands and become fanciful, and so had come too close to the truth for comfort. A pity about her husband too, a nice-mannered young man, who understood that even a very old woman enjoys a friendly chat once in a while. But at least they wouldn't hang him. It would only be life imprisonment.

Letting herself out of the flat, she returned to her own. As she did so, it seemed to her that very faintly she heard a bell ringing. She had often heard it throughout her life, and she knew quite well that it was simply in her own head. But the odd thing was that it still frightened her. One day soon, she felt, it would turn into an imperative summons that she would have to answer, and what would happen then?

The Case of the Parr Children

ANTONIA FRASER

've come about the children.'

The woman who stood outside the door of the flat, her finger poised to ring the bell again, looked desperate. She also looked quite unknown to the owner of the flat, Jemima Shore. It was ten o'clock on Sunday morning; an odd time for anyone to be paying a social call on the celebrated television reporter. Jemima Shore had no children. Outside her work she led a very free and very private existence. As she stood at the door, unusually dishevelled, pulling a dark-blue towelling robe round her, she had time to wonder rather dazedly: Whose children? Why here? Before she decided that the stranger had rung the wrong bell of the flat, and very likely in the wrong house in Holland Park.

'I've come about the children.'

The woman before her was panting slightly as she repeated the words. But then Jemima Shore's flat was on the top floor. It was her appearance which on closer inspection was odd: she looked smudged and dirty like a charcoal drawing which has been abandoned. Her beltless mackintosh had presumably once been white; as had perhaps her ancient tennis shoes with their gaping canvas, and her thick woollen socks. The thin dark dress she wore beneath her mackintosh, hem hanging down, gave the impression of being too old for her until Jemima realized that it was the dress itself which was decrepit. Only her hair showed any sign of care: that had at least been brushed. Short and brown, it hung down straight on either side of her face: in this case the style was too young.

The woman before Jemima might have been a tramp. Then there was the clink of a bottle at her feet as she moved uneasily towards Jemima. In a brown paper bag were the remains of a picnic which had clearly been predominantly alcoholic. The image of the tramp was confirmed.

'Jemima Shore Investigator?' she gasped. 'You've *got* to help me.' And she repeated for the third time: 'You see, I've come about the children.'

Jemima recoiled slightly. It was true that she was billed by this title in her programmes of serious social reportage. It was also true that the general public had from time to time mistaken her for a real investigator as a result. Furthermore, lured by the magic spell of know-all television, people had on occasion brought her problems to solve; and she had on occasions solved them. Nevertheless early on a Sunday morning, well before the first cup of coffee, seemed an inauspicious moment for such an appeal. In any case by the sound of it, the woman needed a professional social worker rather than an amateur investigator.

Jemima decided that the lack of coffee could at least be remedied. Pulling her robe still further around her, and feeling more than slightly cross, she led the way into her elegant little kitchen. The effect of the delicate pink formica surfaces was to make the tramp-woman look grubbier than ever. At which point her visitor leant forward on her kitchen stool, covered in pretty rose-coloured denim, and started to sob loudly and uncontrollably into her hands. Tears trickled between her fingers. Jemima noticed with distaste that the finger-nails too were dirty. Coffee was by now not so much desirable as essential. Jemima proceeded first to make it, and then to administer it.

Ten minutes later she found herself listening to a very strange story indeed. The woman who was telling it described herself as Mrs Catharine Parr.

'Yes, just like the wretched Queen who lost her head, and I'm just as wretched, I'm quite lost too.' Jemima raised her eyebrows briefly at the historical inaccuracy—hadn't Catherine Parr, sixth wife of Henry VIII, died in her bed? But as Mrs Parr rushed on with her dramatic tale, she reflected that here was a woman who probably embellished everything with unnecessary flourishes. Mrs Parr was certainly wretched enough; that went without question. Scotland. She had come overnight from Scotland. Hence of course the mackintosh, even the picnic (although the empty wine bottles remained unexplained). Hence the early hour, for Mrs Parr had come straight from Euston Station, off her sleeper. And now it was back to the children again.

At this point, Jemima Shore managed at last to get a word in edgeways: 'Whose children? Your children?'

Mrs Parr, tears checked, looked at Jemima as though she must already know the answer to that question: 'Why, the *Parr* children of course. Don't you remember the case of the Parr children? There was a lot about it on television,' she added reproachfully.

'The Parr children: yes, I think I do remember something—your children, I suppose.'

To Jemima's surprise there was a pause. Then Mrs Parr said with great solemnity:

'Miss Shore, that's just what I want you to find out. I just don't *know* whether they're my children or not. I just don't *know*.'

'I think,' said Jemima Shore Investigator, resignedly drinking her third cup of coffee, 'you had better tell me all about it from the beginning.'

Oddly enough Jemima genuinely did remember something about the episode. Not from television, but from the newspapers where it had been much discussed, notably in the *Guardian*; and Jemima was a *Guardian* reader. It had been a peculiarly rancorous divorce case. The elderly judge had come down heavily on the side of the father. Not only had he taken the unusual step of awarding Mr. Parr care and custody of the two children of the marriage—mere babies—but he had also summed up the case in full for the benefit of the Press.

In particular he had dwelt venomously on the imperfections of Mrs Parr and her 'trendy amoral Bohemianism unsuitable for contact with any young creature'. This was because Mrs Parr had admitted having an affair with a gypsy or something equally exotic. She now proposed to take her children off with him for the glorious life of the open road; which, she suggested, would enable her children to grow up uninhibited, loving human beings. Mr. Parr responded with a solid bourgeois proposition, including a highly responsible Nanny, a general atmosphere of nursery tea now, private schools later. Columnists had had a field-day for a week or two, discussing the relative merits of bourgeois and Bohemian life-styles for children. On the whole Jemima herself had sympathized with the warm-blooded Mrs Parr.

It transpired that Jemima's recollection of the case was substantially correct. Except that she had forgotten the crucial role played by the so-called Nanny; in fact no Nanny but a kind of poor relation, a trained nurse named Zillah. It was Zillah who had spoken with calm assurance of the father's love for his children, reluctantly of the selfish flightiness of the mother. She had known her cousin Catharine all her life, she said, although their material circumstances had been very different. She pronounced with regret that in her opinion Catharine Parr was simply not fitted to have sole responsibility for young children. It was one of the reasons which had prompted her to leave her nursing career in order to look after the Parr babies.

Since Zillah was clearly a detached witness who had the welfare of the children at heart, her evidence was regarded as crucial by the judge. He contrasted Catharine and Zillah: 'two young women so outwardly alike, so inwardly different'. He made this also a feature of his summing-up. 'Miss Zillah Roberts, who has had none of the benefits of money and education of the mother in the case, has nevertheless demonstrated the kind of firm moral character most appropriate to the care of infants . . . etc. etc.'

In vain Mrs Parr had exploded in court: 'Don't believe her! She's his mistress! They're sleeping together. She's been jealous of me all her life. She always wanted everything I had, my husband, now my children.' Such wild unsubstantiated talk did Mrs Parr no good at all, especially in view of her own admitted 'uninhibited and loving' behaviour. If anything, the judge's summing-up gained in vinegar from the interruption.

Mrs Parr skated over the next part of her story. Deprived of her children, she had set off for the south of Ireland with her lover. Jemima had the impression, listening to her, that drink had played a considerable part in the story—drink and perhaps despair too. Nor did Mrs Parr enlarge on the death of her lover, except to say that he had died as he had lived: 'violently'. As a result Jemima had no idea whether Mrs Parr regretted her bold leap out of the bourgeois nest. All she discovered was that Mrs Parr had had no contact whatsoever with her children for seven years. Neither sought nor proffered. Not sought because Mr Parr had confirmed Mrs Parr's suspicions by marrying Zillah the moment his divorce became absolute: 'and *she* would never have permitted it. Zillah.' Not proffered, of course, because Mrs Parr had left no address behind her.

'I had to make a new life. I wouldn't take any money from him. They'd taken my children away from me and I had to make a new life.'

It was only after the death of Mrs Parr's lover that, destitute and friendless, she had returned to England. Contacting perforce her ex-husband's lawyer for funds of some sort, she had discovered to her astonishment that Mr Parr had died suddenly several months earlier. The lawyers had been trying in their dignified and leisurely fashion to contact his first wife, the mother of his children. In the meantime the second Mrs Parr, Zillah, the children's ex-Nanny and step-mother had taken them from Sussex off to a remote corner of the Scottish Highlands. As she put it to the lawyer, she intended 'to get them and me away from it all'. The lawyer had demurred with the question of the children's future outstanding. But Zillah, with that same quiet air of authority which had swayed the divorce-court judge, convinced him. It might be months before the first Mrs Parr was contacted, she pointed out. In the meantime they had her address. And the children's.

'And suddenly there I was!' exclaimed Mrs Catharine Parr to Jemima Shore, the vehemence returning to her voice. 'But it was too late.'

'Too late?'

'Too late for Zillah. You see, Miss Shore, Zillah was dead. She was drowned in a boating accident in Scotland. It was too late for Zillah.' Jemima sensing the depth of Mrs Parr's bitterness, realized that what she really meant was: Too late for vengeance.

Even then, Mrs Parr's troubles were not over. The encounter with the children had been even more upsetting. Two children, Tamsin nearly nine and Tara nearly eight, who confronted her with scared and hostile eyes. They were being cared for at the lodge which Zillah had so precipitately rented. A local woman from the village, responsible for the caretaking of the lodge, had volunteered. Various suggestions had been made to transfer the children to somewhere less lonely, attended by less tragic memories. However, Tamsin and Tara had shown such extreme distress at the idea of moving away from their belongings and the home they knew that the plan had been abandoned. In the meantime their real mother had announced her arrival.

So Mrs Parr took the sleeper to Inverness.

'But when I got to Scotland I didn't recognize them!' cried Mrs Parr in a return to her dramatic style. 'So I want you to come back to Scotland with me and *interview* them. Find out who they are. You're an *expert* interviewer: I've seen you on television. That programme about refugee children. You talk to them. I beg you, Miss Shore. You see before you a desperate woman and a fearful mother.'

'But were you likely to recognize them?' enquired Jemima rather dryly. 'I mean you hadn't seen either of them for seven years. How old was Tamsin then—eighteen months? Tara—what—six months?'

'It wasn't a question of *physical* recognition, I assure you. In a way, they *looked* more or less as I expected. Fair. Healthy. She'd looked after them all right, Zillah, whoever they are. She always looked after people, Zillah. That's how she got him of course.'

'Then why—' began Jemima hastily.

Mrs Parr leant forward and said in a conspiratorial tone: 'It was spiritual recognition I meant. Nothing spoke to me and said: these are my children. In fact a voice deep in me cried out: Zillah! These are Zillah's children. This is Zillah's revenge. Even from the grave, she won't let me have my own children.' She paused for effect.

'You see Zillah had this sister Kitty. We were cousins, I think I told you. Quite close cousins even though we had been brought up so differently. That's how Zillah came to look after the children in the first place: she wanted a proper home, she said, after the impersonality of nursing. But that didn't satisfy Zillah. She was always on at me to do something about this sister and her family—as though their awful lives were my fault!'

She went on: 'Kitty had two little girls, almost exactly the same ages as my two. Quite fair then, though not as fair as Zillah and not as fair as my children. But there was a resemblance, everyone said so. People sometimes took them for my children. I suppose our relationship acounted for it. Kitty was a wretched creature but physically we were not unalike. Anyway, Zillah thought the world of these babies and was always having them round. Kitty was unhappily married: I believe the husband ran off before the last baby was born. Suddenly, looking at this pair, I thought: little cuckoos. Zillah has taken her own nieces, and put them into my nest—'

'—Which you had left of your own accord.' But Jemima did not say the words aloud. Instead she asked with much greater strength:

'But *why?*'

'The money! That's why,' exclaimed Mrs Parr in triumph. 'The Parr money in trust for them. Parr Biscuits. Doesn't that ring a bell? The money only went to the descendants of Ephraim Parr. *She* wouldn't have got a penny—except what *he* left her. Her nieces had no Parr blood either. But my children, because they were Parrs, would have been, *are* rich. Maybe my poor little children died, ran away, maybe she put them in an orphanage—I don't know. Or'—her voice suddenly changed totally, becoming dreamy, 'Or perhaps these are my children after all. Perhaps I'm imagining it all, after all I've been through. Miss Shore, this is just what I've come all the way from Scotland to get you to find out.'

It was an extraordinary story. Jemima's original impulse had been to give Mrs Catharine Parr a cup of coffee and send her gently on her way. Now the overriding curiosity which was definitely her strongest attribute would not let her be. The appeals of the public to Jemima Shore Investigator certainly fell on compassionate ears; but they also fell on very inquisitive ones. In this instance she felt she owed it to the forces of common sense to point out first to Mrs Parr that lawyers could investigate such matters far more efficiently than she. To this Mrs Parr answered quite reasonably that lawyers would take an age, as they always did:

'And in the meantime what would happen to me and the children? We'd be getting to know each other, getting fond of each other. No, Miss Shore, *you* can settle it. I know you can. Then we can all get on with our lives for better or for worse.'

Then Jemima caved in and acceded to Mrs Parr's request.

It was in this way, for better or for worse as Mrs Parr had put it, that Jemima Shore Investigator found herself the following night taking the sleeper to Inverness.

The sleeping-car attendant recognized Mrs Parr quite merrily: 'Why it's you again Mrs Parr. You'll keep British Rail in business with your travelling.' Then of course he recognized Jemima Shore with even greater delight. Later, taking her ticket, he was with difficulty restrained from confiding to her his full and rich life story which he was convinced would make an excellent television documentary. Staved off, he contented himself with approving Jemima's modest order of late-night tea.

'You're not like your friend, then, Mrs Parr . . .' he made a significant drinking gesture. 'The trouble I had with her going north the first time. Crying and crying, and disturbing all the passengers. However she was better the second time, and mebbe now you'll have a good influence on her now, Miss Shore. I'll be seeing her now and asking her if this time she'll have a late-night cup of tea.' He bustled off, leaving Jemima faintly disquieted. She hoped that Mrs Parr had no drink aboard. The north of Scotland with an alcoholic, probably a fantasist into the bargain . . .

Morning found her in a more robust mood. Which was fortunate since Jemima's first sight of Kildrum Lodge, standing on the edge of a dark, seemingly endless loch, shut in by mountains, was once again disquieting. It was difficult for her to believe that Zillah could have brought the children to such a place out of sheer love for Scottish scenery and country pursuits such as fishing, swimming and walking. The situation of the lodge itself even for Scotland was so extremely isolated. Nor was the glen which led up to the lodge notably beautiful. A general lack of colour except blackness in the water reflected from the skies made it in fact peculiarly depressing. There was a lack of vegetation even on the lower slopes of the mountains, which slid down straight into the loch. The single-track road was bumpy and made of stones. It was difficult to imagine that much traffic passed that way. One could imagine a woman with something to hide—two children perhaps?—seeking out such a location, but not a warm comforting body hoping to cheer up her charges after the sudden death of their father.

The notion of Zillah's sinister purpose, far-fetched in London, suddenly seemed horribly plausible. And this was the loch, the very loch, in which Zillah herself had drowned. No, Kildrum to Jemima Shore did not have the air of a happy uncomplicated place. She looked across at Mrs Parr, in the passenger seat of the hired car. Mrs Parr looked pale. Whether she had passed the night consuming further bottles of wine or was merely dreading the next confrontation with the Parr children, the hands with which she was trying to light a cigarette were shaking. Jemima felt once more extremely sorry for her and glad that she had come to Kildrum.

They approached the lodge. It was surrounded by banks of dark-green rhododendrons, growing unrestrained, which did nothing to cheer the surroundings. There was no other garden, only rough grass going down to the loch. The large windows of the lodge looked blank and unwelcoming. As Jemima drove slowly up the stony road, the front door opened and something white was glimpsed within. It was eerily quiet once the car's engine had stopped. Then the door opened further and the flash of white proved to be a girl wearing jeans and a blue jersey. She had extremely fair, almost lint-white hair, plaited. For a girl of eight she was quite well built—even stocky.

"Tamsin," said Mrs Parr. She pronounced the name as though for Jemima's benefit; but it was once again disquieting that she made no move toward the child. The interior of the house, like the glen itself and the mountains, was dark. Most of the paintwork was brown and the chintz curtains were patterned in a depressing brown and green. Nevertheless some energy had obviously been spent recently in making it cosy. There were cheerful traces of childish occupation, books, a bright red anorak, shiny blue gumboots. Pot plants and an arrangement of leaves bore witness to the presence of a domestic spirit in the house—once upon a time.

In the large kitchen at the back of the house where Jemima insisted on repairing for coffee there was also an unmistakable trace of modern civilization in the shape of a television set. There was a telephone too—but that was black and ancient-looking. Tamsin went with them, still silent. In the kitchen they were immediately joined by Tara, equally silent, equally blonde.

The two sisters stared warily at the women before them as if they were intruders. Which in a sense, thought Jemima, we are. Her eyes caught and held by the two striking flaxen heads, she recalled Mrs Parr's words concerning Zillah's nephew and niece: 'Quite fair too then, but not as fair as Zillah and not as fair as my children . . .' Could children actually become fairer as the years went by? Impossible. No one became fairer with time except out of a bottle. Even these children's hair was darkening slightly at the roots. Jemima felt that she had a first very positive clue that the Parr children were exactly what they purported to be. She was so relieved that a feeling of bonhomie seized her. She smiled warmly at the children and extended her hand.

'I'm Jemima Shore—'

'Investigator!' completed Tamsin triumphantly. And from her back she produced a large placard on which the cheering words: 'Welcome Jemima Shaw Investogater' were carefully inscribed in a variety of lurid pentel colours.

'I did it,' exclaimed Tara.

'I did the spelling,' said Tamsin proudly.

Jemima decided it would be tactful to congratulate her on it. At least fame on the box granted you a kind of passport to instant friendship, whatever the circumstances. In the kitchen too was another figure prepared to be an instant friend: Mrs Elspeth Maxwell, caretaker of the lodge and since the death of Zillah, *in loco parentis* to the Parr children. Elspeth Maxwell, as Jemima quickly appreciated, was a woman of uncertain age but certain garrulity. Instinctively she summed people up as to whether they would make good or bad subjects for an interview. Mrs Parr, madness and melodrama and all, would not in the end make good television. She was perhaps too obsessional at centre. But Elspeth Maxwell, under her flow of anecdote, might give you just that line or vital piece of information you needed to illuminate a whole topic. Jemima decided to cultivate her; whatever the cost in listening to a load of irrelevant gossip.

As a matter of fact Elspeth Maxwell needed about as much cultivation as the rhododendrons growing wild outside the house. During the next few days, Jemima found that her great problem consisted in getting away from Elspeth Maxwell, who occupied the kitchen, and into the children's playroom. Mrs Parr spent most of the time in her bedroom. Her public excuse was that she wanted to let Jemima get on with her task, which had been described to Tamsin and Tara as investigation for a programme about children living in the Highlands. Privately she told Jemima that she wanted to keep clear of emotional involvement with the children 'until I'm *sure*. One way or the other.' Jemima thought there might be a third reason: that Mrs Parr wanted to consume at leisure her daily ration of cheap red wine. The pile of empty bottles on the rubbish dump behind the rhododendrons continued to grow and there was a smell of drink upstairs emanating from Mrs Parr's bedroom. Whenever Mrs Parr chose to empty an ashtray it was overflowing.

On one occasion Jemima tried the door. It was locked. After a moment Mrs Parr called out in a muffled voice: 'Go away. I'm resting.'

It was conclusive evidence of Mrs Parr's addiction that no drink was

le in the rest of the house. Jemima was never offered anything alco-
ac nor was any reference made to the subject. In her experience of
holics, that was far more damning than the sight of a rapidly dimin-
erry bottle in the sitting-room.

th on the subject of the children was interminable: 'Ach, the
things! Terrible for them, now, wasn't it? Their mother drowned
very eyes. What a tragedy. Here in Kildrum.'

other,' corrected Jemima. Elspeth swept on. But the tale was
ic one, whichever way you looked at it.

al accident indeed. Though there's other people been drowned
ch, you know, it's the weeds, those weeds pull you down, right to
ottom. And it's one of the deepest lochs in the Highlands, deeper
than Loch Ness, nearly as deep as Loch Morar, did you know that, Miss
Shore? Then their father not so long dead, I believe, and this lady coming,
their real mother, all on top of it. Then you, so famous, from television . . .'

The trouble was that for all her verbiage, Elspeth Maxwell could not
really tell Jemima anything much about Zillah herself, still less about her
relationship with Tamsin and Tara. It was Elspeth who had had the task
of sorting out Zillah's effects and putting them into suitcases, still lying
upstairs while some sort of decision was reached as to what to do with
them. These Jemima made a mental note to examine as soon as possible.
Otherwise Elspeth had seen absolutely nothing of Zillah during her sojourn at Kildrum Lodge.

'She wanted no help, she told the Estate Office. She could perfectly
well take care of the lodge, she said, and the children. She was used to
it. And the cooking. She wanted peace and quiet, she said, and to fish
and walk and swim and go out in the boat—' Elspeth stopped. 'Ah well,
poor lady. But she certainly kept herself very close, herself and the children. No one knew her in Kildrum. Polite, mind you, a very polite lady,
they said at the Estate Office, wrote very polite letters and notes. But
very close.'

And the children? The verdict was more or less the same. Yes, they
had certainly seemed very fond of Zillah whenever glimpsed in Kildrum.
But generally shy, reserved. And once again polite. Elspeth could only recall one conversation of any moment before Zillah's death, out of a series
of little interchanges and that was when Tamsin, in Kildrum Post Office,

referred to the impending arrival of Mrs Parr. Elspeth, out of motherly sympathy for their apparent loneliness, had invited Tamsin and Tara to tea with her in the village. Tamsin had refused: 'A lady's coming from London to see us. She says she's our Mummy. But Billy and me think Zillah is our Mummy.'

It was, remarked Elspeth, an unusual burst of confidence from Tamsin. She had put it down to Tamsin's distaste at the thought of the arrival of 'the lady from London'—while of course becoming madly curious about Tamsin's family history. As a result of a 'wee discussion' of the subject in her own home, she had actually put two and two together and realized that these were the once famous Parr children. Elspeth, even in Kildrum, had naturally had strong views on *that* subject. How she would now have adored some contact with the household at Kildrum Lodge! But that was politely but steadfastly denied her. Until Zillah's death, ironically enough, brought to Elspeth exactly that involvement she had so long desired.

'I did think: mebbe she has something to hide, and my brother-in-law, Johnnie Maxwell, the ghillie, he thought mebbe the same. Keeping herself so much to herself. But all along, I dare say it was just the fear of the other mother, that one'—Elspeth rolled her eyes to the ceiling where Mrs Parr might be supposed to lie 'resting' in her bedroom—'Fear of her finding the children. Ah well, it's difficult to judge her altogether wrong. If you know what I mean. The dreadful case. All that publicity.'

But Elspeth looked as if she would readily rehash every detail of the case of the Parr children, despite the publicity, for Jemima's benefit.

None of this was particularly helpful. Nor did inspection of Zillah's personal belongings, neatly sorted by Elspeth, bring any reward. It was not that Jemima expected to find a signed confession: 'Tamsin and Tara are imposters. They are the children of my sister . . .' Indeed, she was coming more and more to the conclusion that Mrs Parr's mad suspicions were the product of a mind disordered by alcohol. But Jemima did hope to provide herself with some kind of additional picture of the dead woman, other than the malevolent reports of the first Mrs Parr, and the second-hand gossip of Elspeth Maxwell. All she discovered was that Zillah, like Jemima herself, had an inordinate fondness for the colour beige, presumably for the same reason, to complement her fair colouring; and like a good many other English women bought her underclothes at Marks & Spencer. Jemima did not like to speculate where and when Mrs Parr might have last bought her underclothes.

There were various photographs of Tamsin and Tara but none pre-dating Scotland. There were also some photographs of Zillah's sister Kitty; she did look vaguely like Mrs Parr, Jemima noticed, but no more than that; their features were different; it was a question of physical type rather than strict resemblance. There were no photographs of Kitty's children. Was that sinister? Conceivably. Or maybe she had merely lost touch with them. Was it also sinister that Zillah had not preserved photographs of Tamsin and Tara in Sussex? Once again: conceivably. On the other hand Zillah might have packed away all her Sussex mementoes (there were no photographs of Mr Parr either). Perhaps she came into that category of grief-stricken person who prefers not to be reminded of the past.

From the Estate Office Jemima drew another blank. Major Maclachlan, who had had the unenviable task of identifying Zillah's body, was polite enough, particularly at the thought of a television programme popularizing his corner of the Highlands. But he added very little to the public portrait of a woman whose chief characteristic was her reserve and determination to guard her privacy—her own and that of the children. Her love of country sports, especially fishing, had however impressed him: Major Maclachlan clearly found it unjust that someone with such admirable tastes should have perished as a result of them.

Only Johnnie Maxwell, Elspeth's brother-in-law who was in charge of fishing on the loch, contributed anything at all vivid to her enquiries. For it was Johnnie Maxwell who had been the principal witness at the inquest, having watched the whole drowning from the bank of the loch. To the newspaper account of the tragedy, which Jemima had read, he added some ghoulish details of the pathetic cries of the 'wee girl', unable to save Zillah. The children had believed themselves alone on the loch. In vain Johnnie had called to them to throw in the oar. Tamsin had merely screamed and screamed, oar in hand, Tara had sat quite still and silent, as though dumbstruck in horror. In their distress they did not seem to understand, or perhaps they could not hear him.

Altogether it was a most unfortunate, if not unparalleled accident. One moment Zillah was casting confidently ('Aye, she was a grand fisherwoman, the poor lady, more's the pity'). The next moment she had over-balanced and fallen in the water. There was no one else in the boat except the two children, and no one else to be seen on the shores of the loch except Johnnie. By the time he got his own boat to the children, Zillah had completely vanished and Tamsin was in hysterics, Tara quite mute. Helpers came up from the Estate. They did not find the body till the next morning, when it surfaced in the thick reeds at the shore. There were some bruises on it, but nothing that could not be explained by a fall from the boat and prolonged immersion.

That left the children. Jemima felt she owed it to Mrs Parr to cross-examine them a little on their background. Confident that she would turn up nothing to their disadvantage, she could at least reassure Mrs Parr thoroughly as a result. After that she trusted that her eccentric new contact would settle into normal life or the nearest approximation to it she could manage. Yes, the gentle, efficient cross-examination of Tamsin and Tara would be her final task and then Jemima Shore Investigator would depart for London, having closed the case of the Parr children once and for all.

But it did not work out quite like that.

The children, in their different ways, were friendly enough. Tamsin was even quite talkative once her initial shyness wore off. She had a way of tossing her head so that the blonde pigtails shook, like a show pony shaking its mane. Tara was more silent and physically frailer. But she sprang into life whenever Tamsin felt the need to contradict her, as being her elder and better. Arguing with Tamsin made even Tara quite animated. You could imagine both settling down easily once the double shock of Zillah's death and their real mother's arrival had been assimilated.

Nevertheless something was odd. It was instinct not reason that guided her. Reason told her that Mrs Parr's accusations were absurd. But then nagging instinct would not leave her in peace. She had interviewed too many subjects, she told herself, to be wrong . . . Then reason reasserted itself once more, with the aid of the children's perfectly straightforward account of their past. They referred quite naturally to their life in Sussex.

'We went to a horrid school with nasty rough boys—' began Tara.

'It was a *lovely* school,' interrupted Tamsin. 'I played football with the boys in my break. Silly little girls like Tara couldn't do that.' All of this accorded with the facts given by the lawyer: how the girls had attended the local primary school which was fine for the tomboy Tamsin, not so good for the shrinking Tara. They would have gone to the reputedly excellent school in Kildrum when the Scottish term started had it not been for the death of Zillah.

Nevertheless something was odd, strange, not quite right.

Was it perhaps the fact that the girls never seemed to talk amongst themselves which disconcerted her? After considerable pondering on the subject, Jemima decided that the silence of Tamsin and Tara when alone—no happy or unhappy sounds coming out of their playroom or bedroom—was the most upsetting thing about them. Even the sporadic quarrelling brought on by Tamsin's bossiness ceased. Yet Jemima's experience of children was the sporadic quarrels in front of the grown-ups turned to outright war in private. But she was here as an investigator not as a child analyst (who might or might not have to follow later). Who was she to estimate the shock effect of Zillah's death, in front of their very eyes? Perhaps their confidence had been so rocked by the boating accident that they literally could not speak when alone. It was, when all was said and done, a minor matter compared to the evident correlation of the girls' stories with their proper background.

And yet . . . There was after all the whole question of Zillah's absent nieces. Now was that satisfactorily dealt with or not? Torn between reason and instinct Jemima found it impossible to make up her mind. She naturally raised the subject, in what she hoped to be a discreet manner. For once it was Tara who answered first:

'Oh, no, we never see them. You see they went to America for Christmas and they didn't come back.' She sounded quite blithe.

'Canada, silly,' said Tamsin.

'Same thing.'

'It's not, silly.'

'It is—'

'Christmas?' pressed Jemima.

'They went for a Christmas holiday to America. Aunt Kitty took them and they never came back.'

'They went *forever*,' interrupted Tamsin fiercely. 'They went to Canada and they went *forever*. That's what Zillah said. Aunt Kitty doesn't even send us Christmas cards.' Were the answers, as corrected by Tamsin, a little too pat?

A thought struck Jemima. Later that night she consulted Mrs Parr. If Zillah's sister had been her next of kin, had not the lawyers tried to contact her on Zillah's death? Slightly reluctantly Mrs Parr admitted that the lawyers had tried and so far failed to do so. 'Oddly enough it seemed I was Zillah's next of kin after Kitty,' she added. But Kitty had emigrated to Canada (yes, Canada, Tamsin as usual was right) several years earlier and was at present address unknown. And she was supposed to have taken her two daughters with her.

It was at this point Jemima decided to throw in her hand. In her opinion the investigation was over, the Parr children had emerged with flying colours, and as for their slight oddity, well, that was really only to be expected, wasn't it? Under the circumstances. It was time to get back to Megalith Television and the autumn series. She communicated her decision to Mrs Parr, before nagging instinct could resurrect its tiresome head again.

'You don't feel it then, Jemima?' Mrs Parr sounded for the first time neither vehement nor dreamy but dimly hopeful. 'You don't sense something about them? That they're hiding something? Something strange, unnatural . . .'

'No, I do not,' answered Jemima Shore firmly. 'And if I were you, Catharine'—they had evolved a spurious but convenient intimacy during their days in the lonely lodge—'I would put all such thoughts behind you. See them as part of the ordeal you have suffered, a kind of long illness. Now you must convalesce and recover. And help your children, your own children, to recover too.' It was Jemima Shore at her most bracing. She hoped passionately not so much that she was correct about the children— with every minute she was more convinced of the rightness of reason, the falseness of instinct—but that Mrs Parr would now feel able to welcome them to her somewhat neurotic bosom. She might even give up drink.

Afterwards Jemima would always wonder whether these were the fatal words which turned the case of the Parr children from a mystery into a tragedy. Could she even then have realized or guessed the truth?

The silence of the little girls together: did she gloss too easily over that? But by that time it was too late.

As it was, immediately Jemima had spoken, Mrs Parr seemed to justify her decision in the most warming way. She positively glowed with delight. For a moment Jemima had a glimpse of the dashing young woman who had thrown up her comfortable home to go off with the raggle-taggle-gypsies seven years before. This ardent and presumably attractive creature had been singularly lacking in the Mrs Parr she knew. She referred to herself now as 'lucky Catharine Parr', no longer the wretched Queen who lost her head. Jemima was reminded for an instant of one of the few subjects who had bested her in argument on television, a mother opposing organized schooling, like Catharine Parr a Bohemian. There was the same air of elation. The quick change was rather worrying. Lucky Catharine Parr: Jemima only hoped that she would be third time lucky as the sleeping-car attendant had suggested. It rather depended on what stability she could show as a mother.

'I promise you,' cried Mrs Parr interrupting a new train of thought, 'I give you my word. I'll never ever think about the past again. I'll look after them to my dying day. I'll give them all the love in the world, all the love they've missed all these years. Miss Shore, Jemima, I told you I trusted you. You've done all I asked you to do. Thank you, thank you.'

The next morning dawned horribly wet. It was an added reason for Jemima to be glad to be leaving Kildrum Lodge. A damp Scottish August did not commend itself to her. With nothing further to do, the dripping rhododendrons surrounding the lodge were beginning to depress her spirits. Rain sheeted down on the loch, making even a brisk walk seem impractical. With the children still silent in their playroom and Mrs Parr still lurking upstairs for the kind of late-morning rise she favoured, Jemima decided to make her farewell to Elspeth Maxwell in the kitchen.

She was quickly trapped in the flood of Elspeth's reflections, compared to which the rain outside seemed suddenly mild in contrast. Television intrigued Elspeth Maxwell in general, and Jemima, its incarnation, intrigued her in particular. She was avid for every detail of Jemima's appearance on the box, how many new clothes she needed, television make-up and so forth. On the subject of hair, she first admired the colour of

Jemima's corn-coloured locks, then asked how often she had to have a shampoo, and finally enquired with a touch of acerbity:

'You'll not be putting anything on, then? I'm meaning the colour, what a beautiful bright colour your hair is, Miss Shore. You'll not be using one of those little bottles?'

Jemima smilingly denied it. 'I'm lucky.' She wasn't sure whether Elspeth believed her. After a bit Elspeth continued: 'Not like that poor lady.' She seemed obsessed with the subject. Was she thinking of dyeing her own hair? 'The late Mrs Parr, I mean, when I cleared out her things, I found plenty of bottles, different colours, dark and fair, as though she'd been making a wee experiment. And she had lovely fair hair herself, or so they said, Johnnie and the men when they took her out of the water. Just like the children. Look—' Elspeth suddenly produced two bottles from the kitchen cupboard. One was called Goldilocks and the other Brown Leaf. Jemima thought her guess was right. Elspeth was contemplating her own wee experiment.

'I'm thinking you'll not be needing this on your *natural* fair hair.' There was a faint ironic emphasis in Elspeth's tone. 'And Tamsin and Tara, they'll have lovely hair too when they grow up. They won't need Goldilocks or such things. And who would want Brown Leaf anyway with lovely fair hair like theirs? And yours. Brown Leaf would only hide the colour.' Elspeth put the bottles back in the cupboard as though that settled the matter.

Irritated by her malice—there was nothing wrong with dyeing one's hair but Jemima just did not happen to do it—Jemima abandoned Elspeth and the kitchen for the playroom. Nevertheless, Elspeth's words continued to ring in her head. That and another remark she could not forget. Tamsin and Tara were both reading quietly, lying on their tummies on the floor. Tamsin looked up and smiled.

'When will the programme be, Miss Shore?' she asked brightly. 'When will you come back and film us? Oh, I'm so sad you're going away.'

Jemima was standing by the mantelpiece. It had a large mirror over it, which gave some light to the dark room. In the mirror she gazed back into the room, at the striking blonde heads of the two children lying on the floor. It was of course a mirror image, reversed. The sight was symbolical. It was as though for the first time she was seeing the case of the Parr children turned inside out, reversed, black white, dark fair . . . Lucky children with their mother restored to them. A mother who drank and smoked and was totally undomesticated. But was still their mother. Zillah had done none of these things—but she had done worse: she had tried to keep the children from the mother who bore them. Lucky. Third time lucky.

Jemima stood absolutely still. Behind her back Tamsin smiled again that happy innocent smile. Tara was smiling too.

'Oh, yes, Miss Shore,' she echoed. 'I'm so sad you're going away'. For once Tara was in total agreement with her sister. And in the mirror Jemima saw both girls dissolve into soundless giggles, hands over their mouths to stifle the noise. She continued to stare at the children's blonde heads.

With sudden horrible clarity, Jemima knew that she was wrong, had been wrong all along. She would have to tell the woman resting upstairs that the children were not after all her own. A remark that had long haunted her came to the front of her mind. Catharine Parr: 'Just like the wretched Queen who lost her head, and I'm just as wretched.' And now she knew why it had haunted her. Catharine Parr had not been executed by Henry VIII, but she had been childless by him. Now she would have to break it to Mrs Parr that she too was childless. Would be childless in the future.

It had to be done. There was such a thing as truth. Truth—and justice. But first, however dreadfully, she had to confront the children with what they had done. She had to make them admit it.

Wheeling round, she said as calmly as possible to the little girls: 'I'm just going to drive to the telephone box to arrange with my secretary about my return. This telephone is out of order with the storm last night.' She thought she could trust Tamsin to accept the story. Then Jemima added:

'And when I come back, we'll all go out in the boat. Will you tell your—' she paused in spite of herself, 'Will you tell your Mummy that?'

The children were not smiling now.

'The boat!' exclaimed Tamsin. 'But our Mummy can't swim. She told us.' She sounded tearful. 'She told us not to go in the boat, and anyway we don't want to. She told us we'd never ever have to go in the boat again.'

'Oh don't make us go in the horrid boat, Miss Shore,' Tara's eyes were wide with apprehension. 'Please don't. We can't swim. We never learnt yet.'

'I can swim,' replied Jemima. 'I'm a strong swimmer. Will you give your Mummy my message?'

When Jemima got back, Mrs Parr was standing with Tamsin and Tara by the door of the lodge, holding their hands (the first time Jemima had glimpsed any sign of physical affection in her). She was looking extremely distressed. She was wearing the filthy torn mackintosh in which she had first arrived at Jemima's flat. Her appearance, which had improved slightly over the last few days, was as unkempt and desperate as it had been on that weird occasion.

'Miss Shore, you mustn't do this,' she cried, the moment Jemima was out of the car. 'We can't go out in the boat. It's terrible for the children—after what happened. Besides, I can't swim—'

'I'm sorry, Catharine,' was all Jemima said. She did not relish what she had to do.

Perhaps because she was childless herself, Jemima Shore believed passionately that young children were basically innocent whatever they did. After all, had the Parr children ever really had a chance in life since its disturbed beginnings? And now she, the alleged protector of the weak, the compassionate social campaigner, was going to administer the *coup de grâce*. She wished profoundly that she had not answered the bell to Mrs Parr that fatal Sunday morning.

The rain had stopped. The weather was clearing above the mountains in the west although the sky over the loch remained sullen. In silence the little party entered the rowing boat and Jemima pushed off from the soft ground of the foreshore.

'Come on, Tamsin, sit by me. Row like you did that afternoon with Zillah.'

Mrs Parr gave one more cry: 'Miss Shore! No.' Then she relapsed with a sort of groan into the seat at the stern of the boat. Tara sat beside her, facing Jemima and Tamsin.

After a while Jemima rested on her oar. They were near the middle of the loch. The lodge looked small and far away, the mountains behind less menacing. Following the rain the temperature had risen. Presently the sun came out. It was quite humid. Flies buzzed round Jemima's head and the children. Soon the midges would come to torture them. The water had a forbidding look: she could see thick green weeds floating just beneath the surface. An occasional fish rose and broke the black surface. No one was visible amongst the reeds. They were, the silent boatload, alone on the loch.

Or perhaps they were not alone. Perhaps Johnnie Maxwell the ghillie was somewhere amid the sedge, at his work. If so he would have seen yet another macabre sight on Loch Drum. He would have seen Jemima Shore, her red-gold hair illuminated by the sunlight, lean forward and grab Tara from her seat. He would have seen her hurl the little girl quite far into the lake, like some human Excalibur. He would have heard the loud splash, seen the spreading circles on the black water. Then he would surely, even at the edge of the loch—for the air was very still after the rain—heard Tara's cries. But even if Johnnie Maxwell had been watching, he would have been once again helpless to have saved the drowning person.

Mrs Parr gave a single loud scream and stood up at the stern of the boat. Jemima Shore sat grimly still, like a figure of vengeance. Tamsin got to her feet, wielded her oar and tried in vain to reach out to the child, splashing hopelessly now on, now under the surface of the loch. Jemima Shore continued to sit still.

Then a child's voice was heard, half choking with water: 'Zillah, save me! Zillah!'

It seemed as though the woman standing at the stern of the boat would never move. Suddenly, uncontrollably, she tore off her white mackintosh. And without further hesitation, she made a perfect racing dive on to the surface of the loch. Minutes later Tara, still sobbing and spluttering, but alive, was safely out of the water. Then for the first time since she had thrown Tara into the loch, Jemima Shore made a move—to pull the woman who had called herself Mrs Catharine Parr back into the boat again.

'The police are coming of course,' said Jemima. They were back at the house. 'You killed her, didn't you?'

Tamsin and Tara, in dry clothes, had been sent out to play among the rhododendrons which served for a garden. The sun was gaining in intensity. The loch had moved from black to grey to slate-blue. Tara was bewildered. Tamsin was angry. 'Goodbye, *Mummy*,' she said fiercely to Zillah.

'Don't make her pretend any longer,' Jemima too appealed to Zillah. And to Tamsin: 'I know, you see. I've known for some time.'

Tamsin then turned to her sister: 'Baby. You gave it away. You promised never to call her Zillah. Now they'll come and take Zillah away. I won't ever speak to you again.' And Tamsin ran off into the dark shrubberies.

Zillah Parr, wearing some of her own clothes fished out of Elspeth's packages, was sitting with Jemima by the playroom fire. She looked neat and clean and reassuring, a child's dream mother, as she must always have looked during the last seven years. Until she deliberately assumed the messy run-down identity of Mrs Parr that is. How this paragon must have hated to dirty her finger-nails! Jemima noticed that she had seized the opportunity to scrub them vigorously while she was upstairs in the bath-room changing.

Now the mirror reflected a perfectly composed woman, legs in nice shoes, neatly crossed, sipping the glass of whiskey which Jemima had given her.

'Why not?' said Zillah coolly. 'I never drink you know, normally. Un-like *her*. Nor do I smoke. I find both things quite disgusting. As for pre-tending to be drunk! I used to pour all those bottles of wine down the sink. But I never found a good way of producing cigarette stubs without smok-ing. Ugh, the smell. I never got used to it. But I feel I may need the whiskey this afternoon.'

Silence fell between them. Then Zillah said quite conversationally: 'By the way, how did you know?'

'A historical inaccuracy was your first mistake,' replied Jemima. They might have been analyzing a game of bridge. 'It always struck me as odd that a woman called Catharine Parr, an educated woman to boot, would not have known the simple facts of her namesake's life. It was Catherine Howard by the way who lost her head, not Catherine Parr.'

'Oh really.' Zillah sounded quite uninterested. 'Well I never had any education. I saw no use for it in my work, either.'

'But you made other mistakes. The sleeping-car attendant: that was a risk to take. He recognized you because of all the drinking. He spoke of you being third time lucky, and at first I thought he meant your quick journey up and down from London to Inverness and back. But then I realized that he meant that this was your third journey *northwards.* He spoke of you "going north" the second time and how you weren't so drunk as the first time. She went up first, didn't she? You killed her. Then faked your own death, and somehow got down to London secretly, perhaps from another station. Then up and down again under the name of Catharine Parr.'

"That was unlucky.' Zillah agreed. "Of course I didn't know that he'd met the real Catharine Parr when I travelled up under her name the first time. I might have been more careful.'

'In the end it was a remark of Elspeth Maxwell's which gave me the clue. That, and your expression.'

'That woman! She talks far too much,' said Zillah with a frown.

'The dyes: she showed me the various dyes you had used, I suppose to dye Mrs Parr's hair blonde and darken your own.'

'She dyed her own hair,' Zillah sounded positively complacent. 'I've always been good at getting people to do things. I baited her. Pointed out how well I'd taken care of myself, my hair still blonde and thick, and what a mess she looked. Why, I looked more like the children's mother than she did. I knew that would get her. We'd once been awfully alike, you see, at least to look at. You never guessed that, did you? Kitty never really looked much like her, different nose, different shaped face. But as girls, Catharine and I were often mistaken for each other. It even happened once or twice when I was working for her. And how patronizing she was about it. "Oh no, that was just Zillah" she used to say with that awful laugh of hers when she'd been drinking. "Local saint and poor relation." I was like her but not like.' Zillah hesitated and then went on more briskly.

'I showed her the bottle of Goldilocks, pretended I used it myself and she grabbed it. "Now we'll see who the children's real mother is" she said, when she'd finished.'

'The bottle did fool me at first,' admitted Jemima. 'I thought it must be connected somehow with the children's hair. Then Elspeth gave me the key when she wondered aloud who would ever use Brown Leaf if they had fair hair: "It would only hide the colour."' She paused. 'So you killed her, blonde hair and all.'

'Yes I killed her,' Zillah was still absolutely composed. She seemed to have no shame or even fear. 'I drowned her. She was going to take the children away. I found out that she couldn't swim, took her out in the boat in the morning when I knew Johnnie Maxwell wasn't around. Then I let her drown. I would have done anything to keep the children,' she added.

'I told the children that she'd gone away,' she went on. 'That horrid drunken old tramp. Naturally I didn't tell them I'd killed her. I just said that we would play a game. A game in which I would pretend to fall into the lake and be drowned. Then I would dress up in her old clothes and pretend to *be* her. And they must treat me just as if I *was* her, all cold and distant. They must never hug me as if I was Zillah. And if they played it properly, if they never talked about it to anyone, not even to each other when they were alone, the horrid mother would never come back. And then I could be their proper mother. Just as they had always wanted. Zillah, they used to say with their arms round me, we love you so much, won't you be our Mummy for ever?' Her voice became dreamy and for a moment Zillah was reminded of the person she had known as Catharine Parr. 'I couldn't have any children of my own, you see; I had to have an operation when I was quite young. Wasn't it unfair? That she could have them, who was such a terrible mother, and I couldn't. All my life I've always loved other people's children. My sister's. Then his children.'

'It was the children all along, wasn't it? Not the money. The Parr Trust: that was a red herring.'

'The money!' exclaimed Zillah. Her voice was full of contempt. 'The Parr Trust meant nothing to me. It was an encumbrance if anything. Little children don't need money: they need love and that's exactly what I gave to them. And she would have taken them away, the selfish good-for-nothing tramp that she was, that's what she threatened to do, take them away, and never let me see them again. She said in her drunken way, laughing and drinking together. "This time my fine cousin Zillah, the law will be on my side." So I killed her. And so I defeated her. Just as I defeated her the last time when she tried to take the children away from me in court.'

'And from their father,' interposed Jemima.

'The judge knew a real motherly woman when he saw one,' Zillah went on as though she had not heard. 'He said so in court for all the world to hear. And he was right, wasn't he? Seven years she left them. Not a card. Not a present. And then thinking she could come back, just like that, because their father was dead, and claim them. All for an accident of birth. She was nothing to them, *nothing*, and I was everything.'

And Jemima herself? Her mission?

'Oh yes, I got you here deliberately. To test the children. I was quite confident, you see. I knew they would fool you. But I wanted them to know the sort of questions they would be asked—by lawyers, even perhaps the Press. I used to watch you on television,' she added with a trace of contempt. 'I fooled that judge. He never knew about their father and me. I enjoy fooling people when it's necessary. I knew I could fool you.'

'But you didn't,' said Jemima Shore coldly. She did not like the idea of being fooled. 'There was one more clue. An expression. The expression of triumph on your face when I told you I was satisfied about the children and was going back to London. You dropped your guard for a moment. It reminded me of a woman who had once scored over me on television. I didn't forget that.' She added, 'Besides, you would never have got away with it.'

But privately she thought that if Zillah Parr had not displayed her arrogance by sending for Jemima Shore Investigator as a guinea pig she might well have done so. After all no one had seen Catharine Parr for seven years; bitterly she had cut herself off completely from all her old friends when she went to Ireland. Zillah had also led a deliberately isolated life after her husband's death; in her case she had hoped to elude the children's mother should she ever reappear. Zillah's sister had vanished to Canada. Elspeth Maxwell had been held at arm's length as had the inhabitants of Kildrum. Johnnie Maxwell had met Zillah once but there was no need for him to meet the false Mrs Parr, who so much disliked fishing.

The two women were much of an age and their physical resemblance in youth striking: that resemblance which Zillah suggested had first attracted Mr Parr towards her. Only the hair had to be remedied, since Catharine's untended hair had darkened so much with the passing of the years. As for the corpse, the Parr family lawyer, whom Zillah had met face to face at the time of her husband's death, was, she knew, on holiday in Greece. It was not difficult to fake a resemblance sufficient to make Major Maclachlan at the Estate Office identify the body as that of Zillah Parr.

The truth was so very bizarre: he was hardly likely to suspect it. He would be expecting to see the corpse of Zillah Parr, following Johnnie's account, and the corpse of Zillah Parr, bedraggled by the loch, he would duly see.

The unkempt air of a tramp was remarkably easy to assume: it was largely a matter of externals. After a while the new Mrs Catharine Parr would have discreetly improved her appearance. She would have left Kildrum—and who would have blamed her?—and started a new life elsewhere. A new life with the children. Her own children: at last.

As all this was passing through Jemima's head, suddenly Zillah's control snapped. She started to cry: 'My children, my children. Not hers, Mine—' And she was still crying when the police car came up the rough drive, and tall men with black and white check bands round their hats took her away. First they had read her the warrant: 'Mrs Zillah Parr, I charge you with the murder of Mrs Catharine Parr, on or about the morning of August 6 . . . at Kildrum Lodge, Inverness-shire.'

As the police car vanished from sight down the lonely valley, Tara came out of the rhododendrons and put her hand in Jemima's. There was no sign of Tamsin.

'She will come back, Miss Shore, won't she?' she said anxiously. 'Zillah, I mean, not that Mummy. I didn't like that Mummy. She drank bottles all the time and shouted at us. She said rude words, words we're not allowed to say. I cried when she came and Tamsin hid. That Mummy even tried to hit me. But Zillah told us she would make the horrid Mummy go away. And she did. When will Zillah come back, Miss Shore?'

Holding Tara's hand, Jemima reflected sadly that the case of the Parr children was probably only just beginning.

McLean of Scotland Yard

GEORGE GOODCHILD

cLean was on holiday—a month of well-earned respite from the world of crooks and murderers in which he habitually moved. In relaxation McLean was just as thorough as in the moments of his professional activity. Every morning he left the small hotel in the Highlands, with a book and some sandwiches packed in a rucksack, and tramped to some delectable spot where he could recline and laze away that day. His attire was the very opposite of the well-cut and well-creased clothes which he habitually wore, and few would have recognised the brilliant inspector of the C.I.D. in his shapeless felt hat, baggy trousers and heavy boots.

He had an innate love for nature, and as he walked his observant eyes took in details that most men would have missed. A crawling insect in his path was enough to bring him to a halt, and cause him to stoop down and examine it, catalogue it in its correct species and blow it into mid-air.

In truth he had forgotten the very existence of Scotland Yard. Scotland was quite enough! On this particular day he lounged by a musical stream, read his book, dozed at intervals and let Time have her fling. When the sun declined he walked back to the hotel, with his mind at peace with the world, and a splendid hunger gnawing at his vitals. But on reaching his haven of rest he was informed that a gentleman named Searle wished to see him.

"Searle—Searle! No, I'm not available."

He went upstairs, took a bath, changed into evening dress, as if he were staying at the Ritz instead of a remote hostelry at which he was the sole guest, and came down to dinner. And still the pugnacious Mr Searle was waiting.

"Didn't you tell him I was not available?" he inquired of the waiter.

"Yes, sir, but he said he would wait."

"All right—I'll see him."

It then transpired that his visitor was not named Searle but Tearle—a man known to McLean, and at this moment holding a prominent position in a big Scottish insurance company.

"So it's you," said McLean. "I was told your name was Searle. What's the trouble?"

"I have been trying to find you since yesterday morning. Will you help us? You are the only man to solve—"

"I'm on holiday."

"I know—I met your sister in Glasgow. It was she who put me on your trail. This isn't a police matter—I mean, that I am begging you in a private capacity to save us from being swindled out of ten thousand pounds."

"You think I can perform miracles? Who is the swindler, anyway?"

"A dead man."

"Rather clever of him. Look here, since you've ruined my holiday by distracting my mind, you had better have a meal with me, and run over the points."

Tearle was more than agreeable, having waited with the patience of Job since lunch. They repaired to the small dining-room and the waiter brought an extra plate.

"Now," said McLean, "what's all the fuss about?"

"Did you see yesterday's newspaper?"

"No. I never read newspapers when I'm on holiday."

"Well, a man insured with the Company was found asphyxiated in his garage—an Italian named Lotto. A year ago he took up a life policy for £10,000."

"Most thoughtful of him."

"Very. So far as we can see, the coroner is bound to bring in a verdict of accidental death—in which case we pay up to his nearest relative—in Italy. But suicide is barred in the policy."

"Ah—I get you."

"Wait! The Company is absolutely straight. But there are some curious facts connected with this business. For instance, we have an engineer who swears that the exhaust-pipe of the car was deliberately disconnected under the footboards, thus permitting the dangerous carbon-monoxide gases to escape into the interior of the car. Secondly, the doors of the garage were closed—shut tight."

"Won't the coroner's jury take those facts into consideration?"

"There is contrary evidence. The chauffeur has already stated that the exhaust pipe came adrift two days ago, and that he had intended having it repaired on the day after the tragedy occurred."

"And the closed doors?"

"Both Lotto and the chauffeur were in the habit of entering the garage by the small door in the garden, starting up the car, and letting the engine warm up while they opened the big doors. Anyway, we aren't quite satisfied about it, and you know what these juries are? If they can bring it in 'accidental death' they will—to spare his relatives."

"H'm! What do you want me to do?"

"Come and have a look at the place."

"Great Scott! I'm going fishing to-morrow."

"It isn't far from here—less than twenty miles. I have a car on hand and could run you over there early to-morrow morning. We only want to do the right thing. But we don't feel like being swindled."

"Evidently you have made up your mind that swindling was contemplated?"

"Yes—for various reasons. I know for a fact that Lotto has been living beyond his means—that he has poor relatives in Italy to whom he was greatly attached. The suicide clause was inserted deliberately because he seemed rather a strange fellow. Will you come, and help us through this trouble?"

McLean agreed to do so, without displaying any of the zest that he felt. In truth he could never resist a mystery—and small as this one appeared to be on the surface, experience told him that on innumerable occasions big things emerged from apparently simple cases.

The house of the dead man was remotely situated, and standing in an acre of timbered grounds. McLean had begged Tearle to keep his name and object quiet, and to present him as a friend of Lotto. To the butler he gave his name as Singleton, and expressed a desire to see the corpse.

"Certainly, sir. His death was a great blow to me, for he was the best of masters."

He spoke with an accent that revealed his origin at once—Italian, and was a dark, suave individual of about fifty years of age. He led McLean to the bedroom, and left him alone with the dead man for a few minutes. McLean had seen several asphyxiated men in his time, and Lotto carried all the symptoms. Tearle came in while McLean was nosing around.

"What's the butler's name?" asked McLean.

"Loretti. He has been with Lotto for a number of years, and was devoted to him."

"Did Lotto live alone?"

"Yes. A rather reserved man. I believe he sprang from nothing. Made a little money by some mysterious means and settled down here."

"Any will?"

"I don't know. I think the matter is in the hands of the Public Trustee."

"His private papers are gone?"

"I suppose so. Loretti will know. The chauffeur is outside. Do you want to see him?"

"Yes. Italian?"

"No—English."

The chauffeur was named Spillings, and had been with Lotto for one year—ever since Lotto bought his first car. He was well-spoken, polite, and apparently very upset at what had taken place.

"This gentleman is an old friend of your master's," said Tearle. "He cannot understand how Mr. Lotto came to meet with his misadventure."

"Nor I, sir. I take a good deal of blame upon myself, for not mending the exhaust-pipe sooner."

"Is this the car?" asked McLean.

"Yes, sir."

"Exactly as it was when the tragedy took place?"

"Yes. I have not touched it. I can show you the cause of all the trouble."

He lifted the ill-fitting footboard, and revealed the broken joint.

McLean craned his head forward, and saw the break. It was, as Tearle had said, a little suspicious, for there were a few minute marks which might well have been caused by the use of a tool.

"That was broken on the road?" he said.

"Yes, sir. We hit a big pot-hole and I heard immediately an increase in the sound of the exhaust. I told Mr. Lotto what had happened."

"You told him—and yet he sat in this enclosed car, with all the windows up—on that evening?"

"It was foolish. He must have forgotten."

McLean wandered over to the big doors—and pulled them aside. Then he came back and examined the window.

"Who found Mr. Lotto?"

"I did, sir. It was my evening off and I went into Perth. I returned at eleven o'clock and, to my surprise, heard the engine running. I came in and found Mr. Lotto sitting in the car, with his hands on the steering-wheel—dead."

"Did you detect poisonous gas?"

"The place was full of smoke and the radiator was boiling over. But of course I had opened the big doors—so I wasn't affected by the fumes."

"Did Mr. Lotto have an appointment on that evening?"

"I didn't know he had, or I should have stayed. But Loretti told me he was rung up after I left—about eight o'clock, and he told Loretti he had to run into Perth to see a friend."

McLean shook his head sadly, playing the part of interested and grieved friend.

"I suppose you will be wanted at the inquest to-morrow?" he inquired.

"Yes, sir."

"You think it was all an accident?"

"Why, of course, sir. If you knew Mr. Lotto you must know that he was not the sort of man to take his— That is just a wicked rumour."

"But why didn't he open the doors before he started up the engine?"

"I don't think he paid much attention to what people said about the danger of carbon-monoxide gas. The engine would never run well until it was warmed up. No, sir—there is only one possible verdict."

McLean spent another hour about the place. In the library he found a bureau with some documents in it, and before he left he stuffed some of these into his pocket—while the butler's eagle eyes were elsewhere.

"When does the interment take place?" he asked.

"The day after to-morrow, sir—at Perth."

"I shall try to be present. It is a very sad business, Mr. Loretti."

"Very sad, sir. We have wired to his sister in Italy, but it is doubtful whether she will arrive in time for the interment. He was very fond of her."

"You speak excellent English."

"I have travelled a great deal, sir. Mr. Lotto could scarcely speak a word."

McLean and Tearle ultimately made their departure, and all the way to his hotel McLean was silent. Now and again he would consult the papers and documents which he had taken without permission, and then it was that fishing and lounging were completely forgotten.

"Well," said Tearle at length. "What do you make of it?"

"Interesting—very interesting."

"You don't think it was suicide?"

"I know it wasn't."

"Then you must give evidence—"

"Oh, no. The verdict is a foregone conclusion. You will never get away with the suicide story."

"If we don't—we pay."

"That remains to be seen. I am coming to the Court to-morrow—merely out of interest. But I want you to meet me at Lotto's house to-morrow night at nine o'clock."

"I don't quite understand. Once that verdict is uttered there is nothing left to do but pay up."

"I beg to differ. There are some strange facts in this case. But I have no intention of trying to upset the kindly verdict. Meet me there at nine o'clock, and have two policemen in the offing."

"What!"

"That is my advice."

"Then, by Jove, I'll follow it, though I don't understand what you are driving at."

He went off and McLean spent the rest of the day working up an engrossing theory—nay, more than a theory. Among the things which he had filched was a small photograph—a curious thing that, taken in conjunction with a newspaper cutting, was of the gravest importance.

"Clever!" mused McLean. "Damned clever—if it is true!"

On the following day he motored into Perth and attended the inquest. Things went very smoothly. A jury had been empanelled because of the slight element of doubt as between a verdict of accidental death and suicide, but the evidence supported the former view, and as Mr. Lotto was known and respected locally he was given the benefit of the doubt. As to the cause of death, that left no shadow of doubt. Tearle was slightly dejected despite McLean's absolute composure.

"Accident!" he said. "That was no accident."

"I am inclined to agree."

"Then what—?"

"Nine o'clock," reminded McLean. "I fancy your company will have no need to write that substantial cheque."

Punctually at nine o'clock McLean turned up at the meeting-place, and found Tearle there in the darkness. Close by were two plain-clothes men from the local police. McLean went to them.

"I am Inspector McLean of Scotland Yard," he whispered. "I want you to remain here in the meantime. If what I suspect is true, I may have need of you. If you hear a shot or a whistle, enter the house, without delay."

"Very good, Inspector."

"You have two sets of handcuffs?"

"Yes."

"Good!"

He and Tearle then made up the drive and rang the front-door bell. A long time elapsed before it was answered. Loretti came to the door and blinked at them.

"I find I cannot attend the funeral," said McLean. "But I should like to bid a last farewell to my old friend. Is that convenient?"

"I am afraid not, sir. The undertaker screwed down the coffin this evening."

"Ah. Then I will pay my respects—just the same, if I may?"

Loretti was agreeable. Tearle waited in the hall and McLean entered the library where the coffin lay. Loretti withdrew and McLean immediately went to the window, and slipped back the latch. A minute later he was in the hall—looking distressed.

"Thank you, Mr. Loretti," he said. "I am very sorry to trouble you so late at night. But I have to go to London early in the morning."

"No trouble at all, sir. Good night!"

"Well?" gasped Tearle, when they reached a sheltered part of the garden. "What happened?"

"Nothing much. But something soon will. I have unfastened the library window. We will go through it in a few minutes."

They waited a while, and then stole towards the house. At last McLean reached the window and gently opened it. Tearle followed him into the big room, and shuddered when McLean flashed an electric torch full on to the coffin.

"S-sh! Now we shall know the truth."

He put the torch into Tearle's hand, and produced a screwdriver from his pocket. Then, to Tearle's amazement, he began to remove the many screws. At last the lid was loose. McLean lifted it, and a low exclamation broke from Tearle's lips. *The coffin was filled with—earth.*

"S-sh! You didn't expect that—eh?"

"Great heavens—no! What does it mean? Why is there no body in the coffin?"

"There was when the undertaker screwed it down. But I rather fancy it has been removed—for a certain purpose. I think we will endeavour to locate it. Better remove your shoes. I have rubber on mine."

Tearle did this, but he was a little nervous all the time. Keen as he was to do his duty to his company, this adventure overawed him. But McLean was as eager as a greyhound on the leash. So far everything had transpired as he had expected, and he had no doubt about the finale.

"Tread warily," he whispered. "Mr. Loretti has good ears, if I am any judge."

"Loretti!"

"S-sh! Come!"

They passed into the hall, which was now in darkness, and began to investigate the rooms, one at a time. The ground floor was quite deserted, and on looking through the window McLean saw that the chauffeur's quarters over the garage were unlighted.

"There was a maid," he mused. "Appears to be out. Yes, they would see to that. Let us go upstairs."

The house comprised two stories only, and all the rooms upstairs led from one central corridor. One by one they were entered, and still no living soul was seen. At length McLean came to the end room. It was locked but the key was present. He turned it and switched on the light.

"Ah—Loretti's!"

The butler's clothes were spread over the bed, and on the floor close by was a very large travelling trunk, already half filled with clothing and sundry articles.

"Our friend intends to make an early departure," he mused. "Probably after the funeral."

"I'm still in the dark."

"That is astonishing. I think we have time to make ourselves acquainted with Mr. Loretti's possessions. Leave the door slightly ajar, and if you hear him approaching warn me."

He thereupon commenced to turn out the contents of the trunk. In the bottom of it was a toilet-bag, containing a safety-razor, shaving-brush, and a few oddments. Among the last was a small blue bottle, with a glass stopper. On the side of it was a fragment of red label. McLean removed the stopper and smelt it warily.

"Got it!" he exclaimed.

"Poison?"

"Chloroform. I wish I had the label, but it is not vital. Now we will look up our two friends."

"But where are they?"

"Where is the body? Find that and we find them."

"Great Scott! This is getting gruesome."

"I am afraid it is. I ought to warn you, Tearle, that it is possible they may object to any intrusion on our part. Would you prefer to join the officers outside—until they are wanted?"

"Not likely. I'm going to see this thing through. Lead on, Macduff!"

McLean went down the stairs, and passed through the kitchen. Beyond was a door which gave access to a flight of stone steps. Silently he descended them. They found themselves in a big basement, at the windows of which were bars and shutters—now closed. A door lay on the right, and from the other side of it came the sound of low voices. With an automatic in one hand and the torch in the other, McLean crept towards it. He removed the key and squinted through the key-hole. Then he slipped the torch into his pocket and caught Tearle's arm, indicating the key-hole with the muzzle of the automatic. Tearle bent down and squinted. Inside was a long table, and on it was stretched a human shape—under a sheet. Nearby was Loretti, clad in a long smock, with a knife in his hand—and opposite him the chauffeur, looking pallid.

"My God!" he whispered.

McLean pressed a whistle into his hand.

"Go upstairs and blow it," he whispered. "There is no way out for them."

Tearle mopped his brow and went off. McLean guessed that the door was bolted on the other side, so he went back and put all the strength of his leg into one blow at the lock. The inside staple went, and the door flew open. Loretti swung round, and his face went black with baffled rage.

"You!" he snarled. "What the devil—?"

Quick as lightning a revolver appeared from the pocket of the smock, and a bullet whistled dangerously close to McLean's head. The next moment McLean fired and Loretti dropped his weapon and clutched his right arm with contorted features.

"Put up your hands, Spillings!" rapped McLean. "I shouldn't be surprised if you, too, collected firearms—as well as jewels."

Spillings obeyed and McLean went forward and ran his free hand through the chauffeur's pockets. But he found nothing more dangerous than a knife. Then Tearle's whistle pealed out. Loretti dived for the fallen revolver, but McLean got there first and bowled the Italian over with his foot.

"I arrest you both for murder," he said.

Loretti scowled, but Spillings broke down.

"I didn't do it," he cried. "I only helped carry him— I knew nothing until—"

"Rat!" snarled Loretti.

Through the door came the two officers with Tearle. McLean pointed to his prisoners and in twenty seconds both were handcuffed.

"Take them away," said McLean. "I will come to the station immediately."

Tearle winced as he stared at the form on the table, and the box of surgical instruments on the dresser.

"What—what was the idea?" he inquired.

"A little post-mortem operation."

"But with what object?"

McLean produced an old news-cutting from his pocket. But it was from an Italian newspaper and Tearle could not read it. McLean thereupon translated it.

"To-day the strange case of Signor Lotti came before Judge Matioli at Naples. Signor Lutz, a wealthy diamond merchant of Naples, deposed that on the twentieth instant, Lotti, who was employed by him as a diamond-cutter, swallowed a stone the value of £6,000. The theft was suspected, and Lotti was taken into custody. When the stone failed to appear, an X-ray photograph was taken, and it was shown that the jewel had become lodged in the prisoner's intestine. Signor Lutz now begged that the Judge make an order for an operation to be performed on the man, but this the Judge refused to do. After a long debate the prisoner was sentenced to one year's imprisonment."

"That was twenty years ago," said McLean. "Here is another cutting from the same newspaper—three years later."

"We learn that since his release from prison Signor Lotti, who figured so prominently in the Lutz diamond case, has suffered from attack on the part of professional thieves. Three attempts have been made on his life in order to secure the jewel which he still carries inside his body."

"Well!" gasped Tearle.

"The third document is a receipt from Signor Lutz—dated two years ago. It is a receipt for a sum of money equal to the value of the diamond. Evidently Lotti made enough money to settle that old debt, but he was afraid to go back to Italy. Crooks have long memories. With these docu-ments was an X-ray photograph—taken after Lotti's release, I presume, and attached to a letter from an English surgeon who does not advise an operation. That is the whole grim story."

"By Jove! Who would have dreamed of it! Then they drugged him and carried him into the car—after tinkering with the exhaust pipe?"

"Undoubtedly, and I dare say that they saw to it that he stood no chance of recovering from the drug. Doubtless he lived long enough to in-hale quite a quantity of carbon-monoxide gas, and the smell of the stuff was enough to drown the chloroform. Rather ingenious—what?"

"But what made you suspect them, when there was no question of murder at that time?"

"There were quite a number of suspicious points. In the first place, it is unusual for an Italian to settle down in a climate like Scotland's, when he could scarcely speak a word of the language, and all his interests are in Italy. Obviously he had something to fear—some reason for living a lonely life. Then there was Loretti. He was too eager with his explanations—too free with his assumed emotions. I suspected Loretti from the first. But the first real light came when I found that photographic print of Lotti's inter-nals, with a cross marking the diamond. That and the press-cuttings pro-vided a solid motive."

"It was one that never occurred to me."

"Probably not, but then, my dear Tearle, you have not spent so many years of your priceless youth in the pursuit of the unrighteous. I have come to look upon every person as dishonest until it is proved otherwise. Lord, what a mess-up you have made of my holiday!"

But his twinkling eyes gave that assertion the lie. McLean was a man-hunter all the time. Even fishing and the collection of wee beasties had to take second place.

The Spy and The Healing Waters

EDWARD D. HOCH

When Hastings retired from British Intelligence and moved to Scotland, Rand and his wife Leila had promised to visit him. Thinking about it now, Rand was somewhat ashamed to realize that three months had passed with no attempt to make good on the promise. He turned to Leila one evening after dinner and said, "The weather's supposed to be good this weekend. What say we drive up to Scotland and see old Hastings?"

She put down the archaeology text she was reading and said, "I never thought you'd bring yourself to it."

"I know I've been dragging my feet," Rand admitted. "I'm afraid of what this retirement might have done to him."

Months earlier, Hastings had come under suspicion as a traitor, a Russian mole operating at the highest levels of M.I.6. Rand had been instrumental in clearing his name, but the ordeal had been too much for his former superior. Even though there had been apologies all around, Hastings felt he could never again do an effective job. He'd called it quits and retired to a little holiday home he'd maintained east of Edinburgh along the Firth of Forth.

"He must be very lonely up there," Leila speculated. "It's too bad he never married."

"I think he did, in his university days, but it was short-lived. Ever since I knew him, he devoted himself entirely to his work. When I was heading up Concealed Communications, he took an almost daily interest in the department, even though it was only one of his many responsibilities."

And so it was that Rand and Leila set out for the east coast of Scotland on a Friday morning in May.

They'd phoned Hastings to tell him they were coming, and he had obviously been watching out the window of his cottage. He came out as they turned the car in the gravel driveway, smiling and extending a hand of greeting. "So good of you both to drive all the way up here!"

He had aged in the three months since his retirement, Rand noticed. He walked a little slower and watched the ground, as if fearful of a tumble. In his office overlooking the Thames, he'd always been sure of himself.

"It's a lovely house," Leila marveled as he showed them through the four small rooms.

"Small, though. Very small."

"It's all the space you need."

"Well," Hastings replied, "I have my books, and all my fishing gear. The fishing has always been a delight around here. And my niece in Edinburgh drives out to see me every couple of weeks. It's not a bad life."

Leila had promised during the drive up that she'd be bright and cheerful the whole time of their visit, even though she'd grown to resent Hastings in the years before his retirement. "At least he won't be calling on you with his problems two or three times a year now," she'd said.

"No, those days are over." Rand was surprised that the thought made him a little sad, not only for Hastings but for himself.

Now, seeing Hastings here in his retirement cottage, he felt a little better. His former superior went on about the region at some length, and it was only when Leila went off to use the bathroom that he asked, "Have you been in the Double-C or the other departments since my departure?"

"No, I've had nothing to do with any of them."

"I thought Parkinson might ask you for help."

"He never did before," Rand told him. "You're the only one I ever did work for." Parkinson, who'd moved up to Director of Concealed Communications when Rand retired more than a decade ago, was a by-the-books professional who rarely asked help from anyone. Rand couldn't entirely dislike him, though. It was Parkinson who'd tipped him off that Hastings had been taken to a safe house for questioning on suspicion of treason.

Hastings sighed and gazed out at the water, perhaps following the progress of a large yacht under full sail. "I guess we're both retired, then, after all these years."

"No shop talk," Leila cautioned, returning in time to overhear. "Have you decided how to entertain us for the weekend?" she asked their host.

Hastings took on an impish expression Rand hadn't seen in years. "We might drive over to Foxhart tomorrow. It's not far and there's a rather strange phenomenon there—a spring whose waters are said to heal the infirm."

"You sound like a non-believer."

"Well, I think I'll reserve judgment until I see it. But I don't believe the priests at Lourdes need worry about competition from Foxhart quite yet."

Leila and Rand slept well in the big double bed in the guestroom. Hastings himself prepared breakfast, seeming more relaxed than he had the day before. Then they set off for Foxhart in Rand's car and Hastings warned, "I understood it's crowded on weekends, even though there's been little national publicity about it so far."

"If it's too crowded, we can drive down along the coast," Leila suggested.

When they reached Foxhart shortly before noon, Rand found the traffic being diverted onto a grassy field. A local constable seemed to have things well under control and directed them down a path toward the little stream that was the central attraction. The path itself was crowded with people moving in both directions, some reverently silent while others laughed and chatted like typical tourists. Foxhart was just another stop to them.

At the stream itself, Rand was surprised to see a tall, dark-haired man in clerical garb facing people like some sort of tour guide. "Come, place your hands in this healing water," he told them. "The miracle has happened once, it can happen again. Don't be afraid. Here, Granny, let me give you a hand."

"Is he real?" Leila whispered in Rand's ear.

"Let's see if he takes up a collection."

Most of the people did dip their hands into the swiftly flowing stream, and one elderly man even took off his shoes and socks to immerse his feet. The clergyman spoke again. "I'm the Reverend Joshua Fowler. As you leave, you will note that bottles of the healing water are available for your purchase. All monies raised through their sale goes to continue the Lord's work. Thank you, thank you. Please keep moving. There are other pilgrims anxious to bathe in these waters."

Rand saw that Hastings was no longer looking at the cleric—his gaze had shifted to an attractive woman standing near the edge of the crowd. She wore a fashionable tan raincoat and a scarf to protect her brown hair from the breeze. She was tall, probably in her mid-thirties. Rand judged her to be a business type and wondered what had brought her to this place. Hastings must have wondered, too, because he suddenly left Rand's side and edged his way through the crowd toward her. Rand followed along.

"Hello, Karen," Hastings said as he reached her.

She glanced at him and said, "My name is Monica. You must be mistaking me for someone else." She spoke with a strong American accent.

Hastings hesitated and then tipped the plaid cap he was wearing. "I'm sorry. You looked just like her."

She edged away from them and hurried back up the path to the parking lot. "Who did you think she was?" Rand asked.

"A young woman I met in London last year. Karen Hayes."

"But you were wrong."

"No."

"She's one of ours?"

"CIA, actually. One of their specialists."

"Oh?"

Leila joined them. "What are you up to, huddled here like a pair of thieves? Are you plotting to steal the receipts from the sale of the healing water?"

"Hastings thought he saw someone he knew," Rand explained.

"I'm sorry I dragged you out here," Hastings murmured apologetically. "There wasn't really much to see. Shall we be on our way?"

They were passing a small glass-enclosed concession stand when Leila decided she wanted a souvenir. "I'll catch up with you," she said.

"Just don't bring back a bottle of water," Rand told her.

He and Hastings strolled on toward the parking lot, where a minor traffic jam seemed to have developed. "I suppose she might be on assignment," Hastings said, thinking aloud.

"What?"

"That woman we saw. Karen Hayes."

"You miss the job, don't you?"

"Didn't you, when you retired from Double-C?"

"Well, I had Leila, and I did some writing. And of course you kept me busy over the years."

"I'm not lonely, Rand, if that's what you mean. I just miss knowing what's going on from day to day."

"Surely you could have stayed on. After all their mistaken accusations, they could hardly have forced you out."

"I didn't feel comfortable being back. Parkinson and the others were most friendly and solicitous, but there was something in their eyes that hadn't been there before. I was only two years away from mandatory retirement, anyway, and I found that I could leave now with severance pay and my full pension rights. It seemed the wise thing to do."

Leila came running up the path to join them, carrying a small plastic bag. "The water is three pounds a bottle—can you believe that? I settled for a laminated color photo of the stream with the Reverend Fowler standing beside it."

"I hope you're not planning to hang it in our living room," Rand laughed.

A number of cars were lined up in the car park, attempting to get out. Rand heard the constable blowing his whistle, and then he heard another sound off to his left of almost the same pitch.

It was a woman screaming.

They reached her at the same time as several others. She was a grey-haired woman who looked like somebody's mother. At her feet lay sprawled a woman in a tan raincoat. Blood was soaking through the coat from an unseen wound.

It was the woman Hastings had identified as Karen Hayes and there was no doubt in Rand's experienced eye that she was dead . . .

Neither Rand nor Hastings had been in a line of work where one volunteered information to the police, so they remained on the sidelines during the brief turmoil that followed. Constable Stebbins, the officer who'd been directing traffic in the parking lot, pulled back the raincoat enough to reveal a wound just beneath the left breast. Then he hurried to his patrol car to summon reinforcements on the police radio.

"Keep back, everyone," he urged, using his traffic baton as an extender for his widespread arms. "There's nothing to see here. Keep moving, please!"

Leila tugged on Rand's sleeve. "We don't need to get involved in this, do we?"

"Hastings thinks he knows her," he replied quietly. "Let's just wait until the investigating team arrives."

The Reverend Joshua Fowler had been drawn to the scene by that time and was exhorting the faithful to remain calm. "A woman has been struck down in the prime of her life! Join me in a prayer for her, and a prayer for her attacker, that the Lord might show him some of the mercy that he denied his victim."

Rand took Hastings aside. "You said she was a CIA specialist. What was her field?"

"If that was Karen Hayes, as I believe, she was a disguise technician. Washington loaned her to us last year to help with a particular operation. I assumed she'd gone back by now."

"What sort of operation?"

"That's top secret, Rand."

Their conversation was cut short by the arrival of two police cars. If Rand had expected them to remain on the sidelines, he was mistaken.

The first detective out of the unmarked second car spotted Hastings at once and headed straight for him. "Well, Mr. Hastings, are you involved in this?"

"Not at all," Hastings said. "I'm just showing some friends some of our tourist spots. Jeffrey and Leila, this is Detective Sergeant Scott Winston."

Winston and Rand shook hands and Winston told Hastings, "Stay around. I'll want to see you later about this business." Then he hurried off to the dead woman.

"Now what?" Leila asked.

Hastings said, "I've known Sergeant Winston for as long as I've had my house. I'd see him when I came here to fish. He's a good sort. And this will probably become his case unless he has to ask for help."

"Don't the local police usually summon Scotland Yard for help in murder cases?" Leila looked toward where the police were grouped around the body. "I assume she didn't commit suicide."

"Despite its name," Hastings explained, "Scotland Yard's jurisdiction doesn't normally extend to Scotland. The Scottish courts and legal system are quite separate from ours."

Rand observed that the Reverend Fowler was deep in conversation with Sergeant Winston, gesturing with both hands as he spoke. Perhaps he was disturbed about the business he was losing. "Tell me some more about this place," he urged Hastings. "And about Fowler."

"Well, this is my first visit, of course, but I've read about it in the local papers. It seems that Fowler leased this property from the owner about a year ago. Within months, a young woman who'd been crippled for years because of a hip problem claimed she'd been cured by daily bathing in the stream. This was followed by an elderly man reporting that his arthritis had been cured. That was when Fowler started building the souvenir stand and bottling the water."

"The world is full of charlatans," Rand observed. "What would bring a CIA technician to this place?" he wondered.

"I can't imagine."

Leila, who had been listening enough to grasp the flow of their conversation, suggested, "Perhaps she had a tennis elbow or some such thing—she might have come for the waters herself."

"Then why deny her identity when I greeted her?" Hastings asked.

Leila shrugged. "She was embarrassed," she suggested. "Or you were mistaken."

Sergeant Winston sent the constable to summon them as the body was being removed. "Never had anything like this in Foxhart," Constable Stebbins grumbled. "I've lived here all my forty years and I told them when the tourists started coming in to see the waters that there'd be trouble of some sort. Any time you get this many people, you get trouble."

There was no disagreeing with that, and Winston's refrain was not much different. "It's people from the city who commit these crimes," he declared. "Country people would never stick a stranger with a knife for no reason at all."

"How do you know it was for no reason?" Hastings asked.

"The woman was an American, traveling alone. We've located her rented vehicle in the car park. Apparently she's been touring England and Scotland, judging by the route maps spread out on the passenger seat. She just arrived here this morning. In her bag we found a hotel bill for a single room in Edinburgh last night."

Rand mused. "She was alone at the hotel, and the maps on the passenger seat indicate she was alone in the car as well."

"Exactly," the sergeant confirmed. "A stranger in a strange land, and someone killed her."

"What sort of weapon?" Hastings asked.

"A dagger with a very thin blade, I'd guess. We'll know more after the autopsy. Now tell me what you saw."

"Nothing, really. I had noticed the woman earlier, down by the stream. I suppose she caught my eye because she was younger and healthier than most of the other visitors."

"Did any of you notice someone watching or following her?"

"No," Hastings said. Rand could read in his troubled face the realization that his speaking to Karen Hayes, and calling her by name, might have caused her death.

"What about this man Fowler? Do you know anything about him?"

"Not a thing, except what little I've read in the newspapers about the cures."

"Yes," Sergeant Winston muttered. "Well, he didn't cure *this* woman."

As they were leaving, Rand asked the detective, "Has she been identified yet?"

"She was carrying quite a bit of identification, including an American passport in the name of Monica Camber, and an M.I.5 courtesy card—the sort they issue people on special duty involving travel."

"Interesting," Rand murmured.

Driving back to Hastings' cottage, Rand said, "Perhaps you were wrong. She said her name was Monica, not Karen. She might have been telling the truth. I read once that everyone in the world has a double. This might have been Karen Hayes' double."

"If she was an innocent American tourist, why was she killed?"

"A random act of violence, just as the police believe."

"Hogwash!" Hastings exploded. "I just keep fearing it was my fault that she died."

"Then you're certain it was this Karen Hayes."

"As certain as I've ever been of anything. I spent two entire days with the woman just last year, and I have a very good memory."

"What are you going to do?"

Hastings sighed, as Rand had heard him do so many times in the midst of a particularly troublesome operation. "I suppose I should tell London, pass the word on to the Americans."

"It's none of your affair any more," Rand reminded him.

"The woman is dead, Jeffrey! Someone cares about her—not just the people who employed her but her family and friends!"

"She'll be identified through that M.I.5 travel card."

Hastings was silent for a moment and then he said, "No, I have to tell them now. Otherwise they won't know before Monday."

When they arrived at the cottage, he went directly to the telephone. Rand knew he was dialing a private number of London Central, one that would be manned even on weekends. When he came back to them he said, "Well, I left a top-priority message for Parkinson. It's not Double-C's responsibility, but he's always been decent to me."

They waited, expecting the telephone to ring at any moment, but no call came. Finally Leila walked to the window and stared out at the lush green countryside. "It's so lovely, so peaceful. Why would the CIA have any interest here?"

"I can't imagine," Hastings said. "There's an inactive RAF base near here, but it was mothballed years ago. It's not likely to reopen, either, with peace breaking out across Europe. The cold war is over."

"And the spies are all out of work," Rand said with a smile.

"It's no joke. You know how much of our work has already been taken over by spy satellites, and even those may become obsolete if Russia becomes a completely open society."

"There'll always be spies, Hastings. There'll be little wars and government-backed terrorism."

Leila was growing restless. Her dark hair had streaks of grey in it now, but she was still as lovely as when Rand had first met her down along the Nile River at the height of the cold war, when Russian troops were actually based in Egypt. He remembered his first sight of the high-cheek-boned beauty of her face.

"Well, the healing waters were certainly exciting," she told Hastings. "What have you got to show us next?"

"Would you care for a bite to eat? It's still several hours till dinner."

They agreed on a sandwich, and then a drive into Edinburgh for dinner at a restaurant Hastings favored. On the way they could stop at Inveresk Lodge, a tourist attraction Hastings thought they would enjoy.

As it turned out, their plans were due for a change. They were walking out to the car when a black sedan pulled up in front of the cottage. Rand recognized Parkinson at once, accompanied by a slightly overweight American he'd never seen before. "Glad we caught you!" Parkinson said. "Flew up as soon as I received your message, Hastings. Mr. Camber here is quite concerned about his daughter."

So it's to be more games, Rand decided. The Americans loved games, but no more so than the British. "My name is Rand, Mr. Camber," he introduced himself. "Haven't we met before?"

The American frowned at Rand. "I don't believe so, unless it was back in Richmond. I'm Hugh Camber, Monica's father. I have a construction business back there."

"You spoke with his daughter?" Parkinson asked Hastings.

Rand and Leila both looked at Hastings, who gave one of his sighs and said, "I think we'd better go back indoors."

When they were seated in Hastings' cramped living room, he looked at Camber and said, "The woman I saw this morning at Foxhart was Karen Hayes, a CIA technician. She was not a field operative and to my knowledge never had been. She was a sweet young woman with a particular talent for disguises. Whoever sent her to Foxhart sent her to her death. Which of you is prepared to take responsibility for that?"

The American shifted uneasily. "I think you must be mistaken—"

"Like hell I'm mistaken. You're CIA and everyone in this room knows it. Parkinson here doesn't sacrifice his weekend at home to fly to Scotland with a worried father searching for his daughter."

The man who'd been Hugh Camber got to his feet. "Just tell us what you know, please," he said, his voice softening a bit.

"What's your name?"

"Camber is good enough. Tell me."

Hastings seemed to make a decision. He nodded and started talking, telling them everything that had happened. When he finished, Rand took over. "Now it's your turn, Mr. Camber."

The American gave him a suspicious look. "Does this man have clearance?"

"He was my predecessor at Double-C," Parkinson explained. "I'll vouch for him."

"And the woman, too?"

Leila rose to leave but Rand waved her back to her chair. "My wife stays."

Camber decided not to press the point. "Very well. Does the name Oleg Penkov mean anything to you?"

Rand had been gone too long for the name to register, but Hastings immediately said, "The Limping Man."

"Exactly. And an expert with makeup. They say he can disguise everything but his limp." He showed them a photo of a white-haired man.

"He was at Foxhart?"

"We believe he came to London two weeks ago on some sort of mission."

Rand interrupted. "I thought the cold war was ending. Why would Moscow send someone here?"

"It's not ending as far as industrial espionage goes. They want every secret they can put their hands on."

"Not much industry or espionage in Foxhart," Hastings observed drily.

Camber ignored him and went on. "We brought over Miss—"

"Hayes."

"Well, yes. Miss Hayes was a better disguise technician than anyone London could supply. She knew what to look for, and we felt sure she'd see through Penkov's makeup even if he dressed himself as an old lady. She's been on his tail for the past ten days, ever since he left London."

"Making contacts?"

"Yes. A schoolteacher in Bath, a magistrate in Newcastle, a postman in Blackpool. No one of obvious importance, and no one on any list of suspected agents."

"Perhaps he's selling magazine subscriptions," Rand suggested.

Camber glanced at him distastefully. "Please, Mr. Rand."

"Sorry."

"She called London early this morning and told us she was in Foxhart. Penkov seemed interested in the healing waters here, and she was certain he would make another contact. That's the last we heard."

"When I spoke to her," Hastings said, "I called her by name. It may have blown her cover."

Parkinson thought about it. "I doubt if her name would have meant anything to Penkov—unless she was known to the person he came here to contact."

"But she was dead within minutes."

"A coincidence, possibly," Hugh Camber reassured him.

Still, Rand could see that Hastings was deeply bothered by it. The thought that he might have been responsible for the woman's death, however inadvertently, was beginning to haunt him. "She wasn't an agent, you know," Hastings argued, more to himself than to the others. "I had no reason to believe she might be up here doing field work—and at the Reverend Fowler's healing waters, of all places."

"It's all a bit bizarre," Camber agreed.

Parkinson went to the telephone. "They promised they'd have a preliminary autopsy report by now. Mind if I use your phone?"

"Go ahead."

Parkinson spoke briskly to someone at the other end, asked one or two questions, and then hung up. He returned to report, "Karen Hayes was killed by a single stab wound with a thin-bladed weapon. It penetrated to a depth of about seven inches, going straight to the heart. She died within seconds."

"A thin-bladed weapon," Rand repeated. "And what's the one fact we know about Oleg Penkov's appearance? The single thing he couldn't disguise?"

"His limp," Leila said.

Rand nodded. "If he limps, he probably uses a cane. And that suggests a sword cane."

Parkinson shrugged. "He's probably on his way back to Moscow by now, complete with sword cane."

"Not necessarily," Rand argued. "The limp makes identification fairly easy, especially if he's trying to flee. I'm sure that helped Miss Hayes a great deal while she was on his trail. The safest place for him might be right here in Foxhart, at Fowler's miraculous stream."

"You think he'd return there?" Camber asked.

"Perhaps he never left."

It was after six when they returned to the site of the waters, but this far north in late May there were still hours of daylight remaining. The crowd at the wooded stream seemed even larger than before, swelled no doubt with curiosity-seekers attracted by the news of the killing. The two teenagers working the concession stand were selling bottles of the healing water as fast as they could ring up sales on the cash registers, and Constable Stebbins was doing his best to keep the traffic flowing, jabbing his baton first one way and then another. As they entered the grounds, they spotted Joshua Fowler on the path leading to the stream.

"We'd like to ask you a few questions," Parkinson told him. At Rand's side, Leila was scanning faces as they passed by, searching for someone she might remember from earlier.

"I've already talked with the local police," Fowler said, recognizing them as strangers up from the south. Unfamiliar with jurisdictions, he might have mistaken them for Scotland Yard investigators. "I have nothing more to contribute."

"It's not directly about the killing," Rand explained. "You've been here all day. We're looking for a man with a limp, using a cane, who may have lingered here throughout the afternoon, or left and returned later."

"I didn't notice anyone like that."

Rand believed him, even if the others had doubts. Oleg Penkov hadn't gained his remarkable reputation for disguise by making foolish mistakes. He'd be seen once and only once. If it was necessary for him to return to the scene, it would be in an entirely different guise.

Suddenly Leila tugged at his sleeve. "That man over there!"

"What about him?" Rand followed her gaze to a distinguished-looking white-haired gentleman with a walking stick, starting down the path to the stream.

"Don't you see it? That's the photograph we were just looking at! That's Penkov without his makeup!"

"My God!"

Rand moved forward, stepping between the lines of pilgrims, cutting in front of a blind man and his guide dog. The man with the walking stick was moving faster now, limping only a little. He was almost to the stream before Rand intercepted him.

"Pardon me, Mr. Penkov?"

The face turned toward him, smiling uncertainly, and Rand almost missed the sudden swing of the stick. It was only Leila's shouted warning from behind that alerted him in time, and he lifted his right arm to ward off the half-seen blow, twisting away from it. Then both of them were locked together, toppling down the last few feet of the path into the healing waters of the stream.

It took Camber and Parkinson to pry them apart, restraining the Russian while he and Rand were hauled from the water. Hastings, whose mind had always run to management matters, quickly arranged with Fowler for the use of a small storeroom at the back of the concession stand. It was there that they tried to dry out while awaiting Sergeant Winston's reinforcements and a change of clothes.

"You English are mad!" Oleg Penkov insisted. "What are you trying to do?"

Hugh Camber glowered at him. "Your leaders talk of peace and a new beginning, yet they send you to spy on us."

"No, no—you don't understand! My mission is to dismantle a network of sleeper agents. Some have been in place for twenty years or longer. I am calling on each of them personally, telling them we no longer have a need for them."

"A likely story," Camber snapped. "Then what about the young woman? Why did you kill her?"

"I didn't."

The American picked up the walking stick and broke it over his knee in a dramatic attempt to expose the man's lie.

It was only wood. There was no thin metal blade within.

Hastings and Rand exchanged glances. Parkinson said, trying to keep his voice calm, "Give me the names of the agents you've contacted."

The Russian shivered in his wet clothes. "That would hardly be fair, would it? They have taken no action against your country, and now they will not. Most were recruited during their university days and never used. Why punish them for what might have been?"

"Who killed Karen Hayes?" Camber asked.

"I have no idea. I didn't know the woman."

"She's been on your trail since London."

The Russian's eyebrows raised slightly. "Oh?"

"What about the person you were to meet here?" Rand asked.

"There was no one I was to see here. I stopped off on my way to Edinburgh."

"To take the waters."

"My leg——"

"I know." Rand sighed and went outside, hoping the evening sun would help dry his clothes faster. They would get nowhere with Oleg Penkov.

It was, of course, just possible that he was telling the truth about the purpose of his mission. The cold war was over. Only people like Camber and Parkinson and whoever killed Karen Hayes hadn't heard about it yet.

Hastings followed him out. "What do you want to do?" he asked.

"It's not up to me. Parkinson and the American seem to be running things."

"They need you, Rand. They're backed into a corner. If they tell Sergeant Winston to arrest the Russian, he'll do just that, and we may have an international incident on our hands."

Rand watched the long lines of people moving toward the healing waters, looking for something to believe in. Maybe everyone was. He didn't know why it had happened, but suddenly he thought he knew who had murdered Karen Hayes.

"I'm going to my car," he told Hastings. "Stay here with Leila and back me up."

"What do you want us to do?"

"You'll know when the time comes."

He hurried across the busy parking lot, climbed into his car, backed out of the space, and edged into the exit line heading toward the highway. Camber and Parkinson had come out to watch now, too, and ahead on the highway Rand saw the flashing lights of Detective Sergeant Winston's vehicle arriving at last.

There was a pause in the line to allow the patrol car to enter and Constable Stebbins directed it with a flourish—then he turned back to the exiting line, directing Rand to follow the car ahead. Rand's small sedan almost brushed against Stebbins as it passed, and it was a simple matter for Rand to reach out the window on the driver's side and grab his baton. He saw the color drain from the constable's face, and then Stebbins turned and broke into a run through the rows of vehicles.

Hastings and Parkinson caught him just as he reached the highway.

Later, at the local police station, it was Detective Sergeant Winston who explained the charges against him. "You understand, Stebbins, that we're concerned here strictly with the murder of the American woman, Karen Hayes. Anything else is a matter for these gentlemen. I'm waiting only for the blood test on the grooves of your baton."

"I understand, sir," the constable said, staring at his hands.

Winston nodded and began filling out forms. "But I'm sure we'd all like to hear from Mr. Rand how he was able to deduce that the murder weapon was hidden in your baton."

"That was something of a guess," Rand admitted, "though an educated one. If we believe Penkov's story, and there was no reason to doubt it, he was in this country to contact various sleeper agents, men and women in deep cover who might have surfaced in the event of hostilities between Britain and Russia. These agents were being cut loose, freed of any commitments. Karen Hayes had followed Penkov and recorded his contacts in other cities. Who did he see? A teacher, a magistrate, and a postman—all civil servants or public employees of one sort or another. Then he journeyed to Foxhart, specifically to Joshua Fowler's healing waters, to inform the next person on his list. Was there anyone at Foxhart today who could be classed as a civil servant? Someone working at the healing waters who could be met nowhere else? Certainly not Fowler or the teenagers he employed to sell the bottled water. Only Constable Stebbins, stationed there to direct traffic, seemed to qualify."

Parkinson shook his head in disbelief. "What would the Russians have done with a local constable in a place like Foxhart if war broke out? The idea is ridiculous."

"Is it? Hastings told me earlier of a nearby RAF base in mothballs for years. In the event of war, that base could have reopened. Then would a police constable with a long and perfect record be quite so ridiculous? He might have been just the sort of agent the Russians needed up here."

"Still, you have no proof he killed the Hayes woman."

"No proof at first—only a vague memory. As we were leaving the stream after Fowler's little talk this noon, I was aware of a traffic jam in the parking lot. I thought no more about it at the time, especially after the body was discovered, but what caused that pile-up of cars? We've all seen how efficient Stebbins is at directing traffic. Could it be that he'd left his post for a few moments, to murder Karen Hayes back among those trees? I think it more than likely. The weapon didn't have to be as long as a sword cane—it penetrated only about seven inches. Constables in Britain don't carry guns, but Stebbins had his traffic baton. Suppose it unscrewed to reveal a thin-bladed dagger, like a sharpened knitting needle. He could have walked by Karen Hayes and stabbed her virtually undetected. It was the perfect weapon for a sleeper agent like Stebbins. He might never need it, but it was always with him."

"How did he know about Karen Hayes?" Hastings asked quietly. "He was nowhere near when I spoke her name."

It was Constable Stebbins himself who answered, in a voice full of resignation. "She drove in right after Penkov and wanted to park near him. When I directed her down to the other end of the lot, she flashed a courtesy card from M.I.5 giving her permission to travel anywhere within Britain without delay. I knew she was following him then, and that she was after me, too. I had to kill her."

"What about your meeting with Penkov?"

"I'd received a message that he was coming, but I was on duty today. They assign a constable on weekends to handle all the traffic at Fowler's place. Penkov came there to speak with me when I took a break. After the killing he went away, but he came back. That was when you recognized him."

"He wore no makeup when he returned," Camber said.

"He said once that sometimes no disguise is the best disguise."

"It would have been," Rand agreed, "except that my wife never read the disguise manual. She just looked at the picture and recognized him."

The Cameronian Preacher's Tale

JAMES HOGG

it near me, my children, and come nigh, all ye who are not of my kindred, though of my flock; for my days and hours are numbered; death is with me dealing, and I have a sad and a wonderful story to relate. I have preached and ye have profited; but what I am about to say is far better than man's preaching, it is one of those terrible sermons which God preaches to mankind, of blood unrighteously shed, and most wondrously avenged. The like has not happened in these our latter days. His presence is visible in it; and I reveal it that its burthen may be removed from my soul, so that I may die in peace; and I disclose it, that you may lay it up in your hearts and tell it soberly to your children, that the warning memory of a dispensation so marvellous may live and not perish. Of the deed itself, some of you have heard a whispering; and some of you know the men of whom I am about to speak; but the mystery which covers them up as with a cloud I shall remove; listen, therefore, my children, to a tale of truth, and may you profit by it!

On Dryfe Water, in Annandale, lived Walter Johnstone, a man open hearted and kindly, but proud withal and warm tempered; and on the same water lived John Macmillan, a man of a nature grasping and sordid, and as proud and hot tempered as the other. They were strong men, and vain of their strength; lovers of pleasant company, well to live in the world, extensive dealers in corn and cattle; married too, and both of the same age—five and forty years. They often met, yet they were not friends; nor yet were they companions, for bargain making and money seeking narroweth the heart and shuts up generosity of soul. They were jealous, too, of one another's success in trade, and of the fame they had each acquired for feats of personal strength and agility, and skill with the sword—a weapon which all men carried, in my youth, who were above the condition of a peasant. Their mutual and growing dislike was inflamed by the whisperings of evil friends, and confirmed by the skilful manner in which they negotiated bargains over each other's heads. When they met, a short and surly greeting was exchanged, and those who knew their natures looked for a meeting between them, when the sword or some other dangerous weapon would settle for ever their claims for precedence in cunning and in strength.

They met at the fair of Longtown, and spoke, and no more—with them both it was a busy day, and mutual hatred subsided for a time, in the love of turning the penny and amassing gain. The market rose and fell, and fell and rose; and it was whispered that Macmillan, through the superior skill or good fortune of his rival, had missed some bargains which were very valuable, while some positive losses touched a nature extremely sensible of the importance of wealth. One was elated and the other depressed—but not more depressed than moody and incensed, and in this temper they were seen in the evening in the back room of a public inn, seated apart and silent, calculating losses and gains, drinking deeply, and exchanging dark looks of hatred and distrust. They had been observed, during the whole day, to watch each other's movements, and now when they were met face to face, the labours of the day over, and their natures inflamed by liquor as well as by hatred, their companions looked for personal strife between them, and wondered not a little when they saw Johnstone rise, mount his horse, and ride homewards, leaving his rival in Longtown. Soon afterwards Macmillan started up from a moody fit, drank off a large draught of brandy, threw down a half-guinea, nor waited for change—a thing uncommon with him; and men said, as his horse's feet struck fire from the pavement, that if he overtook Johnstone, there would be a living soul less in the land before sunrise.

Before sunrise next morning the horse of Walter Johnstone came with an empty saddle to his stable door. The bridle was trampled to pieces amongst its feet, and its saddle and sides were splashed over with blood as if a bleeding body had been carried across its back. The cry arose in the country, an instant search was made, and on the side of the public road was found a place where a deadly contest seemed to have happened. It was

in a small green field, bordered by a wood, in the farm of Andrew Pattison. The sod was dinted deep with men's feet, and trodden down and
trampled and sprinkled over with blood as thickly as it had ever been with
dew. Blood drops, too, were traced to some distance, but nothing more was
discovered; the body could not be found, though every field was examined
and every pool dragged. His money and bills, to the amount of several
thousand pounds, were gone, so was his sword—indeed nothing of him
could be found on earth save his blood, and for its spilling a strict account
was yet to be sought.

Suspicion instantly and naturally fell on John Macmillan, who denied
all knowledge of the deed. He had arrived at his own house in due course
of time, no marks of weapon or warfare were on him, he performed family worship as was his custom, and he sang the psalm as loudly and prayed
as fervently as he was in the habit of doing. He was apprehended and
tried, and saved by the contradictory testimony of the witnesses against
him, into whose hearts the spirit of falsehood seemed to have entered, in
order to perplex and confound the judgment of men—or rather that man
might have no hand in the punishment, but that God should bring it
about in his own good time and way. 'Revenge is mine, saith the Lord,'
which meaneth not because it is too sweet a morsel for man, as the
scoffer said, but because it is too dangerous. A glance over this conflicting
testimony will show how little was then known of this foul offence, and
how that little was rendered doubtful and dark by the imperfections of
human nature.

Two men of Longtown were examined. One said that he saw Macmillan insulting and menacing Johnstone, laying his hand on the hilt of his
sword with a look dark and ominous; while the other swore that he was
present at the time, but that it was Johnstone who insulted and menaced
Macmillan, and laid his hand on the hilt of his sword and pointed to the
road homewards. A very expert and searching examination could make no
more of them; they were both respectable men with characters above suspicion. The next witnesses were of another stamp, and their testimony
was circuitous and contradictory. One of them was a shepherd—a reluctant witness. His words were these: 'I was frae hame on the night of the
murder, in the thick of the wood, no just at the place which was bloody
and trampled, but gaye and near hand it. I canna say I can just mind what

I was doing; I had somebody to see I jalouse, but wha it was is naebody's business but my ain. There was maybe ane forbye myself in the wood, and maybe twa; there was ane at ony rate, and I am no sure but it was an auld acquaintance. I see nae use there can be in questioning me. I saw nought, and therefore can say nought. I canna but say that I heard something— the trampling of horses, and a rough voice saying, "Draw and defend yourself." Then followed the clashing of swords and half smothered sort of work, and then the sound of horses' feet was heard again, and that's a' I ken about it; only I thought the voice was Walter Johnstone's, and so thought Kate Pennie, who was with me and kens as meikle as me.' The examination of Katherine Pennie, one of the Pennies of Pennieland, followed, and she declared that she had heard the evidence of Dick Purdie with surprise and anger. On that night she was not over the step of her father's door for more than five minutes, and that was to look at the sheep in the fauld; and she neither heard the clashing of swords nor the word of man or woman. And with respect to Dick Purdie, she scarcely knew him even by sight; and if all tales were true that were told of him, she would not venture into a lonely wood with him, under the cloud of night, for a gown of silk with pearls on each sleeve. The shepherd, when recalled, admitted that Kate Pennie might be right, 'For after a',' said he, 'it happened in the dark, when a man like me, no that gleg of the uptauk, might confound persons. Somebody was with me, I am gaye and sure, frae what took place—if it was nae Kate, I kenna wha it was, and it couldna weel be Kate either, for Kate's a douce quean, and besides is married.' The judge dismissed the witnesses with some indignant words, and, turning to the prisoner, said, 'John Macmillan, the prevarications of these witnesses have saved you; mark my words—saved you from man, but not from God. On the murderer, the Most High will lay His hot right hand, visibly and before men, that we may know that blood unjustly shed will be avenged. You are at liberty to depart.' He left the bar and resumed his station and his pursuits as usual; nor did he appear sensible to the feeling of the country, which was strong against him.

A year passed over his head, other events happened, and the murder of Walter Johnstone began to be dismissed from men's minds. Macmillan went to the fair of Longtown, and when evening came he was seated in the little back room which I mentioned before, and in company with two men of the names of Hunter and Hope. He sat late, drank deeply, but in the midst of the carousal a knock was heard at the door, and a voice called sharply, 'John Macmillan.' He started up, seemed alarmed, and exclaimed, 'What in Heaven's name can *he* want with me?' and opening the door hastily, went into the garden, for he seemed to dread another summons lest his companions should know the voice. As soon as he was gone, one said to the other, 'If that was not the voice of Walter Johnstone, I never heard it in my life; he is either come back in the flesh or in the spirit, and in either way John Macmillan has good cause to dread him.' They listened—they heard Macmillan speaking in great agitation; he was answered only by a low sound, yet he appeared to understand what was said, for his concluding words were, 'Never! never! I shall rather submit to His judgment who cannot err.' When he returned he was pale and shaking, and he sat down and seemed buried in thought. He spread his palms on his knees, shook his head often, then, starting up, said, 'The judge was a fool and no prophet—to mortal man is not given the wisdom of God—so neighbours let us ride.' They mounted their horses and rode homewards into Scotland at a brisk pace.

The night was pleasant, neither light nor dark; there were few travellers out, and the way winded with the hills and with the streams, passing through a pastoral and beautiful country. Macmillan rode close by the side of his companions, closer than was desirable or common; yet he did not speak, nor make answer when he was spoken to; but looked keenly and earnestly before and behind him, as if he expected the coming of some one, and every tree and bush seemed to alarm and startle him. Day at last dawned, and with the growing light his alarm subsided, and he began to converse with his companions, and talk with a levity which surprised them more than his silence had done before. The sun was all but risen when they approached the farm of Andrew Pattison, and here and there the top of a high tree and the summit of a hill had caught light upon them. Hope looked to Hunter silently, when they came nigh the bloody spot where it was believed the murder had been committed. Macmillan sat looking resolutely before him, as if determined not to look upon it; but his horse stopt at once, trembled violently, and then sprung aside, hurling its rider headlong to the ground. All this passed in a moment; his companions sat astonished; the horse rushed forward, leaving him on the ground, from whence he never rose in life, for his neck was broken by the fall, and with a convulsive shiver or two he expired. Then did the prediction of the judge, the warning voice and summons of the preceding night, and the spot and the time, rush upon their recollection; and they firmly believed that a murderer and robber lay dead beside them. 'His horse saw something,' said Hope to Hunter; 'I never saw such flashing eyes in a horse's head;'—'and *he* saw something too,' replied Hunter, 'for the glance that he gave to the bloody spot, when his horse started, was one of terror. I never saw such a look, and I wish never to see such another again.'

When John Macmillan perished, matters stood thus with his memory. It was not only loaded with the sin of blood and the sin of robbery, with the sin of making a faithful woman a widow and her children fatherless, but with the grievous sin also of having driven a worthy family to ruin and beggary. The sum which was lost was large, the creditors were merciless; they fell upon the remaining substance of Johnstone, sweeping it wholly away; and his widow sought shelter in a miserable cottage among the Dryfesdale hills, where she supported her children by gathering and spinning wool. In a far different state and condition remained the family of John Macmillan. He died rich and unincumbered, leaving an evil name and an only child, a daughter, wedded to one whom many knew and esteemed, Joseph Howatson by name, a man sober and sedate; a member, too, of our own broken remnant of Cameronians.

Now, my dear children, the person who addresses you was then, as he is yet, God's preacher for the scattered kirk of Scotland, and his tent was pitched among the green hills of Annandale. The death of the transgressor appeared unto me the manifest judgment of God, and when my people gathered around me I rejoiced to see so great a multitude, and, standing in the midst of them, I preached in such a wise that they were deeply moved. I took for my text these words, 'Hath there been evil in the land and the Lord hath not known it?' I discoursed on the wisdom of Providence in guiding the affairs of men. How He permitted our evil passions to acquire the mastery over us, and urge us to deeds of darkness; allowing us to flourish for a season, that He might strike us in the midst of our splendour in a way so visible and awful that the wildest would cry out, 'Behold the finger of God.' I argued the matter home to the heart; I named no names, but I saw Joseph Howatson hide his face in his hands, for he felt and saw from the eyes which were turned towards him that I alluded to the judgment of God upon his relative.

Joseph Howatson went home heavy and sad of heart, and somewhat touched with anger at God's servant for having so pointedly and publicly alluded to his family misfortune; for he believed his father-in-law was a wise and a worthy man. His way home lay along the banks of a winding and beautiful stream, and just where it entered his own lands there was a rustic gate, over which he leaned for a little space, ruminating upon earlier days, on his wedded wife, on his children, and finally his thoughts settled on his father-in-law. He thought of his kindness to himself and to many others, on his fulfilment of all domestic duties, on his constant performance of family worship, and on his general reputation for honesty and fair dealing. He then dwelt on the circumstances of Johnstone's disappearance, on the singular summons his father-in-law received in Longtown, and the catastrophe which followed on the spot and on the very day of the year that the murder was supposed to be committed. He was in sore perplexity, and said aloud, 'Would to God that I knew the truth; but the doors of eternity, alas! are shut on the secret for ever.' He looked up and John Macmillan stood before him—stood with all the calmness and serenity and meditative air which a grave man wears when he walks out on a sabbath eve.

'Joseph Howatson,' said the apparition, 'on no secret are the doors of eternity shut—of whom were you speaking?' 'I was speaking', answered he, 'of one who is cold and dead, and to whom you bear a strong resemblance.' 'I am he,' said the shape; 'I am John Macmillan.' 'God of heaven!' replied Joseph Howatson, 'how can that be; did I not lay his head in the grave; see it closed over him; how, therefore, can it be? Heaven permits no such visitations.' 'I entreat you, my son,' said the shape, 'to believe what I say; the end of man is not when his body goes to dust; he exists in another state, and from that state am I permitted to come to you; waste not time, which is brief, with vain doubts, I am John Macmillan.' 'Father, father,' said the young man, deeply agitated, 'answer me, did you kill and rob Walter Johnstone?' 'I did,' said the Spirit, 'and for that have I returned to earth; listen to me.' The young man was so much overpowered by a revelation thus fearfully made, that he fell insensible on the ground; and when he recovered, the moon was shining, the dews of night were upon him, and he was alone.

Joseph Howatson imagined that he had dreamed a fearful dream; and conceiving that Divine Providence had presented the truth to his fancy, he began to consider how he could secretly make reparation to the wife and children of Johnstone for the double crime of his relative. But on more mature reflection he was impressed with the belief that a spirit had appeared to him, the spirit of his father-in-law, and that his own alarm had hindered him from learning fully the secret of his visit to earth; he therefore resolved to go to the same place next sabbath night, seek rather than avoid an interview, acquaint himself with the state of bliss or woe in which the spirit was placed, and learn if by acts of affection and restitution he could soften his sufferings or augment his happiness. He went accordingly to the little rustic gate by the side of the lonely stream; he walked up and down; hour passed after hour, but he heard nothing and saw nothing save the murmuring of the brook and the hares running among the wild clover. He had resolved to return home, when something seemed to rise from the ground, as shapeless as a cloud at first, but moving with life. It assumed a form, and the appearance of John Macmillan was once more before him. The young man was nothing daunted, but looking on the spirit, said, 'I thought you just and upright and devout, and incapable of murder and robbery.' The spirit seemed to dilate as it made answer. 'The death of Walter Johnstone sits lightly upon me. We had crossed each other's purposes, we had lessened each other's gains, we had vowed revenge, we met on fair terms, tied our horses to a gate, and fought fairly and long; and when I slew him, I but did what he sought to do to me. I threw him over his horse, carried him far into the country, sought out a deep quagmire on the north side of the Snipe Knowe, in Crake's Moss, and having secured his bills and other perishable property, with the purpose of returning all to his family, I buried him in the moss, leaving his gold in his purse, and laying his cloak and his sword above him.

'Now listen, Joseph Howatson. In my private desk you will find a little key tied with red twine, take it and go to the house of Janet Mathieson in Dumfries, and underneath the hearthstone in my sleeping room you will get my strong-box, open it, it contains all the bills and bonds belonging to

Walter Johnstone. Restore them to his widow. I would have restored them but for my untimely death. Inform her privily and covertly where she will find the body of her husband, so that she may bury him in the churchyard with his ancestors. Do these things, that I may have some assuagement of misery; neglect them, and you will become a world's wonder.' The spirit vanished with these words, and was seen no more.

Joseph Howatson was sorely troubled. He had communed with a spirit, he was impressed with the belief that early death awaited him; he felt a sinking of soul and a misery of body, and he sent for me to help him with counsel, and comfort him in his unexampled sorrow. I loved him and hastened to him; I found him weak and woe-begone, and the hand of God seemed to be sore upon him. He took me out to the banks of the little stream where the shape appeared to him, and having desired me to listen without interrupting him, told me how he had seen his father-in-law's spirit, and related the revelations which it had made and the commands it had laid upon him. 'And now,' he said, 'look upon me. I am young, and ten days ago I had a body strong and a mind buoyant, and gray hairs and the honours of old age seemed to await me. But ere three days pass I shall be as the clod of the valley, for he who converses with a spirit, a spirit shall he soon become. I have written down the strange tale I have told you and I put it into your hands, perform for me and for my wretched parent, the in-structions which the grave yielded up its tenant to give; and may your days be long in the land, and may you grow gray-headed among your people.' I listened to his words with wonder and with awe, and I promised to obey him in all his wishes with my best and most anxious judgment. We went home together; we spent the evening in prayer. Then he set his house in order, spoke to all his children cheerfully and with a mild voice, and falling on the neck of his wife, said, 'Sarah Macmillan, you were the choice of my young heart, and you have been a wife to me kind, tender, and gentle.' He looked at his children and he looked at his wife, for his heart was too full for more words, and retired to his chamber. He was found next morning kneeling by his bedside, his hands held out as if re-pelling some approaching object, horror stamped on every feature, and cold and dead.

Then I felt full assurance of the truth of his communications; and as soon as the amazement which his untimely death occasioned had subsided, and his wife and little ones were somewhat comforted, I proceeded to fulfil his dying request. I found the small key tied with red twine, and I went to the house of Janet Mathieson in Dumfries, and I held up the key and said, 'Woman, knowest thou that?' and when she saw it she said, 'Full well I know it, it belonged to a jolly man and a douce, and mony a merry hour has he whiled away wi' my servant maidens and me.' And when she saw me lift the hearthstone, open the box, and spread out the treasure which it contained, she held up her hands, 'Eh! what o' gowd! what o' gowd! but half's mine, be ye saint or sinner; John Macmillan, douce man, aye said he had something there which he considered as not belonging to him but to a quiet friend; weel I wot he meant me, for I have been a quiet friend to him and his.' I told her I was commissioned by his daughter to remove the property, that I was the minister of that persecuted remnant of the true kirk called Cameronians, and she might therefore deliver it up without fear. 'I ken weel enough wha ye are,' said this worthless woman, 'd'ye think I dinna ken a minister of the kirk; I have seen meikle o' their siller in my day, frae eighteen to fifty and aught have I caroused with divines, Cameronians, I trow, as well as those of a freer kirk. But touching this treasure, give me twenty gowden pieces, else I'se gar three stamps of my foot bring in them that will see me righted, and send you awa to the mountains bleating like a sheep shorn in winter.' I gave the imperious woman twenty pieces of gold, and carried away the fatal box.

Now, when I got free of the ports of Dumfries, I mounted my little horse and rode away into the heart of the country, among the pastoral hills of Dryfesdale. I carried the box on the saddle before me, and its contents awakened a train of melancholy thoughts within me. There were the papers of Walter Johnstone, corresponding to the description which the spirit gave, and marked with his initials in red ink by the hand of the man who slew him. There were two gold watches and two purses of gold, all tied with red twine, and many bills and much money to which no marks were attached. As I rode along pondering on these things, and casting about in my own mind how and by what means I should make restitution, I was aware of a morass, broad and wide, which with all its quagmires glittered in the moonlight before me. I knew I had penetrated into the centre of Dryfesdale, but I was not well acquainted with the country; I therefore drew my bridle, and looked around to see if any house was nigh, where I could find shelter for the night. I saw a small house built of turf and thatched with heather, from the window of which a faint light glimmered. I rode up, alighted, and there I found a woman in widow's weeds, with three sweet children, spinning yarn from the wool which the shepherds shear in spring from the udders of the ewes. She welcomed me, spread bread and placed milk before me. I asked a blessing, and ate and drank, and was refreshed.

Now it happened that, as I sat with the solitary woman and her children, there came a man to the door, and with a loud yell of dismay burst it open and staggered forward crying, 'There's a corse candle in Crake's Moss, and I'll be a dead man before morning.' 'Preserve me! piper,' said the widow, 'ye're in a piteous taking; here is a holy man who will speak comfort to you, and tell you how all these are but delusions of the eye or exhalations of nature.' 'Delusions and exhalations, Dame Johnstone,' said the piper, 'd'ye think I dinna ken a corse light from an elf candle, an elf candle from a will-o'-wisp, and a will-o'-wisp from all other lights of this wide world.' The name of the morass and the woman's name now flashed upon me, and I was struck with amazement and awe. I looked on the widow, and I looked on the wandering piper, and I said, 'Let me look on those corse lights, for God creates nothing in vain; there is a wise purpose in all things, and a wise aim.' And the piper said, 'Na, na; I have nae wish to see ony mair on't, a dead light bodes the living nae gude; and I am sure if I gang near Crake's Moss it will lair me amang the hags and quags.' And I said, 'Foolish old man, you are equally safe every where; the hand of the Lord reaches round the earth, and strikes and protects according as it was foreordained, for nothing is hid from His eyes—come with me.' And the piper looked strangely upon me and stirred not a foot; and I said, 'I shall go by myself;' and the woman said, 'Let me go with you, for I am sad of heart, and can look on such things without fear; for, alas! since I lost my own Walter Johnstone, pleasure is no longer pleasant: and I love to wander in lonesome places and by old churchyards.' 'Then,' said the piper, 'I darena bide my lane with the bairns; I'll go also; but O! let me strengthen my heart with ae spring on my pipes before I venture.' 'Play,' I said, 'Clavers and his Highlandmen, it is the tune to cheer ye and keep your heart up.' 'Your honour's no cannie,' said the old man; 'that's my favourite tune.' So he played it and said, 'Now I am fit to look on lights of good or evil.' And we walked into the open air.

All Crake's Moss seemed on fire; not illumined with one steady and uninterrupted light, but kindled up by fits like the northern sky with its wandering streamers. On a little bank which rose in the centre of the morass, the supernatural splendour seemed chiefly to settle; and having continued to shine for several minutes, the whole faded and left but one faint gleam behind. I fell on my knees, held up my hands to heaven, and said, 'This is of God; behold in that fearful light the finger of the Most High. Blood has been spilt, and can be no longer concealed; the point of the mariner's needle points less surely to the north than yon living flame points to the place where man's body has found a bloody grave. Follow me,' and I walked down to the edge of the moss and gazed earnestly on the spot. I knew now that I looked on the long hidden resting place of Walter Johnstone, and considered that the hand of God was manifest in the way that I had been thus led blindfold into his widow's house. I reflected for a moment on these things; I wished to right the fatherless, yet spare the feelings of the innocent; the supernatural light partly showed me the way, and the words which I now heard whispered by my companions aided in directing the rest.

'I tell ye, Dame Johnstone,' said the piper, 'the man's no cannie; or what's waur, he may belong to the spiritual world himself, and do us a mischief. Saw ye ever mortal man riding with ae spur and carrying a silver-headed cane for a whip, wi' sic a fleece of hair about his haffets and sic a wild ee in his head; and then he kens a' things in the heavens aboon and the earth beneath. He kenned my favourite tune Clavers; I'se uphaud he's no in the body, but ane of the souls made perfect of the auld Covenanters whom Grahame or Grierson slew; we're daft to follow him.' 'Fool body,' I heard the widow say, 'I'll follow him; there's something about that man, be he in the spirit or in the flesh, which is pleasant and promising. O! could he but, by prayer or other means of lawful knowledge, tell me about my dear Walter Johnstone; thrice has he appeared to me in dream or vision with a sorrowful look, and weel ken I what that means.' We had now reached the edge of the morass, and a dim and uncertain light continued to twinkle about the green knoll which rose in its middle. I turned suddenly round and said, 'For a wise purpose am I come; to reveal murder; to speak consolation to the widow and the fatherless, and to soothe the perturbed spirits of those whose fierce passions ended in untimely death. Come with me; the hour is come, and I must not do my commission negligently.' 'I kenned it, I kenned it,' said the piper, 'he's just one of the auld persecuted worthies risen from his red grave to right the injured, and he'll do't discreetly; follow him, Dame, follow him.' 'I shall follow,' said the widow, 'I have that strength given me this night which will bear me through all trials which mortal flesh can endure.'

When we reached the little green hillock in the centre of the morass, I looked to the north and soon distinguished the place described by my friend Joseph Howatson, where the body of Walter Johnstone was deposited. The moon shone clear, the stars aided us with their light, and some turfcutters having left their spades standing near, I ordered the piper to take a spade and dig where I placed my staff. 'O dig carefully,' said the widow, 'do not be rude with mortal dust.' We dug and came to a sword; the point was broken and the blade hacked. 'It is the sword of my Walter Johnstone,' said his widow, 'I could swear to it among a thousand.' 'It is my father's sword,' said a fine dark haired boy who had followed us unperceived, 'it is my father's sword, and were he living who wrought this, he should na be lang in rueing it.' 'He is dead, my child,' I said, 'and beyond your reach, and vengeance is the Lord's.' 'O, Sir,' cried his widow, in a flood of tears, 'ye ken all things; tell me, is this my husband or no?' 'It is the body of Walter Johnstone,' I answered, 'slain by one who is passed to his account, and buried here by the hand that slew him, with his gold in his purse and his watch in his pocket.' So saying we uncovered the body, lifted it up, laid it on the grass; the embalming nature of the morass had preserved it from decay, and mother and child, with tears and with cries, named his name and lamented over him. His gold watch and his money, his cloak and his dress, were untouched and entire, and we bore him to the cottage of his widow, where with clasped hands she sat at his feet and his children at his head till the day drew nigh the dawn; I then rose and said, 'Woman, thy trials have been severe and manifold; a good wife, a good mother, and a good widow hast thou been, and thy reward will be where the blessed alone are admitted. It was revealed to me by a mysterious revelation that thy husband's body was where we found it; and I was com-

missioned by a voice, assuredly not of this world, to deliver thee this treasure, which is thy own, that thy children may be educated, and that bread
and raiment may be thine.' And I delivered her husband's wealth into her
hands, refused gold which she offered, and mounting my horse, rode over
the hills and saw her no more. But I soon heard of her, for there rose a
strange sound in the land, that a Good Spirit had appeared to the widow
of Walter Johnstone, had disclosed where her husband's murdered body
lay, had enriched her with all his lost wealth, had prayed by her side till
the blessed dawn of day, and then vanished with the morning light. I
closed my lips on the secret till now; and I reveal it to you, my children,
that you may know there is a God who ruleth this world by wise and invisible means, and punisheth the wicked, and cheereth the humble of
heart and the lowly minded.

Such was the last sermon of the good John Farley, a man whom I
knew and loved. I think I see him now, with his long white hair and his
look mild, eloquent, and sagacious. He was a giver of good counsel, a sayer
of wise sayings, with wit at will, learning in abundance, and a gift in sarcasm which the wildest dreaded.

Leave It to the River

P. M. HUBBARD

hey say the river takes a life a year, but they say that, or something like it, about half the rivers in these islands. The experts will have it that it all goes back to the days when rivers were gods and, like all gods, potentially destructive unless propitiated by sacrifice. I doubt many people think the river a god now, but a lot still believe in the annual quota, or perhaps the river itself has just got into the habit of it, even though its power for mischief, like that of other gods and natural phenomena, has been much eroded by man's increasing ability to look after himself. I only know that last summer, when a young man employed on the bridge works fell in and was never seen again, there were those who expressed relief that the river had taken its life for the year during the summer (and an Englander at that), and so made life safer for the locals who had anything to do with it during its more dangerous season.

Not being a fisherman or a riparian owner, I myself do not have much to do with the river at any time, but I sail my boat on the salt water of the bay it runs into, and where the river ends and the sea begins is a matter you could greatly exercise your mind on, if you are a man given to mental exercise. A big flood tide when the river itself is in spate can pile the water up till it roars under the soffits of the bridge, and a big ebb can leave the land-water a wee ribbon in the vast expanse of mud which is then the surface of the bay. The fact remains that whatever the river brings down the sea takes and deals with in its own fashion, and if, as it might be once a year or so, the river brings down a human body, it is likely the sea that will do the burying of it, unless someone sees it and fishes it out before it gets that far. It is the sea that will have taken the young Englander from the bridge works. Maybe it took him back to the English coast, so that he came north by land and went south by water, as a lot of people used to do before the ports on the bay silted up, and the regular passenger services to Cumberland stopped operating.

I fancy I know of one life the river was reckoned to have taken but did not take and another it might, in a sense, have taken but would not. But that's some years back. Nichol Mair is well dead now, and his Jeannie safely married and away to another part of the country, and in any case those are not their real names. At the time I kept quiet about it and left it to the river, or maybe it was the sea, to decide the thing, but there seems no harm in speaking of it now. Not, I assure you, to unburden my conscience. I do not find, at my time of life, that my conscience is much given to burdens, and in any case I never had an ill conscience where Nichol Mair was concerned. But I tell it for the interest of the thing, and because the young Englander from the bridge works, disappearing the way he did, has put me in mind of it.

Nichol Mair was a forester, and had been all his working life. By the time I knew him he was employed, like nearly all of them, by the Commission, but he had started in private service in the days when the big estates had their own foresters, and when the foresters still felled with the axe instead of the whining chain-saws that nowadays can make a stretch of hill forest as peaceful in season as a go-kart track on a Saturday afternoon. He was not a tall man—they do not run much to height in these parts—but very broad and strong and red-faced, and he still had his axe and looked after it as a concert violinist looks after his fiddle. If there was axe-work to be done (and there still is at times, even now), it was Nichol they put on to it, and he had no aversion to showing the boys what he could do with his axe, either in the way of business or sometimes, when he had taken a dram or two, just for the hell of it or for a bet, if he could find anyone rash enough to bet against him. I had heard many stories of his accomplishments in that direction, but never saw any of them for myself, not being around at the right times and places.

One other thing Nichol had which he looked after even more carefully than his axe, and took no bets on drunk or sober, and that was his daughter Jeannie, Jeannie's mother having died a while before I first knew him. Whether Jeannie's mother was ever precisely married to Nichol

was a thing you heard different views of, but the technicalities of marriage are not much thought of in these parts, and either way she had lived
with him most of his working life, and had brought up Jeannie as strictly
as if she had been a daughter of the manse or the progeny of a pedigree
saddleback Galloway. By the time I am speaking of there were those who
said that Jeannie was better able to look after Nichol than he was to look
after her, though in the nature of things less forward at it. She was a slender slip of a girl, pale-skinned and dark-haired and a bit slant-eyed, of a
type you see in a while round here, very striking in contrast to the four-
square twopence-coloured women who make up the most of our female
population, and clearly coming from a different stock, which for all I
know may be new-come Irish or prehistoric Pictish, but is certainly, as
I say, very distinctive. The mother I never saw, but she must have been
very much of that sort herself to have produced Jeannie to Nichol
Mair's fathering.

Whether or not Jeannie was capable of looking after Nichol, I would
say (and that was the general view) that she was well capable of looking
after herself. With those looks and the manner of acting and speaking her
mother had somehow given her, the men were round her like wasps round
a beerspill before she was well sixteen, and she handled them with the ef-
fortless composure of an old dog with the daft hoggets, even men much
older than herself. Not that she was standoffish, she was all for a good
time, was Jeannie Mair, and there were those who said she was not above
lending herself whiles to a man she fancied, but never for keeps. That may
have been the plain ill-nature of other girls, or their mothers, or maybe
the men she didn't fancy well enough. There is always plenty of ill-nature
about a girl like Jeannie whatever she does, and I would not say we are
more given to charitable talking than most other rural communities. Certainly she was never in any sort of trouble, but then a girl with her head
screwed on as tight as Jeannie's doesn't get into trouble these days.
Presently she would pick a man she reckoned up to her and settle down,
and there was a good deal of speculation who it would be, with the odds
constantly changing.

Whether Nichol worried about his Jeannie I cannot say. He was proud
of her to the point of daftness and gave her whatever he could she wanted,
and as she had her own money from working in the one smart dress shop,

she was always turned out in a style most of the other girls couldn't hope to match, not with the figures they had and the taste for bright colours which is so marked in these parts. (Jeannie herself wore only simple, plain-coloured clothes, which lit her up like a black candle.) From what came of it, Nichol must have watched over her in a quiet way, but to all outward appearances he let her have her head in most things, if indeed he had even been capable of controlling her, which I would say was doubtful.

At the time I am speaking of (which would be the September of three or four years back) the most favoured claimant to Jeannie's hand was young Macalister, who worked in the bank, no less. Favoured, I mean, by general public estimation. In what way Jeannie favoured him there is no saying, but my guess would be that, whatever she did elsewhere, Jeannie would have no favours, in the more particular sense, to bestow on her chosen man until she had got him publicly signed up in the church with full honours and the white bridal gown of only now negotiable virginity. Young Macalister (Jimmie, he called himself, and a proper Jimmie he looked, too, to my way of thinking) was a posting to our branch from farther east. He was as smooth and smart in his way as Jeannie was in hers, but without the underlying wildness. He wore well-cut dark suits and equally well-cut sandy whiskers, and all but fluttered his eyelashes at you as he cashed your cheque and counted out your dirty notes with his pretty, chopped hands. But he would be a bank manager some day, and that was a far call from a forester's cottage, and he had the added qualification that Jeannie would plainly run rings round him as soon as he had got his ring on her. All that being so, Nichol no doubt favoured him as a son-in-law, whatever he thought of him as a man, and that would have been worth hearing, too, if he could have been brought to say it, only he never said anything, even in his cups, which had any bearing on Jeannie. So at that stage it looked all set for a happy ending, for Nichol and Jeannie at least, and presumably also for Jimmie Macalister if he would be content to take her for richer rather than poorer, but any road for better or worse.

It was then that the villain appeared in the shape of Jack Robson. He was a posting to our parts, too, but from the south, not the east, and he was posted, not to the bank, but to the local division of the Forestry Commission itself; so that if he was not Nichol's actual boss, he had at least a say in what Nichol would be doing and where he would be sent to do it. When

I said Jack Robson was the villain, I used the word in its dramatic or liter-ary sense, but that wasn't the only sort of villain he was, not by a long cast. I do not reckon to be censorious with my fellow creatures now, any more than I do with myself, and I can keep on terms with the generality of people hereabouts, even if there are some I would not buy a pound of potatoes from unless I saw it weighed and many more I would not go drinking with in any circumstances at all. But Jack Robson was a bad man if ever I saw one, and smooth with it in an English way, though he came from no farther south than Carlisle, but with all his smoothness mean and hard and nasty. He was as good-looking as Jimmie Macalister, though dark and sharp-faced instead of soft-faced and sandy, but in other ways he could not well be more different in style. He was what they used to call flash, and for all he spent much of his time in the office or riding round in a Land-Rover, he got himself up like a second-feature lumberjack, with a zipper jacket of black and white woollen check and lace-up boots to the top of his calves. And to my way of judging at least, and it soon appeared not only to mine, he had as much sex-appeal in his little finger as Jimmie had in his whole body from his sandy crown to the soles of his bright black step-in shoes. Nor had this gift of nature gone unnoticed by Jack himself, and as soon as he got settled in, he was off after the local women with the single-minded enthusiasm of a fox in the hen-run.

I say the local women, meaning in general, and to start with that was the way of it, and if half what I heard was true, he had grassed a fair catch of them in his first season among us, including some of the young grilse that hadn't reckoned to be taken by anyone for a while yet, or not until Jack came after them. And if Jack wasn't the only one for the sport in these parts, he was quicker and harder at it than most, and he talked more about it afterwards. But after a bit he seemingly got tired of this promis-cuous ravaging and settled to a serious siege operation, and the target he picked on was inevitably Jeannie Mair. I say inevitably, because for a man who thought he could take his pick, she was the obvious one to pick on, and the fact that she was a girl who made her own decisions and would not be rushed into them was strong drink to a man of his nature. I suppose with an administrative position in what may be called a career service he might be considered as good a matrimonial prospect in economic terms as Jimmie Macalister, but the girl who would consider Jack as a husband in any other terms would need her head examining, which Jeannie certainly did not. As I saw it, the danger was not that Jeannie might marry him, even if he asked her, which was unlikely, but that he might queer her pitch with Jimmie Macalister. But they were two independent creatures and must settle it between them, and the rest of us stood back and held our breath if not in all cases our tongues. What Nichol thought no one knew, because, as always when it was anything to do with Jeannie, he never said, but it is not to be supposed that he was happy about it.

That was the position of things in mid-September, when the big tides came in, and with the rain we had had on the hills northward the river in full spate, and at high water the fields downstream were covered, and in the town itself the water was up to the arches of the bridge and licking at the walls of the gardens that went down to the bank. As it happened, one of these gardens was Nichol's. He had a cottage near the end of the town, which is at best only the one street running parallel with the river, with the bridge taking off in the middle and the houses on one side with their backs to the higher ground and those on the other with their backs, at some remove, to the river. Nobody knows rightly what happened that night except Nichol himself, and he's dead now, though for reasons of my own I have my own idea of it, and I cannot altogether avoid the speculation that Jeannie may have hers too. But officially Jeannie was not there, though admittedly thereby, and I had no reason to say anything then, nor would I if I had, so the only account of the matter was the one Nichol gave to Sergeant Menzies when he knocked him up at the police station a bit after midnight.

Nichol's story was that he had come home at eleven, when the drinking officially stops, and found Jack Robson at one of the back windows of the cottage, the window being in fact that of Jeannie's bedroom and Jeannie herself doucely asleep inside. They had had what he called a bit of an altercation, which seemed natural enough in the circumstances, and Jack had run off down the garden with Nichol after him, and got over the garden wall, maybe thinking to escape along the bank, but instead had slipped on the wet grass and gone into the water. It had been high water a bit after ten, and by then the river was going down as fast as a mill-race only wider and deeper out of all proportion, and what with that and the darkness he had lost sight of Jack at once. For all he knew, he told the sergeant, Jack might have got out of the water somewhere downstream, but on the face of it the chances were on the slender side, so he had thought it right to report the accident in the proper quarter.

Now Sergeant Menzies may well have had his doubts about the precise nature of the altercation Nichol had had with Jack, and it is to be said that although Jack was no doubt agile and strong for his weight, he would have had no chance at all with Nichol if the two of them had actually come to grips, which Nichol swore they had not. But there was likely to be no evidence but that of Nichol himself unless Jack turned up, dead or alive. If he turned up alive, there would be his direct evidence to set against Nichol's, and if dead, there would maybe be some circumstantial evidence indicating the manner of his death, but for the moment there was only Nichol's account of the matter, and with that the sergeant had to be content.

To nobody's surprise, with the river as it was, Jack did not turn up in either condition, and by the next day it was the general view that the river had taken its man, and might well have made a worse choice of it, and if there were maybe one or two among the women who did not altogether agree on the second count, they kept their disagreement to themselves. The police as in duty bound searched the banks downstream when the water allowed them, but found nothing, and that was no great surprise either, the river being in general unwilling to give up its dead once it had them in its keeping, so Jack Robson was presumed dead by drowning, and there the matter rested.

There were two things that happened after that. The first was that a couple of days later a boy was drowned a mile upstream. There had been the three boys fishing where and when they should not have been, and one of them had gone in, and the other two had tried unsuccessfully to get at him from the bank, but had, maybe unheroically but very, very wisely, not tried going in after him. But the river was down a bit by then, and it had been daylight, and they had raised the alarm at once, and the body had been recovered, and a very sad case it was, but boys will be boys, and accidents will happen. Now I would not have it thought that I am a prey to vulgar superstition, but I allow it struck me as unreasonable that the river, with its well-known propensities, should have taken two lives in less than two days, and I had no doubt there were others remarked on it too, but with the tragedy hanging over us, no one was likely to remark on it publicly.

The second thing that happened was that on the day after the boy's death I bumped into Jack Robson myself. I mean bumped into him literally, or rather my boat did. It was time I was getting the boat ashore for the winter, but that day there was sunshine after the rain and a fair wind, and I took her for a last sail on the midday flood and ran down towards the mouth of the bay, and it was there, as I say, that I bumped into Jack Robson. I felt the bump before ever I saw him, but as soon as I did see him, I came up into the wind and stood by to get a better look at him. There was no doubt it was Jack, from the check jacket and the dangling boots, but for the rest the details were unattractive, and I was not inclined to look at them too closely. I wondered, as you may suppose, what I ought to do, but one thing I knew for certain, and that was that I was not having Jack in my boat, not in the state he was in, even if I could have got him into it, which was in any case doubtful. I thought maybe I could get a line on him, though a good long line it would have to be, and tow him ashore, but it was just at that moment that something, it could be the movement of the boat near him, rolled him over in the water, and I saw the back of his head. The scalp was gone back from the bone, not gone away altogether but seemingly drawn back on both sides of the head, so that the whole top of the skull was bare, and along the skull, in a straight line from front to back, there was a long cut clean through the bone and into where the brain had been, and still to some extent was, inside the head.

I thought that, whatever had made that cut (and many people might have ideas on that, including, not least, Sergeant Menzies if he had got a sight of it), it had not in any possible way been made by the river. So the river had taken Jack's body, but it had not taken his life, which meant at least that the boy's death had not been, as it were, wholly unnecessary or unprofitable, though I would not be putting that view forward to the boy's parents, even if I believed it myself, which, as I say, you must not suppose I do. But the river, or it maybe was the sea, had Jack now, and the question was what it would do with him, always supposing I did nothing myself, which I was already much inclined to do. It could send him out to sea until he sank finally, or it could put him ashore on one of the wee, wild beaches down the side of the headland, where a lot of things, driftwood and such, do come ashore, or it could even drift him into the box of one of the fixed salmon nets, which are for ever catching things other than salmon, though not often, I think, as big as Jack. If it put him ashore, I thought it could be reckoned constructively to be taking Nichol Mair's life, or what was worth of it, for all they do not hang people for murder nowadays.

But the more I thought about it, the more I thought it would not do that. There was the boy's death to be considered, if you were to accept that view of things, and I did not see, any more than I had before, why a second life should be necessary, to the river or anyone else. I sat there and thought about it, with the wind flapping the foresail in the quiet sunshine, and the boat going gently down to leeward away from floating Jack, who in the nature of things was less subject to wind pressures than the boat was. The more I thought about it, and the farther I got from Jack, the more I thought I could leave it to the river, and believed, though I use the expression only metaphorically, that the river was to be trusted in the matter. By that time I could no longer even see Jack, though I could not be all that far from him, and that too put heart into me, because there are not many boats on the bay, especially in mid-September, and those that are are mostly intent on their own business.

So in the end I worked the boat's head round with the rudder, and put her across the wind again and made sail for my mooring, and the next day I got her out of the water and reckoned that, if the thing ever came in question, there would be no one likely even to know, let alone swear, that I had not got her out the day before. And I was in the right, too, because no one ever saw Jack Robson again, and Jeannie married Jimmie Macalister in the spring, and he was posted away east again before any real harm could come of it locally, whatever sort of a life she led him elsewhere. And the next year Nichol himself dropped dead, as decent and quiet as you please, while he was at his axe-work after a more than usually hard night, and then there was nothing more to worry about, especially when the river drowned one of the daft caravanners who come in the summer, and the year after that, as I say, it was the Englander from the bridge works. So that you could say the river, whatever its propensities, for the most part looks after its own, that is, if you are of a mind to entertain such way-out beliefs, which I in general am not.

The Body in the Glen

MICHAEL INNES

'Dr Watson,' Appleby said, 'once discovered with some surprise that his friend Sherlock Holmes was uncommonly vague about the workings of the Solar System. Holmes explained that he hadn't much interest in acquiring useless information—useless, that's to say, from his professional point of view, which was that of a dedicated enemy of crime. But the truth is that some scrap of quite out-of-the-way knowledge may turn out uncommonly useful to a detective. For example, there was that Highland holiday of ours. Judith, you remember that? It was when we stumbled upon the mystery of Glen Mervie.'

'The affair that began with my refusing the milk?' Lady Appleby said cryptically. 'It was most obtuse of me.'

I scented a story in this.

'I can't believe,' I murmured diplomatically, 'that Judith would ever be obtuse. But just what happened?'

'My friend Ian Grant,' Appleby began, 'is Laird of Mervie, and the place runs to some uncommonly good shooting in a small way—to say nothing of a trout stream that's a perfect wonder. So I always enjoy a holiday there, and so does Judith. But this particular holiday turned out to be of the bus-man's sort. When, I mean, they found Andrew Strachan's body lying by the Drochet.'

'Ah,' I said. 'Drenched in gore?'

'Certainly.'

'Capital, Appleby. Your reminiscences, if I may say so, tend to be a little on the bloodless side. But here is a certain Andrew Strachan steeped in the stuff. Proceed.'

'Actually, I'll go back a bit—at least to the previous day. Grant and I had been shooting over a neighbour's moor, and Judith came to join us in the afternoon. We drove back to Mervie together, and Grant stopped just outside the village to speak to one of his tenants, an old woman called Mrs Frazer. Mrs Frazer's sole possession seemed to be a cow, and she was milking it when we all went and had a word with her. She wasn't interested in me, but she looked at Judith rather searchingly. And then she offered her a drink of milk straight from the cow. Judith refused it. I think she felt that poor old Mrs Frazer needed whatever dairy produce she could raise, and oughtn't to be giving it away.'

'And that,' I asked, 'was what was obtuse? The old woman was offended that Judith declined her hospitality?'

'It wasn't quite that—as I realised when Grant stepped forward and insisted rather peremptorily that Judith should change her mind. He apologised later. It was a matter, it seemed, of the Evil Eye.'

'The Evil Eye!' I was startled.

'Just that. Didn't the poet Collins write an *Ode on the Popular Superstitions of the Highlands?* The Evil Eye is very much one of them. But, of course, you come on the idea all over Europe.'

'The Italians,' I said, 'call it the *Malocchio.*'

'Quite so. Well, Mrs Frazer had decided that Judith was perhaps the possessor of the Evil Eye. It's widely believed to accompany great physical beauty.' Appleby paused happily on this obvious invention. 'Anyway, the point seemed to be this: Mrs Frazer's cow would die unless the magic was defeated. There are various ways of defeating the Evil Eye, and the surest of them is obliging its possessor to accept a gift. Hence the milk.'

'Superstition of that sort is still widely prevalent in those parts?'

'Most certainly. Grant talked to us very interestingly on the subject that evening. He had a shepherd some way up Glen Mervie whose possession of the Evil Eye was one of the terrors of the region. And there's great belief, too, in various forms of Second Sight—particularly in what's known as Calling—and in family apparitions and so forth. Ian Grant himself would be regarded as no true Laird of Mervie if he admitted that he hadn't in fact seen the spectre of a white horse on the night his father died on the battle-field.'

'And Andrew Strachan,' I asked, 'whose body was found by the Drochet? I suppose the Drochet is a burn?'

'Yes. It rises on Ben Cailie, and runs through the Glen of Mervie to join the Garry. As for Andrew Strachan, I took him to be one of Grant's tenants. But actually he wasn't. His father had been a crofter who bought his own farm. So Andrew Strachan was a landowner himself in a very small way—which was what enabled him to keep his younger brother Donald so harshly under his thumb. If Donald had been a tenant of Grant's he'd have had a square deal. As it was, he worked for his brother Andrew, who was a very hard man. They lived in neighbouring cottages in a clachan a mile beyond the village, which is itself a pretty remote spot. There was only their mother—and she was over eighty—who heard a word of their quarrel.'

'Ought you to tell me they'd had a quarrel? Isn't it giving too much away?'

'You'll find out in a minute. In any case, they *did* have a tremendous quarrel—on that very afternoon, as it happened, that Mrs Frazer gave Judith the milk.

'Donald Strachan's story of what followed was quite simple. The quarrel came to nothing, and later that evening Andrew set off up the glen for Dunwinnie. He was courting there. Or rather, if Donald was to be believed, he was after a woman there who was no better than she should be. It was the sad fact, Donald said, that his brother would often spend half the night in Dunwinnie, drinking a great deal with this ungodly wench, and then he'd come stealing home before daybreak. Such goings-on, you understand, have to be conducted much on the quiet in that part of the world. The kirk and the minister are still powers in the land.'

'And I suppose Donald's suggestion was that Andrew had simply met with an accident?'

'Just that. And all the facts—or nearly all the facts—were such as to make it quite possible. There's a point halfway down the glen where the path forks. One branch climbs imperceptibly, and eventually skirts the verge of some very high rocks overhanging the burn. It was at the foot of these that Andrew Strachan's body was found. His skull was cracked open, and in a way that was a quite conceivable consequence of a perfectly possible fall.'

'In all probability,' Appleby went on, 'there would have been no serious question about what had happened, if it hadn't been for one very queer thing. The lad who found Andrew Strachan dead found Donald Strachan, too—alive and not a couple of hundred yards away. Donald had fractured a thigh, as a man might do who had a bad fall while running blindly among rocks. It seemed a queer coincidence that both brothers should meet with an accident on the same night. And what was Donald doing in the glen, anyway? He had an explanation to offer. It was an uncommonly odd one.'

Appleby paused for a moment. He is rather a practiced retailer of yarns of this sort.

'I mentioned what, in the Highlands, they term Calling. It's supposed that, in some supernatural way, a man may sometimes hear his own name being called out by a relation, or a friend, who at that moment is either dying or in great danger in what may be some quite distant spot. It might be Canada, for example, or Australia.'

'I've heard of it,' I said. 'Indeed, isn't it on record as rather well-attested?'

'Yes, it is—although I don't know what a court of law would make of it. And it looked as if a court of law would have to try. Because Donald Strachan's story was simply that, in the middle of the night, and after their abortive quarrel, he had heard Andrew *calling*. He said he somehow knew at once that it was a *calling* in this rather special sense. And as he was aware that Andrew had gone up the glen to Dunwinnie, he got up and made his way there himself, convinced that there had been an accident or a fatality. And he hurried so recklessly through the darkness that he had his own utterly disabling fall.'

I digested all this for a moment in silence.

'It would certainly have been a hard nut for a judge and jury,' I said. 'But what did you think yourself?'

'I saw another possibility. It wasn't pretty, but at least it had the merit of *not* involving the supernatural. Donald, I supposed, had crept into Andrew's cottage in the night, battered him to death, and then lugged the body to the one spot in the neighbourhood where the appearance of a fatal accident could be made credible. And he'd never have been suspected if he hadn't had his own tumble among the rocks.'

'But had you any evidence?'

'There *was* one piece of evidence.' Appleby paused again. 'And it was I,' he went on rather drily, 'who pointed it out to the local police. The Strachans were both wretchedly poor, and their clothes were little better than rags. And that did rather obscure what was nevertheless clear when one looked hard enough. Andrew's body was fully dressed. But his jacket was on inside out.'

'So you concluded——?'

'I concluded that his body had been shoved into it, and probably into the rest of his clothes, in the dark.'

'It was certainly a fair inference. In fact, my dear Appleby, I can't think of any other explanation.'

'Ah——but remember the Solar System. Holmes *might* conceivably have been caught out by his ignorance of it. And I was being caught out by——well, by my ignorance of those popular superstitions of the Highlands. You remember my telling you that up that glen there was a shepherd whose possession of the Evil Eye was a terror to the district?'

'Certainly I do.'

'Well, it seems there are more ways of averting the Evil Eye than by offering a drink of milk. You can avert it——at least from harming your own person——simply by wearing any of your garments inside out.'

'Widdershins!'

'Yes, indeed——that's the general name for such behaviour. And nobody up there would dream of going through the Glen of Mervie without taking that precaution. So you see the police——and my host, for that matter——distinctly had the laugh on me.'

'It was no laughing matter.'

'That's true. But there was clearly no case against Donald Strachan. He just had to be believed.'

The Milnathort Murder

CHRISTOPHER N. JOHNSTON

I

t was a hundred years ago, and one fine morning in May about seven o'clock (people rose early in those days), Mr Peter Tod, writer and notary-public, Kinross, was busy shaving, when his domestic knocked at his bedroom door and informed him that Miss Beveridge was below and anxious to see him at once. Mr Tod was surprised, and, to tell the truth, just a little annoyed, for a staid old bachelor is not in the way of receiving calls before breakfast from middle-aged spinsters, and Kinross was just as fertile a centre of gossip then as it is at the present day.

But Miss Beveridge was a client of Mr Tod's, and doubtless some business of importance brought her there at that unusual hour—some rascals, perhaps, had stolen her hens. Mr Tod finished his shave with leisurely precision,—he was never in an unreasonable hurry,—adjusted his neck-cloth, donned his coat, and then descended to his business-room. But Miss Beveridge was not there, for, as the servant had been busy dusting out that room when Miss Beveridge arrived, she had shown the lady into the parlour, and so she now informed Mr Tod. The lawyer was provoked, for although he was not a woman-hater, he was a man with whom circumspectness in his relations with the fair sex was carried almost to the extent of eccentricity. So far as his own premises were concerned, these relations were always of a strictly business character, and for many years no female other than his elderly domestic had ever crossed the threshold of his parlour. But here now was Miss Beveridge, a lady of that age and position in life so dangerous to the reputation of a well-to-do elderly bachelor, not merely admitted to the parlour, but introduced to it with the breakfast set upon the table, and left for the last half-hour the witness and doubtless the attentive student of all his bachelor whims and comforts. Mr Tod opened the parlour door with a sudden snap, but instead of finding Miss Beveridge, as he had expected, eyeglass in hand, studying the quality of the sugar or the pattern of the tea-cosy, he beheld her stretched upon a sofa which stood in a recess at the end of the room,—a good old-fashioned horse-hair sofa it was,—with a handkerchief spread over her face. This was worse and worse.

"Really, Miss Beveridge, what is the matter, I pray you?" began the lawyer in his very sharpest tones.

The lady started, looked about her in confusion—for doubtless she had been dosing—and then jumped up and made for Mr Tod.

"Oh, Mr Tod! oh, dear me! oh my dear Mr Tod!" and then, fairly overcome and breaking into sobs, she grasped the lawyer's shoulders.

Had Miss Beveridge been smitten with the plague, Mr Tod could not have started back with greater agility, and it was only by clutching him violently by the sleeve that Miss Beveridge saved herself from being cast upon the floor. As it was, she sank sobbing into an easy-chair that stood by the fireplace.

"Well, upon my word!" exclaimed the lawyer with an acerbity quite unusual with him. "What is the meaning of this extraordinary conduct? Shall I send for a doctor?"

"Oh no, Mr Tod—forgive me, Mr Tod—please don't be angry—I am so upset—if you only knew what I have come through," gasped the poor lady.

"Well, well, for God's sake be composed, and try and explain yourself," said Mr Tod testily.

"Mr Tod," said the lady, rising slowly, and Mr Tod drew back nervously towards the door, expecting a second assault upon his person. But without moving from her place, and with a forced calm, though she was trembling all over, Miss Beveridge continued in a hoarse, gasping whisper, "I saw a man murdered before my eyes this morning."

"Ah!" said the lawyer, with professional interest—he was the local procurator-fiscal, or public prosecutor—"tell me about that; but sit down first. I can't listen to a word until you sit down."

Miss Beveridge sank back upon the easy-chair, and then Mr Tod, deeming himself now secure against any further violence, drew a chair to the table, and leaning forward, with his chin between his palms, he listened to Miss Beveridge's story.

Miss Beveridge, who was a spinster of a certain age, and with a comfortable competency, resided in an old two-storied house, which has long since disappeared, close to the old North Road, on the Glenfarg side of Milnathort, which was then a mere hamlet. The household consisted of Miss Beveridge, who was the only daughter of an old Dr Beveridge, who had practised in Kinross in the middle of the eighteenth century, and Jean, her faithful maid-of-all-work, who had been from time immemorial in the service of the doctor, and after his death in that of his daughter. The story which this lady now told Mr Tod, translated out of the gasping and ejaculatory form in which it was related to him, was as follows:—

About four o'clock that morning she had been awakened by the sound of wheels passing along the road, just under her bedroom window, followed immediately afterwards by a shout. She jumped up, and looking out of her window she saw a closed post-chaise drawn up about sixty or seventy yards from her door, in the Milnathort direction. A bare-headed, middle-aged gentleman, dressed in black, who had apparently dismounted from the conveyance, was running towards her door, closely followed by two other men—the one a slender, gentlemanly-looking man in grey morning clothes, the other a rough, sailor-looking character. The gentleman in black had almost reached the wicket-gate, three or four yards in front of Miss Beveridge's door, when the former of the two pursuers overtook him, and seizing him by the coat-tails, he at once brought him to the ground by a violent side twist. The poor man uttered a loud shriek as he fell, but he was hardly upon the ground ere his captor's fingers were at his throat. The third man had by this time come up, and he at once drew a knife from his waist, which he was apparently about to plunge into the prostrate man's breast. But the other, still holding the throat with one hand, motioned aside the weapon with the other, and then placing his knee upon his victim's chest, and applying both hands again to his throat, he proceeded to strangle him. Miss Beveridge saw no more, and the next thing she remembered was Jean bending over her and mopping her head with a wet sponge. Struggling to her feet, she rushed again to the window, but the men were gone, the carriage too had disappeared, not a vestige or trace remained of the horrible scene which she had just witnessed. Jean, who slept at the back of the house, had not, it appeared, heard the sound of the passing conveyance, but she had been roused by the crash of the looking-glass which her mistress had upset in falling, and she had at once hurried in, to find Miss Beveridge insensible upon the floor.

"And how long did it take her to bring you round?" inquired Mr Tod.

"About four or five minutes, Jean says."

"And you looked out immediately and saw nothing whatever?"

"Yes, everything had disappeared."

"Ah, quite so," and then again, after a longish pause, "quite so."

Mr Tod, as has been stated, was procurator-fiscal, and although he had a strong suspicion that this improbable story was the result of some nightmare, or at most of some hysterical exaggeration of a drunken brawl, he could not allow such a circumstantial narrative to go unsifted. Accordingly he promised to come to inspect the spot immediately after breakfast, and meanwhile he cautioned Miss Beveridge to mention the matter to no one.

"You may depend upon that, Mr Tod. I did not mention what I had seen even to Jean. The poor body would be afraid to bide in the house, so I put it on the cheese."

"On the what?"

"On the cheese. Oh, I beg pardon, I forgot to mention that I had toasted cheese for supper, which may account for my wakening so easily. You knew my Aunt Eliza, you'll remember her? No! Well she was married to an Englishman, and when I stayed with them at Preston we always used to have toasted cheese for supper, and I thought I would like to try—"

"Oh, yes, I understand—that'll do at present—time presses, you know," and the lawyer made a decided motion towards the door.

"H'm!" murmured Mr Tod when he had dismissed his visitor; "these last details cut both ways; it's not like a hysterical woman being so reticent and cautious; but toasted cheese for supper! in a Christian country!"

After breakfast Mr Tod walked up to Miss Beveridge's, and, giving the pretext to Jean of having a new gateway made, he got Miss Beveridge out to show him the spot where the alleged occurrence had taken place. The road was hard and baked, and it was impossible to tell whether the wheel-marks were those of conveyances which had passed the previous night, or whether any vehicle had been that way since daybreak. At the place where the chaise was said to have stopped, it was impossible, from the number of rough stones upon the road, to verify that part of the story. Mr Tod looked in vain for any traces of a struggle at the place near the edge of the road which Miss Beveridge pointed out as the spot where the man had been thrown to the ground. He saw nothing, and he was just turning away when he fancied he noticed something glittering under a tuft of grass at the verge of the roadway.

"See, Miss Beveridge, is there nothing on the other side of the road? They may have rolled over that way."

Miss Beveridge went over to look, and the moment her back was turned Mr Tod stooped and picked up the shining article, which he slipped into his pocket. It was a gentleman's shoe-buckle, of the style usually worn at that period.

"Now, I must see Jean," said Mr Tod at last. "She'll be round at the back, I daresay;" and he went round towards the back of the house.

"Are ye thaur, Jean?" he shouted, on reaching the back premises.

In a minute or two Jean appeared at the scullery door.

"Jean, wumman," began Mr Tod, "this is an awfy biziness aboot the lassie Lawson;" and he mentioned the name of an "unfortunate" who had been to consult him the previous evening.

"Deed ay, sir, it's jist shamefy; her puir mither's like tae break her hert—the hissy!"

"She putts the blame on Jock Lowrie."

"So A' heerd, and A' dinna wunner't; he's an ill loon, that Jock."

"Ye'll a seen them thegither?"

"Ay, twarry times."

"That's jist what A' was gaun tae speer aboot," said the lawyer. "Ye maun tell me a' ye ken;" and he proceeded to take a brief precognition in the cause *Lawson* v. *Lowrie*, in which, as he knew very well, Jean was able to supply him with no assistance which could not have been rendered equally well by any man or woman in the parish of Orwell.

"The Missis is no' lookin' weel the day," said the lawyer at last, making a turn as if to go.

"D'ye think no?" replied Jean, who had been all volubility upon the subject of Miss Lawson's misfortune, but who at once became cautious when the subject of inquiry came nearer home.

"She's no' bin complainin'?"

"She's no' the complainin' kind."

There was no use beating about the bush further, so the lawyer went straight to the point.

"That must hae bin an awfy turn she had i' the nicht, puir body?"

"Oh, she tellt ye aboot that, did she?" replied Jean, whose respect for her mistress at once fell 50 per cent. "Young folks is aye indiscreet."

"Ou ay, she tellt me a' aboot it. Ye maun hae bin awfy skeered. Mind ye, it's a seriis biziness, onybody bein' haf an 'oor in a faintin'-fut."

"Haf an 'oor! wha said onything aboot haf an 'oor? She wasna aboon five minits."

"Ay, was that a'? but hoo d'ye ken that?"

"A' heered her fa', and A' run ben, and she cam' roon' to hersel' in aboot fower minits, or maybe five at maist."

"Puir body! And what did she dae when she cam' roon'?"

"She ran tae the winday, jist as if she war chokin' like."

"Ya didna hear onything afore she fa'd, onything that could maybe hae disturbed her like?"

"Naw, naethin' ava. A' heerd nought till A' waukened wi' the lookin'-gless gaun bang. Man, it's a peety tae see't; that gless cost twa pun' ten jist fower year syne, cum Martinmas."

This was all the information that was to be got out of Jean, and having once more hailed Miss Beveridge, and cautioned her to mention the matter to no one, the lawyer went his way.

Mr Tod was now confirmed in his belief that the story of Miss Beveridge was the result of some nightmare or delusion. It was a most unlikely story to begin with, and no traces of a scuffle were discernible near the place indicated. The statement of Jean, too, made it clear that Miss Beveridge was not more than five minutes absent from the window, and nothing could be more improbable than that at one moment a man should be seen strangling another upon the public highway, and that just five minutes after all traces of victim and assassin should alike have disappeared from view. But there remained the shoe-buckle, and that detail was just sufficient to forbid Mr Tod dismissing the matter altogether without further investigation. Inquiries, however, both at Milnathort and Kinross tended further to discredit Miss Beveridge's story. Nobody in Milnathort had seen or heard anything of a conveyance that morning. The testimony, too, of the groom at the Green Inn, Kinross, was conclusive that no vehicle had passed through Kinross in either direction, for he had been up before four that morning, to supply a relay of horses to an express messenger with despatches from the fleet in the North Seas. The messenger had not arrived,—no doubt the vessel bearing the expected despatches had been unable to make the Moray Firth owing to the westerly winds,— and from half-past three onwards, for many hours, no conveyance had passed Kinross that morning. Mr Tod was able to make all these inquiries without exciting any comment, for in those days, when the road was the only highway, and when serious crime was more frequent in the provinces than is now the case, the public prosecutor had constant occasion to make inquiries concerning passing conveyances and their occupants.

II

On the day following the events above related, Edinburgh was shocked by the news of the brutal murder, on the road near Dunkeld, of Mr Wylie, a well-known Clerk to the Signet. Mr Wylie was agent and factor for a large estate a few miles south of Dunkeld, on the Birnam side of the river, and he had gone north to collect the rents. After the collection he had dined, as was his custom, with the proprietor; he was then put across the river to the Dunkeld side, and he started to walk to the inn at Dunkeld, where he had put up for the two nights of his sojourn in the district. He never reached the inn, and nothing more was heard of him, but his hat was found next morning floating in the river near Delvine. Suspicion fastened upon an Italian who had been seen at Dunkeld the previous day. He was arrested at Perth, and the worst suspicions were fully confirmed by the discovery upon his person of a pocketbook and watch, which were identified as having belonged to Mr Wylie, and of which the Italian could give no better account than the oft-told tale of having found them upon the road. No trace was, however, discovered of the money-bag with £1500 of rent collected that day by Mr Wylie, which the Italian had doubtless *planted* somewhere near at hand.

Four weeks had passed, and nothing had occurred to suggest to Mr Tod that there was any substantial basis for Miss Beveridge's narrative, which indeed now remained in his memory only as a painful recollection of a wasted morning and a striking illustration of the mischievous conse-quences of the disregard of the most elementary laws of health. Mean-while the proofs of the guilt of the Italian accused of Mr Wylie's murder had accumulated with overwhelming force. A blood-stained knife was found in his pocket, and the hairs which adhered to it corresponded in colour to those of Mr Wylie. Blood-stains, too, were found upon the Ital-ian's clothes. Traces of blood were found upon the road near Dunkeld, and there were marks of footprints down to the river near the spot, some of which seemed to correspond with those of the Italian, whilst the mud upon his trousers was of the same colour and quality as the mud upon the edge of the water. Already the *gamins* of Edinburgh and Perth were hold-ing mock hangings of Gasparini.

It happened one day at this time that Mr Thorn, the proprietor of an estate a mile or two to the west of Kinross, was out in the afternoon in quest of a shot at a cushie or a rabbit, for the shooting season proper had not yet begun. He had wandered a little off his ground, but in these days, when game was not much preserved and when the right of shooting was of no commercial value, neighbouring proprietors often indulged one an-other with liberty to shoot over each other's ground. Mr Thorn had wounded a hare, which hobbled away towards a neighbouring covert, now a fir plantation, but then covered with natural scrub and whins. He fol-lowed up, expecting every moment to see the hare drop; but the animal held on wonderfully, and after one or two abortive efforts to cross the dyke, it at last managed to struggle over into the wood. Mr Thorn crept up cau-tiously, hoping to get another shot at it. On gaining the edge of the thicket he saw the hare sitting within easy shot, and he at once raised his gun to give it the *coup-de-grâce*. But just as he was about to pull the trigger some-thing caught his eye away beyond the hare but directly in the line of fire, and he lowered his gun. "Yes," he murmured, peering through the trees, "there's somebody there. By Jove, that fellow has had a lucky let-off, and he's lost me that hare too," for the hare had meanwhile hopped away deeper into the wood.

Mr Thorn determined to cross into the wood to see if he could not get another chance of picking up his wounded quarry. The fence was an awkward one, for he had to descend into a ditch and then to climb up the bank and over the wall at the other side. On gaining the wood Mr Thorn advanced in the direction in which the hare had disappeared, and to his surprise he found that the stranger who had spoilt his sport had meanwhile decamped. Not a trace of him was to be seen. Mr Thorn tried to follow up the hare, but without success, and he returned homewards with none the kindliest of feelings towards the stranger who had robbed him of his soup.

Next day Mr Chalmers, one of Mr Thorn's tenants, came along in the evening to pay his rent. It was always Mr Thorn's custom on these occasions to take a glass of something hot with his tenant; so, after business had been disposed of, he invited Mr Chalmers to partake.

"But A'll be keepin' ye frae yer freens, A' doot," said Mr Chalmers.

"Whaten freens, Jeemes, man?"

"A' thocht ye had companee the noo. A' see a gentleman the day i' the wud by Dirley yont, an A' thocht he'd bin stoppin' here, for a' the ither big folks are awa' the noo, ye ken."

Mr Thorn questioned Chalmers with regard to this stranger, and it appeared that, happening to pass the wood in question in the course of the afternoon, he had seen a stranger of gentlemanly appearance sitting upon the trunk of a fallen tree, and had concluded that he was a visitor of Mr Thorn's out there for an afternoon stroll.

Next morning Mr Thorn was walking about by the side of his house enjoying a whiff, when his eyes fell upon Dirley Wood in the distance, and his thoughts at once reverted to the mysterious stranger who seemed to have made that spot his haunt. Several times he tried to dismiss the subject from his mind, but it always drew over him again with a strange fascination, and his eye wandered away to the wood across the fields. "Let me see," he said at last—"I'm not due at that meeting at Kinross until half-past eleven; I've just time to take a run across and see if our friend is at home this morning." Mr Thorn approached the wood in the same direction in which he had pursued the hare, and reaching the edge he peered in through the branches. "No; he's not there; but, let me see, was that the place? No; it was a little further over. Yes, by Gad, there he is again."

Mr Thorn was looking at the man aslant across the wood, and he perceived that by going along a little way opposite to where the man was sitting he could get a much better view of him. Between the place where Mr Thorn stood and a spot exactly opposite the stranger, where there was another gap, it was impossible to see into the wood owing to the thick growth of underwood along the edge. Mr Thorn paused just before reaching the gap and peered through the verge of the undergrowth. The stranger was sitting upon the trunk of a fallen tree not more than twenty-five paces distant, and looking straight in the direction of the gap.

"Well, he has got little enough to do, I should say," muttered Mr Thorn; "and sitting without a hat, too, this damp morning. I must try and draw him;" and emerging from cover, Mr Thorn planted himself in the gap.

"Good morning, sir," he began.

There was no reply.

"I say, sir—I wish you good morning, sir. It's a very fine day, sir," shouted Mr Thorn.

Still no response.

"Poor fellow," murmured Mr Thorn, "it is quite clear that he is off his head. I must speak to Tod about this at once;" and he turned away, for it was time to bethink himself of the meeting at Kinross.

Later in the forenoon Mr Thorn had an opportunity of speaking to Mr Tod in private, and he inquired whether he had received any information of a lunatic of gentlemanly appearance being at large, and he then went on to explain what had been seen in Dirley Wood. Mr Tod had received no information which threw light upon the matter, but of course he felt bound to look into the affair.

"I'll tell you what it is, Tod. You'll come out and try pot-luck with me; it's Saturday, you know, and I'll show you the gentleman, that you may judge for yourself."

Mr Tod agreed to go.

Dinner was at half-past three, and there was an hour to spare beforehand, so the two gentlemen walked over to Dirley Wood to see if the stranger was again to be found. As they neared the wood Mr Tod hazarded a confident prediction that the stranger would not be forthcoming, and that consequently their walk would be in vain; but, not being a betting man, and being constitutionally cautious, he declined Mr Thorn's invitation to back his opinion to the extent of a crown. Mr Thorn, who knew the exact spot, was at the edge of the wood a moment sooner than his companion. "You've saved that crown," he murmured, as he peered through the branches—"a single step this way and you have him full in view." The two friends placed themselves in the gap, and there, full in front of them, sat the strange gentleman in the same seat as before. He was a man apparently just past middle life, tall and handsome, with a fine open forehead, and a bald head fringed with dark-grey hair. His clothes were black, though, as was natural in view of the kind of life he seemed to be leading, they were much mud-bespattered and bedraggled.

"There's a fine afternoon, sir," said Mr Tod.

The stranger made no response.

"It's of no use, I tell you," said Mr Thorn, "he won't answer."

"Well, at all events, let us go over and stir him up," said the Fiscal.

The two friends descended into the ditch and scrambled up the bank over into the wood.

"Hulloa! I say, he's bolted!" exclaimed Mr Thorn when they had reached the inside of the wood.

The stranger had indeed disappeared the moment the two friends proceeded to cross into the wood, and although they hurried forward he was too agile or too cunning for them, for they were unable to ascertain even the direction he had taken.

"This is a very serious business," said Mr Tod, as they turned to give up the chase; "I must have men out to-morrow to search the wood,—in fact, I don't know but what I ought to go back to Kinross at once for the purpose."

"Oh no! come, my dear Tod; dinner, you know, is dinner, even though that poor chap gets none. He looks wonderfully fresh, and I daresay he will keep for another night."

Mr Tod was constrained.

Mr Thorn's family were from home, so there were just the two friends at dinner. Throughout the meal and the after-dinner potation the conversation again and again reverted to the same subject. The mysterious stranger seemed to exercise a fascinating influence over both gentlemen.

"There is one circumstance," said Mr Tod, as he dismissed a glass of port,—"there is one circumstance from which I infer that, though the stranger haunts the wood, he has access to some civilised place of abode."

"And what is that?" inquired Mr Thorn.

"I had a good look at him—a particularly good look—the sun was just on his face, and, unless I am very much mistaken, he must certainly have shaved within the last forty-eight hours; his chin was quite smooth."

"Tod," said Mr Thorn gravely,—"Tod, you are a born lawyer. Another glass of the port, it will do you no harm; or would you rather have some-thing hot now?"

It was wearing towards seven o'clock when Mr Thorn at length rose.

"I'll tell you what it is, Tod—it's a beautiful evening, and there are still two good hours of light. Let us take a stroll over to Dirley and see if our gentleman is going to roost on his perch, or if he has betaken himself for the night to some more 'civilised place of abode.'"

Mr Tod was quite agreeable, and the two friends started—Mr Thorn for the third time that day—to walk over to Dirley Wood. A glance through the underwood satisfied them that the stranger had resumed his solitary post. Before disclosing themselves at the gap the two friends held a brief consultation. It was agreed that Mr Tod should show himself at the gap as before, in order to attract the man's attention, whilst Mr Thorn should go round and get into the thicket by the other side, and so try to steal up upon him unawares.

"If he breaks cover he will come in your direction," whispered Mr Thorn; "and in any case you will keep a sharp look-out and see which way he takes."

The wood was not a large one, and Mr Thorn soon made the necessary detour. Being familiar with the ground, he then took a beeline for the fallen tree, where the stranger was seated, and stole quietly up towards it. But when he got near the tree Mr Thorn perceived that the man was gone. Mr Tod was at his post.

"Hulloa, Tod," cried Mr Thorn, "where is he?"

"He's gone."

"The deuce he is! but which way did he go?"

"I can't say."

"You can't say! Why, where were your eyes! You haven't been taking a nap, have you?" shouted Mr Thorn, who began to think that after all Mr Tod had been less abstemious than his host had imagined.

"No," replied Mr Tod, looking very foolish, "but he just slipped away somehow, and disappeared amongst the trees. I can't really say which way he took."

"But, dear me, you can see twenty-five yards clear in any direction round the place where he was sitting. You must have seen whether he went to the right or the left. Let me see, where were you standing?" said Mr Thorn, who had now advanced to the dyke, and was quite provoked at the stupidity of the Fiscal. So saying, he scrambled over the dyke, and placed himself in the position Mr Tod had occupied. "Now, don't you see," he continued, pointing to the open spaces round the fallen tree, "how could you fail to—But, why, wha—what the—there the fellow is again!"

The stranger had returned and resumed his seat the moment Mr Thorn quitted the wood.

"Now, Tod," said Mr Thorn, when he had recovered from his extreme surprise, "you'll cross there, and go straight at him. I'll stand here and keep him in view, and follow the moment I see which way he takes."

Mr Tod scrambled over, but ere he had set foot in the wood the man had again disappeared.

"Well, where has he gone?" inquired Mr Tod.

"I'll swear," replied Mr Thorn, "that he hasn't crossed my line of view in any direction. There is an old ditch behind the tree; he must have slipped down there. I think we have him now."

Mr Thorn crossed the dyke, and then the two advanced and proceeded to examine the ditch, which was broad and deep, and full of dead leaves. But nothing was to be seen of the stranger.

"Bah! Pfui! what a horrible smell," said Mr Thorn as they looked about. "He might have been a badger!"

"It's not pleasant certainly," said Mr Tod, poking about in the ditch. "Surely," he added in a moment, "some one has been digging here;" and he thrust his stick into a heap of fresh earth and leaves. "Hulloa, what's this?" His stick had struck something hard. Stooping down, he brushed aside the leaves with his hand, and there was disclosed a shoe which apparently covered a human foot. "Here's our friend at last!"

"Lord bless me! Lord preserve me!" said Mr Thorn, "he must be half mole, half man! How the deuce does he breathe under all that stuff?"

Mr Tod had meanwhile scraped a little further, and disclosed the other foot.

"Come," he said, "you take one foot and I'll take the other, and we'll soon haul him out."

"All right," replied Mr Thorn; "but take care, a brute like this may bite."

Each of the explorers then stooped, and seized a foot. The loose earth and leaves yielded readily, and they drew out from under them the dead body of a man, in a pretty advanced stage of decomposition.

"God help us! God help us!" exclaimed both friends, as they started back and involuntarily clutched each other by the arm.

"You don't know him?" said Mr Tod, after a long pause.

"No; I doubt if his dearest friend could recognise him now."

"He seems to have been a man in a good position of life."

"Yes; his get-up is most correct—complete down to his very shoe-buckles. No; I see, by the way, he has lost one."

"I think I can complete even that," said Mr Tod, for once forgetting his accustomed caution; and he drew a buckle from his fob, and held it beside the one on the poor gentleman's shoe. The buckles were clearly a pair.

"Then you know something about this! You have a clue!"

"That may or may not be," said Mr Tod, biting his lips. "But, meanwhile, pray do not mention this buckle incident to any one."

"It will be necessary," continued Mr Tod in a moment, "to have the body removed to Kinross. Will you kindly go for assistance and a cart, and I shall wait here to see that nothing is disturbed."

"What, will you stay here alone?" inquired Mr Thorn in astonishment.

"Certainly," replied Mr Tod. "I am flesh and blood, and I tell you frankly I don't like it, but it is my duty;" and he seated himself upon the fallen tree.

"Well," replied Mr Thorn, "I used to think myself a bit of a philosopher, but, duty or no duty, I would not stay here alone just now, if you gave me Kinross-shire."

Later in the evening the body was removed to Kinross. Next day it lay exposed to view in the churchyard, but nobody could identify it. Mr Tod brought Miss Beveridge to look at it, but although she thought the clothes and general contour of the body similar to those of the gentleman she had seen assaulted on the road, she was unable, owing to its advanced state of decomposition, positively to identify the body. A medical examination ascertained that the cause of death was asphyxia. The only external injuries were a bruise upon the chest and marks of finger-nails upon the throat. On the day following, the body was buried close to the Arnot burying-ground, in the graveyard beside the lake. Mr Tod, the parish minister, and two grave-diggers, were alone present at the interment.

III

Miss Beveridge was very proud of her father's memory, and she was most anxious to possess a portrait of him. Some time before his death his portrait had been painted, but this was done for a brother of the doctor's, a retired Indian, and was now in possession of his son, a cousin of Miss Beveridge, who was a writer in Edinburgh. Miss Beveridge desired to have a picture based upon this portrait for herself by a skilled hand; and with that view, one day in August, when she happened to be in Edinburgh, she called upon Mr Raeburn, who had already risen to distinction in his profession. After her return home, she waited upon Mr Tod in almost as great a state of nervous excitement as on the memorable morning of the murder, three months before. In Mr Raeburn's studio she had seen a life-size portrait of the poor gentleman she saw strangled on the Great North Road at Milnathort.

"I was so put about," she said, "that I was afraid to ask who it was; and I thought, too, that perhaps I had better say nothing until I had seen you."

Mr Thorn had been up in London for a week or two, and on his way home he stayed for a day in Edinburgh, being anxious to purchase a horse. Crossing St Andrew Square early in the afternoon, he met Mr Tod. The two friends conversed for a few minutes, and then Mr Tod asked Mr Thorn if he happened to be personally acquainted with Raeburn, the portrait-painter.

"Why, yes; I know him very well indeed—a very good fellow!"

"Would it trouble you too much to take me to call upon him? I am anxious to make his acquaintance, for a reason which I shall perhaps explain to you again."

"With the greatest pleasure in the world; but, first of all, you must oblige me. I want your opinion of a horse."

Later in the day, when the horse business had been disposed of, the two friends called upon Mr Raeburn. The painter received his visitors in his parlour, and was all affability—"delighted to make Mr Tod's acquaintance," &c. &c. When they had conversed together for some time, Mr Tod, who seemed fidgety and ill at ease, at last remarked, "Perhaps I am taking too great a liberty, but I have a great desire to see your workshop."

"With the greatest pleasure in the world," said the painter. "Come along," and he led them to the studio. The room was dark, for the blinds were down, and Raeburn went to the window to pull them up. As the light streamed into the room, Mr Tod looked at Mr Thorn, and Mr Thorn looked at Mr Tod, but neither spoke. On a large easel, in the centre of the room, was a full-length portrait of the man they had seen sitting upon the fallen tree in Dirley Wood.

"Ah, you are looking at that," said the painter, turning from the window. "It is the saddest task I ever put my hands to. I hadn't the heart to touch it these three months, until the other day."

"Indeed!" said Mr Thorn. "Then something has happened to the gentleman?"

"Ah! you did not know him! It is poor Wylie, who was murdered at Dunkeld in May last."

Mr Raeburn must have thought the manner of his guests peculiar, for neither of them seemed to give much further heed to his conversation. He directed their attention to several other more or less finished portraits in the studio, but their lack of appreciation was most disappointing. Again and again their eyes wandered back to the portrait in the centre of the room.

"Have you done much to this since his death?" inquired Mr Tod at last.

"Oh no; as I say, I did not touch it until the other day, and I have only given an hour or two to it altogether. Fortunately it was nearly finished at the last sitting, just the day before he left Edinburgh. I was busy with the legs and feet that day: you'll notice he had very neat feet. And the buckles too, luckily I painted them, for he would not be persuaded to leave them with me. It wouldn't have been Wylie without them. They're quite peculiar. You'll notice the Indian work at the edges. His uncle, I believe, got them made in the East."

"They're uncommon then, are they?" inquired Mr Tod.

"Yes, quite; I never saw another pair like them."

"Then I have been lucky," said Mr Tod. "I picked up just such a pair the other day."

So saying he drew a buckle from his pocket, and held it against one of the buckles in the picture. The shape and pattern of the two were indistinguishable.

Next day the buckles, as also the clothes of the man found in Dirley Wood, were identified by Mrs Wylie as those of her deceased husband; and her statement, along with that of Miss Beveridge, having been submitted to the Lord Advocate, a despatch was at once sent up by express to London to secure a reprieve for Gasparini, who at the Perth Autumn Circuit Court had been convicted and sentenced to death for the murder of Mr Wylie. Diligent inquiries were set on foot with reference to conveyances which had been hired in the neighbouring counties on the day before the murder, and the following facts were elicited: Orders had been given by letters from Edinburgh, forged in the name of the Sheriff of Orkney (whose naval dignity was not then so entirely ornamental and picturesque as in these happier times, inasmuch as he was responsible for the transmission of despatches from ships of war in the North Seas), to hostelries at Dunkeld, Perth, and Kinross, to have relays of horses ready for an express messenger with despatches from the north. The horses ordered at Dunkeld and Perth were duly supplied to the supposed messenger, but, as already stated, those ordered at Kinross were never required. On the afternoon of the day of Mr Wylie's disappearance, two men, one a young man of gentlemanly appearance, the other an older man in semi-sailor attire, with rings in his ears, and with a very imperfect command of English, appeared at a posting establishment at Blairgowrie (all inquiries failed to elicit whence or how they came), and hired a post-chaise to take them to Dunkeld. Soon after leaving Blairgowrie, the men offered drink to the driver, who, after taking it, became very ill, and was unable to drive. They put him down, therefore, at a roadside cottage; and the younger of the two travellers mounted the box, and drove to Dunkeld, where they took up the relay of horses. They left Dunkeld about 9:30 P.M., and at one o'clock in the morning they arrived in Perth, where horses were again changed. At Perth there was a third gentleman in the carriage, but he appeared to be asleep, and did not get out. The next trace of the carriage and its occupants was the scene upon the road near Milnathort witnessed by Miss Beveridge at four o'clock in the morning. Apparently the coach had then turned west past Orwell Church, and along the Warroch Road, for it was seen passing Carnbo shortly after five o'clock, and it was next heard of at the inn at the Yetts of Muckhart, nine miles west of Milnathort, which was reached a little before six o'clock. There the two men, for the carriage had now but two occupants, left the horses and conveyance, with directions to have them returned in the afternoon to Perth by the Dunning Road, by which, as they represented, they had themselves come. A gig and driver were hired by the men at the Yetts, and in this they were driven down past Saline to Torryburn on the Firth of Forth, where they dismounted and discharged the trap, at half-past eight o'clock. They were then seen to proceed a short distance along the shore towards Crombie Point, off which a sloop had been lying all morning. In answer apparently to their hail, a boat came off from the sloop and took them on board. The vessel immediately afterwards weighed anchor and made sail down the Firth, and all further trace of her and of the men aboard was lost. These facts, taken together with the story of Miss Beveridge and the discovery and identification of the body, seemed to make it clear that Mr Wylie was waylaid and drugged on his way home to Dunkeld. The kidnappers had thrown out his watch and pocket-book, and put his hat in the river to make it appear that he had been murdered, and they had then driven to Perth, and on past Perth to Milnathort. Here, either on account of careless drugging or of the rebellion of his stomach against attempts to renew the dose, Mr Wylie had recovered and attempted to escape, with the fatal result witnessed by Miss Beveridge. The murderers, unable to dispose of the body before reaching Kinross, were obliged to abandon their intention of changing horses there, and therefore turned west towards the Yetts of Muckhart by the Dollar Road. The body was hid in Dirley Wood, and they then proceeded on to Muckhart.

IV

The necessary steps were being taken to have Gasparini's reprieve converted into a pardon, there being nothing to connect him with the crime on the theory now adopted, and speculation was rife as to whether by inquiries at the ports it would be possible to trace the murderers, when one morning the startling report ran round that Mr Wylie was alive and in Edinburgh.

Nobody in Edinburgh was more generally or more justly respected than Mr William Maxwell Morison, an advocate, who had devoted long years of labour to the compilation of a huge dictionary of the decisions of the Scottish Courts from the earliest times, a work which is still to be found in every law library. Mr Morison, whose studious life had developed in him certain eccentric habits, was in the way of rising very early, and every morning he would take a walk from his house in the High Street down over the fields towards Granton. He now asserted that starting in the morning on one of these strolls, and passing over the open ground north of St Andrew Square (now occupied by the Abercromby Place Gardens), he saw standing a little way off from him, amongst some bushes, Mr Wylie, whom he had known intimately, and whom everybody believed to be dead. Mr Morison hailed his friend, but Mr Wylie apparently desired to avoid an interview, for he made no response, and drew away behind the bushes. Everybody scouted this story. It had been clearly proved that Mr Wylie was murdered; and besides, Mr Wylie was the last man in the world to "get up" a mysterious disappearance. Poor Mrs Wylie, his widow, who had been sorely tried by her sudden bereavement, was painfully shocked by the story, which her knowledge of her husband's character forbade her for one moment to credit. Mr Morison, it was generally remarked, was getting old, and his labours with his dictionary must have unhinged his understanding.

But Mr Morison was very obstinate, and very provoked at the

reception which his tale received, and he determined that if he saw Mr Wylie again he would by no means allow him to escape. The very next morning (it was a Sunday), when setting out for his walk, Mr Morison saw Mr Wylie again near the same spot, and he at once went after him as fast as his old legs could carry him. Mr Wylie, who was still apparently determined to avoid being accosted, withdrew rapidly up the hill in the direction of St Andrew Square. The lexicographer, however, gained upon him, and was close up when Mr Wylie reached the gate of a garden, which at that time ran down from the back of one of the houses on the north side of the Square. Mr Wylie passed through the garden door, and Mr Morison, who recognised the garden as one attached to the house of Mrs Grant, mother of Mrs Wylie, attempted to follow. But the garden door was firmly shut in his face. He at once scrambled up the wall, but Mr Wylie had disappeared. There was no time for him to have gained the house before his pursuer had mounted the wall, and it seemed clear that he must have entered an outbuilding at the foot of the garden, close to the door through which he had passed. Mr Morison scrambled over, and tried the door of the outhouse. It was barred. He peered through the window, but there was no one in the washhouse, for such the building appeared to be. Next he hurried round to see if his friend were lurking behind the building. He was not there, but Mr Morison noticed a window at the back. It appeared that there were two apartments in the outbuilding. Mr Morison looked in at the back window. The room appeared to be a workshop, for there were tools and chips lying about, and there, in a corner, was Mr Wylie upon his knees. He had raised one of the planks of the floor, and was rummaging away underneath it. Mr Morison tried to open the window, but it refused to yield. Then he hurried round again to the door, and endeavoured to stave it in. In vain! Several times he rushed round the building, from window to door and from door to window, seeking an ingress. One may have noticed a dog which has run a rabbit to earth in a small burrow. It feels its prey almost at its nose; it scrapes and tears and gnaws the ground, and every moment it springs from one hole to the other in wild excitement, terrified lest its quarry may make a bolt for it and escape. Even so did Mr Morison rush from back to front of the outhouse, now dash himself against the door of the washhouse, and now shake the window of the toolhouse! Never had the discovery even of the most important decision, hid away unsuspected in some dusty tome of manuscript, thrown the worthy lawyer into such a paroxysm of excitement. When the dog gets tired of scraping and snorting and rushing about, it sometimes sits still for a moment, its nose an inch or two from the mouth of one of the holes, and seems to consider what is to be the next move. So at last Mr Morison, mopping the perspiration from his forehead and heaving all over with exhaustion, sat down upon a chopping log beside the washhouse door, and for a moment considered the situation. Upon one thing he was quite determined: not to quit the building until Mr Wylie was taken from it dead or alive. It was only half-past five of the morning, and nobody seemed to be stirring about. Mr Morison scanned the windows of St Andrew Square, but there was not even an early rising servant-maid to be seen. Then it occurred to him to shout, and he gave several loud hulloas, but still nobody appeared. He took another turn round the building, and tried the window again. It would not yield. "Let me see," he said at last, picking up a stone, "I used to be pretty good at a shy in my day. I wonder if I could put a stone through one of these windows."

Dr James Gregory, a man of mark in his profession, round whose memory still cluster some of the most loving associations of every well-regulated nursery, was Professor of the Practice of Physic in the University of Edinburgh, and resided in one of the houses on the north side of St Andrew Square.

The Professor was in bed enjoying his repose, and filled in his moments of half-wakefulness with a delicious, dreamy consciousness that it was Sunday morning, and that therefore there were still hours of untroubled rest before him, when he was suddenly roused by his wife.

"Are you awake, James?" inquired Mrs Gregory.

"No; what is it?" replied the Professor, with less than his usual urbanity.

"I am sure I heard somebody calling."

"Tuts! tuts! you've been dreaming. Go to sleep."

There was silence for a minute or two, and then Mrs Gregory again roused her husband.

"There, James, didn't you hear that? Three shouts quite distinct."

"I don't care if there were fifty," snarled the Professor. "Get up if you are not going to lie quiet, but don't bother me."

The Professor closed his eyes and turned his face to the wall, and for a few minutes there was again silence in the bedroom. Then a tremendous crash made both the Professor and his wife spring from their pillows and huddle themselves, cowering in the back corner of the bed. Some heavy missile had come smash through the window, knocked over a lamp on a table near the centre of the room, and spent its force in shattering a panel mirror on the wardrobe door.

"The French! my dear, the French!" gasped the Professor, throwing his arm around the frightened woman. "God help us all, I knew it would come to this."

There was silence for a moment as they listened for fresh sounds of violence, and then a foot protruding from under the huddled bed-clothes caught the Professor's eye.

"It would be dreadful, dear, if they came in and found us like this," he whispered.

"Come in! Oh, surely, James, they will not, they dare not come into this room!"

"War is war," said the Professor sadly.

"But you will never let them in here? You will protect me, James?"

"With my life, love. Still, it would be better to have something on."

"Yes, you are quite right, James; but all my things are at the other side of the room. If I had even a petticoat!"

"I shall try and get one," said the Professor, rising in the bed.

"But be careful, James; you might be shot passing the window."

"I shall creep along the floor," replied the Professor.

Dr Gregory descended cautiously from the bed, and on his hands and knees he wended his way past the broken glass and splashes of oil to the other side of the room. Out of range of the window he ventured to rise and secure some garments, which he threw across to his wife, and then he pulled on his own breeches. All was now silent outside, and the Professor's curiosity was rising fast.

"I think I shall just peek and see what they are about."

"Don't—James, don't; you may be hit, and what will become of me with these ruffians?"

The Professor, however, was not to be daunted, and creeping to the edge of the window, he ventured to show half an eye round the corner. At first he saw nothing to account for the recent catastrophe; but growing bolder, and looking a little further round towards the foot of his neighbour's garden, he saw there, not a band of blue-coated Frenchmen, but the learned author of the 'Dictionary of Decisions,' who was wildly gesticulating with his hands.

"Well, upon my word," said the Professor, choking with indignation, "if it isn't that man Morison! I knew he was mad. I said he was mad. I told Hope he was mad; and there he is just raving. Get me that gun at once from the top of the wardrobe."

"Oh, James, you're not going to kill him, surely!"

"No, no; but I shall keep him from further mischief; hand me the gun."

An old rusty blunderbuss, which had belonged to the Professor's grand-uncle, and had seen service in the Low Countries in the wars of King William, lay upon the top of the wardrobe, and this weapon Mrs Gregory now handed to her husband.

"Now go and tell Janet to run for the night-watch," said the Professor, as he laid hold of the murderous instrument.

Mrs Gregory disappeared on the errand, and the Professor threw up the window-sash and leant forward on the sill.

"He is here! He is here! Wylie is here! He cannot escape!" shouted Mr Morison in great excitement.

"Look you here, sir," said the Professor, raising the blunderbuss to his shoulder. "You stay where you are, sir. You don't move a foot, sir, or I'll shoot you down like a dog, sir."

"For God's sake, put that thing down, sir. For God's sake, don't point it here. It's me——Morison!" screamed the lawyer, who saw that the Professor was covering him with the weapon.

"Lie down, then, down on your belly, sir, or I shall certainly fire," replied the Professor, placing his finger upon the trigger.

Mr Morison clapped on the ground like a rabbit, and the Professor congratulated himself on his cleverness, in thus at once disarming the maniac and preventing his escape. For several minutes the two men remained watching each other. Every time that Mr Morison attempted to move or to open explanations, the blunderbuss was again raised to the Professor's shoulder, and the lawyer subsided with trembling limbs. At last

two night-watchmen, who had heard the shouting, and had thus anticipated the servant's summons, appeared behind the wall, and peered over.
The sight they saw was one for which even the varied experience of a
night-watchman had no parallel,—a distinguished legal writer stretched
prone in the dust, cowering under the threatened fire of a learned Professor in his night-shirt at the window above!

When the Professor saw the guardians of the public peace scrambling
over the wall he laid aside his weapon, and hastened down to explain the
unfortunate case. He found Mr Morison eagerly relating to the officers
how he had seen Mr Wylie in the toolhouse, and the Professor at once directed the men to have the poor gentleman removed to the watch-house
until his friends could be communicated with. Meanwhile, a number of
people, roused by the disturbance, were collecting at the spot, and scrambling over into Mrs Grant's gardens. Amongst the new arrivals was Mrs
Grant's housemaid, and that girl suggested that before taking the gentleman away they might as well search the outbuilding. The suggestion took
fire, and the girl was directed to run for the key, notwithstanding the
scornful protests of the Professor, who wanted his prisoner marched off at
once. When the girl returned with the key, the company searched the
washhouse, but found nothing; they searched the toolhouse, but there was
nobody there; they examined the beams and rafters of the roof, but Mr
Wylie was not lurking among them.

"I told you so; take him away, take him away at once!" exclaimed the
triumphant Professor.

"He was here! he was here! I tell you he was here!" protested Mr
Morison, wringing his hands, "here in the toolhouse, not a quarter of an
hour ago, in that corner there close to the wall, and he lifted one of the
planks of the flooring."

"Well, well, sir, you had better come and explain about it to the
Bailie," said one of the watchmen, touching Mr Morison's arm. It would
all have been up, and the most industrious of Scottish lawyers would have
been marched ignominiously away to the lock-up at St Giles, but a girl—
the same who had suggested the search—stooped down and tried the different planks of the flooring near the corner indicated. The fourth plank
from the wall came away readily in her hands. Nothing was to be seen, but

one of the watchmen stooped down, and gave a rummage round under the adjoining planks.

"Here's something, at all events," he said, as he drew out a black handbag.

"Why," exclaimed the girl, "that's Mr Wylie's bag; he used to take it out and in every day when he stayed with us in the country."

The bag was opened. It had two compartments. In the one there was a bundle of notes, and two smaller bags full of coin; in the other there were some writing materials, several opened letters addressed to Mr Wylie, and the lease of a farm on the M———— estate, signed by landlord and tenant on the day of Mr Wylie's disappearance.

V

It was the October Communion in the Tron Church of Edinburgh. The sermon was over; the tables had been "fenced," and the elements brought in for the first table service. There were certain details in the conduct of the service that might in our day be deemed lacking in taste or even reverence. But the uncouthness gave no offence, and there was in it not a trace of real irreverence, for nobody perceived or realised it. There was, too, in the whole service, a solemnity—a sense of reality—which is perhaps not always present nowadays even with a more ornate ritual. The Church of Scotland was then all-powerful, because hardly yet rent by schism; her table was the true meeting-place of the people, for all gathered there, the loftiest with the lowliest, to take from the common board and drink from the common cup the symbols of divine love and sacrifice.

The bread had been handed round, and there was stillness in the church as the cups passed from hand to hand along the tables. But suddenly the silence was broken by a woman's scream and a sound of scuffling. A lady had sprung from her place at the table just as a young man seated nearly opposite her had taken the cup into his hands.

"Don't let him drink, don't let him drink!" she exclaimed, as she tried to dash aside the cup from his lips. There was confusion for a moment, as several elders and the church-officer hurried to the spot. The poor lady was bundled out of her place, and hustled away into the vestry; and then, after a pause, the service was resumed. In the vestry the lady, whose mind seemed to be affected, remained for some time in a very excited state. She was a stranger, nobody knew her, and she seemed too hysterical to give any account of herself or her conduct. By-and-by, however, she became calmer, and the doctor, who had been sent for, gathered from her that she was a Miss Beveridge from Milnathort, and that she had lodgings in the Lothian Road. She declined, however, to give any account of her conduct in the church until she had seen her agent, Mr Tod, writer, Kinross. A chair was got, and the lady was taken home to her lodgings. Next day Mr Tod was advised of the unfortunate state of his client, and requested to come to Edinburgh at once. Mr Tod came to Edinburgh on the Tuesday, and went to the Lothian Road to see Miss Beveridge. He found her wonderfully well and composed, but most anxious to have a private interview with him. When they were alone she told him that, seated at the Communion table and happening to look round, she saw the man who committed the murder on the Old North Road, five months before, in the very act of taking the cup into his hands. Overcome with horror at the sight of one thus deliberately drinking everlasting judgment upon himself, she had sprung up at any cost to prevent the fearful act. Questioned as to her identification of the supposed murderer, Miss Beveridge was not to be shaken. She was positive that the man she saw in the Tron Church was the man she had seen commit the cruel deed upon the Old North Road. On making inquiries as to the identity of this man, Mr Tod learned with astonishment that he was a Mr John Grant, the brother of Mrs Wylie, and that in fact old Mrs Grant and Mrs Wylie had been seated beside him when Miss Beveridge interrupted the service.

Secret but diligent inquiries were now set on foot with reference to Grant's antecedents, and the result was far from satisfactory. John Grant, who was now about thirty years of age, appeared to be one of those men who, to great personal charms, a daring spirit, and much mental acuteness, unite a moral depravity which is almost devilish. He had been expelled from the High School when he was nine years old for theft. Sent next to a school in England, he got into one serious scrape after another; and he was eventually sent home for attempting to set the building on fire. Another English school was tried; but he broke into a drawer in his master's bedroom, and carried off his wife's jewels to the pawnshop. He was expelled again. Next living at home and attending classes at the University was tried; but one day a professor missed a large sum from the drawer into which he collected his fees. Grant was strongly suspected, and although nothing was positively proved against him, his previous reputation was such that, taken together with present suspicion, it soon made the place too hot to hold him. Mr Wylie, who had just married Miss Grant, was now induced to take the lad into his office, and for a year or two Grant seemed to have steadied himself considerably. But in the end bills under Mr Wylie's hand were discovered by the bank to be forgeries, and it appeared that a system of fraud had been going on for several years. John Grant, who was then but eighteen years of age, withdrew from the country. For eleven years he led a roving life abroad. The only communications received from him were calls upon his mother for money, and whatever else was heard of him from other sources there was never in it anything of good. Mr Wylie had strong reason to suspect that on more than one occasion, when the purse of Mrs Grant had an unusually long respite, the silence of her son was due to his acquaintance with the interior of a foreign prison. At last, however, after eleven years' absence, Grant returned home, and he was welcomed back, as such sons always are, by his mother as though he were the very salt of the earth. It was ascertained that after his return home Grant had been anxious to obtain from his mother money to fit out a vessel of marque; but the opposition of Mr Wylie, who managed the old lady's affairs and had great influence with her, defeated this scheme. On more than one occasion Grant had been heard to express his indignation at the conduct of Mr Wylie, and several of his friends had heard him, when in his cups, and talking of the pressgang, utter the wish that he could pack his brother-in-law off for six months on a voyage to the Indies. Still more significant was the fact that after his return home Grant had spent most of his time loafing about Leith in company with foreign sailors, and in particular with the skipper of a Portuguese schooner, whose appearance answered exactly to the description of the sailor seen on the road between Blairgowrie and Torryburn on the night of the murder. Grant, too, it was ascertained, when in Mr Wylie's office, had more than once accompanied his brother-in-law on his rent-collecting journeys to Dunkeld, and he knew exactly what was the course of Mr Wylie's movements on these occasions. From a servant who had quitted Mrs Grant's service it was ascertained that Grant left Edinburgh on the day preceding that of Mr Wylie's disappearance. Two days later he returned in the evening, but he remained at home only for an hour or two, part of the time being spent in the toolhouse on the pretext of mending a box. He did not return home again for more than two months, and during his absence his mother was ignorant of his whereabouts.

All these facts, taken together with the mysterious discovery of Mr Wylie's bag in Mrs Grant's premises, seemed to confirm Miss Beveridge's statement, and the whole constituted a damning array of evidence against Grant. But still there was an indisposition to arrest a man respectably connected, and living quietly at home with his mother, on a charge so horrible as that of the murder of his own brother-in-law, without the most conclusive proof of his guilt. Such a proof, it was thought, could be furnished only by his identification by the men who had seen the two travellers between Blairgowrie and Torryburn on the night of Mr Wylie's disappearance. It was accordingly arranged that on the following Sunday the stablemen from the different inns where the coach had called should have places in the Tron Church in view of the seat where Grant sat regularly with his mother. Arrangements were made to have Grant arrested on leaving the church in the event of the testimony of these men confirming that of Miss Beveridge.

The identification was complete. The men left the church, by arrangement, the moment the benediction was pronounced, and none of them had any difficulty in certifying that Grant was one of the men who had been on the post-chaise on the night in question. As Grant left the church, a man touched his arm and informed him that a certain officer at the Castle was anxious to see him at once. Leaving his mother to find her way home, Grant turned up the High Street towards the Castle. When Mrs Grant was well out of sight, the man who had given Grant the message came up to him in company with another man.

"Well, what is it now? what do you want?" said Grant sharply, when he noticed the men.

"Excuse me, Mr Grant," said the one who had not yet spoken to him, "but I hold here a warrant for your arrest."

"On what charge?" inquired Grant, without changing colour.

"The wilful murder of Andrew Wylie."

"Oh, very well, if that is so, so be it," replied Grant, with extraordinary self-possession; "but you will perhaps permit me first to go home to get some things."

"No, I am sorry I cannot; my orders are imperative to take you to jail at once. Anything you want will be sent for."

"Ah!" said Grant, fumbling in his pocket; "it doesn't matter, you know, only this is a very public place, and I see they are just coming out of the High Kirk. I always like to spare good people's feelings when I can."

The officers did not quite understand the remark, but they had not proceeded a dozen paces when they noticed that Grant was staggering heavily between them, and before they could get out their hands to support him he had fallen backwards on the causeway of the High Street, just in front of the north doorway of St Giles' Cathedral. A small phial slipped from his fingers, and a hoarse, contemptuous laugh rose from his throat. For a moment he lay still, his eyes almost closed, and a crowd of worshippers coming from the church gathered round to see what was the matter. Then his whole frame was racked with frightful convulsions, that caused the group of ladies issuing from church, and attracted by the gathering crowd, to scatter right and left with cries of horror. But the paroxysm was soon over, and he was still for a moment again. Then he stretched himself, as a man stretches himself before rising, a short sigh passed from his white lips, there was a slight shudder, and then the limbs relaxed. John Grant lay dead upon the causeway, and the clock in the crown-steeple above struck one of the afternoon.

The Killing Game

BILL KNOX

ONE

hat's that over—he's safely out of the parish and strictly Central Division's headache for the rest of the day!" Chief Detective Inspector Colin Thane thrust his way into his tiny office in Millside Division's C.I.D. Section, gave a grunt of relief, and tossed his folded raincoat on top of the nearest filing cabinet. His hat followed, then he appealed to the thin, dry-faced figure who leaned against his desk. "How about a cuppa, Phil? I've been trudging round these dam' shipyards till my feet feel ready to fall off."

"Tea?" Detective Inspector Moss gave a cynical grin. "Fancy it Russian style, with lemon?"

"Funny, helluva funny!" Colin Thane scowled, then concentrated on loosening the unfamiliar, stiffly starched white collar his wife had insisted on him wearing. "Last time I used one of these was at a funeral. My neck feels like a slab of raw beef."

"So the guest day's over," mused Phil Moss, pressing the desk buzzer. "What about the 'Ban the Bomb' brigade?"

"There, complete with banners." The collar gave way to brute force. "The uniformed branch had to shovel up about twenty of them who tried a sit-down outside one of the yard gates." Thane moved round the desk and relaxed into the worn leather of the swivel chair set behind it, his feet going up to land unerringly on the one small space not occupied by a debris of overdue paperwork. "Outside of that it was quiet enough."

It had, but—he felt soured as he thought of the way his Thursday morning had been wasted. Acting as nursemaid to any kind of visiting politician wasn't a task the Millside C.I.D. chief could enjoy. When the

politician was General Igor Shashkov, Soviet Minister for Industrial Development, visiting the city of Glasgow as part of a guided tour of Scottish
factories, the nursemaid role had seemed even less attractive than usual.

"A trade and goodwill visit!" Thane snorted. "Phil, give me thief-
catching any day compared with this morning's nonsense. Shake hands,
we're all pals together . . . there were half a dozen Government types
from London with him, secretaries and under-secretaries for this, that,
and the next thing. Not to mention a posse from Special Branch and Home
Office security, with a little firecracker of an Irishman called Donnan running their side of the show. And if that quartet of musclemen Shashkov
has with him are Russian-style civil servants I'll give up my pension!"
Thane stopped as there was a knock, the door opened, and a uniformed orderly looked in. "Sam, we could use some tea—extra sugar in mine and
you're halfway to being a sergeant."

The orderly grinned, nodded, and went out again.

"We've got one or two things on the go, Colin." Moss moved towards
the desk and salvaged a bundle of report sheets lying within a fraction of
Thane's right heel. "You know about the overnight stuff, but the rest came
in while you were showing your pal Shashkov around."

Thane grunted and brought out his cigarettes. "Want one?"

Detective Inspector Moss shook a reluctant head. "Still off them . . .
and I think it's working."

"Makes a change from having the place littered with pills." Thane
chuckled. "Though how the devil the scheme's supposed to work beats
me. What does it come down to? Mind over matter?"

Phil Moss was bleakly unresponsive. He'd long since ceased to expect
sympathy for his stomach ulcer. And he saw nothing particularly humorous in his latest attempt to escape the hands of surgeons who appeared
bent on trimming little pieces off his insides. He'd discovered the new
treatment programme in a health magazine he'd picked up during a raid
on a bookshop which stocked too heavy a percentage of pornographic literature. No smoking, no drinking, a vegetarian diet backed by liberal
helpings of strained arrowroot gruel, half an hour's special exercise in
front of an open window last thing at night . . . maybe mind over matter
wasn't too wide of the mark. He sighed and turned back to the work
at hand.

"First on the list is a slashing over in Creshow Street . . . man attacked as he left home after breakfast to walk across to the local bookie's office. Sergeant MacLeod is handling it, but the fellow who was carved won't talk. Says it was just a 'wee misunderstanding.'"

"Which he'll put right in his own good time," murmured Thane. "What else?"

"Another complaint about Jock Howard's mobile pitch-and-toss school. It was operating on the waste ground behind Profirth's factory last night. Woman says her husband gambled away twenty quid, his week's wages." Moss compressed half an hour's voluble protest into a clipped recitation. "Think we should try paying Jock a visit?"

"With his organisation?" Thane shook his head. "Pinning him down when he's actually operating would amount to a military operation. I want to catch him, not end up the way we did the last time, empty-handed and looking like fools. Anything more?"

"Aye. One I've been working on . . ." Moss broke off as the orderly returned. The uniformed man crossed the room and thumped two heavy tea mugs on the desk, each with a slice of toast balanced precariously on its rim.

"Switchboard was making some, sir," he reported. "I flipped a coin with the radio room for the toast—they lost."

"Thanks." Thane pondered at the sight. "Sam, you're pretty lucky at this sort of thing—"

"Sir?" The orderly hesitated. "Well, I make a bit on the horses now and again, if that's what you mean. But it's research that pays off with the horses, not luck."

"Uh-huh. Sam, I'd like to see you before you go off duty tonight." Thane waited until the man, still puzzled, had departed. Then he gave Moss a slow wink. "Like I said, Phil, let's leave Jock Howard out of the reckoning for the moment." He took a long gulp from the tea mug. "Now, you said you'd been working."

"Somebody has to," said his second-in-command pointedly. "This came in with the despatches from Headquarters. Better see it for yourself." He slid one of the sheets of paper across the desk and sipped his tea as Thane began reading.

An outsider, meeting them for the first time, would have decided that the two men formed an odd study in contrasts. Tall, dark-haired, burly but easy moving, Colin Thane was in his early forties and still close to the peak of his physical condition, apart from a strangely growing tendency to need a larger size in shirt collars. Married, with a bungalow home on the south side of the city, most of his off-duty life revolved around his wife Mary, their two youngsters, an adolescent boxer dog named Clyde and a garden which seemed fated to never receive the attention it required.

His second-in-command differed all along the line. The cherished ulcer apart, Phil Moss was a few years older than Thane, small, wiry, with sparse, sandy hair. Almost round-shouldered, a bachelor given to baggy suits with bulging pockets and crumpled lapels, Moss had lived in one boarding house for almost ten years—during which time his landlady had abandoned all hope and interest in smartening him up.

And there were other contrasts, contrasts which made them a smooth-functioning team whose professional pairing was backed by a solid personal friendship.

Thane was the thruster, the one prepared to back a hunch, then sweat out the result. Thane disliked the documentation, the cross-filing, the indexing which seemed to grow in volume and need every day—disliked it as much as he used it. But he realised it was part of the fine-meshed detail of investigation which landed many of their customers in jail.

In a fight, Thane seldom bothered with his baton and had long ago lost the key to his handcuffs. Phil Moss used both when necessary, could mix it with any company, but was happiest when he could go his own dry, querulous way on some task which called for the absorption of detail, the sifting, grinding pursuit of a problem . . . like now.

"One of the unexpected blessings of the nuclear age." Thane put down the report sheet and lit a fresh cigarette. "Ever heard of it before?"

Moss shook his head. "No, but it's handy."

Handy was the word. Thane drew on the cigarette as he glanced again at the typewritten sequence. The Atomic Weapons Research Establishment's new seismology station in the Perthshire Highlands was primarily intended as one of a growing chain of NATO listening posts, each capable of giving a precise bearing on any nuclear test held anywhere in the world. Their instruments could track down even the most carefully hidden underground blast.

The "bonus" was because the scientist designers had taken the precaution of setting up smaller, automatic units within a fairly tight radius of each main station, allowing an easy check on local, natural disturbances in the lonely, industry-free Highland area. Within its first week of operation the Perthshire post had begun logging and pinpointing various local explosions occurring at isolated places either just off the coast or on quiet upper stretches of certain rivers—salmon poachers dynamiting pools and estuary stretches for quick returns of saleable fish. Now the atom men had a working arrangement with the police, and the dynamite gangs were often being pounced on while still gathering their harvest of stunned, helpless fish.

"But yesterday afternoon the Perthshire cops find a body instead, and think it could belong down here," mused Thane. "In Glen Lyon, near the river—good fishing round there, Phil. Who's handling their end of it?"

Moss grinned. "Our old pal Detective Inspector Roy. Not that he's got much to work on."

"There never is—if you happen to be hugging a few sticks of gelignite when they explode." Thane winced at the report's clinical exactitude. "Appears to have been wearing brown corduroy trousers and a leather jacket . . . any luck with this dry-cleaning mark they mention?"

"I think so." Moss absent-mindedly reached into his pocket for a cigarette, then remembered. "The real reason the job was passed on here was the ballpoint pen they talk about, one with an advertising slogan stamped on it. The pen came from the Redmond garage over in King Street, but they say they hand out hundreds of the things."

"Nothing else on the body?"

"I phoned Roy and asked. Just some other odds and ends that don't give any help. If there was a wallet or anything like that it must have been destroyed in the blast. But this cleaning mark is local all right. I traced it to Langley Laundries' branch shop—also in King Street. They allocated it to someone called G. Shaw who had a pair of corduroys cleaned. No address, the trousers were simply handed in at their counter."

Thane lowered his feet from the desk, reading the expression on his companion's face. "You've found him?"

"There are five G. Shaws listed in the telephone book as living in the division," said Moss carefully. "Number four is a George Shaw, a tobacconist. According to the girl assistant at his shop, he's currently on a fishing holiday in the Highlands. She had a postcard from him yesterday, postmarked Aberfeldy."

"A handful of miles away from the glen," nodded Thane. "Got his address?"

Moss pursed his lips. "He's married, Colin. I was going to send young Beech along—no option. He's the only one free, and I'm on the witness list for the Richmond trial. I'm due at the Sheriff Court in fifteen minutes."

Slowly, Thane rose and began to refasten his shirt collar. "I'll take it." Detective Constable Beech was both young and eager. But more than that was needed when you went round to tell a woman she was probably a widow—then went on to ask her help you prove it.

George Shaw's home was in Wheatlands Avenue, a trim, quiet row of semi-detached villas on the suburban west fringe of Millside Division, a world removed from the industrial grime and tenemented slums which formed Thane's more usual operational area. It was just on noon when the C.I.D. duty car, grey, with an unobtrusive aerial, coasted along the avenue and halted outside Number 42.

"I won't be long—I hope." Thane nodded to the uniformed driver, got out, and walked up the short length of flagstoned path towards the house. He rang the doorbell, heard a dog bark, a woman's voice, and then the sound of an inner door being closed. A moment passed, and then the front door opened.

"Mrs. Shaw?"

She was in her mid-thirties, small, sturdily built, dressed in an old jumper and skirt and obviously midway through the day's housework. The dog barked again from somewhere inside and she smiled. But the smile faded as she looked down the pathway and saw the car parked outside, the uniformed man at the wheel.

"I'm a police officer, Mrs. Shaw. Can I come in?"

She swallowed and hesitated. "Yes, but—what's happened? Is it the shop . . . something wrong there?"

He shook his head. The woman stepped back and he followed as she led him through the hallway to a small lounge where a vacuum cleaner was still plugged to a wall socket.

"If it isn't the shop——" There was a growing fear in her eyes. "Has something happened to George?"

"Better sit down a moment, Mrs. Shaw."

She moistened her lips and obeyed. "What's happened?"

"We're not completely sure, Mrs. Shaw. I'm sorry, but that's how it is. Where is your husband?"

"On a fishing trip, up north. He left last Saturday."

"Do you know where he was going?"

"Nowhere definite——but I had a letter from him yesterday saying he'd been fishing near Aberfeldy. George goes away for a ten-day holiday like this every autumn, just fishing. We——we have our own holiday together earlier." She moistened her lips again. "Would you mind if I had a cigarette?"

"Please . . ." Thane offered her one from his pack and gave her a light. "You haven't heard from him since? By telephone?"

She shook her head.

"Mrs. Shaw, was he wearing a leather jacket and corduroys?"

"Yes." The hand holding the cigarette was quivering, but her eyes remained steady. "Is he dead?"

He nodded, finding silence the best sympathy.

"While he was fishing? I——he couldn't swim. I——I've always been frightened that——"

"It was another kind of accident, Mrs. Shaw." Thane tried to avoid telling her more. "That's why we couldn't be sure, why it was difficult to identify him."

"But——" Her mouth fell open. "What about Peter? You mean they were both——"

"Both?" Thane's voice echoed his surprise. "Your husband wasn't alone?"

"No." She shook her head, bewildered in her imprisoned grief. "George was with a friend, Peter Herrald. They were camping out in George's van. Didn't——didn't you know about Peter?"

It was Colin Thane's turn to shake his head. Another man, and a van——completely missing from the picture. He got up from the chair.

"What happened——how did he die?" Her eyes pleaded an answer.

"There was an explosion." He fumbled for the correct words. "It would be very sudden, Mrs. Shaw. I'll have to ask you more, but that can wait for a little. Is there anyone—?"

She swallowed hard and nodded. "My sister. She lives just along the avenue. It's not far . . . Number 80."

"I'll tell her to come." He put his hand on her shoulder for a moment, then went out. He heard the woman begin to sob as he reached the end of the hallway beyond. At the sound, the unseen dog began whining, claws scratching furiously at the door which separated it from its mistress.

An hour and a half later, the duty car returned Thane to Millside police station, driving through streets where the shoppers were already thinning as they sought cover from the first heavy droplets of a typical September rainstorm. The clouds grew blacker and the drops became a battering downpour as the Jaguar pulled to a halt outside the down-at-heel two-storey stone building which was the divisional office. He made a quick dive across the pavement into the main door, stopped to wipe some of the rain from his forehead, then strode through into the uniformed branch's public office.

The duty sergeant greeted him with a grin. At the last divisional golf outing, uniformed branch versus C.I.D., he had beaten Thane by three and two.

"'Mazing how popular this place is soon as it rains, sir. Cops come popping in from all parts."

Thane glanced round. "Your boss among them?"

"Chief Inspector Craig?" The sergeant nodded. "He's in his room, Mr. Thane."

He spent ten minutes talking with Craig, who ran the uniformed side of the division, then headed up to his own part of the building. The C.I.D. main office was busier than it had been earlier in the day. Five men were at their desks, writing or telephoning. Detective Sergeant MacLeod was in wooden-faced conversation with a fat, twisted-mouthed youngster whose eyes carefully avoided the cloth-wrapped bundle on the table between them.

Thane walked past, jerking his head towards the nearest of the others. "Jim—"

D.C. Sinclair murmured a quick goodbye into the telephone, hung up, and followed Thane through to his office.

"What's young Donny Bruce been up to?"

"Housebreaking, sir."

"Again?" Thane grimaced. "And his brother?"

"Still looking for him as usual, sir. Donny's always the slower when it comes to running." D.C. Sinclair shifted uncomfortably. There was also the point that Vince Bruce could outrun anyone in the Millside Division.

Thane let it pass. "I want you to go to a dentist called Spicer in Glebe Street. Ask him for an exact copy of the dental record of a patient George Shaw. After that, take it to Headquarters—they'll send it on to D.I. Roy at Perth. If there's any difficulty tell Spicer an upper-jaw chart would be enough."

"Sir?"

"There's more of it left," said Thane patiently. "Get moving."

Thane lifted the telephone, then lit a cigarette in the brief seconds before the girl at the downstairs exchange answered.

"Jean, get me Aberfeldy police—D.I. Roy of Perth should be there. If not, ask them to have him call me back." He hung up and was busy spreading a large-scale map of Perthshire across his desk when the office door opened and Phil Moss strolled in.

"Richmond heard the first two witnesses and changed his plea to guilty," said Moss wryly. "Left me with my party piece unsaid, but he got three years. What happened out at Shaw's home?"

"Seems pretty definite it's him. But he had a pal with him, and they had a van. I sent Perthshire a flash report, and I've another call in now." The telephone shrilled and he reached for the receiver, nodding towards the extension earpiece. "Be my guest."

D.I. Roy's gruff voice boomed over the line a moment later and echoed in their ears. "Mr. Thane? It's been a while o' time since we had our last bit o' work together."

"A spell," agreed Thane, winking to his second-in-command. "You got my message?"

"Aye, and we've double-checked most of the glen since then," rumbled Roy. "But there's no' a sign o' another man or a van anywhere around. Mind, we're still lookin'—but if what you say's right there's somethin' damned queer about it."

"I've got more on them now." Thane found his notebook and flipped it open. "They were travelling in a plain red Morris Mini-Van, registration number YGE 670—it belonged to Shaw and there was camping gear aboard. Shaw was thirty-eight, height five foot seven, heavy build, dark brown hair, small moustache. The neighbours say he was the quiet, go-to-church-on-Sunday type and that fishing was his only outside interest. You should have his dental chart this afternoon."

"That'll help," said Roy somberly. "And the other one?"

"Herrald? Height five eight, age about the same, medium build, fair hair but thinning on top, unmarried. Also in business on his own, runs an import-export and manufacturers' agency. His background is pretty sketchy, part from the fact that he lives alone. But I'll have more on him later."

"Maybe by then we'll ha' a bit more ourselves," declared the Perthshire man. But it's a hell o' an area to ask a handful o' polis to cover properly. Mountains, lochs, a sprinklin' o' rivers, and a devil o' a lot o' deer forest—and September is a month when nobody pays much attention to campers or anglers. You'll find 'em wanderin' all over the place. Ach, probably they were tryin' their hand at the poachin', and Herrald got into a panic when his pal was blown up—maybe he just got in that wee red van and went as far an' as fast as he could out o' the place."

"Anything's likely." Thane looked down at the map in front of him. "But this place where Shaw was found doesn't seem particularly close to the river."

"True enough. But there's an old forestry road near it, an' a fairly easy walk from there to one or two good pools." Roy sniffed. "Aye, maybe they were both fine and respectable in Glasgow. But when a man's awa' from home . . . well, about the worst poacher I ever met was a surgeon up from London. He always blacked his face when he went out, an' used a nylon net as if born to the game." He broke off, and the Millside men heard a brief, muffled conversation at the other end of the line. Then Roy's voice boomed again. "Here's a wee bit news we've just heard. Your two started their trip north on Saturday. An' some time over the weekend somebody broke into the explosives magazine at Flenders Colliery near Stirling an' went away wi' a load o' gelignite an' detonators. It was discovered on the

Monday—the Stirlingshire lads thought it was some safeblower stockin'
up for the winter. But Stirling's nice an' handy on the road from Glasgow
north!"

"Interesting!"

"Aye, just so," agreed Roy. "Well, I'm awa' back up the glen. But I'll
keep in touch."

The line went dead. Thane replaced his receiver then grimaced. "So
they're 'our two' now!"

"Ever heard of a county force that didn't claim its local bad hats were
all refugees from the big city?" Moss eyed him thoughtfully. "It's time we
ate. I don't suppose—"

"If you're going to suggest I eat in that fruit-and-nut place you took
me to last time, the answer is no—once was enough!" Thane was emphatic. "Anyway, I'm going to Headquarters. I want to look in at Records
and make sure neither of these two are on the files. I'll eat over there—
the Headquarters canteen always has lamb chops on the menu on Thurs-
days. Meet me there in about an hour, Phil, and we'll go out to Herrald's
office. I was told he has a part-time secretary who works afternoons only,
and I want to see her."

At three P.M. the Millside duty car collected Thane from the Headquarters
building in St. Andrew's Street. He climbed in the back beside Moss and
their driver steered back into the traffic flow, a clogging, crawling mixture
of vehicles moving nose to tail.

"Find out anything back there?" asked Moss.

"Neither has a record and the chops were good." Thane leaned forward. "What the heck's jamming up the traffic?"

Their driver supplied the answer as he inched the car still nearer the
bus ahead. "That Russian V.I.P., sir—he was lunching with the Council at
the City Chambers. Then he was going on down to Ayr to see Burns's Cottage . . . dead keen on Rabbie Burns's poetry, these Russians. Central Division were to keep a route clear for him—the Russian bloke, I mean. This
is the backwash."

"Huh." Thane resigned himself to the situation. "Anything fresh
with you, Phil?"

Moss nodded. "I made a couple of phone calls after I'd eaten. Shaw was a member of an angling club. I located the club secretary and said we'd probably be round to see him. It might be useful."

"Might." Anything might. Thane chewed gently on his upper lip, feeling a growing annoyance at the way in which he somehow found himself refusing to accept the clear-cut conclusions which were so apparently obvious from what facts they had. Yet even the facts seemed wrong in places. The explosion had been in the afternoon. Would any poacher—even two city men who might lack experience—be fool enough to risk the chance of being caught in daylight by a patrolling water bailiff when darkness's shield was only a few hours distant?

And where was Herrald? Hiding somewhere in a panic—or could he be wandering in those hills, concussed, perhaps injured from the same blast which had killed his friend?

It was almost a relief when the car reached St. Enoch's Square, found a parking place, and he had no more time for wandering thought.

Peter Herrald's office was a room on the top floor of one of the squat business blocks which fronted the west side of the square. The elevator, an antiquated self-operated cage, creaked them up and they stepped out on to a rabbit warren of corridors speckled with frosted-glass doors. HERRALD AGENCIES was seventh on the left, there was a light visible through the glass, and they went in.

Two men were already there, talking to an elderly, mousey-haired woman. They turned towards the door, as it creaked open, and the nearest of the men blinked in surprise.

"Didn't expect you here, sir—"

Thane recognised them as d.c.'s from the Central Division. The senior of the two was eyeing him anxiously. This was Central Division territory, but it was always wise to regard visiting chief inspectors as potential trouble.

"The surprise is mutual." Thane's twinkle was disarming. "Just following through a Millside inquiry. And you?"

"The lady here—Miss Douglas—made an emergency call about fifteen minutes back and reported a break-in." The Central Division man frowned. "She says there's some cash missing. Trouble is, the only positive thing we've found so far is a forced lock on a petty-cash box."

"And the mail." Miss Douglas broke in with the shrill dignity of a veteran spinster who finds her word doubted. "I told you, some of the letters had been opened."

Thane nodded soothingly. "I'd like to hear about it, Miss Douglas." He glanced at the Central Division d.c.'s, but they were more than willing to surrender the questioning. "Let's start at the beginning. When did you get here?"

"A little before three o'clock." She flushed a little. "Usually I'm in at two-thirty. But Mr. Herrald is on holiday, and I've very little to do."

Thane looked round the little office with its two desks, chairs, a large cupboard, and a smaller metal cabinet. There was a calendar on the wall but no shade on the solitary electric-light bulb. Miss Douglas had a type-writer, and a kettle and gas ring sat side-by-side in one corner.

"There's only Mr. Herrald and yourself?"

"That's correct," said Miss Douglas firmly. "It's a small business, just orders coming in from customers and Mr. Herrald making sure suppliers meet delivery—that, and some contact with the docks and shipping firms. I'm here every afternoon, but I've told him one day a week would be enough for all the work there is."

"And the break-in?" Thane prompted her on. "These officers can't find any sign of a window forced or the door damaged—"

"But someone has been here," snapped Miss Douglas. "I know. First, there were the morning's letters—some had been opened, then thrown on Mr. Herrald's desk as if the burglar had been looking for money. Then this cash box from my desk—it had ten pounds in it, and that's gone. When I saw that, I telephoned the police then tried Mr. Herrald's desk. He locked it when he left, but it's open now, and—"

"Did he keep any cash there?" Phil Moss broke his silence.

She glared. "Kindly don't interrupt. Mr. Herrald always kept about two hundred pounds inside one of the folders in the bottom drawer—we don't have a safe, and a business like his often has to operate on a cash basis. The money's been taken."

"It was there when he left?"

"He told me it was." Miss Douglas drew herself upright. "I had a key to the desk—if necessary, I'm prepared to be searched." Then her eyes widened. "By a policewoman, of course."

Thane ignored a gurgle from one of the Central men. "I don't think that's needed, Miss Douglas. Isn't there an easy explanation? He's on holiday. Couldn't he have run short of cash, come back here, used his own keys to get in and open his desk—perhaps even had a quick look at the mail while he was at it?"

"Impossible." She gave an emphatic shake of her head. "For one thing, he would have left a note if he'd been here. And the cash box—Mr. Herrald wouldn't touch it. I've got the only key, and the money isn't his or mine. It's for a children's fund. I go round the offices in the block every Monday, collecting from the staffs. If you're suggesting he forced the cash box, then you're accusing him of theft."

Thane didn't press the point. "Does he own a car?"

"Yes, but he can't use it just now. It was in an accident early last week—he said the repairs wouldn't be finished until he got back from holiday."

"And you've no way of contacting him?"

"None." She pursed her lips impatiently. "All he told me was he would be on a fishing trip, camping with a friend. Can't you trace him and tell him what's happened?"

"We're already trying to do that, Miss Douglas—on another matter. Have you a key to his flat?"

"Good heavens, no!" The suggestion brought the mousey-haired spinster close to blushing. "I've never met Mr. Herrald outside of business hours. But I can give you the address . . ."

"We have it." Thane turned to the Central Division twosome. "Sorry, but all this could be caught up in another affair. Get the boffin squad to come over, will you? Tell them I want the place really gone over, no skimping. And I'll need a copy of a full statement from Miss Douglas, soon as you can. Phil—"

"Uh?" Detective Inspector Moss had been looking out the window.

"Come on, let's get over to this flat."

Hands deep in his pockets, Phil Moss nodded gloomily. He was beginning to be infected by a definite premonition of further trouble, trouble which wouldn't cease until Peter Herrald had been located. On second thought, even that might be only a beginning.

He followed Thane out. Behind them, the Central d.c.'s exchanged looks, then one reached for the telephone.

Peter Herrald's flat was small, self-contained, and one of half a dozen service flats situated in an old converted mansion in Highrigg, once part of Glasgow's upper-crust area before rising costs and the servant shortage had sent the original occupants scurrying in search of "mod. cons." and central heating in the new bungalow suburbs. A fifteen-minute drive took them from the city to the mansion, the car swinging off the road and up a short length of wide, gravelled runway to the main door of the ivy-crusted Victorian-style building.

The caretaker, a little man with a scowl and bad breath, answered their hammering knocks on the door—the ancient bell was out of order.

"Herrald? Round the back—'bove what the toffs called the stables." He gave a leering wink. "Polis, eh? What you wantin'?"

"The key." Phil Moss fixed the man with a dyspeptic glare. "When did you see him last?"

The caretaker shrugged. "Can't remember. They come an' they go, mate. Not my job to keep track of 'em—I've enough worries. What d'you want the key for?"

"To open the—" Detective Inspector Moss made an effort. "Just get it, will you?"

The man shuffled off and reappeared a few moments later, the key in his hand. "My boss won't like this happen', you know. The folk here are a complainin' shower at the best."

"Maybe he'd like it better if we kicked the door in. We don't mind, either way," said Thane.

"Ach, polis—" the key was handed over, the caretaker shuffled back inside the building, and the door slammed. The two detectives grinned and walked round to the rear of the mansion, past a one-time vegetable garden which had degenerated into a wasteland of weeds. Herrald's flat seemed the only one with its entrance to the rear, its curtained windows glinting in the sunlight above their heads. The small entrance door was close beside the broad double doors of a lock-up garage.

They went in, and found themselves in a narrow hallway. To the right, an access door opened on the lock-up, which was empty. Ahead, a short flight of carpeted stairs led upwards to the flat. At the top, they found a wider hallway with the apartment's rooms leading off on either side.

The first check took a matter of seconds.

"Either he's an untidy cuss, or he's had visitors," mused Thane, looking round the living room. Like the adjacent bedroom, it was in disorder. Not the disorder they found after a housebreaker had been on the prowl with time at a premium, but a milder, more domestic chaos. A coat lay over a chair back, a sideboard drawer hung open with a miscellany of articles jumbled within, a cupboard door gaped open.

"This must be Herrald." Moss scooped up a framed photograph from the fireplace mantelpiece. The picture showed a plump, fair-haired, mildly good-looking man, a smile on his face as he held a silver trophy aloft. "Wonder where he won that?"

"Here it is." Thane walked over to the window and lifted the cup from the sill. "Highrigg Gold Club Annual Match Play Championship, it says. Hey, he's pretty good too, Phil. Won this with a final round of sixty-four, according to the engraving—over the Highrigg course that's dam' smooth going." He put the cup down again. "Better hang on to that photo—and we'll give the place a going over while we're here."

They got down to the job. Minutes passed, and Thane was exploring the contents of a lean-stocked grocery cupboard when he heard Moss give a sudden shout from the bedroom.

"What's up?"

"This." Phil Moss held out his handkerchief. It was, as usual, grubby. But in the middle of the linen square lay a polished metal cylinder the size of a cigarette stub.

"Watch it—these things can be temperamental." Thane prodded the detonator with a cautious forefinger. "Remember old claw Jackson!" For the Millside Division, it was both a standard warning and grim attempt at humour. Jackson had been a safeblower. He'd lost most of his right hand when he held a detonator for too long and the skin temperature had set it off.

"Found it lying loose among some socks at the bottom of his wardrobe." Moss laid the detonator on the bed cover, then scratched his head. "Looks as if Herrald's an old hand at dynamite poaching—if he kept his stock in the wardrobe, this one could have rolled into a corner and been forgotten. Well, what do you think? Has he done a bunk?"

Thane lit a cigarette and drew on it. "I don't know, Phil. But it's getting difficult to argue against the idea."

Difficult? Between the unsolved visit to Herrald's office and the appearance of the flat, a reasonable inference was that the man had crept back into the city, gathered any money he could, perhaps a change of clothing, and then had got out fast. Reasons? Even discounting the colliery magazine break-in as just a possibility when the detonator pointed to Herrald already having a stock of explosives, there were other penalties waiting the manufacturers' agent when he was located. Unlawful possession of explosives, linked to Shaw's death no matter how accidental that had been, was a charge likely to draw a heavy sentence. In addition, there was the likelihood of another couple of years being added if Herrald could be proved to have been dynamite poaching for salmon.

"Let's make sure there aren't any more of these around." His voice was bleak.

Half an hour later, all they'd uncovered was a little more detail about Herrald's personal background. He seemed to dress well but quietly, smoked both pipe and cigarettes, stocked a good whisky, sent his dirty washing to a laundry. Letters and other papers they discovered in a drawer showed he was thirty-nine, Glasgow born, had been a Royal Army Service Corps captain in World War II, sometimes holidayed abroad and apparently wrote regularly to a married sister living in London. In all, it was the typical pattern of a comfortably established bachelor with no worries either financial or otherwise.

But that was a detonator lying on the bed—and George Shaw was a shattered corpse, George Shaw's wife a widow.

"That looks like the lot for now." Thane threw down the last of the papers. "The boffin squad can give the place a going over once they're finished with his office. I'll leave you to fix it, Phil. Wait here till they come, just in case that caretaker decides to explore. Okay?"

Moss nodded. "Where do we link up, and when?"

"Well—" Thane was uncertain. "Give me that club secretary's address. I'll have a word with him for a start. I'll try to be back at the station in about an hour." He gave a slight grin. "Unless there's more trouble on the go, I'll head home after that and have a meal."

"Might as well pack a bag while you're at it," said Moss pessimistically. "Even money says we're chasing down to London after this character before daybreak."

Gerry Cowan, secretary of the New Anglers Association, was a licensed bookmaker by trade but an angler by inclination. Any attempted jokes about the poor fish he hooked through either occupation had long since died of old age, though his punter clients seemed to be caught regularly, to judge from the fitted cocktail bar, deep fitted carpet and Danish teak furnishings of his private office. Downstairs, the faithful were queuing to put their bob and half-dollar bets on the last race of the day. Upstairs, he toyed with the chrome-plated American casting reel he used as a paperweight and shook his head.

"George Shaw go dynamite poaching, Chief Inspector? Not a chance. I could tell you half a dozen boys who'd do it soon as kiss their mothers. But not our George. He's an angler is George . . . straight up. He's been on the club committee since we got together four years ago. See that fish up there—" He pointed to a massive salmon mounted in a glass case above the bar, and Thane nodded appreciatively. "That's a thirty-pounder, Chief Inspector. George gaffed it for me on the club outing last summer, after I'd had a right ding-dong with it for two hours solid. George go dynamiting?" His tones were shocked.

"What about his friend Herrald?"

The bookmaker screwed up his eyes. "Wouldn't like to quote you odds. The bloke isn't in the club, an' I've only talked to him the odd time George brought him along to a club outing."

"Did he know much about fishing?"

"Herrald? Pretty much of a beginner. First time I saw him fly-cast, he practically hooked his own backside. But I'll tell you why I'm so sure about George. He was fishing up north last year, and saw some blokes cymaging a river pool. Know the stuff? Like cyanide—anyway, a sugar bag full of powder, and you kill everything that swims for miles downstream. Takes the oxygen out of the water and the fish drown. Well, George whistles up the cops and gets a fifty-quid reward from the river owners. Know what he did? Gifted half of it to the club funds and got himself some new tackle with the rest."

One of the telephones at his elbow gave a soft tinkle. The angler answered it, but it was the bookmaker who replaced the phone a moment later.

"Last race coming up, Mr. Thane." He paused suggestively.

"Just one more question." Thane rose to his feet. "Supposing somebody did dynamite a pool and got away with it. What would he clear in hard cash?"

"Depends. A good pool, say twenty–thirty fish, average weight, selling 'em in the right place . . . a couple of hundred quid, maybe less, maybe more."

"A profitable night!"

The New Anglers' secretary stroked the casting reel. "I'll stick to running a book, Chief Inspector. Horses are more reliable."

TWO

Thane was back at his desk by a little after 5 P.M. On the way, he'd paid a brief call at George Shaw's tobacco shop, but the girl assistant behind the counter could tell him only one thing of any value. According to her, Shaw had originally planned the fishing trip as a solo expedition, then had later invited Herrald to join him.

He found a message waiting from Phil Moss. The Scientific Bureau team who'd checked Herrald's office and flat reported there was no sign of a forced entry at either place. If doors had been opened, then keys had been used. On the fingerprint side, only Miss Douglas's "dabs" and one other set had been found at the office, with Miss Douglas's the only clear prints on the rifled cash box. The second set of prints had been repeated throughout Herrald's flat, were the only ones found there, and probably belonged to the missing agent. Phil Moss had mopped up at the two places and had moved on, planning to contact some of Herrald's friends.

Thane sat back and looked at the divisional map on the wall opposite. It sprouted a collection of flags and pins, thin on the outskirts, clustering close near the central area, each a job for his team. The newest of the pins was beside Profirth's factory. A slow grin slid to the corners of his mouth, he reached out, pressed the buzzer button, then waited. In about five seconds flat the door opened and the orderly peered in, his expression hopeful.

"Sam, I've got some work for you. Come in and shut the door."

Constable Sam Newton obeyed with alacrity. Uniformed men attached to the C.I.D. sometimes got the odd spot of plain-clothes work, and that could lead to a permanent transfer.

"Ever played pitch-and-toss, Sam?"

"Now and then." It was a cautious understatement. Sam's home county was Lanarkshire. Out there, a pitch-and-toss school, two pennies flipped skywards from a wooden stick, bets won and lost on how they landed, was a regular recreation for off-shift miners behind every second coalbin.

Colin Thane leaned back, hands behind his head. "I've had a word with Chief Inspector Craig. For the next few days you're off all duties. Draw ten—no, make it fifteen pounds expenses, change into your weekend rig, and see if you can join in Jock Howard's pitch-and-toss school. They change their location every night, and he covers every game with half a dozen 'minders.' You know what that means—the punters scatter any time a cop strays within a quarter of a mile of them. I want to know where they'll be before they get there—and then have a squad waiting. Jock runs a straight game, but it's still against the law and we're getting too many moans from clients' wives."

"I join in the betting, sir?"

"That's the general idea. Any objections?"

Constable Newton had none. Thane gave him a signed chit for the fifteen pounds expense advance and Newton trotted off to draw the money. As the door swung shut behind him the telephone rang and the Millside C.I.D. chief answered it.

"Yes?"

Detective Inspector Roy's voice rumbled over the line. "Just a wee tip-off call, Chief Inspector. I'm back in Perth at the moment, an' just out from a session wi' the Chief Constable, who's no' awful happy right now. Did you know they'd brought that auld devil MacMaster up from Glasgow to do a p.m. on our body?"

"First I'd heard of it." Thane was more interested than surprised. Professor MacMaster, Glasgow University's chief forensic authority, was always happy to launch off anywhere there was an interesting corpse. "What did he make of it?"

"Murder!" The county man barked the word. "Aye, that shakes you, doesn't it?"

Thane whistled his surprise, his grip tightening on the receiver. "He's sure?"

"He howked a bullet out o' what was left o' the man's chest," declared Roy. "It was dam' cleverly done, I'll say that much. The blast destroyed any sign o' an entrance wound, an' a lot more besides. But auld MacMaster found one or two things he didna feel happy about. Things that made him think maybe Shaw had been a dead man when that gelignite went off. He prodded around a bit, an' found he was right."

"The gun?"

"A nine-mil. Mauser pistol, according to ballistics. Was Herrald ever in the army?"

"Last war, Service Corps."

"Aye, just the boys to collect wee souvenirs. It's goin' to be interestin' to meet this fellow. But there's another thing you'd better know . . . the bosses up here have decided to ask Glasgow for help, what wi' the complications and us no' being like some places I'll not name where this happens every other day o' the week. They're askin' for you, seein' you're half involved already."

"Which is my bad luck." Thane scowled into the phone's mouthpiece.

"Aye." The county put a wealth of blunt, grim humour into the word. "You're senior man, Chief Inspector. I don't mind—in fact, you're dam' welcome. See you soon!"

He hung up. Thane did the same, but slowly.

Two men had gone fishing. Two apparently ordinary, friendly individuals, neither with particular worries or cares. Now one was murdered and the other—it looked as though Peter Herrald had a stronger than ever reason for running. Yet what had happened? A quarrel because Herrald had suggested a try at dynamite poaching, maybe produced the explosives, with Shaw threatening to drag in the police?

For the moment, he pushed it from his mind. It looked like being his worry soon enough, and he was going to get at least one decent meal before that began.

On his way out, he stopped at Sergeant MacLeod's desk in the main C.I.D. office. "I'm going home, Mac—while I can. Tell the switchboard, will you? When Phil Moss comes in, he'll have a picture of this character Herrald. Send it straight to Headquarters—we'll need it copied and probably photowired to all forces."

"Sir?" MacLeod raised an eyebrow.

"They've just found a bullet in his pal." He didn't stop for further explanation.

The evening rush-hour traffic was at its peak on the journey out of town, and he cursed the amount of clutch-pedal work involved as he steered his small five-year-old Austin at the tail of one of the snaking queues of vehicles.

At last he won free, left the main road, and a few minutes later drew in at the kerb outside his home. As he got out, a familiar tan-and-white bullet streaked barking towards him down the garden path. Then, tail stump wagging, Clyde escorted him to the front door.

"On time for once!" Mary Thane said it with a twinkle as he came in. "And relax—school homework's done."

Tommy and Kate were in the living room, watching the teatime Western on television. He settled down with them while Clyde sprawled before the fireside—then Mary returned and promptly shepherded them through to the table, leaving the dog in complete possession.

"How was school, Son?"

"The usual, Dad." Tommy concentrated on his bacon and egg.

"Kate?"

"We had fire drill, but there wasn't a fire." His daughter sighed at the educational injustice.

"Mary—anything happen here?" he asked hopefully.

"The sweep came." She chuckled. "He's a new one. Says you arrested him once for housebreaking or something—Jimpy something-or-other."

"Jimpy Donaldson. Always was a ladder man—" The doorbell cut him short.

"I'll go." She went through and returned in a moment, Phil Moss at her side.

"Trouble?" Thane half-rose from his chair.

"No—though I looked in at the office and MacLeod brought me up to

date. You told me you'd be here, remember?" Moss winked at the two children. "How's life, youngsters?"

"We're getting nature study at school now, Uncle Phil," contributed
Kate. "It's fun!"

"If it involves fish, don't tell your father." Moss grinned, then shook
his head as Mary Thane prepared to set an extra place. "Not for me,
Mary—I'll settle for a cup of tea and some bread and butter."

"Still on that diet?" She, at least, was sympathetic. And, reading the
signs, she whisked the children from the room back to the television set as
soon as they'd finished, then left the two men alone in the room.

Thane pushed his chair back and lit a cigarette. "You were right about
the overnight bag, Phil. Perthshire are asking for assistance."

"I'm ready—if you need me." Moss chewed his lip thoughtfully. "For
what it's worth, Herrald's car is definitely out of action. I've seen it at the
garage where they're patching it up, and it's a mess—a bus skidded into
him. And he'd definitely no money worries—his bank says he has plenty
of cash on account. His secretary was right—that business of his needs little effort and has a surprising turnover."

"Plenty of agencies are the same," said Thane. "Have a good list of
contacts and you're made. What about friends, relatives?"

"No relatives here. His father is dead, his mother lives with his sister
in London. I located a couple of people who know him fairly well, but he
seems to have been a pretty quiet type."

"Women?"

"One, a blonde, a receptionist at the Northburn Hotel. Tall, slim,
cool—you know the type." He grimaced. "'Just good friends' according to
her, and she hasn't seen him for over a week. Her name's Barbara Mason.
Want her watched?"

"Better fix it up." Thane shrugged. "Though if Herald is running, he
could be anywhere by now, and that includes being abroad. You know,
Phil, I just don't understand it—"

"Why he did it?" Moss waved aside the forming protest. "All right, I
meant if he did it. We probably won't know the answer to either till we
find him."

They heard a car draw up outside the house. Thane got up, walked
over to the window, and looked out. A police driver was already walking

up the front path. He recognised both car and driver—they were from Headquarters. Chief Superintendent William Ilford, head of the city's C.I.D., believed in direct collection when he wanted one of his divisional chiefs in a hurry.

"Sit down, Colin." "Bhudda" Ilford, a bulky, balding figure, used a second match to get his pipe going to satisfaction, nodded towards the chair opposite him, then tamped down the pipe's glow with one thick thumb.

Thane obeyed, his feet meeting the threadbare section of carpet where a generation of C.I.D. men had rubbed a worn patch while wondering what the man on the other side of the desk had in store for them. The carpet, the faded wallpaper, the heavy, oak-stained bookcase—nothing ever seemed to change in this room, where the city's violence, crookery, and corruption were represented by an untidy bundle of cardboard files perched precariously on one edge of the desk.

The Chief Superintendent took his time, sucking his pipe, his eyes downward in that state of apparent contemplation which had earned him his irreverent nickname.

"I've had a request from Perthshire, Colin. They want me to send you up to help find this fellow Herrald." He sucked the pipe and beamed blandly. "I've also had another request that I keep you right here in Glasgow, where you won't get in the way of some other people who are very interested in what's happened to Mr. Herrald."

"Who? What's going on, sir?" Thane stared at Ilford in amazement.

"Home Office security branch are worried about him, probably with good reason." Ilford sucked his pipe, found it had died, and solemnly relit it. "We had a—well, a discussion let's say. You're still going north, Colin, but the compromise is that you'll co-operate to the limit with the security people. They'll do the same . . . or so they say. All right?"

"Yes, but—"

"You want to know what it's all about. I've got someone here who knows more of the details than I do." Chief Superintendent Ilford flicked the desk's intercom switch. "Ask Colonel Donnan to come through, Peggy."

From the next room, his secretary acknowledged. Ilford closed the switch and gave a slight wink. "You know the name?"

Thane did . . . which made the way things had turned all the more startling. He rose from his chair as the door opened and in came the plump, apple-cheeked little Irishman he'd met only that morning, the man running security arrangements for General Shashkov's tour.

Donnan's handshake was brisk and businesslike. "Try not to look quite so surprised," he pleaded, his soft native brogue sparkling through the words. "And before you ask, I'm still doing the same job, chief nurse-maid to our Redland visitor."

"He's still safe and sound?"

"Tucked up safely in a double-cordoned hotel a handful of miles from Prestwick Airport, but peeved because someone took a shot at him and then got away."

"When?" The news left Thane bewildered. "What happened?"

"This afternoon." Donnan helped himself to a chair and perched on the edge. "We were lucky, in more ways than one. For a start, the shot missed—the range was too long. This fellow pops his head over a wall just as Shashkov is leaving Burns's Cottage. One shot and he was off—he had a motor cycle waiting, stolen in Ayr at noon. We found it again an hour later."

"And are you trying to tell me you think this might have been Peter Herrald?" Thane didn't try to hide his scepticism.

"Lord, no!" It was Colonel Donnan's turn to be surprised. "Look, there's enough confusion right now without making more. What matters is we've got the bullet fired at Shashkov. It came from a nine-millimetre Mauser, and your ballistics people are rushing a comparison with the bullet from that body in Glen Lyon. We think it was very probably the same gun. For the rest—" the security man's face lost its humour "—well, I'm going to tell you a story, the same story I told Chief Superintendent Ilford less than an hour ago. There's been nothing of this in any newspaper, and I'm waving the Official Secrets Act and Defence Regulations like bed-sheets to keep it that way."

Bhudda Ilford relit his pipe for the third time. Thane read the signal, offered Colonel Donnan a cigarette, lit one himself, then sat back while the little Irishman rose from his chair and paced the room, his voice quiet but every word counting.

It had begun a week before, near the little fishing town of Arbroath, on the north-east coast. First, a rowing boat was found dragged up on the beach one morning. Next, a big diesel-powered trawler had come into port, her skipper demanding in agitated, broken English that five of his crew who'd taken the boat and gone ashore should be returned immediately.

"There's always a flock of Iron Curtain trawlers operating in deep water not far off that part of the North Sea," explained Colonel Donnan. "They've got a chain of bigger mother ships with freezing plants for their catches, and mostly stay outside the three-mile limit. We're ninety-nine per cent sure that one or two of these trawlers carry more radar and radio-monitoring equipment than they do fish nets, but that's by the way."

It had happened before, though not often in such numbers. The five trawlermen had taken the chance of their vessel being moored close in-shore, had grabbed the rowing boat in the middle of the night, and had made their personal choice for freedom.

The local police and immigration officials talked to the trawler skip-per, the trawler finally went out to sea again . . . and the police cells at Ar-broath were readied waiting the five trawlermen coming out of hiding. They'd have to be held in routine custody until their expected pleas for po-litical asylum had been formally dealt with.

"Well, they're still waiting on four of 'em," said Colonel Donnan bit-terly. "The fifth turned up a day later and said he'd changed his mind. He had a wife and family back home, and he was worried about what would happen to them. The trawler came back in and picked him up."

But his comrades—using the word loosely—had completely disap-peared ashore. Martin Kelch, Vilkas Stender, Arkan Bretsun, and Taras Serviev, all were Lithuanians. Martin Kelch was the one who had organ-ised their flight from the trawler. Kelch spoke English and knew the Scot-tish north-east—in the chaos at the end of World War II he'd spent a year in a refugee camp not far inland.

"Our fifth man said Kelch had talked 'em out of asking for asylum here. He had some crazy plan about making for London, then stowing aboard a ship bound for America." The security man shrugged. "Well, that's been tried before too. What really worried us happened when our fifth man heard that General Shashkov was coming visiting here. He went into a panic—said that if Kelch got wind of it we'd better look out.

"Kelch's two brothers were purged by the Reds a few years back—knocks on the door at midnight and then never seen again. Like to guess who was the area party boss at the time? General Shashkov."

To Thane, part of the story was now all too clear. "So you believe Kelch and his friends plan to—"

"The dictionary word is 'assassinate,'" interrupted Bhudda Ilford mildly. "Colonel Donnan's theory is that Shaw and Herrald, out on their angling trip, met them, found out too much, that Shaw was killed in some sort of a struggle, and that they may be holding Herrald prisoner until they've—ah—eliminated Shashkov." He used the pipe as a pointer. "He has one rather slender fact to back it—slender, that is, until we know about the comparison result."

Colonel Donnan nodded. "We've picked up the occasional trace of Kelch and his three pals, but always too late. The last was in the public bar of a hotel at Aberfeldy two nights ago. A man answering Kelch's description was seen talking to two men who appeared to be anglers."

Bhudda Ilford grunted. "And from the police side, the last trace we had of either Herrald or Shaw was in the same bar." He gave a heavy sniff.

Thane glanced from one man to the other, a faint twinkle in his eyes. "Who finally meshed the two stories together, sir?"

Colonel Donnan gave a hasty cough and got in first. "The Chief Superintendent has the credit, Thane. Then we had a discussion of the situation and he . . . we agreed that the circumstances warranted a joint-investigation procedure. I want Kelch nailed before he tries again. How or why your two men were involved is fringe detail from my point of view. General Shashkov's visit has three days more to run, and I want to see him safely off the premises at the end of that time. Shashkov is a big man in the Moscow setup. He may be nineteen different kinds of a snake by some standards, but he's over here on a diplomatic mission and qualifies for full V.I.P. protection."

"Snakes usually have fangs of their own," murmured Thane. "He had some tough-looking imports with him this morning. Do they know what's happening?"

"His bodyguard certainly know all about Kelch, and that he's liable to have it in for Shashkov—the fifth trawlerman must have used that information to talk his way out of a possible spell in Siberia." Colonel Donnan flushed. "After this afternoon's potshot, I've been threatened with a top-level Moscow-to-London protest unless we nail all four, and the line it'll take is that we've been morally aiding and abetting them."

The telephone at Bhudda Ilford's elbow rang once, and he lifted it. He listened quietly for a moment, thanked the caller, then replaced the receiver.

"You've got two links now, Colonel," he reported mildly. "Ballistics say the same gun fired both of the bullets we're interested in."

"But Shaw and Herrald—" the information steered Thane back again to his own, earlier, harvest. "What about the raid on the explosives magazine at Stirling? Then we've found a detonator in Herrald's flat, and somebody visited there and at his office, gathering any cash they could find." He rubbed his chin ruefully. "I'll admit the whole situation seemed wildly wrong even before I came here, but—"

"I'm pretty certain Kelch raided the explosives magazine," declared the security man. "All right, I'll be honest. I didn't know a dam' thing about these explosives until I got together with the Chief Superintendent this evening. Sometimes security can be its own worst enemy. As for why Kelch would want explosives—" he gave a faint sigh "—I'd give a lot to know the exact answer. The possibilities have been giving me mental nightmares. And I'll tell you this—don't catalogue Kelch as a simple trawlerman with a vengeance bug. Our information is that there was a time when he was a qualified lawyer, before his family fell foul of the wrong people."

"And lawyers don't think like normal people." Bhudda Ilford struck another match and puffed smoke. "Not in my experience. They specialise in smoke screens. They don't say black is white—they prove it."

Thane gave a slow nod. "Which means Kelch could have planned to make Shaw's death look like an accident, then organised the rest to make it appear that Herrald was making a bolt because of the possible consequences—taking the money, planting the detonator where we'd find it, leaving us floundering in his own particular smoke screen."

It fitted, fitted the pattern of a man who could blend apparently unrelated steps into an organised purposeful campaign.

"Colin—"

"Sir?" He glanced towards Ilford.

"There's a car waiting. Take Phil Moss with you. It's seventy-three miles to Aberfeldy if you take the Sma' Glen road once you get north. I'll expect a call in a couple of hours." He pointed the pipe again as Thane rose. "I'm not going to give you a lecture on how to handle this, but the fewer who know the full story the better."

Colonel Donnan pulled an envelope from his inside pocket and passed it over. "That's what we've got so far on Kelch and company—not much, I'm afraid. I'll have to stick with Shashkov more than ever now, but my people will give you any direct help they can. You'll find contact details in there too."

Shashkov and Kelch, assassination and diplomatic poker play—Thane said goodbye and left. The security man had called George Shaw's death "a fringe detail." Perhaps it was, compared with the threat of another, more successful attack on the Communist leader. But as he boarded the waiting C.I.D. Jaguar and it purred through the old-fashioned stone gate pillars and on to the road beyond, Colin Thane held to another concern. Was Peter Herrald still alive?

It was a concern far simpler to handle than the complexity of sympathising with a killer whose revenge wish was so easy to understand, so hard to condemn.

The car picked up Phil Moss, and fifteen minutes later they'd cleared the city. Their driver glanced at the dashboard clock—just on seven P.M. His foot pressed down on the accelerator, the engine's response sent the speedometer sweeping up and round in a fast curve, and he felt happy. He reckoned on being in Aberfeldy by late dusk, and Thane was one Chief Inspector who didn't mind drivers smoking on duty.

With less than fifteen minutes to go before closing time, the public bar of the Tayman Hotel at Aberfeldy was smoke-filled and busy. Detective Inspector Phil Moss nursed his tomato juice at the little corner table while his Perthshire counterpart took a long swallow from a pint mug of draught beer.

"Beer on duty, whisky for pleasure," declared Detective Inspector Roy, a large, beefy man wearing a dirty fawn waterproof coat and a brown Homburg hat. "You know these parts, Moss?"

Phil Moss shook his head. "Not unless you count being here for two weeks' holiday when I was a youngster." The drive up had been pleasant despite the pace involved. The finest stretch had been across the high, lonely Sma' Glen road where each twisting corner was more likely to disclose a flurry of small game quitting the tarmac than the sight of another vehicle approaching. Then he remembered the swoop down from the moorland into the forested valley, the distant circle of snow-tipped mountain peaks. ". . . nice countryside. I like it."

"Reasonable, reasonable." Roy's regional pride was satisfied. "The river's the thing, though. Where Shaw and Herrald were, on the Lyon, isn't bad. But the real fishin' starts here, on the Tay."

Moss nodded. The talk around the bar seemed equally divided between "the fishin'" and some scandal over the price of a bunch of Blackface sheep sold at the town market the previous week.

"There's a wee stretch o' water I sometimes try mysel'," said Roy. "It's owned by a man I did a bit obligement for once. There's some fine fish waitin' the right rod. The Tay's got the British salmon record—a sixty-four-pounder, man! A clean fifty-four inches long, and caught by a tiny slip o' a girl." He shook his head at the injustice.

"Time's getting on," frowned Moss. "You're sure this man Mac-Lennan will come?"

Roy was positive. "Five minutes to closing time and he'll walk in that door, have two drinks and then be away again," he declared. "You don't know the folk around these parts, but they settle into regular ways. According to the station sergeant, Archie MacLennan's only been missin' twice in the last ten years—that was when they took him to hospital wi' a broken leg an' kept him in over the weekend." He took another gulp at the beer. "Well, that boss o' yours fairly shattered all my pet theories wi' the story he told when you got here. What do you make o' it, eh?"

Moss shrugged. He'd heard the story twice now, first in the car coming up, then when Thane retold it to Roy. Now Colin Thane had gone off in the car on an errand he'd described as "just trying out a hunch," and he was here with Roy, waiting the prophesied arrival of the nearest thing to a witness they seemed to have.

"That's him now." Roy nudged with an elbow, his eyes on the man who had just entered the bar. MacLennan was a tall, sparse figure, white-haired, hollow-cheeked, wearing an old blue-serge suit and heavy boots.

As he reached the counter the barman nodded and passed over a ready-filled glass. Roy rose and winked. "I'll let him ha' that one, for lubrication, then bring him over."

A couple of minutes passed before the Perthshire officer returned, MacLennan by his side, two fresh whiskies in his hand. The introductions over, MacLennan settled down in a vacant chair.

"You're a forestry worker, Mr. MacLennan?" opened Moss politely.

"Aye, at times." MacLennan took the offered glass and held it delicately. "*Slainch*—" The Gaelic toast over, he drained the glass, sucked his lips, and sat silent.

"You look in here most nights?"

"Effery night," corrected MacLennan. "I told Mr. Roy here all about that already this afternoon, and about the two fellows who were in here a couple o' nights back. What else are you after?"

"Just a few more questions about them," said Moss easily. "The barman says he remembers a third man being there, talking to them—but he didn't pay much attention to what was happening. Now we know who the first two were, Glasgow men called Shaw and Herrald. Did you notice this other man?"

"Aye, but nobody effer asked me about him."

Detective Inspector Roy flushed pink. "You could have told us."

"You asked me about two men an' I told you about two men." MacLennan made it matter-of-fact. "You didna mention the foreigner."

"You're sure he was foreign?" Moss leaned forward.

"Foreign or English," said MacLennan stubbornly. "It can be hard to tell, the way they talk at times."

Moss nodded, and D.I. Roy pushed the remaining glass of whisky across the table.

"What did they talk about?"

"Well—" his hand closed round the fresh glass, but this time he merely sipped "—a bit about the fishin', like most. The two Glasgow fellows did most of the talking, but they seemed to know the third one. They called him Martin—"

"Martin Kelch?"

"All I heard was Martin." Their witness glanced at the bar clock. "Then he went out, and the other two had a last drink on their own."

"You said you saw Herrald and Shaw drive off," reminded Roy.

"Aye, chust as the bar closed. I saw them gettin' into a wee red Mini-Van, chust the two of them."

"And that was the last you saw of them?"

"It was." MacLennan frowned. "Are you interested in this other one now, the one they called Martin?"

"Particularly," agreed Moss. Then his eyes widened. "Why? Have you seen him since?"

"No, but I did the day before that," said the forestry worker cautiously. "In the evening to be exact. I was just on a wee walk up Glen Lyon, admiring the scenery along the river—"

"And with a net and gaff hook handy?" growled Roy.

"Admiring the scenery, Inspector," repeated MacLennan doggedly. "Then I heard a wee bit noise, and thought it might be a gamekeeper. Gamekeepers can be as—as misunderstandin' as the police at times, so I turned off the path, thinking I'd take my walk up over the hill instead, preferring to remain anonymous, you might say. Anyway, I was up near the deer fence on the north-east plantation when I saw a bit smoke and took a look to see what it was—campers wi' their picnic fires can burn out a lot o' trees. But it was all right. Only some fellows camping in that old ruin of a shepherd's cottage up there, well clear o' the trees."

"And Martin was there?" Roy's voice was hoarse now.

"He was, though mind you, I never bothered going close enough to have a word wi' them."

"You preferred to remain anonymous," said Moss dryly, conscious of Roy now struggling for control. "Can you describe this man Martin?"

The forestry man finished his drink. "Well, now, he'd be about ordinary height but thin, fair hair cut close . . . in his thirties, I'd say. A good tan on him as if he'd spent a fair time in the open. And when he was in here I noticed he had a big white-metal ring on his left hand." Apologetically, he started to rise. "Now, unless there's anything more, I'll need to be away home—my wife'll have the kettle on."

"That's all we'll need for now," nodded Moss. He asked Roy, "You know where this cottage is?"

"I do." The Perthshire man rumbled the words. "MacLennan, why the devil didn't you tell me this before?"

MacLennan blinked. "You didn't ask me, Inspector, that was all." He pushed back his chair, gave them a vague salute, and stalked his way out of the bar.

"Tight-mouthed, self-preserving . . ." Roy began a low-voiced Technicolor monologue as the bar door closed. "I know—I'm as much to blame. I should have asked him. But of all the . . ."

Phil Moss cut him short. "It happens that way. Look, how do we get up to this cottage?"

"Tonight?" Roy grimaced. "Ach, maybe you're right. We've lost time enough already. We can go most of the way by car, along one of the forestry roads. There's more rut and pothole than surface, but it'll save the best part of a couple of miles walk. When do we start?"

"Now."

They got up and went out, as the bar's closing bell began its clamour and the barman began his first appeal to the rest of his clients to "Drink up, gents . . . time now, please!"

Roy's car was a Ford Consul and he drove it himself with an angry, gear-grating resolve which kept Moss gripping hard on the instrument panel as they roared along the narrow, winding roadway. A handful of miles passed, they crossed a rumbling metal bridge, and then the inspector swung the steering wheel and sent the Ford bounding up a narrow sidetrack. The car's head lamps showed the thick, orderly rows of spruce trees which pressed close on either side, its springs groaned and heaved as the tyres bounced and jarred over the rough surface.

Finally, Roy slowed the car to a gradual halt and switched off the lights. "We'd better walk the rest—it's no' much further."

Phil Moss swallowed hard, relaxed his grip, and nodded.

Half a mile's stumbling progress along the track brought them to the cottage, just beyond a point where the plantation timber thinned and stopped. In the pale moonlight it showed as a grey, almost roofless skeleton.

"No sign of life," said Moss. "Not that I expected any. They'd move on pretty quickly after what happened."

Roy had a wide-beamed pocket torch and they went closer, using its light to thread a path over the soft moorland. The cottage's shell was empty all right—they went through the door space, found dry, cold wood ash in the hearth of the stone fireplace, fresh soot on the solid-built chimney. There were other signs of occupation, scraps of paper, cigarette stubs, a piece of old canvas which appeared to have been used to extend the shelter of the broken roof, a few emptied food tins.

"They picked a good spot," said Roy, shining the torch around the rough stone walls. "Hardly a soul ever comes up this way—it's too far from the river, and the forestry road was only put through as a possible fire-fighting route. Seen enough?"

"Here, yes," said Moss slowly. "The scientific bods can give it a going over in daylight."

"If I'd brought the car up it would have saved us a hike."

"That's what was on my mind." Moss felt his ulcer give a sharp nag and winced at the familiar warning signal that he was both tired and hungry. "But let's make a circle around before we go back."

"Looking for what?" Then Roy understood. "Tyre tracks—aye, the ground's soft enough."

The torch's beam found the tread marks where they left the forestry road about thirty yards south of the cottage. From there the tyres had followed an almost straight course in towards the trees. They crossed the distance, stopping a few yards within the edge, and Roy swung the torch's beam in a slow-moving arc. At first there was only the still, shadowed mass of the trees, then Moss gave a hiss of triumph as the light was suddenly thrown back at them in the glow from a red reflector disc.

The Mini-Van was there, squeezed into the narrow space between two bushy spruce trees, covered in a camouflage of broken branches and leafy scrub.

Phil Moss pushed his way through to the passenger side, opened the door, then reached back for the torch. Roy handed it over, and he played the beam round the interior of the vehicle. The rear space held a miscellany of fishing gear, tumbled together as if disturbed in a hasty search. But the front compartment showed signs still easier to read. The driver's window was shattered by a neat bullet hole, there was a dark red stain on the grey upholstery fabric.

"Well, that's the van," murmured Roy. "An' I half-expected another body wi' it."

"Did you want one?" Moss's voice was acid.

"Ach, don't be daft." Roy grinned ruefully in the torch-light. "But man, you've got to admit—it would ha' made things that wee bit simpler!"

THREE

Colin Thane drew his coat a little closer round his body and gave an involuntary shiver. The temperature was only partly to blame, though there was a nip of frost in the air on this mid-September night and the country road where he stood was both high and exposed. For the rest, the cold, ramshackle gloom of the scene illuminated by the police car's headlights was reason enough.

The derelict and abandoned Dunspar Refugee Centre, on the Perthshire side of the boundary between that county and Angus, had originally been built as a World War II camp for an army anti-aircraft battery. When the army withdrew, a fresh coat of paint, a few extra stoves for the Nissen huts, and some clothespoles on an ash-surfaced drying green had readied it for its next phase, living quarters for about fifty DPs from Europe, families and individuals still trying to adjust to the future—or to the fact that there might be a future.

Years had passed since the last of the refugees had left Dunspar Centre, most back to their homelands, others abroad, a few settling in Scotland. The Nissen huts had been bought and removed by a scrap merchant, only the concrete bases, isolated walls of brick, a few forgotten coils of barbed wire and a scattering of other flotsam, remained as dreary reminders of the place which had once been "home" to Martin Kelch.

The scanty file handed over by Colonel Donnan didn't help very much.

There were the brief, basic descriptions of the four men. Martin Kelch, late thirties, fair hair, thin face and build, medium height, white-metal ring on his left hand. Taras Serviev, a few years older, stocky build, medium height, close-cropped grey hair, small moustache. Arkan Bretsun, youngest, about twenty-eight, brown hair, dark complexion, slim build, smaller than the others. Vilkas Stender, mid-thirties, brown hair, height about five-ten, medium build, finger missing from his left hand . . . four men from the sea, four men who'd managed to elude every attempt to locate them. The two main items in Donnan's file showed just how completely these attempts had come to a dead end.

The first, a detailed report from Arbroath, only repeated what Thane had been told before and added a few adornments. When it had been discovered that Kelch had once lived in the area, his name had been found in old records of Dunspar Camp's occupants. Three ex-refugee families from the camp, now settled locally, had each been questioned but claimed they'd had no contact with the runaways.

The second report, from Donnan's main agent for the North East, was equally unhappy. Discovering Martin Kelch had been seen in Aberfeldy had been pure luck. Donnan's man had gone there on another task, a standard background screening of an Admiralty employee being transferred to a new secret project. He'd asked around about Kelch and his companions as a matter of routine, believing them long since gone from his territory. When he stumbled on the truth, it was too late. The trawlermen had vanished again.

But from Arbroath, the North Sea fishing port, to Aberfeldy, the Highland tourist centre, was more than sixty miles. Somebody must have helped them cross that distance—which was the slender reason why Thane had left Moss and Roy at Aberfeldy and had made the hour-long drive to Dunspar Camp.

He took a last look at the camp, turned on his heel, and walked back to the Jaguar. The driver wriggled into a more upright position behind the wheel and restarted the engine as Thane swung aboard.

"According to the map, there's a village called Greenbank about half a mile on. I want the local police force—he'll probably be at home in his slippers, watching telly."

The driver grinned and slid the Jaguar into gear.

Greenbank was little more than a score of cottages clustered in a hollow which was protected from the east wind by a sturdy belt of larch trees. Its single street was deserted, but a few yards past the one and only general store and just across the road from its tiny hall-church, a blue lamp with the sign POLICE marked their destination.

The small, brick-built house was both home and office for the village constable. Thane knocked, and the man came promptly enough to the door, fastening his tunic buttons with redoubled speed the moment he saw his visitor's warrant card. Thane looked down at the village man's feet—just as he'd said, thick, comfortable carpet slippers. There were compensations in being posted to the backwoods.

"Come in, sir!" The constable was young, probably in his mid-twenties. Too young for Thane's purpose.

The "office" room of the house was partly occupied by a clothes-horse filled with rows of children's clothing. The constable flushed scarlet and bundled it into a corner.

"I'm trying to find out about the old refugee camp along the road," Thane told him. "Who lived there, who they knew in the village, that sort of thing. Can you help?"

The younger man shook his head. "Not much, sir. I only came here a couple o' years back when old Willie Murray retired from the force." He frowned. "I had a visit from the district sergeant a few days back, and he was asking about the camp too. Wanted to know if any strangers had been seen around—but there've been no reports so far."

"What about Murray? Does he still live in the village?"

"Two cottages down the road, sir—but he's in the next room right now. He often looks in for a blether—my wife was just getting a wee cup o' tea for us when you came. I'll get him to come through . . ."

He went out and returned with ex-Constable Murray, plump, bald, wearing old, frayed police-issue trousers with a heavy roll-necked wool jersey and obviously delighted to be summoned.

"Aye, I was here when the first batch o' they refugees reached Dunspar," he confirmed. "They'd had a pretty rough time, most o' them, a rough time. Despair Camp, some o' the locals used to call it."

"Remember any of the people at the camp?" asked Thane.

The ex-cop nodded. "A few. They were here for a year or so, most of them. Folk in the village used to ask them home for a meal, that sort of thing."

"How about one in particular, a man called Martin Kelch, a Lithuanian? He's in his late thirties, fair-haired, medium height, thin build. Wears a white-metal ring."

"Kelch?" Murray pondered. "Well, it's going back about fifteen years, sir. He'd be in his early twenties then. Wait though—that ring! Aye, I remember him all right." He chuckled. "He made a good few o' those rings up at the camp and sold them in the village. Nearly landed in trouble when I found out where he'd been getting the metal—stripping bits o' plumbing fitments out o' the church hall. But the minister didn't want to prosecute."

"Had he any friends around the village—close friends?"

The ex-policeman's eyes narrowed. "I heard the sergeant was around asking about the camp the other day. You mean the kind o' friends a man could come back to after a long spell, is that it, sir?"

Thane nodded.

"And it's important?" The ex-policeman seemed to hesitate. "Things change, you know, Chief Inspector. Some folk might find it awkward to be reminded of what happened a few years back."

"And the friend could be a woman," Thane guessed the rest of the reason. "I don't want to drag skeletons from cupboards, Murray. But whether it's going to embarrass the lady or not, I'll have to see her."

"That's what I thought you'd say." Murray scratched his chin unhappily. "All right, her name's Moira Brendon, her husband is Big Jock Brendon who runs Greynan farm—just up beside the old campsite. Back at the time we're talking about, her name was Moira Paul and she ran around quite a bit with young Kelch."

"I'll take it easy with her," promised Thane.

"It's no' her I'm worrying about, at least not the way you think," said Murray gloomily. "Jock Brendon didn't come here until after the camp was closed. There were only one or two folk like mysel' who knew just how close Kelch and Moira were—putting it politely. And if Jock Brendon ever found out, he'd belt that wife o' his from here to yonder and back again."

A cat darted into the shadowed darkness as the Jaguar pulled into the farmhouse yard a few minutes later. Greynan farm was modest in size, a big barn and a few outbuildings grouped round the side and rear of the single-storey farmhouse where lights showed at the curtained windows.

Thane ignored the front door—in the farming counties, front doors are strictly reserved for weddings, funerals, and similar occasions. The cat scurried off again as he walked from the car to the kitchen door and rapped on the brass knocker.

He heard the clack of high-heeled shoes on a stone floor, a light blinked on above him, and then a woman's voice asked, "Who's there?"

"Police, Mrs. Brendon."

The door was unlocked and opened a few inches, still held secure by a guard-chain. Moira Paul, now Brendon, looked round the edge. She was small, a red-head, a little too plump, and wore more make-up than he'd expected. From her looks, fifteen years back she must have rated as the belle of Greenbank village.

"My name's Thane—Chief Detective Inspector." He held his warrant card into the stream of light.

"My husband's out." She stared at him, panic in her eyes. "If you want him, you'll need to come back."

"I've come to see you, Mrs. Brendon. I can come back if you want, but you—well, you might prefer to get this over while you're on your own. I'm looking for Martin Kelch." He jammed his foot in the door as she tried to close it again. "That's not being sensible. There's your husband to consider—" It was a nasty piece of arm-twisting, but it got results. The pressure eased on his foot, she slowly unchained the door.

"You'd better come in." Her voice was flat and resigned. He followed her into the farm kitchen, a big warm room which smelled fresh and looked clean. A table was ready for supper, a pot simmered on the old-fashioned black cooking range, and two armchairs were set one on either side of a crackling log fire. She gestured him towards the nearest of the chairs, took a cigarette from an opened packet on the table and lit it in quick, nervous fashion.

"Why did you come here?"

"I told you—I'm looking for Martin Kelch." There was a big grandfather clock in one corner of the room and he saw her eyes flicker towards it. "How long till your husband comes home, Mrs. Brendon?"

"Ten minutes, maybe less. He . . . he's at a farmers' meeting over at Alyth." She drew in a breath. "Martin isn't here."

"But he's been, hasn't he?"

She didn't answer.

"Listen to me, Mrs. Brendon." Thane's manner changed, his words rapped across the room. "I'll spell it out for you. Tell me the truth and I can be out of here in five minutes. Your husband needn't know anything about this visit—or about what you and Kelch were to each other. As far as I'm concerned that'll be your part finished. But if you even as much as bend the truth then I'll be back, at a time which may not be so—well, let's say convenient.

"Now try again. Has Kelch been here?"

She nodded.

"When?"

"Last Thursday—two days after he got away from the trawler."

"How many others with him?"

"Three. He . . . Martin said there had been another one, but that he'd been too scared to go on." She sat on the arm of the chair opposite and faced him squarely. "Jock doesn't know anything about it."

"Tell me from the beginning."

She took a puff at the cigarette. "It was on the Thursday evening. Jock had gone out to an N.F.U. committee meeting. He'd hardly gone before Martin knocked at the door, just like you did."

"You recognised him?"

She gave a faint half-smile. "Time doesn't really alter people when you've . . . when you've known them well, Chief Inspector. He told me he'd seen me earlier in the day, when I'd come back to the farm from shopping in the village. He and the others had been hiding in the fields up near the old campsite."

"And you helped them?"

"They aren't criminals." She was calmer now. "I gave them a meal, made up sandwiches, and found them one or two old bits of clothing of Jock's they could wear—I told Jock the next day that I'd given the stuff away at the door."

"What about money—and where did they sleep?"

"All I had was a few shillings from the housekeeping. I said they could hide in the barn for the night, but Martin wanted to move on—" She stopped suddenly and a spark of defiance showed in her eyes. "Why do you have to chase them like this? What wrong have they done, getting away from the kind of life people have where they come from?"

"Don't spoil it now," Thane told her quietly. "Did he say where they were going?"

She turned away from him, staring into the fire, thinking maybe of two young people who'd once shared a summer in the warm haven of those rolling, high-grassed Perthshire fields. Then the grandfather clock in the corner gave a sudden asthmatic rumble and struck the half-hour. Ten-thirty. She bit her lip, then nodded.

"He'd come to Greenbank to try to contact Lady Dunspar. Not me."

"Who's she?" Thane made no pretence of being well briefed on county society circles.

"She founded Dunspar Camp—she used to live in Dunspar House, about a mile away from here. When the refugees were here she worked practically full time at the camp, helping out. Once things had settled she helped most of them either get home again or start up somewhere fresh."

"Including Martin?"

'Yes, she—Martin was the same age as her son would have been. He was killed in the Pacific. Martin was one of her favourites, and he thought she could help him. But he didn't know she'd sold Dunspar House about a year back—not till he got there and found it's being run as a children's home."

"Where does she live now?"

"I looked it up in the phone book for him. She moved to a smaller place, Creave Cottage, just outside Dunkeld."

It fitted. Dunkeld was another twenty miles inland, almost midway between the village and the Glen Lyon area. Thane got up to leave.

"That's . . . all?" She eyed him anxiously.

"If it's the truth, Mrs. Brendon."

She saw him to the door and waited there until he'd boarded the Jaguar. As the car drew out of the farmyard she was still there, framed by the glow of light from the kitchen.

Half a mile along the road a pair of head lamps grew towards the car. The other vehicle passed seconds later, a mud-spattered Land-Rover travelling towards the farm, the shadowed outline of a tall, broad-shouldered man hunched behind the steering wheel.

Thane's driver wondered at the smile which flickered over the detective's face. But there was no explanation offered, and he went back to concentrating on the dark, twisting road ahead.

*   *   *

It was eleven-twenty P.M. when the police car reached Dunkeld, by which time another nagging concern was troubling Thane. He'd been out of touch with Phil Moss for two hours, long enough for plenty to have happened—and although the Jaguar's R.T. transmitter had one of the new change-net frequency switches, reception in the Highland fringe was too often a matter of faith, a hopeful bellowing into the microphone, and charity towards the poor devil trying to understand at the other end.

A lighted telephone box ahead made up his mind. A couple of minutes later he was speaking to the police station at Aberfeldy.

"Colin—am I glad you called in!" Detective Inspector Moss had practically jumped to take the telephone.

"Things happening?"

"Roy and I found Herrald's van and the place where our trawlermen seem to have been camping out. But that can wait. Bhudda Ilford was on the line less than five minutes back, wanting to know where the devil you'd got to and why."

"I've got what could be a nice strong lead to Kelch," Thane told him. "I'm on my way there now."

"Better leave it," advised Moss. "Bhudda left a message. You've to shove over to Lochearnhead—"

"But that's—"

"Forty-four miles, to be exact." There was urgency in Phil's voice. "Since nine tonight there's been an all-areas 'wanted for questioning' request out for Kelch and his pals. Two men who don't speak much English and who match up on description were picked up at Lochearnhead half an hour back."

Midnight had passed by the time the travel-stained Jaguar reached the mountain-hemmed Highland village, and the first person Thane saw as he pushed his way through the door of Lochearnhead police station was Colonel Donnan.

The gloom on his face was message enough.

"False alarm?"

"With good intent." The little Irishman shrugged. "Just one of these things—I came rocketing up here as soon as I heard, and arrived just as the apologies were beginning. They were two Belgians over here on a walking holiday, and it was just their bad luck they matched up in appearance with the descriptions put out for Vilkas Stender and Arkan Bretsun. Anyway, they came out of it all right, and the local cops have promised them a guided tour as compensation." He gave a weary yawn. "Well, a wasted trip for both of us, Thane, and time I was getting back to make sure General Shashkov's sleeping peacefully. What about you?"

"There was someone I wanted to see but—" It was already late and it would be later before Thane got back, too late to go knocking on an elderly widow's door then expect a friendly reception. And Thane had a feeling that Lady Elizabeth Dunspar would need careful handling. "No, I'll head for Aberfeldy, check with Moss, and settle for an early start in the morning. One thing, though—I'd like to know Shashkov's programme for the rest of his visit."

"That's simple enough," said Donnan. "Tomorrow is Friday—hell, that's today now. He drives through to Edinburgh and inspects an electronics factory . . . they've been busy all week shoving the things he shouldn't see into dark corners. Then he has lunch with the Lord Provost, visits Edinburgh Castle, the usual tourist stuff. Dinner in the evening with the Secretary of State for Scotland."

"Which should be a merry meal." Thane had read that Cabinet member's last pronouncement—blast was a better word—on the evils of communism. "What's the menu? Pistols for two, coffee for one?"

"They'll sit down like the best of pals and spend all evening assuring each other of unshaken confidence in their ability to work for peace together," was Donnan's cynical forecast. "Be happy you're a thief-catcher, Thane. They're more honest than some."

"I've believed that for a long time." Thane chuckled. "What happens on Saturday?"

"Don't you ever read the papers? The whole programme was published in advance—which doesn't make me any happier. He's over on the east coast for most of the day, starting off with a visit to St. Andrews and a game of golf over the Old Course. The solid sportsman touch—he's scheduled to win by two and one. From there, he goes on to inspect a coal mine in Fife and he winds up the day by giving a private dinner back in Glasgow. First thing on Sunday he flies home from Prestwick—one of

Aeroflot's planes, a turbojet TU-104, is coming in to collect him." Donnan sighed. "Once he's aboard I can relax and have a nice, quiet breakdown."

"If he's aboard—"

"Thank you and good night, Chief Inspector." Donnan gave a sour smile, shoved past him, and went out into the night. A moment later, Thane heard the sound of a car start up and then draw away.

He stayed long enough in the police station to commiserate with the duty officers and telephone Bhudda Ilford to explain the position.

"It sounded too good to be true." Ilford's disappointment echoed over the wire as he heard Thane's report. "Well, what's your next move?"

"Finding out more about the people who've helped them," said Thane. "I don't pretend it's a particularly brilliant way to tackle it, but right now there's little else we can do."

"All right, but keep in touch. G'night."

Thane heard the receiver slam down at the other end before he could reply. Bhudda was obviously anxious to get to bed. Well, there were worse ideas.

Phil Moss was still up and waiting at the Tayman Hotel when the Jaguar reached Aberfeldy. They talked, Moss confirmed that the Scientific Bureau team were making a dawn start to be with them and then the few hours of sleep ahead seemed more welcome than ever.

A six A.M. rap on the door dragged Thane back to wakefulness. He rubbed the sleep from his eyes while the hotel porter brought in his morning tea and the news that it was "no' too bad a morning." The tea helped, so did his first cigarette. Then he went down to breakfast.

Phil Moss was already in the hotel dining room, all alone, munching toast and sipping milky-white coffee. D.I. Roy, cautiously conserving his expense allowance, had gone off to stay with friends in the village.

"Sir?" The one waitress on duty offered Thane the menu, took his order, yawned, and disappeared again.

"How d'you feel, Phil?" Thane settled in his chair.

"Horrible," complained his companion. "I've got the room with the plumbing running through it. Nothing but ruddy rumbles, grumbles, and clonks all night." He tried to look on the brighter side. "Wonder how Dan Laurence and his boys liked their early morning start?"

"Dan wouldn't. The language would be interesting." Thane brightened as the waitress returned with his order—coffee, bacon and eggs—and began to eat.

Detective Superintendent Laurence, head of Glasgow C.I.D.'s Scientific Branch, was due to arrive at the cottage at about seven A.M.—a big, bulky, untidy bear of a man whose white hair seemed permanently tousled. Laurence was a master of many strange skills, and his team could be counted on to search out and explore any traces left which might throw some kind of light on what had happened in the glen.

"What about Lady Dunspar?" Moss finished the last of his coffee and helped himself from Thane's pot.

"Try and leave a little—" the sarcasm was wasted. "We'll wait until Dan has had a chance to look around. After that, you and I'll take a trip over to Dunkeld and see how far we can get her to talk."

"Going to be difficult?"

"Probably. Kelch seemed pretty sure that she'd be on his side. He was always her favourite among the refugees, and if he did reach her, she's likely to try hard to cover it up."

"If she thinks of him as just a plain, honest trawlerman who wants to get away to a new life, that's one thing." Moss frowned. "But won't she probably change her mind when she hears what's been going on?"

"I wouldn't bet on it." Thane shook his head.

Breakfast over, they walked the short distance from the hotel to the police station. Their car was parked outside, and Moss guided the driver on the twisting route to the cottage, finding acid amusement in the way the uniformed man at the wheel winced each time the Jaguar's wheels splashed a way through the muddy pools of the forestry track.

Two vehicles were already parked at the edge of the clearing. One was a county car, the other was the big sand-coloured van which was the Scientific Bureau's mobile-lab unit. They parked in line, then the two detectives walked over to the group of figures at work by the cottage.

"'Morning." Dan Laurence, a cigarette drooping from one corner of his mouth, stumped across to meet them. His heavy overcoat was unbuttoned, tobacco ash strewed the front of his jacket. "About time you got here—we may need someone to run errands. Not you, though, Moss. You're too dam' fragile."

Thane grinned. "Any luck yet, Dan?"

"For the——" Laurence groaned at the way in which non-specialists seemed to expect instant miracles. "I've got the lads on a general examination of the place. We've got the photographic side buttoned up, and we're finding any amount of fingerprints, mostly on old food tins. But they won't mean much until we get something or somebody to compare them against—unless you can produce a nice bundle of two-hand record cards for this bunch."

"Can't oblige," said Thane dryly. "Dan, you've already got sample prints of Herrald from his flat and office——"

"Prints we think belong to Herrald," corrected the Bureau chief. "I'm ahead of you, Colin. I left word for a man to go round to Shaw's home and do the same there, and Perth have done their best at the mortuary."

"Seen the van yet?"

"On my way there now. Willie!" Laurence gave a bellow towards the cottage and a young, camera-laden detective hurried towards him. "Right, son, we're going over to the Mini. Nip on first and get a picture o' those tyre marks before somebody's big feet squash them flat."

The photographer hurried off, and they crossed at a more leisurely pace to where the little red vehicle still lay undisturbed. Two county men stood guard beside it, and D.I. Roy pushed his way into view from the trees beyond. He was tired-eyed. For him, the job was now forty hours old, with sleep a tiny fraction of that time.

"Nothing's been touched," he assured the Bureau chief.

"That makes a change, anyway," grunted Laurence. "Once we're finished, I'll want the van moved to a garage, somewhere private where we can take it apart if we need to—can you fix that?"

"Easily enough."

"Well, I won't mess around too much for the moment." Laurence touched the bloodstain on the driver's seat in experimental fashion, peered at the bullet-holed window, grunted again, and took a jeweller's glass from his pocket for a closer inspection. "Aye, the angle's about right. MacMaster took the bullet out of Shaw's chest, didn't he?"

"Wait a moment and you can ask him yourself." Thane nodded towards the track, where a big, old-fashioned Rolls-Royce was purring to a halt beside the other vehicles. Professor MacMaster crossed towards them, the legs of his immaculately creased black trousers tucked into the tops of a pair of stout Wellington boots.

"Busy, gentlemen?" He looked around and gave a sniff. "I thought I'd come over and see what was happening—but I won't interfere, Superintendent."

A glint of devilry appeared on Dan Laurence's face. "Just stay and watch as much as you want, Professor. There's no harm in a man learning."

"I think I'll get back to the cottage," said Thane hastily. He'd seen the university expert and Laurence become embroiled before . . . they worked best when scoring points off one another, but it was no place for an innocent bystander. "Roy, there's a job I'd like you to tackle. You told Moss this track is more or less a fire-fighting road from this point on. Does that mean it comes to a dead end?"

The county man nodded. "It's on that map I gave Moss last night. There's only one way a vehicle can get out o' here, an' that's back the way we came."

"So anything coming up would have to make a turn, which would probably mean driving off the road." Thane pressed one foot into the soft, muddy soil and examined the result. "It might leave tyre marks—and I want this section of road checked for them."

"What's the idea?" demanded Moss.

"Nothing spectacular, Phil. I'd just like to know if the Mini was the only vehicle to come this way and, if it was, whether it travelled the route more than once."

Detective Inspector Roy scratched one ear. "I think I know what you mean. I might as well take care o' it now—I've nothing else on my plate."

"Let's split it," suggested Moss. "I'll take one side of the track, you take the other. Right?" He glanced for Thane's approval.

"It'll save time," agreed Thane. He watched them set off, then continued on his own towards the cottage.

Nothing spectacular, he'd said. Checking out a possibility which might mean anything or nothing—it happened all the time, the gathering, sorting, storing, and rejecting. How had Kelch reached the ruined cottage in the first instance? Had he stumbled on it, known of it from those earlier days, or been told about it? Had he and the others hitchhiked, walked, or been taken by some outside friend who could supply a car?

Maybe Lady Dunspar would supply some of the answers. He stopped at the door of the old cottage and found himself scowling at the weathered stonework. The cottage knew—but Thane dealt in people, he'd have to wait on Laurence and MacMaster to tell him what, if anything, they could learn within its walls.

He went in, to find one of the Scientific Branch men busy gathering his equipment together.

"We've almost finished here, sir," greeted the man. "Just don't touch what's left of that window frame in the corner wall until I've had a look at it, will you?"

"I'll keep clear." Powder spray and camel's-hair brushes had been busy, light grey smudges of fingerprint powder were all around showing the work completed. Another of Laurence's men was over by a now neat and orderly line of opened tins and debris of various kinds collected from about the cottage.

The man looked up, his face wrinkled in disgust. "They weren't short of groceries anyway, sir. And what they've left behind has gone well and truly bad—some of it even has the beginnings of mould sprouting. Makes trying to get dabs from the stuff pretty awkward."

Thane came closer, took one sniff, and retired before the mixture of rancid odours which hit his nostrils. Over by the fireplace the situation was easier, a collection of cigarette butts laid out for laboratory tests aimed at saliva grouping. He took out a cigarette of his own, lit it, then frowned and knelt as he caught sight of a scrap of blue paper lying between the edges of two of the damp stone slabs which formed the cottage floor.

The paper slipped free, a torn fragment less than two inches in length. He felt its texture and hardly needed the fraction of printed lettering just short of the torn edge to know where it had come from. He'd seen too many similar pieces of coloured paper after too many safeblowings to fail to recognise part of the outer wrappings from a stick of gelignite.

"Better take care of this." He handed the paper to the nearest of Laurence's men, who slipped it into a small plastic envelope for safe keeping. It was a mere thread of evidence, circumstantial evidence pointing to explosives having been kept in the cottage. On its own it would mean nothing in a court. Side by side with other facts, other threads, it could help weave a net of circumstantial truth no jury could ignore.

Thane walked back to the doorway and looked out. Now and again a bright quiver of light came from the direction of the trees, the police photographer's electronic flash at work lighting the gloom around the red Mini-Van. As he watched, Professor MacMaster's gaunt figure stepped out of the trees and loped awkwardly towards him.

"Waiting and hoping, Chief Inspector?" The forensic expert gave the equivalent of a smile. "Little assistance I can give you for the moment, I'm afraid—though I always enjoy these field-study expeditions. A chance to get out into the fresh country air, good for the lungs. If the average citizen had any idea of the appearance of his lungs, the view I get of them, he'd come rushing out to a place like this, away from the soot."

"The thought's enough for me," said Thane dryly. "You're finished, Professor?"

"Apart from a glimpse here. I've asked Laurence to let me have certain items for laboratory examination, of course . . . a sample of the blood staining on the van seat among them. Tell me, do you know if the missing man—"

"Herrald?"

"Is that his name? Ah well, do you know if he has any record of hospital admission? If he has, their records should contain his blood group and I may need that if the sample doesn't match against—ah—Shaw."

"We can find out for you."

"Good. Well, I won't keep you back." He gave a brief nod and went into the cottage. Thane took another long draw on his cigarette, then set off towards the parked line of cars at the track's edge. His driver saw him coming, broke off the conversation he'd been having with his opposite numbers from the other vehicles, and hovered warily beside the Jaguar's bonnet.

"Anything fresh, sir?"

"Only the air, according to the professor," said Thane regretfully. "Better stay around—I'll need the car in a minute or two." He turned away as Phil Moss and D.I. Roy trudged into sight, returning from their search of the track's verges. One look at their faces was enough.

"Out of luck, Colin," declared his second-in-command. "There's a turning place about a hundred yards on, hard rock and gravel wide enough to swing a truck. If anyone did drive up here they knew about it and used it—we checked a clear quarter mile up and down from it, but there's no sign of tyre marks."

"The forestry commission build a lot o' these turning places," contributed Roy gloomily. "If they didn't, their vehicles would be bogged down in the winter."

"Instead, we're bogged down." Thane took it fairly philosophically. "I'd like you to stay here and keep an eye on things, Roy—oh, and Professor MacMaster has a query you'd better pass on to Glasgow as soon as you get a chance. He wants to know Herrald's blood group. If you need us in a hurry, we'll be visiting Lady Dunspar."

Roy hesitated. "Eh . . . don't take this the wrong way, either o' you. But, well, she's a woman that's liked around these parts. She does a lot o' good for folk, without makin' a fuss about it."

"Which is exactly why I think she'll know more than anyone about Martin Kelch. But I'll go easy with her . . . as easy as she allows." Thane glanced at his watch. "We should be there by ten-thirty—and let's hope she's in a friendly mood."

FOUR

Lady Elizabeth Dunspar's home was a small, slightly old-fashioned villa with white walls, a red-tiled roof and a setting straight from a chocolate-box lid. It's front faced on to a long stretch of rich, carefully mown lawn reaching down to the very bank of the River Tay, at that point a silver-smooth, fast-flowing sheet of water. To the rear of the house, a high hedge shielded the kitchen garden from the main road and a short, rhododendron-lined driveway ran from the road to a wide, gravelled parking place. All around, the mountains and forests had edged back to form a fringe to a valley of rich, cattle-filled grazing land.

Thane's car crunched to a gentle halt on the gravel and the two men went on together the last few yards.

"Nicely kept." Thane ran an envious eye over the weeded, well-raked, carefully pruned beds of roses which flanked either side of the front porch.

"By a full-time gardener, I'll bet," said Moss. "This lot would do me when I start drawing pension."

They heard a soft chuckle of laughter and turned. The slim, sun-tanned woman standing behind them where she'd stepped from the bushes was probably about sixty. Her iron-grey hair was covered by a large flop-brimmed hat, she wore gardening gloves, slacks, and a dark-green sweater.

"I'm the gardener." She smiled again. "Was the rest a prelude to a proposal?"

Thane grinned. "Lady Dunspar?"

"Well, at least you didn't take me for the odd-job woman—that's the usual reaction." The smile lingered. "Can I help you?"

He carried out the introductions and watched the smile fade to mere politeness.

"You'd better come inside—use the doormat, please."

They obeyed meekly and followed her through a small hallway and into the villa's lounge, L-shaped, gaily decorated, with wide french windows looking straight out on to the lawn and the river beyond.

"Sit down, please." She gestured them towards two of the several teak-framed armchairs which were placed round a copy Adam fireplace in pink marble. The polished wood floor had most of its area covered by a Persian carpet in lime green, and a big radio-stereogram unit, framed in teak, occupied a length of wall to one side.

Phil Moss gave the room a casual, appreciative inspection, then glanced at the two portraits hung on the wall behind the stereo unit. One showed a dark-haired youngster in R.A.F. uniform, pilot's wings on the tunic, the other was an equally dark-haired schoolgirl who, despite her chubbiness and broad, teen-age grin, seemed vaguely familiar. He'd seen her somewhere, decided Moss—probably in newspaper photographs or within the covers of one of the glossy magazines he sampled in the waiting room at his doctor's surgery.

Yet . . . he postponed the puzzle as Lady Dunspar sat down opposite them.

"Well, Chief Inspector?" Firm and assured, she turned towards Thane.

"I think you know why we're here, Lady Dunspar—"

"Do I?" She blinked deliberately and this time the smile was even colder. "Perhaps you'd better tell me."

"In that case . . ." Thane switched his approach. "Would it save time if I said we know Martin Kelch and three companions tried to locate you at Greenbank? That they were told you now lived near Dunkeld and left Greenbank to come here?"

She was silent for a moment, then gave a slight shrug. "I don't need to ask where you got that information—and I can guess one way in which you'd obtain it. An unpleasant way. Well, I'm not a young woman who kept a secret from her husband, Chief Inspector. I'm a widow, reasonably independent, and I've never given a twopenny damn for authority. If I have to make a decision I let my own mind and heart tell me what to do."

"Did they tell you to help Martin Kelch?"

She drew herself a little more upright in the chair. "Have I said he was here?"

"You've more or less admitted it, Lady Dunspar. It would be a natural enough reaction to help him, just the way you did before when he was a young refugee. You always had—well, a soft spot for him, didn't you?" He watched her closely.

"That's true." Her face softened. "He was the same age as—as my son would have been. Martin had the same kind of nature too—affectionate, a little reckless, sure of his own ability. He was all on his own in that camp, and when word finally did come that his family had been located and that he could go back to Lithuania I asked him not to do it. I wanted him to stay with me—be more or less an adopted son. He refused, Chief Inspector. He told me his place was back with them. Once he'd gone I had one or two letters then silence, no word—"

"Until he arrived at this house a few nights ago?"

"Yes, he was here." Lady Dunspar glimpsed the notebook appearing in Phil Moss's hand and shook her head. "Put that away, please. I'm prepared to talk about this in a civilised fashion, but I point-blank refuse to make anything approaching a statement."

Thane gave a faint nod and Moss tucked the notebook back in his pocket.

"Martin arrived here on the Friday afternoon . . . his friends hid in one of the fields outside until he signalled them it was safe. I live alone, Chief Inspector, except for a housekeeper who lives out and has Saturday and Sunday off, so as soon as she had gone they were quite safe."

"And they stayed in this house?"

"Yes."

"For how long?"

She shook her head. "I've said enough—except that Martin and his friends came here in need of help and I did all I could to give them that help."

"Help for what purpose, Lady Dunspar?" A new, harder note underlined his question. "To get to America—or did they know then about General Shashkov's visit, and have a different purpose?"

Lady Dunspar rose to her feet. "I don't know what that's supposed to mean. But unless you intend to bring some charge against me, I suggest you leave."

He shook his head. "Not yet. I didn't come north just to round up a bunch of trawlermen who've jumped from a ship, Lady Dunspar. I'm trying to find four men who now have a small arsenal of gelignite in their possession, four men who've already had one try at killing a visiting diplomat. All right, maybe you don't care about Shashkov, or what the consequences could be. Maybe you feel that men like Kelch are justified if they see killing the man as a mixture of retribution and justice, and to hell with the consequences . . ."

"Martin would have nothing to do with—"

"Wouldn't he?" Thane walked over and stood directly in front of her. "There's more, Lady Dunspar. I'm thinking of two anglers who came north for a holiday. On Wednesday one of these men was shot dead. His friend is missing. We found their van a short distance from an old cottage where we know Kelch and the others had been hiding. Let's forget Shashkov, Lady Dunspar. But what about an ordinary little man called George Shaw? And what about his wife? I was the one who had to tell her that he'd been killed, that he wouldn't be back from that fishing trip." He took a deep breath and let his hands fall by his sides. "Or do they make no difference, Lady Dunspar?"

Suddenly, she seemed to have aged. She spoke in a near daze, making no attempt to hide the tremour in her voice. "This cottage—where was it?"

"Near Glen Lyon, beside a forestry road. You know it?"

She bit her lip, and when she spoke it wasn't to answer. "But—but it happened on Wednesday, you said! Martin couldn't have been responsible, in any way. On Wednesday he was—" she stopped short and bit her lip again.

"He was what, Lady Dunspar?"

"I'm sorry—" It came out as a near whisper. "All I'm prepared to say at this moment is that neither Martin nor his friends are in this house and that I personally no longer know their whereabouts. You're at liberty to search my home if you don't believe me . . . that's all, Chief Inspector. I— I would like a little time to consider what you've told me."

Thane looked at her for a long moment, then nodded. "I'll take your word they aren't here. But time's a precious factor as far as we're concerned, Lady Dunspar—don't waste too much of it making up your mind what to do. Other lives could depend on it."

"This afternoon—early?"

"All right." He nodded across to Moss, who rose from his chair. "I've taken your word on one point. Will you give it on another—that you won't try to contact them by telephone or any other way?"

"I won't." She straightened her shoulders a little. "I—I'll see you to the door."

Still curious, Phil Moss began to follow them, then stopped beside the portrait of the girl. There was something nudging his mind about that face, the same and yet different from another he'd known. He gave a mild courtesy cough.

"Lady Dunspar, this girl—is she your daughter?"

A surprise flicker of what could have been either panic or anger crossed her face. "Yes. Why?"

"I just wondered."

She led them the rest of the way to the house door, said goodbye, and closed it quickly behind them.

"What the heck made you ask about that painting?" demanded Thane as they crunched their way back across the gravel to the car. "Since when were you interested in family portraits?"

"I don't really know," admitted his companion. "Just a feeling I've seen that face somewhere, and recently. Yet it was different somehow— ach, I give up."

"Her son was killed over fifteen years ago," reminded Thane. "The girl's portrait was probably painted at the same time as her brother's— your schoolgirl will be a woman by now."

They reached the car and climbed aboard. As the Jaguar's door closed again, the driver gave an inquiring glance.

"It's your turn to play detective," Thane told him. "I want to locate the local telephone exchange—the phone in that house was non-automatic, so we shouldn't have far to go."

"Thinking of arranging a phone tap?" asked Moss as the car pulled away. "That can mean trouble—and if she knows where they are she could be calling them right now."

"She gave her word, Phil." Thane took out his cigarettes, lit one, and leaned back as the car started off. "With that kind of woman, her word is her bond. And I'm pretty certain that what she told us was the absolute truth—as far as it goes. No, I want to have a look through the exchange's list of trunk calls passed from her number. There may be a lead there, a lead to the type of help she gave to Kelch—and before we go back to see her, I'd like to have some idea of what she's able to tell us."

The telephone exchange was located in a small back room behind a shop which combined the role of post office, news-agent, and grocery store for a tiny clachan of houses about two miles distant. The grocer's wife, who also acted as switchboard girl, took care of a customer's order for two tins of diced fruit and a bottle of detergent, then lifted the counter flap and ushered the two C.I.D. men through to the rear.

"Lady Dunspar's telephone?" she showed instant amazement. "Is something wrong up at the house?"

"Nothing to concern yourself about," Thane reassured her. "Have you got the list of numbers?"

"Aye, it's in this book." She lifted a black ledger from beside a stacked tray of bread then paused unhappily. "You won't mind if I make a wee call to the district supervisor at Dunkeld exchange, just to make sure it's all right to show you it?"

Thane told her to go ahead. They heard only her side of the brief conversation, but when she'd finished and unplugged the line on the board she was satisfied.

"Help yourselves," she invited.

Thane reached for the ledger then stopped as the driver from their car came through the counter flap and into the room.

"Something up?"

"Looks that way, Chief Inspector," said the driver. "The car radio's still crackling like the devil was inside it, but the message was you've to call Edinburgh City headquarters—they've a priority call for you."

"Thanks." He turned to the grocer's wife as the man went back towards the car. "Can you get me through?" She set to work, and he frowned, then handed the ledger to Moss. "Phil, find any numbers called from that house since last Friday. Once I've spoken to Edinburgh we can contact Post Office Information and match addresses against her calls."

Moss pushed his way further into the back shop, found a seat on a sack of potatoes, and began flicking the trunk lists. At the board, the grocer's wife looked up. "I've got them on the line now, sir." She pointed to an extension receiver mounted on the wall. "Will you take it there?"

He nodded, then touched her on the arm. "Mind going outside?"

"But the switchboard—"

"I won't be long."

She wasn't pleased, but she went. As the door closed behind her, he lifted the receiver. "Thane . . ."

"Where the hell have you been hiding?" Colonel Donnan's voice came faint and despairingly over the line. "It's taken me dam' near fifteen minutes to get hold of you—where are you anyway?"

"In a midget-sized telephone exchange near Dunkeld. Why?" Thane refused to be ruffled, but the temptation was there.

"You'd probably be a dam' sight nearer to Kelch if you were here in Edinburgh." The security chief's Irish brogue thickened and betrayed his tension. "It's just forty minutes since somebody had a good try at blowing General Shashkov sky-high—a bomb in a pillarbox just opposite the electronics factory he was visiting. The box went up with a bang exactly as Shashkov's car passed it!"

"What's the casualty list?" Thane rapped the query while Moss crowded closer, straining his ears to catch the distant end of the conversation.

"Five, but the devil still seems to be looking after his own," snarled

Donnan. "The car was damaged a little, the driver cut by flying glass, but Shashkov came out of it without a mark. One motor-cycle cop is in hospital with a fractured skull—he was between the car and the bomb, and he's on the danger list. One of my boys and two beat cops are in the same hospital having chunks of pillarbox picked out of them. It was cast iron, Thane—you know what that means."

"As good as an anti-personnel bomb," said Thane grimly.

"Correct. We'd kept the crowd well back as a security precaution, so they were all right—just minor cuts and fainting women. There's damage, but the damage that's worrying me is happening now!" Donnan groaned at the thought. "We can't keep this one quiet—it's already going out as a news flash on radio and TV. The evening papers will be chucking everything else out of their front pages, not just here but over most of Europe. I've had the Home Secretary, the Foreign Secretary, my own bosses, even the ruddy Post Office, all jumping on me and asking what I'm doing about it. By tonight the propaganda machines will have started grinding on the other side of the Curtain, and who'll be left holding the baby? Me!"

Thane made a sympathetic noise. "Think it was a time bomb?"

"No. Too accurate for that. Shashkov arrived five minutes late, yet it still popped off exactly as he drove past. The army bomb-disposal types are still there, but they're betting on some type of short-range radio control. We've got one lead—a beat cop, one of the squad on crowd control, says he remembers noticing a small parcel being shoved in the slot of the mail box by a man who drove up in a grey Ford Zephyr. The cordon boys were just arriving for duty, it was almost a couple of hours before Shashkov was due, and he thought nothing of it at the time."

"Any description?"

"Medium height, raincoat—that's all." Donnan paused hopefully. "The car wouldn't mean anything to you, would it?"

"Not a thing."

"Well, it was just a long shot. For what it's worth, there's a priority warning going out to all forces. But we've no registration number for the car, and we can't throw the driver of every grey Zephyr into jug just so that we can sort things out." An even more bitter note crept into his voice. "The only person who isn't worried is Shashkov. Last time I saw him he growled like a bear—then grinned when he thought I wasn't watching.

Probably thinks that being on the receiving end of an imperialist-type plot will give his popularity a big boost back home. But look, Thane, there's always a chance this car could be heading north—"

"We'll do our best," Thane assured him, then hung up after Donnan had said a mournful goodbye. The unattended switchboard was already buzzing like an angry bee, with four calls waiting to be answered, two of them showing angrily flashing signal discs. He opened the door and the grocer's wife hurried back to duty.

Kelch and Serviev, Stender and Bretsun—still on the loose, probably with another plan ready to put into action once they learned their second bid had failed . . .

"Well, as I always say, third time lucky," said the woman by his side.

"Eh?" He blinked.

"Mrs. MacDonald in the village." She connected the last of the waiting calls and sat back. "She's just had a son, and her with two daughters before him—her sister was on the line just now."

"Nice for her—the mother, I mean," said Thane absently. "Phil, you heard most of Donnan?"

"Enough."

"Not much we can do except keep on our own course. Let's see that trunk-call list." He skimmed over the entries for Lady Dunspar's number. "Kelch reached her last Friday night—there's a call to Galsgow listed, then another to the same number the following morning, followed by two to somewhere in Perth. What's this one?" He showed the book to the grocer's wife, who was still at the switchboard.

"A telegram, Mr. Thane."

"Got a copy handy?"

She shook her head. "For telegrams, I just put the caller through to Dunkeld. They'll have it there."

He checked through the rest of the list, but after the Saturday it seemed Lady Dunspar had had no more need of trunk telephone conversations.

"Phil, get on to Information and dig up names and addresses for these numbers—then try and find out what was in that telegram." He gave the woman a chance to handle Moss's call and deal with a couple of waiting village subscribers, then asked her, "Any way of knowing details about local calls made from Lady Dunspar's phone?"

"No." She saw his disappointment and relented. "Well, not officially, if you know what I mean. But in a wee place like this you soon get a fair idea of the numbers people will call regularly. And I can usually remember if they've asked for anyone out of the ordinary, like the minister or the doctor."

It was a slender hope, but Thane grabbed for it. "How about Lady Dunspar, then? Think hard—it's important."

The grocer's wife frowned in an effort of concentration. "No, she didn't have the doctor—that was Mrs. Douglas, with her breathlessness. Wait now—" she gave a snap of her fingers "—yes, she wanted one of the garages in Dunkeld."

"When? What day?"

"I'm trying." She frowned again. "First thing on Sunday morning, that was it. Aye, I'm sure now, because I kept on ringing for a solid three minutes before they answered. With most folk, I'd simply have told them there was no reply. But with Lady Dunspar, it's different." The grocer's wife toyed with the board's plug lines, a frown gathering. "She's not in trouble herself is she—I mean, with you asking all these questions about her?"

Thane shook his head. "Don't worry about it. And don't talk about it either, if you really want to help her. Now, can you remember which garage she telephoned?"

She had flushed a little. "Och, it was young Tommy Harton's place. That's why she had to wait so long for an answer—he's on there by himself on a Sunday, and he never gets out of bed on time."

Sunday morning and a garage—it added up, added up all too well. "How do I get there?"

"Straight along the Dunkeld road for about two miles, and you can't miss it," she assured him.

He was ready to go, but Phil Moss was still apparently tied to the telephone, his expression and the irate snap in his voice as he talked to the unfortunate at the other end of the line showing that all wasn't going smoothly.

"Trouble, Phil?"

"Trouble?" Moss clasped his hand over the instrument's mouthpiece.

"I've been shuffled between three operators up till now, but the one I've got right now seems more or less intelligent. Why? Going somewhere?"

Thane explained, then left him to resume the battle and went out of the little store.

Harton's Garage consisted of two petrol pumps, a little wooden hut used as an office and, at the rear, a brick-built repair shop and garage area new enough to still have only primer paint over the wood of the door frames. The office hut was empty but, his coat collar turned up against a sudden downpour, Thane crossed over to the repair shop.

"Petrol, mister?" A young, freckle-faced mechanic left the tyre he'd been repairing and came towards him.

"I'm looking for Tommy Harton," Thane told him, glancing over to where two older men were wrestling with the innards of a mud-spattered tractor.

"That's me." The youngster grinned. "If you've got car trouble—"

Thane shook his head. "Police."

"Oh!" Harton pulled a rag from his overall pocket, wiped his hands, and jerked his head in the direction of the hut. "If it's private, we'd better go into the office."

Thane followed him out through the rain and into the little building. There were two chairs, a table, an unlit stove, and the rest of the area was occupied by cartons of vehicle spares.

"Fag?" Harton offered his battered pack, took one after Thane, and accepted a light. "What's the trouble?"

"You had a telephone call on Sunday morning from Lady Dunspar." Thane drew on the cigarette, watching the youngster's face. "I'd like to know what she wanted."

"Why?" Harton made it a challenge.

"Because I'm interested."

The youngster shook his head. "Sorry, that's not good enough. This place is mine, mister—but I don't hide it from anybody that the reason is she gave me help to get going, the kind of help banks don't give you unless you give them the kind of security that shows you don't need the money anyway." He swept a place clear on the table and perched himself on the edge, waiting.

Thane took a gamble. "She telephoned about a car, didn't she—a grey Ford Zephyr?" The youngster's slightly tightened expression was answer enough. "Keep quiet if you want, Harton. Nobody can force you to co-operate, but you're only heading into a mess of trouble. I'm not trying to nail a charge on the woman, but I may have to unless I find someone who'll give me some sensible answers."

"How . . . how serious is it?"

"Among other things, murder." The words came hard and cold from Thane's lips. "Is that enough?"

Harton swallowed and nodded. "All right—if you mean it about her not being involved. She phoned here on Sunday, about a car."

"Whose car is it?"

"Mine." Harton came off the table, went over to the stove, and flipped his half-smoked cigarette into the open front. "She has a car of her own, but her daughter has been using it most of the time, and she lives away from home. When Lady Dunspar rang me, she said she needed some form of transport right away, for a few days. Some friends had arrived, and she wanted to drive them around." He shrugged. "Well, I helped out."

"And gave her the Ford."

"Why not?" demanded Harton defensively. "She did me a good turn. The Ford's mine, and I told her she could have a loan of it till today."

"You mean—" it was Thane's turn to be surprised "—you mean you've got it back?"

"Not yet," said the youngster patiently. "Look, I need the car tonight. I'm hiring it out to a Yank who's coming up for the fishing, and he's due to arrive in Dunkeld this evening. I've got the letter he sent—" He began to paw through the papers on the table.

"Never mind it," snapped Thane. "What's the arrangement for re-turning the car?"

"I'm collecting it from her home this afternoon." Harton scratched his head. "When I gave her the Ford I told her I'd need it back today, and that I'd fix up something else to take its place. I'm giving her an old Austin, not as good a car, but the only thing I've got available."

"I don't think she'll need it somehow." Thane pursed his lips. "What's the Ford's registration number?"

"QYO 302, but—"

Colin Thane was already on his way to the car outside. A moment later, as it sped back through the rain towards the grocery store and Phil Moss, he was calling control on the Jaguar's radio. The control operator's voice answered, faint but distinct, giving him a strength-three reading.

He flicked the "send" switch again. "Add to special search message and with direct advise to Colonel Donnan through Edinburgh City headquarters—" He passed on the Ford's number, had it acknowledged, and moments later heard the girl putting out the message on the general net wave length.

Phil Moss was lounging in the doorway of the village store, sheltering from the last drops of the fading rainstorm. Thane threw open the car's rear door as it braked to a halt alongside.

"Get in—quick."

Moss tumbled aboard and slammed the door as the car began rolling again, tyres hissing on the wet road.

"Colin, I've—"

"We're heading back to Lady Dunspar's place," Thane cut across him. "That grey Ford, Phil. She borrowed it from a local garage, and it's due to be returned this afternoon."

Moss blinked. "And I thought I had news! I traced the call she made to Glasgow on the Friday evening. She telephoned Peter Herrald, his number anyway." He gave a bitter grimace of satisfaction. "The other thing is I can tell you where I saw the girl before—"

"What girl?" Thane growled it, still trying to absorb the implication of a link to the missing angler.

"The girl in the painting in her house. It was the dark hair that threw me—but Herrald's name triggered it. She may be Lady Dunspar's daughter, but her hair is blond now and she calls herself Barbara Mason."

"The hotel receptionist you spoke to—Herrald's girl friend!"

"The same." Moss grabbed for support as the car swung round the next corner, the back end sliding first one way then the other as the driver calmly controlled the skid. "What's the rush? You don't imagine these boys are going to be kind and considerate enough to bring the old girl her car back the way they promised, do you?"

"I'd do it, Phil—make a point of it, in fact. Look, Kelch is no fool. His bunch have been using a car which in theory is out on loan to a quiet, elderly woman. It wouldn't be easy to trace back unless somebody managed to catch the registration number."

"And they may have false plates rigged," admitted Moss.

"Right. Still, Kelch won't want to hang on to the one car for too long, and bringing the Ford back gives them an equally easy chance to switch cars—leaving everybody looking for a grey Ford while they're actually running around in another car which nobody is going to report as being either stolen or hired!"

He'd satisfied Moss, and now, as the car rushed on, Thane had a puzzle of his own . . . Herrald and Lady Dunspar's daughter. "Phil, what about the other phone calls, and that telegram?"

"The two Perth calls were to her bank, the Central Scottish. The telegram was to a woman friend on the other side of Dunkeld telling her she couldn't keep a date they had for the Sunday." Moss winced as the Jaguar flirted round another corner on the thickly hedged road, and glanced anxiously towards the speedometer. "Do we have to go so fast right now?"

A faint smile suppressed in the corners of his mouth, their driver took a fraction of pressure off the accelerator but Thane nodded him on again.

"We do. It's only a two-hour drive from Edinburgh to this part of the world. If the Ford left the city soon after the bombing, it should be getting pretty close to us right now. And we've got to get it, Phil. We've got to get whoever is in it."

Four men, three, two, one—just as long as he had one of the group, a chance to lay his hands on something or somebody at the heart of the situation, somebody or something more tangible than the present maze of half-innocent helpers who seemed to surround Kelch's every move. Thane stared along the road ahead, the rain drumming louder on the car roof, the wipers sweeping their regular beat.

The car's radio came to life at the same instant as the red roof of Lady Dunspar's home appeared in the distance ahead. He grabbed the microphone and acknowledged.

"Glasgow car one-eleven, Chief Inspector Thane." The merest fraction of a pause as the girl operator drew breath, and then she went on, "Grey Ford QYO 302 reported seen heading north on the main A.9 road near Bankfoot, one occupant. Report is from Bankfoot constable and traffic car six-two is heading south on A.9 to intercept. Over."

"Roger. Also in area and closing. Out." Thane tossed the microphone into its cubbyhole. "Phil?"

Moss already had the map unfolded.

"He could branch off for here about three miles north of Bankfoot."

"How far from here to the junction?"

"Maybe another three. Unless the traffic car gets him, he should be heading straight for us."

As the Jaguar whipped past the red-roofed villa, their driver glanced at them through his mirror. "Do I keep going, sir, or do you want to block him?"

Thane chewed his lower lip. Nine chances out of ten the Ford was coming their way. But there was the tenth chance, and only one other mobile unit in the area. "Keep going, but be ready for trouble," he ordered. "He's liable to try anything, but stop the car any way you can—I'll carry the can if the result is a pileup."

They'd topped a slight rise and were notching seventy down the long straight of the reverse slope, down to where a smaller service road branched off to the right, when they saw the Ford. The grey car, a rain-distorted blur at first, was driving towards them at a more sedate pace but the first sign of the approaching Jaguar seemed to warn the other driver. The Ford slowed, then accelerated violently, tackling a slithering, tyre-screaming turn which shot it into the side road.

"Take him."

The two men grabbed for support as their driver obeyed.

Six cylinders bellowed as the car dropped down a gear for maximum acceleration and jerked forward. The uniformed figure at the wheel settled into a tight-shouldered crouch, half-crooning as he coaxed the 220 horsepower of the sleek projectile under his control. They took the branch-road's angle in a bouncing slide, and the car stayed in third gear until every last safe rev had been pulled from its power unit.

The Ford ahead was moving fast and being handled well over the narrow, hedge-lined service road—but Thane's car had engine advantage, controlled by a professional.

The grey car reached a wheel-hopping, desperate pace, yet the gap between them closed with such a rush that its pursuer had to ease up to avoid nosing into its rear.

"Road's too narrow, sir," reported Thane's driver, letting the gap widen again. "Corner ahead—once we're round it I'll try giving him a nudge."

The Ford's driver looked back at them once before the corner, a quick, jerking glance before he wrestled the grey car into a wildly braking turn which spelled torture for suspension and transmission. Rubber screamed again, then as the car's tail disappeared from view there was a sudden thunder of impacting metal and shattered glass. As the Jaguar slithered to a skidding halt Thane had a momentary glimpse of a round black object hurtling skywards. Then he was being jerked forward in his seat, and Phil Moss was thrown against him as their car came to a final stop, angled across the roadway and half distance round the corner.

"Hell, he's really copped it, sir!" Their driver spoke with awe, shaken at their own narrow escape.

A handful of yards ahead, the crumpled wreck of the grey car was almost wrapped round what had once been a farm tractor but was now an equally twisted tangle of metal. The savage impact on the wet surface had swept both vehicles off the road and tumbled them sideways into the deep drainage ditch which ran a few feet in from the verge. One of the Ford's front wheels was still spinning, the other, the wheel Thane had seen going into the air as it was torn loose, lay about twenty yards further on.

"There's someone—" Moss threw open the door and they scrambled out into the steady downpour as a man struggled to his feet on the opposite side of the road from the wreckage. He staggered and almost fell again as they reached him, the glaze of pure shock still in his eyes.

"Came straight at me, man—straight at the tractor—" the farm worker's limbs trembled jerkily "—I jumped for it. Straight at me, he was comin'."

They left him to the driver's care and sprinted over to the Ford. The rain spattered and hissed against the car's exposed exhaust as Thane clambered on to the tilted side and managed to wrench open the buckled metal of the driver's door. He threw it back, looked inside the car and felt sick. Stocky build, medium height, age about forty, close-cropped grey hair, and a small moustache—the description tallied with the one Colonel Donnan had passed on.

But Taras Serviev was both trapped and dying. The steering wheel had taken him in the chest, glass splinters had drawn blood from half a dozen cuts on his face and hands, and his legs were pinned beneath the shattered engine bulkhead, leaving him lying at an angle against the wide bench seat.

The man's head turned slowly, painfully, and his lips parted in an attempt at a cynical welcome. Thane pulled himself into a better position and nodded to Moss. "We'll need help, Phil—ambulance and a breakdown crew." While Moss sprinted back through the rain towards the Jaguar, he eased his head and shoulders inside the wreckage. "It won't take long, Serviev."

"Any time ... too long." Serviev gave a faint shake of his head. "You ... know me?"

Thane nodded. "And the others. Where are they, Serviev? Where's Kelch?"

The trapped man moistened his lips. "Cigarette ..."

Thane sniffed the reek of petrol in the air and shook his head. "Too risky."

"Life is ... risk." Serviev tried to move, and gave a moaning gasp of pain.

Thane eased himself still closer. "Serviev, where's Martin Kelch? And where's Peter Herrald—what's happened to him?"

"Safe." The trapped man drew a wheezing, shallow breath. "Shashkov will ... die before you ... find." He seemed to come close to losing his slender grip on consciousness, then drew on some last source of energy and looked up again. He ran his tongue over his lips and gave a bare-toothed grimace. "Drink ..."

"All right." Thane raised himself up and saw Phil Moss coming back from the Jaguar. "Phil, can you find some water?"

"Water." Moss brushed the trickles of rain from his face and gave a gloomy nod. He went back to the police car and returned in a moment carrying the water bottle from the emergency kit.

"Thanks." Thane unscrewed the cap, gripped the bottle with his right hand and eased back into the wreck. "Here it is, Serviev."

As the water touched his lips, Serviev tried to swallow. His eyes met Thane's and he struggled to speak for a moment.

"Take your time." The chief leaned still further forward as Serviev tried to reach up with one hand. "Just sip—I'll worry about the bottle."

"Bottle . . ." Serviev twitched and he stared at Thane. Then suddenly his face twisted into the start of a laugh, a strangely taunting laugh. "You . . ."

He died before the chuckle had been more than shaped on his lips. Thane waited a moment, then climbed back down from the wreckage. As he did, he became freshly aware of the beating rain, the cold wet feel of the metal on which he'd been lying, the way the rivulets of water ran down the front of his coat, soaking into the damp, clinging cloth.

One accounted for—but three to go, plus Peter Herrald still to be found. And all he'd learned towards that was that Herrald was alive.

He was still standing by the wreck when the county traffic car arrived. Another twenty minutes went by before the ambulance and breakdown truck reached the scene.

FIVE

It was mid-afternoon before Thane paid his second call on Lady Dunspar. When he arrived, a small blue-and-white Triumph coupe was parked on the driveway and the front door was opened by a girl whom he knew immediately. Phil Moss had been right. Except that the dark hair had been dyed blond, that a pretty school child develops into an attractive woman, and Lady Dunspar's daughter hadn't really changed so much since her portrait had been painted.

"Come in please, Chief Inspector." Barbara Mason was slim, smaller than her mother, neat in waist and bust, dressed in a sheath dress of dark-grey jersey wool. Her eyes were a hazel brown and worried, her voice had the neutral warmth of the trained receptionist. She closed the door once he'd entered, then showed him into the lounge. Lady Dunspar sat by the fireside, the small table next her chair set for afternoon tea . . . and she'd changed from her gardening clothes into a plain, expensively tailored navy-blue costume.

"You're alone, Chief Inspector?" She motioned him to the chair opposite while her daughter hovered restlessly in the background. "Barbara, is this—?"

"No, it was another one," said the girl cautiously. "I can't remember his name."

"Detective Inspector Moss," Thane told her. "He was with me this morning, when we came to see your mother. But we didn't link you with her until later."

"I'm a widow, Chief Inspector." She gave the wedding ring on her left hand a nervous twist. "My husband's name was Mason."

"And let me save a little of your time, Mr. Thane." Lady Dunspar's voice was quiet and steady. "Barbara knows why you were here. In return, she told me something I didn't know this morning. You said a man called Shaw had been killed. But you didn't tell me that his companion—the man who disappeared—was named Herrald. That might have made a difference."

Thane nodded. "He's still missing, Lady Dunspar—the same Peter Herrald you telephoned on Friday evening." He saw her surprise and gave a tight smile. "It's my turn to say that was something I didn't know this morning. But a lot has happened since. For a start, you're wondering why a certain car wasn't returned on schedule, aren't you?"

The two women exchanged glances, then Lady Dunspar gave a soft sigh. "You've discovered quite a lot in a very short time, Mr. Thane. I suppose I should congratulate you."

He was fairly certain now that they were going to talk, but it was a moment for shock tactics, a final blow to smash any remaining reluctance. "The car crashed about two hours ago, during a chase on a farm road not far from here. The driver died." As the colour ebbed from her face he shook his head. "Martin Kelch wasn't aboard. The driver's name was Serviev—he was responsible for a bomb explosion in Edinburgh this morning, an explosion just as General Shashkov was arriving at a factory."

"Was he—"

"Killed? No Shashkov's all right. But there are five other men in hospital, at least one critically ill. Policemen, Lady Dunspar. One of their jobs was to hold back the crowd that had gathered . . . a crowd of men, women, children." His words came flat and level, yet were eloquent in their muted anger. "Your opinion may be different. But for my money anyone who'll explode a bomb like the one this morning rates as a mad dog, and no matter how fond you've been of a dog, when he goes mad he has to be hunted down."

There was pain as well as dignity in her nod. "I understand."

"Good." Thane looked at mother and daughter in turn. "I came here alone for a reason. Down in England one policeman's evidence of what he sees or hears is enough on its own. But not in Scotland—up here, any statement must have two witnesses. In other words, if you answer my questions I can use the information. But because I'm alone, I couldn't prove in court that you'd said a word. I thought you might find that— well, easier."

"What you really mean is that you'll learn more from me if I'm not worried about being dragged off to a cell in the local police station." Lady Dunspar showed a brief twinkle of her more usual humour. "Barbara—" she beckoned her daughter forward "—Mr. Thane might like some tea while we talk."

"You're sure, Mother?" The girl crossed over and laid a hand on her mother's shoulder. She bit her lip. "It's your decision, but—"

"It's my decision." Lady Dunspar was firm. "Just one thing, Mr. Thane. Barbara at no time played any part in what has happened . . . at no time."

"Then why did she come here?" Thane watched the slim blonde pour tea into the cups, "Why this afternoon?"

"I'll answer for myself." The girl jerked round. "Yesterday I was questioned about Peter—no reasons given, just asked if I knew where he was, how long I'd known him, other things. Then this morning I discovered I was being followed, and not very cleverly, Mr. Thane. Well, I knew Peter had been planning a fishing holiday near here with a friend called Shaw. So I dodged my policeman and drove up to find out if my mother knew anything about what was happening." She turned back to the cups. "Sugar?"

"Thanks." Thane rubbed his chin. "Couldn't you have telephoned?"

"I once operated a hotel switchboard." She handed him his cup. "I've never felt quite the same about telephones since."

Thane gave in. "All right. Supposing we start at the beginning—with Peter Herrald."

It was one of the strangest interviews he'd ever coped with, sitting there balancing the delicate Royal Doulton cup and saucer on his knee, refusing a biscuit, nodding as Lady Dunspar answered his questions, her daughter coming in occasionally to supplement the older woman's replies.

Barbara Mason and Peter Herrald had met at a party in Glasgow about two months before and Herrald, whose business apparently left him with both time and a reasonable amount of money to spare, had begun dating her regularly. On the third week, a drive north into the Highlands had ended in their visiting Lady Dunspar—and they'd been back at the house together twice more since then.

"A close friendship?"

"We weren't in love, if that's what you mean." The young widow flushed. "We liked each other's company, but that's as far as it went. I'm not hunting for a new husband—and Peter liked coming here, even though most of the time Mother kept telling him about the work she'd done at that refugee camp."

"He was interested in it," protested Lady Dunspar. "In a way, that's why all this has happened—why I'm to blame." She set down the cup, her manner weary. "You see, I told him about Martin. Martin always wanted to go abroad, Mr. Thane. But it wasn't always easy for refugees, and he couldn't get the necessary permissions . . . if he had, he wouldn't have gone back to his own country."

The rest of the sequence fell into place. Herrald had listened and sympathised. He'd talked about his own interests, the import-export contacts which were part of his business, his nodding acquaintance with Glasgow's sprawling dockland.

"And that's why—"

"Why I thought of him when Martin arrived here needing help," nodded Lady Dunspar.

Thane listened. She'd telephoned Peter Herrald at his home on the Friday evening, asking if he knew any way in which the four runaway trawlermen could be got aboard a ship towards their goal.

"He said he wasn't sure, but that he'd certainly do what he could—

then he told me he was coming north anyway, and that the best idea might be for him to meet Martin and the others."

"You telephoned him again the next morning?"

"Yes. Martin had been worried about the idea, but he'd agreed by then. He spoke to Peter, and they arranged a meeting for the Tuesday."

"Where? At the old cottage?"

She shook her head. "No. It was to be at Aberfeldy, in the evening."

"Did your 'guests' know about General Shashkov's visit by then?"

"Yes. I—I told Martin myself. I don't know why, I just—just thought it was something that would interest him."

"It looks as though it did," said Thane, his expression grim. "How did they react?"

"They were bitter." Lady Dunspar looked up at him. "Yes, especially Martin, Chief Inspector—people who have suffered have a right to their feelings. But these men were only interested in getting away, getting right out of Europe. Not one of them hinted at anything else."

It was after Herrald's call that she'd first suggested the old cottage as a hide-out. Then she'd despatched a shaved, cleaned-up Kelch into Perth carrying a cheque drawn on her bank—telephoning first to make sure it would be cashed on the spot, then again to satisfy herself there had been no hitch. By the time he'd returned, the three other trawlermen had helped her lay out a stock of tinned food from her own household stores.

"The car came last, of course," she told Thane. "I knew young Tommy Harton would give me one, but I thought leaving it till the last minute looked more natural."

"When did they leave?"

"A little before noon on Sunday, and I haven't seen them since." She held her head high. "That's my story, Mr. Thane."

He swung towards her daughter. "And you knew nothing about any of this—Herrald didn't call you to tell you what was happening?"

The girl shook her head. "Neither Peter nor my mother wanted me to be involved—she told me nothing until today." She took a cigarette from a box on the table, lit it with a quick, nervous snap of the matching table lighter, and asked, "What do you think has happened to him? Do you . . . do you think he's been killed too?"

"Not according to Serviev. About the only thing he did tell me was that Herrald was safe." Thane shrugged. "We won't really know until we've found him—" another point still puzzled him "—Lady Dunspar, why did you believe that Kelch couldn't have been involved in Shaw's death if it had happened on Wednesday?"

She kneaded her fingers together on her lap. "Because Martin telephoned here on Tuesday night. He said he was going with Peter Herrald to Glasgow the next morning, and that it looked as if their troubles were just about over."

"Anything else?"

She said no. Patiently, Thane backtracked over the story, seeking any possible lead to where Kelch and his companions might have gone to once they had to leave the cottage. He drew a blank. No, they'd left nothing behind them—he was welcome to search if he chose, and no need for a warrant. No, there had been no further contact since the Tuesday call—she'd been hoping that Martin Kelch himself might return for the change-over of cars and she could have found out what had happened.

"One last point." Thane plugged on patiently. "When Kelch was a refugee over here, did he know anyone from the Stirling area?"

"I suppose so." She frowned. "It's possible. He was given a job working in a coal mine—a lot of the refugees got the chance. But like most of them, his health didn't stand up to it."

"Flenders Colliery?"

She concentrated for a moment. "I think that was the name. Why?"

Routine, he told her. Barbara Mason showed him out, her mother sitting in the chair beside the Adam fireplace, a hurt, bewildered look on her face.

"Will you be back?" Her manner made it plain she hoped for a negative answer.

"Probably."

"I suppose you'll have men watching here." Her face was tight and angry.

"They started just before you arrived, Mrs. Mason."

She paused at the doorway and looked out across the green of the grass towards the river. "My mother doesn't go in for emotional scenes,

Chief Inspector. You heard her say she blames herself for most of this. If Peter—if he's dead, she'll feel that's her fault too." She shrugged. "I don't suppose it matters—the police don't trust anyone very much, do they?"

"Goodbye, Mrs. Mason." He said nothing more, though he was tempted. The door slammed shut, and he walked back down the driveway to his car.

The arranged rendezvous was back at Aberfeldy, and he arrived there at an awkward moment—Phil Moss and Colonel Donnan stood inside the main office of the little police station, Donnan flushed and angry, Moss with a stubborn, determined glower on his thin, lined face. In the background, one of the local police was self-consciously fixing his attention on writing a report.

The sudden silence as he entered was warning enough. Thane looked from one man to the other and sighed. "All right, what's up?"

The two men bristled, each waiting for the other to speak.

"Visitors first, then," declared Thane. "Colonel?"

The Irishman drew himself erect. "I've half a mind—" he ignored the quick, cynical twist which glinted on his opponent's lips "—I've half a mind to report him for insubordination, insulting language and . . ."

"And common sense," suggested Moss acidly.

Thane threw a frown towards him. "Quiet, Phil—you'll have your turn."

Moss shrugged. "Sorry."

"What was the trouble, Colonel?"

Donnan scowled. "I come dashing up here as soon as I hear about Serviev's crash. Then Moss tells me about the link between Herrald and Lady Dunspar's daughter—yet when I ask him to have Glasgow police pick her up for requestioning he gives me a flat refusal. I make a second request—that he turn over to me any papers found on Serviev—and again he refuses."

"What about the insulting language?" probed Thane.

"Well—" Donnan pursed his lips. "Maybe there was some on both sides. But nobody calls me a—a bog-trotting Mick and gets away with it."

"Barbara Mason is with her mother—I've just come from talking to them both," said Thane. "Anyway, I'd have turned down your idea. Some people you pull in, and they talk. Others you get more from by leaving them to think things over. Her mother admits contacting Herrald and asking him to help, but says the girl knew nothing—I'm inclined to believe her. She also says Martin Kelch once worked at Flenders Colliery—"

"Where the explosives were stolen!" Donnan temporarily forgot his feud. "That explains one part of the puzzle." Then he scowled again, though not quite so angrily. "There are still these papers—"

"Serviev's pockets were empty," said Thane.

Moss cleared his throat. "Colin, we did find a couple things in the car, after you'd gone. They were under the front seat. I thought you'd better see 'em first, before they . . . disappeared. They've been checked for prints. Negative apart from Serviev." He turned to a paper-wrapped bundle on the table at his side. "Ever seen one of those?"

Thane took the small, metal-framed box and examined it. A factory-made unit, fairly similar to the speed-control unit on his youngster's electric-train set, it was different in that there were no outlet terminals, only a small socket at one end and a single, calibrated knob.

"I have," said Donnan. "It's a remote-control unit for one of those fancy toy speedboats. The box is an elementary short-range transmitter—its signal varies the boat's rudder control. Well, the idea's simple enough—the bomb-disposal boys found some fragments in the letter-box wreckage which were probably the other end of the system."

Buy the two sections of the remote control in a toy shop, fit one into a package with gelignite and an electrically fired detonator, the electric circuit completed when the rudder control was swung by the transmitter's action, the transmitter operator a safe distance away . . . they saw now how the blast could have been so perfectly timed by men who had had only a few days and limited resources available to rig a package of potential death.

"What else?" Thane leaned over the table, his curiosity mounting.

Moss flipped a golf tee along the table. The little wooden shape spun to a gradual halt as he lifted out the last of his finds. "The tee was jammed under the carpeting, as if it had fallen from somebody's pocket. But this little piece of work was tied under the seat springs, held so that it would stay nice and handy."

The knife had a six-inch blade, the steel stone-honed down to half its original thickness, a needle point backed by two razor-keen edges. Thane ran his thumb lightly along the cold metal. It didn't take much imagination to realise how effective a weapon it would have been. He'd seen knives like it before, but used for a more peaceful purpose. "Once upon a time this was a fish-gutting knife, Phil. Most deep-sea fishermen have one—but not worked into this fashion."

"It's still a gutting knife," agreed Donnan soberly. "But not for fish, Thane." He turned to Phil Moss, a grudging respect back in his eyes. "Well, if Kelch and his men are still in business tomorrow, that golf tee tells us where they're going to make their next try."

"The Old Course?"

"At St. Andrews," nodded the security man. "Can I have the transmitter box now? I'd like the army bomb-disposal people to see it. They may be able to rig some sort of a jamming device."

"It's an idea," agreed Thane. "If Kelch has another little package ready, the same as today's, it would give him quite a surprise if you jammed the wave length, maybe even caused a premature bang. But where could he plant the bomb this time?"

"Your guess is as good as mine." Donnan shrugged. "The course is closed for all play tomorrow until General Shashkov has completed his round. Every step he takes he'll be covered by a security screen. I've got cops, some of my own men, a bunch of R.A.F. police drafted over from Leuchars air station—and precautions will be stiffer than ever after today. I'd like to see him cancel the rest of his programme, but the old devil's insisting on carrying it out to the letter, and saying it is up to us to keep him in one piece. He's almost enjoying the situation."

"Will he have a gallery following him around?"

"Bound to have—and a big one. Maybe several hundred people." Colonel Donnan's unhappiness was complete. "We can keep them fairly well back, outside ropes. The stewards and the guard force have orders that only a picked entourage group of reporters and camera men get inside the cordon. But we can't do more. If we sealed the course off from the outside world it would be an admission of complete and absolute ruddy fright, and Moscow's propaganda factories would make us look like a bunch of red-nosed comics—that, or blood-stained capitalistic lackeys keeping the Soviet's hero isolated from making friendly contact with the eager, downtrodden Scottish peasantry."

"You've a fair grasp of the language," Thane told him. "What's he like anyway?"

"The lingo is infectious when part of your daily chore is reading translated extracts from *Pravda* to find out which way the wind's blowing," grunted Donnan. "Shashkov? He's one of the bunch who grabbed their chance when Joe Stalin's day ended. Tough as nails—though he's supposed to be out of favour with some sections of the Moscow clique, who think he's wearing the velvet gloves too often nowadays. He's one of the divide-and-conquer brigade, strictly a Cold War merchant with sense enough to know his side would get just as hurt as anyone if the cold ever turned to hot."

"Better the devil you know than the devil you don't," mused Thane, laying the knife back in the parcel, then reaching in again to take out a folded newspaper which had been lying at its foot. "What about this, Phil?"

"It was in the glove compartment. Yesterday's edition of the *Bugle*— I looked through it, but there's no marking of any kind." Moss stuck his hands in his pockets. "Still, I thought I'd better leave it with the rest."

"Made any arrangement about Serviev's clothing?"

"A car's bringing the stuff from the mortuary."

Thane glanced at his watch. "Well, there doesn't seem to be much else we can do around here. Unless—you said you had a complaint to lodge, Colonel. Want to make it official?"

"Oh, the hell with it." Donnan grinned. "I've got the jitters, that's all—anyone seems to be rubbing me the wrong way, and I react."

"It could be a potential ulcer." Thane's eyes twinkled with a mixture of humour and relief. "Ask Moss—he's an authority. But not now. You're going back to Shashkov?"

"As usual. This is the night he eats with the Secretary of State." Colonel Donnan shook his head. "The way things are going, they'll want me to taste the soup before it's served."

Thane had already given him his ration of sympathy. "Have fun," he nodded. "Phil, I want you to go over to St. Andrews. Say hello to the local police, then start asking around the Old Course staff—starter, greenskeepers, ticket rangers, anyone like that. If that golf tee means what we think, then Kelch or Serviev or one of the others has been recce-ing that golf course. Better try the local golf-equipment shops too. With Lady Dunspar's money in their pockets, plus what they took from Herrald's office, they'd be able to outfit themselves for the game."

"Hotels have already been checked," contributed Colonel Donnan. "We drew a blank. But—no, we didn't inquire too closely on casual golfers. The Old Course is public, pay your money and play your game— there must be scores of players going over it every day."

"Then we'll just have to hope that our trawlermen were spectacular enough to be remembered." Thane bundled the package together, pushing the control device towards Donnan. "I'm taking these and Serviev's clothing back to Glasgow, to let Dan Laurence's boffins have a look at them. He should be able to tell us more about what he found at the cottage while I'm at it . . . and with luck, I may get MacMaster's contribution at the same time."

"Aye." Moss put an edge into the word. "You'll be back tonight?"

"Depends on what happens, and that's up to the boffins."

"I don't grudge you an evening at home. That's one of the privileges of rank. I just wish you'd put more polish into the excuses." He reached for his hat. "I'll keep in contact with the St. Andrews station—and give Mary my love." He had followed Donnan out of the door before Thane could muster a reply.

By early evening, Thane was back in the city. His driver took the car straight into the parking yard at Police Headquarters, stopped, and waited hopefully.

"That's all for a spell," nodded Thane, then thumbed towards the packages on the rear seat. "But take these up to the Scientific Bureau before you disappear. Tell 'em I'll be along soon."

Policy dictated his first call, on Bhudda Ilford. But the city's C.I.D. boss was out. The duty man at the Central C.I.D. bar wasn't sure where or why, only that it involved a runaway bank cashier and that Chief Superintendent Ilford wouldn't be back for a couple of hours.

"You know the old man." He winked. "Every now and again he gets up off his backside, takes over a job, and goes out into the big, bad world."

Thane had experienced it before. Bhudda's brief excursions back to working detection formed a type of safety valve, one the C.I.D. boss claimed help keep him sane in the face of his usual round of desk-bound activities.

"When he comes in, I'd like to know."

"You will." The duty man turned back to monitor the radio, which was beginning to brisken with messages to the mobile units. As Thane left, the first of the night-shift squads were beginning to drift in . . . Friday night was pay night, and they'd have a busy evening once the pubs closed at nine-thirty and their customers scattered around the streets.

"Chief Inspector—" the hail came as he crossed the street again to the main Headquarters building. He slowed to let the hurrying figure of Detective Sergeant MacLeod catch up with him. The sergeant puffed a little after his sprint. "Didn't expect to see you here, sir!"

"Makes a change from chasing my tail up north," Thane told him. "Anything happening in the division?"

"Nothing desperate," said MacLeod thankfully. "I'm along to have a word with Records office—three complaints of a con man working a television-maintenance racket came in today, and I thought they could maybe match the method on the m.o. files and give us a lead."

"What about Vince Bruce?"

The sergeant shook his head. The young housebreaker was still on the run. "But brother Donny has admitted five other break-ins," he volunteered. "We've recovered some of the stuff."

"Donny's share?" Thane was unimpressed. "Vince always keeps the best. He's the one I want." He rattled the coins in his trouser pocket and remembered his other interest. "Any word from Sam Newton?"

"Millside's pitch-and-toss expert?" MacLeod gave an involuntary twinkle. "Aye, he phoned in. He's made contact with some of the bunch in Jock Howard's game, and says he'll be playing tonight."

"Good." Constable Newton was likely to enjoy the experience of being paid to gamble. "Tell him to stick with it—there's usually a bigger turnout on a Saturday, and then the real school get together on Sundays. If we can nail Jock Howard on a Sunday so much the better." Thane's dry chuckle heralded misfortune for the pitch-and-toss organiser. "Gambling on the Sabbath always looks that little bit meatier on a charge sheet."

He said goodbye to the sergeant and went into the Headquarters building. The elevator took him to the second floor, the Scientific Branch's area, branded as either hallowed or unholy precincts depending on the results produced and the effect they had on some hard-hoping divisional C.I.D. man's theories.

Thane knocked on the opened door of Dan Laurence's room and went in, just as Laurence stuck his head round the connecting door leading to the main laboratory area beyond.

"It's you, is it?" The Scientific Branch chief gave a grunt. He was in his shirt-sleeves, the usual ash-tipped cigarette smouldered between his lips, its smoke making him peer through half-shut eyes. "Hell, man, it's no' ten minutes since that last load of yours was dumped on my lap."

"I just thought I'd make sure you got it all right," soothed Thane.

"Well, we did." Dan Laurence was at his gruffest. "And if characters would stop telephoning me to remind me anything connected with Martin Kelch has to have absolute priority I might have more of a chance to do something about it. Hell, Colin, show some ruddy humanity—away and lose yourself in the canteen, go home, go to the pictures, any damn thing, but leave us alone for a couple of hours."

"You'll be ready by then?"

"With your stuff, yes. The lads I left up north are sending down some scrapings and fingerprint samples from the Ford your pal Serviev crashed, but it'll be nearer midnight before we've got the stuff sorted out." He rummaged on his desk. "Here's something while you're waiting—the report on what we got between the Mini-Van and the cottage this morning."

Thane took the half-dozen stapled sheets of close-typed quarto paper and scanned through the top-page summary which gave the bare bones of the fuller detail within. When the Scientific Branch put its name to a report the apparent confusion in which they worked died into cold, carefully marshalled fact, and this one was no exception.

It started off quietly enough. Latent prints found aboard the van matched samples from Shaw's home and Herrald's flat. But there were others, still unidentified, which matched up with some of the four sets of prints each labelled "unknown" which had been found in the cottage. Traces of Shaw's prints had also been found in the building, as had those of Herrald—or, as the Branch report stubbornly phrased it, "were similar to fingerprints believed to be those of the men concerned."

Next came the Mini-Van. Thane raised an eyebrow. "The bullet hole in the driver's window showed the shot had been fired from close range, at a slightly downward angle, and from outside the van . . . Dan?"

"Just what it says." Laurence displayed his usual contempt for the non-technical mind. "I wanted to make sure the bloke in the passenger seat didn't pull the trigger—two shots, one through the glass, the other into Shaw. But fire a bullet through glass and it punches a hole, an anything but clean hole. Put the microscope on it, and on one side there are always wee flakes o' glass blown away. The bullet is always fired from the opposite side to where the flakes are kicked loose." The Scientific Branch chief liked his little lectures. He lit a fresh cigarette from the stub of the old and went on. "The clean entry punch shows the bullet was fired from close up—there's a trace o' powder anyway, to tell the truth. And more flakes being punched off from the bottom o' the exit hole than the top tells us the angle. Happy?"

"Deliriously." The last section was a report on an analysis of mud scrapings from the van's tyres and underside—local soils, stone chips, road grit, the same repeated in the dirt samples taken from the little vehicle's rubber floor mats.

"Hmm." Laurence gazed at him quizzically. "You're no' exactly the picture o' a satisfied customer, Colin."

"Sorry." Thane folded the report and put it in his pocket. "But there's not much for me in this lot."

"Aye, we'll maybe have better news for you when you come back," said Laurence pointedly. "Hey—" he snapped his fingers in sudden recollection "—old MacMaster left a message for you. The blood on the van's seat was Group C, the same as Shaw's. Herrald's blood is Group AB. One of the Central Division lads found Herrald had his appendix taken out about a year back, and the hospital still had his card on file."

"So Herrald should still be in one piece—Serviev said the same thing." Thane turned toward the door, then stopped. "Dan, I'll be back in those two hours. Anyone wants me in between, I'll either be at the *Bugle* office or at home."

Dan Laurence shook his head as the burly chief went out. He liked Thane, and at that moment didn't envy him his task. But then, he didn't particularly envy any cop outside his own test-tube kingdom. Professor MacMaster's motto was that dead men could tell any amount of tales. Dan Laurence went further, and declared his laboratory could coax speech from any material.

He took the cigarette from his mouth and gave a bellow. "Willie! Away down to the canteen and bring up some sandwiches. We've got work to do, but a man's got to eat!"

The youngest member of his team, busy at a bench in the main laboratory, heard the shout and groaned. He had a date with the little blond policewoman who'd recently arrived on the staff down in Lost Property. He just hoped she'd understand—again.

The *Evening Bugle* office, a cream-stone building which looked more like a church than the headquarters of a high-geared money-making newspaper group, was situated a stone's throw away from the City Chambers, the centre of Glasgow's municipal administration. The stone's-throw distance was apt—the *Bugle* took as poor a view of the efficiency of the city fathers as they did of the *Bugle*'s activities, and a daily barrage of verbal missiles formed a regular trade between the two forces.

Peace apparently reigned, however, as Thane entered the main door of the *Bugle* office and asked at the reception desk for Jock Mills, the paper's crime reporter. The last edition of the day was being run off in a muffled thunder of presses from the basement below, a covey of young messenger boys were playing cards with their bus-fare money as stakes.

The commissionaire, a thin-faced ex-soldier with a rash of medal ribbons on his tunic, spoke into the internal phone for a moment, then called over the nearest of the youngsters. The boy came over, somewhat annoyed at the interruption.

"Mr. Mills, up in the interview room." The commissionaire thumbed towards Thane. The boy gave a brief nod and led their visitor towards the elevator.

"Been here long?" asked Thane.

"Two months."

"Going to be a reporter?" encouraged Thane.

"Me?" The boy was shocked. "Work round the clock and no overtime? That's for mugs, mister."

The elevator halted before he could detail his own life plan, and he guided Thane along the door-lined corridor to the interview room, a frosted-glass cubicle furnished with a handful of armchairs and an extension phone.

Jock Mills was already there. The *Bugle*'s crime reporter, a cheerful, red-haired young man, greeted him warmly.

"I'll take it this isn't a social call," he grinned. "And I haven't trod on anybody's toes lately—so that means you want something."

Thane looked around him warily. "This room used to be wired for sound, Jock. You told me about it once, remember?"

The reporter flushed. "That's only when we want a tape of an interview—some people go pale at the sight of a notebook, you know that. Others have a nasty habit of calling you a liar once their story is in print and they think they can sue."

Thane accepted it. Jock Mills had built up his police contacts on trust, and that took too long, offered the chance of too many exclusive stories over the average year, to throw away for a one-day sensation.

"What can you tell me about this, Jock?" He took a thick manilla envelope from his pocket and waited while the reporter opened out the folded newspaper it contained—the paper Phil Moss had found in the Ford's glove box.

"Yesterday's—an early edition." The younger man gave Thane a shrewd glance. "It's important?"

"Maybe."

"Something to do with the Shashkov affair?" He chuckled at the Millside chief's stony-faced reaction. "We're splashing the Edinburgh bomb attempt—everybody is. But still not one whisper about the four gents from a certain trawler."

"Which is probably wise," growled Thane.

"No comment." The reporter gave a sardonic shake of his head. "We've been on to the trawlermen angle for days. Our local cor tipped us off the day after they got ashore, just about the time the fifth man gave himself up. The story was set and ready when the editor was handed a Ministry 'D' notice. He didn't fancy a spell in jail, so the story was killed." Mills shrugged. "We've a free press, as long as it behaves itself. Anyway, what about this paper?"

"Does the *Bugle* circulate as far north as Aberfeldy?"

"No . . ." Jock Mills turned its pages casually, then stopped at the centre spread, a new interest dawning. "But this edition would go even further north. Mind if I bring the circulation manager in on this? His name's Vaughan—he's all right."

Thane nodded agreement and waited while Mills used the telephone. The *Bugle*'s circulation manager, a portly, bow-tied bustler, joined them within a minute. Once Jock Mills had shown him the paper he displayed the same interest.

"We call this a 'slip' edition," he explained. "The *Bugle* loses a lot of circulation in the summer and autumn, readers going off on holiday— and to try and hold on to some of it we send the paper after them. These slip editions are identical with our regular issues except for one inside page. We slip a new page in for a limited run, maybe a thousand copies, maybe more for each of a dozen or so holiday centres . . . you know the sort of thing, happy family groups on the beach, what's on at the local cinema, lucky prizewinners in our promenade competitions." He grimaced. "It costs money, the return is small and the page layout is usually a mess. But it keeps the circulation figures looking a little brighter."

"And this one?"

"Went to Aberdeen." The circulation manager pointed to the picture page before him. "Horrible, isn't it?"

"You mean this paper couldn't be bought anywhere else?"

"Definitely no."

"But some copies would be kept here?"

"One or two." The man hesitated. "Then, of course, the delivery driver might hand out a few on the way north." He fingered his bow tie and gave Thane a sly glance. "Ever known a police station that didn't have a free supply of papers for the men on office duty? It always helps when one of our boys gets booked for speeding—"

Thane made a diplomatic retreat. "This paper didn't come from a police station. Where else?"

"Level-crossing operators get them, cafés where the drivers stop for a meal—look, I'll try and locate the man who did yesterday's Aberdeen run."

It took a few minutes. The driver concerned was out, and they had to wait until he returned. But when Thane left the newspaper office he had a list of half a dozen places where spare copies of the Aberdeen slip edition had been handed out.

The three which mattered most were all in the Fife area. The *Bugle* van had been on a two-stage run, one half of its papers due to be off-loaded at Kirkcaldy, a regular-edition delivery point. From there, the special slip edition had travelled north through Fife, crossed the River Tay by vehicle ferry, and then rejoined the main road for Aberdeen. It was far away from the Glen Lyon district, but a route which passed only a double handful of miles distant from both St. Andrews and Sunbury Colliery, General Shashkov's two Saturday stopping places!

He halted at the pavement's edge and glanced at his watch. In just over an hour he was due to see Dan Laurence again. The three places in Fife where the driver had handed over slip editions were a café, a filling station, and a shop where he'd stopped to buy cigarettes. The sooner Phil Moss had the addressees and could check them out the better.

Thane said a sad goodbye to his hopes of a meal at home and settled for a telephone at Headquarters and egg and chips in the police canteen.

SIX

Hunched in the front seat of a Fife county patrol car, Detective Inspector Moss eyed the brightly lit shop across the roadway in jaundiced gloom. Since Thane's telephone message had finally reached him, he'd tracked down two of the three slip-edition copies of the *Bugle*—and that apparently simple task had taken him nearly two hours.

On the surface, it had seemed simple enough—certainly better than the job of plodding around questioning the Old Course greenskeeping staff. They were used to visiting strangers arriving, treated them as commonplace, and could only shake their heads over the descriptions he kept repeating.

The county car and driver were waiting on him, and he'd left the course right away. This same little general store they were now parked opposite had been the nearest and first on his list, about ten miles from St. Andrews, on the outskirts of Cupar, one of the many small towns in the area. But on the first visit the shop assistant had known nothing about the newspaper, and the owner was out on a delivery run and not due back for sometime.

He'd moved on. The two other places, the filling station and the café, were both at Glenrothes, another ten miles south. The filling station's copy was easy enough to trace—torn into squares, it was hanging on a nail in the mechanics' washroom. At the café, he thought he'd struck better fortune when the proprietor remembered giving his copy away. The snag was that half a dozen "regulars" had been in the place at the time and he couldn't remember which of them had taken it. Moss had found out for him, the hard way, had scored the café off his list—and now the general store represented the last chance.

"Think you'll have better luck here, sir?" His driver, a bulky Fifer with a neat, bristling moustache, was beginning to feel equally disgruntled.

"Huh!" Moss glared again at the shop's beacon-like windows. Dusk had faded into darkness on their return trip to the town, and the car's side-lights cast their own dull glow by the kerbside. "He's probably using the paper to wrap up groceries." A twinkle of lights a little way along the road caught his eye. "What's that place?"

"The huts?" The driver relaxed a little behind the wheel. "Sort of a holiday camp, sir—pre-fab chalets, home-made huts, that sort of thing. Used to be a couple of converted buses too, but the council said that was a bit much, and they had to move on."

Moss nodded. He'd vaguely noticed the collection on their first visit—the Fife holiday coast and its neighbouring inland had several similar spots.

"Here goes." He got out of the car and crossed over.

The *ting* of the shop bell as he opened the door brought a small fat butterball of a man hurrying from the room at the rear. The shopkeeper beamed across the counter, one chubby hand resting lightly on a mound of pre-packed cheese.

"Police." Moss slapped his warrant card on the counter.

"The girl told me you'd been." The man chuckled. "She thought it was something to do with a newspaper, but she always gets things tangled."

"This time she was right," Moss told him. "A van driver says he gave you a copy of the Glasgow *Bugle* yesterday, when he stopped off for cigarettes."

"That's right." The moon-shaped face reddened a little. "Why? He's stopped here before, that bloke—always gives me one. Says he always has a few spares."

"Nothing wrong with him giving you it," Moss reassured him. "What matters is, do you still have it?"

The shopkeeper's fingers rapped a soft, thoughtful tattoo on the cheese. "Well . . . no." Like most fat men, when his smile died the expression which remained was almost lugubrious. "You see, we don't get evening papers around here—not normally, anyway. You've got to go further into town for them. One of the fellows from the huts came in for a message—pound of cooked ham, it was—and he happened to see the paper on the counter. He asked me if he could have it. Surprised me a bit, but I said yes."

"Surprised you?"

"Well, him being some kind of a foreigner."

"Medium height, sturdy build, grey hair, small moustache—about my age?" Moss reeled off Serviev's description and felt a sudden thrill of tension.

"Younger maybe, but that's him—a decent bloke. They all are."

"All? You mean there are more of them in one of the huts?"

"Four of them, though he's the only one I've really spoken to at all." The shopkeeper pulled the loose skin of one cheek. "I wondered about renting them the hut, but they're a quiet bunch, and there've been no complaints from any of the other families."

It took another half-dozen questions to squeeze out that the shopkeeper owned three of the huts on the holiday ground and rented them out as a handy extra income. He'd had a "vacancy" sign hanging three days before, the result of a last-minute cancellation, and the men had arrived out of the blue and taken the booking.

"Ten quid a week, power and television thrown in." He was worried now. "They . . . they seemed all right."

"Did they have a car, a grey Ford?" Moss took the man's nod in his stride. "And they're still living in the hut?"

"Well, they've paid till the end of the week—though I haven't seen the car around tonight."

"It won't be back," said Moss dryly. "Which hut?"

Second chalet on the left in the rear row, the shopkeeper told him—and was still pulling at his cheek as Moss went out. As the door clanged shut, the thin, wiry cop stopped on the pavement for a moment, looking along at the holiday ground, then made up his mind. He crossed to the waiting car and gave a brief nod as the driver looked out of his opened window.

"We're on to something this time." He thumbed back over his shoulder. "I'm going to have a scout round one of those huts—while I'm doing it, call control and ask 'em to stand by for a possible assistance call. If there's anyone at home over there we'll need help before we knock on the door."

"You said there would only be three of them, sir." The Fifer stroked his moustache. "I don't mind a wee bit o' a roughhouse."

"You're more likely to get a stick of gelignite shoved down your throat if these laddies play rough," growled Moss. "Get on with it."

The driver winced a little and reached for the microphone, making a mental note that this particular terrier had teeth. Satisfied, Moss tucked his hands deep into the pockets of his flapping dirty-white raincoat and headed for the holiday huts, his pace neither fast nor slow, walking through the entrance with the air of a visitor who knew where he was going but was in no desperate rush to get there.

In all, there were about forty huts in the collection, scattered in rough, unplanned rows. The main pathway was a mixture of rough tarmac and rougher road chips, dimly lit by one meagre line of weak electric bulbs strung between wires. Every few yards, an unlit side path led off to either side. He took the third path to the left, strolling into its darkness, hands still in his pockets. A few of the huts around had lights burning behind their drawn curtains, he heard music coming from one and the ghostly blue-white flicker of a television screen varied its intensity through another lightly veiled window.

He left the path beside one dark, silent structure which appeared to owe its basic creation to a variety of packing cases and took to the darker shadows, moving quietly, striking towards the rear of the camp area.

There were six huts in the rear row, and the storekeeper's chalet was easily recognisable for two reasons. It bulked the largest, and it was the only one without lights.

Moss eased forward, his footsteps muffled by the soft turf. At the chalet door he stopped, listened, pressed his ear against the wood, still heard nothing, and tried the handle. It turned. With his free hand he drew out the sawn-off, lead-loaded, strictly non-regulation baton from his inside pocket. The door creaked a little as he pushed it open, but the house remained still. He waited another long moment then, decision made, fumbled for the light switch and the bulb in the little hallway blazed to life. The baton still at the ready, he began a cautious search.

The chalet was empty, but it hadn't been that way for long. The glowing stove, the smell of tobacco smoke in the air, the greasy dishes piled in the tiny kitchen sink, the still-tepid coffee pot, all emphasized the point. The place had been kept reasonably tidy, but then, the men who'd been using it had travelled light—and trawlermen, living in confined space, soon learn the elementary rules of housekeeping.

Moss frowned uneasily. Had Kelch and his two companions taken fright at Serviev's non-return and decided to move on? He stopped beside the stove as a glint of metal caught his eye. Some scraps of sheet tin, a soldering iron, and a length of wire solder lay side by side in an old cardboard shoebox.

There was something wrong, something very wrong—he sensed it rather than realised anything positive. On a sudden hunch, he crossed to the television set in one corner and laid his hand on the cabinet. It was warm to the touch—only minutes could have passed since it had been in use.

Moss headed for the door. He reached it, switched out the hall light, and stepped into the dark of the night. It took his eyes a brief second to re-adjust, and that was long enough. A vague shape detached itself from the wall at his side and he was still turning, still raising the baton, when the blow fell.

Detective Inspector Moss slumped down, his mind blanking red midway through a half-formed curse at his own stupidity.

Two other men joined his assailant, stepping silently from the shadows. The tallest chuckled, then joined his companions in dragging the unconscious figure back into the chalet.

"Belt them on the skull—that's an old-fashioned philosophy. The trouble with today's average cop is that he doesn't realise that he needs brain, not brawn." Detective Superintendent Laurence was once again happily mounted on his pet hobby-horse.

"All right, Dan, I'm not arguing." Colin Thane gave a sigh and looked hopefully at the pair of shoes on the laboratory table between them. He'd returned to the Scientific Branch exactly on schedule. Dan Laurence had agreed he was ready, but so far was showing no inclination to hurry. "You said there was something interesting about Serviev's shoes. . . ."

"Uh? Oh, aye—aye, that's right. Well, for a start we found the odd fleck o' grass an' grass seed on them. Then there was some sand engrained around the soles and in the welt o' the uppers. The sand had a trace or two o' bone meal, Colin—and the microscope showed one or two grains o' the same combination around the tip o' yon wee golf tee you brought in. Which leads me to the inspired deduction that he'd been walking, probably playing, over a seaside golf course . . . it was shore sand, not inland stuff, and bone meal's a regular top dressing for many a golf course." He held the shoes closer to the light, satisfaction in his eyes. "But we're no' finished. Take a look at the leather at the toes. See how it's pretty badly scuffed?"

Thane rubbed his thumb lightly over the leather, feeling the rough scoring which marred its surface. "What about it?"

"It's good and bad." Laurence shook his head. "Sorry, Colin, I know you're thinkin' about Shashkov's game o' golf tomorrow. But you'd maybe better keep an open mind. We got fragments o' coal and sandstone grit out o' those cuts, and more o' both from his clothes and shoes."

"Which came first?" Tight-lipped, Thane saw his hopes tangle and crash.

"Well . . ." The Scientific Branch chief frowned and absent-mindedly lit a cigarette. "On the shoes, the coal grit and sandstone covered the sand and bone-meal traces here an' there, so if I had to plump for a choice I'd say he'd been prowlin' around a colliery or a coal yard o' some kind after he'd been at the golf." He put down the shoes and sat on the table, legs dangling. "Another thing, you wouldn't take a rope with you if you were having a game o' golf, would you? Yet we found a whole lot o' wee rope fibres on his clothes."

"Why take a rope to a colliery?"

"Hell, how should I know?" protested Laurence. "But he's been rubbin' against rope, Colin—and by the amount o' fibres we found, it was no casual contact."

On what facts they had, Dan Laurence had made the only choice he could. Perhaps Kelch and his comrades had examined the Old Course, then rejected it as posing too many problems, turned their attention instead to Sunbury Colliery, the next stop on Shashkov's Saturday programme.

The rope—it could mean anything or nothing. It could be an ingredient in Kelch's next move—for the moment, Thane tucked it aside in his mind.

"Anything else, Dan?"

"Nothing that matters—not yet, anyway." He nodded his shaggy head towards the next bench, where two of his "lads" were at work. "We're having a wee look at what came down from the crashed Ford, but so far there's been nothing spectacular."

Thane glanced at his watch. "Then I'd better move. Bhudda Ilford should be back by now, and you can guess what he's going to ask."

"Well, it won't be the state of the weather," nodded Laurence wryly. "The best of British luck, friend—you'll need it."

It was a mild, starlit night outside, but the chill in Chief Superintendent Ilford's office had no connection with the weather. He waved Thane to the chair opposite, lit his pipe with slow, deliberate care, and took a few puffs in absolute silence.

"I've been out for the last two hours. Any idea why?"

"The duty man said you'd got a line on a bank embezzlement," said Thane cautiously.

"That's one side of the coin," Ilford set down his pipe in the big ash-tray beside him. "The other is I wanted to hide from this ruddy telephone. You know why?" He gave a rumbling bark. "Because since noon today it's been ringing non-stop, one dam' fool official after another, right up the ladder—everyone but the ruddy Prime Minister, all wanting to know why we haven't nailed Kelch and his pals. 'Do we realise how serious it all is?'" He mimicked officialdom in a vicious, squeaking parody, then scowled. "All right, now it's my turn, Colin. What the hell's happening—or when is it going to? Do I have to wait for the newspapers?"

Thane met the city C.I.D. chief's glare and felt his own temper rise. "We're trying—you know that," he replied stubbornly. "We got Serviev this afternoon, Phil Moss is checking another lead right now, the Scientific Branch and plenty others have been working their guts out—" In the same deliberate, coldly factual voice he catalogued the situation through every detail. "That's how it stands, sir. Unless—" the ice in his manner matched Ilford's "—unless, of course, you've any fresh approach in mind."

A slow, twitching grin began in one corner of Bhudda Ilford's mouth and spread. "All right, we've snarled at each other. Let's leave it. If it helps, one bright Whitehall type suggested we should have a Scotland Yard team flown north. I told him we were already co-operating to the full with Home Office security, that Scotland Yard, whether he knew it or not, was a purely English firm and had no powers in Scotland, that we'd never needed their help in my lifetime and that we didn't propose to start now."

He struck another match for his pipe, watched Thane over the flame, and mused half to himself. "A few flecks of coal dust aren't sufficient on their own to satisfy me the next try will be at the colliery."

"They could easily have given both places a looking over before they made any decision," agreed Thane. Inwardly, he was indignant. Had Bhudda imagined he was going to thump all his eggs in one basket? "I'd grant that the odds might have swayed a fraction against the Old Course, sir—but nothing more."

Satisfied, Ilford thumbed through the memos on his desk until he found the one he wanted. "Probably academic now, but the army came through with Herrald's service record. Called up in 1941, commissioned in the Royal Engineers in '42, wounded and transferred to the Royal Army Service Corps in '44, demobbed as a captain. No decorations, no black marks. As for this story of Lady Dunspar's that he suggested he could smuggle Kelch and his friends out of the country, there's a strong chance he could have done it. I put a couple of men on checking round some of his business contacts."

"They confirmed?"

"They did more than that. Herrald has—or maybe had—some pretty good connections in the shipping business thanks to his import-export trading. A couple of them admitted he telephoned them last Friday evening, wanting to know sailing dates on the Atlantic run and hinting he might be trying for a rather special favour." Ilford stopped as the telephone at his side gave a double ring. He looked at the instrument with something close to loathing then, as it rang again, sighed and answered.

"Ilford here—" As the C.I.D. chief spoke, Thane began to relax back in his chair then leaned forward again at Bhudda's next words. "Yes, he's with me. What's happening at your end?"

The voice at the other end of the line spoke for almost a minute. Ilford grunted from time to time, his face gradually changing from interest through disbelief to despair. At last, he gave a groan. "All right—tell him yourself." He practically threw the receiver across the desktop. "It's Moss. He's not only lost them, he's gone and lost his ruddy car into the bargain!"

Thane took over the call. "Phil?"

"I heard him." Phil Moss's voice came sad and weary over the line. "I'll keep it brief, Colin. The newspaper angle paid off. They were living in a hut in a holiday camp outside Cupar, and I went there to have a look. But they must have been edgy because of Serviev—probably had somebody keeping an eye on the camp gate. The hut was empty when I went in, but when I came out somebody belted me on the skull."

Thane could do little more than commiserate with the rest of Moss's tale. When he'd come round, he'd been lying in the chalet and his raincoat was missing. He'd staggered back to the main gate, and tripped over the county police driver lying unconscious between two of the huts.

Finding their car had been taken completed Moss's burden of humiliation. When the driver came round, all he could tell was that he'd seen someone whom he'd taken to be Moss, somebody wearing the same dirty-white raincoat, beckoning to him from the camp gate. He'd got out of the car and sprinted over—while the figure in the raincoat moved back inside the camp, waiting beside a darkened hut. Then someone had stepped out behind him and he too had been thumped on the head.

"Any trace of the car yet, Phil?"

"None," said Moss unhappily. "There's a radio alert out for it, which should have made interesting listening. And some of the county blokes are here now. How's Bhudda?"

Thane flickered a glance across the desk. "The forecast mentioned a deep depression—possible storms. Stay put, Phil. I'll be up as soon as I can."

"Right." He heard his second-in-command sigh and then the click as the faraway telephone was replaced.

Bhudda Ilford had a suspicious frown on his broad, normally placid face as Thane turned towards him. "What was that about storms?" he demanded.

"It looks like being another all-night session up there," said Thane easily. "Phil wanted to know what the weather would be like."

Ilford gave a snort of only part belief. "Well, you'd better get moving. I'll contact Colonel Donnan and bring him up to date . . . which will be another happy little interlude. When you see Moss, tell him . . . tell him . . . no, leave it. That's going to be my pleasure." He struck another match for his pipe, scraped the wood too savagely, and cursed as the blazing match head snapped and landed in his correspondence tray. Tamping out the potential bonfire, he totally ignored Thane's departure.

The Headquarters driver had eaten, rested, and was in fine fettle for the journey north. The Jaguar sang its way over the long, quiet miles of road and it was barely ten P.M. by a church clock as it slowed to a purring crawl through the streets of Cupar and finally halted at the holiday ground.

"Get it over with," begged Moss, coming forward from the camp entrance as Thane left the car. "What did Bhudda say, Colin?"

"He's saving it for later." Thane fell into step with him. "Found your car yet?"

"No." Moss kicked a loose stone ahead of him. "They've probably dumped it by now and acquired something different."

"How's the head?"

"Sore—in more ways than one." His thin face was bitter in the dull glow from the wire-strung path lights. "I feel a ruddy idiot. How were things in Glasgow?"

Thane told him as they neared the chalet door.

Moss gave a sad shake of his head. "Well, I can't add much. I've talked with people in the other huts, and had another session with the shopkeeper. They're vague on descriptions, only certain that four men were here and that the Ford was parked outside. They left early in the morning and weren't usually back till late evening." Moss nodded to the uniformed constable on duty outside the chalet and waved his companion on. "Welcome to Kelch's Castle," he punned viciously. "After tonight, the county boys will probably rename it Moss's Misery."

They went in through the little hallway to the main room, where two Fife C.I.D. men were already in occupancy.

"We've done the usual, sir," said the older of the two as Moss finished the introductions. "Plenty of dabs all over the place, but we've still to sort 'em out."

"They're not worrying about leaving traces." Thane glanced towards the two doors leading from the room. "What's behind those?"

"Bedrooms," contributed Moss. "Left a couple of dirty shirts behind in one, a few bits and pieces in the other. Here's the collection." He crossed over to the sideboard close by the stove. The results of the search were piled on its top . . . a comb and a handkerchief, a half-used tube of toothpaste, all the other minor, anonymous items which men might overlook or abandon when they prepared to quit in a hurry.

Thane raked through the heap with scant enthusiasm.

"That's the lot?"

"Apart from a few magazines and this soldering kit." Phil Moss lifted the cardboard box from its place beside the stove and dumped it in front of Thane. "Looks as if they've been passing the time by building another little surprise package."

"Uh-huh." The scraps of tinplate, rough-cut by metal shears, were assorted in shape and size. One or two bore traces of pencilled lines where shears had cut slightly off their marked path. Thane pieced a few together and whistled gently through his teeth as he examined the result. "Not much help, are they? Could be trimmings from a box, a canister, any dam' thing."

"And guaranteed both nasty and clever." Moss ran one hand tenderly over the top of his head.

Thane moved over to the stove, lifted its lid, glanced in at the glowing coals, then closed it again and nodded to the county men. "Better have this fire extinguished and the ashes fine-riddled. . . .

"Clever to a point, Phil, but that's all they've been so far. A revolver shot at long range—that's the idea of an optimistic amateur. The pillar-box bomb was different, but to be any way sure of the result they'd have needed a hell of a sight more explosives than they could get through that letter slot in one small package."

"They're trying hard, give them that much." Moss scowled, went over to the sink, ran some water from the tap into a glass, and used it to wash down a pill. "Agh. Well, what next?"

Thane eyed him closely. Phil Moss's normal pallor was intensified by the lines of strain around his eyes, the tight set of his lips. "You look as though you could use something stronger than tap-juice, Phil. And some food, decent food. After that, we move over to St. Andrews—nice and handy to welcome Donnan when he brings up Shashkov and company in the morning. We'll base ourselves in the local cop shop, have them lay on two telephones, and then we start dredging. Every village cop, every garage, every pub we can wake to life. . . . Kelch hasn't been wasting his time. He's pretty certainly been having a good look around, doing his homework so that nothing is left to chance. Where he's been and when, that's what we've got to find out."

They were high and dry, stranded, with little more than ten hours to go before Shashkov's visit to Fife got under way. Stranded, without any real lead to follow and left with only the angry helplessness, the gnawing frustration of having found yet another trail only to have it once more peter out to nothing.

Thane looked again at the little fragments of scrapped tinplate, frag-ments which held a secret of their own. Another radio-controlled bomb? Donnan had promised he'd organise some form of jamming device. But Martin Kelch was unlikely to try the same idea twice, and a shop-to-shop dragnet still hadn't been able to trace the sale of the first, let alone a second, radio-controlled set in the period since the trawlermen had landed. He shrugged and brushed the tinplate fragments back into a heap.

"Come on . . . food."

By eleven-fifteen they'd eaten, were installed in St. Andrews police station, and the operators at the local telephone exchange were handling the first of the torrent of calls ahead. At eleven-forty, the missing police car was found abandoned in a lane near the village of Kennoway, eight miles from where it had been stolen. Ten minutes later, the police office at Kennoway was back on the line again. A local vet, preparing to answer an emergency call from one of the farms around, had discovered that his blue Wolseley 1500 saloon had been whisked away from the garage behind his house.

By midnight, Moss knew his switchboard operator's first name was Maisie and that she worked nights because her fiancé was a merchant seaman. On the practical side, he'd located the owner of a village pub a mile or so from Sunbury Colliery. The man had a vague recollection of two strangers being in his bar at noon two days before, and thought they'd driven off in a grey car. Tourists, he'd guessed from their accents. Descriptions? No, he couldn't remember what they'd been like.

To balance, Thane had an indignant St. Andrews garageman whom he had roused from sleep. He'd filled the tank of a grey Ford Zephyr the previous day, one man aboard it. But he'd been too busy to do more than work the pump and take the money, and the customer was only the vaguest of memories.

Outside the warmth of the station, the same quest was occupying the energies of a considerable section of the strength of three county forces around them . . . mobile units searching for the blue Wolseley, village cops dragged from their beds to their bicycles in a prowling search for strangers, town beatmen checking hotels and vacant buildings, campsites and bed-and-breakfast bungalows. Two squads had more specific tasks— one to guard the entrances to Sunbury Colliery, the other to patrol in pairs the sprawling expanse of the Old Course.

Thirty minutes after Saturday had begun, Dan Laurence telephoned through from Glasgow, spent considerable wrath describing how every blanking telephone line into St. Andrews police station seemed to have been engaged for the last few blanking hours, then finally came round to the reason for his call.

"If you're still interested, here's what we've got from the crashed Ford," he rumbled. "Underwing and tyre examination show only shore sand and road grit, no traces of coal or sandstone. But the grit we vacuumed up from the car floor had one or two flakes o' coal among it, the same sandstone grains and rope fibre. That's from both back and front seats, Colin."

An aimless doodle spread across Thane's pad of scrap paper as he listened. A little man and a big bomb, both surrounded by what could have been a floral wreath. One day he'd save some of these doodles and thump them down in front of a psychiatrist. No, maybe he wouldn't. The findings might be too close for comfort. He tapped the ballpoint for a moment.

"Colin?" Laurence's voice came grumphing over the wire.

"Still here, Dan." He drew a golf ball, then added a smouldering fuse. "You found sand on his shoes—"

"And on the car floor. The odd bit o' grass and a speck or two o' bone meal as well. Fingerprints are pretty much as you'd expect—one set identified as Serviev's, three others matching the ones tabbed 'unknown' from the cottage."

Coal and grass, the colliery or the Old Course—the same puzzle as before. More and more Thane's instincts pulled against the first possibility, despite the evidence of the dust layers.

There was that hint of the spectacular in setting the next attempt on Shashkov's life at the Old Course, before a massed audience. It was a touch more in keeping with what he'd learned of Kelch's character than a killing amid the grime of a colliery.

"Any more word from Professor MacMaster, Dan?" He asked more from habit than hope.

"Aye, he looked in about an hour back," said Laurence. "He'd heard you'd been around Headquarters—wanted to tell you something about the mould on those food tins he collected from the cottage. Called it an 'interesting phenomenon.'" The Scientific Branch chief gave a sardonic chuckle. "Anyway, you'll see him in the morning. He's driving up to St. Andrews—for a week-end rest, according to him. You know what that means. If anyone gets killed, the bald-headed old buzzard wants to be nice and near."

They said goodbye and Thane hung up. The station sergeant had been brewing tea, and the taste of that strong, almost scalding liquid had seldom been sweeter. He looked over the top of the mug toward Phil Moss and mustered a grin. "It could be worse, I suppose. At least we don't have to foot the phone bill." He lit a cigarette, and left the pack on the desk.

Moss watched for a moment, then crossed over and silently helped himself to one.

"Thought you'd stopped." Thane tossed him the matches.

"———" The word wasn't usually heard outside of Glasgow, but it was superbly tailored to fit the feelings of one tired, soreheaded, particularly miserable detective inspector.

They had their first break an hour later, and almost simultaneously a surprise visitor. The break was a radio message from one of the mobile units. The stolen Wolseley had been found abandoned, half-hidden under a railway culvert two miles from St. Andrews. Unless the little group of men they hunted were trying a final bluff—Thane's craggy face hardened. No, if there was any bluff intended it was a double measure, the kind dreamed up by a mind which could expect the police to ponder beyond the obvious and which was prepared to exploit that very possibility. The other facet, of course, was that Kelch might feel his plans were now so well laid that nothing could go wrong.

The visitor was Colonel Donnan, a weary-eyed, blue-stubbled figure who gulped a mug of tea then peeled off his coat and slumped into a chair. "After Ilford told me what was happening I thought I'd better gallop up and join you," he told them. "Anything more I should know?"

Thane talked and he listened, nursing a cigarette. When Thane had finished, Donnan looked away from him for a moment, staring at the plain, cream-painted wall, gnawing gently on his lip. Then he nodded. "The golf course it is—and there's no sense trying to persuade Shashkov to cancel the game. I've tried. But the publicity he's been getting is doing just what we guessed—making him a hero back home. He's loving it." He reached for the telephone. "Well, I didn't want to do this, but I've no option. Whether we look dam' fools or not, there'll be no public gallery following him around—and anyone found on the Old Course while he's there lands in a cell until it's over." As the operator answered, he placed a priority call to Army Scottish Command in Edinburgh then, hand over the mouthpiece, made his own weary comment. "Why couldn't he have stuck to chess, like all the rest of his mob?"

The call came through and he got busy. But it was already too late. Fate's carefully constructed rendezvous was out there in the darkness, positioned and ready just as it had been since an hour before midnight.

SEVEN

When the sun shines, the Old Course at St. Andrews, readily acknowledged the most famous and oldest golf course in the world, lays claim to a third title—the most beautiful. Starting as a narrow neck of flawless green turf, fringed on one side by the grey-blue waters of the North Sea, on the other by the tall, calm, stone-built dignity of the university town, it broadens beyond into a plump, tempting expanse of rolling fairways which are ridged and bounded by whin and gorse, their greens unique in their cunning, baize-smooth hills and valleys.

Plump, tempting—and deadly, as even the most experienced practitioner of the art of club-swinging has discovered to his shaken cost. To play the Old Course is a love-hate ordeal which begins from the very moment the player stands on what has been called the loneliest spot in the world, the first tee. Ahead lies his challenge and his first obstacle, the shallow, gentle-flowing Swilcan Burn. To one side, the austere clubhouse of the Royal and Ancient Golf Club seems to sneer at his bravado in coming here. Behind, deadliest of all, wait the constant, silently critical audience of golfing addicts whose cold appraisal knows neither warmth nor kindness. At the first tee, even steel-nerved low-handicap men have swung, missed the ball, and carved chunks from the sacred turf in their moment of nervous tension.

Out beyond, where the gorse flaunts its flanking threats, another danger lies hidden—the yawning, trap-mouthed sand bunkers with menace in their very names. The Beardies and Coffins, Nick's and the Pulpit, Hell and the Grave, Cat's Trap and Lion's Mouth, Principal's Nose and the Wig are constant and ready.

The Old Course, in short, is a disease. A fatal, irresistible infection 6545 yards long with a standard scratch score of seventy-three and a casualty rate measured in husbandless wives and fat, happy traders who sell golf balls, tees, aspirins, instruction books, and similar aids.

That it was closed to play for the morning had been publicised before—with a fresh reminder in the screaming headlines with which every morning paper in the country followed up the Shashkov bomb-attempt story and spun webs of conjecture round the security precautions to be taken during the Communist leader's visit to St. Andrews.

But sportsmen usually start at the back of their newspaper and seldom reach page one's contents. Before breakfast the first straggling, club-laden arrivals had already been turned away by the police patrols on duty around the starter's box.

At nine-thirty A.M., a cold-edged wind blowing in from the sea despite the cloudless sky, the young policeman on duty at the main entrance shivered a little as he tried to ram the point home.

"Sorry, dad, but it's final. You'll have to wait till afternoon if you want a game." He grinned sympathetically. "Look, why not go and get yourself a nice cup o' coffee, eh?"

"Blast your coffee and I'm not your father!" Mr. William Wallace, a stout, elderly figure in an old Norfolk jacket, antiquated plus-fours and tweed cap, his much repaired pencil golf bag and its collection of wooden-shafted clubs slung over one shoulder, was becoming angry. It showed in the violent red hue gathering over his face, in the way his false teeth clicked to emphasize each word. "I'm a ratepayer of this town, I know my rights, and no fluffy-faced young—young dressed-up school boy is going to rob me of them!"

The constable flushed. He only needed a quick mow with an electric razor once a week, but—"Now listen, dad. . . ."

"You listen!" William Wallace stormed on with all the valour of the Scottish hero whose name he bore. "Every Saturday morning for the last forty-six years I've had my round over the Old Course. Every Saturday, bar the time I got married and had to go away for the honeymoon! This is a public course, isn't it?"

"Yes, but—"

"And any citizen of St. Andrews has the right to use it, provided he's paid his greens fees? Isn't there a parchment covenant which guarantees it?"

"I know, dad. Signed in 1552—we had it thumped into us at school."
The youngster tried another tact. "But there've been other Saturdays like
this now and again, haven't there? Say the Open Championship is on, you
don't expect to go bashing your way out through the field, do you? Or if
the course is closed because of the weather—"

"There isn't a championship and the weather's fine." William Wallace glared around at the bustle of blue and khaki uniforms around.
"There's just a damned awful fuss about some Bolshevik who'd more
likely been thrown in jail in my young days." He gave a final, angry clack
of his teeth. "Now, do I get my rights or not?"

The youngster shook his head. "Sorry, not till the afternoon."

A sergeant and another constable were ambling towards them, attracted by the row. William Wallace jerked his golf bag higher on his
shoulder with a defiant rattle of clubs, gave a loud sniff in the direction of
the reinforcements, and stumped off. If they thought they'd heard the last
of this—he scowled again, then headed for the nearest coffee shop.

Behind him, the uniformed men exchanged grins. The sergeant
sucked a peppermint, glanced at his watch, then murmured a warning as
he spotted the quartet walking along the shore road towards them.

A shave, a fresh shirt, and a good breakfast had refuelled Colin
Thane's energies. Colonel Donnan was by his side, Phil Moss a pace or two
behind with the local police superintendent, who was arrayed in his best
uniform complete with neck-rubbing stiff white collar.

"All quiet, sergeant?" The superintendent swept the scene, his worries
evident in the only half-attentive way he returned the sergeant's snapped
salute.

"So far, sir. All uniformed men in position."

"Fine—fine." The superintendent turned to Thane and the others.
"Time I had a last word with the club people. Any of you want to come
along?"

They shook their heads.

"Well now—" Colonel Donnan watched the superintendent stride
off, and drew in deep lungfuls of the sea-spiced air. "Half an hour till
Shashkov arrives. Any last-minute bright ideas?" His expression was grim
as he rested his hands on the painted wooden railing which was the
course's boundary. "Or do we just stand here and wait for it to happen?"

A steady, nearing throb of rotor blades pulled their attention sky-wards. The big R.A.F. helicopter, its body silver, nose and rotor blades yellow, was coming in over the course about fifty feet up. The nose dipped a fraction, it hovered, then, as the rotor beat changed, it began to move away again, gaining height.

"There's another one around somewhere." Donnan pursed his lips.

"Over there, out to sea." Thane spotted the second approaching speck. "How'll you communicate?"

"Direct walkie-talkie link—we'll be in constant touch."

Donnan had marshalled his resources with care. Colin Thane ran through the details again—details the little Irishman had formulated to final pattern only a short time before dawn.

The helicopter patrol was only a beginning. The Old Course perimeter was now under the guard of police, a full infantry company from the Black Watch, and an R.A.F. Regiment dog-handling squad. Within their cordon other R.A.F. guard dogs and their handlers were already covering the gorsed and bunkered grassland in regular search patterns.

Another, equally purposeful sweep had already been completed. At dawn, two truckloads of Royal Engineers had arrived, unloaded their sensitive mine-detector gear, and had launched a slow, steady search of the tees, main paths, greens, all the other places where a bomb might have been planted. While they'd worked, a smaller team had been busy in the clubhouse, setting up a compact but powerful transmitter jamming unit which they guaranteed would block any attempt to repeat the radio-controlled bang of the previous day.

And for the game itself, while the two helicopters prowled overhead, Donnan's final force would operate—thirty picked Special Branch and W.D. security men operating as a screen around and ahead of the two golfers.

Thane pulled his cigarettes from his pocket, found three left, handed them round, then tossed the crumpled, empty pack into a litter bin. "You've done your share, Donnan. It seems watertight." He shrugged. "I wish I could say the same, but what's left for us to chew on?"

"Nothing." Phil Moss sourly beat the security man to a reply. "Absolutely nothing—you know it." There were police still on their routine of search throughout the town, others on roadblocks on the routes leading into it, but beyond that their entire investigation seemed to have come to a grinding halt.

"There's always this report old MacMaster's bringing up, but it sounds pretty useless." Thane shook his head in a dull stubbornness. "Yet I've a feeling about it all—a feeling we've had a chance somewhere and missed it. If we'd had more time. . . ."

But they hadn't. Bhudda Ilford had hammered around that same theme when Thane had spoken to him by telephone before breakfast. Outside of that, the city C.I.D. chief had passed on the only cheering piece of information of the day—the police motor cyclist injured in the Edinburgh bomb blast was improving, should recover all right.

The minutes passed. Gradually the grass bank on the opposite side of the road from the course began filling as a crowd gathered, held well back by a line of blue-uniformed police and khaki-clad army men.

The cavalcade bringing the Soviet Minister for Industrial Development arrived exactly on schedule—five large black cars, the first and last filled with security men. Two of the other three vehicles contained a covey of the Russian's broad-shouldered, dark-suited personal entourage and a handful of accredited pressmen. In the middle car, its CD plates gleaming, Shashkov sat with his golf partner, a portly senior Treasury Minister from London who'd been chosen for the occasion by reason of his indifferent game and professional charm.

"Our boy seems happy enough," muttered Moss as Shashkov bounced from his car, already dressed for action in a violent green windcheater, beige slacks, and white shoes, a beige cap rammed squarely on his heavy, close-shaven head.

"Glad somebody is." Thane watched their V.I.P. charge wave a greeting to the crowd and appear unabashed by the cold, dour silence. They were spectators, most of them, nothing more, along to see Shashkov in the same spirit they might have viewed a circus parade—or a funeral. Over to the left, two bearded students unfurled a ban-the-bomb banner and were promptly submerged as plain-clothes men closed in.

Now the golf bags were produced from the cars. Shashkov's, brand new and complete with matched irons and an orange umbrella, came first and was taken charge of by the veteran Old Course caddy who'd been allocated to the job. The Treasury Minister's bag was smaller, in leather, with little hand-knitted woollen caps covering each clubhead.

Other golf bags, equally bulky, were being dragged out. Thane's expression became a wintery smile. He knew their contents, repeater shotguns and light automatic carbines, all the rest of the arsenal of items which would accompany the twosome on their eighteen-hole sporting amble.

"Aye, it's funny sir." The county sergeant misread Thane's smile as Shashkov disappeared into the clubhouse. "From the look of him, he'd be better at howkin' up coal wi' thon clubs than hittin' a poor wee ball."

"If you'd a coal mine handy." Thane said it idly. "Well, he'll see a mine this afternoon—if he gets there in one piece." He'd just spotted Professor MacMaster trying to find a way through the cordon opposite and having an argument with a burly infantryman in the process.

"We've got coal all right." The sergeant chuckled. "But no' in a mine, sir—more like in a bottle, you might say. There's a coal seam along at the rocks by the old castle."

Thane took a half-step forward, ready to go to MacMaster's aid, then stopped where he was as the county man's words sank home. "What do you mean, in a bottle?"

The sudden snap in the Millside detective's voice took the other man by surprise and jerked both Moss and Donnan's attention towards them.

"It's—well, it's just the local name for the dungeon at the castle, sir," said the sergeant, embarrassed at being the centre of so much interest. "We call it the bottle dungeon—it's carved out o' the rock in the shape o' one. That's where you'll find the coal seam."

"Has it been checked?" Thane glanced at Phil Moss and saw swift realisation dawning. Taras Serviev had died with a taunting laugh on his lips, a laugh at Thane saying he'd "worry" about the bottle he was trying to hold to the trapped man's lips. And the toes of Serviev's shoes had been scuffed and scraped by contact with rock and coal—rock and coal which, till that moment, Thane had automatically linked with the colliery next on General Shashkov's programme of visits. If Serviev had found a last, twisted joke in the bottle thrust before him. . . . "Well, what about it? Has the castle been checked?"

"No." The sergeant bit his lip. "At least, I don't think so, sir. It's closed up just now—one o' the inside walls is dangerous, and they've stopped visitors going through on tours until it's been repaired a bit."

They'd seen the castle—it was hard to be in St. Andrews for any length of time without catching a glimpse of the old stronghold. On the shore road, but at the opposite end of the town from the golf course, it was a massive, ruined, roofless stone shell surrounded by a high metal fence. To the rear, what was left of its gaunt fortress walls perched on the edge of a drop of close on a hundred feet of jagged rock to the sea below. Once, it had been an imposing structure. Now, it was one of the many, widely scattered ancient monuments maintained by the Ministry of Works.

"But—" Donnan's mouth opened and closed again.

For once, Thane ignored the little Irishman. "Where do we find keys to the place, Sergeant?"

"The caretaker, sir—he lives fairly near."

There was a fresh rustle of interest from the crowd in the background. General Shashkov and his partner had reemerged from the clubhouse and were walking in businesslike fashion towards the first tee.

"Let's go and get them." Thane saw MacMaster still struggling to reach their party, but the professor would have to wait. "Phil, you'd better come along too—we'll let you know what happens, Colonel." He hustled Moss and the sergeant over to the nearest of the waiting police cars, the sergeant gave directions to the startled driver, and the car roared on its way.

The caretaker was at home, listening to the radio. As soon as he'd pulled on his shoes, produced his keys, and joined them in the car they were off again, tyres screaming as they rounded a corner and took one of the narrow streets leading back to the shore.

"When did you inspect the place last?" demanded Thane.

The caretaker gripped the seat edge as the car swayed round the last bend. "Not since Monday—I was told once a week would do until the builders were ready to start."

The rest of the journey took only a couple of minutes. As the car pulled up outside the locked entrance gate, the castle's skeleton shape silent and apparently empty of life, Thane glanced back for a moment in the direction of the Old Course. Shashkov's game would be under way by now—and with it Colonel Donnan's personal ordeal. Then he was out of the car, standing with the others while the caretaker used the largest of his bunch of keys and swung open the gate.

"Colin—" Phil Moss tapped the lock with his fist "—this wouldn't take much work to open. A bent nail would practically do the job."

Thane nodded. "Any other ways in?"

"Well, yes—there's a path down to the shore." The caretaker frowned unhappily. "Look, Chief Inspector, don't blame me if somebody's got in here—the fence is only meant to keep youngsters an' drunks out. There's nothing worth thieving and nobody's going to try to flog the ruddy castle, are they?"

"Forget it." Thane led the way along the narrow pathway laid out across the grass of the filled-in moat, Moss, the sergeant, and the caretaker following at his heels. A thin gust of wind stirred the dust underfoot as they went through the broad, gloomy arch of the castle's main entrance and into the open space beyond, laid out as a grass lawn with benches for visitors and flanked all around by the broken remnants of the great, thick walls which had first been begun over seven hundred years before, to stand through war and siege and bombardment then gradually crumble in the face of time.

"The bottle dungeon's over there—" The caretaker pointed to a low stone structure guarded by a heavy door over in the far left corner of the courtyard and selected another key from his jingling ring as they crossed in its direction.

They were two-thirds of the way across when the door ahead suddenly swung open and a figure dived out, heading for the opposite wall. At the same moment, a hoarse, muffled shout reached their ears.

"Look out for more—I'll take him!" Thane barked the warning as he charged to cut off the runaway.

The man ahead, small, slim, his grey raincoat flapping as he ran, realised a moment later that he wouldn't make his goal, a low, almost levelled part of the outer wall leading to a rough scramble down the cliffs below. He hesitated, then spun on his heel and headed for a short flight of worn stairs leading to a higher platform. His right hand darted into a pocket of the coat and there was a knife clasped tight in it as he reached the top.

Thane didn't slow. His feet clattered on the stone slabs as he bounded towards the man above who had stopped and now stood panting, that right arm with the knife held far out from his side, its blade bright and waiting. As the burly detective's rush carried him on to the platform, the knife arm slashed and even as he twisted to avoid the steel Thane felt a rake of pain across his shoulder.

The knife arm swung back for another wild stroke, but this time Thane was under it. Forefinger rigid, his right hand slammed out towards the man's throat . . . slightly off balance, he missed the nerve centre he'd aimed for but the blow still sent the other man reeling, the knife waving ineffectually, the runaway dazed by the unarmed combat tactic Thane had first learned in a dockside brawl.

He gathered himself for a final pounce, just as the runaway made another desperate scramble, pulling himself from the platform on to a higher portion of wall. Thane grabbed the man's left foot with both hands, twisted, then let go and threw himself back as the knife flashed towards him, thrown with all the strength his opponent possessed. The knife missed, clattering on the platform at his feet—but the effort of the throw cost the climber his grip on the worn stone blocks. He clawed wildly, trying to pull himself upwards, then as Thane came on again he tried to twist his body out of the detective's reach. He failed. Instead, he tumbled from his perch, skidding down the opposite side of the stonework, then falling backwards.

The man didn't fall far—less than fifteen feet. But the railings were below, the railings with their long, blunt spikes.

Thane felt the man's scream hit him like a blow to the stomach. He looked down, then turned quickly away, the pain in his shoulder burning again, the long slash through the cloth of his jacket and the shirt below red and sticky with blood.

"Colin—" Phil Moss panted up the stairway to his side and winced as he saw the wound. "Hell, he meant business."

"Aye." Thane picked up the knife. It was a twin to the thin, razor-edged fish-gutting knife they'd found in Serviev's car after the crash. "Damn the things."

"There's somebody down that dungeon." Moss looked around, his face grim. "I thought he could keep for a moment—the caretaker's standing by."

From below, they heard a shout. The county sergeant, joined by the driver from the police car, had reached the railings and their grotesquely draped burden. His voice was strained as he hailed them again.

"He's still alive, but only just—we canna lift him clear on our own, though. He's unconscious."

"Don't try it," Thane shouted back. "Get what help you need, and a doctor. One of you stay and try to ease him." If the man below had any chance, it depended on the right care, skilled care, being there as he was lifted clear.

The sergeant nodded, had a quick consultation with his companion, then trotted off at a ponderous run.

"What about you?" Phil Moss eyed Thane anxiously.

"I'll hold together." Thane knew he'd been lucky. The thickness of his jacket cloth had taken the worst of the knife slash. He explored the wound with his other hand. The cut seemed to run for about six inches, but the bleeding was too regular, the pain when he moved sufficiently subdued for any real damage to have been caused. "Let's get over to this dam' dungeon."

"Right." Moss followed him down the stone stairway. "Which one was he?" He nodded in the direction of the hidden railings.

"From what I saw of him, Arkan Bretsun—the description matches—small, slim, dark-haired." Two down now, two to go, and if they were lucky—he increased his pace across the centre courtyard to where the caretaker was standing nervously at the entrance to the dungeon doorway. The caretaker's face was white with shock as he stood back to let them enter.

"Watch the roof, sir—" The warning came just as Thane hit his head on the low stone archway. He cursed, staggered blindly for a step or two, then halted, hardly believing what he saw.

The caretaker had already switched on the electric lights which a thoughtful Ministry of Works had installed so that visitors could savour in maximum comfort the horrors of the little room. It was a small, windowless cell with a vaulted roof, the middle of the floor a dark hole rimmed by a waist-high wall.

"Down there?" Thane's voice echoed the disbelief on his face. There was a damp chill in the air, an ancient, evil staleness in his nostrils. Modern steel hooks were set in the wall, and there was a rope ladder lying bundled to one side. "Can't you light it?"

The caretaker nodded. "I did—he asked me to put them off again. He's been used to the dark—the lights hurt his eyes."

Thane strode over to the dark hole and looked down into its gaping black unreality. "Down there . . . we're going to get you out. We're putting on the lights first. All right?"

"Yes—yes, I'm ready." The voice was shaky, with a near hysterical edge of relief to it.

"Now, then." Thane nodded to the caretaker. The man flicked a switch beside him, and a circle of bare electric bulbs snapped to life in the pit below. In the foot of the bottle, the man who crouched on the rock threw up an arm to cover his eyes. But the momentary glimpse was enough for the two detectives above . . . they'd found Peter Herrald.

With practised ease the caretaker came forward, fitted the rope ladder to its hooks, and let it uncoil down into the pit. Phil Moss was first down its swaying length, the caretaker gave Thane a steadying hand over the rim of the edging wall, and in seconds all three were down beside the prisoner.

Gently, Moss drew the man's arm away from his face. "It's over now, Mr. Herrald."

Peter Herrald kept his eyes closed against the light. His face had a thick stubble of beard beneath its grime, his thinning fair hair was unkempt, and he kept his hands clasped tight against the crumpled cloth of his soiled grey sports jacket. He licked his lips and took a deep, sighing breath. "I—" He stopped and shook his head. "How did you find me?"

"Mostly luck." Thane stared around him in fascination. Plenty of old castle fortresses in Europe could still show examples of the savagery with which prisoners had been treated in the Dark Ages of history, places now seen only occasionally by the student or the tourist who went poking beyond the bright lights of the holiday centres. But this one—to a native Scot it was a sobering revelation of the ways of his ancestors.

The bottle dungeon had been hacked out of the living rock on which the castle was built. It's "neck" was a circular shaft some eight feet in depth and five feet across, the black band of the coal seam clearly visible against the paler sandstone. Then below the neck, the bottle widened, its sides flaring outwards all around for another fifteen feet, the final pit being fifteen feet across—and its floor sloping in from the walls to form a shallow, cone-shaped depression. Once down here, no man living could ever have escaped again unaided . . . down here, in the dark and the damp and the silence.

The castle caretaker had seen the same reaction many a time before.

"Aye, it's no' a very pleasant place," he mused. "And many a poor devil found that out. A few years and they'd go blind or daft or both." There was worry on his face as he looked back to Herrald. "What's going to happen about—about him?"

"A lot." Thane bent down beside Herrald, who had now opened his eyes a fraction but still shielded them against the light. "When did they bring you here?"

"The same day they killed George Shaw." Herrald shuddered and swallowed hard. "You know about that?"

"Most of it." Thane studied him for a moment. Over three days in this damp blackness of a pit—Peter Herrald appeared to have paid heavily for his quixotic offer to help these runaway trawlermen. "Can you tell me where they are now? Did you hear them talk?"

"Talk?" Herrald's laugh trembled as it echoed round the stone walls. "Since they put me here, I've been alone most of the time. They'd come and feed me, that's about all. Sometimes there was one of them just standing up above, listening—" His voice sank to a near whimper. "I tried shouting at first, then pleading with them. But it didn't make any difference."

Phil Moss gave a grunt. "Half a dozen men could shout their heads off down here and they wouldn't be heard outside. Come on, let's try you on your feet." The castle caretaker helped him bring Herrald up from his crouch.

"Did they tell you they were going to kill Shashkov?" Thane probed on, still hopeful that this crumpled, unshaven figure might be able to give him some lead.

"Kelch said so—that was after George found the gelignite and wanted to turn them in to the police. That—that was why they killed him, to stop him." He looked round the three rescuers. "Could one of you give me a cigarette?"

Thane fumbled in his pocket, then remembered he'd none.

The caretaker filled the gap, and Herrald cupped his grimy hands round the match as it flared.

"Thanks. I—they took mine. Took everything." He drew in a long pull of the smoke and let it trickle slowly from his nostrils.

"General Shashkov is still intact. Right now he's playing golf about a mile from here." Thane rubbed his chin. "Listen, Herrald, this is vital. Did you hear anything, anything at all, about what they were going to do?"

"Me?" Slowly, Herrald shook his head. "Don't you understand? I don't know anything." There was an open pleading in his voice. "Don't you understand? I don't know where this place is, I don't know what time it is except that it's probably still Saturday. The one who was here just before you came—Bretsun, I think it was—he told me they were going away, and that I'd be found in a day or so. He was starting to say something else, then he seemed to realise something was wrong. He went out, I heard voices, and I began shouting again . . . that's all I know."

"All right, take it easy." Thane tried to hide his disappointment. "Can you make it up that ladder if we help?"

Herrald gave a twisted smile. "I—I'll make it. If it gets me out of here, I'll make it."

The caretaker went up first. Herrald came next, with Phil Moss close behind, helping him from rung to rung. Thane came last of all, grunting at the twinging pain from his shoulder, grateful for the heave of assistance his wiry second-in-command gave him as he reached the top.

"The light still hurts." Peter Herrald screwed his eyes shut as he looked out at daylight for the first time.

"It'll pass." Thane urged him gently through the outer door, and breathed deeply the fresh salt sea air like nectar after the stagnating atmosphere of the pit. "A bath, a shave, a change of clothes, and a decent meal and you'll feel a darned sight better." He could see an ambulance drawn up outside the castle, and a second police car. As they walked slowly out into the courtyard a small procession came from the opposite side of the old building, a stretcher carried in their midst.

One of the men detached himself from the group and hurried over.

The county sergeant gave a hasty salute as he approached. "We've got him off now, sir. But the doctor says he hasn't much chance."

"Still unconscious?"

"And likely to stay that way, it seems." The sergeant ran a finger round the inside of his shirt collar. "He's in a bit o' a mess, sir. Eh—should you no' be seeing about that shoulder o' yours? We're taking him to the hospital. You could come along too an'—" he glanced significantly at Herrald "—it might be an idea to take him along while we're at it."

Thane rubbed his shoulder, thought for a moment, then nodded. "Take him with you. I'll come as soon as I've got word to Colonel Donnan. All quiet on the course?"

"So far, sir." The sergeant gave a flickering grin. "I heard one of our lads on the car radio while I was waitin' for the ambulance, an' it's quite a game. Thon Russian took nine strokes at the first hole and a ten at the second—he's thumping that wee ball as if it was the original enemy of the people!" He stepped over to Herrald and took him by the arm. "Now then, come an'—" He froze, the rest of it dying on his lips as a low, flat thunder-like roar split the quiet of the courtyard.

They turned instinctively, though the castle's tumble-down walls and the curve of the shore line both cut off any chance of seeing the Old Course. Thane had a momentary glimpse of one of the helicopters beating a hurried way across the sky, then it too was gone from view.

Phil Moss gave a soft sigh. "That was a big 'un!"

Thane gave a slow nod, all expression wiped from his face, a tight ball of tension gripping within him. Then, moving by sheer instinct, they were both sprinting towards the castle gateway.

It took their car two minutes in a flat-out siren-wailing rush to reach the Old Course, and just over that time to push on down the road which bounded the first leg of its landward side, where every few yards blue-uniformed police or khaki-clad army men stood staring towards the green horizon line. As the road petered out at the side of a collection of railway sheds, the driver licked his lips and glanced sideways at Thane.

"Keep going!"

The man nodded, dropped his speed, changed gear, and swung the wheel as he saw his chance. Heaving and swaying, the car bucked a way over the fringe of rough ground bordering the road. Springs thudded a protest, and then the tyres were running in a soft whisper over the smooth turf of the course. They gained speed again, threading their swaying path past bunkers, leaving the fluttering flag of the second hole behind, braking hard at the top of one rise at the side of the fold in the ground beyond. The car's tyres spun for a moment as it was urged in a new direction and then they were on their way once more.

General Shashkov's golfing expedition were gathered in a group at the fourth tee . . . and apart from the guns in the hands of the tense, grim-faced ring of security guards there was no sign of trouble in the party. Thane could see the Soviet Minister's green windcheater moving among a small, closely clustered group of figures standing to one side of the ring.

As the car stopped, Thane threw open his door and leaned out. "Where's Colonel Donnan?"

The nearest of the guards, a thin, ginger-haired six-footer with a straggling moustache, used the muzzle of his loosely held Patchett gun as a pointer. "On his way back now . . . he went on up to have a look at whatever it was that went bang."

Thane got out of the car and followed the line of the gun muzzle. One of the helicopters was whirring back towards them, its rotors scything a shimmering disc against the blue sky. A moment later it came in low, hovered noisily, then swept a miniature dust storm to life as it settled to land about fifty yards away. While the rotors slowed to a quieter tickover, Colonel Donnan's small plump form jumped from the cabin and came trotting over.

He gave them the briefest of nods. "Hold on—I'll be right back."

He passed Thane at the same steady trot, heading straight for General Shashkov's waiting group. An interested spectator, Phil Moss emerged from the car and stood beside Thane to watch what followed. Whatever Donnan was saying, Shashkov obviously didn't like it. A young, anxious-faced interpreter standing between them, the little Irishman and the bulky, gaily attired Communist engaged in a growing rumble of conversation, both brushing aside any interruptions from the others around.

At last, it ended. General Shashkov spun on his heel, barked at his followers, and the entire party began trekking back the way they had come—all, that was, except his opponent who was left standing, idly swinging a club in undecided fashion. After a moment, he too began to walk slowly away.

"And that's ruddy well that." There was a look of grim-jawed satisfaction on the security chief's face as he stumped over to the police car. Then he stopped short as, for the first time, he noticed Thane's arm. "Hey, what happened to you?"

"One of Kelch's pals—Arkan Bretsun. We've recovered Peter Herrald too. They had him stowed away in a hellhole corner of that castle."

Donnan gave a mild curse, his mind only half-occupied by the information. "The obvious again—so obvious everybody dam' well overlooks it," he said bitterly. "The same on ahead. A squad of men check over every conceivable place with mine detectors, straining for the slightest signal that there's any metal buried—and come back with half a dozen ancient horseshoes and a load of old iron. Yet they miss a bomb planted right under their ruddy noses!"

"What happened?" It was Thane's turn to ask.

Donnan shrugged. "Come and see for yourself. I'm going back up anyway. Shashkov's heading straight for the clubhouse. I told him he either went back under his own steam or we ruddy well carried him."

"Diplomatically, or just like that?" Phil Moss raised one cynical eyebrow.

"More or less like that." Donnan scuffed one foot on the turf. "There's a harmless old character lying dead out there just because our ruddy V.I.P. wouldn't take 'niet' for an answer till now." He gestured towards the helicopter. "Well, coming Thane? You too, Moss, if you like."

Phil Moss shook his head. "Not in that thing. Unless—" he looked questioningly at Thane and relaxed as his chief shook his head.

"Take the car back, Phil. Make sure the roadblocks stay on their toes, and start organising another comb-out of the town. If Kelch and Stender know they've failed, then find we've located Herrald and knocked off Bretsun they're liable to try to make a break for it."

"If they haven't done it already." Resigned to his task, Moss watched the two men go over to the helicopter and scramble aboard. Then, as the rotors quickened and the machine rose, he turned back to the car.

*   *   *

The copter pilot, a gum-chewing R.A.F. man, swung his machine in a tight turn as it climbed, then sent it heading north only a hundred feet or so above the ground.

"First time?" bellowed Donnan above the beating roar.

Thane nodded, watching the smooth fairways ripple past below like some giant, close-woven carpet. "Where are we heading?"

"The tenth hole—what's left of it." Donnan pointed over to his right, down to where the Old Course's fringe of rough merged with the longer grass and sand dunes leading to the shore, where the waves were coming in white-capped and steady. "But take a look over there first. This old boy—his name was Wallace—had a set-to with the police on duty at the first tee earlier this morning. I know that part because the cop concerned mentioned it to one of my men and described the old fellow. Treated it as a joke, which is all it was then. Anyway, he chased him off. But it looks as though the old fellow had a stubborn streak in him, and sneaked out along the shore with his clubs—there's a road running right along, and we couldn't close the beach to holidaymakers, not without having a riot on our hands. Doing it to the course was bad enough!"

"But you'd a cordon—" protested Thane.

"Who were too busy watching for an organised invasion to spot one old man who knew his way around." Donnan scowled. "Anyway, he got on to the course at the ninth hole, just where it starts to turn and come back. The first we knew he was there was when one of the helicopters radioed that there was a character happily golfing his way along the tenth fairway! I chased the nearest squad I had towards him, but they were too late." He slammed one clenched fist into the other. "Too late, Thane—and the shame of it is I should be glad they were, glad the old gent blew himself sky-high!"

"Otherwise it might have been Shashkov who went up." Thane said it quietly. It wasn't his job to hold the scales, but it was easy enough to sympathise with the practical viewpoint. "Where was the bomb?"

"In the hole—in the ruddy hole." Donnan moaned at the thought. "And there's the result." He pointed below again, at the same time as the helicopter began to lose height.

The tenth green, set higher than the fairway which led to it and with

a tricky backward slope which had beaten many a championship expo-
nent, was now disfigured by a dark brown crater of dislodged earth eighteen to twenty feet from edge to ragged edge. A handful of men, some in
civilian clothes, two in khaki with an Alsatian dog beside them, stood
watching the helicopter descend. A coat was spread over the face and
upper body of the dead man lying near them.

Thane and Donnan left the machine as soon as it touched down and
crossed over to the others, who waited with a professional lack of curiosity.

"Found anything more?" asked Donnan.

"Just this, sir." One of the dog-handlers showed a round, blackened
object, barely recognisable as a golf ball. "It was over by those whin
bushes, about forty yards away."

"You saw it happen?" Thane had bent down beside the body. Now he
replaced the coat and rose. From the extent of his injuries, the old man
must have been killed instantly.

"That's right, sir." The dog-handler scratched his charge lightly behind one ear. "We got a message someone was over here and started across.
When we saw the bloke, my mate gave a shout, but the bloke just played
his next shot on to the green as if he'd never heard us."

"And a minute later the thing blew up," said Donnan wearily.

The dog-handler nodded. "He'd chipped his ball fairly close to the
pin, maybe four or five feet away. While we were still coming over, he took
the flag pin from the hole, picked up his putter, and knocked the ball in—
a perfect putt. The place exploded the same second."

"And the ball came out of that can again as if it had been shot from a
gun." The Alsatian cocked its ears as Thane whistled tunelessly through
his teeth. "I see what you mean, Colonel. They took out the regular can at
the hole, dug down a bit more, then replaced the can with their own version, complete with gelignite attached beneath. It could have been done
any time last night, and in theory—"

"In theory, the first golfers to reach the hole today should have been
Shashkov and his partner," said the little security chief. "It took a stubborn old man to upset the apple-cart."

The only tricky part of the scheme would be building the firing mech-
anism, and even that would have posed no major problem to a handy-
man, decided Thane. Given a few simple tools, the type of materials which

could be obtained in almost any bicycle shop, and a few hours for trial-and-error experiment, the finished product could be guaranteed almost foolproof. It had probably been a two-stage system: stage one, a "safety-catch" released when the flag pin was removed from the hole; stage two, a spring-balanced bottom plate with the battery-electric contact, the circuit to the detonator completed by the sheer weight of the golf ball dropping into the hole.

Of course, a fluke long-distance putt could have wrecked the scheme. But neither Shashkov nor his opponent were in the Ben Hogan class . . . yes, the basic courtesies of the game would have taken care of the rest. Both men would have been within the killing circle when the blast occurred.

"We'll keep an eye on things here until your boffin squad can get here." Donnan's voice cut across his thoughts. "Anything else you'll need?"

"Statements—but there's no hurry. And the course will have to stay closed for the rest of the day."

"That's a police job now." Donnan shook his head. "I've got troubles enough—and the Press Relations boys at Whitehall are going to have nightmares over this one."

The helicopter whisked them back to the clubhouse and from there a car took Thane on to the local hospital. Twenty minutes later, his shoulder wound cleaned and bandaged, wearing a fresh shirt and a sports jacket loaned by one of the hospital residents to replace his own slashed and blood-stained garments, a fresh pack of cigarettes in his pocket, he felt ready for work again.

"A simple enough wound." Professor MacMaster, an interested observer throughout the treatment, seemed almost disappointed. The forensic expert was still smarting at the way he'd been handled before he'd been able to get through the cordon at the clubhouse. "A week or two should be enough for complete healing, which is more than can be said for the man who caused it."

"I heard." Arkan Bretsun was dead. Still unconscious when he reached the hospital, he'd lasted barely minutes thereafter—no medical skill could have saved him.

"No sense in blaming yourself." MacMaster mellowed a little. "None at all. Why isn't Inspector Moss around?"

"There are still two of them on the loose," reminded Thane. "He's trying to find them."

"Well, I've a task of my own waiting—" MacMaster rose to go "—a visit to the golf course before they remove Wallace's body. I'd better leave you this." He produced one of his familiar wax-sealed envelopes. "It's the report I mentioned to Laurence, fingerprints found at the cottage."

"Thanks." Thane moved his arm experimentally. It was stiff, and the bandages were restricting, but he felt little pain. Once MacMaster had left, he put the envelope in his pocket and rose to his feet. It was time for a talk with Peter Herrald.

A nurse in the corridor outside the casualty office guided him along to the room where Herrald was a restless patient. The hospital's opinion was that he needed a spell of rest and quiet, but he had a different view. Sitting up in bed, wearing a heavy, hospital-issue dressing gown over pyjamas, the promised bath, shave, and hot meal seemed to have considerably raised his spirits.

"You're looking better, anyway," Thane agreed.

"I'm fine, just a bit weak at the knees." The other man grimaced. "And I don't like hospitals—don't ask me why, I just don't. The sergeant who brought me here promised he'd find me some clean clothes. As soon as he does, I'm getting out—no matter what they say." He hesitated. "Eh . . . I hope you don't mind, Chief Inspector, but I made a phone call a few minutes ago."

"Depends who you were calling." Thane sat on the edge of the bed and took out his cigarettes. "Lady Dunspar and her daughter Barbara?"

"That's right." Herrald gave a slightly sheepish grin. "I felt—well, you know. . . ." He took one of the cigarettes, then a light, and settled back against the pillows.

"I know you're pretty friendly with them." Thane lit his own cigarette and found an ashtray. "What I want to do now is fill in some of the gaps. We know Lady Dunspar telephoned you on the Friday evening and told you Kelch and the others had turned up at her home. What happened then?"

Herrald sighed. "I said I'd help, which was the biggest mistake I've ever made—but it seemed right at the time."

"Why'd you ask her not to tell her daughter?"

"Just wanted to keep her out of it." Herrald shrugged. "You know, in case there was . . . well, trouble later. Not that I thought there would be. I'd pretty well worked out how to do it when her mother phoned again on the Saturday. Freighter on one of the South American runs—easier to get ashore at the other end, and they could work their own way north from there."

Thane rubbed his chin. "Did Shaw know what you were up to?"

"No. Not at first. We'd fixed up the fishing trip, we were going north anyway." Herrald shifted uncomfortably, then drew hard on the cigarette. "All I planned to do was help some poor devils out of their troubles."

"Right. Let's take it stage by stage. When Lady Dunspar phoned again on the Saturday, before you left, you arranged to meet Kelch. Where and when?"

"On the Tuesday evening, outside the Tayman Hotel at Aberfeldy."

"Where were you till then?"

"Fishing." Herrald appeared puzzled. "Why?"

"I'm just trying to fill in the picture," said Thane patiently. "Where did you camp the first night? Near Stirling?"

"No, we drove right up to Loch Tay and camped there, in a clearing just off the road—George Shaw had been there before."

"When did you tell him what was going on?"

"On the Tuesday afternoon. He—well, he wasn't very happy about it at first, but I told him he didn't need to get involved to any real extent and he said it would be all right as long as his wife didn't find out." Herrald bit his lip. "We treated it as a bit of a lark."

"So the first time you met Kelch was that evening. What happened?"

"Well, he seemed a decent enough character, bitter at times, but we expected that. We arranged to drive up to the old cottage where they were hiding out first thing the next morning. I'd a camera with me, and I wanted to get their photographs and some other details—"

"Fake travel documents?"

"Well, passes, that sort of thing." Herrald's voice was becoming slightly strained. "Look, I haven't done this before, if that's what you're hinting. But you get to know the ropes. Anyway, we went up as arranged and they were friendly enough. We talked it over and had some food with them—and then George found the explosives. Two boxes of the stuff and some detonators—it was an accident the way it happened. They had them wrapped up in sacking and lying in a corner. George was nosing about, and saw what the stuff was before they could stop him."

Thane nodded. So far, the story was falling pretty well into the shape he'd expected. "And the row began," he prompted.

"That's right. George—well, he began asking questions, wanting answers. Kelch told him to forget what he'd seen—"

"What about you?"

Herrald shook his head. "I kept quiet. George was doing enough talking for us both, anyway. Then he marched across to the van and shouted to me to come too, that he was going for the police. That was when Kelch pulled the gun—but George must have thought he was bluffing, because he got in and slammed the door. Next second Kelch fired at him through the window."

"What happened to you?"

"They shoved me back in the cottage and kept me there. When they brought me out again they told me how—what they'd done about George, and that they were making it look as if I'd panicked and made a bolt for it."

"I see." Thane stubbed his cigarette, rose from the bed and walked across to the window. The hospital gardens were in full bloom, a riot of colours. "That's when they told you about Shashkov?"

"Kelch did. He was running the show—though the others didn't need much pushing. As far as Kelch was concerned, nothing else seemed to matter."

"Not even losing his chance to get abroad?" Thane turned from the window. "How did he hope to get away? Still use you?"

"It didn't seem to matter any more. I told you." Herrald took a last, nervous puff at his cigarette. "Then they took my keys, my wallet, everything. Kelch said he knew a place where they could keep me out of the road and lie low themselves if they had to—he'd found it when he was looking over the places Shashkov would visit. They gathered their kit together, tied me up, and shoved me in the boot of the Ford. Then the car drove off. Hours it seemed to last, and there must have been either fumes getting in, or the air became used up. Anyway, I passed out. When I came to I was in that—that pit. That's all I know."

Thane nodded. "And that's all I'll ask for now. Oh . . . except this. In case we want to contact you, what are your plans once these clothes arrive?"

"Get out of here, have a couple of stiff whiskies, then wait for Barbara and her mother to arrive—they're driving over. They want me to go back with them and rest up for a few days."

"Sounds sensible." Thane gave him a brief farewell nod and left the room, closing the door behind him. He walked on along the corridor, towards the main door of the hospital—then stopped short as it swung open and Phil Moss strode in.

"I hoped you'd still be here." Moss's voice was grey and colourless, his manner tired and yet somehow relieved. "We don't need to look for Martin Kelch any more."

"He's been picked up?" Thane's first reaction was surprise. "Where?"

"He's been found." Moss chose the words with professional care. "A couple of youngsters found him down by the harbour, Colin. He was lying in a corner, behind a pile of old fish boxes—and the gun was still in his hand."

"Suicide?" Thane winced. All else apart, he somehow hadn't pictured the young trawlerman taking that way out.

"A good try at it. Maybe good enough yet." Moss jerked a thumb over his shoulder. "The ambulance is bringing him in now. He's got a bullet through his head, but he's still alive—for the moment, and only just." He pursed his lips. "I'd say the rest is a formality, but they're going to try to operate."

Make him well enough to hang was what he meant, and they both knew it. Thane cursed softly and blindly. "Can he talk?"

Moss shook his head. "The only way you'd know he was still with us is via a stethoscope. I've kept the search going for Stender."

Three down now, and one to go. But Stender was small beer compared with Martin Kelch.

"What now, Colin?" Moss asked it for a second time before Thane came back to realities.

"You've got someone with him?"

"One of the local C.I.D. men—with orders to stick beside him right through."

"Right." They were part of a machine, a machine with a job to do, one it had done hundreds of times before, often enough to be second nature to all its individual parts. "Let's go and have a look at the place, Phil."

They left the hospital just as the ambulance arrived.

EIGHT

It was quiet, almost peaceful down by the tiny, old-fashioned harbour. The ambulance's arrival and departure had been seen by only a handful of people and, the excitement apparently over, most of them had drifted away.

"Over here—" Moss led the way as they left the car and walked along the quayside. It was low tide, and most of the collection of fishing boats and small pleasure craft were either high and dry on the exposed sandy bottom or sitting at an angle in the shallow water. The harbour itself was little more than a long stone breakwater and a flanking quayside, a base for motor-boat trips round the bay and a haven from the waves which could batter so furiously along that stretch of the North Sea coastline.

The uniformed man left on guard saluted as they approached the small mountain of fish boxes lying near the junction of breakwater and quay. Beside him, two youths in heavy roll-necked jerseys and faded blue jeans showed immediate interest.

"These are the lads who found him," explained Phil Moss. "Johnny MacVey and—"

"Sandy Porter," nodded the second of the pair, a brief grin crossing his freckled face. "Who's your pal, Inspector?"

"My name's Thane." He took an immediate liking to the pair—their easy, frank appearance made a welcome, refreshing contrast to the average run of the past few days. "You've told the story before, I know. But I'd like to hear it myself."

The two youngsters glanced at one another and Porter scratched his head. "It's not much of a story. We're up from Edinburgh for the weekend, to do a spot of skin-diving. Our gear's over in the car." He gestured towards an old but well-polished Vauxhall, parked a little way along the quayside. "Anyway, we reached the harbour about twenty minutes ago— the idea was to try exploring along the outer line of the breakwater. Changing into underwater kit in a car is possible but pretty cramping—so we thought we'd try and find a sheltered spot around here."

"And this was it?"

"We thought so." The youngster grimaced. "Instead, we found the bloke lying in behind the boxes. Johnny waited here and I went off to phone the police. But I didn't have to—I bumped into a couple of 'em before I reached a telephone."

"Two of the local men," explained Moss. "I had them keeping an eye around the harbour, just in case Kelch and his pal tried to pinch a boat."

"One way of getting round the roadblocks," acknowledged Thane. He turned back to the skin-divers. "Did either of you hear any noise, see anything before you found him?"

The two youngsters shook their heads.

"But the gun was still in his hand," volunteered the hitherto silent partner.

"Constable?"

The uniformed man cleared his throat. "We've asked around, sir. With the tide out, the harbour was pretty well deserted. But there were some folk on one of those boats—the cabin cruiser with the yellow hull lying across the harbour. They say they heard some kind of a bang, and from their story it would be about ten or fifteen minutes before these lads came along. That's all they know, sir. They looked out, right enough— they'd heard the bang from the Old Course beforehand and were wondering what was happening. But they didn't see anything."

"Nobody did," said Moss, his face tight with annoyance. "It was the same story from the bunch I asked before I went up to the hospital."

Thane shrugged his acceptance. "We'll need you along at the police office later, for a formal statement, but that's all for now," he told the two skin-divers.

They nodded, then headed towards their car, their expedition temporarily abandoned.

"Got the cartridge case, Phil?" Thane knelt to examine the dark red pool of blood staining part of the worn stone of the quayside in the shadowed space behind the crates.

"In my pocket," Moss confirmed. "It was lying beside one of the boxes—I've marked the place. But the bullet must still be around."

"Exit wound?" Thane anticipated his companion's nod of agreement. At such close range, a nine-millimetre bullet's velocity was savage to behold.

Together, they made a gradually widening search for the missing metal slug. They finally located it, flattened and almost beyond recognition—the obvious result of a ricochet from part of the stonework around.

From the harbour, they went back to the hospital and arrived at its entrance just as Peter Herrald was about to step into a waiting taxi. He was leaning shakily on the arm of a nurse, but there was a look of determination on his face. He saw them, stopped, and gave a smile as they approached.

"I told you I'd be out of here as soon as I got some clothes."

Colin Thane ran an eye over the new but ill-fitting suit Herrald was wearing. "How is he, Nurse?"

The nurse gave a shrug. "The doctor wanted him to stay, sir, but Mr. Herrald has voluntarily discharged himself—"

"And they can't keep me. But thanks for what you've done." Herrald ran one hand over the sleeve of his jacket. "As soon as I get some cash I'll need to settle up with the outfitter who supplied this."

"Better take some money while you're at it—pay me back later." Thane took out his wallet and gave Herrald four of the one-pound notes it contained.

"Thanks." Herrald gratefully pocketed the cash. "I've already borrowed something from the doctor who tried to keep me in—add this, and I'm solvent for the moment." He ran his tongue lightly over his lips. "I—I heard about Kelch. Is that why you're back?"

Thane nodded.

"Seems they don't think much of his chances. Well, personally I won't lose any sleep over it." Herrald gave a tight grin. "Do you blame me?" Without waiting for an answer he got aboard the taxi. The door slammed shut and in a moment it was driving off.

As the vehicle swung out through the hospital gates the two detectives followed the nurse into the building. The young doctor who'd dressed Thane's shoulder wound was still on duty—and could tell them right off that their trip had been a waste of time.

"They're working on him in the theatre, and probably will be for about another hour," he declared.

"How does it look?"

"Nasty. But beyond that I don't know what the chances are."

"We'll come back. But if anything happens before we do . . ."

"We'll whistle you up, don't worry," he assured them.

When they got back to the police station, a waiting swarm of figures descended on the car.

"Gentlemen of the press," said Moss wryly. "Like flies round a honeypot." Reluctantly, he opened the car door and was first out. A moment later, he gave an indignant hoot. "Get these ruddy cameras out from under my nose!"

The cameramen fell back, their task completed. As they went, the notebook brigade swung forward.

"Sorry boys." Thane glanced round the circle, recognising several familiar faces. "There's no statement coming from me. Maybe later—"

"From a Ministry spokesman?" The cynical query, from a tall, rabbit-jawed character he recognised as Scottish stringer for one of the London nationals, brought a sardonic chuckle from the others. "General Shashkov's put out a statement about the bomb attempt, Chief Inspector. It roasts everybody from the British Government downwards." He flipped through the pages of his notebook. "What about this? 'It is hard to see how such an outrage could have occurred unless there had been definite and perhaps even deliberate negligence of elementary safeguards.' Don't you want to answer it?"

"That's not my job at the moment." Thane began to push his way through the clustering group, his face expressionless. It probably wouldn't be long before the pressmen got their first hint of what had been happening away from the Old Course, and when that happened the real hue and cry would begin. But this was one time when his usual reputation for being reasonably co-operative with the press was going to take a drastic beating.

Inside the police station, Phil Moss gave a sigh of relief as he slammed the door, shutting out the last protests from their pursuers. "Another load of trouble round our necks." His expression was gloomy.

"What else?" asked Thane. "Shashkov was bound to make the most of it. But at least we'll get rid of him in one piece now."

"There's still Stender left."

"It's finished, Phil." Thane was optimistic. "All we've got now is one very frightened trawlerman, hiding somewhere and wondering how long it'll be before he's rounded up."

They checkèd with the station duty officer, but that harassed individual had nothing fresh to report.

"Not unless you're interested in a character who couldn't remember where he left his car," he grumbled. "First he phones and says it's gone from where he left it last night, in the street round the corner from where he lives. I let the roadblocks know and put out a general alert . . . that was quarter of an hour ago. Now he's just phoned again. He just found it, further along the same street."

"Intact?" asked Thane.

"Yes. But he left it unlocked. Interested?"

"Better check on it, just in case," Thane told him.

The duty officer could supply something more welcome—a mug of tea and a sandwich each.

"Ah . . . " Thane settled back in a chair in the same room they'd used most of the night, took a long gulp of the tea, then a first bite at the thick-cut bread. "Twisted luck, that's all it's been, Phil. Twisted one way, then the other. Yet it wouldn't have happened at all if those four had jumped ship at any other time than when Shashkov was due here. They'd either have been whisked out of the country by Herrald or would have ended up walking into a police station somewhere and asking for a bed for the night."

"I wonder why Kelch did it—shoot himself, I mean." Moss tasted the tea and winced. It was strong and tarry, and what it was going to do to his digestive acids he hated to imagine.

"Looks plain enough." Thane chewed for a moment. "The Old Course must have been their last big effort—the one that wouldn't fail. But it did, which was a big enough blow for him. On top of that, supposing Kelch had a rendezvous with the others down at the harbour once the blast was over and they'd gathered an idea of what happened. Your own idea fits, that they were planning to pinch a boat. If he passed the castle and saw the place cluttered with cops he'd know we'd found Herrald. Then Bretsun doesn't turn up, and he gets worried. Supposing Stender is missing too, because he's too busy dodging our patrols to be able to make it?"

"Leaving Kelch alone with a complete failure and a double indictment for murder hanging over him," murmured Moss. "Not a pleasant future."

"Plus one thing more," said Thane, running his fingers round the edge of the tea mug. "It was low tide, Phil . . . a damn-fool mistake for a fisherman to make, but that's how it happens. The odds were that any of the boats he could handle on his own were stuck high and dry."

"And so to a bullet in the head." Moss finished his sandwich, abandoned the tea, and lit a cigarette. "What's that?"

Ruefully, Thane contemplated the envelope in his hand. "A present from Professor MacMaster. Well, we won't have much need of it now, but let's see anyway." He ripped open the flap, took out the folded, typewritten sheets within, and glanced through them. Suddenly he stopped, frowned, then went back to the beginning of the report and read it through again from start to finish. The frown deepened. Then he passed the sheets across to his second-in-command. "Read it, Phil. Carefully."

Detective Inspector Moss obeyed. When he was finished, he was just as puzzled as he'd been at the start.

"Bacterial activity, chemical change—" He shook his head in bewilderment. "Old MacMaster's been having fun, but what's it all about?"

Thane took back the papers. "One point, Phil. A small one, but one I can't understand." He glanced at the report again. "Translated into plain English, MacMaster got hold of those emptied tins and other junk we found in the cottage where Shaw was killed."

"I can read," grunted Moss. "Dan Laurence's boys found fingerprints on them, but that didn't surprise anyone."

"It's the next part that matters, Phil." Thane eyed him patiently. "Some of the food they'd dumped was going bad."

"And smelled like it." Moss wrinkled his nose in remembered disgust.

"Belt up and listen for a minute, will you?" Thane rubbed his chin.

"MacMaster examined each item. Now listen. 'Bacterial activity commences the moment any foodstuff is exposed to the air, as does chemical change . . . blah, blah . . . an interesting specimen was a glass jar which appeared to have contained a variety of meat paste.'" He grinned to himself. "That's what the ruddy label said, anyway. Here's what matters—'smeared traces of paste on the outer surface of the jar had been exposed for sufficient time to allow development of a characteristic mould growth.' The rest of it. . . ."

"Says that the mould grew over a part of the jar where Dan Laurence's boys found a fingerprint, or at least part of one," nodded Moss, still uncertain but his interest growing. "The print was partly eaten over by the mould but—" he broke off, mouth open in surprise as the situation percolated through.

"But could still be identified." Thane's voice was a low murmur. MacMaster's report said the mould would have needed approximately four days to develop. Four days back from the time the jar had been collected by him meant the Monday.

Yet how could that whiskering blue-grey growth have been spreading across a fingerprint identified as Peter Herrald's when Herrald had told him that his first visit to the cottage hadn't been until the Wednesday?

As always, MacMaster's report was a masterpiece of caution. Temperature, humidity, a wide variety of factors could have influenced the mould's exact rate of development—but still left that four-day barrier. He summed up the situation as "one of interesting research possibilities, so far untested by the courts."

"Maybe Herrald picked up the jar on Wednesday, when it had already been used?" Phil Moss strove for an easy explanation.

"No, that's out." Thane rejected the suggestion with a degree of reluctance. "According to MacMaster, the mould structure would show if that had happened—something to do with reaction on the sweat deposit from the skin pores."

"Then Herrald either lied to you or was confused. Which?"

"He seemed certain enough." Thane chewed his lip. "We could go and ask him outright but—no, leave it just now. I'm more interested in Kelch."

The hour crawled round with still no trace of Stender. The last of the runaways had performed a most efficient vanishing trick, and all Thane could do was make sure the local roadblock pattern was maintained and that the regular search network was in full operation in the areas beyond. Colonel Donnan telephoned from the manager's office at Sunbury Colliery. . . . General Shashkov's visit there was going smoothly and without hitch, but the security chief was more interested in filling in the background to the fragmentary reports he'd been receiving.

Thane told him. When he'd finished, he heard the little Irishman give a sigh.

"I'll tell Shashkov. It won't make much difference to the build-up he's giving the whole affair, but I'll tell him. Once this visit is over we're heading back for Glasgow. You'll keep in touch?"

Thane promised and hung up. He looked at his watch, nodded to Phil Moss, and rose from his chair.

There was another visitor at the hospital when they arrived. Lady Dunspar, a lightweight fawn raincoat buttoned over her tweed costume, sat stubbornly in a chair in the waiting room a little way inside the entrance hall. Her face calm and determined, she glanced up as Thane's burly figure entered the room.

"There's little sense in being here," he told her, his voice firm but sympathetic. "I can't let you see him."

"I know. The hospital staff said the same—that even if I did he wouldn't know I was there." She shook her head. "It doesn't matter. I—well, I can't explain, but I'll stay in this room until—well, until I'm forced to leave."

"That's a matter for the hospital." Thane understood, understood to a deeper extent than this proud, lonely woman would have believed. "But if you're staying here, what about your daughter and Herrald?"

"I've told them." Her eyes were troubled for a moment. "It was difficult, very difficult, Chief Inspector. After what Martin did to Peter Herrald it may seem wrong for me to feel like this. Barbara said—" She pursed her lips. "Anyway, they've changed their plans. Barbara is driving Peter back to Glasgow. They asked me to let you know."

"I'll come back." Thane left her and went out into the corridor. Phil Moss had apparently vanished, but as he glanced around, undecided, he heard footsteps and the small, wiry d.i. came round a corner towards him. At his side was an older, silver-haired man wearing a loose-hanging white hospital coat over an immaculate dark grey suit.

"Chief Inspector Thane?" The newcomer spoke with an underlying trace of North Country accent. "I'm Gransden—surgical consultant. Your colleague tells me you want to hear anything I can tell you about the man Kelch's condition."

"Anything possible," agreed Thane.

"At this stage it doesn't amount to much." The surgeon gestured them to follow and led the way back along the corridor. "In here, I think——" He ushered them into a small, sunlit office and waited until they'd perched themselves on the long black-leather couch which, with a desk and its chair plus a couple of filing cabinets, was the room's quota of furnishings. "Now, how can I help?"

"The obvious question first. Will he live?"

"That would be in the nature of the type of gambling forecast I abhor, Chief Inspector." Gransden ran his thumbs over the tips of his scrubbed, close-cut fingernails and frowned. "For the moment, the man's condition is critical. All we've done is—ah—what you might term a basic tidying up, emergency treatment. If we can and as soon as we can, we'll require to move him to a specialised neuro-surgical hospital. But to attempt that at the moment would be tantamount to killing him."

"But you think he has a chance of pulling through?"

The surgeon shrugged. "There's always a chance." He gave a brief, frosty twinkle. "You know, a bullet through the head isn't nearly as reliable a way of procuring death as the layman believes."

"And in this case?" Thane gave a faint nod to his companion and Phil Moss dredged out notebook and pencil.

"The entry wound was in the temporal region, approximately here——" Gransden pointed with one forefinger to a spot just in front of and a little above his right ear "——and the shot was fired at probably almost direct contact with the weapon. It was possible to see the muzzle outline in the powder tattooing on the skin. The bullet's passage from there was downwards and slightly forward, with the exit wound below the left antrum." He gave the same wintery twinkle at Moss's slowing pencil. "Below the cheekbone, Mr. Moss. There's considerable damage around the region of the exit wound of course—always is. And it's impossible yet to say what if any damage has been done to the optic nerves for a start."

"But the brain is undamaged—" Thane raised a hopeful eyebrow.

"Apparently." The surgeon was in pedantic mood. "Even if it had been, the result wouldn't necessarily be fatal. There are certain—ah— spare areas in the cerebrum. But that's by the way. If he pulls through, a certain amount of repair work will be necessary."

"He's still unconscious?"

"And likely to remain that way for some time to come," confirmed Gransden. "If you are really asking when, if he lives, you can have a chance at questioning him and getting any sort of a reply, then the answer could be several days." He lost a little of his patience. "The man's fighting for his life, Chief Inspector. The wound in itself would be bad enough without complications."

"Sir?" Moss glanced up from his notebook. Colin Thane's face showed identical surprise.

The surgeon gave a tut of annoyance. "The fellow was ill enough by any standard even before the gunshot wound." He noticed their continued bewilderment and put the situation as simply as he could. "Kelch is suffering from pneumonia, gentlemen. A fairly advanced case—pneumonic consolidation with a pleural effusion."

It hit Thane with all the force of a blow to the stomach. "How far advanced, Mr. Gransden?"

"He must have been as weak as a kitten, running a very high temperature. My guess—only a guess, of course—is that the condition has been building for anything up to three days. He's in an oxygen tent at this moment, and in normal circumstances he should have been under medical care long before now."

Colin Thane swallowed hard. "I'd like as positive an answer as you can give me to this, sir. Could—could a man in that condition have been taking an active part in—well, in strenuous activities?"

Gransden chewed his lip and deliberated for a moment. "That's difficult to say, damned difficult. Some people can keep going to the point of collapse. I'd say it would be possible but—" He shook his head.

"Can we see him?"

"No reason why not." The surgeon began heading for the door.

"And one other request, sir. I'd like permission to have a paraffin-wax test made of his right hand."

The surgeon's eyes narrowed with fresh, thoughtful interest. "Like that, is it? All right. But it's only fair to warn you I don't claim any vast experience, but the angle of the head wound, everything about it, is perfectly in accord with an attempted suicide. A little awkward, perhaps. But a last-second, involuntary movement of the head would account for both angle and failure."

Once again they followed him.

The room where Martin Kelch was lying was one floor up. Outside the door, the county C.I.D. man rose from his chair as they approached.

"Nothing yet, sir."

Thane nodded. Then, as the surgeon opened the door, he went in, Phil Moss just behind him.

Martin Kelch's bed was partly enveloped by the transparent cloak of the oxygen tent. As they entered, a nurse turned from the cylinders and controls placed to one side of the bed and glanced at Gransden.

"Carry on," he told her. "We'll only be a moment."

The two detectives moved forward and for the first time Thane saw the man he'd pursued so desperately . . . the man about whom he now had gathering doubt.

Bandages and heavy padded dressings framed and obscured Martin Kelch's pale, thin, clean-shaven face. It was a delicately boned face, with wide mouth, firm chin, and aquiline nose. His eyes were closed, the only sign that life still clung to him the almost imperceptible rise and fall of his chest.

"Satisfied?" The surgeon fidgetted impatiently.

"Yes." Thane turned away from the bed. "What happened to the clothes he was wearing?"

"Kept to one side, as Inspector Moss requested the ambulance team."

The clothing was in a cupboard in a small ward utility room nearby. Gransden had his own work schedule to maintain and was quite thankful to say goodbye as soon as he saw that they were finished with him. Once he'd gone, Thane turned to the little bundle.

"Just the pockets for now, Phil."

By the time the last pocket had been emptied, the collection was slender, but still interesting.

The trousers yielded a heavy clasp knife, matches, a comb, and some loose change. The overcoat added only a packet of cigarettes to the heap. But with the jacket Phil Moss had better luck. From the inside pocket he produced a thick bill-fold, and he whistled as he checked its contents. "There's almost eighty quid here, Colin—and Herrald's driving license!" He finished the other pockets, added a handkerchief, a ballpoint pen, and some more loose change to the pile, then scratched his thinning hair. "Well, what now? Look, it doesn't need a genius to guess what's on your mind, Colin. But even if we had twice as much to go on as we actually have, we'd still need to go easy, very, very easy."

He waited, well aware of the struggle going on inside his burly, dark-haired friend—a struggle to weigh fact fairly against conviction, to balance a tight-rope path between the urge to act on intuition and the knowledge that that could be just as dangerous as moving too slowly.

At last, Thane stirred. "Phil, I want you to stay here for a spell. Organise the paraffin-wax test and keep an eye on Kelch."

"And you?"

"I'm heading for Glasgow. General Shashkov will be on his way there by now, and where Shashkov goes Colonel Donnan isn't far behind."

"There's also the point that Peter Herrald will be back home this evening." Moss's voice was dry and humorless. "Thinking of having another little chat with him?"

A slow, equally humorless grin twisted one corner of Thane's mouth. "Not yet, Phil. But I'm going to make sure that I know exactly where to find him if the time does come." He pulled the bundle of clothing together. "I'll take these with me—anything happens, contact me through Headquarters or the Division."

"What about Lady Dunspar?"

"I promised I'd see her before I left. She's not likely to budge, Phil—it might be an idea to have a word with the matron and try to find her a more comfortable place."

"I'll fix it." As Thane left, Moss slowly lit a cigarette. A thought struck him. It was almost two hours now since he'd last felt a twinge from his ulcer. It meant something, it always did. But he'd never yet managed to work out what or why.

Lady Dunspar was still sitting in the same chair in the downstairs waiting room. She got up as Thane entered, her eyes searching his face.

"You've—you've seen him, Mr. Thane?"

"A few minutes ago," he told her. "He's still unconscious, and likely to stay that way—and there's no sense pretending he isn't in a pretty bad way."

"That's what they told me before." She bit her lip. "But . . . there's a chance, isn't there?"

"There always is." Thane took the jacket from the bundle of clothing over his arm. "Do you recognise this, Lady Dunspar?"

She glanced at it and shook her head.

"Do Herrald and your daughter know Martin Kelch is unconscious—how bad his condition is?"

"Yes. They—that was why Barbara was angry about my waiting. When the doctor told me it might be days before he came round, even if he won through, she—well, she said I was mad to stay, that it was unnatural after all that had happened."

He left it at that, said goodbye, and went out. A few minutes later he was relaxing in the passenger seat of the same police Jaguar which had brought him north the night before. As the car ate the miles back towards Glasgow, the uniformed driver took a guarded glance towards his apparently sleepy-eyed passenger. The Millside C.I.D. chief was usually a friendly, talkative character on a journey . . . well, he'd been putting in his share of overtime lately, he supposed.

It was late afternoon when the car reached the city. Thane spent a few minutes at Headquarters, just long enough to drop off the load of clothing at the Scientific Branch's outer office and to make a quick check through their file on the case. When he came out again, there was a new confidence in his step.

"Over to Millside now," he told his driver. "And let's get moving—I don't want to be grabbed by Bhudda Ilford in search of explanations."

The man grinned and obeyed, turning the car on to the fast dockside route across the city. In under ten minutes the Jaguar pulled to a halt outside the familiar, grimy bulk of the divisional police office.

Thane got out, headed non-stop through the public office, and climbed the stairs to the C.I.D. section. He nodded a greeting to the men on duty, but didn't slow until he'd reached the sanctuary of his own office. Once there, he back-heeled the door shut behind him, tossed his hat on to its peg, and dropped thankfully into the worn leather of the chair behind his desk. The hands of the clock on the opposite wall had still ten minutes to travel before they reached five P.M.—Saturday tea and television time in practically every home throughout the city. The Saturday sports editions of the evening newspapers would be starting their run on the presses as usual . . . except that for once, their football news would have a challenge for front-page supremacy in the Shashkov story.

There was one last cigarette left in his pack. He lit it, flicked the match away, then pulled a pad of scrap paper towards him and began writing, marshalling into order the stepped sequence of moves he'd mentally roughed on the journey to the city.

When he'd finished, he stubbed the cigarette and lifted the telephone. The station switchboard girl came on the line almost immediately, surprise in her voice.

"Aye, I'm back," he told her. "But keep quiet about it. I'm still up north as far as most of the outside world is concerned." He heard her chuckle, then went on. "You're going to be kept pretty busy for a spell. First off, I want you to locate a Colonel Donnan—he's Home Office security and Headquarters should be able to tell you where he is about now. After that, get me a line through to the army records section at Scottish Command."

"Right, sir."

"Oh—Jean." He caught her just before she went off the line. "Two other things, top priority. Give me a call to my home, will you? And any tea on the brew down in that cubbyhole of yours?"

"I'll cope—but we're low on sugar."

Thane heard a buzz and a click, the pulse of the ringing tone over the line, then his wife's voice answered.

"Just me, Mary. I'm back in town."

"In one piece?" There was a strained brightness in her query. He'd heard it before—most cops did when the pressure was on and things, unpleasant things, were happening. "I've been listening to the radio—the news bulletins have been leading off with the bomb attempt, Colin."

"I'm fine. Well—" he glanced down at his shoulder "—I've got a natty piece of bandaging as a decoration and you've got one shirt less to launder in future. How it happened was something separate. I'm telling you just in case you hear a different version."

"Will you be home?"

"Tonight?" He knew she'd already guessed the answer. "Not a chance, dear. But tomorrow, before noon. Kids okay?"

"They're both out playing." She hesitated. "Colin—"

"Don't bother saying it," he assured her. "The rough stuff's over. Okay now?"

"If you mean it." Which meant she wasn't convinced. They said goodbye and he replaced the receiver. Was the rough stuff really over? He'd said the same thing to Phil Moss, but then he'd been talking about Shashkov's safety. The rest—that would probably depend on exactly how carefully he handled what lay ahead.

A double knock sounded on the door of his room, and he looked up as it opened and Sergeant MacLeod came in.

"Spare a moment, sir?" MacLeod was cautious, with the memory of past experience of crisis times.

"Not much more than that, Mac." He leaned back in the chair. "But if you hadn't come I was on my way out to find you. How many men are free right now—or on jobs that can wait for a spell?"

The C.I.D. sergeant pursed his lips. "Three, four including myself, sir—it's been reasonably quiet all day. Beech and Mahone will be clear as soon as they've booked in Vince Bruce."

"Vince!" Thane gave a slow grin of appreciation at the news that the fleet-footed young burglar had finally been nailed. "Who's our sprint star—Beech or Mahone?"

"Well, neither sir." MacLeod deliberately shifted his gaze towards the window. "They were in the duty car when there was an emergency call to a housebreaking in Finlay Street. Vince made a break for it as they turned up, and jumped the back garden wall. But he landed badly, and sprained his ankle—they had to carry him in."

Thane's grunt was comment enough. "Anything else I should know?"

"The pitch-and-toss school, sir—Constable Newton reported in. He played last night, and he's going to be in the game again this evening. He says there's definitely another big game set for Sunday, but he won't know where it'll be until tonight. Do you still want the raid scheduled for tomorrow?"

"That's what I said and that's what I meant." Thane struggled against impatience. Being a divisional C.D.I. called for octopus-like abilities at any time, but right at that moment he could hardly have cared less about the pitch-and-toss gamblers. "Did Newton say anything more?"

MacLeod gave a gloomy nod. "He lost ten pounds last night, sir. But he reckons he'll collect some cash this time—something about a system he's trying."

"That means he'll probably land the division in the bankruptcy court." Thane sighed. "Right, Mac, now here's—" he broke off with a frown as the telephone rang, shrugged, and answered it. But he brightened as he heard Colonel Donnan's voice sounding over the line.

"Unless it's important keep it brief, will you?" pleaded the little security man. "I'm in Shashkov's suite at the Southern Hotel—and he's just announced he wants to go out for a drive around town."

"It's important. How soon can you get over to Millside?"

"Eh?" Donnan was bewildered.

"I said how soon can you get over." Thane rammed each word over the wire. "And the quicker the better. I don't think Kelch is the man we want." He brushed aside the splutter which crackled over the line. "I'll tell you why when I see you."

He hung up on that, a smile wisping on his lips. Donnan would come all right. He glanced back to Sergeant MacLeod, standing patiently, his face expressionless.

"Your turn now, Mac." He gave the C.I.D. man a brief, elementary sketch of the situation. "I want a tail put on Herrald and the Mason girl. Use two men in case they split up later tonight." He grunted at MacLeod's sardonic expression. "Don't worry—they probably will. Tell whoever are on it we'll relieve them if and when we can, but I'll have their guts if they lose contact, and a double helping if they're spotted." He gave MacLeod the number of Barbara Mason's car, the hotel where she both worked and lived, Herrald's address. The rest boiled down to routine.

"I'll get them moving." MacLeod turned towards the door.

"Not yet." Thane pulled the scrap pad towards him again. "We're just getting started."

It was another ten minutes before Detective Sergeant MacLeod finally emerged from Thane's room, ten minutes interrupted only by the arrival of an orderly with the promised tea from the switchboard, the same orderly's return with two packs of cigarettes, and a brief break when Thane's call to army records came through.

Outside, MacLeod closed the door gently behind him, then looked around the main C.I.D. room, pursing his lips. Then he waved the half-dozen expectant, waiting men to gather around him. "Tonight, just for once, you're going to have to work for your ruddy money," he informed them. "By tomorrow, most of you are going to wish you'd been drowned at birth. Now, let's get on with it."

Colonel Donnan wasted a minimum of time in getting to Millside. But even so, only one detective was still in the main C.I.D. room when he arrived, an unfortunate d.c. trying to speak on two telephones at the same time while a third instrument pealed indignantly in the background. Donnan stalked past the confusion, rapped on Thane's office door, and barged in.

The Millside C.I.D. chief tossed down the pencil he'd been using and swung round in his chair to greet the security man.

"Well, you didn't waste time," he declared, stoppering a chuckle as he saw Donnan's ruffled indignation. "Sit down—cigarette, Colonel?"

The security chief ignored the offered pack and gave a sound close to a snarl. "Never mind the social chit-chat, Thane. What the hell did you mean when you said Kelch wasn't the man we wanted? And if you thought it funny hanging up on me like that, I didn't . . . I'm damned if I did!"

"Couldn't think of a better way to get you here in double-quick time." Thane met Donnan's glare, held it, and saw it die down a little as the man opposite recognised the iron-hard purpose which lay beneath the burly detective's outward calm.

"Well. . . ." He took the cigarette and a light. "All right, I'll listen."

"Start off with two factors, one of them a fingerprint." Carefully, deliberately, Colin Thane etched out the substance of Professor MacMaster's report, then the interview he'd had with the hospital surgeon. Gradually, Colonel Donnan's remaining hostility thawed and gave way to reluctant interest.

"But what does it prove?" he complained. "Maybe Herrald did lie, and maybe Kelch was as ill as you say. But how far does it take you?" A last puff at the cigarette, and he stubbed it on the desk ashtray. "Just that Herrald may want to hide an earlier meeting because of what happened later. And you told me yourself—medically, Kelch might have been able to keep going, even with the pneumonia in full flame."

Thane knew the argument. He'd used it against himself when he first tried to analyse the new maze of possibilities which had sprouted up before him.

"Yet here's something you told me," he countered. "You said General Shashkov was squeezing every drop of publicity out of the situation because it not only made us look foolish but helped build up his public image back home—that he'd been 'out of favour' with some of his Party pals. How much out of favour?"

"How much?" Donnan found it hard to answer straight off. "That has to be two-thirds guesswork. It's the old, old story, pressure groups at work, charges of what they call ideological variation, hell knows what else. If Shashkov was out of the way well—" he shrugged "—he wields a lot of influence. That's probably his main value to the top boys. They'd find him hard to replace."

"And supposing this get-tough brigade decided to arrange things so that he was completely out of the way?" Thane's fingers closed hard round the pencil again. "Where would be the best place to try it? At home, where things could be nasty if anything went wrong—or abroad, where it would be easy to shift the blame away from themselves? Wouldn't it be ideal for them to get rid of Shashkov and at the same time set him up as a martyr, use the situation to stoke up their own line, force the top boys to turn on the pressure again?"

Incredulous, Donnan started to laugh then changed his mind. He sat back, shaking his head. "Now take it easy, Thane. This is—"

"Madness? Is it?" The pencil snapped, but Thane ignored it. "I'm a cop—I'm supposed to deal in facts, nothing else. Right, I'll give you facts. How long is it since Shashkov's visit to Britain was announced as being scheduled? A little over three months. How long is it since Peter Herrald met Barbara Mason at a party he 'just happened to go along to with a friend'? Two months. Herrald ended war service as an R.A.S.C. captain. Before that he was in the Royal Engineers. But do you know what his unit was before he was commissioned? A demolition section—explosives experts, trained for the job. I got that from army records twenty minutes ago."

He saw Donnan's flickering frown and knew that, at least, had scored.

"If that's not enough, explain this away," Thane plunged on. "Four men were seen around the holiday chalet where Phil Moss was clubbed. Three of them left fingerprints all over the place—couldn't have cared less. But not the fourth, Colonel. A fourth man's prints were at the old cottage, on the car Serviev crashed—so what was so special about the chalet? Was it he didn't go there, that the fourth man people caught a glimpse of was somebody else altogether, somebody who couldn't take chances?"

Colonel Donnan sat silent for a long moment, his mouth narrowed, a new, thoughtful look in his eyes. When he spoke, the words came slowly.

"Anything more?"

"Only little things. I've got men out, but they need time."

Donnan nodded, his voice dulled. "All it would need would be the right man in a high-up position over there. They know Shashkov is going to Scotland . . . Martin Kelch is on their files and working on the trawler fleet. He has a built-in motive, friends who'd shelter him, in fact he could have been made for the purpose. Plant some other 'freedom lovers' on the trawler, give them time to work on him, then make sure they get the chance to make what looks like a genuine break, and the rest follows on."

"With Herrald already waiting ashore." Thane slid the cigarettes across the table again. "That import-export business could make an ideal cover for a very different type of agency."

"And provided the orders came from the usual source, he wouldn't query them." Donnan lit his cigarette and drew heavily. "The contact man, the man who could have gathered all the local knowledge they would need." A thought struck him. "Where is he now?"

"In town. Being watched." A grey humour wisped over Thane's lips. "As long as Martin Kelch is unconscious and looks like dying, Herrald will sit things out. Why not? Right now everyone feels sorry for him. He's the poor devil who saw his pal killed, the man who was kept in the bottle. When the story makes the papers, he'll be a minor hero. Stolen explosives, home-made bombs—the whole thing was rigged, Donnan, all part of the play-acting with Herrald as stage manager!"

The security man cleared his throat. "Could you use some help?" The words meant more than they said, his complete acceptance of the turnabout.

Thane had been saving his final long-shot hunch for this moment. "You could take Vilkas Stender off my hands, for a start."

"You know where he is?" The little Irishman was taken completely by surprise. "I thought he'd simply vanished—"

"I think I know where he'll head," said Thane softly. "There's one place nobody in his right mind would go searching for an Iron Curtain refugee—a ship that's ready to sail back there." He picked up one of the scrawled notes on his desk. "There are three due to sail from Scottish ports in the next forty-eight hours. Want the sailing times?"

Donnan's hand closed on the paper. "As of now, this is mine. What else?"

Thane grinned at the other man's enthusiasm. "I'll let you know," he promised. "It's going to be a long night."

It was. Till three A.M., to be precise. But when Colin Thane finally surrendered to the canvas-sprung comfort of a brief sleep in the folding camp bed kept stowed in his office he knew he'd been right, knew that only one last factor was needed to complete the pattern he'd sought to reconstruct. And Phil Moss had it, was bringing it down with him when he left St. Andrews at dawn.

The big silver-grey TU 104 turbojet carrying General Shashkov back to Moscow howled down the Prestwick Airport runway at exactly 0:800 hours on a Sunday morning, a lumbering, clumsy giant which transformed into a great but graceful metal bird as it became airborne and found its own element. It gained height, vapour trailing, the sun glinting to give the watchers below a last glimpse of the red hammer-and-sickle emblem on its nose. Then, within seconds, it was a dwindling shape fading to a dot lost among the clouds.

One hour later, Colin Thane telephoned from his office in Millside to Peter Herrald's flat. When Herrald answered, Thane kept his manner apologetic while he asked the man to come over and give the signed statement he'd promised.

"Seen the Sunday papers yet?" Thane trailed all the bait necessary. "General Shashkov's been kicking up blazes—headlines all the way. Now we've heard they've found out about Kelch. The only part of the story they don't know yet is your own—and the press brigade will probably be on to that by noon. And I've got my orders—" Thane winked across his desk at Phil Moss and Donnan "—we've to have your statement in full before there's as much as a sniff of a reporter around. Can I send a car to collect you in half an hour?"

Herrald grumbled, then agreed and hung up.

Exactly on time, two detective constables arrived at his flat. They were polite, they were cheerful, their car was outside—and they didn't mention that since five that morning, when they took over from the previous duty team, they'd been within constant watching distance.

A few minutes before ten A.M. Peter Herrald came strolling into Thane's office. He wore a neat, tailored sports jacket and whipcord slacks and returned Thane's greeting with a lazy ease.

"How's the shoulder, Chief Inspector?"

"A little stiff, that's all." Thane glanced at the others in the room. "You know Inspector Moss—this is Colonel Donnan, Home Office security."

Herrald nodded, then took the chair Phil Moss pushed forward. He was in front of the desk, with Thane in his usual chair opposite. Donnan sat over by the window and Phil Moss stationed himself casually by the door, notebook in hand.

"You had a pretty rough time of it from what I've heard," said Donnan sympathetically.

"Back here, it seems like a nightmare." Herrald shook his head. "I don't know how long it takes to forget that kind of thing. Barbara said"—he broke off and glanced at Thane—"you know she drove me down yesterday?"

Thane nodded. "Her mother told me. You know Lady Dunspar's still at the hospital?"

"I know." Herrald pursed his lips. "I telephoned her there this morning, just after you called. The woman's beyond reasoning with, but I felt I had to try. She said there was no change in Kelch." He ran a hand over his thinning fair hair. "I still feel . . . well, every now and again I get the shakes." He fumbled in his pocket and brought out a narrow leather cigarette case. "Mind?"

"Go ahead." Thane pushed the ashtray towards him and struck a match for the man. Herrald cupped a steady hand over the flame, then sat back.

"Thanks. Well, do you want to get this statement over?"

"Might as well." Casually, Thane flicked over the papers before him. "These are my own notes of what you said yesterday. They'll save us going over too much old ground. You left Glasgow with George Shaw on the Saturday. When did you first meet Martin Kelch?"

"On the Tuesday night, outside the Tayman Hotel in Aberfeldy." Herrald fingered the lapel of his jacket as he sat back in the chair, his eyes straying round the room. "That was the arrangement we'd made."

"And the first time you visited the cottage was the next day?"

Herrald nodded.

From his stance by the door, Phil Moss gave a sigh. "Sorry, Mr. Herrald—but do you mind giving answers?"

Herrald looked round, saw the notebook, and grimaced. "For the record? All right, put down 'answered yes.'"

"You said things were friendly at first when you arrived up there." Thane fiddled with the papers again. "You had a meal with them."

"Well, a pretty rough and ready one," agreed Herrald. "They were living on tinned stuff mostly."

"Did you give them any food?"

"Us?" Herrald blinked. "No. Why?"

"Just building the picture," Thane assured him. "You were camping, you might have had spare supplies. Now, when George Shaw found the gelignite and said he'd go for the police, you say Kelch was the one who fired the shot that killed him. I can fill in the details—but I'd like to tell you one thing." Thane leaned forward, the smile wiped from his face, his voice ice-flecked. "You're a liar, Mr. Herrald."

Herrald jerked in his chair. "What do you mean?"

"A pretty good liar." Thane strode round the desk and stood towering over the man. He reached out, took the cigarette from Herrald's fingers, and stubbed it out on the ashtray. "But not quite good enough."

A red flush spread over Herrald's smooth, plump face. "Have you gone crazy, Chief Inspector? You pulled me out of that pit yourself! Colonel— look, I can't remember your name, but do you know what this is all about?"

The security chief remained impassive. "Most of it. If it helps, I had three men at the dockside when Vilkas Stender tried to board the freighter *Dubrova* at Leith Docks at two o'clock this morning. Funny thing—she was due to sail with the tide at four, bound for the Baltic, first port of call Riga." He ran one hand lightly round his collar. "Funny thing. After all the trouble he went to getting off that trawler you wouldn't think he'd want to go back behind the Curtain again, would you?"

"What's Stender got to do with me?" Herrald started to rise from his chair. "He was one of the four—that's all I know about him."

"Is it?" Thane pushed him back down again. "Herrald, your job was to meet up with these four and play Kelch and Lady Dunspar along as far as possible. The knight in shining armour coming to help those poor run-away sailormen—" He gave a growl. "You could have kept the fiction going until it was time to put Kelch out of the way and let your three pals get to work. All you'd have to do was tell Lady Dunspar that all four of them had rejected your help and disappeared—you could be certain she wouldn't talk, and George Shaw would probably be the same. In fact, George Shaw was a perfect alibi—because if he ever did tell what he thought was the truth, you still emerged as just a fellow who'd tried to help and been shoved aside. Only the thing blew up in your face when he found out too much!"

"The whole thing's ridiculous!" Herrald saw his protest fall on deaf ears.

"Who killed Shaw?"

"I told you—Kelch."

Thane sighed. "There's a little point about Scottish law you maybe don't know. If a group of people join together in acts which add up to murder, then the law says they're all equally guilty. And Herrald—murder by shooting, murder by use of explosives both carry a death sentence."

"But you're wrong—completely wrong!" Herrald ran one hand over his head, his eyes bright with what could have been fear but was nearer to a fighting despair.

Thane leaned back against the desk, watching the man all the time. "I'm tired, Herrald. We're all tired. So I'm going to tell you just a few of the things we've got against you. You said you didn't go to the cottage till the Wednesday. We can prove you were there on the Monday, prove it positively."

"I—all right, that's true." Herrald chewed his lower lip. "But just to talk to them. That doesn't make me a murderer, does it?"

"How'd you know where to find them?"

"Kelch told me—when we spoke on the phone the second time Lady Dunspar called me."

"She says differently. But we've traced a record of another trunk call to your number, from a phone box less than half a mile from her home." Thane's smile was cold. "That was one of the things we kept working on overnight—checking telephone exchanges all along the area from where Kelch and the others first came ashore, inland to the Dunkeld area. One phone call a night, always late at night, always to your number, always a different exchange. You knew exactly how they were getting on—you had to, to play your part in the game."

"The killing game," grunted Donnan from his corner by the window.

Herrald sat silent now, the colour gone, his hands clenched in his lap.

"There's plenty more." Thane's voice went on in a remorseless monotone. "A shop assistant who remembers an 'uncle' buying a radio-controlled toy launch for his 'nephew'—two months back, and the description is vague. But it still fits. Two months back, Herrald. Just about the time you became the sudden friend of a man who happened to work in the same hotel as Barbara Mason, then persuaded him to take you along to a party where you knew you'd meet her."

The telephone on his desk gave a double ring and he broke off, nodding to Moss, who crossed over and answered the call, listened for a moment, thanked the voice at the other end, then hung up.

"Kelch's condition"—as Herrald's head snapped up in his direction he gave a faint grin—"slight improvement, Colin. Still unconscious, but he may make it now."

"Thanks." Thane ran a thumb along his chin and contemplated Herrald again. "You pulled a nice double bluff with those fake raids on your office and flat after Shaw was killed. Left it to us to decide that somebody was trying to make us believe you were on the run. You scored there—but you came a cropper when it came to Martin Kelch."

Herrald struggled to find his voice. "Another crazy idea, Chief Inspector? Kelch shot himself—everyone knows that."

"Then maybe they're wrong." Thane stared him down. "You didn't know Kelch had a galloping case of pneumonia, did you? Hiding out in fields at night probably started it. Being dumped into that damp-walled stone pit fanned it on. You kept him there until you needed him, didn't you? Then gave him a clean-up and fresh clothes—but didn't you notice how weak he was? Did you think he'd just been down there too long?" The Millside chief leaned back. "But that's only part of it—tell him, Phil."

Moss gave an acid scowl. "We took a paraffin test of Kelch's right hand. He'd fired a gun all right. But the doctors were already wondering about a bruise at the back of his head, a bruise which meant he could have been out cold at the time—his finger on the trigger, but someone else supplying the muscle power." He gave a soft, comfortable belch. "Then we found something else, when we tried to take his prints. The finger tips were raw, grazed, full of little cuts, the kind of cuts a half-delirious man might get if he was trying to claw his way out of that pit, Herrald. We tried the paraffin test again—and got sandstone particles from those cuts."

Peter Herrald sat motionless in his chair for a moment, then opened his hands and looked down at them. When he raised his head again he tried to force a smile but failed.

"You win with that one, Chief Inspector. Kelch was the man in the bottle. You've guessed the rest?"

Thane nodded. "You raided the explosives magazine?"

"First night out. Shaw didn't know a thing until he found the stuff under the van's spare wheel just after we got to the cottage on Wednesday." He shrugged. "I'd been there earlier—sneaked up on the Monday while he was fishing and the others had made sure Kelch wouldn't be around. But I couldn't move the gelignite that time. Shaw had the van keys with him."

"Who shot him?"

"Doesn't matter much now, does it?" He didn't look for an answer. "I did. That was when we had to put Kelch on ice—he tried to make a break for it, tumbled to what was going on. We would have to have done it that night anyway. Shashkov dead and a nice, convenient suicide by a man who'd done what he wanted and was tired of running—it would have made a neat package." He gave a slow, regretful shake of his head.

Colonel Donnan stirred by the window. "The two other tries?"

"Just part of the build-up. I'd scheduled the job for the Old Course, and hopped down the bottle once things got under way." Herrald gave a weak grimace. "Well, it flopped. But you'd found me, and Stender had already taken Kelch down to the harbour." He gave a pale ghost of a smile. "No problem. We'd 'borrowed' a car. Stender's job was to get rid of Kelch half an hour after he heard the bomb go off, then get out." The words were bold, but there was a tremor creeping into his voice and his hands were clenched tight again.

"Want to tell us more?" Donnan spoke coaxingly. "I've got men searching your flat right now."

"They won't find much that matters—not the kind of thing you're after." Herrald stood up. "Maybe later, Colonel—maybe not. I've done enough talking for a spell."

Thane gave a faint nod. Phil Moss came forward and took a light finger-and-thumb grip on Herrald's sleeve. They went out of the room and the door closed.

Colin Thane felt suddenly tired. But one last thing remained. "What about Stender, Colonel? When will you deliver him?"

The security chief sucked hard on his teeth, a harsh, unpleasant sound. "I held out on you, Thane, I'm sorry, but sometimes I have to play dirty. My men saw him all right, but they were under orders to do nothing to prevent him boarding the ship. He sailed on it."

Thane stared at him, dumbfounded.

"This is why." Donnan pulled a long white envelope from his inside pocket. "I told Shashkov the whole story before he left for the airport this morning. Told him if Stender was picked up when the ship docks at Riga that's his affair. Shashkov will take care of his end of the business, you've got Herrald and I've got this." He nodded towards the envelope. "It's a letter from Shashkov for release to the press. His thanks to the British Government for their swift action in stamping out 'hired assassins from an outside agency.' There won't be another propaganda cheep about the whole business."

"A diplomatic agreement?" Thane didn't try to hide his feelings. "What about Herrald? You can't hush up his story when he comes to court."

"Nobody will try to." Donnan walked towards the door, then turned. There was a strange expression on his face, almost a pleading for understanding. "But the law needs only certain evidence to find a man guilty, Thane. What doesn't affect the verdict doesn't need to be given, does it?" He went out, closing the door quietly behind him.

Chief Inspector Thane went over to the window and stood looking out at the grey tenements around. Martin Kelch should pull through now—and the elderly woman waiting at his bedside could be counted on to help him mould that new life he craved. Well, it was one dividend, perhaps the only one.

He glanced at his watch. He had time to go home for lunch, maybe even take the dog for a walk before he ate. And afterwards he could give MacLeod a hand on the scheduled raid on the pitch-and-toss school. It suddenly seemed very important, a return to ordinary things.

He took his hat from its peg and headed for the door.

Concrete Evidence

IAN RANKIN

t's amazing what you find in these old buildings," said the contractor, a middle-aged man in safety helmet and overalls. Beneath the overalls lurked a shirt and tie, the marks of his station. He was the chief, the gaffer. Nothing surprised him anymore, not even unearthing a skeleton.

"Do you know," he went on, "in my time, I've found everything from ancient coins to a pocket watch. How old do you reckon he is then?"

"We're not even sure it *is* a he, not yet. Give us a chance, Mr. Beesford."

"Well, when can we start work again?"

"Later on today."

"Must be gey old though, eh?"

"How do you make that out?"

"Well, it's got no clothes on, has it? They've perished. Takes time for that to happen, plenty of time. . . ."

Rebus had to concede, the man had a point. Yet the concrete floor beneath which the bones had been found . . . *it* didn't look so old, did it? Rebus cast an eye over the cellar again. It was situated a storey or so beneath road-level, in the basement of an old building off the Cowgate. Rebus was often in the Cowgate; the mortuary was just up the road. He knew that the older buildings here were a veritable warren; long narrow tunnels ran here, there, and, it seemed, everywhere, semicylindrical in shape and just about high enough to stand up in. This present building was being given the full works—gutted, new drainage system, rewiring. They were taking out the floor in the cellar to lay new drains and also because there seemed to be damp—certainly there was a fusty smell to the place—and its cause needed to be found.

They were expecting to find old drains, open drains perhaps. Maybe even a trickle of a stream, something which would lead to damp. Instead, their pneumatic drills found what remained of a corpse, perhaps hundreds of years old. Except, of course, for that concrete floor. It couldn't be more than fifty or sixty years old, could it? Would clothing deteriorate to a visible nothing in so short a time? Perhaps the damp could do that. Rebus found the cellar oppressive. The smell, the shadowy lighting provided by portable lamps, the dust.

But the photographers were finished, and so was the pathologist, Dr. Curt. He didn't have too much to report at this stage, except to comment that he preferred it when skeletons were kept in cupboards, not confined to the cellar. They'd take the bones away, along with samples of the earth and rubble around the find, and they'd see what they would see.

"Archaeology's not really my line," the doctor added. "It may take me some time to bone up on it." And he smiled his usual smile.

It took several days for the telephone call to come. Rebus picked up the receiver.

"Hello?"

"Inspector Rebus? Dr. Curt here. About our emaciated friend."

"Yes?"

"Male, five feet ten inches tall, probably been down there between thirty and thirty-five years. His left leg was broken at some time, long before he died. It healed nicely. But the little finger on his left hand had been dislocated and it did *not* heal so well. I'd say it was crooked all his adult life. Perfect for afternoon tea in Morningside."

"Yes?" Rebus knew damned well Curt was leading up to something. He knew, too, that Curt was not a man to be hurried.

"Tests on the soil and gravel around the skeleton show traces of human tissue, but no fibres or anything that might have been clothing. No shoes, socks, underpants, nothing. Altogether, I'd say he was buried there in the altogether."

"But did he die there?"

"Can't say."

"All right, what did he die *of*?"

There was an almost palpable smile in Curt's voice. "Inspector, I thought you'd never ask. Blow to the skull, a blow of considerable force to the back of the head. Murder I'd say. Yes, definitely murder."

There were, of course, ways of tracing the dead, of coming to a near-infallible identification. But the older the crime, the less likely this outcome became. Dental records, for example. They just weren't *kept* in the fifties and sixties the way they are today. A dentist practising then would most probably be playing near-full-time golf by now. And the record of a patient who hadn't been in for his checkup since 1960? Discarded, most probably. Besides, as Dr. Curt pointed out, the man's teeth had seen little serious work, a few fillings, a single extraction.

The same went for medical records, which didn't stop Rebus from checking. A broken left leg, a dislocated left pinkie. Maybe some aged doctor would recall? But then again, maybe not. Almost certainly not. The local papers and radio were interested, which was a bonus. They were given what information the police had, but no memories seemed to be jogged as a result.

Curt had said he was no archaeologist; well, Rebus was no historian either. He knew other cases—contemporary cases—were yammering for his attention. The files stacked up on his desk were evidence enough of that. He'd give this one a few days, a few hours of his time. When the dead ends started to cluster around him, he'd drop it and head back for the here and now.

Who owned the building back in the 1950s? That was easy enough to discover: a wine importer and merchant. Pretty much a one-man operation, Hillbeith Vintners had held the premises from 1948 until 1967. And yes, there was a Mr. Hillbeith, retired from the trade and living over in Burntisland, with a house gazing out across silver sands to the grey North Sea.

He still had a cellar, and insisted that Rebus have a "wee taste" from it. Rebus got the idea that Mr. Hillbeith liked visitors—a socially acceptable excuse for a drink. He took his time in the cellar (there must have been over 500 bottles in there) and emerged with cobwebs hanging from his cardigan, holding a dusty bottle of something nice. This he opened and set on the mantelpiece. It would be half an hour or so yet at the very least before they could usefully have a glass.

Mr. Hillbeith was, he told Rebus, seventy-four. He'd been in the wine trade for nearly half a century and had "never regretted a day, not a day, nor even an hour." Lucky you, Rebus thought to himself.

"Do you remember having that new floor laid in the cellar, Mr. Hillbeith?"

"Oh yes. That particular cellar was going to be for best claret. It was just the right temperature, you see, and there was no vibration from passing buses and the like. But it was damp, had been ever since I'd moved in. So I got a building firm to take a look. They suggested a new floor and some other alterations. It all seemed fairly straightforward and their charges seemed reasonable, so I told them to go ahead."

"And when was this, sir?"

"Nineteen sixty. The spring of that year. There you are, I've got a great memory where business matters are concerned." His small eyes beamed at Rebus through the thick lenses of their glasses. "I can even tell you how much the work cost me . . . and it was a pretty penny at the time. All for nothing, as it turned out. The cellar was still damp, and there was always that *smell* in it, a very unwholesome smell. I couldn't take a chance with the claret, so it became the general stockroom, empty bottles and glasses, packing cases, that sort of thing."

"Do you happen to recall, Mr. Hillbeith, was the smell there *before* the new floor was put in?"

"Well, certainly there was *a* smell there before the floor was laid, but the smell afterwards was different somehow." He rose and fetched two crystal glasses from the china cabinet, inspecting them for dust. "There's a lot of nonsense talked about wine, Inspector. About decanting, the type of glasses you must use, and so on. Decanting can help, of course, but I prefer the feel of the bottle. The bottle, after all, is part of the wine, isn't it?" He handed an empty glass to Rebus. "We'll wait a few minutes yet."

Rebus swallowed drily. It had been a long drive. "Do you recall the name of the firm, sir, the one that did the work?"

Hillbeith laughed. "How could I forget? Abbot & Ford, they were called. I mean, you just don't forget a name like that, do you? Abbot &

Ford. You see, it sounds like Abbotsford, doesn't it? A small firm they were, mind. But you may know one of them, Alexander Abbot."

"Of Abbot Building?"

"The same. He went on to make quite a name for himself, didn't he? Quite a fortune. Built up quite a company, too, but he started out small like most of us do."

"How small, would you say?"

"Oh, small, small. Just a few men." He rose and stretched an arm towards the mantelpiece. "I think this should be ready to taste, Inspector. If you'll hold out your glass—"

Hillbeith poured slowly, deliberately, checking that no lees escaped into the glass. He poured another slow, generous measure for himself. The wine was reddish-brown. "Robe and disc not too promising," he muttered to himself. He gave his glass a shake and studied it. "Legs not promising either." He sighed. "Oh dear." Finally, Hillbeith sniffed the glass anxiously, then took a swig.

"Cheers," said Rebus, indulging in a mouthful. A mouthful of vinegar. He managed to swallow, then saw Hillbeith spit back into the glass.

"Oxidisation," the old man said, sounding cruelly tricked. "It happens. I'd best check a few more bottles to assess the damage. Will you stay, Inspector?" Hillbeith sounded keen.

"Sorry, sir," said Rebus, ready with his get-out clause. "I'm still on duty."

Alexander Abbot, aged fifty-five, still saw himself as the force behind the Abbot Building Company. There might be a dozen executives working furiously beneath him, but the company had grown from *his* energy and from *his* fury. He was chairman, and a busy man, too. He made this plain to Rebus at their meeting in the executive offices of ABC. The office spoke of business confidence, but then in Rebus's experience this meant little in itself. Often, the more dire straits a company was in, the healthier it tried to look. Still, Alexander Abbot seemed happy enough with life.

"In a recession," he explained, lighting an overlong cigar, "you trim your work force pronto. You stick with regular clients, good payers, and don't take on too much work from clients you don't know. They're the ones who're likely to welch on you or go bust, leaving nothing but bills. Young businesses . . . they're always hit hardest in a recession, no backup, you see. Then, when the recession's over for another few years, you dust yourself off and go touting for business again, rehiring the men you laid off. That's where we've always had the edge over Jack Kirkwall."

Kirkwall Construction was ABC's main competitor in the Lowlands, when it came to medium-sized contracts. Doubtless Kirkwall was the larger company. It too was run by a "self-made" man, Jack Kirkwall. A larger-than-life figure. There was, Rebus quickly realised, little love lost between the two rivals.

The very mention of Kirkwall's name seemed to have dampened Alexander Abbot's spirits. He chewed on his cigar like it was a debtor's finger.

"You started small though, didn't you, sir?"

"Oh aye, they don't come much smaller. We were a pimple on the bum of the construction industry at one time." He gestured to the walls of his office. "Not that you'd guess it, eh?"

Rebus nodded. "You were still a small firm back in nineteen sixty, weren't you?"

"Nineteen sixty. Let's think. We were just starting out. It wasn't ABC then, of course. Let's see. I think I got a loan from my dad in nineteen fifty-seven, went into partnership with a chap called Hugh Ford, another self-employed builder. Yes, that's right. Nineteen sixty, it was Abbot & Ford. Of course it was."

"Do you happen to remember working at a wine merchant's in the Cowgate?"

"When?"

"The spring of nineteen sixty."

"A wine merchant's?" Abbot furrowed his brow. "Should be able to remember that. Long time ago, mind. A wine merchant's."

"You were laying a new floor in one of the cellars, amongst other work. Hillbeith Vintners."

"Oh aye, Hillbeith, it's coming back now. I remember him. Little funny chap with glasses. Gave us a case of wine when the job was finished. Nice of him, but the wine was a bit off as I remember."

"How many men were working on the job?"

Abbot exhaled noisily. "Now you're asking. It was over thirty years ago, Inspector."

"I appreciate that, sir. Would there be any records?"

Abbot shook his head. "There might have been up to about ten years ago, but when we moved into this place a lot of the older stuff got chucked out. I regret it now. It'd be nice to have a display of stuff from the old days, something we could set up in the reception. But no, all the Abbot & Ford stuff got dumped."

"So you don't remember how many men were on that particular job? Is there anyone else I could talk to, someone who might—"

"We were small back then, I can tell you that. Mostly using casual labour and part-timers. A job that size, I wouldn't think we'd be using more than three or four men, if that."

"You don't recall anyone going missing? Not turning up for work, that sort of thing?"

Abbot bristled. "I'm a stickler for time-keeping, Inspector. If anyone had done a bunk, I'd remember, I'm pretty sure of that. Besides, we were careful about who we took on. No lazy buggers, nobody who'd do a runner halfway through a job."

Rebus sighed. Here was one of the dead ends. He rose to his feet. "Well, thanks anyway, Mr. Abbot. It was good of you to find time to see me." The two men shook hands, Abbot rising to his feet.

"Not at all, Inspector. Wish I could help you with your little mystery. I like a good detective story myself." They were almost at the door now.

"Oh," said Rebus, "just one last thing. Where could I find your old partner, Mr. Ford?"

Abbot's face lost its animation. His voice was suddenly that of an old man. "Hugh died, Inspector. A boating accident. He was drowned. Hell of a thing to happen. Hell of a thing."

Two dead ends.

Mr. Hillbeith's telephone call came later that day, while Rebus was ploughing through the transcript of an interview with a rapist. His head felt full of foul-smelling glue, his stomach acid with caffeine.

"Is that Inspector Rebus?"

"Yes, hello, Mr. Hillbeith. What can I do for you?" Rebus pinched the bridge of his nose and screwed shut his eyes.

"I was thinking all last night about that skeleton."

"Yes?" In between bottles of wine, Rebus didn't doubt.

"Well, I was trying to think back to when the work was being done. It might not be much, but I definitely recall that there were four people involved. Mr. Abbot and Mr. Ford worked on it pretty much full time, and there were two other men, one of them a teenager, the other in his forties. They worked on a more casual basis."

"You don't recall their names?"

"No, only that the teenager had a nickname. Everyone called him by that. I don't think I ever knew his real name."

"Well, thanks anyway, Mr. Hillbeith. I'll get back to Mr. Abbot and see if what you've told me jogs his memory."

"Oh, you've spoken to him then?"

"This morning. No progress to report. I didn't realise Mr. Ford had died."

"Ah, well, that's the other thing."

"What is?"

"Poor Mr. Ford. Sailing accident, wasn't it?"

"That's right."

"Only I remember that too. You see, that accident happened just after they'd finished the job. They kept talking about how they were going to take a few days off and go fishing. Mr. Abbot said it would be their first holiday in years."

Rebus's eyes were open now. "How soon was this after they'd finished your floor?"

"Well, directly after, I suppose."

"Do you remember Mr. Ford?"

"Well, he was very quiet. Mr. Abbot did all the talking, really. A very quiet man. A hard worker though, I got that impression."

"Did you notice anything about his hands? A misshapen pinkie?"

"Sorry, Inspector, it *was* a long time ago."

Rebus appreciated that. "Of course it was, Mr. Hillbeith. You've been a great help. Thank you."

He put down the receiver. A long time ago, yes, but still murder, still calculated and cold-blooded murder. Well, a path had opened in front of him. Not much of a path perhaps, a bit overgrown and treacherous. Nevertheless . . . Best foot forward, John. Best foot forward.

*   *   *

Of course, he kept telling himself, he was still ruling possibilities out rather than ruling them in, which was why he wanted to know a little more about the boating accident. He didn't want to get the information from Alexander Abbot.

Instead, the morning after Hillbeith's phone call, Rebus went to the National Library of Scotland on George IV Bridge. The doorman let him through the turnstile and he climbed an imposing staircase to the reading room. The woman on the desk filled in a one-day reader's card for him and showed him how to use the computer. There were two banks of computers being used by people to find the books they needed. Rebus had to go into the reading room and find an empty chair, note its number, and put this on his slip when he'd decided which volume he required. Then he went to his chair and sat, waiting.

There were two floors to the reading room, both enveloped by shelves of reference books. The people working at the long desks downstairs seemed bleary. Just another morning's graft for them; but Rebus found it all fascinating. One person worked with a card index in front of him, to which he referred frequently. Another seemed asleep, head resting on arms. Pens scratched across countless sheets of paper. A few souls, lost for inspiration, merely chewed on their pens and stared at the others around them, as Rebus was doing.

Eventually, his volume was brought to him. It was a bound edition of the *Scotsman*, containing every issue for the months from January to June, 1960. Two thick leather buckles kept the volume closed. Rebus untied these and began to turn the pages.

He knew what he was looking for, and pretty well where to find it, but that didn't stop him browsing through football reports and front-page headlines. 1960. He'd been fifteen, preparing to leave school and go into the army. He'd been busy trying to lose his virginity and supporting Hearts. Yes, a long time ago.

The story hadn't quite made the front page. Instead, there were two paragraphs on page three.

"Drowning Off Lower Largo." The victim, Mr. Hugh Ford, was described as being twenty-six years of age (a year older than the survivor,

Mr. Alex Abbot) and a resident of Duddingston, Edinburgh. The men, on a short fishing holiday, had taken a boat out early in the morning, a boat hired from a local man, Mr. John Thomson. There was a squall, and the boat capsized. Mr. Abbot, a fair swimmer, had made it back to the shore. Mr. Ford, a poor swimmer, had not. Mr. Ford was further described as a "bachelor, a quiet man, shy according to Mr. Abbot, who was still under observation at the Victoria Hospital, Kirkcaldy." There was a little more, but not much. Apparently, Ford's parents were dead, but he had a sister, Mrs. Isabel Hammond, somewhere out in Australia.

Why hadn't Abbot mentioned any of this? Maybe he wanted to forget. Maybe it still gave him the occasional bad dream. And of course he would have forgotten all about the Hillbeith contract precisely because this tragedy happened so soon afterwards. So soon. Just the one line of print really bothered Rebus; just that one sentence niggled.

"Mr. Ford's body has still not been recovered."

Records might get lost in time, but not by Fife Police. They sent on what they had, much of it written in fading ink on fragile paper, some of it typed—badly. The two friends and colleagues, Abbot and Ford, had set out on Friday evening to the Fishing-Net Hotel in Largo, arriving late. As arranged, they'd set out early next morning on a boat they'd hired from a local man, John Thomson. The accident had taken place only an hour or so after setting out. The boat was recovered. It had been overturned, but of Ford there was no sign. Inquiries were made. Mr. Ford's belongings were taken back to Edinburgh by Mr. Abbot, after the latter was released from hospital, having sustained a bump to the head when the boat turned over. He was also suffering from shock and exhaustion. Mr. Ford's sister, Mrs. Isabel Hammond, was never traced.

They had investigated a little further. The business run jointly by Messrs. Abbot and Ford now became Mr. Abbot's. The case notes contained a good amount of information and suspicion—between the lines, as it were. Oh yes, they'd investigated Alexander Abbot, but there had been no evidence. They'd searched for the body, had found none. Without a body, they were left with only their suspicions and their nagging doubts.

"Yes," Rebus said quietly to himself, "but what if you were looking for the body in the wrong place?" The wrong place at the wrong time. The work on the cellar had ended on Friday afternoon, and by Saturday morning Hugh Ford had ceased to exist.

The path Rebus was on had become less overgrown, but it was still rock-strewn and dangerous, still a potential dead end.

The Fishing-Net Hotel was still in existence, though apparently much changed from its 1960 incarnation. The present owners told Rebus to arrive in time for lunch if he could and it would be on the house. Largo was north of Burntisland but on the same coastline. Alexander Selkirk, the original of Defoe's Robinson Crusoe, had a connection with the fishing village. There was a small statue of him somewhere which Rebus had been shown as a boy (but only after much hunting, he recalled). Largo was picturesque, but then so were most, if not all, of the coastal villages in Fife's "East Neuk." But it was not yet quite the height of the tourist season and the customers taking lunch at the Fishing-Net Hotel were businessmen and locals.

It was a good lunch, as picturesque as its surroundings but with a bit more flavour. And afterwards, the owner, an Englishman for whom life in Largo was a long-held dream come true, offered to show Rebus round, including "the very room your Mr. Ford stayed in the night before he died."

"How can you be sure?"

"I looked in the register."

Rebus managed not to look too surprised. The hotel had changed hands so often since 1960, he despaired of finding anyone who would remember the events of that weekend.

"The register?"

"Yes, we were left a lot of old stuff when we bought this place. The storerooms were chock-a-block. Old ledgers and what have you going back to the nineteen twenties and thirties. It was easy enough to find nineteen sixty."

Rebus stopped in his tracks. "Never mind showing me Mr. Ford's room, would you mind letting me see that register?"

He sat at a desk in the manager's office with the register open in front of him, while Mr. Summerson's finger stabbed the line. "There you are,

Inspector, H. Ford. Signed in at eleven-fifty P.M., address given as Duddingston. Room number seven."

It wasn't so much a signature as a blurred scrawl and above it, on a separate line, was Alexander Abbot's own more flowing signature.

"Bit late to arrive, wasn't it?" commented Rebus.

"Agreed."

"I don't suppose there's anyone working here nowadays who worked in the hotel back then?"

Summerson laughed quietly. "People do retire in this country, Inspector."

"Of course, I just wondered." He remembered the newspaper story. "What about John Thomson? Does the name mean anything to you?"

"Old Jock? Jock Thomson? The fisherman?"

"Probably."

"Oh, yes, he's still about. You'll almost certainly find him down by the dockside, or else in the Harbour Tavern."

"Thanks. I'd like to take this register with me if I may?"

Jock Thomson sucked on his pipe and nodded. He looked the archetype of the "old salt," from his baggy cord trousers to his chiselled face and silvery beard. The only departure from the norm was, perhaps, the Perrier water in front of him on a table in the Harbour Tavern.

"I like the fizz," he explained after ordering it, "and besides, my doctor's told me to keep off the alcohol. Total abstinence, he said, total abstinence. Either the booze goes, Jock, or the pipe does. No contest."

And he sucked greedily on the pipe. Then complained when his drink arrived without "the wee slice of lemon." Rebus returned to the bar to fulfill his mission.

"Oh aye," said Thomson, "remember it like it was yesterday. Only there's not much to remember, is there?"

"Why do you say that?"

"Two inexperienced laddies go out in a boat. Boat tips. End of story."

"Was the weather going to be bad that morning?"

"Not particularly. But there *was* a squall blew up. Blew up and blew out in a matter of minutes. Long enough though."

"How did the two men seem?"

"How do you mean?"

"Well, were they looking forward to the trip?"

"Don't know, I never saw them. The younger one, Abbot was it? He phoned to book a boat from me, said they'd be going out early, six or thereabouts. I told him he was daft, but he said there was no need for me to be on the dockside, if I'd just have the boat ready and tell him which one it was. And that's what I did. By the time I woke up that morning, he was swimming for the shore and his pal was food for the fish."

"So you never actually saw Mr. Ford?"

"No, and I only saw the lad Abbot afterwards, when the ambulance was taking him away."

It was fitting into place almost too easily now. And Rebus thought, sometimes these things are only visible with hindsight, from a space of years. "I don't suppose," he ventured, "you know anyone who worked at the hotel back then?"

"Owner's moved on," said Thomson, "who knows where to. It might be that Janice Dryman worked there then. Can't recall if she did."

"Where could I find her?"

Thomson peered at the clock behind the bar. "Hang around here ten minutes or so, you'll bump into her. She usually comes in of an afternoon. Meantime, I'll have another of these if you're buying."

Thomson pushed his empty glass over to Rebus. Rebus, most definitely, was buying.

Miss Dryman—"never married, never really saw the point"—was in her early fifties. She worked in a gift shop in town and after her stint finished usually nipped into the Tavern for a soft drink and "a bit of gossip." Rebus asked what she would like to drink.

"Lemonade, please," she said, "with a drop of whiskey in it." And she laughed with Jock Thomson, as though this were an old and cherished joke between them. Rebus, not used to playing the part of straight man, headed yet again for the bar.

"Oh yes," she said, her lips poised above the glass. "I was working there at the time all right. Chambermaid and general dogsbody, that was me."

"You wouldn't see them arrive though?"

Miss Dryman looked as though she had some secret to impart. "*Nobody* saw them arrive, I know that for a fact. Mrs. Dennis who ran the place back then, she said she'd be buggered if she'd wait up half the night for a couple of fishermen. They knew what rooms they were in and their keys were left at reception."

"What about the front door?"

"Left unlocked, I suppose. The world was a safer place back then."

"Aye, you're right there," added Jock Thomson, sucking on his sliver of lemon.

"And Mr. Abbot and Mr. Ford knew this was the arrangement?"

"I suppose so. Otherwise it wouldn't have worked, would it?"

So Abbot knew there'd be nobody around at the hotel, not if he left it late enough before arriving.

"And what about in the morning?"

"Mrs. Dennis said they were up and out before she knew anything about it. She was annoyed because she'd already cooked the kippers for their breakfast before she realised."

So nobody saw them in the morning either. In fact . . .

"In fact," said Rebus, "nobody saw Mr. Ford at all. Nobody at the hotel, not you, Mr. Thomson, nobody." Both drinkers conceded this.

"I saw his stuff though," said Miss Dryman.

"What stuff?"

"In his room, his clothes and stuff. That morning. I didn't know anything about the accident and I went in to clean."

"The bed had been slept in?"

"Looked like it. Sheets all rumpled. And his suitcase was on the floor, only half unpacked. Not that there was much *to* unpack."

"Oh?"

"A single change of clothes, I'd say. I remember them because they seemed mucky, you know, not fresh. Not the sort of stuff *I'd* take on holiday with me."

"What? Like he'd been working in them?"

She considered this. "Maybe."

"No point wearing clean clothes for fishing," Thomson added. But Rebus wasn't listening.

Ford's clothes, the clothes he had been working in while laying the floor. It made sense. Abbot bludgeoned him, stripped him, and covered his body in fresh cement. He'd taken the clothes away with him and put them in a case, opening it in the hotel room, ruffling the sheets. Simple, but effective. Effective these past thirty years. The motive? A falling-out perhaps, or simple greed. It was a small company, but growing, and perhaps Abbot hadn't wanted to share. Rebus placed a five-pound note on the table.

"To cover the next couple of rounds," he said, getting to his feet. "I'd better be off. Some of us are still on duty."

There were things to be done. He had to speak to his superior, Chief Inspector Lauderdale. And that was for starters. Maybe Ford's Australian sister could be traced this time round. There had to be someone out there who could acknowledge that Ford had suffered from a broken leg in youth, and that he had a crooked finger. So far, Rebus could think of only one person—Alexander Abbot. Somehow, he didn't think Abbot could be relied on to tell the truth, the whole truth.

Then there was the hotel register. The forensics lab could ply their cunning trade on it. Perhaps they'd be able to say for certain that Ford's signature was merely a bad rendition of Abbot's. But again, he needed a sample of Ford's handwriting in order to substantiate that the signature was not genuine. Who did he know who might possess such a document? Only Alexander Abbot. Or Mr. Hillbeith, but Mr. Hillbeith had not been able to help.

"No, Inspector, as I told you, it was Mr. Abbot who handled all the paperwork, all that side of things. If there is an invoice or a receipt, it will be in his hand, not Mr. Ford's. I don't recall ever seeing Mr. Ford writing anything."

No through road.

Chief Inspector Lauderdale was not wholly sympathetic. So far all Rebus had to offer were more suppositions to add to those of the Fife Police at the time. There was no proof that Alexander Abbot had killed his partner. No proof that the skeleton was Hugh Ford. Moreover, there wasn't even much in the way of circumstantial evidence. They could bring in Abbot for questioning, but all he had to do was plead innocence.

He could afford a good lawyer; and even bad lawyers weren't stupid enough to let the police probe too deeply.

"We need proof, John," said Lauderdale, "concrete evidence. The simplest proof would be that hotel signature. If we prove it's not Ford's, then we have Abbot at that hotel, Abbot in the boat, and Abbot shouting that his friend has drowned, *all* without Ford having been there. That's what we need. The rest of it, as it stands, is rubbish. You know that."

Yes, Rebus knew. He didn't doubt that, given an hour alone with Abbot in a darkened alley, he'd have his confession. But it didn't work like that. It worked through the law. Besides, Abbot's heart might not be too healthy. BUSINESSMAN, 55, DIES UNDER QUESTIONING. No, it had to be done some other way.

The problem was, there *was* no other way. Alexander Abbot was getting away with murder. Or was he? Why did his story have to be false? Why did the body have to be Hugh Ford's? The answer was: because the whole thing seemed to fit. Only, the last piece of the jigsaw had been lost under some sofa or chair a long time ago, so long ago now that it might remain missing forever.

He didn't know why he did it. If in doubt, retrace your steps . . . something like that. Maybe he just liked the atmosphere. Whatever, Rebus found himself back in the National Library, waiting at his desk for the servitor to bring him his bound volume of old news. He mouthed the words of "Yesterday's Papers" to himself as he waited. Then, when the volume appeared, he unbuckled it with ease and pulled open the pages. He read past the April editions, read through into May and June. Football results, headlines—and what was this? A snippet of business news, barely a filler at the bottom right-hand corner of a page. About how the Kirkwall Construction Company was swallowing up a couple of smaller competitors in Fife and Midlothian.

" 'The nineteen sixties will be a decade of revolution in the building industry,' said Managing Director Mr. Jack Kirkwall, 'and Kirkwall Construction aims to meet that challenge through growth and quality. The bigger we are, the better we are. These acquisitions strengthen the company, and they're good news for the work force, too.' "

It was the kind of sentiment which had lasted into the 1980s. Jack

Kirkwall, Alexander Abbot's bitter rival. Now there was a man Rebus ought to meet. . . .

The meeting, however, had to be postponed until the following week. Kirkwall was in hospital for a minor operation.

"I'm at that age, Inspector," he told Rebus when they finally met, "when things go wrong and need treatment or replacing. Just like any bit of well-used machinery."

And he laughed, though the laughter, to Rebus's ears, had a hollow centre. Kirkwall looked older than his sixty-two years, his skin saggy, complexion wan. They were in his living room, from where, these days, he did most of his work.

"Since I turned sixty, I've only really wandered into the company headquarters for the occasional meeting. I leave the daily chores to my son, Peter. He seems to be managing." The laughter this time was self-mocking.

Rebus had suggested a further postponement of the meeting, but when Jack Kirkwall knew that the subject was to be Alexander Abbot, he was adamant that they should go ahead.

"Is he in trouble then?"

"He might be," Rebus admitted. Some of the colour seemed to reappear in Kirkwall's cheeks and he relaxed a little further into his reclining leather chair. Rebus didn't want to give Kirkwall the story. Kirkwall and Abbot were still business rivals, after all. Still, it seemed, enemies. Given the story, Kirkwall might try some underhand tactic, some rumour in the media, and if it got out that the story originally came from a police inspector, well. Hello, being sued and goodbye, pension.

No, Rebus didn't want that. Yet he did want to know whether Kirkwall knew anything, knew of any reason why Abbot might wish, might *need* to kill Ford.

"Go on, Inspector."

"It goes back quite a way, sir. Nineteen sixty, to be precise. Your firm was at that time in the process of expansion."

"Correct."

"What did you know about Abbot & Ford?"

Kirkwall brushed the palm of one hand over the knuckles of the other. "Just that they were growing, too. Of course, they were younger than us, much smaller than us. ABC still is much smaller than us. But they were cocky, they were winning some contracts ahead of us. I had my eye on them."

"Did you know Mr. Ford at all?"

"Oh yes. Really, he was the cleverer of the two men. I've never had much respect for Abbot. But Hugh Ford was quiet, hardworking. Abbot was the one who did the shouting and got the firm noticed."

"Did Mr. Ford have a crooked finger?"

Kirkwall seemed bemused by the question. "I've no idea," he said at last. "I never actually met the man, I merely knew *about* him. Why? Is it important?"

Rebus felt at last his meandering, narrowing path had come to the lip of the chasm. Nothing for it but to turn back.

"Well," he said, "it would have clarified something."

"You know, Inspector, my company *was* interested in taking Abbot & Ford under our wing."

"Oh?"

"But then with the accident, that tragic accident. Well, Abbot took control and he wasn't at all interested in any offer we had to make. Downright rude, in fact. Yes, I've always thought that it was such a *lucky* accident so far as Abbot was concerned."

"How do you mean, sir?"

"I mean, Inspector, that Hugh Ford was on our side. He wanted to sell up. But Abbot was against it."

So Rebus had his motive. Well, what did it matter? He was still lacking that concrete evidence Lauderdale demanded.

". . . Would it show up from his handwriting?"

Rebus had missed what Kirkwall had been saying. "I'm sorry, sir, I didn't catch that."

"I said, Inspector, if Hugh Ford had a crooked finger, would it show from his handwriting?"

"Handwriting?"

"Because I had his agreement to the takeover. He'd written to me personally to tell me. Had gone behind Abbot's back, I suppose. I bet Alex Abbot was mad as hell when he found out about that." Kirkwall's smile was vibrant now. "I always thought that accident was a bit too lucky where Abbot was concerned. A bit too neat. No proof though. There was never any proof."

"Do you still have the letter?"

"What?"

"The letter from Mr. Ford, do you still have it?"

Rebus was tingling now, and Kirkwall caught his excitement. "I never throw anything away, Inspector. Oh yes, I've got it. It'll be upstairs."

"Can I see it? I mean, can I see it now?"

"If you like," Kirkwall made to stand up, but paused. "*Is* Alex Abbot in trouble, Inspector?"

"If you've still got that letter from Hugh Ford, then yes, sir, I'd say Mr. Abbot could be in very grave trouble indeed."

"Inspector, you've made an old man very happy."

It was the letter against Alex Abbot's word, of course, and he denied everything. But there was enough now for a trial. The entry in the hotel's ledger, while it was *possibly* the work of Alexander Abbot, was *certainly* not the work of the man who had written the letter to Jack Kirkwall. A search warrant gave the police the powers to look through Abbot's home and the ABC headquarters. A contract, drawn up between Abbot and Ford when the two men had gone into partnership, was discovered to be held in a solicitor's safe. The signature matched that on the letter to Jack Kirkwall. Kirkwall himself appeared in court to give evidence. He seemed to Rebus a different man altogether from the person he'd met previously: sprightly, keening, enjoying life to the full.

From the dock, Alexander Abbot looked on almost reproachfully, as if this were just one more business trick in a life full of them. Life, too, was the sentence of the judge.

The Night of Kirk O' Field
The Murder of Darnley

RAFAEL SABATINI

erhaps one of the greatest mistakes of a lifetime in which mistakes were plentiful was the hesitancy of the Queen of Scots in executing upon her husband Darnley the prompt vengeance she had sworn for the murder of David Rizzio.

When Rizzio was slain, and she herself held captive by the murderers in her Palace of Holyrood, whilst Darnley ruled as king, she had simulated belief in her husband's innocence that she might use him for her vengeful ends.

She had played so craftily upon his cowardly nature as to convince him that Morton, Ruthven, and the other traitor lords with whom he had leagued himself were at heart his own implacable enemies; that they pretended friendship for him to make a tool of him, and that when he had served their turn they would destroy him.

In his consequent terror he had betrayed his associates, assisting her to trick them by a promise to sign an act of oblivion for what was done. Trusting to this the lords had relaxed their vigilance, whereupon, accompanied by Darnley, she had escaped by night from Holyrood.

Hope tempering at first the rage and chagrin in the hearts of the lords she had duped, they had sent a messenger to her at Dunbar to request of her the fulfilment of her promise to sign the document of their security.

But Mary put off the messenger, and whilst the army she had summoned was hastily assembling, she used her craft to divide the rebels against themselves.

To her natural brother, the Earl of Murray, to Argyll, and to all those who had been exiled for their rebellion at the time of her marriage—and who knew not where they stood in the present turn of events, since one of the objects of the murder had been to procure their reinstatement—she sent an offer of complete pardon, on condition that they should at once dissociate themselves from those concerned in the death of the Seigneur Davie.

These terms they accepted thankfully, as well they might. Thereupon, finding themselves abandoned by all men—even by Darnley in whose service they had engaged in the murder—Morton, Ruthven, and their associates scattered and fled.

By the end of that month of March, Morton, Ruthven, Lindsay of the Byres, George Douglas, and some sixty others were denounced as rebels with forfeiture of life and goods, while one Thomas Scott, who had been in command of the guards that had kept Her Majesty prisoner at Holyrood, was hanged, drawn, and quartered at the Market Cross.

News of this reached the fugitives to increase their desperate rage. But what drove the iron into the soul of the arch-murderer Ruthven was Darnley's solemn public declaration denying all knowledge of or complicity in Rizzio's assassination; nor did it soothe his fury to know that all Scotland rang with contemptuous laughter at that impudent and cowardly perjury. From his sick-bed at Newcastle, whereon some six weeks later he was to breathe his last, the forsaken wretch replied to it by sending the Queen the bond to which he had demanded Darnley's signature before embarking upon the business.

It was a damning document. There above the plain signature and seal of the King was the admission, not merely of complicity, but that the thing was done by his express will and command, that the responsibility was his own, and that he would hold the doers scatheless from all consequences.

Mary could scarcely have hoped to be able to confront her worthless husband with so complete a proof of his duplicity and baseness. She sent for him, confounded him with the sight of that appalling bond, made an end to the amity which for her own ends she had pretended, and drove him out of her presence with a fury before which he dared not linger.

You see him, then, crushed under his load of mortification, realizing at last how he had been duped on every hand, first by the lords for their own purpose and then by the Queen for hers. Her contempt of him was now so manifest that it spread to all who served him—for she made it plain that who showed him friendship earned her deep displeasure—so that he was forced to withdraw from a Court where his life was become impossible. For a while he wandered up and down a land where every door was shut in his face, where every man of whatsoever party, traitor or true, despised him alike. In the end, he took himself off to his father, Lennox, and at Glasgow he sought what amusement he could with his dogs and his hawks, and such odd vulgar rustic love-affairs as came his way.

It was in allowing him thus to go his ways, in leaving her vengeance—indeed, her justice—but half accomplished, that lay the greatest of the Queen's mistakes. Better for her had she taken with Darnley the direct way that was her right. Better for her, if acting strongly then, she had banished or hanged him for his part in the treason that had inspired the murder of Rizzio. Unfortunately, a factor that served to quicken her abhorrence of him served also to set a curb of caution upon the satisfaction of it.

This factor that came so inopportunely into her life was her regard for the arrogant, unscrupulous Earl of Bothwell. Her hand was stayed by fear that men should say that for Bothwell's sake she had rid herself of a husband become troublesome. That Bothwell had been her friend in the hour when she had needed friends, and knew not whom she might trust; that by his masterfulness he seemed a man upon whom a woman might lean with confidence, may account for the beginnings of the extraordinary influence he came so swiftly to exercise over her, and the passion he awakened in her to such a degree that she was unable to dissemble it.

Her regard for him, the more flagrant by contrast with her contempt for Darnley, is betrayed in the will she made before her confinement in the following June. Whilst to Darnley she bequeathed nothing but the red-enamelled diamond ring with which he had married her—"It was with this that I was married," she wrote almost contemptuously. "I leave it to the King who gave it me"—she appointed Bothwell to the tutelage of her child in the event of her not surviving it, and to the government of the realm.

The King came to visit her during her convalescence, and was scowled upon by Murray and Argyll, who were at Holyrood, and most of all by Bothwell, whose arrogance by now was such that he was become the best-hated man in Scotland. The Queen received him very coldly, whilst using

Bothwell more than cordially in his very presence, so that he departed again in a deeper humiliation than before.

Then before the end of July there was her sudden visit to Bothwell at Alloa, which gave rise to so much scandal. Hearing of it, Darnley followed in a vain attempt to assert his rights as king and husband, only to be flouted and dismissed with the conviction that his life was no longer safe in Scotland, and that he had best cross the Border. Yet, to his undoing, detained perhaps by the overweening pride that is usually part of a fool's equipment, he did not act upon that wise resolve. He returned instead to his hawking and his hunting, and was seldom seen at Court thereafter.

Even when in the following October, Mary lay at the point of death at Jedburgh, Darnley came but to stay a day, and left her again without any assurance that she would recover. But then the facts of her illness, and how it had been contracted, were not such as to encourage kindness in him, even had he been inclined to kindness.

Bothwell had taken three wounds in a Border affray some weeks before, and Mary, hearing of this and that he lay in grievous case at Hermitage, had ridden thither in her fond solicitude—a distance of thirty miles—and back again in the same day, thus contracting a chill which had brought her to the very gates of death.

Darnley had not only heard of this, but he had found Bothwell at Jedburgh, whither he had been borne in a litter, when in his turn he had heard of how it was with Mary; and Bothwell had treated him with more than the contempt which all men now showed him, but which from none could wound him so deeply as from this man whom rumour accounted Mary's lover.

Matters between husband and wife were thus come to a pass in which they could not continue, as all men saw, and as she herself confessed at Craigmillar, whither she repaired, still weak in body, towards the end of November.

Over a great fire that blazed in a vast chamber of the castle she sat sick at heart and shivering, for all that her wasted body was swathed in a long cloak of deepest purple reversed with ermine. Her face was thin and of a transparent pallor, her eyes great pools of wistfulness amid the shadows which her illness had set about them.

"I do wish I could be dead!" she sighed.

Bothwell's eyes narrowed. He was leaning on the back of her tall chair, a long, virile figure with a hawk-nosed, bearded face that was sternly handsome. He thrust back the crisp dark hair that clustered about his brow, and fetched a sigh.

"It was never my own death I wished when a man stood in my road to aught I craved," he said, lowering his voice, for Maitland of Lethington—now restored to his secretaryship—was writing at a table across the room, and my Lord of Argyll was leaning over him.

She looked up at him suddenly, her eyes startled.

"What devil's counsel do you whisper?" she asked him. And when he would have answered, she raised a hand. "No," she said. "Not that way."

"There is another," said Bothwell coolly. He moved, came round, and stood squarely upon the hearth, his back to the fire, confronting her, nor did he further trouble to lower his voice. "We have considered it already."

"What have you considered?"

Her voice was strained; fear and excitement blended in her face.

"How the shackles that fetter you might be broken. Be not alarmed. It was the virtuous Murray himself propounded it to Argyll and Lething-ton—for the good of Scotland and yourself." A sneer flitted across his tanned face. "Let them speak for themselves." He raised his voice and called to them across the room.

They came at once, and the four made an odd group as they stood there in the firelit gloom of that November day—the lovely young Queen, so frail and wistful in her high-backed chair; the stalwart, arrogant Both-well, magnificent in a doublet of peach-coloured velvet that tapered to a golden girdle; Argyll, portly and sober in a rich suit of black; and Mait-land of Lethington, lean and crafty of face, in a long furred gown that flapped about his bony shanks.

It was to Lethington that Bothwell addressed himself.

"Her Grace is in a mood to hear how the Gordian knot of her mar-riage might be unravelled," said he, grimly ironic.

Lethington raised his eyebrows, licked his thin lips, and rubbed his bony hands one in the other.

"Unravelled?" he echoed with wondering stress. "Unravelled? Ha!" His dark eyes flashed round at them. "Better adopt Alexander's plan, and cut it. 'Twill be more complete and—and final."

"No, no!" she cried. "I will not have you shed his blood."

"He himself was none so tender where another was concerned," Bothwell reminded her—as if the memory of Rizzio were dear to him.

"What he may have done does not weigh upon my conscience," was her answer.

"He might," put in Argyll, "be convicted of treason for having consented to Your Grace's retention in ward at Holyrood after Rizzio's murder."

She considered an instant, then shook her head.

"It is too late. It should have been done long since. Now men will say that it is but a pretext to be rid of him." She looked up at Bothwell, who remained standing immediately before her, between her and the fire. "You said that my Lord of Murray had discussed this matter. Was it in such terms as these?"

Bothwell laughed silently at the thought of the sly Murray rendering himself a party to anything so direct and desperate. It was Lethington who answered her.

"My Lord Murray was for a divorce. That would set Your Grace free, and it might be obtained, he said, by tearing up the Pope's bull of dispensation that permitted the marriage. Yet, madame, although Lord Murray would himself go no further, I have no cause to doubt that were other means concerted, he would be content to look through his fingers."

Her mind, however, did not seem to follow his speech beyond the matter of the divorce. A faint flush of eagerness stirred in her pale cheeks.

"Ah, yes!" she cried. "I, too, have thought of that—of this divorce. And God knows I do not want for grounds. And it could be obtained, you say, by tearing up this papal bull?"

"The marriage could be proclaimed void thereafter," Argyll explained.

She looked past Bothwell into the fire, and took her chin in her hand.

"Yes," she said slowly, musingly, and again, "yes. That were a way. That is the way." And then suddenly she looked up, and they saw doubt and dread in her eyes. "But in that case—what of my son?"

"Aye!" said Lethington grimly. He shrugged his narrow shoulders, parted his hands, and brought them together again. "That's the obstacle, as we perceived. It would imperil his succession."

"It would make a bastard of him, you mean?" she cried, demanding the full expansion of their thoughts.

"Indeed it would do no less," the secretary assented.

"So that," said Bothwell, softly, "we come back to Alexander's method. What the fingers may not unravel, the knife can sever."

She shivered, and drew her furred cloak the more closely about her.

Lethington leaned forward. He spoke in kindly, soothing accents.

"Let us guide this matter among us, madame," he murmured, "and we'll find means to rid Your Grace of this young fool, without hurt to your honour or prejudice to your son. And the Earl of Murray will look the other way, provided you pardon Morton and his friends for the killing they did in Darnley's service."

She looked from one to the other of them, scanning each face in turn. Then her eyes returned to a contemplation of the flaming logs, and she spoke very softly.

"Do nothing by which a spot might be laid on my honour or conscience," she said, with an odd deliberateness that seemed to insist upon the strictly literal meaning of her words. "Rather I pray you let the matter rest until God remedy it."

Lethington looked at the other two, the other two looked at him. He rubbed his hands softly.

"Trust to us, madame," he answered. "We will so guide the matter that Your Grace shall see nothing but what is good and approved by Parliament."

She committed herself to no reply, and so they were content to take their answer from her silence. They went in quest of Huntly and Sir James Balfour, and the five of them entered into a bond for the destruction of him whom they named "the young fool and proud tiranne," to be engaged in when Mary should have pardoned Morton and his fellow-conspirators.

It was not until Christmas Eve that she signed this pardon of some seventy fugitives, proscribed for their participation in the Rizzio murder, towards whom she had hitherto shown herself so implacable.

The world saw in this no more than a deed of clemency and charity befitting the solemn festival of good-will. But the five who had entered into that bond at Craigmillar Castle beheld in it more accurately the fulfilment of her part of the suggested bargain, the price she paid in advance to be rid of Darnley, the sign of her full agreement that the knot which might not be unravelled should be cut.

On that same day Her Grace went with Bothwell to Lord Drummond's, where they abode for the best part of a week, and thence they went on together to Tullibardine, the rash and open intimacy between them giving nourishment to scandal.

At the same time Darnley quitted Stirling, where he had lately been living in miserable conditions, ignored by the nobles, and even stinted in his necessary expenses, deprived of his ordinary servants, and his silver replaced by pewter. The miserable youth reached Glasgow deadly sick. He had been taken ill on the way, and the inevitable rumour was spread that he had been poisoned. Later, when it became known that his once lovely countenance was now blotched and disfigured, it was realized that his illness was no more than the inevitable result of the debauched life he led.

Conceiving himself on the point of death, Darnley wrote piteously to the Queen; but she ignored his letters until she learnt that his condition was improving, when at last (on January 29th) she went to visit him at Glasgow. It may well be that she nourished some hope that nature would resolve the matter for her, and remove the need for such desperate measures as had been concerted. But seeing him likely to recover, two things became necessary, to bring him to the place that was suitable for the fulfilment of her designs, and to simulate reconciliation with him, and even renewed and tender affection, so that none might hereafter charge her with complicity in what should follow.

I hope that in this I do her memory no injustice. It is thus that I read the sequel, nor can I read it in any other way.

She found him abed, with a piece of taffeta over his face to hide its disfigurement, and she was so moved—as it seemed—by his condition, that she fell on her knees beside him, and wept in the presence of her attendants and his own, confessing penitence if anything she had done in the past could have contributed to their estrangement. Thus reconciliation followed, and she used him tenderly, grew solicitous concerning him, and vowed that as soon as he could be moved, he must be taken to surroundings more salubrious and more befitting the dignity of his station.

Gladly then he agreed to return with her to Holyrood.

"Not to Holyrood," she said "At least, not until your health is mended, lest you should carry thither infection dangerous to your little son."

"Wither then?" he asked her, and when she mentioned Craigmillar, he started up in bed, so that the taffeta slipped from his face, and it was with difficulty that she dissembled the loathing with which the sight of its pustules inspired her,.

"Craigmillar!" he cried. "Then what I was told is true."

"What were you told?" quoth she, staring at him, brows knit, her face blank.

A rumour had filtered through to him of the Craigmillar bond. He had been told that a letter drawn up there had been presented to her for her signature, which she had refused. Thus much he told her, adding that he could not believe that she would do him any hurt; and yet why did she desire to bear him to Craigmillar?

"You have been told lies," she answered him. "I saw no such letter; I subscribed none, nor was ever asked to subscribe any," which indeed was literally true. "To this I swear. As for your going to Craigmillar, you shall go whithersoever you please, yourself."

He sank back on his pillows, and his trembling subsided.

"I believe thee, Mary. I believe thou'ld never do me any harm," he repeated, "and if any other would," he added on a bombastic note, "they shall buy it dear, unless they take me sleeping. But I'll never to Craigmillar."

"I have said you shall go where you please," she assured him again.

He considered.

"There is the house at Kirk o' Field. It has a fine garden, and is in a position that is deemed the healthiest about Edinburgh. I need good air; good air and baths have been prescribed me to cleanse me of this plague. Kirk o' Field will serve, if it be your pleasure."

She gave a ready consent, dispatched messengers ahead to prepare the house, and to take from Holyrood certain furnishings that should improve the interior, and render it as fitting as possible a dwelling for a king.

Some days later they set out, his misgivings quieted by the tenderness which she now showed him—particularly when witnesses were at hand.

It was a tenderness that grew steadily during those twelve days in which he lay in convalescence in the house at Kirk o' Field; she was playful and coquettish with him as a maid with her lover, so that nothing was talked of but the completeness of this reconciliation, and the hope that it would lead to a peace within the realm that would be a benefit to all. Yet many there were who marvelled at it, wondering whether the waywardness and caprice of woman could account for so sudden a change from hatred to affection.

Darnley was lodged on the upper floor, in a room comfortably furnished from the palace. It was hung with six pieces of tapestry, and the floor was partly covered by an Eastern carpet. It contained, besides the handsome bed—which once had belonged to the Queen's mother—a couple of high chairs in purple velvet, a little table with a green velvet cover, and some cushions in red. By the side of the bed stood the specially prepared bath that was part of the cure which Darnley was undergoing. It had for its incongruous lid a door that had been lifted from its hinges.

Immediately underneath was a room that had been prepared for the Queen, with a little bed of yellow and green damask, and a furred coverlet. The windows looked out upon the close, and the door opened upon the passage leading to the garden.

Here the Queen slept on several of those nights of early February, for indeed she was more often at Kirk o' Field than at Holyrood, and when she was not bearing Darnley company in his chamber, and beguiling the tedium of his illness, she was to be seen walking in the garden with Lady Reres, and from his bed he could hear her sometimes singing as she sauntered there.

Never since the ephemeral season of their courtship had she been on such fond terms with him, and all his fears of hostile designs entertained against him by her immediate followers were stilled at last. Yet not for long. Into his fool's paradise came Lord Robert of Holyrood, with a warning that flung him into a sweat of panic.

The conspirators had hired a few trusted assistants to help them carry out their plans, and a rumour had got abroad—in the unaccountable way of rumours—that there was danger to the King. It was of this rumour that Lord Robert brought him word, telling him bluntly that unless he escaped quickly from this place, he would leave his life there. Yet when Darnley had repeated this to the Queen, and the Queen indignantly had sent for Lord Robert and demanded to know his meaning, his lordship denied that he had uttered any such warning, protested that his words must have been misunderstood—that they referred solely to the King's condition, which demanded, he thought, different treatment and healthier air.

Knowing not what to believe, Darnley's uneasiness abode with him. Yet, trusting Mary, and feeling secure so long as she was by his side, he became more and more insistent upon her presence, more and more fretful in her absence. It was to quiet him that she consented to sleep as often as might be at Kirk o' Field. She slept there on the Wednesday of that week, and again on Friday, and she was to have done so yet again on that fateful Sunday, February 9th, but that her servant Sebastien—one who had accompanied her from France, and for whom she had a deep affection—was that day married, and Her Majesty had promised to be present at the masque that night at Holyrood, in honour of his nuptials.

Nevertheless, she did not utterly neglect her husband on that account. She rode to Kirk o' Field early in the evening, accompanied by Bothwell, Huntly, Argyll, and some others; and leaving the lords at cards below to while away the time, she repaired to Darnley, and sat beside his bed, soothing a spirit oddly perturbed, as if with some premonition of what was brewing.

"Ye'll not leave me the night," he begged her once.

"Alas," she said, "I must! Sebastien is being wed, and I have promised to be present."

He sighed and shifted uneasily.

"Soon I shall be well, and then these foolish humours will cease to haunt me. But just now I cannot bear you from my sight. When you are with me I am at peace. I know that all is well. But when you go I am filled with fears, lying helpless here."

"What should you fear?" she asked him.

"The hate that I know is alive against me."

"You are casting shadows to affright yourself," said she.

"What's that?" he cried, half raising himself in sudden alarm. "Listen!"

From the room below came faintly a sound of footsteps, accompanied by a noise as of something being trundled.

"It will be my servants in my room—putting it to rights."

"To what purpose since you do not sleep there tonight?" he asked. He raised his voice and called his page.

"Why, what will you do?" she asked him, steadying her own alarm.

He answered her by bidding the youth who had entered go see what was doing in the room below. The lad departed, and had he done his errand faithfully, he would have found Bothwell's followers, Hay and Hepburn, and the Queen's man, Nicholas Hubert—better known as French Paris—emptying a keg of gunpowder on the floor immediately under the King's bed. But it happened that in the passage he came suddenly face to face with the splendid figure of Bothwell, cloaked and hatted, and Bothwell asked him whither he went.

The boy told him.

"It is nothing," Bothwell said. "They are moving Her Grace's bed in accordance with her wishes."

And the lad, overborne by that commanding figure which so effectively blocked his path, chose the line of lesser resistance. He went back to bear the King that message as if for himself he had seen what my Lord' Bothwell had but told him.

Darnley was pacified by the assurance, and the lad withdrew.

"Did I not tell you how it was?" quoth Mary. "Is not my word enough?"

"Forgive the doubt," Darnley begged her. "Indeed, there was no doubt of you, who have shown me so much charity in my affliction." He sighed, and looked at her with melancholy eyes.

"I would the past had been other than it has been between you and me," he said. "I was too young for kingship, I think. In my green youth I listened to false counsellors, and was quick to jealousy and the follies it begets. Then, when you cast me out and I wandered friendless, a devil took possession of me. Yet, if you will but consent to bury all the past into oblivion, I will make amends, and you shall find me worthier hereafter."

She rose, white to the lips, her bosom heaving under her long cloak. She turned aside and stepped to the window. She stood there, peering out into the gloom of the close, her knees trembling under her.

"Why do you not answer me?" he cried.

"What answer do you need?" she said and her voice shook. "Are you not answered already?" And then, breathlessly, she added: "It is time to go, I think."

They heard a heavy step upon the stairs and the clank of a sword against the rails. The door opened, and Bothwell, wrapped in his scarlet cloak, stood bending his tall shoulders under the low lintel. His gleaming eyes, so oddly mocking in their glance, for all that his face was set, fell upon Darnley, and with their look flung him into an inward state of blending fear and rage.

"Your Grace," said Bothwell's deep voice, "it is close upon midnight."

He came no more than in time; it needed the sight of him with its reminder of all that he meant to her to sustain a purpose that was being sapped by pity.

"Very well," she said. "I come."

Bothwell stood aside to give her egress and to invite it. But the King delayed her.

"A moment—a word!" he begged, and to Bothwell: "Give us leave apart, sir!"

Yet, King though he might be, there was no ready obedience from the arrogant Border lord, her lover. It was to Mary that Bothwell looked for commands, nor stirred until she signed to him to go. And even then he went no farther than the other side of the door, so that he might be close at hand to fortify her should any weakness assail her now in this supreme hour.

Darnley struggled up in bed, caught her hand, and pulled her to him.

"Do not leave me, Mary. Do not leave me!" he implored her.

"Why, what is this?" she cried, but her voice lacked steadiness. "Would you have me disappoint poor Sebastien, who loves me?"

"I see. Sebastien is more to you than I?"

"Now this is folly. Sebastien is my faithful servant."

"And am I less? Do you not believe that my one aim henceforth will be to serve you and faithfully? Oh, forgive this weakness. I am full of evil foreboding to-night. Go, then, if go you must, but give me at least some assurance of your love, some pledge of it in earnest that you will come again to-morrow nor part from me again."

She looked into the white, piteous young face that had once been so lovely, and her soul faltered. It needed the knowledge that Bothwell waited just beyond the door, that he could overhear what was being said, to strengthen her fearfully in her tragic purpose.

She has been censured most for what next she did. Murray himself spoke of it afterwards as the worst part of the business. But it is possible that she was concerned only at the moment to put an end to a scene that was unnerving her, and that she took the readiest means to it.

She drew a ring from her finger and slipped it on to one of his.

"Be this the pledge, then," she said; "and so content and rest yourself."

With that she broke from him, white and scared, and reached the door. Yet with her hand upon the latch she paused. Looking at him she saw that he was smiling, and perhaps horror of her betrayal of him overwhelmed her. It must be that she then desired to warn him, yet with Bothwell within earshot she realized that any warning must precipitate the tragedy, with direst consequences to Bothwell and herself.

To conquer her weakness, she thought of David Rizzio, whom Darnley had murdered almost at her feet, and whom this night was to avenge. She thought of the Judas part that he had played in that affair, and sought persuasion that it was fitting he should now be paid in kind. Yet, very woman that she was, failing to find any such persuasion, she found instead in the very thought of Rizzio the very means to convey her warning.

Standing tense and white by the door, regarding him with dilating eyes, she spoke her last words to him.

"It would be just about this time last year that Davie was slain," she said, and on that passed out to the waiting Bothwell.

Once on the stairs she paused and set a hand upon the shoulder of the stalwart Borderer.

"Must it be? Oh, must it be?" she whispered fearfully.

She caught the flash of his eyes in the half gloom as he leaned over her, his arm about her waist drawing her to him.

"Is it not just? Is it not full merited?" he asked her.

"And yet I would that we did not profit by it," she complained.

"Shall we pity him on that account?" he asked, and laughed softly and shortly. "Come away," he added abruptly. "They wait for you!" And so, by the suasion of his arm and his imperious will, she was swept onward along the road of her destiny.

Outside the horses were ready. There was a little group of gentlemen to escort her, and half a dozen servants with lighted torches, whilst Lady Reres was in waiting. A man stood forward to assist her to mount, his face and hands so blackened by gunpowder that for a moment she failed to recognize him. She laughed nervously when he named himself.

"Lord, Paris, how begrimed you are!" she cried; and, mounting, rode away towards Holyrood with her torch-bearers and attendants.

In the room above, Darnley lay considering her last words. He turned them over in his thoughts, assured by the tone she had used and how she had looked that they contained some message.

"It would be just about this time last year that Davie was slain."

In themselves, those words were not strictly accurate. It wanted yet a month to the anniversary of Rizzio's death. And why, at parting, should she have reminded him of that which she had agreed should be forgotten? Instantly came the answer that she sought to warn him that retribution was impending. He thought again of the rumours that he had heard of a bond signed at Craigmillar; he recalled Lord Robert's warning to him, afterwards denied.

He recalled her words to himself at the time of Rizzio's death: "Consider well what I now say. Consider and remember. I shall never rest until I give you as sore a heart as I have presently." And further, he remembered her cry at once agonized and fiercely vengeful: "Jamais, jamais je n'oublierai."

His terrors mounted swiftly, to be quieted again at last when he looked at the ring she had put upon his finger in pledge of her renewed affection. The past was dead and buried, surely. Though danger might threaten, she would guard him against it, setting her love about him like a panoply of steel. When she came to-morrow, he would question her closely, and she should be more frank and open with him, and tell him all. Meanwhile, he would take his precautions for to-night.

He sent his page to make fast all doors. The youth went and did as he was bidden, with the exception of the door that led to the garden. It had no bolts, and the key was missing; yet, seeing his master's nervous, excited state, he forbore from any mention of that circumstance when presently he returned to him.

Darnley requested a book of Psalms, that he might read himself to sleep. The page dozed in a chair, and so the hours passed; and at last the King himself fell into a light slumber. Out of this he started suddenly at a little before two o'clock, and sat upright in bed, alarmed without knowing why, listening with straining ears and throbbing pulses.

He caught a repetition of the sound that had aroused him, a sound akin to that which had drawn his attention earlier, when Mary had been with him. It came up faintly from the room immediately beneath: her room. Some one was moving there, he thought. Then as he continued to listen, all became quiet again, save his fears, which would not be quieted. He extinguished the light, slipped from the bed, and, crossing to the window, peered out into the close that was faintly illumined by a moon in its first quarter. A shadow moved, he thought. He watched with increasing panic for confirmation, and presently saw that he had been right. Not one, but several shadows were shifting there among the trees. Shadows of men, they were, and as he peered, he saw one that went running from the house across the lawn and joined the others, now clustered together in a group. What could be their purpose here? In the silence, he seemed to hear again the echo of Mary's last words to him:

"*It would be just about this time last year that Davie was slain.*"

In terror, he groped his way to the chair where the page slept and shook the lad vigorously.

"Afoot, boy!" he said, in a hoarse whisper. He had meant to shout it, but his voice failed him, his windpipe clutched by panic. "Afoot—we are beset by enemies!"

At once the youth was wide awake, and together—the King just in his shirt as he was—they made their way from the room in the dark, groping their way, and so reached the windows at the back. Darnley opened one of these very softly, then sent the boy back for a sheet. Making this fast, they descended by it to the garden, and started towards the wall, intending to climb it, that they might reach the open.

The boy led the way, and the King followed, his teeth chattering as much from the cold as from the terror that possessed him. And then, quite suddenly, without the least warning, the ground, it seemed to them, heaved under their feet, and they were flung violently forward on their faces. A great blaze rent the darkness of the night, accompanied by the thunders of an explosion so terrific that it seemed as if the whole world must have been shattered by it.

For some instants the King and his page lay half stunned where they had fallen, and well might it have been for them had they so continued. But Darnley, recovering, staggered to his feet, pulling the boy up with him and supporting him. Then, as he began to move, he heard a soft whistle in the gloom behind him. Over his shoulder he looked towards the house, to behold a great, smoking gap now yawning in it. Through this gap he caught a glimpse of shadowy men moving in the close beyond, and he realized that he had been seen. The white shirt he wore had betrayed his presence to them.

With a stifled scream, he began to run towards the wall, the page staggering after him. Behind them now came the clank and thud of a score of overtaking feet. Soon they were surrounded. The King turned this way and that, desperately seeking a way out of the murderous human ring that fenced them round.

"What d'ye seek? What d'ye seek?" he screeched, in a pitiful attempt to question with authority.

A tall man in a trailing cloak advanced and seized him.

"We seek thee, fool!" said the voice of Bothwell.

The kingliness that he had never known how to wear becomingly now fell from him utterly.

"Mercy—mercy!" he cried.

"Such mercy as you had on David Rizzio!" answered the Border lord.

Darnley fell on his knees and sought to embrace the murderer's legs. Bothwell stooped over him, seized the wretched man's shirt, and pulled it from his shivering body; then, flinging the sleeves about the royal neck, slipped one over the other and drew them tight, nor relaxed his hold until the young man's struggles had entirely ceased.

Four days later, Mary went to visit the body of her husband in the chapel of Holyrood House, whither it had been conveyed, and there, as a contemporary tells us, she looked upon it long, "not only without grief, but with greedy eyes." Thereafter it was buried secretly in the night by Rizzio's side, so that murderer and victim lay at peace together in the end.

The Two Drovers

SIR WALTER SCOTT

1

t was the day after Doune Fair when my story commences. It had been a brisk market, several dealers had attended from the northern and midland counties in England, and English money had flown so merrily about as to gladden the hearts of the Highland farmers. Many large droves were about to set off for England, under the protection of their owners, or of the topsmen whom they employed in the tedious, laborious, and responsible office of driving the cattle for many hundred miles, from the market where they had been purchased, to the fields or farm-yards where they were to be fattened for the shambles.

The Highlanders, in particular, are masters of this difficult trade of driving, which seems to suit them as well as the trade of war. It affords exercise for all their habits of patient endurance and active exertion. They are required to know perfectly the drove roads, which lie over the wildest tracts of the country, and to avoid as much as possible the highways, which distress the feet of the bullocks, and the turnpikes, which annoy the spirit of the drover; whereas, on the broad green or grey track, which leads across the pathless moor, the herd not only move at ease and without taxation, but, if they mind their business, may pick up a mouthful of food by the way. At night, the drivers usually sleep along with their cattle, let the weather be what it will, and many of these hardy men do not once rest under a roof during a journey on foot from Lochaber to Lincolnshire. They are paid very highly, for the trust reposed is of the last importance, as it depends on their prudence, vigilance, and honesty, whether the cattle reach the final market in good order, and afford a profit to the grazier. But as they maintain themselves at their own expense, they are especially economical in that particular. At the period we speak of, a Highland drover was victualled for his long and toilsome journey with a few handfuls of oatmeal, and two or three onions, renewed from time to time, and a ram's horn filled with whisky, which he used regularly, but sparingly, every night and morning. His dirk, or *skene-dhu* (black-knife), so worn as to be concealed beneath the arm, or by the folds of the plaid, was his only weapon, excepting the cudgel with which he directed the movement of the cattle. A Highlander was never so happy as on these occasions. There was a variety in the whole journey, which exercised the Celt's natural curiosity and love of motion; there were the constant change of place and scene, the petty adventures incidental to the traffic, and the intercourse with the various farmers, graziers, and traders, intermingled with occasional merrymakings, not the less acceptable to Donald that they were void of expense—and there was the consciousness of superior skill for the Highlander, a child amongst flocks, is a prince amongst herds, and his natural habits induce him to disdain the shepherd's slothful life, so that he feels himself nowhere more at home than when following a gallant drove of his country cattle in the character of their guardian.

Of the number who left Doune in the morning, and with the purpose we described, not a *Glunamie* of them all cocked his bonnet more briskly, or gartered his tartan hose under knee over a pair of more promising spiogs (legs) than did Robin Oig M'Combich, called familiarly Robin Oig, that is, Young, or the Lesser, Robin. Though small of stature as the epithet Oig implies, and not very strongly limbed, he was as light and alert as one of the deer of his mountains. He had an elasticity of step which, in the course of a long march, made many a stout fellow envy him; and the manner in which he busked his plaid and adjusted his bonnet, argued a consciousness that so smart a John Highlandman as himself would not pass unnoticed among the Lowland lasses. The ruddy cheek, red lips, and white teeth, set off a countenance which had gained by exposure to the weather a healthful and hardy rather than a rugged hue. If Robin Oig did not laugh, or even smile frequently, as indeed is not the practice among his countrymen, his bright eyes usually gleamed from under his bonnet with an expression of cheerfulness ready to be turned into mirth.

The departure of Robin Oig was an incident in the little town, in and near which he had many friends, male and female. He was a topping person in his way, transacted considerable business on his own behalf, and was entrusted by the best farmers in the Highlands in preference to any other drover in that district. He might have increased his business to any extent had he condescended to manage it by deputy; but except a lad or two, sister's sons of his own, Robin rejected the idea of assistance, conscious, perhaps, how much his reputation depended upon his attending in person to the practical discharge of his duty in every instance. He remained, therefore, contented with the highest premium given to persons of his description, and comforted himself with the hopes that a few journeys to England might enable him to conduct business on his own account, in a manner becoming his birth. For Robin Oig's father, Lachlan M'Combich (or *son of my friend* his actual clan-surname being M'Gregor), had been so called by the celebrated Rob Roy, because of the particular friendship which had subsisted between the grandsire of Robin and that renowned cateran. Some people even say that Robin Oig derived his Christian name from one as renowned in the wilds of Loch Lomond as ever was his namesake Robin Hood, in the precincts of merry Sherwood. 'Of such ancestry,' as James Boswell says, 'who would not be proud?' Robin Oig was proud accordingly; but his frequent visits to England and to the Lowlands had given him tact enough to know that pretensions, which still gave him a little right to distinction in his own lonely glen, might be both obnoxious and ridiculous if preferred elsewhere. The pride of birth, therefore, was like the miser's treasure, the secret subject of his contemplation, but never exhibited to strangers as a subject of boasting.

Many were the words of gratulation and good luck which were bestowed on Robin Oig. The judges commended his drove, especially Robin's own property, which were the best of them. Some thrust out their snuff-mulls for the parting pinch—others tendered the *doch-an-dorrach* or parting cup. All cried—'Good luck travel with you and come home with you.—Give you luck in the Saxon market—brave notes in the *leabhar-dhu*' (black pocket-book) 'and plenty of English gold in the *sporran* (pouch of goatskin).

The bonny lasses made their adieus more modestly, and more than one, it was said would have given her best brooch to be certain that it was upon her that his eye last rested as he turned towards the road.

Robin Oig had just given the preliminary *'Hoo-hoo!'* to urge forward the loiterers of the drove, when there was a cry behind him.

'Stay, Robin—bide a blink. Here is Janet of Tomahourich—auld Janet, your father's sister.'

'Plague on her, for an auld Highland witch and spaewife,' said a farmer from the Carse of Stirling; 'she'll cast some of her cantrips on the cattle.'

'She canna do that,' said another sapient of the same profession— 'Robin Oig is no the lad to leave any of them without tying St. Mungo's knot on their tails, and that will put to her speed the best witch that ever flew over Dimayet upon a broomstick.'

It may not be indifferent to the reader to know that the Highland cattle are peculiarly liable to be *taken,* or infected, by spells and witchcraft; which judicious people guard against by knitting knots of peculiar complexity on the tuft of hair which terminates the animal's tail.

But the old woman who was the object of the farmer's suspicion seemed only busied about the drover, without paying any attention to the drove. Robin, on the contrary, appeared rather impatient of her presence.

'What auld-world fancy,' he said, 'has brought you so early from the ingle-side this morning, Muhme? I am sure I bid you good-even, and had your God-speed, last night.'

'And left me more siller than the useless old woman will use till you come back again, bird of my bosom,' said the sibyl. 'But it is little I would care for the food that nourishes me, or the fire that warms me, or for God's blessed sun itself, if aught but weel should happen to the grandson of my father. So let me walk the *deasil* round you, that you may go safe out into the foreign land, and come safe home.'

Robin Oig stopped, half embarrassed, half laughing, and signing to those near that he only complied with the old woman to soothe her humour. In the meantime she traced around him, with wavering steps, the propitiation, which some have thought has been derived from the Druidical mythology. It consists, as is well known, in the person who makes the *deasil* walking three times round the person who is the object of the ceremony, taking care to move according to the course of the sun. At once, however, she stopped short, and exclaimed, in a voice of alarm and horror, 'Grandson of my father, there is blood on your hand.'

'Hush, for God's sake, aunt,' said Robin Oig; 'you will bring more trouble on yourself with this Taishataragh' (second sight) 'than you will be able to get out of for many a day.'

The old woman only repeated, with a ghastly look, 'There is blood on your hand, and it is English blood. The blood of the Gael is richer and redder. Let us see—let us—'

Ere Robin Oig could prevent her, which, indeed, could only have been done by positive violence, so hasty and peremptory were her proceedings, she had drawn from his side the dirk which lodged in the folds of his plaid, and held it up, exclaiming, although the weapon gleamed clear and bright in the sun, 'Blood, blood—Saxon blood again. Robin Oig M'Combich, go not this day to England!'

'Prutt, trutt,' answered Robin Oig, 'that will never do neither—it would be next thing to running the country. For shame, Muhme—give me the dirk. You cannot tell by the colour the difference betwixt the blood of a black bullock and a white one, and you speak of knowing Saxon from Gaelic blood. All men have their blood from Adam, Muhme. Give me my skene-dhu, and let me go on my road. I should have been half-way to Stirling Brig by this time.—Give me my dirk, and let me go.'

'Never will I give it to you,' said the old woman. 'Never will I quit my hold on your plaid, unless you promise me not to wear that unhappy weapon.'

The women around him urged him also, saying few of his aunt's words fell to the ground; and as the Lowland farmers continued to look moodily on the scene, Robin Oig determined to close it at any sacrifice.

'Well, then,' said the young drover, giving the scabbard of the weapon to Hugh Morrison, 'you Lowlanders care nothing for these freats. Keep my dirk for me. I cannot give it to you, because it was my father's; but your drove follows ours, and I am content it should be in your keeping, not in mine.—Will this do, Muhme?'

'It must,' said the old woman—'that is, if the Lowlander is mad enough to carry the knife.'

The strong Westlandman laughed aloud.

'Goodwife,' said he, 'I am Hugh Morrison from Glenae, come of the Manly Morrisons of auld langsyne, that never took short weapon against a man in their lives. And neither needed they. They had their broadswords, and I have this bit supple,' showing a formidable cudgel—'for dirking ower the board, I leave that to John Highlandman.—Ye needna snort, none of you Highlanders, and you in especial, Robin. I'll keep the bit knife, if you are feared for the auld spaewife's tale, and give it back to you whenever you want it.'

Robin was not particularly pleased with some part of Hugh Morrison's speech; but he had learned in his travels more patience than belonged to his Highland constitution originally, and he accepted the service of the descendant of the Manly Morrisons without finding fault with the rather depreciating manner in which it was offered.

'If he had not had his morning in his head, and been but a Dumfriesshire hog into the boot, he would have spoken more like a gentleman. But you cannot have more of a sow than a grumph. It's shame my father's knife should ever slash a haggis for the like of him.'

Thus saying (but saying it in Gaelic) Robin drove on his cattle, and waved farewell to all behind him. He was in the greater haste, because he expected to join at Falkirk a comrade and brother in profession, with whom he proposed to travel in company.

Robin Oig's chosen friend was a young Englishman, Harry Wakefield by name, well known at every northern market, and in his way as much famed and honoured as our Highland driver of bullocks. He was nearly six feet high, gallantly formed to keep the rounds at Smithfield, or maintain the ring at a wrestling match; and although he might have been overmatched, perhaps, among the regular professors of the Fancy, yet, as a yokel, or rustic, or a chance customer, he was able to give a bellyful to any amateur of the pugilistic art. Doncaster races saw him in his glory, betting his guinea, and generally successfully; nor was there a main fought in Yorkshire, the feeders being persons of celebrity, at which he was not to be seen, if business permitted. But though a *sprack* lad, and fond of pleasure and its haunts, Harry Wakefield was steady, and not the cautious Robin Oig M'Combich himself was more attentive to the main chance. His holidays were holidays indeed; but his days of work were dedicated to steady and persevering labour. In countenance and temper, Wakefield was the model of old England's merry yeomen, whose clothyard shafts, in so many hundred battles, asserted her superiority over the nations, and whose good sabres in our own time are her cheapest and most assured defence. His mirth was readily excited; for, strong in limb and constitution, and fortunate in circumstances, he was disposed to be pleased with everything about him; and such difficulties as he might occasionally encounter were, to a man of his energy, rather matter of amusement than serious annoyance. With all the merits of a sanguine temper, our young English drover was not without his defects. He was irascible, sometimes to the verge of being quarrelsome; and perhaps not the less inclined to bring his disputes to a pugilistic decision, because he found few antagonists able to stand up to him in the boxing ring.

It is difficult to say how Harry Wakefield and Robin Oig first became intimates; but it is certain a close acquaintance had taken place betwixt them, although they had apparently few common subjects of conversation or of interest, so soon as their talk ceased to be of bullocks. Robin Oig, indeed, spoke the English language rather imperfectly upon any other topics but stots and kyloes, and Harry Wakefield could never bring his broad Yorkshire tongue to utter a single word of Gaelic. It was in vain Robin spent a whole morning, during a walk over Minch Moor in attempting to teach his companion to utter, with true precision, the shibboleth *Llhu,* which is the Gaelic for calf. From Traquair to Murder-cairn, the hill rang with the discordant attempts of the Saxon upon the unmanageable monosyllable, and the heartfelt laugh which followed every failure. They had, however, better modes of awakening the echoes; for Wakefield could sing many a ditty to the praise of Moll, Susan, and Cicely, and Robin Oig had a particular gift at whistling interminable pibrochs through all their involutions, and what was more agreeable to his companion's southern ear, knew many of the northern airs, both lively and pathetic, to which Wakefield learned to pipe a bass. This, though Robin could hardly have comprehended his companion's stories about horse-racing, and cock-fighting or fox-hunting, and although his own legends of clan-fights and *creaghs,* varied with talk of Highland goblins and fairy folk, would have been caviare to his companion, they contrived nevertheless to find a degree of pleasure in each other's company, which had for three years back induced them to join company and travel together, when the direction of their journey permitted. Each, indeed, found his advantage in this companionship; for where could the Englishman have found a guide through the Western Highlands like Robin Oig M'Combich? and when they were on what Harry called the *right* side of the Border, his patronage, which was extensive, and his purse which was heavy, were at all times in the service of his Highland friend, and on many occasions his liberality did him genuine yeoman's service.

2

Were ever two such loving friends!—
How could they disagree?
O thus it was, he loved him dear,
And thought how to requite him,
And having no friend left but he,
He did resolve to fight him.
—DUKE UPON DUKE

The pair of friends had traversed with their usual cordiality the grassy wilds of Liddesdale, and crossed the opposite part of Cumberland, emphatically called The Waste. In these solitary regions, the cattle under the charge of our drovers derived their subsistence chiefly by picking their food as they went along the drove-road, or sometimes by the tempting opportunity of a *start and owerloup,* or invasion of the neighbouring pasture, where an occasion presented itself. But now the scene changed before them; they were descending towards a fertile and enclosed country, where no such liberties could be taken with impunity, or without a previous arrangement and bargain with the possessors of the ground. This was more especially the case, as a great northern fair was upon the eve of taking place, where both the Scotch and English drover expected to dispose of a part of their cattle, which it was desirable to produce in the market, rested and in good order. Fields were therefore difficult to be obtained, and only upon high terms. This necessity occasioned a temporary separation betwixt the two friends, who went to bargain, each as he could, for the separate accommodation of his herd. Unhappily it chanced that both of them, unknown to each other, thought of bargaining for the ground they wanted on the property of a country gentleman of some fortune, whose estate lay in the neighbourhood. The English drover applied to the bailiff on the property, who was known to him. It chanced that the Cumbrian squire, who had entertained some suspicions of his manager's honesty, was taking occasional measures to ascertain how far they were well founded, and had desired that any inquiries about his enclosures, with a view to occupy them for a temporary purpose, should be referred to himself. As, however, Mr. Ireby had gone the day before upon a journey of some miles' distance to the northward, the bailiff chose to consider the check upon his full powers as for the time removed, and concluded that he should best consult his master's interest, and perhaps his own, in making an agreement with Harry Wakefield, Meanwhile, ignorant of what his comrade was doing, Robin Oig, on his side, chanced to be overtaken by a good-looking smart little man upon a pony, most knowingly hogged and cropped, as was then the fashion, the rider wearing tight leather breeches and long-necked bright spurs. This cavalier asked one or two pertinent questions about markets and the price of stock. So Robin, seeing him a well-judging civil gentleman, took the freedom to ask him whether he could let him know if there was any grass-land to be let in that neighbourhood, for the temporary accommodation of his drove. He could not have put the question to more willing ears. The gentleman of the buckskin was the proprietor with whose bailiff Harry Wakefield had dealt or was in the act of dealing.

'Thou art in good luck, my canny Scot,' said Mr. Ireby, 'to have spoken to me, for I see thy cattle have done their day's work, and I have at my disposal the only field within three miles that is to be let in these parts.'

'The drove can pe gang two, three, four miles very pratty weel indeed,' said the cautious Highlander; 'put what would his honour be axing for the peasts pe the head, if she was to tak the park for twa or three days?'

'We won't differ, Sawney, if you let me have six stots for winterers, in the way of reason.'

'And which peasts wad your honour pe for having?'

'Why—let me see—the two black—the dun one—yon doddy—him with the twisted horn—the brockit—How much by the head?'

'Ah,' said Robin, 'your honour is a shudge—a real shudge—I couldna have set off the pest six peasts petter mysell, me that ken them as if they were my pairns, puir things.'

'Well, how much per head, Sawney?' continued Mr. Ireby.

'It was high markets at Doune and Falkirk,' answered Robin.

And thus the conversation proceeded, until they had agreed on the *prix juste* for the bullocks, the squire throwing in the temporary accommodation of the enclosure for the cattle into the boot, and Robin making, as he thought, a very good bargain, provided the grass was but tolerable. The squire walked his pony alongside of the drove, partly to show him the way, and see him put into possession of the field, and partly to learn the latest news of the northern markets.

They arrived at the field, and the pasture seemed excellent. But what was their surprise when they saw the bailiff quietly inducting the cattle of Harry Wakefield into the grassy Goshen which had just been assigned to those of Robin Oig M'Combich by the proprietor himself! Squire Ireby set spurs to his horse, dashed up to his servant, and learning what had passed between the parties, briefly informed the English drover that his bailiff had let the ground without his authority, and that he might seek grass for his cattle wherever he would, since he was to get none there. At the same time he rebuked his servant severely for having transgressed his commands, and ordered him instantly to assist in ejecting the hungry and weary cattle of Harry Wakefield, which were just beginning to enjoy a meal of unusual plenty, and to introduce those of his comrade, whom the English drover now began to consider as a rival.

The feelings which arose in Wakefield's mind would have induced him to resist Mr. Ireby's decision; but every Englishman has a tolerably accurate sense of law and justice, and John Fleecebumpkin, the bailiff, having acknowledged that he had exceeded his commission, Wakefield saw nothing else for it than to collect his hungry and disappointed charge and drive them on to seek quarters elsewhere. Robin Oig saw what had happened with regret, and hastened to offer to his English friend to share with him the disputed possession. But Wakefield's pride was severely hurt, and he answered disdainfully, 'Take it all, man—take it all—never make two bites of a cherry—thou canst talk over the gentry, and blear a plain man's eye—Out upon you, man—I would not kiss any man's dirty latchets for leave to bake in his oven.'

Robin Oig, sorry but not surprised at his comrade's displeasure, hastened to entreat his friend to wait but an hour till he had gone to the squire's house to receive payment for the cattle he had sold, and he could come back and help him to drive the cattle into some convenient place of rest, and explain to him the whole mistake they had both of them fallen into. But the Englishman continued indignant: 'Thou hast been selling, has thou? Ay, ay,—thou is a cunning lad for kenning the hours of bargaining. Go to the devil with thyself, for I will ne'er see thy fause loon's visage again—thou should be ashamed to look me in the face.'

'I am ashamed to look no man in the face,' said Robin Oig, something moved; 'and moreover I will look you in the face this blessed day, if you will bide at the clachan down younder.'

'Mayhap you had as well keep away,' said his comrade; and turning his back on his former friend, he collected his unwilling associates, assisted by the bailiff, who took some real and some affected interest in seeing Wakefield accommodated.

After spending some time in negotiating with more than one of the neighbouring farmers, who could not, or would not, afford the accommodation desired, Harry Wakefield at last, and in his necessity, accomplished his point by means of the landlord of the ale-house at which Robin Oig and he had agreed to pass the night, when they first separated from each other. Mine host was content to let him turn his cattle on a piece of barren moor, at a price little less than the bailiff had asked for the disputed enclosure; and the wretchedness of the pasture, as well as the price paid for it, were set down as exaggerations of the breach of faith and friendship of his Scottish crony. This turn of Wakefield's passions was encouraged by the bailiff (who had his own reasons for being offended against poor Robin, as having been the unwitting cause of his falling into disgrace with his master), as well as by the innkeeper, and two or three chance guests, who stimulated the drover in his resentment against his quondam associate,—some from the ancient grudge against the Scots which, when it exists anywhere, is to be found lurking in the Border counties, and some from the general love of mischief, which characterizes mankind in all ranks of life, to the honour of Adam's children be it spoken. Good John Barleycorn also, who always heightens and exaggerates the prevailing passions, be they angry or kindly, was not wanting in his offices on this occasion; and confusion to false friends and hard masters was pledged in more than one tankard.

In the meanwhile Mr. Ireby found some amusement in detaining the northern drover at his ancient hall. He caused a cold round of beef to be placed before the Scot in the butler's pantry, together with a foaming tankard of home-brewed, and took pleasure in seeing the hearty appetite with which these unwonted edibles were discussed by Robin Oig M'Combich. The squire himself lighting his pipe, compounded between his patrician dignity and his love of agricultural gossip, by walking up and down while he conversed with his guest.

'I passed another drove,' said the squire, 'with one of your countrymen behind them—they were something less beasts than your drove, doddies most of them—a big man was with them—none of your kilts though, but a decent pair of breeches—D'ye know who he may be?'

'Hout aye—that might, could, and would be Hughie Morrison—I didna think he could hae peen sae weel up. He has made a day on us; but his Argyleshires will have wearied shanks. How far was he pehind?'

'I think about six or seven miles,' answered the squire, 'for I passed them at the Christenbury Crag, and I overtook you at the Hollan Bush. If his beasts be leg-weary, he will maybe be selling bargains.'

'Na, na, Hughie Morrison is no the man for pargains—ye maun come to some Highland body like Robin Oig hersell for the like of these—put I maun pe wishing you goot night, and twenty of them let alane ane, and I maun down to the clachan to see if the lad Harry Waakfelt is out of his humdudgeons yet.'

The party at the alehouse was still in full talk, and the treachery of Robin Oig still the theme of conversation, when the supposed culprit entered the apartment. His arrival, as usually happens in such a case, put an instant stop to the discussion of which he had furnished the subject, and he was received by the company assembled with that chilling silence which, more than a thousand exclamations, tells an intruder that he is unwelcome. Surprised and offended, but not appalled by the reception which he experienced, Robin entered with an undaunted and even haughty air, attempted no greeting as he saw he was received with none, and placed himself by the side of the fire, a little apart from a table at which Harry Wakefield, the bailiff, and two or three other persons were seated. The ample Cumbrian kitchen would have afforded plenty of room, even for a larger separation.

Robin, thus seated, proceeded to light his pipe, and call for a pint of twopenny.

'We have no twopence ale,' answered Ralph Heskett, the landlord; 'but as thou findest thy own tobacco, it's like thou mayest find thy own liquor too—it's the wont of thy country, I wot.'

'Shame, goodman,' said the landlady, a blithe bustling housewife, hastening herself to supply the guest with liquor—'Thou knowest well enow what the strange man wants, and it's thy trade to be civil, man. Thou shouldst know, that if the Scot likes a small pot, he pays a sure penny.'

Without taking any notice of this nuptial dialogue, the Highlander took the flagon in his hand, and addressing the company generally, drank the interesting toast of 'Good markets', to the party assembled.

'The better that the wind blew fewer dealers from the north,' said one of the farmers, 'and fewer Highland runts to eat up the English meadows.'

'Saul of my pody, put you are wrang there, my friend,' answered Robin, with composure, 'it is you fat Englishmen that eat up our Scots cattle, puir things.'

'I wish there was a summat to eat up their drovers,' said another; 'a plain Englishman canna make bread within a kenning of them.'

'Or an honest servant keep his master's favour, but they will come sliding in between him and the sunshine,' said the bailiff.

'If these pe jokes,' said Robin Oig, with the same composure, 'there is ower mony jokes upon one man.'

'It is no joke, but downright earnest,' said the bailiff. 'Harkye, Mr. Robin Ogg, or whatever is your name, it's right we should tell you that we are all of one opinion, and that is that you, Mr. Robin Ogg, have behaved to our friend, Mr. Harry Wakefield here, like a raff and a blackguard.'

'Nae doubt, nae doubt,' answered Robin, with great composure; 'and you are a set of very petty judges, for whose prains or pehaviour I wad not gie a pinch of sneeshing. If Mr. Harry Waakfelt kens where he is wranged, he kens where he may be righted.'

'He speaks truth,' said Wakefield, who had listened to what passed, divided between the offence which he had taken at Robin's late behaviour, and the revival of his habitual feelings of regard.

He now arose, and went towards Robin, who got up from his seat as he approached, and held out his hand.

'That's right, Harry—go it—serve him out,' resounded on all sides— 'tip him the nailer—show him the mill.'

'Hold your peace all of you and be——,' said Wakefield; and then addressing his comrade, he took him by the extended hand, with something alike of respect and defiance. 'Robin,' he said, 'thou hast used me ill enough this day; but if you mean, like a frank fellow, to shake hands, and make a tussle for love on the sod, why I'll forgie thee, man, and we shall be better friends than ever.'

'And would it not pe petter to be cood friends without more of the matter?' said Robin; 'we will be much petter friendships with our panes hale than proken.'

Harry Wakefield dropped the hand of his friend, or rather threw it from him.

'I did not think I had been keeping company for three years with a coward.'

'Coward pelongs to none of my name,' said Robin, whose eyes began to kindle, but keeping the command of his temper. 'It was no coward's legs or hands, Harry Waakfelt, that drew you out of the fords of Frew, when you was drifting ower the plack rock, and every eel in the river expected his share of you.'

'And that is true enough, too,' said the Englishman, struck by the appeal.

'Adzooks!' exclaimed the bailiff—'sure Harry Wakefield, the nattiest lad at Whitson Tryste, Wooler Fair, Carlisle Sands, or Stagshaw Bank, is not going to show white feather? Ah, this comes of living so long with kilts and bonnets—men forget the use of their daddles.'

'I may teach you, Master Fleecebumpkin, that I have not lost the use of mine,' said Wakefield, and then went on. 'This will never do, Robin. We must have a turn-up, or we shall be the talk of the country-side. I'll be d——d if I hurt thee—I'll put on the gloves gin thou like. Come, stand forward like a man.'

'To pe peaten like a dog,' said Robin; 'is there any reason in that? If you think I have done you wrong, I'll go before your shudge, though I neither know his law nor his language.'

A general cry of 'No, no—no law, no lawyer! a bellyful and be friends,' was echoed by the bystanders.

'But,' continued Robin, 'if I am to fight, I've no skill to fight like a jackanapes, with hands and nails.'

'How would you fight, then?' said his antagonist; 'though I am think-ing it would be hard to bring you to the scratch anyhow.'

'I would fight with proadswords, and sink point on the first plood drawn, like a gentleman.'

A loud shout of laughter followed the proposal, which indeed had rather escaped from poor Robin's swelling heart, than been the dictate of his sober judgement.

'Gentleman, quotha!' was echoed on all sides, with a shot of unextin-guishable laughter; 'a very pretty gentleman, God wot—Canst get two swords for the gentlemen to fight with, Ralph Heskett?'

'No, but I can send to the armoury at Carlisle, and lend them two forks, to be making shift with in the meantime.'

'Tush, man,' said another, 'the bonny Scots come into the world with the blue bonnet on their heads, and dirk and pistol at their belt,'

'Best send post,' said Mr. Fleecebumpkin, 'to the squire of Corby Cas-tle, to come and stand second to the *gentleman*.'

In the midst of this torrent of general ridicule, the Highlander in-stinctively griped beneath the folds of his plaid.

'But it's better not,' he said in his own language. 'A hundred curses on the swine-eaters, who know neither decency nor civility!'

'Make room, the pack of you,' he said, advancing to the door,

But his former friend interposed his sturdy bulk, and opposed his leaving the house; and when Robin Oig attempted to make his way by force, he hit him down on the floor, with as much ease as a boy bowls down a nine-pin.

'A ring, a ring!' was now shouted, until the dark rafters, and the hams that hung on them, trembled again, and the very platters on the *bink* clattered against each other. 'Well done, Harry'—'Give it him home, Harry'—'Take care of him now—he sees his own blood!'

Such were the exclamations, while the Highlander, starting from the ground, all his coldness and caution lost in frantic rage, sprang at his an-tagonist with the fury, the activity, and the vindictive purpose of an in-censed tiger-cat. But when could rage encounter science and temper? Robin Oig again went down in the unequal contest; and as the blow was necessarily a severe one, he lay motionless on the floor of the kitchen. The landlady ran to offer some aid, but Mr. Fleecebumpkin would not permit her to approach.

'Let him alone,' he said, 'he will come to within time, and come up to scratch again. He has not got half his broth yet.'

'He has got all I mean to give him, though,' said his antagonist, whose heart began to relent towards his old associate; 'and I would rather by half give the rest to yourself, Mr. Fleecebumpkin, for you pretend to know a thing or two, and Robin had not art enough even to peel before setting to, but fought with his plaid dangling about him.—Stand up, Robin, my man! all friends now; and let me hear the man that will speak a word against you, or your country, for your sake.'

Robin Oig was still under the dominion of his passion, and eager to renew the onset; but being withheld on the one side by the peace-making Dame Heskett, and on the other, aware that Wakefield no longer meant to renew the combat, his fury sank into gloomy sullenness.

'Come, come, never grudge so much as it, man,' said the brave-spirited Englishman, with the placability of his country, 'shake hands, and we will be better friends than ever.'

'Friends!' exclaimed Robin Oig, with strong emphasis—'friends!—Never. Look to yourself, Harry Waakfelt.'

'Then the curse of Cromwell on your proud Scots stomach, as the man says in the play, and you may do your worst, and be d—; for one man can say nothing more to another after a tussle, than that he is sorry for it.'

On these terms the friends parted; Robin Oig drew out, in silence, a piece of money, threw it on the table, and then left the alehouse. But turning at the door, he shook his hand at Wakefield, pointing with his forefinger upwards, in a manner which might imply either a threat or a caution. He then disappeared in the moonlight.

Some words passed after his departure between the bailiff, who piqued himself on being a little of a bully, and Harry Wakefield, who, with generous inconsistency, was now not indisposed to begin a new combat in defence of Robin Oig's reputation, 'although he could not use his daddles like an Englishman, as it did not come natural to him.' But Dame Heskett prevented this second quarrel from coming to a head by her peremptory interference. 'There should be no more fighting in her house,' she said; 'there had been too much already.—And you, Mr. Wakefield, may live to learn,' she added, 'what it is to make a deadly enemy out of a good friend.'

'Pshaw, dame! Robin Oig is an honest fellow, and will never keep malice.'

'Do not trust to that—you do not know the dour temper of the Scots, though you have dealt with them so often. I have a right to know them, my mother being a Scot.'

'And so is well seen on her daughter,' said Ralph Heskett.

This nuptial sarcasm gave the discourse another turn; fresh customers entered the tap-room or kitchen, and others left it. The conversation turned on the expected markets, and the report of prices from different parts both of Scotland and England—treaties were commenced, and Harry Wakefield was lucky enough to find a chap for a part of his drove, and at a very considerable profit; an event of consequence more than sufficient to blot out all remembrances of the unpleasant scuffle in the earlier part of the day. But there remained one party from whose mind that recollection could not have been wiped away by the possession of every head of cattle betwixt Esk and Eden.

This was Robin Oig M'Combich.—'That I should have had no weapon,' he said, 'and for the first time in my life!—Blighted by the tongue that bids the Highlander part with the dirk—the dirk—ha! the English blood!—My Muhme's word—when did her word fall to the ground?'

The recollection of the fatal prophecy confirmed the deadly intention which instantly sprang up in his mind.

'Ha! Morrison cannot be many miles behind; and if it were a hundred, what then?'

His impetuous spirit had now a fixed purpose and motive of action, and he turned the light foot of his country towards the wilds, through which he knew, by Mr. Ireby's report, that Morrison was advancing. His mind was wholly engrossed by the sense of injury—injury sustained from a friend; and by the desire of vengeance on one whom he now accounted his most bitter enemy. The treasured ideas of self-importance and self-opinion—of ideal birth and quality, had become more precious to him (like the hoard to the miser) because he could only enjoy them in secret.

But that hoard was pillaged, the idols which he had secretly worshipped had been desecrated and profaned. Insulted, abused, and beaten, he was no longer worthy, in his own opinion, of the name he bore or the lineage which he belonged to—nothing was left to him—nothing but revenge; and, as the reflection added a galling spur to every step, he determined it should be as sudden and signal as the offence.

When Robin Oig left the door of the alehouse, seven or eight English miles at least lay betwixt Morrison and him. The advance of the former was slow, limited by the sluggish pace of his cattle; the last left behind him stubble-field and hedge-row, crag and dark heath, all glittering with frost-rime in the broad November moonlight, at the rates of six miles an hour. And now the distant lowing of Morrison's cattle is heard; and now they are seen creeping like moles in size and slowness of motion on the broad face of the moor; and now he meets them—passes them, and stops their conductor.

'May good betide us,' said the Southlander. 'Is this you, Robin M'Combich, or your wraith?'

'It is Robin Oig M'Combich,' answered the Highlander, 'and it is not.—But never mind that, put pe giving me the skene-dhu.'

'What! you are for back to the Highlands—The devil!—Have you selt all of before the fair? This beats all for quick markets!'

'I have not sold—I am not going north—May pe I will never go north again.—Give me pack my dirk, Hugh Morrison, or there will pe words petween us.'

'Indeed, Robin, I'll be better advised before I gie it back to you—it is a wanchancy weapon in a Highlandman's hand, and I am thinking you will be about some barns-breaking.'

'Prutt, trutt! let me have my weapon,' said Robin Oig, impatiently.

'Hooly, and fairly,' said his well-meaning friend. 'I'll tell you what will do better than these dirking doings—Ye ken Highlander, and Lowlander, and Border-men, are a' ae man's bairns when you are over the Scots dyke. See, the Eskdale callants, and fighting Charlie of Liddesdale, and the Lockerby lads, and the four Dandies of Lustruther, and a wheen mair grey plaids, are coming up behind, and if you are wranged, there is the hand of a Manly Morrison, we'll see you righted, if Carlisle and Stanwix baith took up the feud.'

'To tell you the truth,' said Robin Oig, desirous of eluding the suspicions of his friend, 'I have enlisted with a party of the Black Watch, and must march off to-morrow morning.'

'Enlisted! Were you mad or drunk?—You must buy yourself off—I can lend you twenty notes, and twenty to that, if the drove sell.'

'I thank you—thank ye, Hughie; but I go with good will the gate that I am going,—so the dirk—the dirk!'

'There it is for you then, since less wunna serve. But think on what I was saying.—Waes me, it will be sair news in the braes of Balquidder, that Robin Oig M'Combich should have run an ill gate, and ta'en on.'

'Ill news in Balquidder, indeed!' echoed poor Robin. 'But Cot speed you, Hughie, and send you good marcats. Ye winna meet with Robin Oig again, either at tryste or fair.'

So saying, he shook hastily the hand of his acquaintance, and set out in the direction from which he had advanced, with the spirit of his former pace.

'There is something wrang with the lad,' muttered the Morrison to himself, 'but we'll maybe see better into the morn's morning.'

But long ere the morning dawned, the catastrophe of our tale had taken place. It was two hours after the affray had happened, and it was totally forgotten by almost every one, when Robin Oig returned to Heskett's inn. The place was filled at once by various sorts of men, and with noises corresponding to their character. There were the grave low sounds of men engaged in busy traffic, with the laugh, the song, and the riotous jest of those who had nothing to do but enjoy themselves. Among the last was Harry Wakefield, who, amidst a grinning group of smock-frocks, hobnailed shoes, and jolly English physiognomies, was trolling forth the old ditty,

> *What though my name be Roger,*
> *Who drives the plough and cart . . .*

when he was interrupted by a well-known voice saying in a high and stern tone, marked by the sharp Highland accent, 'Harry Waakfelt—if you be a man, stand up!'

'What is the matter?—what is it?' the guests demanded of each other.

'It is only a d——d Scotsman,' said Fleecebumpkin, who was by this time very drunk, 'whom Harry Wakefield helped to his broth the day, who is now come to have his *cauld kail* het again.'

'Harry Waakfelt,' repeated the same ominous summons, 'stand up, if you be a man!'

There is something in the tone of deep and concentrated passion, which attracts attention and imposes awe, even by the very sound. The guests shrank back on every side, and gazed at the Highlander as he stood in the middle of them, his brows bent, and his features rigid with resolution.

'I will stand up with all my heart, Robin, my boy, but it shall be to shake hands with you, and drink down all unkindness. It is not the fault of your heart, man, that you don't know how to clench your hands.'

But this time he stood opposite to his antagonist; his open and unsuspecting look strangely contrasted with the stern purpose, which gleamed wild, dark, and vindictive in the eyes of the Highlander.

'''Tis not thy fault, man, that not having the luck to be an Englishman, thou canst not fight more than a schoolgirl.'

'I *can* fight,' answered Robin Oig sternly, but calmly, 'and you shall know it. You, Harry Waakfelt, showed me to-day how the Saxon churls fight——I show you now how the Highland Dunnièwassel fights.'

He seconded the word with the action, and plunged the dagger, which he suddenly displayed, into the broad chest of the English yeoman, with such fatal certainty and force, that the hilt made a hollow sound against the breast-bone, and the double-edged point split the very heart of his victim. Harry Wakefield fell and expired with a single groan. His assassin next seized the bailiff by the collar, and offered the blood poniard to his throat, whilst dread and surprise rendered the man incapable of defence.

'It were very just to lay you beside him,' he said, 'but the blood of a base pick-thank shall never mix on my father's dirk with that of a brave man.'

As he spoke, he cast the man from him with so much force that he fell on the floor, while Robin, with his other hand, threw the fatal weapon into the blazing turf-fire.

'There,' he said, 'take me who likes——and let fire cleanse blood if it can.'

The pause of astonishment still continuing, Robin Oig asked for a peace-officer, and a constable having stepped out, he surrendered himself to his custody.

'A bloody night's work you have made of it,' said the constable.

'Your own fault,' said the Highlander. 'Had you kept his hands off me twa hours since, he would have been now as well and merry as he was twa minutes since.'

'It must be sorely answered,' said the peace-officer.

'Never mind that—death pays all debts; it will pay that too.'

The horror of the bystanders began now to give way to indignation; and the sight of a favourite companion murdered in the midst of them, the provocation being, in their opinion, so utterly inadequate to the excess of vengeance, might have induced them to kill the perpetrator of the deed upon the spot. The constable, however, did his duty on this occasion, and with the assistance of some of the more reasonable persons present, procured horses to guard the prisoner to Carlisle, to abide his doom at the next assizes. While the escort was preparing, the prisoner neither expressed the least interest nor attempted the slightest reply. Only, before he was carried from the fatal apartment, he desired to look at the dead body, which, raised from the floor, had been deposited upon a large table (at the head of which Harry Wakefield had presided but a few minutes before, full of life, vigour, and animation) until the surgeons should examine the mortal wound. The face of the corpse was decently covered with a napkin. To the surprise and horror of the bystanders, which displayed itself in a general *Ah!* drawn through clenched teeth and half-shut lips, Robin Oig removed the cloth, and gazed with a mournful but steady eye on the lifeless visage, which had been so lately animated that the smile of good-humoured confidence in his own strength, of conciliation at once and contempt towards his enemy, still curled his lip. While those present expected that the wound, which had so lately flooded the apartment with gore, would send forth fresh streams at the touch of the homicide, Robin Oig replaced the covering with the brief exclamation—'He was a pretty man!'

My story is nearly ended. The unfortunate Highlander stood his trial at Carlisle. I was myself present, and as a young Scottish lawyer, or barrister at least, and reputed a man of some quality, the politeness of the Sheriff of Cumberland offered me a place on the bench. The facts of the case were proved in the manner I have related them; and whatever might be at first the prejudice of the audience against a crime so un-English as that of assassination from revenge, yet when the rooted national prejudices of the prisoner had been explained, which made him consider himself as stained with indelible dishonour when subjected to personal violence; when his previous patience, moderation, and endurance were considered, the generosity of the English audience was inclined to regard his crime as the wayward aberration of a false idea of honour rather than as flowing from a heart naturally savage, or perverted by habitual vice. I shall never forget the charge of the venerable judge to the jury, although not at that time liable to be much affected either by that which was eloquent or pathetic.

'We have had,' he said, 'in the previous part of our duty' (alluding to some former trials) 'to discuss crimes which infer disgust and abhorrence, while they call down the well-merited vengeance of the law. It is now our still more melancholy task to apply its salutary though severe enactments to a case of a very singular character, in which the crime (for a crime it is, and a deep one) arose less out of the malevolence of the heart, than the error of the understanding—less from an idea of committing wrong, than from an unhappily perverted notion of that which is right. Here we have two men, highly esteemed, it has been stated, in their rank of life, and attached, it seems, to each other as friends, one of whose lives has been already sacrificed to a punctilio, and the other is about to prove the vengeance of the offended law; and yet both may claim our commiseration at least, as men acting in ignorance of each other's national prejudices, and unhappily misguided rather than voluntarily erring from the path of right conduct.

'In the original cause of the misunderstanding, we must in justice give the right to the prisoner at the bar. He had acquired possession of the enclosure, which was the object of competition, by a legal contract with the proprietor, Mr. Ireby; and yet, when accosted with reproaches undeserved in themselves, and galling doubtless to a temper at least sufficiently susceptible of passion, he offered notwithstanding to yield up half his acquisition for the sake of peace and good neighbourhood, and his amicable proposal was rejected with scorn. Then follows the scene at Mr. Heskett the publican's, and you will observe how the stranger was treated by the deceased, and, I am sorry to observe, by those around, who seem to have urged him in a manner which was aggravating in the highest degree. While he asked for peace and composition, and offered submission to a magistrate, or to a mutual arbiter, the prisoner was insulted by a whole company, who seem on this occasion to have forgotten the national maxim of "fair play"; and while attempting to escape from the place in peace, he was intercepted, struck down, and beaten to the effusion of his blood.

'Gentlemen of the jury, it was with some impatience that I heard my learned brother, who opened the case for the crown, give an unfavourable turn to the prisoner's conduct on this occasion. He said the prisoner was afraid to encounter his antagonist in fair fight, or to submit to the laws of the ring; and that therefore, like a cowardly Italian, he had recourse to his fatal stiletto, to murder the man whom he dared not meet in manly encounter. I observed the prisoner shrink from this part of the accusation with the abhorrence natural to a brave man; and as I would wish to make my words impressive when I point his real crime, I must secure his opinion of my impartiality, by rebutting everything that seems to me a false accusation. There can be no doubt that the prisoner is a man of resolution—too much resolution—I wish to Heaven that he had less, or rather that he had had a better education to regulate it.

'Gentlemen, as to the laws my brother talks of, they may be known in the bull-ring, or the bear-garden, or the cockpit, but they are not known here. Or, if they should be so far admitted as furnishing a species of proof that no malice was intended in this sort of combat, from which fatal accidents do sometimes arise, it can only be so admitted when both parties are *in pari casu*, equally acquainted with, and equally willing to refer themselves to, that species of arbitrament. But will it be contended that a man of superior rank and education is to be subjected, or is obliged to subject himself, to this coarse and brutal strife, perhaps in opposition to a younger, stronger, or more skilful opponent? Certainly even the pugilistic code, if founded upon the fair play of Merry Old England, as my brother alleges it to be, can contain nothing so preposterous. And, gentlemen of the jury, if the laws would support an English gentleman, wearing, we will suppose, his sword, in defending himself by force against a violent personal aggression of the nature offered to this prisoner, they will not less protect a foreigner and a stranger, involved in the same unpleasing circumstances. If, therefore, gentlemen of the jury, when thus pressed by a *vis major,* the object of obloquy to a whole company, and of direct violence from one at least, and, as he might reasonably apprehend, from more, the panel had produced the weapon which his countrymen, as we are informed, generally carry about their persons, and the same unhappy circumstance had ensued which you have heard detailed in evidence, I could not in my conscience have asked from you a verdict of murder. The prisoner's personal defence might, indeed, even in that case, have gone more or less beyond the *Moderamen inculpatae tutelae,* spoken of by lawyers, but the punishment incurred would have been that of manslaughter, not of murder. I beg leave to add that I should have thought this milder species of charge was demanded in the case supposed, notwithstanding the statute of James 1 cap. 8, which takes the case of slaughter by stabbing with a short weapon, even without malice prepense, out of the benefit of clergy. For this statute of stabbing, as it is termed, arose out of a temporary cause; and as the real guilt is the same, whether the slaughter be committed by the dagger, or the sword or pistol, the benignity of the modern law places them all on the same, or nearly the same footing.

'But, gentlemen of the jury, the pinch of the case lies in the interval of two hours interposed betwixt the reception of the injury and the fatal retaliation. In the heat of affray and *chaude mêlée,* law, compassionating the infirmities of humanity, makes allowance for the passions which rule such a stormy moment—for the sense of present pain, for the apprehension of further injury, for the difficulty of ascertaining with due accuracy the precise degree of violence which is necessary to protect the person of the individual, without annoying or injuring the assailant more than is absolutely requisite. But the time necessary to walk twelve miles, however speedily performed, was an interval sufficient for the prisoner to have recollected himself; and the violence with so many circumstances of deliberate determination, could neither be induced by the passion of anger, nor that of fear. It was the purpose and the act of predetermined revenge, for which law neither can, will, nor ought to have sympathy or allowance.

'It is true, we may repeat to ourselves, in alleviation of this poor man's unhappy action, that his case is a very peculiar one. The country which he inhabits was, in the days of many now alive, inaccessible to the laws, not only of England, which have not even yet penetrated thither, but to those to which our neighbours of Scotland are subjected, and which must be supposed to be, and no doubt actually are, founded upon the general principles of justice and equity which pervade every civilized country. Amongst their mountains, as among the North American Indians, the various tribes were wont to make war upon each other, so that each man was obliged to go armed for his protection. These men, from the ideas which they entertained of their own descent and of their own consequence, regarded themselves as so many cavaliers or men-at-arms, rather than as the peasantry of a peaceful country. Those laws of the ring, as my brother terms them, were unknown to the race of warlike mountaineers; that decision of quarrels by no other weapons than those which nature has given every man, must to them have seemed as vulgar and as preposterous as to the noblesse of France. Revenge, on the other hand, must have been as familiar to their habits of society as to those of the Cherokees or Mohawks. It is indeed, as described by Bacon, at bottom a kind of wild untutored justice; for the fear of retaliation must withhold the hands of the oppressor where there is no regular law to check daring violence. But though all this may be granted, and though we may allow that, such having been the case of the Highlands in the days of the prisoner's fathers, many of the opinions and sentiments must still continue to influence the present generation, it cannot, and ought not, even in this most painful case, to alter the administration of the law, either in your hands, gentlemen of the jury, or in mine. The first object of civilization is to place the general protection of the law, equally administered, in the room of that wild justice, which every man cut and carved for himself, according to the length of his sword and the strength of his arm. The law says to the subjects, with a voice only inferior to that of the Diety, 'Vengeance is mine.' The instant that there is time for passion to cool, and reason to interpose, an injured party must become aware that the law assumes the exclusive cognizance of the right and wrong betwixt the parties, and opposes her inviolable buckler to every attempt of the private party to right himself. I repeat, that this unhappy man ought personally to be the object rather of our pity than our abhorrence, for he failed in his ignorance, and from mistaken notions of honour. But his crime is not the less that of murder, gentlemen, and, in your high and important office, it is your duty so to find. Englishmen have their angry passions as well as Scots; and should this man's action remain unpunished, you may unsheath, under various pretences, a thousand daggers betwixt the Land's-end and the Orkneys.'

The venerable judge thus ended what, to judge by his apparent emotion, and by the tears which filled his eyes, was really a painful task. The jury, according to his instructions, brought in a verdict of Guilty; and Robin Oig M'Combich *alias* M'Gregor, was sentenced to death and left for execution, which took place accordingly. He met his fate with great firmness, and acknowledged the justice of his sentence. But he repelled indignantly the observations of those who accused him of attacking an unarmed man. 'I give a life for the life I took,' he said, 'and what can I do more?'

The Murder Hole

CATHERINE SINCLAIR

Ah, frantic Fear!
I see, I see thee near;
I know thy hurried step, thy hagard eye!
Like thee I start, like thee disorder'd fly!
—COLLINS

In a remote district of country belonging to Lord Cassillis, between Ayrshire and Galloway, about three hundred years ago, a moor of apparently boundless extent stretched several miles along the road, and wearied the eye of the traveller by the sameness and desolation of its appearance; not a tree varied the prospect—not a shrub enlivened the eye by its freshness—nor a native flower bloomed to adorn this ungenial soil. One 'lonesome desert' reached the horizon on every side, with nothing to mark that any mortal had ever visited the scene before, except a few rude huts that were scattered near its centre; and a road, or rather pathway, for those whom business or necessity obliged to pass in that direction. At length, deserted as this wild region had always been, it became still more gloomy. Strange rumours arose, that the path of unwary travellers had been beset on this 'blasted heath,' and that treachery and murder had intercepted the solitary stranger as he traversed its dreary extent. When several persons, who were known to have passed that way, mysteriously disappeared, the inquiries of their relatives led to a strict and anxious investigation; but though the officers of justice were sent to scour the country, and examine the inhabitants, not a trace could be obtained of the persons in question, nor of any place of concealment which could be a refuge for the lawless or desperate to horde in. Yet, as inquiry became stricter, and the disappearance of individuals more frequent, the simple inhabitants of the neighbouring hamlet were agitated by the most fearful apprehensions. Some declared that the death-like stillness of the night was often interrupted by sudden and preternatural cries of more than mortal anguish, which seemed to arise in the distance; and a shepherd one evening, who had lost his way on the moor, declared he had approached three mysterious figures, who seemed struggling against each other with supernatural energy, till at length one of them, with a frightful scream, suddenly sunk into the earth.

Gradually the inhabitants deserted their dwellings on the heath, and settled in distant quarters, till at length but one of the cottages continued to be inhabited by an old woman and her two sons, who loudly lamented that poverty chained them to this solitary and mysterious spot. Travellers who frequented this road now generally did so in groups to protect each other; and if night overtook them, they usually stopped at the humble cottage of the old woman and her sons, where cleanliness compensated for the want of luxury, and where, over a blazing fire of peat, the bolder spirits smiled at the imaginary terrors of the road, and the more timid trembled as they listened to the tales of terror and affright with which their hosts entertained them.

One gloomy and tempestuous night in November, a pedlar boy hastily traversed the moor. Terrified to find himself involved in darkness amidst its boundless wastes, a thousand frightful traditions, connected with this dreary scene, darted across his mind—every blast, as it swept in hollow gusts over the heath, seemed to teem with the sighs of departed spirits— and the birds, as they winged their way above his head, appeared, with loud and shrill cries, to warn him of approaching danger. The whistle with which he usually beguiled his weary pilgrimage died away into silence, and he groped along with trembling and uncertain steps, which sounded too loudly in his ears. The promise of Scripture occurred to his memory, and revived his courage. 'I will be unto thee as a rock in the desert, and as an hiding-place in the storm.' *Surely,* thought he, *though alone, I am not forsaken;* and a prayer for assistance hovered on his lips.

A light now glimmered in the distance which would lead him, he conjectured, to the cottage of the old woman; and towards that he eagerly bent his way, remembering as he hastened along, that when he had visited it the year before, it was in company with a large party of travellers, who had beguiled the evening with those tales of mystery which had so lately filled his brain with images of terror. He recollected, too, how anxiously the old woman and her sons had endeavoured to detain him when the other travellers were departing; and now, therefore, he confidently anticipated a cordial and cheering reception. His first call for admission obtained no visible marks of attention, but instantly the greatest noise and confusion prevailed within the cottage. They think it is one of the supernatural visitants of whom the old lady talks so much, thought the boy, approaching a window, where the light within shewed him all the inhabitants at their several occupations; the old woman was hastily scrubbing the stone floor, and strewing it thickly over with sand, while her two sons seemed with equal haste to be thrusting something large and heavy into an immense chest, which they carefully locked. The boy, in a frolicsome mood, thoughtlessly tapped at the window, when they all instantly started up with consternation so strongly depicted on their countenances, that he shrunk back involuntarily with an undefined feeling of apprehension; but before he had time to reflect a moment longer, one of the men suddenly darted out at the door, and seizing the boy roughly by the shoulder, dragged him violently into the cottage. 'I am not what you take me for,' said the boy, attempting to laugh, 'but only the poor pedlar who visited you last year.' 'Are you *alone?*' inquired the old woman, in a harsh deep tone, which made his heart thrill with apprehension. 'Yes,' said the boy, 'I am alone *here;* and alas!' he added, with a burst of uncontrollable feeling, 'I am alone in the wide world also! Not a person exists who would assist me in distress, or shed a single tear if I died this very night.' '*Then* you are welcome!' said one of the men with a sneer, while he cast a glance of peculiar expression at the other inhabitants of the cottage.

It was with a shiver of apprehension, rather than of cold, that the boy drew towards the fire, and the looks which the old woman and her sons exchanged, made him wish that he had preferred the shelter of any one of the roofless cottages which were scattered near, rather than trust himself among persons of such dubious aspect. Dreadful surmises flitted across his brain; and terrors which he could neither combat nor examine imperceptibly stole into his mind; but alone, and beyond the reach of assistance, he resolved to smother his suspicions, or at least not increase the danger by revealing them. The room to which he retired for the night had a confused and desolate aspect; the curtains seemed to have been violently torn down from the bed, and still hung in tatters around it—the table seemed to have been broken by some violent concussion, and the fragments of various pieces of furniture lay scattered upon the floor. The boy begged that a light might burn in his apartment till he was asleep, and anxiously examined the fastenings of the door; but they seemed to have been wrenched asunder on some former occasion, and were still left rusty and broken.

It was long ere the pedlar attempted to compose his agitated nerves to rest; but at length his senses began to 'steep themselves in forgetfulness,' though his imagination remained painfully active, and presented new scenes of terror to his mind, with all the vividness of reality. He fancied himself again wandering on the heath, which appeared to be peopled with spectres, who all beckoned to him not to enter the cottage, and as he approached it, they vanished with a hollow and despairing cry. The scene then changed, and he found himself again seated by the fire, where the countenances of the men scowled upon him with the most terrifying malignity, and he thought the old woman suddenly seized him by the arms, and pinioned them to his side. Suddenly the boy was startled from these agitated slumbers, by what sounded to him like a cry of distress; he was broad awake in a moment, and sat up in bed,—but the noise was not repeated, and he endeavoured to persuade himself it had only been a continuation of the fearful images which had disturbed his rest, when, on glancing at the door, he observed underneath it a broad red stream of blood silently stealing its course along the floor. Frantic with alarm, it was but the work of a moment to spring from his bed, and rush to the door, through a chink of which, his eye nearly dimmed with affright, he could watch unsuspected whatever might be done in the adjoining room.

His fear vanished instantly when he perceived that it was only a *goat* that they had been slaughtering; and he was about to steal into his bed again, ashamed of his groundless apprehensions, when his ear was arrested by a conversation which transfixed him aghast with terror to the spot.

'This is an easier job than you had yesterday,' said the man who held the goat. 'I wish all the throats we've cut were as easily and quietly done. Did you ever hear such a noise as the old gentleman made last night! It was well we had no neighbour within a dozen of miles, or they must have heard his cries for help and mercy.'

'Don't speak of it,' replied the other; 'I was never fond of bloodshed.'

'Ha! ha!' said the other, with a sneer, 'you say so, do you?'

'I do,' answered the first, gloomily; 'the Murder Hole is the thing for me—*that* tells no tales—a single scuffle—a single plunge—and the fellow's dead and buried to your hand in a moment. I would defy all the officers in Christendom to discover any mischief *there*.'

'Ay, Nature did us a good turn when she contrived such a place as that. Who that saw a hole in the heath, filled with clear water, and so small that the long grass meets over the top of it, would suppose that the depth is unfathomable, and that it conceals more than forty people who have met their deaths there?—it sucks them in like a leech!'

'How do you mean to dispatch the lad in the next room?' asked the old woman in an under tone. The elder son made her a sign to be silent, and pointed towards the door where their trembling auditor was concealed; while the other, with an expression of brutal ferocity, passed his bloody knife across his throat.

The pedlar boy possessed a bold and daring spirit, which was now roused to desperation; but in any open resistance the odds were so completely against him, that flight seemed his best resource. He gently stole to the window, and having by one desperate effort broke the rusty bolt by which the casement had been fastened, he let himself down without noise or difficulty. This betokens good, thought he, pausing an instant in dreadful hesitation what direction to take. This momentary deliberation was fearfully interrupted by the hoarse voice of the men calling aloud, *'The boy has fled—let loose the blood-hound!'* These words sunk like a death-knell on his heart, for escape appeared now impossible, and his nerves seemed to melt away like wax in a furnace. Shall I perish without a struggle! thought he, rousing himself to exertion, and, helpless and terrified as a hare pursued by its ruthless hunters, he fled across the heath. Soon the baying of the blood-hound broke the stillness of the night, and the voice of its masters sounded through the moor, as they endeavoured to accelerate its speed,—panting and breathless the boy pursued his hopeless career, but every moment his pursuers seemed to gain upon his failing steps. The hound was unimpeded by the darkness which was to him so impenetrable, and its noise rung louder and deeper on his ear—while the lanterns which were carried by the men gleamed near and distinct upon his vision.

At his fullest speed, the terrified boy fell with violence over a heap of stones, and having nothing on but his shirt, he was severely cut in every limb. With one wild cry to Heaven for assistance, he continued prostrate on the earth, bleeding, and nearly insensible. The hoarse voices of the men, and the still louder baying of the dog, were now so near, that instant destruction seemed inevitable,—already he felt himself in their fangs, and the bloody knife of the assassin appeared to gleam before his eyes,—despair renewed his energy, and once more, in an agony of affright that seemed verging towards madness, he rushed forward so rapidly that terror seemed to have given wings to his feet. A loud cry near the spot he had left arose on his ears without suspending his flight. The hound had stopped at the place where the pedlar's wounds bled so profusely, and deeming the chase now over, it lay down there, and could not be induced to proceed; in vain the men beat it with frantic violence, and tried again to put the hound on the scent,—the sight of blood had satisfied the animal that its work was done, and with dogged resolution it resisted every inducement to pursue the same scent a second time. The pedlar boy in the meantime paused not in his flight till morning dawned—and still as he fled, the noise of steps seemed to pursue him, and the cry of his assassins still sounded in the distance. Ten miles off he reached a village, and spread instant alarm throughout the neighbourhood—the inhabitants were aroused with one accord into a tumult of indignation—several of them had lost sons, brothers, or friends on the heath, and all united in proceeding instantly to seize the old woman and her sons, who were nearly torn to pieces by their violence. Three gibbets were immediately raised on the moor, and the wretched culprits confessed before their execution to the destruction of nearly fifty victims in the Murder Hole which they pointed out, and near which they suffered the penalty of their crimes. The bones of several murdered persons were with difficulty brought up from the abyss into which they had been thrust; but so narrow is the aperture, and so extraordinary the depth, that all who see it are inclined to coincide in the tradition of the country people that it is unfathomable. The scene of these events still continues nearly as it was 300 years ago. The remains of the old cottage, with its blackened walls, (haunted of course by a thousand evil spirits) and the extensive moor, on which a more modern *inn* (if it can be dignified with such an epithet) resembles its predecessor in every thing but the character of its inhabitants; the landlord is deformed, but possesses extraordinary genius; he has himself manufactured a violin, on which he plays with untaught skill,—and if any *discord* be heard in the house, or any *murder* committed in it, *this* is his only instrument. His daughter (who has never travelled beyond the heath) has inherited her father's talent, and learnt all his tales of terror and superstition, which she relates with infinite spirit; but when you are led by her across the heath to drop a stone into that deep and narrow gulf to which our story relates,—when you stand on its slippery edge, and (parting the long grass with which it is covered) gaze into its mysterious depths,—when she describes, with all the animation of an *eye-witness,* the struggle of the victims grasping the grass as a last hope of preservation, and trying to drag in their assassin as an expiring effort of vengeance,—when you are told that for 300 years the clear waters in this diamond of the desert have remained untasted by mortal lips, and that the solitary traveller is still pursued at night by the howling of the blood-hound,—it is *then only* that it is possible fully to appreciate the terrors of THE MURDER HOLE.

Muruer So Cool

GUY N. SMITH

e're probably wasting our time." Detective Chief Inspector Brown pulled the brim of his hat down in an attempt to shield his dour features from the rain which lashed down from the surrounding mountains. "My guess is that it's just an unfortunate accident. But it happens to be a high profile tragedy soon after the opening of Glendower, Scotland's answer to Silverstone. The owners' ambition is that Glendower will be to motor racing what Gleneagles is to golf. This business is in the public eye, on the front page of every newspaper and we have to be seen to be doing something, Odell, because the Masterson team is claiming that Jim Tracy's car was sabotaged by the Caliari team. I was praying that the forensic examination of the wrecked car would unearth some mechanical fault that had caused Tracy to go out of control. But it didn't and the buck has been passed on to us. One paper is even claiming that there's a hoodoo on Glendower, that the laird who owned the land before the turn of the century has put a curse on it—when the estate went bankrupt the land was sold to the highest bidder. Sure, this was once the home of red deer and the race track has driven the herds to seek new pastures but that's the way of the world today. Anyway, I'll feel easier knowing that you've investigated the case. The last thing I want is some piece of damning evidence coming to light at a later stage."

"Well, I'll see what I can do." Raymond Odell was tall and lean. It was difficult to judge his age from those lived-in aquiline features. He had worked with Brown in the Glasgow Force years ago before taking early retirement. But retirement had proved dull and Odell had returned to his old job in a private capacity. The official force were jealous of him, even

Brown sometimes, he guessed. But they were glad enough of his help when they came up against something they couldn't handle. Like the Glendower tragedy.

A much younger fair-haired man watched and listened intently. Tommy Bourne had worked with Odell since qualifying for a criminology degree at college. Jobs were not easy to come by north of the border and Tommy's uncle, a police sergeant at Inverness, had known Odell well. So Odell had taken the young man on a six month trial period. The situation had become permanent and the two men now worked as a team. They had an impressive record of successes, often cases that the police had consigned to their unsolved files. This might be just another of those.

Odell was on his hands and knees examining the burned out remains of what had been claimed to be the most up-to-date Formula 1 car ever to go on circuit. It had lasted a mere three laps.

Tommy gazed in awe from Pit 1 out across the famous circuit, standing on an elevated platform outside the entrance which commanded an unrestricted view of the track, a position usually occupied by one of the maintenance crew where, as well as monitoring the race, a fault which was not yet obvious to the driver might be spotted as the car approached. He had watched the first ever competition held at Glendower on television. It had been hyped as a new era in motor racing, certainly a boost for the Scottish economy. Never in his wildest dreams had he anticipated standing right here in what, for himself, had already become a shrine. It was exactly like it had been on television, he experienced a momentary sense of unreality. He recalled every detail, even the charred patch, barely fifty yards from the pit, where former world champion Jim Tracy had crashed attempting to regain his crown. That had been shown on the evening news yesterday. Just looking across from here sent shivers up Tommy's spine. With an effort he forced himself back to reality. If there had been sabotage, even murder, then he and Odell would need to draw upon every reserve of their powers of deduction to solve it.

The pit had a touch of luxuriousness amidst its oil and grease. An adjacent room was fitted with easy chairs and a table, there were cooking facilities and a small cooler where team members could fix themselves iced drinks.

"Well, the experts have gone through the remains of the car with a fine tooth comb," Odell straightened up, wiped his hands on a piece of rag, "so there's little point in a layman wasting his time trying to unravel mechanical technicalities. Now, let's have a look around the pit . . ."

Tools and equipment hung from hooks, others were laid out on benches in a neat array in readiness for when they were needed to carry out a split second repair or to change a set of wheels. On the nearest bench lay a pair of powerful binoculars. The Glasgow detective picked them up, examined them. "Doubtless kept here for the purpose of scrutinizing the team car," he murmured to himself. "Hmm, what's this?"

Tommy and Brown peered over Odell's shoulder, saw a circular scratch that had scored the surface of the binoculars just below the lens adjustment.

"It looks like some kind of attachment has been screwed to it at some stage," Raymond Odell muttered, scrutinized it with the aid of his powerful lens before returning it to the bench. "Interesting," he turned back to his companions, "I think before we go any further I'd better have a word with the Masterson team, Frank Masterson himself and then the mechanics. Then I'll talk to the Caliari team. I think we need to hear both sides of the story in this bitter feud, don't you?"

"He was a brilliant driver," Frank Masterson spoke scathingly, "but he hit his peak and after that there was only one way he was going—downhill. There was no way he would ever be world champion again. I tried to tell him that but he wouldn't listen. Head's too big for his helmet, always was. Downright snob, too. He was gutted when his daughter, Claire, started going out with one of the mechanics." Masterson laughed. "Just imagine it, a world champion's daughter going to marry a mechanic out of the pit! Claire was so besotted with young Sam Wyman that for maybe the first time in her life she actually stood up to her father. There was a row and she walked out of the family home. Personally, I wish the couple well, good luck to the girl for sticking to her principles even though her father threatened to cut her out of his will. He wanted me to fire Sam Wyman. No way! What the team do in their own time is their business. Then I poured salt in the wound by telling Jim Tracy that I wasn't keeping him on after the end of the season. He went beserk at first, then settled back down to racing with even more determination than before. He was out to show me and the rest of the world that he could make it back to world champion again. I wished him luck but I knew damned well that there was no way he would ever hit that kind of form again. Of course, the Caliari team still regarded Jim as their most serious rival and, to be honest, it wouldn't surprise me if in some way they were responsible for Jim's death, something so clever that it left no trace and it will always go down in the records as just another accident." Masterson shrugged his shoulders in resignation.

"Had there been any threats?" Odell's eyes narrowed.

"Aye, a couple," the other nodded. "Telephone threats to Jim's home a week or so ago. Somebody somehow got hold of his ex-directory number. Guy with an Italian accent. That doesn't necessarily mean that it was one of the Caliari team, it could just have been a deranged fan of theirs and nothing at all to do with them personally. There's plenty of Italians living in Britain, not to mention those who have come over here specially to watch the heats. But the team were using the media, trying to drum up publicity, and there's nothing the public likes better than hostile rivalry. It was all a bit over the top. Agnelli, their manager, was quoted as saying that Jim Tracy was likely to kill himself trying to regain his world title. Which gets me thinking . . ."

"How long has Wyman worked with the team?" Odell asked.

"Four years. Prior to that he was apprenticed to the gun trade in Edinburgh. He was an all-round first class mechanic, he might even have set up as a clockmaker, he was that versatile. Anything technical and Sam could adapt to it, he had that kind of brain. As I've already said, I think that somehow the Caliari team are responsible for Jim's death, they've fixed it so that it looks like an accident, done something that even the forensic guys won't be able to rumble."

"We mustn't jump to conclusions," Raymond Odell smiled. "Now, I'd like to talk to Sam Wyman. From what you tell me he probably knew Jim Tracy as well as anybody, for better or for worse."

Sam Wyman was in his mid-twenties, fair-haired and with blue eyes that met the detective's gaze unwaveringly. "Yes," he replied to Odell's question, "I'm going to marry Claire Tracy but we're going to wait a little while in view of her father's tragic death. She's upset, all the more so because they parted on such bad terms. Me, I don't bear Jim a grudge, there's no point. He thought his daughter was marrying beneath her but she stuck to her guns. Whether Jim lived or died it would have made no difference. Anyway, knowing Jim as I did, I guess he would have come round to it and accepted me in due course. He was that kind of fella, hot-headed. I let it all wash over me. I'm a member of the Masterson team and Jim was still their number one driver. It was my duty to do everything I could to make sure he won."

"Was there a rivalry between you and Jim Tracy at work?"

"No, we were both professionals, we kept our grievances to our private lives. Professionally, we were both part of a team. I didn't have a lot to do with him, just helped change the wheels or do whatever was necessary when he came into the pit. Apart from that, in recent weeks I rarely saw him."

"Do you mix with the Caliari team at all?"

"You gotta be joking!" Wyman laughed. "They'd cut our throats as soon as look at us. Imagine returning to Italy if you'd lost. That time they lost the World Cup there were crowds waiting at the airport, baying for the blood of the manager and the team. The Caliari team are out to win, by fair means or foul. And if they could get away with killing Jim Tracy, they wouldn't think twice about it."

"You witnessed the accident?"

"Yeah," Wyman grimaced. "I was standing up on the observation platform as Tracy approached. He looked to be doing fine, nothing amiss as far as I could see although there must've been. Then, suddenly, he seemed to lose control and within seconds the car was an inferno. I'll never forget it as long as I live. I guess it could happen to any driver at any level, and there's not a thing he can do about it. I tell you, next time I do a couple of laps it'll be uppermost in my mind."

"You've ambitions of your own on the circuit," it was a statement, not a question, for Odell knew that there were few mechanics without aspirations that went beyond working in the pits.

"I guess so," Sam Wyman grinned, "I've done a few fair laps this year but I've a long way to go. Four years ago I was working in the gun trade but it was a dead end job. Motor racing was always my first love. High profile, if you know what I mean. Now that they've banned handguns you don't even have the hope of winning a Gold Medal pistol shooting at the Olympics but, in any case, it's nowhere near as glamorous as winning on the race track. There's nothing like motor racing to get the adrenalin pumping. So I thought I'd use my mechanical skills in the pits and take every opportunity I could to get behind the wheel and see how it went from there."

"A sensible approach," Odell turned away, addressed Brown. "Now, I think I'll speak with Agnelli, the Caliari manager. I'd be interested to discover whether this rivalry between the teams is all just hot-air hype or whether he does really hate the opposition."

Agnelli was a small, excitable man, gesticulating as he spoke. He clearly resented being interrupted during his preparations for the morrow's heats. "Tracy was too old for racing," he waved his hands. "As you people in Britain say, he was . . . 'over the hill'. He would not have won, anyway, so why should my team want to kill him?"

"But he was still one of the top racing drivers in the world," Odell regarded the other closely. "He *might* just have won, his experience telling where it counted."

"*Pah!*" Agnelli snapped. "Three years ago, yes. Today, tomorrow, no. No chance."

"Yet, by what you told the newspapers, your vitriolic attacks on Tracy, you still regarded him as a serious rival."

"Because it is what the public want to hear, bitter rivalry," the Italian retorted. "The Caliari team will qualify tomorrow, in first place. Tracy would have been no threat to us. But these accusations are upsetting the team," the other began shouting, "and I cannot tolerate them. I shall sue for a lot of money if they continue!"

"'He protesteth too much'," Brown quoted wryly as they left the Caliari headquarters, "which makes me think that there may not be smoke without fire."

"Perhaps, but it's his way," Odell answered. "We mustn't jump to conclusions. Now, if it's possible, I should like to look at Tracy's body."

"As you wish. I should think that the postmortem will be completed by now and the body will be in the hospital mortuary. However, the pathologist will have missed nothing, I can assure you. I have worked with Colin Douglas too long to doubt his capabilities."

"All the same, I'd still like to take a look," Odell walked briskly towards their parked car, Brown and Tommy at his heels.

"As you can see for yourself, Mister Odell," Colin Douglas was tall with greying hair, an austere man who was not accustomed to having his work questioned, "the body is scarcely recognizable—badly burned and with multiple injuries, several of which on their own could have been responsible for his death. Which ever one he died from, death was instantaneous, I can assure you."

"I'm merely looking for my own satisfaction," Odell was undeterred as he leaned over the charred corpse. Tracy had innumerable cuts and lacerations, limbs were broken, his flesh was blackened by the intense heat. Douglas spoke the truth. If murder had been committed then the means would surely have been in the car itself and forensic tests had so far failed to come up with anything.

"Be my guest," the pathologist's sarcasm was undisguised. "If you find anything I've missed, then you're welcome to my job. I retire next year."

"What's this?" Odell's finger probed the neck, pushed at the charred flesh.

"Just one of many small injuries which in itself is of no consequence," Douglas was at the detective's side instantly, studying the small neat hole which Odell's finger had opened up. "It was probably made by a sliver of metal or glass."

"Just too neat," Odell murmured. "In fact, it's the kind of wound a bullet would leave."

"Except that there is no bullet lodged in the body," Douglas sneered. "If there was, I would have found it. See," his fingers pushed past Odell's, "the hole is only a few millimetres in depth, there is no lodged bullet. There are many ways in which that hole could have been made in that terrible accident. I really do think that you are wasting everybody's time, Mister Odell."

"If so, then I apologize," Raymond Odell was unruffled by the other's scathing comments as he straightened up. "But I don't think I need to take up any more of your time, Mister Douglas. I have seen all that I need to see. Now, Brown, let us proceed to our next call. With a bit of luck we may be on to something."

Neither Brown nor Tommy enquired further. They both knew Raymond Odell only too well. He would explain when he had the full facts and not until.

Sam Wyman lived in a small white-washed cottage on the edge of the rolling moorland, the habitat of grouse and deer, fox and badger, a landscape of purple heather with rugged mountains looming in the background.

"An idyllic retreat," Odell murmured as the three of them walked up the path towards the front door, "and judging by the smoke coming from the chimney there is somebody at home."

But nobody answered their persistent knocking.

"He's maybe lit the fire and gone out . . ." Brown stiffened as the unmistakable sound of a gunshot shattered the rural stillness.

"Come on," Odell turned and led the way round to the rear of the building. "It would seem that our man isn't very far away, after all."

The small rear garden was dominated by a rectangular shed constructed of corrugated tin sheets. Even as the three stood staring at it another shot rang out from within, somewhat muffled by the building.

"But . . . but there was no bullet in Tracy's body," Brown's train of thought was accelerating.

"No, there wasn't," Odell's expression was grim. "That's why we're here now. Let's see what Sam Wyman has to say for himself."

They pushed open the shed door and gazed upon an indoor shooting range. At the far end a number of targets were set in a sandpit. Wyman, wearing ear defenders and totally oblivious of the presence of the detectives, was aligning his pistol for yet another shot.

Crack! He obliterated the bullseye in target No. 3. He was about to swing his sights on to the fourth target when he sensed, rather than heard, his visitors.

"At least we can arrest him for being in possession of an illegal handgun," Brown's officialdom, his training to uphold the law to its very letter, dominated. Odell's upraised hand silenced him. There were far more serious matters at stake.

"*Mister Odell!*" There was both surprise and alarm on Wyman's features. He laid the pistol down on a nearby bench, ripped off his ear defenders. "I didn't expect . . ."

"Of course you didn't," Raymond Odell smiled mirthlessly. "A secret pistol range, hidden from the eyes and ears of the law, eh? But I would have thought that you had done all the shooting you needed to do by now."

"I'm planning to emigrate to the States," Wyman's voice was loaded with panic, "handguns are legal there. I can shoot all I want and . . ."

"Perhaps," Raymond Odell stepped forward, picked up another weapon which was lying on a bench. "Ah, now everything fits!" His tone was one of satisfaction. "My word, this one still has an attachment fitted to it so that it can be screwed to another object such as . . . *a pair of binoculars!*"

"How . . . how could you possibly know?" The other was white and trembling.

"I half guessed at the outset when I found marks on those binoculars that could only mean that some kind of attachment had been fitted to them at some time," Odell was examining the pistol intently, pursed his lips. "An air pistol, .22 calibre. Also a repeater, works on compression. Still, I suppose it had to be a repeater because, however good a shot you are, and I have already witnessed your superb marksmanship, you could not rely on a single shot finding its mark. See," Odell extracted a flexible tubular clip from the weapon, "BB shot, much easier and more effective for your purpose than the standard 'waisted' airgun pellets. I knew that the murder weapon could not possibly be a cartridge-firing one and that left only one other possibility—this!"

"But there was no bullet in Tracy's body," Brown muttered in disbelief.

"So it can't possibly be murder," Wyman shrieked, beginning to panic. "All right, I shouldn't be in possession of handguns but that's all you can get me for."

"You knew very well that no bullet would be found in the corpse," Odell continued. "But there was one originally, and you know that as well as I do. It wasn't powerful enough to kill but it wasn't supposed to be. It was just enough to cause momentary pain and distraction, like a bee sting, enough to make Jim Tracy lose control at high speed. The crash and the ensuing inferno did the rest, killed him and *melted the ice pellet which you had shot him with!*"

Sam Wyman swayed unsteadily on his feet. Brown's supporting hand was firm, held him upright as well as ensuring that the mechanic did not make a dash for the door. Tommy Bourne moved close. Just in case.

"Let me explain fully," these were the moments which Raymond Odell lived for, the final assembly of a jigsaw puzzle and the explanation of detail to a dumbfounded audience. "You were going to marry Claire Tracy in spite of her father's objections. You could have lived with that but not with your future wife losing her considerable inheritance. You saw a way to change all that, to kill Jim Tracy before he altered his will. That way Claire would have her inheritance much sooner than expected. Her mother had died during Claire's childhood and there were no other beneficiaries of Jim's estate. You almost became a rich man. Almost."

Wyman closed his eyes. He did not speak.

"I have no doubt that it was you who phoned Jim Tracy and made those death threats, imitating an Italian accent. That way you added to the suspicion which would undoubtedly fall on the Caliari team if murder was suspected. Two things aroused my suspicions when I examined the Masterson team pit. First, Tracy's accident had occurred within fifty yards of the pit, close enough for him to have been shot from the pit itself. But, if that had happened, then how would the marksman go undetected by other members of the team? The only possible place that would provide him with enough privacy to carry out the shooting was that platform by the entrance. Here the murderer would not only be screened from view but he also had an added field of vision, a vantage point from which to take his time and make sure of his shot. And his target would be getting nearer with every split second."

Detective Chief Inspector Brown pursed his lips in a silent whistle.

"All you required was a few seconds," Odell went on. "Doubtless you resorted to rapid fire with your BB repeater but all you needed was for one pellet to find its mark. Which it did, in Tracy's neck, and that was enough to bring about his death. You had fixed the air pistol to your binoculars; crowds at race tracks are accustomed to seeing team members using binoculars, they would not look twice. The report of an air pistol would go unheard above the roar of the cars. You were pretty safe. If it didn't work today, it would tomorrow. You had time on your side because you knew that Tracy would not go and change his will for a few days. All he had on his mind was the burning desire to win the world championship again."

"But there was no bullet," Wyman protested weakly.

"Yes and no," Odell reached across the bench on which lay cleaning equipment for pistols and a number of other accessories. "You used *this!*" He held up a metal object with a slim cup-shaped end. "A bullet mould. As a gunsmith you had been used to making your own ammunition, moulding bullets for all calibres. So you adapted a .22 bullet mould to make BB pistol pellets, ball bearings, in layman's terms. That was when you hit on the idea of the 'vanishing' bullet. A bullet fashioned out of ice would have exactly the same striking velocity as a lead one and, in any case, the victim's body temperature would melt it. For a trained gunsmith and pistol shot, the task was a relatively simple one. There were even ice cubes in the cooler in the pit rest room for you to use. You didn't have to aim for a bullseye, you only had to hit Jim Tracy somewhere on his body, enough to make him lose control. If you missed, nobody would be any the wiser, you could try again. You could be unlucky time after time but your victim could only be unlucky once. And I think that just about sums it all up."

"If you only knew what he was like, the life he gave Claire," Sam Wyman groaned, "then you'd understand." He did not offer any resistance as Brown clicked the handcuffs.

"If you had killed for that reason alone then I might have some sympathy for you," Raymond Odell snapped. "But your motive was greed. All the same, I have to credit you with ingenuity. It was a clever plot and it was almost the perfect murder. Almost . . . but not quite."

The Body-Snatchers

ROBERT LOUIS STEVENSON

very night in the year, four of us sat in the small parlour of the George at Debenham—the undertaker, and the landlord, and Fettes, and myself. Sometimes there would be more; but blow high, blow low, come rain or snow or frost, we four would be each planted in his own particular armchair. Fettes was an old drunken Scotsman, a man of education obviously, and a man of some property, since he lived in idleness. He had come to Debenham years ago, while still young, and by a mere continuance of living had grown to be an adopted townsman. His blue camlet cloak was a local antiquity, like the church spire. His place in the parlour at the George, his absence from church, his old, crapulous, disreputable vices, were all things of course in Debenham. He had some vague Radical opinions and some fleeting infidelities, which he would now and again set forth and emphasize with tottering slaps upon the table. He drank rum—five glasses regularly every evening; and for the greater portion of his nightly visit to the George sat, with his glass in his right hand, in a state of melancholy alcoholic saturation. We called him the doctor, for he was supposed to have some special knowledge of medicine, and had been known, upon a pinch, to set a fracture or reduce a dislocation; but, beyond these slight particulars, we had no knowledge of his character and antecedents.

One dark winter night—it had struck nine some time before the landlord joined us—there was a sick man in the George, a great neighbouring proprietor suddenly struck down with apoplexy on his way to Parliament; and the great man's still greater London doctor had been telegraphed to his bedside. It was the first time that such a thing had happened in Debenham, for the railway was but newly open, and we were all proportionately moved by the occurrence.

'He's come,' said the landlord, after he had filled and lighted his pipe.

'He?' said I. 'Who?—not the doctor?'

'Himself,' replied our host.

'What is his name?'

'Dr. Macfarlane,' said the landlord.

Fettes was far through his third tumbler, stupidly fuddled, now nodding over, now staring mazily around him; but at the last word he seemed to awaken, and repeated the name 'Macfarlane' twice, quietly enough the first time, but with sudden emotion at the second.

'Yes,' said the landlord, 'that's his name, Dr. Wolfe Macfarlane.'

Fettes became instantly sober; his eyes awoke, his voice became clear, loud, and steady, his language forcible and earnest. We were all startled by the transformation, as if a man had risen from the dead.

'I beg your pardon,' he said; 'I am afraid I have not been paying much attention to your talk. Who is this Wolfe Macfarlane?' And then, when he had heard the landlord out, 'It cannot be, it cannot be,' he added; 'and yet I would like well to see him face to face.'

'Do you know him, doctor?' asked the undertaker, with a gasp.

'God forbid!' was the reply. 'And yet the name is a strange one; it were too much to fancy two. Tell me, landlord, is he old?'

'Well,' said the host, 'he's not a young man, to be sure, and his hair is white; but he looks younger than you.'

'He is older, though; years older. But,' with a slap upon the table, 'it's the rum you see in my face—rum and sin. This man, perhaps, may have an easy conscience and a good digestion. Conscience! Hear me speak. You would think I was some good, old, decent Christian, would you not? But no, not I; I never canted. Voltaire might have canted if he'd stood in my shoes; but the brains'—with a rattling fillip on his bald head—'the brains were clear and active, and I saw and made no deductions.'

'If you know this doctor,' I ventured to remark, after a somewhat awful pause, 'I should gather that you do not share the landlord's good opinion.'

Fettes paid no regard to me.

'Yes,' he said, with sudden decision, 'I must see him face to face.'

There was another pause, and then a door was closed rather sharply on the first floor, and a step was heard upon the stair.

'That's the doctor,' cried the landlord. 'Look sharp, and you can catch him.'

It was but two steps from the small parlour to the door of the old George Inn; the wide oak staircase landed almost in the street; there was room for a Turkey rug and nothing more between the threshold and the last round of the descent; but this little space was every evening brilliantly lit up, not only by the light upon the stair and the great signal-lamp below the sign, but by the warm radiance of the barroom window. The George thus brightly advertised itself to passers-by in the cold street. Fettes walked steadily to the spot, and we, who were hanging behind, beheld the two men meet, as one of them had phrased it, face to face. Dr. Macfarlane was alert and vigorous. His white hair set off his pale and placid, although energetic countenance. He was richly dressed in the finest of broadcloth and the whitest of linen, with a great gold watch-chain, and studs and spectacles of the same precious material. He wore a broad folded tie, white and speckled with lilac, and he carried on his arm a comfortable driving coat of fur. There was no doubt but he became his years, breathing, as he did, of wealth and consideration; and it was a surprising contrast to see our parlour sot—bald, dirty, pimpled, and robed in his old camlet cloak— confront him at the bottom of the stairs.

'Macfarlane!' he said somewhat loudly, more like a herald than a friend.

The great doctor pulled up short on the fourth step, as though the familiarity of the address surprised and somewhat shocked his dignity.

'Toddy Macfarlane!' repeated Fettes.

The London man almost staggered. He stared for the swiftest of seconds at the man before him, glanced behind him with a sort of scare, and then in a startled whisper, 'Fettes!' he said, 'you!'

'Ay,' said the other, 'me! Did you think I was dead, too? We are not so easy shut of our acquaintance.'

'Hush, hush!' exclaimed the doctor. 'Hush, hush! this meeting is so unexpected—I can see you are unmanned. I hardly knew you, I confess, at first; but I am overjoyed—overjoyed to have this opportunity. For the present it must be how-d'ye-do and goodbye in one, for my fly is waiting, and

I must not fail the train; but you shall—let me see—yes—you shall give me your address, and you can count on early news of me. We must do something for you, Fettes. I fear you are out at elbows; but we must see to that for auld lang syne, as once we sang at suppers.'

'Money!' cried Fettes; 'money from you! The money I had from you is lying where I cast it in the rain.'

Dr. Macfarlane had talked himself into some measure of superiority and confidence, but the uncommon energy of this refusal cast him back into his first confusion.

A horrible, ugly look came and went across his almost venerable countenance, 'My dear fellow,' he said, 'be it as you please; my last thought is to offend you. I would intrude on none. I will leave you my address, however—'

'I do not wish it—I do not wish to know the roof that shelters you,' interrupted the other. 'I heard your name; I feared it might be you; I wished to know if, after all, there were a God; I know now that there is none. Begone!'

He still stood in the middle of the rug, between the stair and doorway; and the great London physician, in order to escape, would be forced to step to one side. It was plain that he hesitated before the thought of this humiliation. White as he was, there was a dangerous glitter in his spectacles; but, while he still paused uncertain, he became aware that the driver of his fly was peering in from the street at this unusual scene, and caught a glimpse at the same time of our little body from the parlour, huddled by the corner of the bar. The presence of so many witnesses decided him at once to flee. He crouched together, brushing on the wainscot, and made a dart like a serpent, striking for the door. But his tribulation was not yet entirely at an end, for even as he was passing Fettes clutched him by the arm and these words came in a whisper, and yet painfully distinct, 'Have you seen it again?'

The great rich London doctor cried out aloud with a sharp, throttling cry; he dashed his questioner across the open space, and, with his hands over his head, fled out of the door like a detected thief. Before it had occurred to one of us to make a movement the fly was already rattling toward the station. The scene was over like a dream, but the dream had left proofs and traces of its passage. Next day the servant found the fine gold spectacles broken on the threshold, and that very night we were all standing breathless by the barroom window, and Fettes at our side, sober, pale, and resolute in look.

'God protect us, Mr. Fettes!' said the landlord, coming first into possession of his customary senses. 'What in the universe is all this? These are strange things you have been saying.'

Fettes turned toward us; he looked us each in succession in the face. 'See if you can hold your tongues,' said he. 'That man Macfarlane is not safe to cross; those that have done so already have repented it too late.'

And then, without so much as finishing his third glass, far less waiting for the other two, he bade us goodbye and went forth, under the lamp of the hotel, into the black night.

We three turned to our places in the parlour, with the big red fire and four clear candles; and, as we recapitulated what had passed, the first chill of our surprise soon changed into a glow of curiosity. We sat late; it was the latest session I have known in the old George. Each man, before we parted, had his theory that he was bound to prove; and none of us had any nearer business in this world than to track out the past of our condemned companion, and surprise the secret that he shared with the great London doctor. It is no great boast, but I believe I was a better hand at worming out a story than either of my fellows at the George; and perhaps there is now no other man alive who could narrate to you the following foul and unnatural events.

In his young days Fettes studied medicine in the schools of Edinburgh. He had talent of a kind, the talent that picks up swiftly what it hears and readily retains it for its own. He worked little at home; but he was civil, attentive, and intelligent in the presence of his masters. They soon picked him out as a lad who listened closely and remembered well; nay, strange as it seemed to me when I first heard it, he was in those days well favoured, and pleased by his exterior. There was, at that period, a certain extramural teacher of anatomy, whom I shall here designate by the letter K. His name was subsequently too well known. The man who bore it skulled through the streets of Edinburgh in disguise, while the mob that applauded at the execution of Burke called loudly for the blood of his employer. But Mr. K—— was then at the top of his vogue; he enjoyed the popularity due partly to his own talent and address, partly to the incapacity of his rival, the university professor. The students, at least, swore by his name, and Fettes believed himself, and was believed by others, to have laid the foundations of success when he had acquired the favour of this meteorically famous man. Mr. K—— was a *bon vivant* as well as an accomplished teacher; he liked a sly illusion no less than a careful preparation. In both capacities Fettes enjoyed and deserved his notice, and by the second year of his attendance he held the half-regular position of second demonstrator or sub-assistant in his class.

In this capacity the charge of the theatre and lecture-room devolved in particular upon his shoulders. He had to answer for the cleanliness of the premises and the conduct of the other students, and it was a part of his duty to supply, receive, and divide the various subjects. It was with a view to this last— at that time very delicate—affair that he was lodged by Mr. K—— in the same wynd, and at last in the same building, with the dissecting rooms. Here, after a night of turbulent pleasures, his hand still tottering, his sight still misty and confused, he would be called out of bed in the black hours before the winter dawn by the unclean and desperate interlopers who supplied the table. He would open the door to these men, since infamous throughout the land. He would help them with their tragic burden, pay them their sordid price, and remain alone, when they were gone, with the unfriendly relics of humanity. From such a scene he would return to snatch another hour or two of slumber, to repair the abuses of the night, and refresh himself for the labours of the day.

Few lads could have been more insensible to the impressions of a life thus passed among the ensigns of morality. His mind was closed against all general considerations. He was incapable of interest in the fate and fortunes of another, the slave of his own desires and low ambitions. Cold, light, and selfish in the last resort, he had that modicum of prudence, miscalled morality, which keeps a man from inconvenient drunkenness or punishable theft. He coveted, besides, a measure of consideration from his masters and his fellow pupils, and he had no desire to fail conspicuously in the external parts of life. Thus he made it his pleasure to gain some distinction in his studies, and day after day rendered unimpeachable eye-service to his employer, Mr. K——. For his day of work he indemnified himself by nights of roaring, blackguardly enjoyment; and when that balance had been struck, the organ that he called his conscience declared itself content.

The supply of subjects was a continual trouble to him as well as to his master. In that large and busy class, the raw material of the anatomists kept perpetually running out; and the business thus rendered necessary was not only unpleasant in itself, but threatened dangerous consequences to all who were concerned. It was the policy of Mr. K—— to ask no questions in his dealings with the trade. 'They bring the body, and we pay the price,' he used to say, dwelling on the alliteration—'*quid pro quo.*' And, again, and somewhat profanely, 'Ask no questions,' he would tell his assistants, 'for conscience sake.' There was no understanding that the subjects were provided by the crime of murder. Had that idea been broached to him in words, he would have recoiled in horror; but the lightness of his speech upon so grave a matter was, in itself, an offense against good manners, and a temptation to the men with whom he dealt. Fettes, for instance, had often remarked to himself upon the singular freshness of the bodies. He had been struck again and again by the hangdog, abominable looks of the ruffians who came to him before the dawn; and, putting things together clearly in his private thoughts, he perhaps attributed a meaning too immoral and too categorical to the unguarded councils of his master. He understood his duty, in short, to have three branches: to take what was brought, to pay the price, and to avert the eye from any evidence of crime.

One November morning this policy of silence was put sharply to the test. He had been awake all night with a racking toothache—pacing his room like a caged beast or throwing himself in fury on his bed—and had fallen at last into that profound, uneasy slumber that so often follows on a night of pain, when he was awakened by the third or fourth angry repetition of the concerted signal. There was a thin, bright moonshine; it was bitter cold, windy, and frosty; the town had not yet awakened, but an indefinable stir already preluded the noise and business of the day. The ghouls had come later than usual, and they seemed more than usually eager to be gone. Fettes, sick with sleep, lighted them upstairs. He heard their grumbling Irish voices through a dream; and as they stripped the sack from their sad merchandise he leaned dozing, with his shoulder propped against the wall; he had to shake himself to find the men their money. As he did so his eyes lighted on the dead face. He started; he took two steps nearer, with the candle raised.

'God Almighty!' he cried. 'That is Jane Galbraith!'

The men answered nothing, but they shuffled nearer the door.

'I know her, I tell you,' he continued. 'She was alive and hearty yesterday. It's impossible she can be dead; it's impossible you should have got this body fairly.'

'Sure, sir, you're mistaken entirely,' said one of the men.

But the other looked Fettes darkly in the eyes, and demanded the money on the spot.

It was impossible to misconceive the threat or to exaggerate the danger. The lad's heart failed him. He stammered some excuse, counted out the sum, and saw his hateful visitors depart. No sooner were they gone than he hastened to confirm his doubts. By a dozen unquestionable marks he identified the girl he had jested with the day before. He saw, with horror, marks upon her body that might well be taken as violence. A panic seized him, and he took refuge in his room. There he reflected at length over the discovery that he had made; considered soberly the bearing of Mr. K——'s instructions and the danger to himself of interference in so serious a business, and at last, in sore perplexity, determined to wait for the advice of his immediate superior, the class assistant.

This was a young doctor, Wolfe Macfarlane, a high favourite among the reckless students, clever, dissipated, and unscrupulous to the last degree. He had travelled and studied abroad. His manners were agreeable and a little forward. He was an authority on the stage, skilful on the ice or the links with skate or golf club; he dressed with nice audacity, and, to put the finishing touch upon his glory, he kept a gig and a strong trotting horse. With Fettes he was on terms of intimacy; indeed, their relative positions called for some community of life; and when subjects were scarce the pair would drive far into the country in Macfarlane's gig, visit and desecrate some lonely graveyard, and return before dawn with their booty to the door of the dissecting room.

On that particular morning Macfarlane arrived somewhat earlier than his wont. Fettes heard him, and met him on the stairs, told him his story, and showed him the cause of his alarm. Macfarlane examined the marks on her body.

'Yes,' he said with a nod, 'it looks fishy.'

'Well, what should I do?' asked Fettes.

'Do?' repeated the other. 'Do you want to do anything? Least said sooner mended, I should say.'

'Some one else might recognize her,' objected Fettes. 'She was as well known at the Castle Rock.'

'We'll hope not,' said Macfarlane, 'and if anybody does—well, you didn't, don't you see, and there's an end. The fact is, this has been going on too long. Stir up the mud, and you'll get K—— into the most unholy trouble; you'll be in a shocking box yourself. So will I, if you come to that. I should like to know how anyone of us would look or what the devil we should have to say ourselves, in any Christian witness box. For me, you know, there's one thing certain—that, practically speaking, all our subjects have been murdered.'

'Macfarlane!' cried Fettes.

'Come now!' sneered the other. 'As if you hadn't suspected it yourself!'

'Suspecting is one thing—'

'And proof another. Yes, I know; and I'm as sorry as you are this should have come here,' tapping the body with his cane. 'The next best thing for me is not to recognize it; and,' he added coolly, 'I don't. You may, if you please. I don't dictate, but I think a man of the world would do as I do; and, I may add, I fancy that is what K—— would look for at our hands. The question is, Why did he choose us two for his assistants? And I answer, Because he didn't want old wives.'

This was the tone of all others to affect the mind of a lad like Fettes. He agreed to imitate Macfarlane. The body of the unfortunate girl was duly dissected, and no one remarked or appeared to recognize her.

One afternoon, when his day's work was over, Fettes dropped into a popular tavern and found Macfarlane sitting with a stranger. This was a small man, very pale and dark, with coal-black eyes. The cut of his features gave a promise of intellect and refinement which was but feebly realized in his manners, for he proved, upon a nearer acquaintance, coarse, vulgar, and stupid. He exercised, however, a very remarkable control over

Macfarlane; issued orders like the Great Bashaw; became inflamed at the least discussion or delay, and commented rudely on the servility with which he was obeyed. This most offensive person took a fancy to Fettes on the spot, plied him with drinks, and honoured him with unusual confidences on his past career. If a tenth of what he confessed were true, he was a very loathsome rogue; and the lad's vanity was tickled by the attention of so experienced a man.

'I'm a pretty bad fellow myself,' the stranger remarked, 'but Macfarlane is the boy—Toddy Macfarlane I call him. Toddy, order your friend another glass.' Or it might be, 'Toddy, you jump up and shut the door.' 'Toddy hates me,' he said again. 'Oh, yes, Toddy, you do!'

'Don't you call me that confounded name,' growled Macfarlane.

'Hear him! Did you ever see the lads play knife? He would like to do that all over my body,' remarked the stranger.

'We medicals have a better way than that,' said Fettes. 'When we dislike a dead friend of ours, we dissect him.'

Macfarlane looked up sharply, as though this jest were scarcely to his mind.

The afternoon passed. Gray, for that was the stranger's name, invited Fettes to join them at dinner, ordered a feast so sumptuous that the tavern was thrown into commotion, and when all was done commanded Macfarlane to settle the bill. It was late before they separated; the man Gray was incapably drunk. Macfarlane, sobered by his fury, chewed the cud of the money he had been forced to squander and the slights he had been obliged to swallow. Fettes, with various liquors singing in his head, returned home with devious footsteps and a mind entirely in abeyance. Next day Macfarlane was absent from the class, and Fettes smiled to himself as he imagined him still squiring the intolerable Gray from tavern to tavern. As soon as the hour of liberty had struck, he posted from place to place in quest of his last night's companions. He could find them, however, nowhere; so returned early to his rooms, went early to bed, and slept the sleep of the just.

At four in the morning he was awakened by the well-known signal. Descending to the door, he was filled with astonishment to find Macfarlane with his gig, and in the gig one of those long and ghastly packages with which he was so well acquainted.

'What?' he cried. 'Have you been out alone? How did you manage?'

But Macfarlane silenced him roughly, bidding him turn to business. When they had got the body upstairs and laid it on the table, Macfarlane made at first as if he were going away. Then he paused and seemed to hesitate; and then, 'You had better look at the face,' said he, in tones of some constraint. 'You had better,' he repeated, as Fettes only stared at him in wonder.

'But where, and how, and when did you come by it?' cried the other.

'Look at the face,' was the only answer.

Fettes was staggered; strange doubts assailed him. He looked from the young doctor to the body, and then back again. At last, with a start, he did as he was bidden. He had almost expected the sight that met his eyes, and yet the shock was cruel. To see, fixed in the rigidity of death and naked on that coarse layer of sackcloth, the man whom he had left well clad and full of meat and sin upon the threshold of a tavern, awoke, even in the thoughtless Fettes, some of the terrors of the conscience. It was a *cras tibi* which re-echoed in his soul, that two whom he had known should have come to lie upon these icy tables. Yet these were only secondary thoughts. His first concern regarded Wolfe. Unprepared for a challenge so momentous, he knew not how to look his comrade in the face. He durst not meet his eye, and he had neither words nor voice at his command.

It was Macfarlane himself who made the first advance. He came up quietly behind and laid his hand gently but firmly on the other's shoulder.

'Richardson,' said he, 'may have the head.'

Now, Richardson was a student who had long been anxious for that portion of the human subject to dissect. There was no answer, and the murderer resumed: 'Talking of business, you must pay me; your accounts, you see, must tally.'

Fettes found a voice, the ghost of his own: 'Pay you!' he cried. 'Pay you for that?'

'Why, yes, of course you must. By all means and on every possible account, you must,' returned the other. 'I dare not give it for nothing, you dare not take it for nothing; it would compromise us both. This is another case like Jane Galbraith's. The more things are wrong, the more we must act as if all were right. Where does old K—— keep his money?'

'There,' answered Fettes hoarsely, pointing to a cupboard in the corner.

'Give me the key, then,' said the other calmly, holding out his hand.

There was an instant's hesitation, and the die was cast. Macfarlane could not suppress a nervous twitch, the infinitesimal mark of an immense relief, as he felt the key between his fingers. He opened the cupboard, brought out pen and ink and a paper book that stood in one compartment, and separated from the funds in a drawer a sum suitable to the occasion.

'Now, look here,' he said, 'there is the payment made—first proof of your good faith: first step to your security. You have now to clinch it by a second. Enter the payment in your book, and then you for your part may defy the devil.'

The next few seconds were for Fettes an agony of thought; but in balancing his terrors it was the most immediate that triumphed. Any future difficulty seemed almost welcome if he could avoid a present quarrel with Macfarlane. He set down the candle which he had been carrying all this time, and with a steady hand entered the date, the nature, and the amount of the transaction.

'And now,' said Macfarlane, 'it's only fair that you should pocket the lucre. I've had my share already. By the by, when a man of the world falls into a bit of luck, has a few extra shillings in his pocket—I'm ashamed to speak of it, but there's a rule of conduct in the case. No treating, no purchase of expensive class books, no squaring of old debts; borrow, don't lend.'

'Macfarlane,' began Fettes, still somewhat hoarsely, 'I have put my neck in a halter to oblige you.'

'To oblige me?' cried Wolfe. 'Oh, come! You did, as near as I can see the matter, what you downright had to do in self defence. Suppose I got into trouble, where would you be? This second little matter flows clearly from the first. Mr. Gray is the continuation of Miss Galbraith. You can't begin and then stop. If you begin, you must keep on beginning; that's the truth. No rest for the wicked.'

A horrible sense of blackness and the treachery of fate seized hold upon the soul of the unhappy student.

'My God!' he cried, 'but what have I done? and when did I begin? To be made a class assistant—in the name of reason, where's the harm in that? Service wanted the position; Service might have got it. Would *he* have been where *I* am now?'

'My dear fellow,' said Macfarlane, 'what a boy you are! What harm *has* come to you? What harm *can* come to you if you hold your tongue? Why, man, do you know what this life is? There are two squads of us—the lions and the lambs. If you're a lamb, you'll come to lie upon these tables like Gray or Jane Galbraith; if you're a lion, you'll live and drive a horse like me, like K——, like all the world with any wit or courage. You're staggered at the first. But look at K——! My dear fellow, you're clever, you have pluck. I like you, and K—— likes you. You were born to lead the hunt; and I tell you, on my honour and my experience of life, three days from now you'll laugh at all these scarecrows like a High School boy at a farce.'

And with that Macfarlane took his departure and drove off up the wynd in his gig to get under cover before daylight. Fettes was thus left alone with his regrets. He saw the miserable peril in which he stood involved. He saw, with inexpressible dismay, that there was no limit to his weakness, and that, from concession to concession, he had fallen from the arbiter of Macfarlane's destiny to his paid and helpless accomplice. He would have given the world to have been a little braver at the time, but it did not occur to him that he might still be brave. The secret of Jane Galbraith and the cursed entry in the day book closed his mouth.

Hours passed; the class began to arrive; the members of the unhappy Gray were dealt out to one and to another, and received without remark. Richardson was made happy with the head; and, before the hour of freedom rang, Fettes trembled with exultation to perceive how far they had already gone toward safety.

For two days he continued to watch, with an increasing joy, the dreadful process of disguise.

On the third day Macfarlane made his appearance. He had been ill, he said; but he made up for lost time by the energy with which he directed the students. To Richardson in particular he extended the most valuable assistance and advice, and that student, encouraged by the praise of the demonstrator, burned high with ambitious hopes, and saw the medal already in his grasp.

Before the week was out Macfarlane's prophecy had been fulfilled. Fettes had outlived his terrors and had forgotten his baseness. He began to plume himself upon his courage, and had so arranged the story in his mind that he could look back on these events with an unhealthy pride. Of his accomplice he saw but little. They met, of course, in the business of the class; they received their orders together from Mr. K——. At times they had a word or two in private, and Macfarlane was from first to last particularly kind and jovial. But it was plain that he avoided any reference to their common secret; and even when Fettes whispered to him that he had cast in his lot with the lions and forsworn the lambs, he only signed to him smilingly to hold his peace.

At length an occasion arose which threw the pair once more into a closer union. Mr. K—— was again short of subjects; pupils were eager, and it was a part of this teacher's pretensions to be always well supplied. At the same time there came the news of a burial in the rustic graveyard of Glencorse. Time has little changed the place in question. It stood then, as now, upon a crossroad, out of call of human habitations, and buried fathom deep in the foliage of six cedar trees. The cries of the sheep upon the neighbouring hills, the streamlets upon either hand, one loudly singing among pebbles, the other dripping furtively from pond to pond, the stir of the wind in mountainous old flowering chestnuts, and once in seven days the voice of the bell and the old tunes of the precentor, were the only sounds that disturbed the silence around the rural church. The Resurrection Man—to use a byname of the period—was not to be deterred by any of the sanctities of customary piety. It was part of his trade to despise and desecrate the scrolls and trumpets of old tombs, the paths worn by the feet of worshippers and mourners, and the offerings and the inscriptions of bereaved affection. To rustic neighbourhoods where love is more than commonly tenacious, and where some bonds of blood or fellowship unite the entire society of a parish, the body-snatcher, far from being repelled by natural respect, was attracted by the ease and safety of the task. To bodies that had been laid in earth, in joyful expectation of a far different awakening, there came that hasty, lamplit, terror-haunted resurrection of the spade and mattock. The coffin was forced, the cerements torn, and the melancholy relics, clad in sackcloth, after being rattled for hours on moonless byways, were at length exposed to uttermost indignities before a class of gaping boys.

Somewhat as two vultures may swoop upon a dying lamb, Fettes and Macfarlane were to be let loose upon a grave in that green and quiet resting place. The wife of a farmer, a woman who had lived for sixty years, and been known for nothing but good butter and a godly conversation, was to be rooted from her grave at midnight and carried, dead and naked, to that faraway city that she had always honoured with her Sunday's best; the place beside her family was to be empty till the crack of doom; her innocent and always venerable members to be exposed to that last curiosity of the anatomist.

Late one afternoon the pair set forth, well wrapped in cloaks and furnished with a formidable bottle. It rained without remission—a cold, dense, lashing rain. Now and again there blew a puff of wind, but these sheets of falling water kept it down. Bottle and all, it was a sad and silent drive as far as Penicuik, where they were to spend the evening. They stopped once, to hide their implements in a thick bush not far from the churchyard, and once again at the Fisher's Tryst, to have a toast before the kitchen fire and vary their nips of whisky with a glass of ale. When they reached their journey's end the gig was housed, the horse was fed and comforted, and the two young doctors in a private room sat down to the best dinner and the best wine the house afforded. The lights, the fire, the beating rain upon the window, the cold, incongruous work that lay before them, added zest to their enjoyment of the meal. With every glass their cordiality increased. Soon Macfarlane handed a little pile of gold to his companion.

'A compliment,' he said. 'Between friends these little damned accommodations ought to fly like pipelights.'

Fettes pocketed the money, and applauded the sentiment to the echo. 'You are a philosopher,' he cried. 'I was an ass till I knew you. You and K—— between you, by the Lord Harry! but you'll make a man of me.'

'Of course we shall,' applauded Macfarlane. 'A man? I tell you, it required a man to back me up the other morning. There are some big, brawling, forty-year-old cowards who would have turned sick at the look of the damned thing; but not you—you kept your head. I watched you.'

'Well, and why not?' Fettes thus vaunted himself. 'It was no affair of mine. There was nothing to gain on the one side but disturbance, and on the other I could count on your gratitude, don't you see?' And he slapped his pocket till the gold pieces rang.

Macfarlane somehow felt a certain touch of alarm at these unpleasant words. He may have regretted that he had taught his young companion so successfully, but he had no time to interfere, for the other noisily continued in this boastful strain:

'The great thing is not to be afraid. No, between you and me, I don't want to hang—that's practical; but for all cant, Macfarlane, I was born with a contempt. Hell, God, devil, right, wrong, sin, crime, and all the old gallery of curiosities—they may frighten boys, but men of the world, like you and me, despise them. Here's to the memory of Gray!'

It was by this time growing somewhat late. The gig, according to order, was brought round to the door with both lamps brightly shining, and the young men had to pay their bill and take the road. They announced that they were bound for Peebles, and drove in that direction till they were clear of the last houses of the town; then, extinguishing the lamps, returned upon their course, and followed a byroad toward Glencorse. There was no sound but that of their own passage, and the incessant, strident pouring of the rain. It was pitch dark; here and there a white gate or a white stone in the wall guided them for a short space across the night; but for the most part it was at a foot pace, and almost groping, that they picked their way through that resonant blackness to their solemn and isolated destination. In the sunken woods that traverse the neighbourhood of the burying ground the last glimmer failed them, and it became necessary to kindle a match and reillumine one of the lanterns of the gig. Thus, under the dripping trees, and environed by huge and moving shadows, they reached the scene of their inhallowed labours.

They were both experienced in such affairs, and powerful with the spade; and they had scarce been twenty minutes at their task before they were rewarded by a dull rattle on the coffin lid. At the same moment, Macfarlane, having hurt his hand upon a stone, flung it carelessly above his head. The grave, in which they now stood almost to the shoulders, was close to the edge of the platform of the graveyard; and the gig lamp had been propped, the better to illuminate their labours, against a tree, and on the immediate verge of the steep bank descending to the stream. Chance had taken a sure aim with the stone. Then came a clang of broken glass; night fell upon them; sounds alternately dull and ringing announced the bounding of the lantern down the bank, and its occasional collision with the trees. A stone or two, which it had dislodged in its descent, rattled behind it into the profundities of the glen; and then silence, like night, resumed its sway; and they might bend their hearing to its utmost pitch, but naught was to be heard except the rain, now marching to the wind, now steadily falling over miles of open country.

They were so nearly at an end of their abhorred task that they judged it wisest to complete it in the dark. The coffin was exhumed and broken open; the body inserted in the dripping sack and carried between them to the gig; one mounted to keep it in its place, and the other, taking the horse by the mouth, groped along by wall and bush until they reached the wider road by the Fisher's Tryst. Here was a faint, diffused radiancy, which they hailed like daylight; by that they pushed the horse to a good pace and began to rattle along merrily in the direction of the town.

They had both been wetted to the skin during their operations, and now, as the gig jumped among the deep ruts, the thing that stood propped between them fell now upon one and now upon the other. At every repetition of the horrid contact each instinctively repelled it with the greater haste; and the process, natural although it was, began to tell upon the nerves of the companions. Macfarlane made some ill-favoured jest about the farmer's wife, but it came hollowly from his lips, and was allowed to drop in silence. Still their unnatural burden bumped from side to side; and now the head would be laid, as if in confidence, upon their shoulders, and now the drenching sackcloth would flap icily about their faces. A creeping chill began to possess the soul of Fettes. He peered at the bundle, and it seemed somehow larger than at first. All over the countryside, and from every degree of distance, the farm dogs accompanied their passage with tragic ululations; and it grew and grew upon his mind that some unnatural miracle had been accomplished, that some nameless change had befallen the dead body, and that it was in fear of their unholy burden that the dogs were howling.

'For God's sake,' said he, making a great effort to arrive at speech, 'for God's sake, let's have a light!'

Seemingly Macfarlane was affected in the same direction; for, though he made no reply, he stopped the horse, passed the reins to his companion, got down, and proceeded to kindle the remaining lamp. They had by that time got no farther than the crossroad down to Auchenclinny. The rain still poured as though the deluge were returning, and it was no easy matter to make a light in such a world of wet and darkness. When at last the flickering blue flame had been transferred to the wick and began to expand and clarify, and shed a wide circle of misty brightness round the gig, it became possible for the two young men to see each other and the thing they had along with them. The rain had moulded the rough sacking to the outlines of the body underneath, the head was distinct from the trunk, the shoulders plainly modelled; something at once spectral and human riveted their eyes upon the ghastly comrade of their drive.

For some time Macfarlane stood motionless, holding up the lamp. A nameless dread was swathed, like a wet sheet, about the body, and tightened the white skin upon the face of Fettes; a fear that was meaningless, a horror of what could not be, kept mounting to his brain. Another beat of the watch, and he had spoken. But his comrade forestalled him.

'That is not a woman,' said Macfarlane, in a hushed voice.

'It was a woman when we put her in,' whispered Fettes.

'Hold that lamp,' said the other. 'I must see her face.'

And as Fettes took the lamp his companion untied the fastenings of the sack and drew down the cover from the head. The light fell very clear upon the dark, well moulded features and smooth-shaven cheeks of a too familiar countenance, often beheld in dreams of both of these young men. A wild yell rang up into the night; each leaped from his own side into the roadway: the lamp fell, broke, and was extinguished; and the horse, terrified by this unusual commotion, bounded and went off toward Edinburgh at a gallop, bearing along with it, the sole occupant of the gig, the body of the dead and long dissected Gray.

Iceman

PETER TURNBULL

TUESDAY—07:30

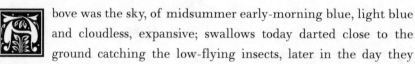 bove was the sky, of midsummer early-morning blue, light blue and cloudless, expansive; swallows today darted close to the ground catching the low-flying insects, later in the day they would be wheeling two or three hundred feet above the ground after the day's thermal currents had pushed their prey skywards. But now they skimmed and wheeled on wing tip above the meadow wort and sedge. Below the sky was a rich foliage of green of trees and shrubs and fields in which blackbird and thrush sang. A path of cracked brown soil wound through the landscape and an onlooker would notice first the man, a man in late middle age, a full and pleasant face, a round stomach. The man wore a white shirt with sleeves rolled up and he carried a light summer jacket; he wore white slacks and trainer shoes which, given his years, looked somewhat odd, somewhat out of place. In his other hand he carried a dog chain. The onlooker would also notice a springer spaniel, a mature but youthful dog, trotting contentedly along the path in front of the man. Behind, as a backdrop, beyond a belt of golden corn, the grey tower blocks of Airdrie, Lanarkshire.

The man walked away from the tower blocks, in front of him was a vista of green fields beneath a blue sky and a rising sun. The man enjoyed the walk because his dog enjoyed the walk. The man enjoyed the walk with his dog; without his dog, the walk would be without meaning for him. In fact, he doubted if he would have risen early from his bed had it not been for the dog, and so would have missed the best part of the day and the great sense of achievement, which stays with one throughout the day, that an early rise confers. He enjoyed the walk each morning, winter

and summer, just as many years earlier he had enjoyed Christmas, only because his children had enjoyed it, tearing open their presents. And he had
enjoyed Saltcoats or Burntisland for two weeks a year again only because
his children had enjoyed them. Without children he would have hiber-
nated during Christmas week, and without children he would happily
have stayed home during the Fair. The man had travelled when younger,
when in the army, and now he was no longer young and had long since
stopped feeling the so-called wanderlust and wouldn't willingly travel
anywhere, save perhaps once every year or two to visit an old friend. But
travelling to visit places was a thing of the past. When it came down to it,
he wasn't very good at travelling at the best of times. He was of Airdrie
and at home in this town. Why, he thought, why travel when you've already arrived?

He walked and kicked a rotten branch off the path. In the distance,
but out of sight, was the M8 to and from Edinburgh. He could hear the
rumble of the rush-hour traffic. The man was in his late fifties, his dog
was eight years old. They were an equivalent age, he and his dog. Two old
pals enjoying each other's company.

One man and his dog, in the fields, in the early morning.

The children were up and gone with children of their own. Mrs. Toulson, God rest her, had gone before him, and so now it was just him and
Mick and the grandchildren at Sunday lunchtime, two sets leapfrogging
each other, Sunday over Sunday.

He walked on. He liked the walk out, but on the way back he couldn't
seem to take his eyes off the flat, up there, centre block, twenty-second
floor. Mick too seemed to know when the homeward leg had begun, then
he would saunter where before he had gambolled.

Jack Toulson swung at a prominent blade of grass with the dog chain;
he caught it but the blade bent with the blow and survived. He thought,
as he had thought before, that his relationship with Mick was deeper,
more poignant, more trusting, more pure somehow than the relationships
he had had with any human being, even his family, no, especially with his
family, with the ups and downs they had had. But him and Mick . . .

He saw the woman close to the path.

He saw her because Mick had seen her, and had stopped as springers
will, looking at a quarry, head and tail in a line, front paw raised and bent,

pointing. Nothing alarming, Mick did that when he saw a rabbit, but Jack Toulson followed his dog's point, the practice of an ancient relationship between man and beast.

"Ha!" he said, because the first fleeting impression was of a woman lying in the sun, basking in the rays. But the impression was fleeting even before it was an impression, less than a second in fact, as if his brain had wished the impression upon him, so as to deliberately soften the impact of seeing a dead body lying beside a path, and not just any path but *his* path, and there welled up in him a strange sense of resentment that his territory had been violated, and he knew immediately that his walk, the walk belonging to him and Mick, would never be the same. Each morning they would come by this location and think . . . The woman lay on her back, fully clothed, smart clothing too, he saw, evening wear. She lay as if laid out, as Mrs. Toulson had been when he last saw her and had kissed her cheek: arms and legs straight, head face up.

He saw a blue cord round her neck, a cord of strong nylon rope in which was entwined a stick to tighten the cord.

A bird sang.

Traffic rumbled unseen. Traffic on "the top road" could be seen, though heard less than rumbling motorway commuters.

There, all around, life was going on. Here life had been snuffed out, cut off in the bud, for she was still a young woman. He walked up to his dog, caught the collar, and snapped the lead on. He knelt and patted the springer's flank. "We'll need to go and get the polis, you and me, pal," he said.

"Thought she was sunbathing." Jack Toulson cast a glance of horrific fascination over his shoulder and then turned back to Richard King. "I mean, it sounds stupid, but that's what I thought. I know it's a wee bit early in the day for sunbathing but that's the first thought that came into my head. I mean, see women, what they won't do for a tan, and getting out early in a quiet field like this is less stupid than laying under one of they sun beds. I look across at the next block some nights and I tell you there's four or five of them on at any one time, especially in the spring because they women don't want to go to Benidorm looking pale, they want to go looking as though they've always been there. They glow blue, do you know, the sun beds at night."

"I know." King looked beyond Jack Toulson to the locus of the crime, uniformed officers, a blue and white ribbon hanging limp in the still air. The corpse, originally thought by the member of the public to be a woman sunbathing, was now covered by a green plastic sheet, which lay inside the ribbon.

"Did you go near the body, sir?"

"I told the other officers."

"Tell me."

"Well no, old Mick saw her first."

"Mick?"

"My dog. Didn't you, pal?" Toulson rattled the chain. Mick barked. "He pointed."

"I see." King was not unversed in the ways of the gun dog and having said what he said had then the immediate impression that he had robbed Jack Toulson of the pleasure of explaining what he meant by a dog "pointing."

"But no, I didn't go near. I knew she was dead."

"Oh . . . ?"

Toulson nodded. "I'm an undertaker. I was until I took early retirement. The company was trimming back and they offered me a decent enough package. So I took it. I've got little outgoings now, just me and Mick really."

"I don't see how that means you . . ."

"I could tell, son. See me, I've been in the death business since I was fifteen, that's the best part of half a century. I don't know how I can do it, but I can, I can tell a corpse from a sleeper at some distance, and I knew she was 'off.'"

"Off?"

"Dead. Mick knew too. He wouldn't have pointed at a sleeper. But even without Mick I would have known she was off. Tell you something else, I can look at a living person who looks and feels healthy and I know that they'll be off in six months' time. It's what the death business does to you. So no, I didn't go near. Me and Mick ran back over the fields to the road and dialled three nines at the call box. Didn't we, Mick? Quite a crowd puller."

"Sorry," said King. He was a chubby, bearded cop, twenty-five years old.

"Yon crowds." Toulson nodded to the end of the path, at the road, where the public had gathered, from where TV cameras were filming the scene. A bus slowed as it drove by, the driver and passengers on both decks peered towards King and Toulson and the uniformed officers and sheet of green plastic: something to talk about at work, something to tune into the news broadcasts for, something to read about in the *Evening Times,* and tomorrow's *Record* and *Herald.*

"It happens." King followed Toulson's gaze. "We call it the 'ogle factor'; wherever there's a really bad pile-up there's always minor accidents surrounding it as drivers ogle instead of keeping their eyes on the road."

"Aye, I can imagine."

"Apart from the body, you saw nothing amiss?" Toulson shook his head. "I wasn't really looking, you see, but no, I saw nothing at all that didn't look right. It was just another morning, particularly fine and pleasant, height of summer. It definitely wasn't there yesterday morning, me and Mick come this way each morning, don't we, Mick?"

King nodded. "She would have been noticed if she had been left there during the day. Plenty of folk cut across these fields and anyway, as you've noticed, she's easily seen from the road. What happened to her happened in the night, that's for sure, and before five A.M. It's dark up until five A.M. I should know, I've been on duty all night."

"Aye, we did shifts at the undertakers. Folk pop into the world at odd times and they don't mind when they go either. I've lifted corpses from houses at two, three A.M. I could never get used to shifts. That's another thing, she was laid out."

King looked at Toulson.

"She was laid out. She didn't die of natural causes, otherwise she would have crumpled, and she wasn't attacked here. She was laid out, somebody took a lot of trouble to lay her out. That's how they were when we picked them up from folks' houses. The doctor calls, certifies death, and lays them out. Then we call and pick them up. They're always in that position. Have to go into the box like that."

"Your employment hasn't affected you, has it?"

"Can't afford to let it, son. It's like going into a supermarket, it's easy to pick a joint of beef off the shelf, but behind it is a man who's prepared to kill and cut up the cow. Graveyards are pleasant and tranquil places but behind each one is a man or men who are prepared to work with corpses."

"Still couldn't do your job," said King.

"And I couldn't do yours. Anyway, yon was laid out."

"You didn't see anybody else about?"

Jack Toulson shook his head. "Not here in the fields. I did see one or two folk in the street after I left the flats, but just the usual, the milkman, the postie. After I made the call I stayed at the start of the path and stopped a lassie from taking her own dog down, told her there was a body all laid out and the polis were on their way."

"Then?"

"Then I identified myself to the officers and offered to show them the corpse, but they told me to direct them instead, which I did. They came back pretty quickly and took a plastic sheet and a roll of tape from the boot of their car. Then they went back down the path and asked me to wait to speak to you."

It was one of those rare occasions when the telephone did not awaken her. It was one of those rare occasions when she did not have to pretend to be asleep when her husband, disturbed from his slumber by the softly purring phone, had groped for the handset, pulled it under the duvet, and murmured, "Reynolds." It was one of those occasions when she could enjoy rising with her husband and see him off to work. Conventionally wifely. Perhaps she thought it was the sort of action likely to invite scathing comments from feminists, but nonetheless, she found it hugely enjoyable, hugely rewarding; wifely.

Janet Reynolds suffered insomnia. That is to say that throughout her early life she had seen herself as a "sufferer" of that condition. Now in her early thirties, she had long referred to herself as "benefitting" from the condition. It gave her more waking hours in each twenty-four than is enjoyed by the average person. Once her attitude had changed, she began to use the time to study, consume vast novels, learn foreign languages.

"Yes . . ." Reynolds continued to talk as his slender wife slid out of bed and opened the curtains.

"Coffee?" she asked.

"Please . . . no, sorry . . . carry on, I was speaking to my wife . . . Airdrie? Very well. It may take an hour from now. I'm coming from Pollokshields in the rush hour. But I'll be there as quick as I can."

In the kitchen his wife smiled at him in her housecoat. The room smelled of toast and percolated coffee.

"Got to have something inside you. You've always said that."

"Certainly, have to." Reynolds slid into his jacket. "The human body is an engine and all engines need food. Oh . . . the first cup of coffee in the morning . . . heaven . . . we're all allowed our addictions, even members of the medical profession."

"Two slices?"

"Please. Where's Gustav?"

"I let him out, he's in the garden with a bone. Why?"

"No reason, just that he usually shares my toast."

"Going to Airdrie?"

"Aye, but that's where these things tend to happen. In Milngavie and Bearsden and points north and west, they use solicitors to spill blood, out east they use knives."

"Oh, unfair on the good people of the east, I'd say. Toast, two slices for the consumption of. I mean, speaking as a lassie from Tollcross, that is."

"Point taken, but that's just the way it seems. Still, we'll see what we find. Every corpse tells a story, and no two stories are ever the same."

"And what do you know about this story?"

"Adult female, strangled with a ligature. Seems straightforward, but you never know. I have the easy job, it's the poor old polis that fight in the trenches—who she is, why she was murdered, by whom; rather them than me. Right, I'll see you when I see you."

King kept a respectful distance as Reynolds knelt by the corpse, peeled back the sheet, and conducted a preliminary examination. Occasionally he scribbled a note on his pad. Behind King were the three blocks of high-rise flats, at the living room window of each stood a person, or a couple, or a family, each unknown to the others, all the way to the twenty-fifth floor, each staring down at the unfolding drama in the field in the middle distance. A movement to King's right caught his eye. He turned and watched a plum-coloured Rover sliding to a halt beside the flashing blue lights of Tango Delta Foxtrot, which less than one hour previously had responded to Jack Toulson's three nines call and then radioed in a Code 41. King watched as Donoghue got out of his car. He was, to King's eyes, immaculately dressed in a light grey suit. Donoghue paused to light his pipe and then began to walk along the footpath towards the locus. King knew what would happen. Donoghue would approach, nod in response to the salute of the senior constable, stand next to King, fix him with eye contact, and then raise one eyebrow. King knew the script and began to rehearse his lines.

Donoghue approached. A sudden zephyr, short-lived as it was sudden, carried a whiff of his tobacco smoke before him. King nodded to Donoghue as Donoghue approached and raised an eyebrow.

"Female deceased, sir, adult white European. Dr. Reynolds, as you see, is at the locus, he's just arrived, in fact. The deceased was found by a member of the public when he was walking his dog. Ligature round the neck of deceased indicates murder by strangulation. I have not looked for identification yet."

"I see." Donoghue pulled on his pipe and watched Reynolds slip the sheet over the body and stand.

Reynolds turned away from the corpse and walked to where Donoghue and King stood. "Mr. Donoghue."

"Dr. Reynolds, good morning."

"A fine day for it." Reynolds brushed dirt from his hands. "A fine sunny morning and in the country. Usually it's a scheme in February."

"What can you tell us, sir?"

"I can tell you a lot. And I can tell you little. I can tell you that she is deceased, possibly murdered."

"The ligature . . . ?" King interrupted. "I . . ."

"A smoke screen, gentlemen, and as such that does suggest foul play, though that's your department, but it is not a very good smoke screen. The preliminary examination always gives a cascade of information, so, point by point, and not in any order of importance, the first thing that I have to tell you, she wasn't strangled. The rope round her neck is nylon, quite strong enough to strangle her, but the stick in the rope is rotten: it would have snapped in twain had any pressure been applied to it. My guess is that it was picked up from hereabouts and shoved in the rope as an afterthought before the felons made their getaway."

"Felons?"

"I'll come to that. But I can immediately discard strangulation as a cause of death. If she had been strangled by the rope, or by a pair of meaty hands, there would be massive bruising about the neck which would have remained after death. It takes living tissue to make bruising subside. A corpse can be bruised, especially if death is recent, but only living tissue can recover from bruising. I would also expect there to be other indications of strangulation: bleeding from the ears, and a congestion of blood in the face, giving the face a puffed-out and mottled appearance. There is none of that. Further, I would have expected there to be collateral damage to the hands, caused when she fought off her attacker, or bruising to her wrists caused by her being restrained prior to or during strangulation."

"None of that?"

"Not a mark upon her that I can see. Further, her clothing is not in disarray, which I would have expected had she met a violent death. The problem now encountered is that I can't guess her time of death. The body is too cold."

"Cold?"

"It's frozen. Literally. In fact, there is evidence that it's thawing rapidly. There is ice under the lips and still small particles of ice in the hair. They would not occur normally, given the time of year. My guess is they brought her here in the night in a deep-frozen state and she immediately began to thaw. The nights are warm, top soil retains heat and has been heated by two weeks of very hot weather. Once the sun rose the thawing became rapid. In fact, the soil under the corpse is a little damp."

"So." Donoghue pulled on his pipe. "She was placed here in the night, but could have been murdered . . . ?"

"Ten years ago."

"Ten years ago!"

"Or twenty, or ten days ago. What I can tell you is that she didn't freeze to death. There's no frostbite on the extremities; frostbite is caused by a living body fighting to keep itself warm. The lady here, she died instantly, at least quickly. And she was deep-frozen immediately after death.

Once on ice at a sufficiently low temperature, no biological degradation will occur. It's that very principle that causes lunatic Americans to have their bodies deep-frozen upon natural death so that when in two hundred years' time scientists have found a cure for heart disease or whatever, the body can be thawed out, revived, and repaired. Any scientist will tell you that that is complete nonsense, quite impossible, because if we could cure heart disease we could only cure it before the long goodbye and not after. But that doesn't stop Yanks with more money than sense having their earthly remains frozen. Anyway, I'll take her back to the G.R.I. Look at her heart, that'll point me in the right direction. I'd put her age at death as being about thirty years. She was a natural brown-haired woman, but her hair was dyed blond."

"She died blond," said King. "They have more fun."

Donoghue glared at him.

"Sorry, sir," mumbled King. "Not in the best taste."

"Unlike you, too," Donoghue said. "Not the sort of crack I'd expect from you."

"But it gives an insight into her lifestyle," said Reynolds quickly. "A woman who liked the good life. Her clothing doesn't come from Paddy's Market and she has some serious rocks on her fingers, held there by some serious metals. But, once again, I venture into your territory."

"Venture all you like, Dr. Reynolds." Donoghue looked at his pipe, verifying that it had indeed gone out.

"She was, or at least had been, married."

"The rings you mentioned?" Donoghue lit his pipe.

"*In absentia*," Reynolds nodded. "In their case, *in absentia*. Whether she removed those two particular rings upon divorce, or whether they were taken from her upon death in an attempt to disguise her identity as another form of smoke screen is for you gentlemen to find out. But nonetheless, second finger, left hand, clear impression of two rings having been in constant presence. But, whatever, with your permission I'll have the body removed to the G.R.I. and commence the postmortem."

"Could you let us have the clothing as soon as possible?"

"Certainly."

"Thanks. Oh, Dr. Reynolds, you mentioned felons."

"In the plural, yes, I did. Just a common-sense observation really, just that one person can dispose of the body of another more easily if it is pliable, if it can be folded up into the boot of a car, for example. But in this case, the deceased was stiff as a length of wood and covered in ice. Difficult for one person to manhandle on his own, no sign of her being dragged along the path, though in fairness the ground is concrete hard, little if any trace would be left. Yet again I find myself moving into your territory. The other thing that occurs to me is that in order to freeze a corpse you would need access to an industrial-scale refrigeration plant. She was a tall woman, five ten I measured, it's not the sort of freezing job you can do at home, and that would seem to imply conspiracy. But if you'll excuse me, I'll carry on. I'll phone the results to you at P Division and fax the complete report as soon as I've written it."

"Thank you, sir. Richard."

"Yes, sir."

"A sweep of this entire area, around the locus but especially from the locus to the road and anywhere where a motor vehicle would have parked. I don't know what you're looking for, but you'll know it when you see it. I'll leave that in your capable hands."

"Very good, sir."

"Sounds good," said the woman, high cheekbones, blue eyes, natural blond hair tied up in a bun. "I read the reviews and I haven't been to live theatre for long enough."

"Most cops don't like the theatre." The man stood with an upright posture, balancing his weight evenly between two slightly spread feet. "Their day-to-day life is endless street theatre, they get all the drama they can use at work, but occasionally, once in a blue moon . . ."

"Listen, I said I'd love to go . . ." The phone rang. The woman picked it up. "Uniform bar . . . Yes sir, he's here." She handed the phone to the man. "It's a slave driver, for you."

"Oh . . . and I was hoping for a quiet day, what's this going to be about?"

"It'll be the Code Forty-one that came in this morning, right at the beginning of the day shift. Go on, take it, he's waiting."

"Detective Sergeant Sussock . . . Yes, right away." He put down the phone. "See that guy, he's young enough to be my son and no wonder he's got so far so fast. The job, the job, and nothing but the job."

"On you go, old Sussock, and stop your carping."

Sussock leaned forward and stole a kiss.

"Ray!"

Sussock shrugged.

"Look, I'm angry." She looked quickly about her. "We made an agreement, a contract. We said we'd keep this discreet. If you do that again, we're finished. I'm not a bloody tart to be pecked at in public."

"There's nobody about," said Sussock meekly.

"How do you know, how do you know? Working here's like living in a village. Nothing goes unnoticed."

"I wouldn't have done it if I thought there was even the slightest . . ."

"On you go, Fabian's waiting. And I'm going to think again about that theatre date."

"Elka . . ."

The phone rang. She snatched it up. "Uniform bar. WPC Willems speaking . . . Yes, if you'll just give me the details, madam . . ."

Sussock went upstairs to the CID corridor and tapped reverently on Donoghue's door.

"Come," Donoghue said after an imperious pause. He looked up and smiled as Sussock entered his office. "Oh, Ray, thanks for coming up, take a pew."

"Thanks."

"You look upset, Ray?"

"It's nothing. Just wish I hadn't done something, that's all."

"So join the rest of humanity, Ray. We all have regrets like that. All we can do is learn from them, use them to help us proceed onwards and upwards, that's the ticket, ever onwards, ever upwards."

"Aye." Sussock sank into the "pew," unable to share Donoghue's spirited enthusiasm. It seemed like a lifetime of regrets had brought him here, sinking into a chair in front of the desk of a man twenty years his junior and feeling just as battered and misshapen as his trilby, which, if memory served him, was itself secondhand when he bought it from a charity shop. Or was that the winter fedora? Could have been the fedora he used in wintertime . . .

Donoghue leaned back in his chair and pulled Sussock's wandering mind back to reality. "You may have heard that we have a murder inquiry in progress. I'm anxious to keep up the momentum."

"Of course, sir. What do we have?"

And Donoghue told him in a leisurely manner, pausing at times to relight his pipe, which seemed to refuse to kindle. All very rich, thought Sussock, who, if he recalled, had been summoned as a matter of urgency. "So that's it, Ray. She was iced up and now she's thawed out, cause of death to be determined, just thought I'd put you in the picture, since you're on the day shift."

"Aye." Sussock shifted his position in the chair and glanced out of the window at the sun glinting off the angular concrete and glass buildings of Sauchiehall Street.

"I've asked the collator to press a couple of buttons on his computer of which he is so proud to come up with the names of female m.p.'s of about thirty years of age."

"Aye." Sussock fidgeted with his hat. "The deceased, now, how tall would she be?"

"Five ten approx. You said that as though you know something, Ray."

"I could well. You know, it might be worth asking the collator to search for female m.p.'s of about forty-five years. He could alternatively search for a file in the name of Reissmann."

"Tell me more."

"She disappeared eighteen months ago. I remember it because it was allocated to me. It's still unsolved. It's that my ears pricked up when you mentioned that she had been kept in a frozen state. Her husband is in the refrigeration business. He's fond of calling himself 'Reissmann the Iceman.'"

"Ray, you interest me. No, you don't, you intrigue me."

"He owns a refrigerated warehouse. Food distributers rent refrigerated storage space from him. He also has a government contract, keeps deep-frozen meat as part of the EEC meat mountain, so-called."

"What manner of man is he?"

"A bit like a pub landlord. Flashy dresser, gold-crown smile for everyone, but the slightest thing annoys him, at which point he turns into the human equivalent of a rattlesnake, except you don't get the warning rattle before he strikes. I didn't take to him. I don't wish to be unkind to publicans, but that's the way I felt about the guy. You know the feeling you get. I felt all the time that there was more to his wife's disappearance than he was letting on. He overacted a bit, too much of the anxiety and concerned partner."

"Did you quiz him?"

"Aye, we did that right enough. Hard enough, too. Gave his house and garden a good going-over with the sniffer dogs, kept him in the cells overnight. Had to let him go because of lack of evidence. I remember him looking pleased, as though he believed that he'd got away with something. I very nearly told him we'd see each other again but I kept it zipped; I didn't want him to cover too many tracks. I felt it was in our interests to let him think he'd got away with it; you know how it is, opening your mouth makes you feel good at the time but at the end of the day you're just digging a hole."

"Shrewd, Ray. Because we all know what happens to people who dig holes." Donoghue leaned forward and picked up the phone on his desk. He dialled a two-figure internal number. "Collator . . . DI Donoghue . . . The search I asked you to do for female m.p.'s of about thirty years, I'd like you to widen it to include female m.p.'s of about forty-five years, and if it throws up the name Reissmann . . . R—E—I—S—S—M—A—N—N, then that's the file we want to see first. . . . I'll ask. . . . Ray, what was the lady's first name?"

Sussock clicked his fingers. "Shirley . . . Cindy . . . Susan . . . began with an 'S,' sorry."

"The initial 'S,'" Donoghue said. "There can't be too many missing Reissmanns of about forty-five years, it's not what you'd call a common name . . . but I think you could use some common sense. If there are two files on people called Reissmann bring them both up here." He replaced the phone. "New man, keen as mustard but little imagination. Where were we?"

"Mrs. Reissmann."

"Did you search the business premises?"

Sussock shook his head. "No, no we didn't. When we drew a blank we requested advice from the Home Office major local enquiry computer, and it sent back a printout advising us to check outbuildings, cellars, and drains."

"And?"

"He owns a large house in Busby, close to his warehouse; we had already checked the outbuildings and so we left. The house has no cellarage, there was nothing blocking the drains, we lifted the floorboards, again nothing. But there was something. You know, I was watching Reissmann when the boys were lifting the carpets and the floorboards and again he acted, he pretended to be indignant, but beyond the indignation was a sense of smugness, his mouth was making the sort of noise you'd expect, but his eyes were saying, You won't find her down there."

"Ray, I look to you for guidance. I think your m.p. has been found, and found deceased, as are most m.p.'s who don't turn up within forty-eight hours."

Sussock sat back in his chair. "I'd be inclined to go and talk to her mother."

"Her mother?"

"Aye. They were very close. Mrs. Reissmann was forty-five, her mother was eighteen when she was born. The mother is still only in her sixties. Very much alive, and was convinced that Reissmann did her daughter in."

"Motive?"

"She couldn't have children. At least one of them couldn't and he blamed her apparently. As I recall, Mrs. Reissmann had had all the tests done and had even undergone exploratory operations to see if anything was blocked inside. She got a clean bill of health each time. He, on the other hand, would have no tests done and persisted with the insistence that the problem lay with her. Her mother reckons he filled her in so as to replace her with a younger model who could provide him with a son and heir to his empire."

"His empire being a warehouse in Busby." Donoghue laid his pipe in the ashtray. "Ray, it's lunchtime. Grab some feed and then go and see Mrs. Reissmann's—"

A knock on the door.

"Come in . . . ah . . . good man."

"The files you requested, sir." The collator handed Donoghue a number of files. "Only one Reissmann forty-five years of age, Sandra by name."

"Sandra." Sussock stood. "That's it. Sandra Reissmann."

"Thank you. As I said, Ray. Grab some fodder and then go and have a chat to Sandra Reissmann's mother. I'll familiarise myself with the file."

"It was the doctors at the hospital who eventually said no." The woman ground a nail into the ashtray. Behind her, out of her kitchen window, three floors up, Sussock could see the black tenements of Shettleston. "See, our Sandra, my wee girl, she'd nae life wi' him. He blamed her all the time for no getting pregnant and she got to thinking she was to blame, and she had these operations to see if anything was blocked inside but it wisnae and it all just made her weak and ill. The doctors had a fancy way of putting it, what did they say, 'We're undermining her health,' that's what they said. She was badgered into having more tests and operations by that monster, and it was the doctor who eventually said, 'Look, hen, it's no you. There's nothing wrong with you, it must be your man.' He didn't take kindly to that and he threw a maddy so he did, but he wouldn't go and get himself tested, not our Mr. Reissmann the Iceman with a smile for everybody and a knife in each hand, also for everybody. See, my nice wee angel with him and him so much older than her. He's nearly as old as me so he is. I don't know what she saw in him but she must have thought, 'Here I am a woman of thirty with nae man, I'd best grab what I can,' and she grabbed him. She was a bonny lass and could have done better than him; maybe she couldn't stop thinking that I was married from a gymslip and a mother at eighteen. I was divorced when I was twenty-three right enough, but, aye . . . so you've found my wee girl, aye, Mr. . . . ."

"Sussock. Yes, I'm afraid we believe we have. At some point we may ask you to identify her."

"But no just yet."

"No."

"She's not being cut up!"

"Her face won't be touched."

"Oh, Sandra . . ."

"We have to determine the cause of death. It's vital we do that, we can't proceed unless we do that."

"No, I suppose . . . So how can I help you?" She lit another cigarette. Sussock coughed. "Does this bother you?"

"Just a wee bit, my chest . . ."

"Oh, aye, well it's my daughter. I knew she was dead, eighteen months with no word from my wee girl when she's the one to phone you every day . . . could only mean she was dead . . . but aye . . . your chest . . . I'll make this the last one."

"I'm obliged."

"Perhaps we'll make it the last one. See how I feel. So how can I help you?'

"When did you last see your daughter?"

"See her to speak to, see . . . Wait here, will you, Mr. Sussock?"

Mrs. Gallagher stood, a pale, thin woman, and seemed to Sussock to scurry out of the kitchen, the sides of her slippers sticking briefly to the tacky vinyl floor. Sussock waved his arm in an attempt to clear the smoke. Mrs. Gallagher returned too soon for comfort for Sussock's lungs.

"See, me, son. I keep a diary. Always have done. Do you want to know what I was doing twenty-five years ago, name a day and I can tell you. All my diaries are next door in my room."

"No, I just want to know when you last saw your daughter."

The woman flicked over the pages of a pocket diary. "I marked it, so I did. Aye . . . aye . . . here we are, Tuesday, February second, last year. I recall it well; she said her man was acting strange and had started talking about children again. I said, 'Again!' See, all the operations she had were done before she was thirty-five, after that they just stopped trying, and he didn't mention children again. Then he started talking about wanting a son and he was getting cold and distant towards her. But he was keen to take her for a meal that Saturday, so she phoned and said she was going to Loon Fung Restaurant, Chinese, but really posh. Anyway, she didn't phone the day after, so in the evening I phoned her. Her man said she was no there, she'd gone to visit me. I knew then something was wrong, because she didn't drive and would have had to travel from Busby to Shettleston on a bus in winter, Sunday service at that, and last winter was a bad one."

"I recall," said Sussock, his lungs hurting.

"So next day when she still hadn't phoned, I told him to report her missing."

"You told him?"

"Insisted. So I did." She dogged the nail and to Sussock's relief didn't reach for another. "I did some wee checking. I phoned the restaurant and the owner told me that they were there, sounded embarrassed. Said Mr. and Mrs. Reissmann had attended the restaurant and Mrs. Reissmann had been taken ill. He was a very polite Chinese gentleman, so I said, 'How?' and he said she had fallen down, and I said, 'Oh my God, did Sandra have a drink in her?' and he said that she did. That's the strangest thing because Sandra's a dried-out alcoholic. She can't afford to touch a drop, once she gets the taste in her, and her man kept her off, he did that for her, but the reason he did was to help her get pregnant, at least in the early days. So here, he takes her to a restaurant and plies her with drink. It just doesn't add up and deliver."

"Can I take a note of the date they went to the restaurant?" Sussock took his pad from his pocket.

"Saturday second February. The Loon Fung. Top of Maryhill Road, almost in Bearsden. But I told all this to the polis that called on Monday fourth February," she added, checking her diary. "See here, Monday, polis called about Sandra." Mrs. Gallagher toyed with the butts in the ashtray. "You'll be arresting him?"

"Arresting who?"

"Reissmann the Iceman, everybody's wee pal. He murdered my wee angel, so he did."

"Oh?"

"Had to. He wanted a son, started to want a son again, after stopping trying for ten years. He had a notion and so he had to trade my wee angel in for another bit of stuff. After all they'd tried before, by then she was too old, and divorce is just not his style. Too costly, and he's a good man with a knife."

Sussock noticed a slight glint in her eye. He thought the woman was about to tell him something. He said so.

"I met him through my man. They were laid up in Barlinnie together. My second man, that is."

"He's got form?"

"Aye. He did two years for malicious wounding, carved a boy up good, they say. But it's not what the polis wanted him for."

"No?"

"No. They wanted him for the murder of his first wife. There was a scuffle on the bridge, they say, you know the wee suspension bridge near The Green, that bridge. It was dark, a winter's night, not many witnesses, but a couple did say it was a lassie struggling with a man. But no one was close enough to see which man and she went into the water so she did, when it was close to zero. So he walked, after a 'not proven' verdict. He married our Sandra a year later. And see, the wedding, it was in January. Reissmann, see him, it's more than his line of work that makes folk call him the Iceman. He's got this thing about ice and snow. You married, Mr. Sussock?"

Sussock stood. "Separated. We live apart. Thank you for your time."

"Separated," sighed Mrs. Gallagher. "Best way."

Donoghue listened attentively, pressing the phone to the side of his head, and scribbled as he listened. Then he said, "Ray, that's a good bit of work. Come back in and we'll go and see Reissmann together." He replaced the phone and picked it up instantly and punched a two-figure internal number. "Collator, can you let me have another file on Reissmann? Yes, same name, this time it's a male about sixty-five years of age, he'll have track for malicious wounding and a charge of murder. Now, yes please." He replaced the phone. It rang as soon as he put it down. "Is there no rest . . ." He snatched it up. "DI Donoghue."

"Reynolds, G.R.I. here."

"Ah, Dr. Reynolds, excellent."

"I've completed the p.m. on the young lady I first saw in a field this morning. Not so young in fact. I'll have the report written up and faxed to you, but I thought you'd like to know the nuts and bolts ASAP."

"Certainly would."

"Well, you know the nice thing about ice is that it can work for us as well as against us. I can't tell you when she was murdered but her last moments of life have been frozen for us, a time bracket of a few hours, captured forever, or until she started to thaw. Well, her age: after examination

I'd say she was in her mid forties. I dissected a tooth, that gives the most accurate reading of age. The age I estimated this morning was an appearance diagnosis. She just looked younger than she was. She hadn't been aged by childbearing, though not for want of trying, going by the operation scars on her abdomen."

"That accords with our findings."

"Well, in her last hour of life, she consumed a Chinese meal, bean shoots by the look of it, and she consumed large quantities of alcohol, still frozen in her blood, and she died from carbon monoxide poisoning, also still frozen in her bloodstream. But exactly when . . ."

"It happened on the night of Saturday second, Sunday third February last year. Sandra Reissmann was reported missing on the Monday after she was seen in a Chinese restaurant on the Saturday evening badly under the influence of alcohol."

"It all begins to fit together," Reynolds said. "It's my guess that she lay slumped in the rear of the car comatose with alcohol and was allowed to inhale the exhaust fumes of the car. If the car was left in an enclosed space like a garage, or had a pipe running from the exhaust to the interior of the car, death would be rapid, within fifteen minutes, probably much less. Her body was then laid out and deep-frozen. Can't imagine why anyone would want to go to those lengths, keep her in a deep-frozen state, hidden for eighteen months, and then leave her in the open, with a daft smoke screen of a rope round her neck and a rotten stick, allegedly used to twist it. That's really your department, but to me it smacks of somebody panicking."

"Doesn't it just." Donoghue smiled. "Could be useful to us, very useful indeed."

"He's not here, sorry. Can I help you?"

"Can I ask who you are, please?"

"If I can ask who you gentlemen are?"

Donoghue smiled. "Quite right, sorry, we should have introduced ourselves." He showed the woman his ID. "DI Donoghue and this is DS Sussock."

"Oh, I'm Mrs. Joyce, the under manager." Donoghue thought the woman to have an honest face and Sussock was grateful she didn't smoke.

Her office had glass windows and looked out onto endless banks of white freezers. Men in smocks drove forklift trucks or pulled a chain of trollies behind electrically powered tugs. "Mr. Reissmann has gone home, he complained of the heat."

"The heat! It's quite cold in here really."

"Oh, Mr. Reissmann has a poor tolerance of heat."

"I see," said Donoghue. "So this is what a refrigerated warehouse looks like?"

"Certainly is." Mrs. Joyce looked pleased in a genuine, proud manner, so thought Donoghue, a humility which induced pride about something that to others might seem matter of fact, pleased about a job that others would resent or view as tedious. "We rent out freezer space by the cubic metre, we have two million cubic metres of freezer space."

"Business good?"

"Booming. The food industry has survived the recession, as it does every recession."

"People have to eat."

"Exactly. In fact, Mr. Reissmann has told me to fill the tubs."

"Tubs?"

"Freezers. We call them 'tubs.' Mr. Reissmann has told me to fill the tubs beyond the makers' recommended limits. If you overfill a fridge it reduces its efficiency."

"I'm aware of that. They also need defrosting. I presume that this is what is going on down there, third line of tubs at the bottom of the shed."

Mrs. Joyce followed Donoghue's gaze to where three young men appeared to be chopping at ice with small axes. "Yes, in fact that tub hasn't been used for nearly two years now. Mr. Reissmann hung an Out of Order sign on it, which happens from time to time, but he usually has them repaired within a matter of hours. That one he seemed to forget about. Then he put a lock on it, a wee padlock. We couldn't understand that, there we were turning away business and overfilling tubs and there's a tub sitting there doing nothing, twenty foot long, six feet wide, and four feet deep."

"Really?" said Donoghue. "Really?"

"Aye, and to tell you the truth there was some talk among the crew.

Mr. Reissmann's wife, she disappeared some months ago, and the gossip was that she was in there, but it was only gossip, see she was seen after the tub was taken out of use."

"She was?"

"Aye. That tub went out of use on the day my son got married, two years ago last month. I'm a grandmother now."

"Congratulations."

"Aye, well, the tub had an Out of Order sign hung on it in the June, and Mrs. Reissmann didn't go missing until the winter, about January I think."

"When did the padlock appear on the tub?"

"About the same . . . oh . . ." Mrs. Joyce paled.

"What are those lads doing to the tub?"

"Well . . . as you see, chopping at the ice to speed up the defrosting. When it's defrosted we'll drain it and let it freeze up again. Same process as domestic fridges."

"But you haven't drained it yet?"

"No. We came in this morning and Mr. Reissmann was there, started early. The lid was up and it was defrosting. It had been empty . . . well . . . we get a slack period after lunch so I asked the boys to start chopping the ice, better than having them standing around."

"Don't."

"Don't what?"

"Drain it," said Donoghue. "Don't drain it; in fact, take the crew off and refreeze it. And then leave it."

"Oh . . ."

"There's a gentleman we know, we'd like him to have a look at the ice, or maybe what's in the ice. The sort of thing that you or I might not even notice, but would tell him a whole story. Please, freeze it, put the lid down, and leave it."

"Yes . . . yes . . . of course . . ."

The house said new money. Long, squat, light sandstone under red tile, clipped lawn, imitation stagecoach lamps each side of an imitation oak door. An ice-blue sports car stood in the drive looking like a thoroughbred

with an impeccable pedigree from Italy or Germany but on closer inspection proved to be made in Japan. Donoghue halted his Rover behind
the Japanese imitation but remained in his seat. Sussock glanced at him
questioningly.

"Let's let caution be our watchword, Ray. It occurred to me that Mr.
Reissmann, who evidently keeps his house 'just so' like this house is,
would be the sort of man who keeps the company of rottweilers."

"Nothing moving."

"Very well, let's pay our respects, but proceed with caution."

The doorbell sounded the Westminster chimes. It was opened on the
second ring by a young woman. She wore a short cheesecloth shirt over a
yellow bikini, bronzed endless pins stopped in yellow high heels. She had
a yellow band in her hair. She wore sunglasses.

"Sunny inside, is it, miss?" said Donoghue. The woman's hand went
involuntarily up to her sunglasses. "I . . . er . . . I'm on the sun bed," she
stuttered, but the excuse sounded hollow to both cops. "Can I . . ."

"Police."

"Oh!"

"You sound surprised."

"I . . . Mr. Reissmann's by the pool. . . ."

"Very interesting, but who said we wished to speak with him?"
Donoghue thought the woman to be nineteen, maybe twenty.

"I thought . . . the police . . . I mean . . . well, it's his house. . . ." Then
the woman calmed and gathered herself. "Mr. Reissmann is by the pool,
I'll tell him you're here. If you'd wait here." She turned and walked away,
wobbling on too-high heels on deep pile carpet.

"One frightened young lady, I'd say, Ray."

"Oh, I think so, sir, I think so. Someone with a tale to tell."

The two cops waited by the door. The house, so far as they could tell,
was as Donoghue had said: "just so," everything neatly in its place, the
sort of house where the books, if there were books at all, would be
arranged with the ones with the tallest spines at the ends of the shelves,
sinking down to those with the shortest spines in the centre of the shelves.
Donoghue had been in such houses. Gentle, superficial music played from
somewhere, irritating, all-pervading, as in a modern bar.

Presently the woman returned. It seemed to both cops that she was still nervous. She still wore the sunglasses. "Mr. Reissmann will see you now."

Donoghue thought, Damn right he will, but said coldly, "That's good of him."

The woman led the way through the house. The cops' initial impression was not belied by the walk. New furniture, fitted carpets, all very "new money," everything still in its place and the irritating music filling the house.

Reissmann sat beside a large indoor pool. The woman stopped at the entrance to the swimming pool, said, "Mr. Reissmann," turned, and departed.

"Gentlemen," Reissmann said with a glinting smile. He remained inclined on a wooden poolside chair, dressed in yellow trunks. Donoghue noted him to be a small man, with a swarthy complexion, muscular, and suffering from a chronic hirsute state which appeared not to cause him to be self-conscious. He made no attempt to hide the mass of hair which covered his body from neck to ankles; his swimming trunks were, to the cops, distastefully brief for a man of his years. A metal champagne bucket stood beside the chair; it contained ice cubes and was three-quarters empty. Reissmann had ice cubes on his head, his chest, and stomach. "Can I help you?"

"I do hope so, Mr. Reissmann. My name's DI Donoghue and this is . . ."

"Detective Sergeant Sussock, we've met."

The steel-cold smile was fixed. "It cost me a lot of money to repair the damage you had your men do to my house."

"Well, we won't have to do that again, Mr. Reissmann," said Donoghue. "Mr. Reissmann, we believe we have found your wife. She still has to be identified, but that I feel will be a formality."

"Is she dead?" Reissmann's jaw sagged and Donoghue knew immediately what Sussock had that morning meant about Reissmann's tendency to overact. It just didn't come off.

"She was found in a field in Airdrie, by a man walking his dog."

"Sandra . . . how dreadful . . . , but you know, after eighteen months, I began to fear the worst so you've not surprised me. She had no reason to leave. Things were not too bad between us. How did she die, exposure?"

"No. She was murdered."

"Murdered! How? Strangled?"

"No, but it is interesting that you should say that."

"Well, I just thought that most women are strangled, I mean those that are murdered ... you know, hands around the neck, length of rope ... that's normal, isn't it?"

"No. It's not normal. Most female victims of murder are battered to death or knifed. It's either the famous blunt instrument or a regular kitchen knife that accounts for most murders, male or female."

"Perhaps I've been watching too many detective films."

"Perhaps you have."

Reissmann dipped a paw into the metal bucket and scooped up a fistful of ice cubes and laid them on his scalp. A second fistful was distributed on his chest and stomach. "Some like it hot," he said, "but only some." He tested the weight of the bucket and looked up at Sussock. "Would you do me a wee favour?"

"Perhaps," said Sussock after a pause.

"Could you press the button there. On the wall." Sussock did so. A bell rang far off in the recesses of the house.

"It rings in the kitchen." Reissmann smiled. "That's where she'll be."

"She?"

"The girl, Rosie. She'll be in the kitchen. I need more ice, Rosie will bring it. She knows what that bell's for. —So our Sandra. She's dead right enough, aye?"

"She is. You don't seem so upset."

"Aye well, like I said, after eighteen months there can only be one result. —Where's that girl?"

"Where were you this morning?"

"This morning?"

"This morning."

"Slept late. Got up at ten. Went up to the warehouse, worked till lunchtime."

"Not bad for a businessman."

"The warehouse is doing well, ticking along nicely, and it always will while people need food. I came back to keep cool by the pool. Could you press the bell again?"

Sussock did so, but only after a pause.

"See, women. She knew I was running out of ice."

"She's probably on the sun bed."

"We don't have one. Wouldn't allow one in the house."

"Interesting," said Donoghue.

"Why?"

"Nothing, nothing. Tell me, what is your relationship with the girl, Rosie?"

"Is that anything to do with you?"

"Yes. I think it is. Since your wife's death is of what we term suspicious circumstances, everything to do with you is something to do with me. So, the girl?"

"We have a relationship."

"A relationship?"

"A man needs a woman. Sandra didn't seem to be coming back. Can't get married; Sandra can't be presumed dead, officially, that is, for another six months. But there's a formality, marriage I mean, you can do everything you want to do without a ring and a certificate. We're trying for a family."

"Anybody with you in the house this morning?"

"Rosie. Rosie was with me all the time. You can ask her."

"We will."

"She'll be in the kitchen. She's a good girl." Reissmann plunged his hand into the pail. "See, I can touch the bottom now. I need ice, see women, they're useless. Press the bell, pal."

"No," said Sussock.

Reissmann glared at him. Then forced a smile. But it was too late, the glare had been a flash of insight into Reissmann's nature and both cops had seen it. He levered himself effortlessly out of the chair and jabbed the bell.

"Do you know anybody who'd want to harm your wife?"

"No, right! No!" He sank back in the chair and looked with a look almost akin to disbelief at the few remaining cubes of ice in the pail. "I can't believe this. Do I have to fetch my own ice now?"

"There's just you and Rosie in the house?"

"Aye. Mind you, you'd think I was on my own." He banged the pail down hard on the tiles. "Women!"

"You're not planning to go anywhere, are you, Mr. Reissmann?"

"No. Why?"

"Because," said Donoghue, "we'll be back to have another chat."

"Oh yes. About what?"

"About your wife's murder. Let's just say that right now we want to meet as many people as possible."

"By means of introduction," added Sussock.

"I know how you work. You know fine well I've got a wee history. Talk about giving a dog a bad name."

"We'll go and talk to Rosie," Donoghue said calmly, "then we'll see ourselves out."

"Tell her I want some ice."

"We'll ask her. When we've finished speaking to her, of course."

The kitchen was empty. A half-drunk mug of coffee stood on the table in front of an open magazine. On the working surface a coffee percolator bubbled and hissed.

"Sort of reminds you of the nursery rhyme," Sussock said. "You know the one, 'Who's been sitting in my chair?'"

"More like the *Marie Celeste* if you ask me," Donoghue replied, surveying the kitchen. "Pity, I would have liked to have spoken to her. We didn't get her surname. We'll either see her soon or not at all. My guess, not at all. She's cleared the pitch. I bet she saw all this coming and had a running-away pack all made up ready to grab and go."

The bell rang angrily, loudly jarring the ears of Donoghue and Sussock.

"Let's go, Ray. Leave Mr. Reissmann the Iceman to find he's on his own in his own time."

Outside, the Japanese car had been driven away. Tyre tracks over the flowerbed and on the lawn showed the route taken by Rosie as she skirted Donoghue's Rover to make good her escape into leafy, civilised Busby.

Donoghue and Sussock returned to P Division police station, entered the building by the rear Staff Only door, and signed in at the uniform bar.

"Lady to see you, sir," said Phil Hamilton, duty bar officer. He indicated the public waiting area. Donoghue and Sussock turned. The woman stood as they turned. She had donned a long yellow cotton skirt and carried a yellow handbag, but otherwise she was dressed as she was when she had opened the door of Reissmann's house. She walked towards Donoghue and Sussock. "I want to make a statement," she said.

The woman sat in Donoghue's office. Sussock sat in the adjacent chair. Donoghue sat behind his desk pulling gently on his pipe. The young woman seemed to him to be relaxing and held her sunglasses in her hand. Both her eyes were deeply bruised, one eye with noticeably older bruising than the other.

"They're caused by slaps to the side of the head," she said, noting Donoghue looking at her eyes. "If you slap someone hard enough at the side of the head, blood flows into the orbit of the eye and looks like the person has been punched in the eye. But it's a good slapping."

"I know that, Miss Smythe," said Donoghue. "Carry on, please."

"Well, there's not much to tell. I wasn't with him when he topped his wife but I found out about it over time; he wanted a wean and she couldn't get pregnant. He seemed to accept it and they lived together for another ten years without mentioning it. Then last winter he decided he wanted a wean, him a man of sixty-five, wants to be a daddy. So he got shot of her. Since then he's been trying with me, but see, me, I think it's him, he's the one that can't do it. Then last night he had had a good drink, him and his mates, and he suddenly blurted out, 'We've got to move her.'" Rosie Smythe took a deep drag on a nail. "He was so persistent, so me and him and two mates . . ."

"You don't know their names?"

Rosie Smythe smiled. "Would you believe, 'Jimmie'? Called each other 'Jimmie' all the time. We went to the warehouse. I had to drive the van because they three were half cut. He did it on a whim. Said the workforce were gossiping and it only needed one of the workforce to prize off the padlock and we'd all be in the pokey. I don't know what he meant 'cos I never . . ."

"Not until last night, you didn't," said Donoghue.

"Aw, listen, Mr. . . ."

"Just carry on."

"Aye, well, so I drove the van to the rear of the warehouse. He knocks off the alarm and we went in. They guys arrived, hatchets and ice picks. He opens up a tub and in the name of God there's a woman in there, stiff, all her clothes, all her jewellery, everything. Just like she was sleeping. They chopped her out of the ice. I've never seen anything like it. . . ."

"And you went along with it?"

"Look mister, I'm nineteen, they were heavy guys, they were mad in the drink, they had hatchets and ice picks, I was scared for my life and I did what I was told."

"All right."

"So they carried her out, stiff as a board, and put her in the back of the van. Told me to turn the heater on to melt her as much as we could. Told me to look for a field. I found myself on the M8 and Reissmann, he looks at where we're going and says, 'You daft wee bitch, you should have gone to Ayreshire from Busby, not through the town,' so I just drove on and got off the M8 and drove down a road and another and another. Saw a gate leading into a field and stopped. They three took her out and carried her into the field. I waited till they came back. I was too scared to drive off alone. But when you called this afternoon, I knew then I had to leave and tell the polis. The van's in the garage at the side of the house."

"I see." Donoghue leaned back in his chair. "Well, Mr. Sussock here will take a full statement from you, tell him all you know."

"What will happen to me?"

"You'll be charged with conspiracy to murder. But in the light of your assistance . . . and extenuating circumstances, I doubt the Fiscal will proceed with the charge. But we have to charge you and detain you."

The woman stood slowly. "He killed his first wife, too," she said. "He told me once when he was drunk."

"Just add that to your statement."

"This way, Rosie." Sussock stood and opened the door.

Donoghue picked up the phone on his desk and tapped a two-figure internal number. "Uniform bar? Good. DI Donoghue here . . . I'd like a sergeant and four constables and a van . . . As soon as you like. We're going to Busby to make an arrest in connection with a Code Forty-one. And we'll need to recover a van. It'll be in the garage of the house."

He glanced up at the clock on the wall of his office just as the display changed from 16:40 to 16:41. He would be late home, but, he thought, within acceptable limits. He replaced the phone and dialled an Edinburgh number and spoke briefly to his wife, who sighed and said she'd keep his supper warm.

Acknowledgments

Grateful acknowledgment is made to the following for permission to reprint their copyrighted material.

"The Dancing Bear," by Doug Allyn. Copyright © 1994 by Doug Allyn. Reprinted by permission of the author and his agent, James Allen, Literary Agent.

"Vanishing Point," by Hugh B. Cave. Copyright © 1994 by Hugh B. Cave. Reprinted by permission of the author.

"The Adventure of the Callous Colonel," by Basil Copper. Copyright © 1993 by Basil Copper. Reprinted by permission of the author.

"The Dreadful Bell," by Elizabeth Ferrars. Copyright © 1980 by Elizabeth Ferrars. Reprinted by permission of the author and her agent, David Highham Associates, Ltd.

"The Case of the Parr Children," by Antonia Fraser. Copyright © 1987 by Antonia Parr. Reprinted by permission of the author.

"McLean of Scotland Yard," by George Goodchild. Copyright © 1929 by George Goodchild. Reprinted by permission of the Executrix for the author's Estate, Sonia Roberts.

"The Spy and the Healing Waters," by Edward D. Hoch. Copyright © 1990 by Edward D. Hoch. Reprinted by permission of the author.